MW01015375

Creekbanks

by
Tim Richardson

Amazon Kindle

Plexis Publishing, USA

Amazon Kindle
Plexis USA

ISBN: 978-1726-6722-69

PRINTED IN THE UNITED STATES OF AMERICA

About the Author

Tim Richardson, was born and raised in Burlington, NJ. He still lives there with his wife of 46 years Pamela. They have two sons, and six grandchildren. Tim is a retired police officer, and a US Navy veteran. He has always had a love of writing, and history, especially local history, and the Civil War. In his first book, Creekbanks, he combines those loves to tell the story of an American family. It is a story about where they came from, why they came, how they got here, and how they lived once they arrived. Creekbanks is a work of fiction, but tells a story that, in reality, could be about any one of us.

Dedication

It is only fitting that this work should be dedicated to family, for without family there is nothing. There is no sharing of life or lives, of laughter or tears, of dreams or experiences, or of love.

And to my wife Pam, who is the earth on which I walk, the air that I breathe, and the sun, the moon, and the stars that adorn my sky. Love seems such an inadequate word when I think about what she means to me.

And to my late mother-in-law, Mom. Her encouragement and support were priceless.

Introduction

Michael McBride was a farmer. His family's farm overlooked the Rancocas Creek just east of the Village of Rancocas, and except for his service during America's Civil War, he had never ventured far from its banks. He was born and raised here, and expected that he would live out his life and be buried on this land that had been home to the McBride's for nearly 150 years.

Though there had been a time, when the Rancocas and everyone he loved, and everything it meant to him was lost, and may have been lost forever had it not been for the persistence and perseverance of a mother's love. A mother assisted by Julia Grant, a caring neighbor, and the wife of General Ulysses S. Grant.

Now, nearly 75 years after the Civil War, his granddaughter, Katherine Rosemary McBride, named after her grandmother, cares for him, and runs the family farm. Her older brother Evan is a US Naval officer serving aboard the *USS Lexington* in the south Pacific. They had been raised by their grandparents after losing their father, Colin McBride, in the First World War, and their mother, Diana, shortly thereafter.

Katy Rose, as Michael McBride calls his granddaughter, knows little about the history of the McBride family, and even less about her grandmother's family, the Calhoun's. The little she does know about her own family came from the large well-worn family Bible. All she really knows about the Calhoun's was that they were from Maryland.

Her grandparents had often told stories about how they had met, but each time the story was different, and although the stories were always enjoyable and full of love and laughter, Katy was convinced that the real story had never been told. She knew that they had been married in 1865, immediately after the war, and that her grandfather had served, and had been wounded. Perhaps the true story of their meeting was somehow tied to the war, and perhaps the memories of it were too painful, and contained demons they did not wish to awaken.

However, on an autumn morning in 1938, Michael McBride, now 92 years old, begins to tell his granddaughter the story of the McBride and the Calhoun families. It is a story that begins along the banks of the River Ballynaclough near Limerick, Ireland, in 1789, and ends alongside the New Jersey Turnpike in 1974. A span of 185 years.

There are shipmates, friends, in-laws, cousins, and convertibles. All with a role to play. Advice from an aging Benjamin Franklin, an encounter with a US President, and assistance in pulling off a wedding provided by a US Senator by the name of Harry S. Truman.

A house that sits at the intersection of I-295 and the Beverly-Rancocas Road outside the Village of Rancocas was the inspiration for this story, but Creekbanks was never meant to be a story about a house, but a story about people's lives, and where and how they lived them. From the banks of the Ballynaclough, the Delaware, the Catoctin, and the Rancocas, to the divided City of Baltimore, Beverly's Camp Cadwallader, Philadelphia's Union Volunteer Refreshment Saloon, provost duty in the coalfields of Pennsylavania, the Union Supply Depot at City Point, VA, and the battlefields of the Wilderness, and the Shenandoah Valley, Creekbanks is not just the story of the McBride's or the Calhoun's, it is a story about America, it is a story about us.

Though a work of fiction, many of the people, places, and events, within these pages are real. The *Loving Union*, for example, regularly sailed between the ports of Philadelphia, Charleston, Liverpool, and Limerick, during the late 18th Century. William Powell, City Tavern, The Indian Queen Inn and its proprietor Mrs. House, were all real as well. Samuel Finley, was the Constable of Newville, PA, in 1860. Colonel George Thomas commanded the 2nd US Cavalry at Carlisle Barracks, though there is nothing to indicate they were dispatched to Baltimore to escort Abraham Lincoln as he was secreted through that city, and LCDR George Cooper was the Captain of the *USS Rhind* , during its construction at the Philadelphia Navy Yard in 1938. These are just examples, there are many others. License has been taken with the words, the actions, and some of the timelines to make them fit the story. I apologize in advance for any offenses, and hope that you find in these pages what was intended, an enjoyable story, and not a history lesson.

(Note: Where dialogue begins with the first line written in the ancient Irish it can be assumed that the dialogue that follows is also being spoken in the Irish. When those characters who might speak in the Irish don't do so, the dialogue is generally written with them having a brogue.)

The McBride Family

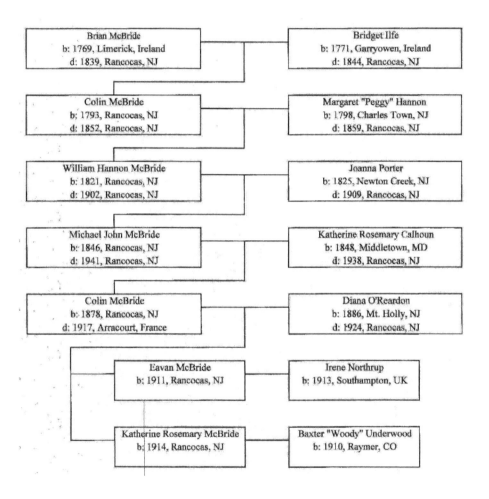

Brian McBride
b: 1769, Limerick, Ireland
d: 1839, Rancocas, NJ

Bridget Ilfe
b: 1771, Garryowen, Ireland
d: 1844, Rancocas, NJ

Colin McBride
b: 1793, Rancocas, NJ
d: 1852, Rancocas, NJ

Margaret "Peggy" Hannon
b: 1798, Charles Town, NJ
d: 1859, Rancocas, NJ

William Hannon McBride
b: 1821, Rancocas, NJ
d: 1902, Rancocas, NJ

Joanna Porter
b: 1825, Newton Creek, NJ
d: 1909, Rancocas, NJ

Michael John McBride
b: 1846, Rancocas, NJ
d: 1941, Rancocas, NJ

Katherine Rosemary Calhoun
b: 1848, Middletown, MD
d: 1938, Rancocas, NJ

Colin McBride
b: 1878, Rancocas, NJ
d: 1917, Arracourt, France

Diana O'Reardon
b: 1886, Mt. Holly, NJ
d: 1924, Rancocas, NJ

Eavan McBride
b: 1911, Rancocas, NJ

Irene Northrup
b: 1913, Southampton, UK

Katherine Rosemary McBride
b: 1914, Rancocas, NJ

Baxter "Woody" Underwood
b: 1910, Raymer, CO

The Calhoun Family

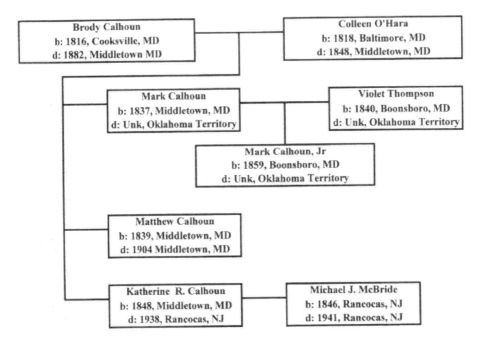

Map of the Village of Rancocas

(circa 1835)

Chapter 1

The Rancocas
1938

The rattle of musket fire, the distant sound of cannon, coming closer and closer, getting louder and louder. The ground begins to shake, then the trembling begins, the awful uncontrollable trembling. The terror. The panic. The grey mist drifts towards him relentless in its mission, and from somewhere within its deafening silence, their terrible battlecry, muted to all but him. The mist keeps coming until it is right in front of him, and in it he can see the face.

It is always the same face, the face in the cemetery. It is so close that in its eyes he can see his own reflection. It is the reflection of a madman. He continues to stare at it until the light in the eyes fades and goes dark, and the eyes are dead, and it is he who has killed them.

Then the face becomes many faces. The tortured pleading faces of other men he has killed, of the men he has seen killed, wounded, and maimed. The faces of the enemy, of friends, of comrades in arms, and the marching column upon column of countless others. They roll by in an ugly silent parade, and the only scream that can be heard is his own. It has been nearly 75 years, and the nightmare of the faces still comes. He knows it will never stop, because he knows, as all men who have gone to war know, that war wounds men's souls, and those wounds do not easily heal.

His name was Michael. Michael J. McBride, an entry in the large well-worn family Bible said that he was born on March 21, 1846, in the Village of Rancocas, in the County of Burlington, in the State of New Jersey. He was the proud son of a proud man, who like his father before him, grew corn. But, once… once he had been a soldier, a soldier who went to war, a war that ended, but even now denies him its peace.

He was floating, suspended in that dark safe place through which you must pass as you go from being asleep to awake. This was one of his favorite places. It hadn't always been, at one time it was a place that terrified him. It was a place where the faces came to visit him, but that had changed, now it is the place where she comes to visit him, and the faces are no match for her love.

As he floated he took advantage of this magical place to move freely between his dreams and memories of her, and to avoid the real world that waited just beyond. The real world wasn't a bad place, it was just that it had become such a lonely place now that she was no longer there. He knew she would come to him just before he awoke, and as he floated and waited he smiled as he remembered the things he loved most about her; the deep emerald green of her eyes, the smell of her hair, the warmth of her touch, and that faint, "I know a secret smile" that she always wore. That she came to him here was a secret that he shared with no one. These fleeting moments were his and his alone and were more precious to him than life itself, and he knew that when she

1

stopped coming, the faces would come for him, they would overwhelm him, and like the others, his scream too would finally be silenced.

She had quietly crept into the room trying very hard not to wake him. The knifelike rays of the mid-morning, early autumn sun seemed to search desperately for a break in the plain woolen curtains so that their light could explode into the room. The heavy well-worn woolens had been hung for the express purpose of delaying this intrusion for as long as possible.

She peered around the edge of the curtain and out the window to the farmyard below. The big wooden barn was directly opposite the window. The large heavy center doors were wide open so she knew that the foreman and his crew were busy somewhere on the property.

She didn't recall hearing the loud roar of the tractor this morning but knowing it was in use pretty much every day assumed she had just missed it. She had purchased the two year old used tractor the previous winter for $420.00, in an effort to modernize and make the farm more efficient. This time of year, in addition to the tractor, eight of their twelve mules would be put to work as well. They tried to rest four of the mules every third day whenever they could in an effort to keep them as strong and as healthy as possible.

With the purchase of the tractor they now had three motorized vehicles on the farm. The 1932 Ford Model B truck that she had purchased two years ago, and the 1923 Model T that had belonged to her brother Evan. Her grandfather had been opposed to the purchase of the truck and the tractor. He felt they were too noisy and smelly and would scare the mules. He wasn't against progress, he just really preferred the mules.

She could drive every one of them, and when she did have to drive somewhere she usually used the truck. The Model T was too unreliable and rode worse than a horse-drawn wagon. Lately, she had been giving some thought to buying herself a new car. She was really taken with the new Plymouth convertibles and felt maybe it was time she treated herself to something special. But, with the way the economy was, now was probably not the best time to make such a purchase.

As her thoughts drifted between the luxurious Plymouth and managing the farm she recalled how when he was still able he would have had as much as four to five hours of work in by this time of day. He didn't like sleeping late, and when he awoke he seemed almost embarrassed and ashamed that he had allowed so much good day light to go to waste. Still, she knew that when he did sleep it was mostly fitful and it was rare that she ever awakened him.

Everyone called her Katy. Everyone that is except for her grandfather, he called her Katy Rose. She had been named for her grandmother; Katherine Rosemary McBride.

She looked over at her grandfather, now in his nineties, as he peacefully slept in the old featherbed he had shared with her grandmother for over 70 years. She smiled as she remembered when, as a little girl, she used to jump into this bed and sink into the softness of its feathery stuffing to snuggle with them or to just wrap herself in one of the many handmade quilts that adorned it and take a warm nap on a chilly winter afternoon.

How she loved those wonderful well-worn quilts with their unusual geometric patterns and unique fabrics. Her grandmother had handcrafted each and every one of them. Some her grandmother had made by herself, others with friends, and even a few with her granddaughter Katy. Her grandmother used to say that every square of fabric in her quilts held a special memory of someone, someplace, or something, even the squares that were made from grandfather's old work shirts.

Katy remembered when, as children, she and her older brother Evan used to help with the annual re-stuffing of the mattress. One of her grandfather's favorite jokes that he had played on his young grandchildren. Her grandfather, knowing that when she learned that the mattress was stuffed with feathers she would be concerned about the little birds who were now without them, had convinced her at an early age that when the birds came north in the spring they took off their winter feathers because they were too hot and put on cooler summer feathers. He explained that he and the birds had entered into a long standing agreement that they would give him their winter feathers and in exchange he would allow them to build their nests in the trees on his farm. At some point as she grew older she of course came to realize that her grandfather had told her a fairy tale. That the "feathers" that were used to re-stuff the mattress were store bought and the feathers she and her brother happily gathered were carefully and secretly discarded. But even now, as a young woman, she preferred her grandfather's story to the truth.

He still lived on the family farm, and the room in which he now slept was in the house on that farm. The farm had been in the family since the 1790's. The original house, a two room log cabin, had been joined by this house in 1816.

She turned and looked out the window again. About 100 yards to the left of the barn was Hilyard's Lane. This narrow road, just a little under a mile in length, connected the farm and the creek with the Beverly Mt. Holly Road, the main east-west road to the north. At the southern end of the road was Hilyard's landing. Katy had always found it curious that the lane and landing were named for a man who had never worked the land, or lived on the land, and in fact had sold the land nearly 150 years ago.

Through the trees beyond the barn she could just make out the waters of the creek shimmering in the sunlight about a quarter mile in the distance. It was still early fall. In another month or so most of the leaves would be down. Then she would have a much better view of the creek from this room.

The Rancocas flowed west into the Delaware River about 12 miles north of Philadelphia and about six miles south of Burlington. It was a busy navigable waterway. It was barely 100 feet wide in some places and as much as a quarter mile wide in others. It provided access to the busy inland ports of Mt. Holly and Lumberton, and like Rancocas and Hilyard's, there were also a number of other smaller stops, or landings, along its banks.

Hilyard's landing was eight miles upstream from the river and was on the north branch of the creek just upstream from the forks. The forks was where the creek split. The north branch provided access to the port of Mt. Holly five miles further upstream, and the south fork provided access to Lumberton, upstream about the same distance.

Up until about ten years ago just about everything that came from Philadelphia or points south came by water via the Rancocas. Even with the building of the Centerton Bridge at the old Rancocas landing, the creek was still the area's primary commercial thoroughfare. But, as the road system improved as well as access to the railroads, more and more produce began to move overland, and shipping along the Rancocas began to dwindle.

When Katy had been a child, it was not unusual to have a ship stop at Hilyard's two or three times a week. Now it was once or twice every couple of months at most. The pier, the dock, and the small warehouse that had been used to store incoming and outgoing cargo, were still there, but due to the decline in their use, they were no longer as well maintained as they perhaps should have been.

Katy remembered how she and Evan used to rush to the landing when a ship was expected and try to be the first to see the ship and identify it. They knew every ship that plied the Rancocas and would call out the name as soon as they recognized it. They made a game out of being the first to call out the name of not only the ship but of its master as well, for they knew all of their names too.

They would often board the ships as soon as they docked and pretend to be pirates or John Paul Jones as they played on and about the decks. On occasion, if the ship was making the return trip on the same day, they would be permitted to remain onboard for the trip up to Mt. Holly or Lumberton and back. They would dream that maybe someday they could stay on board and go all the way to Philadelphia, or perhaps actually be hired as members of the crew, but that never happened.

She smiled as she recalled the countless hours they had spent together playing, fishing, and swimming along the creek's banks. Sometimes she saw it as her moat, keeping at bay the things that might hurt her or those she loved. At other times it seemed an ocean that hid from her the wonders of the world beyond. What was it like, the Rancocas, she wondered when Brian McBride built a log cabin and began to farm and work this land so long ago.

All she knew of Brian was what she learned from the family Bible. In 1793, Bridget, Brian's wife, had given birth to a son, Colin. Bridget would later bear two more children, only one of who would survive to adulthood, a daughter, Colleen, who would marry a Philadelphia shopkeeper.

Michael J. McBride's grandfather, and Katy's great-great grandfather, Colin McBride, built this 2½ story 7-room brick house she now shared with her grandfather, a project that had taken over two years, to impress the girl with whom he had fallen in love, and to convince her father, a prominent local property owner, that despite being a simple farmer, he could provide for her. The father was still unconvinced, but unable to withstand the pressure brought by his wife and daughter, as well as the friends and supporters of the young and energetic Colin McBride, he reluctantly consented to the marriage. So, in 1817 Colin McBride married Margaret "Peggy" Hannon of Charles Town.

In 1821, Peggy McBride gave birth, in this house, to a son, the second of five children, who Colin named, William Hannon McBride, as he continued to attempt to earn his father-in-law's approval. William would marry Joanna in 1844. She would eventually give birth in this house to Michael, their only child, in 1846, who would marry Katherine in 1865.

Katherine would give birth to Katy's father, named Colin for his grandfather, in the house in 1878, after five previous children had died in infancy. He would marry his teen-age bride Diana in 1905, and Katy's older brother Evan would be the fourth generation of McBride babies to be born in the house in 1911, followed by Katy in 1914.

Katy had no memory of her father. He had a deep sense of patriotism, and despite his age, 36, he volunteered and left Rancocas to fight the "War to End All Wars" when she was barely three. He never returned. He had risen to the rank of Captain, but was missing and presumed dead after an artillery barrage outside the French town of Arracourt. His body was never recovered.

Her mother, Diana, would never recover from the loss of her husband. She died in 1924 from what doctors described as "Medical Complications". Katy's grandmother was convinced that Diana had simply died of a broken heart.

So Katy and Evan had been raised by their grandparents, in this house, on this farm. Evan had decided against being a farmer. He had always loved being on and around the water. So, despite the misgivings of his grandparents, he applied for and received an appointment to the US Naval Academy at Annapolis. An outstanding student and athlete, he graduated in 1933, and was currently serving on board the *USS Lexington* in the Pacific.

Katy envied her older brother. He had always been the adventurous one. His letters were always full of new places he had seen, exotic foods he would try, and the different people and customs he would encounter. He had seen and done more in the nearly ten years he had been gone than she could ever hope to see or do.

Katy, who was much older than her age of 24, never left the farm, which had now more than tripled in size from the original 1790's acreage. She had nearly married a few years ago but the young man heard opportunity calling his name and felt they should go west in search of the promised land. Despite how much she thought she loved him she could not bring herself to leave the place and the people she loved more.

Like her grandmother she could best be described as petite. She was a little less than average height and working on the farm throughout her life had kept her trim. She had an attractive figure but nothing about her would be considered voluptuous.

With Katy it was her eyes. Like her grandmother's they were a deep almost hypnotizing emerald green. They could radiate with joy and almost be heard to laugh, or they could flash with an anger that those who knew her knew it was best to avoid.

Her shoulder length auburn hair normally hung loose to frame a cute to pretty face that featured a little bit of a pugged nose with quick to smile lips above a dimpled chin. She knew how to dress and could make herself into a beauty when the mood or occasion required, but when on the farm she usually would wear men's work jeans with a blouse, work boots, and an old hat. Unless you were up close she could easily be mistaken for a young boy.

From time to time ladies from the village would drop in. They usually made little effort to hide their shock at her appearance. She was sure she was the subject of some scandalous gossip around their tables. Was it shameful that she took a little pleasure in knowing this, and that she found it humorous? She had decided long ago that she didn't care if it was or not, she had a farm to run, which was hard to do in dresses and nylons.

From its very beginning the McBride farm had generally prospered. Brian, the first McBride to farm the property, had taken the advice of some very wise men and learned to grow corn. Through trial and error, and with the assistance of other local farmers, the McBride's had become quite adept at growing corn both in quantity and quality.

Through the years they had also produced rye, wheat, some tobacco, and grew apples and peaches in a small orchard. Now it was primarily corn, with tomatoes and soy beans as their rotation crops. The orchards were still there but were not much larger than they had been 100 years ago. They were pretty much left unattended and any fruit they bore was either used by the family or eaten by the deer and other wildlife that also thrived on the farm.

As she reflected on the history of the farm and this house's storied past, she walked over to the bed and looked down on her grandfather's leathery, weather beaten old face and remembered how handsome, vibrant, and strong he had always seemed to her. She tried to remember when it was that he had suddenly gotten so old. The easy answer was that it had started eight months ago when he had lost his beloved Katherine. But she felt there was something more.

Her grandfather had never spent much time away from the farm, except for the years during the Civil War when he had fought for the Union. Her grandmother had once told her that he had served with distinction and in fact had been seriously wounded. She had also told her that it was not something her grandfather liked to talk about, and that even if she asked him about it, in all likelihood, he wouldn't tell her anything. Katy suspected, as she stood there, that perhaps some old demons from that time in his past had returned to haunt him.

As she watched an oh so familiar smile formed upon his lips and she couldn't help but smile herself, and be a little envious, because she knew he was visiting with his Katherine, her grandmother. He thought their visits were a secret but Katy knew about them, she had figured it out from watching him sleep. She had noticed that often, just before he awoke, he would wistfully sigh her name and, for a brief second there would be such a look of sadness on his face. Then the smile would return. Katy figured that that was when her grandmother would promise him that she would visit his dreams again. Katy would then smile herself, knowing that her grandmother would never break a promise to her beloved husband.

Then, he would awaken. Usually hungry, and call out for Katy Rose. Despite being weakened by age, he could get around pretty well with a cane but he needed help getting out of bed and with the stairs. So, she would be there to help and get him down to the kitchen, which was added around the turn of the century along with another first floor bedroom, and within the last year, a first floor bathroom with running water, a tub, and a toilet. Despite how much easier it would be on him, and Katy, if he were to move to the first floor bedroom, he insisted on remaining in the second floor room he had shared with his beloved Katherine. Once she got him to the kitchen she would fix him something to eat and they would sometimes talk for hours. She loved her grandfather very much, and would sorely miss him when he was gone.

Today was different, she waited but he did not wake up. She noticed that the smile was gone, replaced by a look of longing, and as she watched she saw that tears were flowing down the tributary like wrinkles that now covered his once strong and handsome face. She reached out and took his hand in hers and with her other hand lovingly wiped away the tears.

He opened his eyes releasing still more tears, and he looked deep into Katy's eyes. "Katherine," he said. "I'm no good here alone. Take me with you."

As Katy looked into his eyes it was almost as if she was looking through them and directly into his soul where she could see the depth of the love he had for her grandmother. Tears were beginning to fall onto her face now as well as she too remembered how her grandmother's love had filled this house, and how her passing had left such a void.

She hoped as she listened to her grandfather's plea that someday someone could feel for her half the love this poor tired old man felt for the woman with whom he had shared his life and now wanted only to be reunited with in death.

"It's me Poppa," she said, "and I'm not ready to give you up to Nana just yet. So, I'm afraid you'll just have to stay here with me."

He closed his eyes and then slowly reopened them. They were focused now and he was back from wherever he had been.

"I miss her Katy Rose," he sighed.

"I know Poppa, me too."

"You know you're a lot like your grandmother. You remind me of her in so many ways," he sighed. "So, although I never believed it could have happened, as it seems it is destined that another woman come between my Katherine and me, I am so very happy that it is you!" He laughed. A familiar laugh, a laugh she had not heard in a long time, a laugh that she had missed.

"Me too!" She replied and laughed through her tears.

He looked down at where their hands were joined, smiled slightly and said, "You know this reminds me of how I met your grandmother." He looked back at her, gave her hand a squeeze and asked, "Did I ever tell you that story?"

Now, throughout her life Katy had heard a variety of stories about how her grandparents had met more times than she could count. They were all wonderful stories, and which one, if any of them, was true was anybody's guess, but he always took such delight in telling them. When her grandmother was alive and they would tell the stories together they were always told with playful and loving jabs, and teasing, and arguing, and lots and lots of laughter as they relished in sharing the wonderful memories of their love. It was as if every time they told one of the stories they got to start all over again.

She was having trouble holding back the tears now and as the tears and memories continued to flow she shook her head and with what was partially a sob and partially a laugh she said, "No, I don't think so."

He laughed again, even more heartily than last time and she couldn't help but join in. He brought her hand to his lips and kissed it. Then, as he held it against his cheek he smiled and said, "Katy Rose I believe you're telling a fib, and as a punishment for doing so I hereby sentence you to having to listen to me tell the story, the true story, of not only how I met your grandmother but of a journey. A journey from the banks of the Ballynaclough to the banks of the Rancocas. Now stop your crying."

"Okay," she squeaked as the sobs subsided and the tears stopped, and she wondered, what journey, and what was a Ballynaclough?

Amazingly, without any assistance, he sat up in the bed, brought his face up close to hers tilted his head, smiled and said, "Okay to the story, or okay that you'll stop crying?"

She laughed and said, "Okay to both."

"Excellent!" He said.

Then, again without any assistance, he propped himself on two pillows he easily placed against the old wrought iron headboard, took the other two pillows, the ones her grandmother had always slept on, tossed them towards the bottom of the bed and said, "Now get comfortable, it's a long story, but it's worth the listen."

"Don't you want to eat first?" She asked.

She walked back over to the window and opened the heavy woolen curtains. As soon as she did the bright autumn sun exploded into the room filling every exposed space with its light.

"No, no, no," he said as he dismissed the idea of eating with a wave of one hand as he shaded his eyes with the other. "We'll eat later. I want to begin telling you this story. For some reason or other today all my memories seem so vivid and I want to release them and let them flow like the waters of that muddy old creek out there."

"Okay," she said as she returned to the bed and arranged the pillows against the wrought iron at the foot of the bed so that she could face him. She was certain that the story she was about to hear was going to be quite different from anything she had heard in the past. She also felt that this was a story that was not going to be told in a single afternoon, and that when this story was over things would be different, but she didn't know why, or how.

She was no longer crying. She wiped the last of the tears away, settled herself in, looked at him, smiled, and said, "Ready."

He fixed his eyes on her and she noticed that they were clear and focused and that they were bluer than she had ever remembered. He began to speak in a strong clear voice that did not sound as if it belonged to a man whose body and mind time and life had hammered at for over nine decades. It was as if the events would be told with the voice that was there as they happened.

"I was born in this very room, raised in this house, and now sooner than later expect that I will die and be buried in the family plot on this very farm. And, while like everyone else my life began at birth the story of my life, or anyone's life cannot be told based on the calendar of a life. For there are times in every life when through happenstance, coincidence, or perhaps even divine intervention, we may be granted the unique opportunity of having our lives start anew, of having what might be considered a rebirth.

"The difference is that there are those of us who have recognized that opportunity and seized upon it, and others of us who have ignored that opportunity. Throughout our history, the McBride's have, whenever given the chance, eagerly snatched up every such opportunity with both hands.

"For me the most significant, and perhaps most divine, being the first time I ever saw your grandmother. I was at a very bad point in my life. I was alive, but I was not really living. You cannot understand how so like a miracle your grandmother was to me and in fact to all of us unless you know not only her story, but the whole story. The story of all of us."

Now Katy knew that her grandmother was from Maryland and knew some things about her life before she became the wife of Michael J. McBride, but something in the old man's voice and eyes lead her to believe she was about to hear a story that perhaps had never been told before. A story that went far beyond her grandfather, her grandmother, and herself. As he started to speak she realized that he wasn't telling this story for her, he was telling the story for himself.

"Katy Rose," he began. "Do you know why you are here?"

"I do," she said with a smile. "Because I used coming up here to see you as an excuse to get away from that monstrous pile of red hot cast iron in the kitchen, and now have fallen victim to your charms and am about to spend the better part of my day listening to you tell me a story." She crossed her arms. "That's why I am here," she said with a laugh, always the smart aleck.

He spread his arms, looked around the room, and said, "Well, if there's something you need to do that is more pressing I would of course understand." Then he winked.

She put her hand under her chin, pretended to think very hard and said, "Nope. I think I'm good."

They both laughed.

"Poppa," she said leaning forward. "There's no place else in the whole world I'd rather be right now than right here."

"Katy Rose," he began again. "Your being here has nothing remotely to do with anything in the kitchen, in this house, or anywhere else for that matter. You are here because my great-grandfather, Brian McBride, did not wish to hang."

Katy looked at her grandfather in disbelief.

"Hang?" Was all she could say.

"Hang," he repeated as he nodded.

She adjusted the pillows behind her back and wriggled around to get into a more comfortable position. She had never heard this before. A McBride hanged? This was going to be much more interesting than she originally thought.

He was staring out the window towards the banks of the Rancocas Creek as he began to speak.

"From the time he was a small boy, my great-grandfather, Brian McBride wanted to be a farmer. He was very bright, well read, could work numbers, and could probably have been anything he set his mind to. But, he wanted to own his own land, to till his own ground, raise his own crops, and tend to his own livestock.

And his dream nearly came true...

Chapter 2
The Ballynaclough
1789

Brian McBride, along with his wife Bridget, owned and worked a small farm on the banks of the River Ballynaclough, a small tributary of the River Shannon near Limerick, Ireland. The Ballynaclough was more of a creek than a river. It was quite shallow, and barely 50 feet wide in most places, as it wound its way several miles through the Irish countryside.

The nine acre tract had been bequeathed to Brian by his maternal grandfather who had died when Brian was 15. The terms of the inheritance required that Brian be 18, before he could take possession of the property. His grandfather had also set two other conditions which needed to be met before the property would become Brian's.

First, like his grandfather, he was to become a Freemason. This caused Brian no hardship as he had always had a keen interest in this mysterious but well respected society and had intended to petition for membership as soon as he was old enough anyway. Only a few months after his eighteenth birthday he was raised in Limerick Lodge #271, thereby satisfying the first of the conditions.

The second condition was that Brian be married. That same year Brian was buying some tobacco at Sheehy's Mercantile in Limerick. One of Sheehy's clerks, knowing he had recently become a member of the Lodge, was trying to interest him in a new suit of clothes. Brian spied a pretty young girl peering at him from behind a stack of dry goods. He smiled, she laughed. He excused himself, walked over to the blushing redhead and introduced himself. Her name was Bridget Ilfe, she was from Garryowen, and she was sixteen years old. The very next day "arrangements" were made, and the courtship began. So, less than a year after being raised to the sublime degree, Brain satisfied the second of his grandfather's conditions.

Several weeks later, without much fanfare, and after having paid a few government fees, and signed some documents and a register book, Brian became a property owner. With the help of some friends and a few neighbors they built a small two room cottage out of white washed stone, and a small sod barn on the property. They then began to farm.

Working alone Brian figured he would be able to plow, plant, raise, and harvest perhaps four acres of potatoes, and two acres of grain per season. Anything they did not use themselves he would sell at market. In addition, Bridget would keep a vegetable and herb garden, and they would keep a few pigs for butchering, some chickens for eggs, a cow or two for their milk, and a small number of sheep for the wool and meat. With only six acres being planted there was still plenty of room for the cows and sheep to graze. Brian knew that this was not something that would happen right away but expected he could reach this level within the first two to three years.

Brian and Bridget expected that they would spend the bulk of their lives on this land and that soon they would begin to raise a family here.

They had been living on the farm for a little over six months. Brian was eating his noon meal when there was a rap at the door of the cottage. Brian and Bridget exchanged glances.

"*A thagann ar cuairt ag an am seo den la*?" asked Brian in the Irish. They could both speak English quite well, with a bit of a brogue, but they preferred the language they grew up with when alone or in the company of like-minded Irishmen.

"Who comes calling at this time of day?"

"I'm sure I don't know," answered Bridget, also in the Irish, as there was a second rap, "but we won't know if you don't answer it, will we?"

Brian went to the door and opened it. Standing there was an impressively attired footman. Brian was speechless as he stood there gaping. Why was there a footman at his door?

"His Lordship would like a word," said the footman who then turned smartly and walked away.

Brian turned and looked at Bridget who was also gaping. She shrugged and gestured for him to go outside.

"O' course," Brian said in his brogue as he turned back to the door, but the footman was no longer there.

Brian noticed that just a dozen yards or so outside his door was a very finely appointed open coach. It was being pulled by a matching pair of beautiful chestnuts who were being handled by a coachman who was as impressively dressed as was the footman. The footman was now standing near the door of the coach at the ready in the event the door should need to be opened.

Seated in the coach was an elegantly dressed man who Brian guessed was perhaps in his late twenties. Brian smiled slightly as it occurred to him that this man was actually, "pretty". The man was staring straight ahead and seemed unaware that there was anyone else around.

"Can I be o' service Sir?" Brian asked.

"I am Lord Northrup of Hampshire," the man said as he turned his head to look in Brian's direction. He held a small lace handkerchief under his nose as he spoke.

"Honored yer Lordship," said Brian as he bowed slightly. "I am Brian McBride and dis here is me wife Bridget." Bridget curtsied. "We're atcher service."

"Yes, indeed," the man said with a nod as he looked around at the farm as if he had suddenly become aware it was there. Silence. Brian glanced at Bridget and then turned back to the coach.

"Would yas like ta come in m'Lord?" Brian asked as he extended his arm towards the cottage.

"What?" He stammered as he looked in Brian's direction. "Um, no, no, but thank you, thank you, I'm fine here," he said but the look on his face made it clear that entering the cottage would have been well beneath him.

Again, there was an awkward silence.

"Is dere sometin' I can get fer ya m'Lord?" Brian asked. "Sometin' ta drink, some food mebbe?"

"What? No, no, thank you." The man was slowly looking around as if he was searching for something.

Prompted by his fraternal affiliation, Brian extended his right hand and took a few steps towards the coach.

"Would ya honor me den by takin' me hand? We may find we share a common bond," Brian said with a smile.

"My God no!" Exclaimed the nobleman who looked almost frightened as he leaned away from Brian. "I'm sure you touch animals with that hand and it's likely to be infested with any number of plagues." He brought the handkerchief up nearly covering the entire lower half of his face.

Brian didn't know whether to be offended or to laugh as he looked at his hand and then dropped it back down to his side. He did notice however that it was a little dirty.

The coachman coughed to get Brian's attention and when Brian looked at him he discreetly gave Brian a sign so that while it was obvious His Lordship knew nothing of the fraternity, the coachman did. Brian nodded to the coachman.

"My apologies, I did not mean to offend," his Lordship said still holding the handkerchief at his nose, as he looked in Brian's direction. "It is just that a man of my position is not usually exposed to any of this." And he waved his handkerchief indicating his surroundings. "So, I am sensitive, as it were, to any number of maladies that one such as yourself might encounter or have about you. I'm sure you understand."

"O' course m'Lord," Brian replied as he looked down to keep from laughing right out loud at this very dandy gentleman.

"Besides," he continued. "I'm sure we have nothing even remotely in common Mr. ...McBrian was it?"

"McBride," Brian corrected.

"Yes, of course, McBride," the man said. "Except perhaps an appreciation for a fine parcel of land. It is rather lovely here," he said looking around.

"Tanks m'Lord. T'is home ta us."

Another awkward silence as Brian and Bridget again exchanged glances.

"Curious m'Lord," Brian finally said, "and I'm sure at some point ya plan on sayin' so, but what is da purpose o' yer visit?"

"Oh yes, of course, let me get to it," he said as he stood and turned to face Brian and Bridget.

Brian noticed for the first time that the man was holding a highly polished ebony walking stick topped by a very large and ornate gold knob. That stick must be worth more than this entire farm, and several others, he thought.

As Lord Northrup stood the footman reached across and opened the coach door. Startled His Lordship quickly rapped the upper edge of the door with the walking stick bringing the door and the footman to an immediate stop.

"Carlton!" He nearly shrieked. "I've no intention of stepping down. Close the door."

"My Lord," the footman, whose name was apparently Carlton, said as he closed the door and resumed his station.

Now standing, Lord Northrup turned to face Brian and Bridget, closed his eyes, rolled his head around, and flexed his neck. He took a deep breathe, opened his eyes, and looked at them. Here was a man who gave every appearance of preparing to give a rehearsed speech.

"I've come to change your lives," he said as he spread his arms wide and beamed a large but insincere smile.

"Ave ya?" Brian said with just as large a smile as he placed his hands on his hips and bent slightly forward at the waist. This was becoming quite curious.

"I have," he continued. "I am Lord Northrup of Hampshire." Brian started to speak, but Lord Northrup held up his hand stopping him. Apparently he hadn't rehearsed interruptions. Another deep breath and he continued.

"I am Lord Northrup of Hampshire. I am of Ireland to see to my father's business interests. Since these interests are primarily related to shipping, it is important that I am proximate to the ports of Limerick." A breath.

Brian now had his arms crossed, his head tilted, and was trying very hard not to laugh at this pompous ass.

"In my native Hampshire there are a number of very fine houses. It is possible, that even here," and he waved the handkerchief, "you may have heard of Highclere or Stanstead House. Well, I intend to build a residence whose grandeur and opulence will exceed even theirs." A breath.

"I have surveyed every piece of property for miles around and have determined that the loveliest spot on which to build my house is here." He banged the floor of the coach twice with the walking stick to emphasize that he meant this very spot. "I shall call it Meadow Hill." He placed both hands on top of the walking stick in front of him, beamed his insincere smile, and bowed his head. The performance was over.

Brian was dumbfounded. This was something he had not even remotely expected. This man wanted his farm.

"I'm sorry m'Lord," Brian stammered, "but, da land ain't fer sale."

"My good man," Lord Northrup taken aback continued. "I will be paying you a very generous amount for the property. You will have plenty to go elsewhere and have the same "things"," he said the word as if it left a bad taste in his mouth, "that you have here."

Elsewhere? Things? Brian was getting angry, and it showed. He started walking towards the coach.

"Carlton," said His Lordship calmly, and the footman stepped in front of Brian blocking his path.

"Dis is our home," Brian said trying but not doing a very good job of keeping the anger out of his voice. "I inherited dis land from me grandfather. T'is not fer sale. Not now, not ever. Now, since we 'ave nothin' more ta discuss. I'll bid ya g'day m'Lord and ask dat ya leaves me farm."

"At least hear me out," Lord Northrup said again beaming his insincere smile. "I am willing to pay 20 shillings for the property just as it is." He held his hands up to keep Brian from speaking. "You must realize, it is a very generous offer, and a lot of money for a man of your station."

Now Brian was seething.

"Generous offer? Man o' my station?" Brian nearly shouted.

Bridget had moved to his side. She touched his arm and whispered, "Temper, Brian."

13

It was Brian's turn to take a deep breath.

"Lord Northrup," he began having regained most of his composure. "T'is flattered I am dat ya find me land to yer likin'. Me grandfather was a prominent Protestant and a man o' business in Limerick. Ta be sure, he was legally entitled ta own and ta bequeath land. He bequeathed dis land ta me. Me and me wife are also o' da Church so t'is legal fer us ta own land as well. We own dis land and t'is not fer sale. Our business derefore is truly finished. So's again, I'll say g'day, and ask dat ya leaves me farm."

"You are quite an adept negotiator Mr. McBride," said his Lordship coolly. "Alright then, I will pay two pounds and not a farthing more." His stared at Brian with eyes that seemed to have gone cold and said, "Now, to my mind, our business is concluded."

Brian could restrain himself no longer.

"Get off me land ya pompous English arse," he said menacingly as Bridget gripped his arm to keep him from charging the coach.

Lord Northrup no longer played the role of the insincere dandy, he was much more threatening now. He glared at Brian.

"Flattered are you?" He began. "Prominent Protestant? Legally entitled? Not for sale? You pitiful little peasant. Did you actually think I was asking your permission to acquire this land? I was paying you to go away so I could wipe away the shit stains you have left on this land and begin to build a house suitable for civilized people. But what would you know of that? In my experience most Irishmen are no more civilized than their beloved sheep and usually smell worse."

Brian stared at the ground and kept taking deep breaths to keep his temper in check so he would not hang for killing an English lord. "Ya will not 'ave dis land," he said hoarsely.

"Oh yes, I will have this land. It will take a little longer than I expected. And I'm sure it will be more expensive than I expected as now there will be additional fees, and bribes, and government officials to satisfy. But, make no mistake. It will be mine."

Brian glared.

"Ya bastard," he said.

"Don't be unpleasant," Lord Northrup scolded. "Your last chance. You can have the twenty shillings and a few weeks to gather your belongings and find some place to go, or you can continue to pretend that as an Irishman you matter and in a few months lose everything to the tax collector."

"If'n ya don't leave now I will kill ya," Brian said deliberately without looking up.

"So," the Englishman sighed, "it does in fact appear our business is concluded… for now. I will take my leave then and bid you good day, not because of your hollow threat, but because I choose to." He doffed his elegantly feathered tri-corner cap. "A pleasure to have made your acquaintance Mrs. McBride," he said. As he turned and sat he looked at Brian and said, "You must learn to accept your place and, when in your best interests, to submit to those above you." He tapped the side of the coach with the walking stick and as the footman jumped up alongside the driver he said, "Limerick, and let's try to get there before dark."

14

Brian and Bridget just stood there and stared after the coach until long after it had disappeared from sight. Bridget was crying. Brian placed his arm around her shoulders, turned, and led her back into the cottage.

Brian, completely at a loss, sat at the table with his head in his hands. Bridget cleared away what was left of the noon meal. No one spoke. Well over an hour passed.

"Ta se seo fos ar feirme, agus ta me ag obair le deanamh."

"This is still our farm, and I have work to do," he said as he gathered himself and stood up.

Bridget walked over and stood before him. She had stopped crying but her eyes were red and her cheeks still moist from her tears. She looked up at her husband.

"What is to become of us?" She asked in the Irish.

Brian put his arms around her and pulled her to him and they embraced. He rested his cheek on top of her head. Her soft red hair smelled of rain water and lilacs. He kissed the top of her head and silently thanked God for bringing Bridget Ilfe into his life.

She nestled the side of her face against Brian's chest. She could hear his heart beat. It was the beat of a troubled heart. She leaned back and looked up at her husband.

"I love you," she said with a smile, "and, I trust that whatever you decide we must do will be right for us. I am your wife, and whither thou goest, I will go, and where thou lodgest, I will lodge."

She stood on tiptoe, placed her hand behind his neck, pulled him to her and tenderly kissed his lips. When the kiss ended he held her even more tightly as tears began to form in his eyes.

"I love you Bridget Ilfe," he whispered.

"McBride please," she said with a soft laugh. "The way you pronounce Ilfe makes it sound like I should be one of the little people." She broke the embrace, playfully slapped him on the chest and said, "Now go get some work done. There'll be no supper for anyone who doesn't work." With that she turned from him.

Brian reached out and playfully smacked her on the bottom. She squealed and turned but he was already halfway out the door and putting on his cap.

"I'll call you when the supper's ready!" She called after him and feeling much better set about her chores in the house.

As Brian walked across the yard he began to formulate a plan. Tomorrow he would go to Limerick and call on Mr. Thomas Goodwin, the Worshipful Master of Limerick Lodge #271, maybe there was something he could do or suggest that might help.

The next morning Brian walked the two miles into Limerick and that afternoon was warmly welcomed at the home of Worshipful Brother Goodwin on Barracks Street. Though the Worshipful Master was quite comfortable with the Irish, he preferred that English be spoken in his home. Brian described in as much detail as he could recall his encounter with Lord Northrup of Hampshire.

"Yes, unfortunately I too am familiar with Lord Northrup," said WB Goodwin, with only a hint of a brogue, as they sat in the parlor. "He has a reputation fer ruthlessness, not only in how he conducts his business but in his manner as well. He cares fer no one but himself and will go ta any length ta destroy any man, especially an Irishman, who does not agree with him, opposes him, or otherwise stands in his way. I'm afraid Brother McBride dat ya 'ave squared off against a man who has da means and da resolve ta carry out his trets. Did ya really call him a pompous arse and treten ta kill him?"

"Yes, I'm afraid I did," Brian said as he hung his head and slowly shook it back and forth.

"Well good fer yew!" The WM said as he reached across and slapped Brian on the knee. "He is da one fer sure, and probably deserves da other," he said with a laugh.

The parlor door opened and Mrs. Goodwin entered carrying a tray. She set it on a nearby sideboard turned to her husband and said, "Tae when yer ready, Thomas."

"Tank ya m'dear," he said as she left the room and closed the door.

He stood and gestured towards the sideboard. Brian stood as well and after pouring themselves some tea they returned to their chairs. "Da Lodge, and o' course da fraternity, will stand by ya. I will reach out fer da other Worshipful Masters in da district, inform 'em o' what is goin' on, and see what, if anyting, we can do on yer behalf."

He sipped his tea and then turned and set it down on a small table beside his chair. He leaned forward with his elbows on his knees and his hands clasped in front of him and looked Brian in the eye.

"I'll not be a lyin' ta ya, Brother. Dis man is dangerous and his father, who is his benefactor, has da ear o' King George as well as da Prime Minister. Good King George may be mad but yer Lord Northrup may be even worse? We will do what we can, but I can be makin' no promises."

"I understand, and I tank ya fer seein' me and fer whatever help ya might see yer way to be givin'."

"I will get busy on dis and let's meet again in say five days' time. Is dat agreeable?"

"It t'is Worshipful Master," Brian said as they stood and shared an ancient but familiar grip. "*Go raibh maith agat.*"

"Thank you."

"Yer welcome, Brian."

Brian returned to the farm and told Bridget about his meeting with WB Goodwin. They tried to go about their lives as normally as they could but the shadow of Lord Northrup and his threats often darkened their thoughts.

Five days later Brian again sat in the parlor of the house on Barracks Street. After exchanging greetings and some unrelated small talk, the Worshipful Master shared some news from the docks at the Port of Limerick with Brian.

"It seems since we last spoke," the Worshipful Master began, "dat dere has been a problem with our friend's ships gettin' off-loaded. I'm sure t'is nothin' more den some sort o' minor illness dat is making da dock workers sluggish, but t'is causin' quite a problem. Other ship owners and masters are gettin' angry with our friend 'cause da delay in getting' his ships unloaded has caused 'em ta lay off 'til dock space becomes available. Some o' dese ships are carryin' perishable cargoes and der owners and masters are afraid da delay may cost 'em dearly.

"Someone has even suggested ta dese owners and masters dat da problem may in some small way be related ta our friend's recent attempts at acquiring large amounts o' propity with no regard fer da Irish families what owns it. I understands dat dis probability has also been conveyed to our friend."

"Do ya tink dis will do any good?" An encouraged Brian asked.

"I don't know," WB Goodwin continued, "but, it never hurts ta 'ave wealthy Englishmen angry with each other now does it. Also, I do know dat money is very, very important ta dis man and his father, and dat anyting dat interferes with da makin' o' money will 'ave ta be given his full attention. We can only hope dat dis will cause him ta 'ave ta focus on his business interests. Den, perhaps, he'll lose interest in stealing Irish farms fer da buildin' o' his fancy house."

"Bridget and me cannot tank yew and da others enough fer what yer doin' fer us," Brian said.

The Worshipful Master placed his hand on his chest and looked at Brian with feigned offense and surprise.

"Ya can't believe dat I or anyone with whom I may be associated could be responsible fer dis illness dat has afflicted our poor dock workers can ya?" He said with a smile.

"O' course not," Brian said also with a smile, "and please accept me apology fer it was not me intent ta make it seem so."

"Yer apology is accepted," The Worshipful Master said with a nod of his head. "I will keep ya informed Brother." And the two men stood and bid each other a Masonic farewell.

The news about the problems with Lord Northrup's business was encouraging to Brian and Bridget and they began to feel as if there might actually be a chance that their farm would be saved.

Nearly three weeks had passed since Brian's meeting in Limerick when in the afternoon, while clearing fieldstones from a meadow along the Ballynaclough, Brian saw a horse and rider approaching from the east. While somewhat concerned, Brian doubted very much that Lord Northrup was the kind of man who would ride the two miles from Limerick, and it was even more doubtful that he would come to see Brian alone.

As the horse drew closer, Brian recognized the rider as WB Thomas Goodwin. The horse was coming at a trot and WB Goodwin waved his hat indicating that Brian should meet him down at the water's edge. Brian waved to acknowledge that he understood and began walking in that direction.

When Brian got there WB Goodwin had already dismounted and was standing on the bank while the horse was leisurely drinking from the river several feet away. The Worshipful Master removed his plain tri-corner hat, wiped his brow, sat down in the grass, and motioned for Brian to do the same. They sat looking across the stream and watching the horse for several minutes before WB Goodwin spoke.

"Ar bplean chuma abheith ag obair."

"Our plan seemed to be working," WB Goodwin said in the Irish. "Lord Northrup has been so busy trying to make peace with the other ship owners, and negotiating with the dock workers that he's had no time to acquire property or even think about building anything."

"That's good isn't it?" Asked Brian also in the Irish.

"Yes, it is. But there's been a development," the Worshipful Master sighed. "Two days ago," he continued. "One of Northrup's ships arrived here from Liverpool."

"Did it get unloaded?"

"It didn't have to, it unloaded itself."

"I'm not sure I understand," said Brian.

"The cargo was men," said WB Goodwin. "Fifty men, dock workers from Liverpool hired by Northrup to come here and unload his ships."

"Can he do that?" Brian asked.

"The point is, he has. There has of course been protests by local merchants and officials, and there have been rioting between Northrup's men and the local dock workers. But, his problem has been solved. The ships are getting unloaded and we're no longer getting a lot of support."

"What does this mean?"

"It means," the Worshipful Master said as he turned to look at Brian and placed his hand on Brian's shoulder. "That Lord Northrup has won. We cannot ask the dock workers to continue to jeopardize their jobs, and quite frankly I don't know what other course of action may be open to us."

"So, it's over," Brian said and hung his head.

"Not necessarily. We must have rattled Northrup to cause him to go to the expense of bringing in his own men all the way from Liverpool. He may now think that it best he stay in the city where he can keep a better eye on his interests instead of trying to oversee the building of an estate several miles away."

"Perhaps," said Brian

"In any event," WB Goodwin said as he slapped Brian on the back and stood. "Let's not give up hope just yet."

Brian stood and watched the Worshipful Master walk over to the horse and take it by the reins. He shook his head as if trying to wake himself up.

"I'm sorry Worshipful Brother Goodwin," he said. "Where are my manners? You rode all the way out here and I haven't so much as offered you a drink of water. It would be an honor if you would join us for supper."

"Have you any mead?" He asked with a smile.

"I have."

"Then your invitation is accepted. Actually, I was beginning to think you'd never ask," WB Goodwin said with a laugh, "and for this evening," he said as he looked at Brian, "let us talk no more of Lord Northrup or dock workers. Tonight we shall be Thomas, Bridget, and Brian. Three dear old friends sharing a meal and the local gossip. Agreed?"

"Agreed Worshipful..., agreed, Thomas. But only after we tell Bridget the latest news or else we'll never get a moment's peace," said Brian with a smile.

"Ah, yes," Thomas said as he nodded. "Very well then, very well." And he put his arm around Brian's shoulders as they started for the cottage with the horse following behind.

Bridget was thrilled that they were to have a guest for supper and set out the good china from the sideboard. Both the china and sideboard had been part of her dowry. Brian and Thomas, after making it clear that it was not to be a topic for further discussion that evening, told Bridget what had transpired on the docks at Limerick over the last several weeks. She listened, but said nothing.

When they were finished, she walked over to Thomas, who was more than a few inches taller than Brian, put her hands on his chest, stood on tiptoe, and kissed him on the chin. As that was as high as she could reach.

"What was that for?" Asked Thomas aware that her actions had caused him to blush brightly.

"For what you have done," said Bridget as Brian laughed.

"But, we might not have succeeded," he said as he laughed too.

"Well, that's for the trying," she said.

"Well, what if we do succeed?" He exclaimed. "What do I get then?"

Now it was Bridget's turn to blush.

"Oh, my!" She said. She quickly turned to the sideboard and pretended to be busy with the china.

Both men laughed.

They had a good meal, a good long visit, and consumed a lot of mead. So much in fact that Thomas ended up staying the night, sleeping on straw Brian brought in from the barn.

In the morning after a light breakfast, Thomas thanked them for their hospitality, urged them to continue to believe that they had seen the last of Lord Northrup, and took his leave. When he was gone Brian and Bridget discussed how it did in fact appear as if they were going to get to keep their farm.

Chapter 3

The Catoctin
1848

He, like so many of his countrymen, was a farmer. It wasn't a bad life, but it was a hard life, perhaps too hard for some. He wondered if today had happened because it had gotten too hard for her.

He looked around the room, it had been her favorite room in the house. He had argued against even building this room that he felt was an unnecessary waste of materials and time, but she had insisted that the home of a successful landowner must have a proper parlor. Landowner? He chuckled quietly at their little private joke. He was and always would be just a farmer and at times wondered whether in fact it was actually he that owned the land or the land that owned him. But he could never deny her and had added the parlor when they built their house.

He couldn't help but smile as he recalled how she always used to kid him about being a "landowner". It had started when they had bought the farm.

The previous owner was a transplanted Englishman who found he did not like life in the "colonies", as he called them, despite America having been independent for nearly seventy years. Now he wished to return home to England. He obviously considered himself a bit of a fancy but was probably no more an aristocrat than the two milk cows that were included in the purchase price of the farm. Though he sure did dress and talk pretty.

"Congratulations my good man," he had said after the sale as they shook hands. "The first step to the higher levels of society is property. You are now a landowner. If you make the most of this investment and use your resources wisely you may find yourself a man of prominence 'ere long. A landowner," he repeated as he nodded and stared off into space. "Yes, a landowner, how very good."

A landowner? A tract of 45 acres, give or take, hardly qualified as a plantation. Although a good portion of the land had been cleared and there was a small rustic cabin and large partially built barn on the property.

He sighed as he realized he would never hear her call him a landowner again.

It was good land. It was situated near the National Road on the Catoctin Creek just about a mile west of Middletown, Maryland. The peaceful green valley was bordered by the Catoctin Mountains to the east, and South Mountain to the west. The Catoctin Creek flowed down out of the mountains from which it got its name and eventually emptied into the Potomac about nine miles south of Middletown, and about two and a half miles upstream from the important transportation center at Point of Rocks.

He brought himself back to this room in which, except for the last few days, he had never spent much time. He never really understood the need for it. But, every Sunday, after mass, she would serve tea and her small homemade breads and cakes to her friends, neighbors, and anyone else who might happen to stop by. It was while receiving her guests at her impromptu parties that she always seemed to be her happiest.

It was not a large room, and in fact over the last few days it had suddenly seemed extremely small. He sat on one of her prized store-bought straight back wooden chairs. Leaning forward, his elbows on his knees, his hands clasped together, staring at a little dark spot on the wooden floor between his feet. Wondering what traumatic event in the life of the tree the plank had been cut from caused the spot to form. It was a safe place for his mind to be, inside that tree.

He wore his best suit of clothes. Faded, well-worn, and just a little on the small side. It was the suit he would wear on those rare occasions when he would accompany her to mass and then join her in this parlor to welcome visitors.

She did not like him working on the Sabbath and it was a rare Sunday indeed that she did not remind him of it while trying but not succeeding in looking stern. But, he knew that she knew that the farm was like a delicate living thing. It needed constant care and attention if it was to survive, and their survival depended on it. He wasn't a banker, or a merchant, or a tradesman, or a landowner. He was a farmer and farmers did not get Sunday's off.

As he stared at that spot on the floor he wondered if God understood about farmers and the Sabbath. He must, he thought, for wasn't it God that created both? Or, was she gone because he did not understand? Was the Sabbath so important to God that He would punish him for not observing it by taking her?

His mind began to search for a way to fix this. Perhaps if he stopped farming and spent every day as if it were the Sabbath, maybe he could make up for his failures to strictly observe it in the past and then maybe God would give her back to him. He sighed, he was grieving and he supposed like all men who grieved, in his grief he was looking for ways to reverse the irreversible. She was gone and there was nothing he could ever do that would bring her back.

He once again focused on the dark spot on the floor. It was shimmering. It was then he realized it was because he was crying and that his tears were falling on that spot. He wondered again about the spot and whether or not it was possible that trees grieved. Could it be that trees could have dark spots in their lives just like people and was it ordained that those dark spots would never fade or go away?

He lifted his head and looked around the room. Except for the several chairs, some of which belonged to friends and neighbors, all the furniture had been pushed back against the walls. The chairs had once been arranged in neat rows facing the fireplace that was on the wall opposite the entrance to the room.

In front of the fireplace were two saw horses. They had once been in perfect alignment, but like the chairs were now askew. It was on those saw horses that her coffin had rested.

The floor was littered with the petals and pieces of the wildflowers that their friends and neighbors who knew of her love of flowers had adorned the room with. The thought angered him. Whatever would make them think they could make the scene less ugly or tragic with a few flowers? They could fill the room top to bottom with them and it wouldn't change a damned thing!

He dropped his head again looking for his safe dark spot. As he did the sun, which, rightfully so in his mind, had been hidden by low thick gray clouds until now broke through. It took him a moment to realize what it was. Why would the sun shine if she were not here to share it?

The sunlight made the spot not seem so dark. Was that how trees with dark spots survived and made the spots seem not so dark? By letting the sun back in? He guessed it could be possible.

One thing he knew for sure. He was a farmer and the sun meant there was work to be done. He didn't get Sundays off, or the day she died, or the day of her funeral, or to grieve. He would grieve alone during sleepless nights in a room and bed that would never again know light, warmth, joy, or love.

For the second time in a week he considered leaving. This place would never hold anything for him now. How could it? She was gone. This little farm in western Maryland was where they had chosen to live. It did not pick them. He could leave now. It was 1848 and America was nothing if not a land of opportunity. He could go west.

He even considered joining her in death but knew that would not work. Taking your own life was a great sin in God's eyes and if he did so he had no hope of ever seeing her again in the heaven in which she so faithfully believed.

A shadow fell across his little dark spot. Actually it was two shadows, side by side. They were outside looking through the window. They were talking. He couldn't hear their voices or what they were saying but he knew they were talking.

How dare they, how dare they interrupt his self-imposed solitude. They had no right. They had no idea what he was going through. He had lost his wife.

They had lost their mother. He in fact had no idea what they were going through. How sad, frightened, and confused they must be. How selfish of him not to realize it. This was not the father she would have expected him to be. He felt shame.

As he continued to stare at the spot there was another sound, this one was unmistakable. It was a baby's cry.

It was the baby girl she had died giving birth to. He did not know how to feel. If the baby had died would she have lived? Did he hate this baby? Did he resent her? How could he be expected to love someone who had taken so much from him? Truly God would not ask so much of him, not now, not after this.

He thought about the first time he had seen the baby. He had in fact been holding her when he learned that his wife had died. He had immediately set the baby down and had not looked at her since and was trying very hard not to even think about her now.

Her death had been unexpected. It was supposed to be a normal birth, something that happened countless times every day around the world. But, she had started to bleed and they couldn't stop it. His wife had bled to death while he was having his heart melted by the baby he now blamed it on.

He remembered telling the midwife who had handed him the baby that her barely opened eyes were emerald green. She had smiled and reminded him that all new-born babies had blue eyes. He replied that maybe so, but hers would soon be emerald green just like her mother's. How could he have known that never again would he see the light of life in his wife's beautiful eyes?

The shadows were still there, the baby was still crying, and the spot was still a safe place to hide. He sat up and brought the heels of his hands up to his eyes wiped away the tears and rubbed them vigorously. He placed his hands on his head, tilted his head back and looked straight up at the ceiling. In a barely audible voice he said, "I'm sorry my love, please forgive me my cowardice."

Sitting almost straight up he placed his hands back on his knees, looked down at the spot, and said softly, "I have no time or room in my life for darkness now. The only woman I can ever imagine loving has died, but I know that as long as I continue to love her, her spirit will continue to live in this room, in this house, and in my heart, and most importantly in the souls of the three lives she has entrusted to me. I will not let her down. So, no more hiding, I have two sons who need me, a farm to work, and a newborn daughter to learn to love."

He stood up walked over to the window and looked out at the two boys. Mark, the oldest at 11, had his father's pale blue eyes and thick unmanageable brown hair. He was tall and thin for his age and his calm demeanor and sense of responsibility belied his young age. His brother, Matthew, was 9. He was as tall as a nine year old was expected to be but was already developing the muscular frame of his father. He had the same blue eyes but sandy hair. He was a happy adventurous risk taker whose mischievous smile always gave him away.

They were often by his side, helping out as best they could while he worked the farm. In fact he had almost stopped thinking of them as children and more as small men, but as he looked through the glass at them now he realized they were only little boys, little boys who needed him now almost as much as he needed them.

He reached down and opened the window. He got down on his knees, put his forearms on the sill, rested his chin on the back of his hands, and looked out at his sons. They had changed out of their good clothes and he couldn't help but notice how frightened they looked.

Mark spoke first, "You okay Pa?"

"No son, I don't think I am. How 'bout you two, how you doing?"

Mark shrugged and Matthew who was closely watching his older brother did the same.

"Don't know," Mark said. He glanced at his brother and said, "Don't know how we're supposed to feel. Ma always told us about what happens after somebody dies so we figure she's watchin'. We wanna do what's right, you know, for Ma. Will you tell us what to do, or how to feel?"

"Oh son, I can't tell you how to feel. Nobody can. Everybody who loses someone feels differently."

"How do you feel?" Asked Matthew.

"Well, I'm sad. Very, very sad, confused, because I don't know why this happened, afraid because I don't know how my life will be now without your mother in it, and angry because something I love very much and did not want to lose was taken away from me."

Matthew crossed his arms in front of his chest and proclaimed, "That's how I feel too then."

He nodded at his youngest son, smiled and said, "Well alright then."

"I feel lonely," Mark said softly. "Feels like a kinda lonely that might not never go away. Is that okay?"

"Mark, you are wiser than your years, and, it is okay. But, someday when the pain of what's happened here has faded you won't feel so lonely, and, me and Matthew promise we'll do everything we can to help you, won't we Matthew."

Matthew nodded.

"When something like this happens," he told his sons. "It makes your heart feel sick."

"Does your heart feel sick?" Matthew asked.

"Yes Matthew it does, very sick."

"Are you gonna die Pa?"

"Yeah, I am, someday. But not today, and I promise both of you that I will do everything I can to live as long as I can so that we can all be together for a long, long time. We're gonna get through this. We'll never stop missing or loving your mother, but most of the pain will go away, you'll see."

Then he thought, is this the place where we should be having this conversation? His two young sons were standing outside on the porch of their farmhouse looking in a window, while he kneeled inside leaning out that window. Then he realized that years later when they collectively or individually thought about or talked about this conversation, and he was sure they would, it wouldn't be important where or how it took place, but that it had taken place.

"Are we gonna keep her?" Mark suddenly asked.

"Did we have to trade her for Ma? She don't even got a name," said Matthew.

He was taken completely by surprise. He just stared at his sons and knew that the way he answered this question was going to have a major impact on all of their lives. And, Mark was right. He had been so absorbed in his own grief and anger that he had never even given his daughter a name.

"Don't go anywhere," he said. He stood up, closed the window, turned around and looked around the room. Then he left the room and went out the front door to join his sons.

As he was leaving the room he looked down at the dark spot that had seemed so important a short time ago. As he passed over it he said to himself, "No more hiding."

He walked across the porch and sat down on the top step. He motioned to his sons to sit down beside him, one on each side. He put his arms around their shoulders and held them.

He could feel their resistance. He was usually not this demonstrative. He decided this too would have to change.

"First of all, we didn't trade your mother for the baby. Please don't feel that way. Babies are a gift God gives to people who truly love one another. He figures people who have that much love should be able to share it with babies. That's why the baby is here. God saw that your mother and I had so much love that he sent us another baby to share it with, just like he sent us both of you to love when you were babies. This baby is a very special gift from God and your mother. It is the last gift your mother will ever give to us. How can we not love this baby?"

"Since Ma is gone will there still be enough love to go around?" Matthew asked.

"Well Matthew, it's true your mother is gone, but her love is still here. It's in all of us. She always gave us all her love. So yeah, there's more than enough love to go around for you, Matthew, me, and the baby."

The two brothers leaned forward and turned their heads to look at each other. When they straightened up Mark asked, "Do we just call her Baby, or will she have a name?"

He smiled. "She'll have a name. But she should be the first one to hear it don't you think? Come on, let's go tell your sister her name."

They stood up, walked around to the back of the house, and entered the large country kitchen. There were four adults in the kitchen talking in hushed tones. Two men were seated at the table, one woman was at the cupboard looking out a window, and the other younger woman was seated in a rocking chair holding the baby.

He could feel the tension build when he walked into the room. These people were family and they were concerned about him, the boys, and the baby. The older couple were his in-laws and the younger were his brother and his wife.

When they entered the older woman standing at the cupboard turned to face him, looked at her husband, then back at him and began to speak, "We've been talking about it and we think the baby should come to Baltimore to be with us."

Her husband who was holding an unlit pipe in his hand continued looking straight ahead and said nothing but it was clear that what was being proposed had not been arrived at easily. He appreciated how hard it had been for these folks to even consider such a thing, and how hard it was for her to say it to him.

"Thank you," he said, "but, the boys and I talked it over and think the baby's place is here with us, with her family."

The woman turned back towards the cupboard and with a hint of anger and frustration in her voice said, "You haven't even bothered to name her. What do you know about taking care of a baby? Especially a baby girl?"

He turned to the younger man, his brother.

"What was the name of Ma's aunt? The one who worked as a cook on the ship that brought her over from Ireland to pay her passage? Everybody always talked about her. They said she was scandalous, but determined and tough. What was her name?"

His brother looked up at the ceiling and smiled. "Katherine," he said. "Aunt Katherine Rosemary." He shook his head and chuckled. "Last I heard she was an innkeeper somewhere outside of Washington City."

He walked over, took the baby from the younger woman, held her up in his outstretched arms and said, "Ladies and gentleman, allow me to introduce Katherine Rosemary Calhoun. Beloved daughter of Colleen and Brody Calhoun, and sister of Mark and Matthew Calhoun," and he winked at his two smiling sons. "Katherine Rosemary is going to need to be determined and tough just like her namesake, because she is going to grow up on this farm with her brothers and father." He turned to his mother-in-law. "You're right I know nothing about taking care of a baby girl but there must be a woman somewhere around Middletown who does and will help me. Until I find that person I was hoping baby Katherine's grandmother and aunt would be willing to stay around."

The silence seemed to go on forever as the four adults looked at each other. Then finally, "For as long as it takes," the grandmother said with a sob, smiling through her tears she wiped them away with her apron and turned to the younger woman who nodded and was also smiling as tears began to run down her face as well.

Brody Calhoun walked across the kitchen carrying his tiny ten day old daughter. He kissed her forehead, and gently handed her off to her grandmother.

"Colleen's love is in this house and in us. This is where we belong. This is where Katherine belongs." He kissed the grandmother on the cheek.

She nodded and said, "I know. God bless you Brody."

"Now," he said, turning to face the others. "The boys and I have some chores to do and would appreciate the help of Grandfather O'Hara and Uncle Kevin. After that, ladies, we will all be hungry."

This was followed by a lot of hugging and crying as the men made their way out the kitchen door and the ladies set about preparing a meal.

Later that evening after the boys had gone off to bed and the baby had been settled, Brody, his father-in-law, and brother sat on the back porch of the farmhouse enjoying a smoke and mugs of hard cider. The women having cleaned up the kitchen had extinguished the lanterns and candles and turned in as well.

Brody excused himself and took a stroll around the house to stretch his legs and noticed that there were candles burning in the parlor. He went up onto the porch and looked through the window and saw that his mother-in-law was cleaning the room where earlier that day her daughter's funeral had been held. He did not want to intrude but at the same time felt that what she was doing was probably causing her a great deal of sadness and pain, and somehow felt responsible for that.

He entered the house and as quietly as he could entered the parlor. She was sweeping up the remnants of the flowers and she was crying.

"I'm sorry," he said quietly. "I should be doing that."

"Nonsense," she said without looking up.

"I'm also sorry about Colleen," he said barely above a whisper.

"Sorry about Colleen?" She asked, stopped sweeping, and lifted her head to look at him as tears streamed down her face. "Exactly what are you sorry about Brody? Are you sorry that she loved you and you her? Are you sorry that you granted every wish she ever made? Are you sorry that the love the two of you shared created two wonderful little boys and a beautiful baby girl? Or, are you sorry that you made her so happy? What is it Brody? What is it that you're sorry for?" Immediately she regretted everything she had said.

"I'm sorry she's dead," he sobbed and sat heavily in the same chair he had occupied earlier that day and once again with his elbows on his knees held his head in his hands and wept.

She leaned the broom against the wall and came to him. She sat down beside him, put her arms around him, and hugged his head to her chest.

"Oh Brody darling," she whispered. "That wasn't your fault. Please don't blame yourself or that little girl. Our faith teaches us that it is God who decides when we should be called from this life to live eternally with him in his house. None of us could have known that God had decided that now was going to be Colleen's time. Our faith tells us that as those who are left behind we must accept God's decision and rejoice in our loved one's deliverance into heaven. But, what it doesn't tell us is how much that loss will hurt and how difficult it will be to get over or to understand. There is no one to blame Brody, there's only today, and then tomorrow, and then the day after that, and the day after that, and the day after that, and forever. And love, because that's what is going to see us through darling that is what is going to see us through." She kissed him on the head and slowly began to gently rock him back and forth.

He had no idea how long they sat like that, but eventually together they finished cleaning up the room and putting it back in order. They spoke only occasionally while doing so and when they had finished they held each other for a few minutes, she then pulled his face to hers and kissed him softly on the lips. He went out onto the porch, and she went off to bed.

Brody and his mother-in-law never spoke of that time they had spent together in Colleen's parlor but there was no need to, their hearts had said everything that would ever need to be said about it.

Chapter 4

The Ballynaclough
1789

It had been nearly six weeks since Mr. Goodwin's visit, and almost four months since Lord Northrup had paid a visit to their farm, when they received a visit from a rotund little man who arrived in a jaunting cart being pulled by an old but healthy enough looking draft horse. From his appearance he could have been a clerk in Sheehy's Mercantile.

"Henry Owen is me name," he said as Brian approached the cart. "I am da tax collector fer da Munster Commissioner." He doffed his cap. "Are yew Brian McBride?"

Was this it? Had the nightmare finally come true? Or was it nothing? Was this just the course of normal business? As these thoughts rushed through Brian's mind he could do nothing but stare at the man.

"Yew dere me good man," he asked again sounding a little irritated. "Would ya be bein' Brian McBride would ya?"

Brian slowly nodded. "*Ta me*," he answered in the Irish. "I am."

"In da English if'n ya please," said Mr. Owen. "T'is against da rules ta be conductin' me business in da Irish."

Brian nodded.

"And are ya da proprietor o' dis here propity?"

"I am," Brian said, in the English.

"May I be steppin' down den?"

Brian had by now regained most of his wits.

"O' course Mr. Owen, forgive me," he said. "Ya caught me off me guard. Please, won't yas come in and share a cup o' tae?"

"I will, tank ya Mr. McBride," he said as he stepped down and retrieved a journal from beneath the seat of the cart.

Bridget was kneeling at the fireplace tending to a Dutch oven when they entered the cottage. She stood and turned and was about to speak when she noticed that Brian wasn't alone. Before she even knew who he was, like Brian, she too thought the worst.

"Mr. Owen, dis is me wife," Brian said. "Bridget, dis is Mr. Owen, da Munster tax collector." He paused seeing the look of dismay on Bridget's face. "I've invited him fer tae."

"Welcome Mr. Owen," she managed to say as she curtsied. "I will prepare us some."

"A pleasure to be meetin' ya it is Mrs. McBride, and tank ya. T'is not usually with such hospitality dat I am greeted," he said as he removed his cap.

They sat down, and as Bridget went about preparing the tea Mr. Owen opened his journal.

"I'm assumin' ya knows why I'm here," the man said.

"Yer da tax collector," Brian said with a grin. "So, t'is here to collect taxes ya are I would tink."

"Yes, yes, dat's right taxes," he said as he looked at Brian as if he were disappointed that Brian had been right about the purpose of his visit. "If ya would be kind enough to just give me a minute," he said as he began leafing through the journal studiously running his finger down the pages as he slowly turned each one.

The man did not look up but continued flipping pages as Bridget served the tea. When finished serving she took a seat opposite Brian. Brian reached across the table and took her hand.

"Ah yes," the tax collector announced as he stopped turning pages. "Here we are." He looked up at Brian. "Now, yew are Brian McBride, and ya are da proprietor o' dis here propity?"

"I taught we settled dat out in da yard," Brian said.

"Hmm? Yes, yes o' course we did," he said as he nodded. "As such ya know dat yew are responsible fer da payment o' all taxes, liens, and levies against da propity?" He continued without looking up.

"I do," said Brian. He was becoming anxious. He looked across at Bridget who was biting her lower lip.

"And how long 'ave ya owned da propity?"

"I inherited it from me grandfather a little over a year ago."

"Says here," the man said without looking up from his journal. "Dat da owner was a Mr. Michael Endicott o' Limerick?"

"Yes sir," Michael said. "Dat was me grandfather."

"Mr. Endicott was?" Said Mr. Owen as he turned his head slightly and looked at Brian.

"Yes sir. He was me mother's father." Brian's anxiety was growing.

"Ah, yer mother's father he was, I see," the man said as he picked up his cup, blew across the rim, and took a few sips of the now lukewarm tea. "Dis is very good, very good tae," he said as he nodded in Bridget's direction. "Tank ya Mrs. McBride."

Bridget still biting her lip could only nod.

"Our records say dat Mr. Endicott acquired da property in 1778, as payment ta satisfy a debt," the man said in a very officious tone. "At da time da tax on da propity was ten shillings."

And Lord Northrup wanted to buy the property for 20, thought Brian.

"Unfortunately…," the man continued.

Brian and Bridget exchanged glances and then looked back at the man. Was their nightmare coming true?

"…da tax was not paid at da time o' transfer."

Ten shillings? Brian thought. Is that all? We have that.

"In fact, no tax has been paid on da propity since da Endicott acquisition, meanin' dat da taxes are over 12 years in arrears." The man looked up, looked at Brian, then Bridget, took another sip of his tea, and returned his attention to the journal.

Brian was doing some quick calculations in his head. Ten shillings times 12 years would be six pounds. They could still afford to pay that. He hoped that that was all there was.

"O' course, since yer acquisition o' da propity, improvements 'ave been made so's quite natural dat da tax has gone up."

Brian could not breathe, it felt as if there was no air in the room.

"Da commissioner has set da tax at six pounds."

Brian breathed a sigh of relief. Six pounds. It would use up most all of everything they had saved, but they would pay the six pounds if it meant keeping the farm.

"So, we pays da six pounds and everyting is square?" Asked Brian as he squeezed Bridget's hand.

"Six pounds?" The man asked as he looked at Brian as if he'd grown another head. "Oh, me goodness no!" He continued. "With da arrears, liens, and levies, as we discussed earlier, not ta mention dat da taxes were not satisfied at da time o' yer acquisition o' da propity, and da new rate o' six pounds, which is already in arrears, six pounds will come nowhere near ta satisfyin' da debt."

"I was not aware dat der was a debt at da time I acquired da propity," Brian said.

"Well sir, as da acquiring party, I'm afraid t'was yer responsibility ta inquire."

There was a lump in Brian's throat, he could feel himself beginning to tremble. He let go of Bridget's hand. It was happening. It was happening right now, and there was nothing he could do to stop it.

"So," he was finally able to get out. "How much will it be ta be satisfyin' da debt?"

The man, who had made the previous announcements as if he were doing nothing more than telling Brian and Bridget that the sky was blue, again turned his attention to the journal.

"Well, let's see," he said running his finger down the page. "Da Commissioner has set da total debt at 24 pounds," he calmly announced as he looked up at Brian.

24 pounds? 24 pounds? That was more than they earned in an entire year. There was no way they were going to be able to come up with that much money. No one in Ireland, except the English, had that much money.

Brian looked at the tax collector, then at Bridget. There was a dull ringing in his ears, he could hear nothing but the ringing. If they were saying anything he couldn't hear it. His vision was blurred, everything was out of focus.

Bridget looked like she was shrinking. She had brought her apron up to her face and was crying into it. She was bent over so far that her face was almost even with the top of the table.

Brian was sweating, he felt dizzy and nauseous. He was afraid he was going to pass out. He took a couple of deep breaths, he had to get control. He had to!

"Are ya alright?" He heard Mr. Owen ask.

It sounded as if he were under water. He closed his eyes and squeezed them shut, vigorously shook his head, and reopened his eyes.

"No, Mr. Owen!" He shouted. "No, I am not alright!"

He stood so quickly that his chair went flying, he slammed both hands down on the table, bent over, and glared at the little man who had been sent to not only take his farm, but to take his heart. Mr. Owen looked terrified, he turned his head and ducked as if he expected Brian to strike him.

Brian could hear nothing but his own voice, and his pulse pounding in his head like a drum. The man looked at Brian but Brian no longer saw the tax collector instead he saw Lord Northrup and he was beaming that offensive insincere smile. Brian wanted to reach out and with both hands choke the life out of him.

Through his rage Brian heard a voice calling his name. It sounded as if it was coming from a great distance, or perhaps from down a well.

He turned his head and saw Bridget standing beside him. She had both her hands wrapped around his right arm and was shaking him. She was saying something. He couldn't understand her. What was she saying?

"Brian, Brian, get hold o' yerself, Brian." Bridget was trying desperately to get her husband to listen.

Then he realized it was her, it was her that was calling his name. Suddenly Brian was back from the dark recesses of his rage. Bridget saw the focus come back into his eyes and felt his trembling stop.

His look changed from one of rage to one of absolute defeat. She had never seen anyone who looked so sad. She let go of his arm.

Brian walked over and picked up the chair he had sent flying. He leaned on the back of the chair with both hands and with his back to Bridget and Mr. Owen he took several deep breaths, then with the heels of his hands vigorously rubbed his eyes.

He turned, carried the chair back to the table, and sat down again. He placed his hands on the table, intertwined his fingers and fixed his eyes on them. He did not have to look but he knew Bridget was standing beside him.

He turned and looked at the cowering tax collector with a sheepish grin.

"Forgive me Mr. Owen," he said, "but I'm afraid I found yer news ta be a bit unsettlin'."

"So's it would appear," Mr. Owen said with a sigh of relief as he sat up and with his sleeve wiped away the sweat that had appeared on his brow. He reached out and lifted the tea cup to his lips and seemed surprised that it was empty. He looked at Bridget, then back at the cup, and then at Bridget again.

A strange chirping noise came from Bridget and when Brian looked up at her he saw that she had her hand clasped over her mouth and it appeared that she was struggling very hard to keep from laughing. She was pointing and nodding in Mr. Owen's direction but seemed incapable of speaking. To Brian's amazement Mr. Owen, apparently understanding Bridget's chirping and sign language, stood, picked up his cup and saucer and with a bow of his head handed them to Bridget who then walked to be fireplace and refilled the cup from the kettle.

After Mr. Owen had sat down again he turned to Brian and said, "Ya has ta understand Mr. McBride. I don't set da rates or determine da amount o' any debt, da Commissioner does all a dat. I simply delivers da message."

Brian reached out placed his hand on the tax collectors forearm and said, "If'n ya don't mind my sayin' so Mr. Owen, yer delivery needs a bit o' work."

With that Bridget could restrain herself no longer. She burst into laughter that soon had tears running down her cheeks. Brian and Mr. Owen looked at her as if she'd gone mad. But, her laughter was contagious and within moments they were laughing as well.

Catching his breath, Brian turned to Mr. Owen, and said, "Would yas be doin' us da honor o' joinin us fer supper?"

"I'd be delighted," he replied surprised, but still laughing.

Once everyone had calmed down Brian and Mr. Owen went out to tend to Mr. Owen's cart and horse while Bridget prepared the meal.

It was time to face reality. They didn't have 24 pounds, neither did they have any way to get 24 pounds. Even if they sold all of their possessions and borrowed from family and friends the best they could do was maybe a little more than half of that.

"So what 'appens now Mr. Owen?" Brian asked during supper. "We can't pay da debt."

"Well," he began, between bites. "Ordinarily dere are options. Sometimes dere's a grace period dat is granted dat can be as long as 90-days. Sometimes da Commissioner will hold a lien against da propity and allow da debt ta be paid over time as long as it t'is satisfied within a specified period, and sometimes da propity owner is given time ta sell da propity with da proceeds o' da sale being used ta satisfy da debt."

"Ya said, ordinarily. Our situation t'is not ordinary den?" Brian asked.

Mr. Owen set down his fork, laid his hands beside his plate, turned to Brian, and said, "At da risk o' unsettlin' ya once again Mr. McBride. I was instructed by da Commissioner ta make it very clear ta ya dat ya has ten days ta pay da debt. If not paid da propity would be seized and sold fer da amount o' da debt on da eleventh day."

Brian looked across the table at Bridget. They did not have to speak, there was no doubt Northrup's hand was in this.

"Mr. Owen, are ya familiar with a man by da name o' Lord Northrup?" Brian asked as he turned to the tax collector.

"I am," he replied. "I find him ta be a rather unpleasant man. He is a friend o' da Commissioner."

"Well, no surprise der den," Brian said.

"I don't know if ya know, but he has been very busy o' late."

"What do ya mean?" Brian asked.

"Over da course o' da last few months," he began. "Lord Northrup has acquired over 100 acres o' propity here along da southern banks o' da Ballynaclough either by direct purchase, intimidation really, or payin' da debt after seizure or foreclosure. Yer propity is one o' only two others along da river dat he has yet ta acquire. T'is me understandin' dat himself is lookin' ta acquire over 200 acres fer ta build a grand house on."

"Lord Northrup paid us a visit a few months back," Brian said. "He tried ta buy our farm offerin' far less den t'is worth. When I refused ta be sellin' it he tretened ta do exactly what has 'appened here t'day."

"Lord Northrup is not only unpleasant," said the tax collector, "but he is powerful, and he hates da Irish someting awful."

Brian could only nod.

When the supper was done Brian accompanied Mr. Owen out to the barn and helped him with his horse and cart.

As Mr. Owen climbed up onto the cart, Brian asked, "Ya said der were two other propities along da Ballynaclough dat Northrup had yet ta get hold o'. Can ya tell me what der about?"

The tax collector held up the journal and tapped the cover with his fingers. "I'm ta visit da both o' dem tomorrow," he replied with a hint of sadness in his voice.

"Try not ta be unsettlin' 'em," Brian said with a smile as he shook the man's hand.

"I'll mind me delivery," he said returning the smile as he brought his other hand up and grasped Brian's hand in both of his. "I'm sorry fer da role I 'ave played in yer misfortune me friend, and I tank ya fer yer kindness and hospitality." Then he very easily switched to the Irish, "*Go bhfuil tu cad ta se fos go maith faoi Eirinn mo chara, agus mar chomhalta Eireannach, ba mhaith liom tu ach an chuid is fear.*"

"You are what is still good about Ireland my friend, and as a fellow Irishman I wish you only the very best."

There was a lump in Brian's throat as the man released his hand. Brian could only nod. He stood there staring as the cart slowly disappeared down the lane.

He did some things around the yard and in the barn before returning to the house. When he did return to the house he found that Bridget had finished clearing away the supper and was sitting at the table mending what appeared to him to be an apron. Brian went to the fireplace, took a clay pipe off the mantel, filled it with tobacco, and lit it with a match. He walked over and took a seat opposite Bridget.

Bridget looked up and for several minutes nothing was said. The time for tears had passed. A powerful tyrant had used his position and his means to take away their home, and in the world they lived in there was nothing they could do about it.

"*Ni doigh liom gur feidir liom maireachtail anseo nios mo.*"

"I don't think I can live here anymore," he finally said.

"You can for another ten days," Bridget replied in the Irish as she returned to her sewing.

"No, I don't mean here on this land," he said. "I mean in Limerick, or Munster, or maybe even Ireland itself."

Bridget looked across at her husband, set aside her sewing, and said, "I'll make us some tea."

"Northrup is going to own everything from the Dock Road to Ballincurra along the Ballynaclough, and south as far as the bogs. There's no room for us, and I won't be a tenant farmer for Northrup or anybody else. How can I stay here and not have my heart broken every time I walk past any of the properties he has stolen for his grand estate. I can't do it, and I won't do it."

"That's fine," she said as she poured the tea, "but Ireland's a pretty big place."

"But, don't you see?" Brian continued. "No matter where we go in Ireland there will be another Lord Northrup. Ireland will not be a place for the Irish until the English are gone. The English have got to go!"

"You'll be joining the Whiteboys then?" Bridget asked.

"What?" Brian replied, a puzzled look on his face. "No, no, of course not. What I'm saying, I think, is that I can't stay in Ireland as long as the English are here."

"Okay then. Let's leave."

"What?"

"Let's leave,"

33

"What do you mean?"

"I mean, let's leave."

"Where will we go?" Brian asked.

"That's the question isn't it Brian? Where will we go?"

"Why, we could go anywhere we wanted to," he said smugly. "Anywhere in the world."

"Okay Brian, let's talk about where we can go," Bridget said as she jumped to her feet. "How about England Brian? No, that's no good, there are lots of Englishman there. I know, I know, Scotland, Scotland would be good! No, that's no good either, it's just Ireland a little further north." She was walking around the room bowing and throwing her arms about as if she were lecturing somewhere in a great hall. "How about France? We could stay there until another war with England breaks out, after all they'll know we're not on England's side right? We only talk like them. Or Spain! You speak Spanish don't you Brian?"

Brian threw up his hands. "Alright, alright, enough, enough!"

Bridget flopped down in the chair across from him and dropped her head and arms as if she were exhausted.

"What happened to where thou goest, and where thou lodgest?" Brian asked.

She lifted her eyebrows, peeked up at Brian and smiled. "Need a place to goest and lodgest first," she said. They both broke out in laughter.

"We must be mad," Brian said. "Here we are ten days from losing everything and it seems all we can do about it is laugh."

"My darling," Bridget began, reaching across to take his hand. "Neither one of us can really deny that we knew the day Lord Northrup left here that sooner or later the farm was going to be his. Yes, there were some glimmers of hope and we prayed that our fate might change, but all along in our heart of hearts, we knew, we knew, we were going to lose our home. We laugh because laughter is all we've got left, and as Irishmen, of that we have an endless supply. Besides to do anything else would be admitting defeat, and I'll not give that pompous ass the satisfaction." She folded her arms in front of her, gave a demonstrative nod, and winked.

Brian stood up and applauded.

"All told we have around eight pounds," Brian said sitting back down. "We can sell off everything and maybe come up with another two. But, it's going to take a lot more than ten pounds to begin a new life somewhere. Probably take at least five times that. Any suggestions?"

"Well, I'm told I have certain talents," she said with a wink. "How are you at pillaging?"

"Be serious," he said.

"Brian, we will work. We will work day and night. We will do whatever it takes, but we will get the money we need and we will start a new life somewhere."

"How can you be so sure?"

"Because I love you, and I know that together we can do anything."

He smiled. "I believe you may be right. Now, about those talents," he said.

She squealed with laughter and ran into the bedroom with him right behind her.

In the following days, they sold everything they could. Brian had expected they could make about two pounds, but they made just a touch over one. They sold everything except their clothes, the table and chairs, plates, mugs, and cookware, and the sideboard and china which made up the bulk of Bridget's dowry.

They left the farm nine days after Mr. Owen's visit. Brian had made arrangements for them to live in a small one-room tenant's shed on a cousin's farm near the village of Mungret, about two miles southwest of where their farm had been. Bridget found work in the village as a laundress, and Brian worked in the mill. When he was not at the mill he helped out on the local farms and did all manner of other odd jobs to earn money. On days when there was nothing available he would walk the three miles into Limerick to find a few hours work on the docks. They figured they needed 50 pounds, and their goal was to have it in less than two years.

On the eleventh day, following an elegant lunch at his townhouse in Limerick, Lord Northrup paid the Munster Commissioner 24 pounds to satisfy the debt on the McBride property along the Ballynaclough, plus an additional and unrecorded 12 pounds, "in appreciation for his service to the crown," is how his Lordship put it. It galled him that he had had to pay over 35 pounds to get a property that he should have been able to acquire for 20 shillings. But, he had destroyed another Irish life, and that made it all worthwhile.

Five days later, Brian, having been alerted by tax collector Henry Owen, stood behind a tree on the banks of the Ballynaclough, on ground that had once belonged to him, and watched from a distance as the house and barn were razed and everything that could be burned was set to the torch. His Lordship was there, Brian recognized the finely appointed coach that carried him. Brian didn't recognize any of the five men who actually destroyed what had been his home. Who they were really didn't matter.

Brian couldn't help but think, as he stood there openly weeping, that maybe Lord Northrup had made the trip from Limerick for no other reason than to gloat. The truth was that that was exactly why he was there.

Chapter 5

The Rancocas
1938

It was after noon and Katy had finally convinced her grandfather Michael that he should stop and have something to eat. She would have made him stop sooner but the story was so interesting and he was telling it with such enthusiasm and clarity that she too had lost track of time. For the first time in her life she understood that the names she had read so often in the family Bible weren't just names, they were real people. People who were related to her. They were the people who made her possible.

Despite the fact that they had a full modern bathroom on the first floor, her grandfather still insisted on using the pitcher and a wash basin in his room to freshen up every morning. He would wash up, get dressed, and call for Katy when he was ready to come downstairs. Then he would usually use the indoor bathroom to attend to the other necessities of life, conceding to its advantages over their previous outdoor facilities.

Katy was gathering the things she would need to prepare her grandfather a meal when she heard a slight rap on the back door. When she went to the door she saw Mikey. Mikey was a nine year old black boy who lived up on the Burlington Road. He was a nephew to Mr. Davenport, the foreman on the McBride farm.

It seemed Mikey was always on the farm somewhere, trying to help his uncle or doing odd jobs for Katy. More often than not he was just in the way, but he was such a happy and fun little fellow that everyone made allowances. Usually Katy would pay him a few pennies for some of the tasks she would ask him to perform. She was sure that doing so made him feel more like he was part of the crew.

"Well, hello Mikey, how are you?" She greeted the young boy as she opened the door and motioned for him to come in. "I'm just fixing some lunch for Mr. Pop," which is how Mikey referred to her grandfather. "Would you like something?" She asked.

"Is it okay to have a glass of milk?" He answered as he entered and removed his battered flat cap.

"Certainly," she said. "Have a seat at the table and I'll get it." As Katy was removing the glass milk pitcher from their GE monitor-top electric refrigerator and getting a glass out of the cupboard, she noticed that Mikey was carrying a small bundle that looked to be the mail. He took a seat at the table and very carefully placed his cap and the bundle on his lap.

"What have you got there?" She asked.

"The mail," he said as he took a big drink from the glass she had placed in front of him. "Post man gave it to me and tol' me to bring it directly to you," he continued with a very serious look and tone. "He said if I didn't bring it directly to you

I would be in volition of feral post man relations and could be sent to prison." He nodded, took another drink from his glass, and wiped his mouth with his sleeve.

"Well we certainly wouldn't want that would we," Katy said with a big smile as she leaned back against the counter opposite the table with her arms crossed in front of her.

"No ma'am," he answered slowly shaking his head.

"Well?"

"Ma'am?"

"If you don't want to be in violation of any federal postal regulations don't you think you should deliver me my mail?"

"Oh! Yes Ma'am," Mikey said as he got up and walked around the table and handed her the bundle.

"Thank you," Katy said. "I'll be sure and tell the postman how well you carried out your assignment."

"Welcome," he said with a nod as he beamed a big smile and returned to his seat at the table.

"I'll bet this mail delivery business is pretty thirsty work huh," she said.

Mikey nodded and smiled.

"Probably builds up an appetite too," she continued. "Why don't you refill your glass while I get you a cookie or two," she said as she turned to the cupboard, took out a plate and then took the lid off a large jar containing the cookies.

"Thank you Miss Kate," Mikey said enthusiastically as she set the plate with the two large sugar cookies on it down in front of him.

"Welcome," she said imitating Mikey as best she could with a smile as she patted him on the head.

"Where's Mr. Pop?" He asked as he savored his delicious rewards.

"He's still upstairs," she said as she casually began to go through the bundle Mikey had delivered. "He'll be calling for me soon and I'll go give him a hand with the stairs," she continued not looking up at the youngster who was already into his second cookie.

She noticed that among the advertisements, catalogs, farm journals, and of course the bills, was a letter with an FPO San Francisco postmark. It was from her brother Evan and she felt herself flush a little. She restrained herself from immediately tearing into it and set it on the counter with the rest of what had been in the bundle. She turned and looked out the window over the sink.

"Anything interesting?" He asked.

She spun around quickly, and there standing in the kitchen doorway was her grandfather. He was completely dressed, and although he had his cane, he did not appear to be leaning on it for support.

"How did you get down here?" She asked alarmed and a little more than surprised.

"Floated," he said extending his arms out to his sides like wings, "like a big old cloud." He looked at Mikey with a wink, and said, "You saw me didn't you?"

Mikey just shook his head and stared wide eyed and open mouthed.

"Are you crazy?" Katy nearly shrieked as she rushed to his side. "You could have fallen down the stairs and broke your neck or anyone of a hundred other bones."

She tried to take him by the arm but he gently shrugged her off and said, "I'm fine. Now just let me be." He made his way to the table on his own and as he sat down asked, "What's to eat?"

"Vegetable soup and left over chicken," an uneasy and flustered Katy said as she returned to preparing his meal.

"Sounds good," he said. "Is there fresh bread too?"

"Sure," Katy said still not sure about what was going on.

"Even better," he said. "I'm starved."

He turned to Mikey and said, "Do I know you? What's your name?"

"You know me Mr. Pop!" Mikey said with a big smile. "My name's Mikey!"

"Mikey? Hey, wait a minute," he said. "That's my name! What's your other name?"

Mikey was confused but laughingly replied, "I'm Mikey, I don't got no other name."

"You must have another name," the old man said. "I do. It's McBride."

Katy watched the exchange between these two and couldn't help but smile as she remembered how her grandfather used to tease with her and her brother Evan when they were Mikey's age.

"Oh, you don't mean my other name, you mean my last name," said Mikey still beaming that smile. "It's Simmons!"

"Simmons is it?" He said. "Good thing it's different than McBride otherwise I don't know how they'd ever tell us apart!" And he reached over and rubbed Mikey's head.

"You crazy Mr. Pop!" Squealed Mikey. "They could tell us apart 'cause I'm just a little boy, and you... well, you's old!"

Katy couldn't help but laugh right out loud.

"Old? Why I think that after I have my soup I'll have to take you out there to the lane and challenge you to a race to the landing. Then we'll see who's old!" There was a moment of silence as Mikey just stared, but then Michael McBride broke into laughter, and everyone joined in, especially Mikey.

There was a light rap at the backdoor, and Mr. Davenport, the foreman, opened it and came in. He removed his well-cared for wide brimmed western style hat, and Katy noted that as always for a man who made his living working in the fields he was neat and well groomed. He nodded to Katy and her grandfather, and it was obvious he was surprised at seeing the grandfather.

"There you are," he said to Mikey. "I've been looking all over for you. Your mama will skin me alive if I don't get you home soon. Have you been troubling these people?"

"No, Mr. Davenport," Katy said. "Actually, Mikey was performing an official government function."

"Is that right?" Mr. Davenport said tilting his head and looking at Mikey.

"I brung the mail," he said.

"Brought," corrected his uncle.

"And, did such a good job of it that he earned himself a glass of milk and a couple of cookies," Katy added. "Would you like anything Mr. Davenport?"

"Now that sounds like Mikey," Mr. Davenport said with a smile. "No thank you Miss Kate, I'm fine," he answered. "Did you say thank you?" He asked turning back to Mikey.

"Yes sir," he said as Katy nodded and smiled.

"Well finish up then and we'll be going."

"We'll have to schedule our race for another day," said the grandfather to Mikey with a wink.

"Race?" Asked Mr. Davenport.

"Poppa's been teasing poor Mikey," explained Katy.

"Oh." Mr. Davenport just nodded, not sure what was going on.

"How's the work going Davenport?" Asked Michael McBride turning his attention to the foreman.

"Good, Mr. McBride, real good, that tractor Miss Kate bought is a real godsend," he said nodding at Katy. "If we had another one of those we wouldn't need any mules at all."

"A farm without mules?" Laughed Michael McBride, "What is this world coming to?"

"Progress they call it Mr. McBride, progress," chuckled Davenport.

"How're the gloves?" Asked Michael, "Everybody's gloves okay? Man doing hard work needs good gloves."

For as long as Katy could remember her grandfather had insisted on buying everyone who worked on the farm a pair of quality leather gloves, and if they wore out they were quickly replaced. No one seemed to know why gloves were so important to her grandfather, and he never would say, so Katy had stopped asking a long time ago.

"The gloves are fine, Mr. McBride," said Davenport looking down at the pair he had clutched in his left hand. "Just fine. Now come on Mikey, let's get you home." He nodded to Katy and her grandfather and motioned Mikey towards the door.

"Goodbye Mr. Pop," said Mikey as he got up from the table. "Thank you for the cookies and milk Miss Kate."

"Goodbye," they said. "And you're welcome," said Katy.

"I think I'd a won," said Mikey to his uncle as he went out the door.

"You know we're lucky to have a man like Davenport, and that little Mikey is one precious little boy," said her grandfather.

"Yeah, well I suppose that is true," said Katy, "but, just what do you mean by coming down those stairs all by yourself and waltzing in here like you were some... some..."

"Some normal person?"

"No, that's not what I meant," a frustrated Katy said. "It's just that..."

"Soup's ready," interrupted her grandfather.

"What? Oh," she said and she turned back to the stove just in time to stop the soup from boiling over. Shaking her head she poured the hot soup into a bowl, put the chicken and bread on a plate, and set it on the table in front of her grandfather. "It's just that I worry about you."

"I know Katy Rose," he said, "and I love you for it. But, I just feel so alive today. Better than I've felt in months."

"So it appears," said Katy as she poured him a glass of milk, pulled out a chair and sat down opposite him. "But...why? How?" She asked.

"I don't know," he said, "but, as long as I do, I intend to take advantage of it."

Katy noticed that his hands were not trembling as they normally did when he fed himself, and he seemed to be eating as if he were enjoying the food and not only eating because he had to. She didn't know what to think, but he sure seemed happy.

"Okay," she said, "but, promise me you won't try to do anything crazy like…"

"Like run a race against Mikey?" He asked as he looked up with a wink and a smile.

"Yes, exactly!" She laughed. "And don't do anything without letting me know first."

He looked up at her again.

"I promise I won't try to stop you or interfere, I just want to be there in case you need help."

"Deal," he said and stuck out his hand. She took it and with a large exaggerated shake the bargain was struck.

"When I finish," he said as he returned to his meal. "I think I'd like to walk down and visit your grandmother. I haven't called on her in quite some time, and I don't want her to think I've forgotten her. Then maybe we can stop at the landing. I haven't been down there since early summer."

She started to object but then remembered their deal so instead said, "How about this? You go in and have a seat in the parlor while I clean this up and then afterwards we'll walk down to together."

"How about this?" He smiled. "I'll sit out on the back porch and enjoy the afternoon sun while you clean up, and then we'll go together."

Katy shook her head, smiled, and said, "You are a pain in my…"

"Aht, aht,ahh," he said as he shook his finger at her.

"You win," she laughed as she began clearing the table.

When he had finished her grandfather, like it was something he did everyday stood up with very little difficulty and started for the backdoor.

"Don't forget your cane," she said.

He gave her a look.

"Just in case. Please?" She gave him her best spoiled little granddaughter look.

He smiled, retrieved the cane, bowed to Katy and exited out the backdoor.

"Make sure you wait for me now," she hollered after him.

"Yes Granny," he teased. Katy chuckled to herself and returned to her kitchen duties. While she was cleaning up she thought about an article she had read about the elderly and how it was not unusual for them to have periods of unusual energy and lucidness especially when their time was drawing near. She immediately vanquished these thoughts from her mind. She was sure that it was a combination of rest, the season, and his memories and storytelling that had him feeling so well.

Michael McBride seated himself on the porch, placed his cane between his feet, put both of his hands on top of the cane, and rested his chin on the backs of his hands. He looked across the yard and admired the large barn. The original barn had been built in 1818, just two years after the house. It had been enlarged since then and undergone a number of other renovations, but the original stone foundation still supported most of the building.

The largest and most prominent stone in the foundation was on the corner facing Michael. The northeast corner of the building. Carved into this large stone was the date it had been placed, April 4, 1818, and the letter G, surrounded by the Masonic square and compasses. Family records indicated that the Grand Master of Masons, James Giles, of Brearly Lodge #9, in Bridgeton, and Matthew McHenry, Worshipful Master of Mt. Holly Lodge #18, were in attendance when the stone was placed, as well as a number of other Brothers, friends, and neighbors. Apparently it had been quite an affair. It saddened him that he couldn't remember the last time he had attended a lodge meeting.

As she was drying the last of the dishes she remembered the letter from Evan. She thought about telling her grandfather about the letter but decided that she would read the letter first in case it contained bad news. Then she would share with her grandfather whatever news she thought would not upset him. While, even to her, this might not seem fair, there were no lengths she would not go to, to protect him. When she was finished she sat down at the table with the letter. She kept turning it in her hands as she tried to decide whether to read it now or wait for later. The decision was made for her.

"Probably be a good idea to get down to the creek and back before it freezes over," her grandfather hollered from the porch.

"Coming," she answered.

She took the letter and put it in the cupboard alongside the sink and went out the door to join her grandfather. There was a rocking chair and a wooden bench on the porch. Her grandfather was sitting in the rocker so she sat down on the bench stretched her arms out to her side, and tilted her head as far back as it would go.

"Ahhhh," she sighed. "This is nice." She looked over at her grandfather.

"Are you purposely trying to keep me from going for my walk?" He asked with a grin.

"No," she lied with as much innocence in her voice as she could muster. "I just wanted to rest for a few minutes."

"Okay," he sighed and leaned forward in the chair resting his hands and chin on top of his cane again. Without turning his head he looked at her out of the corner of his eye.

"Oh alright," she said. "Let's go." She stood and went to him so she could help him to his feet, but stopped when he put his hand up.

"We have a deal." He smiled.

She exhaled. "Right," she said.

With the help of the cane he made it down off the porch and started across the farmyard. He was a little unsteady at first but soon was moving quite well with minimum use of the cane. She stayed close to him but made an honest effort not to hover or interfere.

"Wish the tractor was here," he said. "I'd like to climb up on it and try it out."

She started to say no, but caught herself and instead said, "I'll let Mr. Davenport know and maybe you could try that tomorrow."

"Really?" He said, surprised because he had not been serious but was not now going to miss the opportunity. "That would be nice."

When they got to Hilyard's Lane at the edge of the farmyard they turned south and started towards the creek. He was still moving pretty well.

"You know, it's a quarter mile just down to the landing, with a side trip to the cemetery, and then back up to the house, the whole thing is going to be close to a mile," Katy said as matter-of-factly as she could. "Why don't we take the Model A, or the truck?"

"Is it really that far?" He said as he gave Katy a side long glance. "I always wondered about how far it might be." He reached out and touched her arm bringing both of them to a stop. "I know how far it is Katy Rose, I've been walking these lanes my whole life. I feel too good, and it's too nice a day not to walk. Don't worry, if I begin to feel tired or don't think I can make it I'll turn back. Okay?"

"Alright," she said, "but I can't help but worry."

As they walked slowly along they shared memories about the places and things they passed. Many of the memories included the two people who were no longer on these creek banks but were always in the forefront of their thoughts and hearts; his wife and her grandmother Katherine Rosemary McBride, and her brother and his grandson Evan McBride.

They decided they would take the path that went to the right along the creek just before the landing and visit the family cemetery first. The well cared for cemetery was on a small hill overlooking the creek and was surrounded by a white iron fence. The grave of Katherine Rosemary McBride was in the left hand corner on the far side of the cemetery.

"I placed her here," said Michael as he stood looking down at her headstone, "because it has the best view of the creek, and it was as close to Maryland as I could get her." He turned to his granddaughter, "I wonder if I might have some time alone with her?"

"Certainly," whispered Katy as she reached out and squeezed his arm, and with a tear in her eye turned and walked away.

Katy walked amongst the other headstones and markers stopping and reading the engraving on many of them as she did so. The oldest was that of Caleb McBride, who had died in 1797, at the age of two. Among the twenty or so other graves, were those of Caleb's parents Brian and Bridget McBride, Katy's great-grandparents William and Joanna McBride, and her mother Diana McBride. There was a monument dedicated to her father who had died in France, and whose body had never been recovered.

In the back corner furthest from the creek was a lone headstone. In previous visits Katy, knowing it wasn't a member of the family, had never paid that much attention to it. She walked over to it, knelt down, and wiped away the dirt and mold that hid most of the engraving.

"Frank Jefferson," she whispered as she read the engraving, "born June 10, 1845, died October 19, 1864."

"He was the best friend I ever had," her grandfather, who had walked up behind her said. "He's back here away from the creek," he continued with a smile, "because he couldn't swim, and was deathly afraid of the water."

"Did you know him long?"

"A little over six months," answered her grandfather, "but it seemed like we had known each other our entire lives."

"1864, he was killed in the war?"

"Yes, he was, at Cedar Creek, in a cemetery."

"Were you there?"

"Yes," her grandfather answered. "Yes, I was there." He turned and started walking away.

Katy stood and walked after him. "Will you tell me about it?" She asked as she caught up to him, "about him, about the war?"

"Yes," he said without looking at her. "Yes, I believe I might." Then he continued back down the path towards the landing.

"Be careful," she said, as they walked out onto the wooden dock just a few minutes later. "It doesn't get used very much anymore and there may be some loose or rotted boards."

"I will," he said and reached out and took her hand. "Just in case." He smiled.

They walked out about halfway onto the dock and stopped. He stood there and looked up and down the creek. She noticed the moisture in his eyes and couldn't help but wonder if, like her, he was thinking that this might well be the last time he'd ever look out on the body of water that had played such a major role in not only his life, but in the history of the McBride family. She also thought about the future.

Not only had Katy never married, but neither were there any prospects in the foreseeable future. Even if she did marry and have children they would not bear the McBride name. Unless Evan had a son who came home to Rancocas, Michael J. McBride would be the last of the McBride men to ever live along the banks of the Rancocas Creek. There was a short rail that ran along the western edge of the dock to their right. He pointed.

"Let's go sit for a minute," he said.

She smiled trying but not doing a very good job of hiding her concern.

"I'm fine. I just want to enjoy the view."

"Okay," she said and they walked over and sat down on the rail.

The rail sagged a bit under their weight but was pretty stable. They sat and watched the rapid flow of the outgoing tide and the little eddies and whirlpools that formed around the pilings that supported the dock.

"When was the last time a ship was in?" He asked.

"Couple of months ago at least," she answered. "June, maybe July. I expect it won't be long before they stop coming at all."

"When I was a boy," he said. "Captain John Gardner used to bring his *Norristown* up from Philadelphia and was a frequent visitor to this landing. He was gruff and profane, and always seemed larger than life to me. He drooled and spit tobacco everywhere." He paused as if lost in his thoughts. "I wanted to grow up to be just like him." He laughed.

"Thank God you didn't!" Laughed Katy.

"You know," he said. "We used to keep a log that had the name of every ship that ever called here, the name of its master, and its cargo. The *Barclay*, the *Independence*, wonder where they are now. Probably tied to some forgotten old dock like this one, and gone to rot. I wonder where that log is." He asked wistfully. "It might be fun to look at."

Katy just nodded, hearing but not listening as she studied the flowing waters of the creek. Then it occurred to her.

"We used to keep it in the desk in the warehouse," she said surprising even herself at having remembered.

They looked at each other, then at the little warehouse at the head of the dock. The building was showing its age and the effects of not having been maintained over the last several years, but it still stood. They smiled at each other, shrugged, and walked over to the long abandoned building.

The front of the building, which faced the creek had a door and a window. They tried to look through the window but it was so caked with dirt and mud that they couldn't see a thing. The door was intact but dirt had piled up against the bottom of it and mold, grass, and weeds held it closed as well as any lock would have.

Using her hands and feet, Katy cleared away the dirt. She looked at her grandfather and extended her hand towards the door latch indicating that he should try and open it. With a broad smile he reached out and after several tugs was able to lift the latch. He pulled on the door but it would not budge.

Even with Katy's help the door, swollen by moisture and time, would only give a few inches. Pulling on the door she put her face to the crack and tried to look into the warehouse.

"Must be a leak in the roof," she said. "It looks awfully wet in there. I can see the desk though," she said as she backed away from the opening.

"We need something to pry it with," her grandfather said. Then he picked up his cane, held it up in front of his eyes and looked down the length of it smiled and said, "I think this will work."

"But what if we break it?' Katy asked. "What will you walk with?"

"I'll have to rely on my own two feet and legs, and if they fail me I guess you'll just have to carry me."

"I don't know," she said shaking her head.

"Look," he said. "You want to get me back to the house, but I want to see inside. Now, I'm not leaving here until I do. So, I don't see where we have any other choice. Do you?"

"Okay," she sighed, "but I'll do it. Give me the cane." And she held out her hand.

He lifted the cane so that it was horizontal and then held it out to her as if he was presenting her with Excalibur itself. She curtsied as she accepted the offering, and he bowed reverently. They laughed.

Katy took the cane and wedged it between the door and the jamb about waist high. She pulled on the cane but not as hard as she could have because she was still afraid of breaking it. The door did not budge.

"You can do better that that," kidded her grandfather.

"I don't know," she said, holding the cane in position but no longer pulling.

"Go on," he chided her. "Put some strength behind it don't pull on it like some girl."

"I'll give it one more try," she said.

With that she pulled on the cane as hard as she could. The cane bowed, but it did not break. Then... the door gave a little. She looked at her grandfather and they exchanged smiles.

"Keep going, you've got it now," he said.

Katy got a good strong grip on the cane. She lifted her right leg and placed her foot against the side of the building for leverage. Then with a loud grunt, she pulled with her upper body, and pushed with her leg as hard as she could. That, "pull like a girl", crack had ticked her off just a bit.

Whatever it was that had been holding the door gave way. The door flew open, and Katy and the cane went flying. Katy ended up about halfway down the dock flat on her back with the cane lying nearby. And, there she stayed.

"Are you alright?" He asked, standing over her.

She looked up at him. She had had the wind knocked out of her and her backside was a little sore, but other than that everything seemed okay. She nodded and sat up.

He tried not to but he couldn't help himself and he burst out laughing. His laughter angered her at first, but imagining what she must have looked like hurtling backwards and ending up on her rear end on the wet dock overcame her anger as she too burst into laughter.

"It's open," he said with a broad smile as their laughter subsided. "Shall we?" And he held out his hand.

Katy took his hand, and being very careful not to pull him over, stood up. Then together they walked to the open door of the small warehouse. The door was indeed open, but it did not appear to be damaged.

Holding hands they entered the dark building. The first thing they noticed was the musty smell and the dampness. There were several areas of the roof that indicated the roof had been leaking in a number of places for a long time.

They also noticed that areas of the floor were slippery and spongy, either from a buildup of mold due to the moisture, or wood rot. There were three crates and two barrels stacked against the far wall. "What do you suppose is in those?" asked her grandfather.

"I don't know," she said, "and, I don't care, and we're not going to try and find out today. The desk should be over here by the window."

They turned to their right, and there just a few feet away was the desk. It was a desk only because that was what they called it. It was not really a piece of furniture, nor was it designed to be sat at.

The desk was about four feet in height with a smooth slanted top for writing. Above the writing area was a flat shelf with an inkwell and places in which to place writing utensils and other small items. There were two drawers beneath the writing surface, and below that were two doors behind which were additional shelves. It was a homemade very utilitarian piece.

When they reached the desk they stood looking at it for a moment. Then Katy reached out and tried to lift the hinged writing service. When she did the damp rotted wood split, and she was left holding the bottom half while the top half stayed put.

They could see that there was a journal in the space beneath the writing surface, but it was also obvious that the space, and the journal, had been affected by standing water. They tried to open the drawers and the two doors but like the writing surface they fell apart the moment any force was used. Katy gathered up the journal as best she could, and they left the warehouse.

Back on the dock in the light of day they could see that the journal was ruined and that any information that had ever been recorded in it had been lost to the water the leaking roof had exposed it to.

"I'm sorry Poppa," Katy said.

"Yeah, me too," he said sadly. "It would have been nice to see the names of some old friends, might have kindled some nice memories."

"You okay?"

"Yeah." He smiled. "I'm fine. Let's head back"

Katy went and retrieved his cane, as she handed it to him she asked, "Are you going to be able to make it back alright?"

He smiled as he took the cane. "You wanna race?"

"No," she said. "I think I'll make you take your time so I can keep up."

They joined arms and slowly started up the lane back towards the house.

"So," Katy said, in an effort to brighten her grandfather's mood. "What happens after Great-great-great-grandfather McBride loses the farm?"

"A chance encounter," he said without turning to face Katy, "that turns an honest man into a criminal."

Chapter 6

The Ballynaclaugh

1789

Brian and Bridget set about quickly acquiring as much money as they could. They begged, they borrowed, and they stole. Brian found robbing the English gentry along Ireland's country roads an unusual experience but it seemed to come easier after his first couple of encounters. Until a likeness of him appeared on a Wanted Poster, and they received an unexpected visit.

Brian's first experience as a criminal was not a well-planned act. It wasn't even an expected encounter.

Brian was walking along one of the many country roads south of Limerick about mid-morning on a cold crisp day in early November, on his way to the docks to see if he could find a few hours work. As he rounded a bend, he saw a man stopped in the road about 50 yards ahead of him. The man was alone, fairly well dressed, and appeared to be struggling to repair a wheel on an overloaded spring cart being pulled by an old tired looking grey horse. Brian continued walking towards the man with the intention of offering to help the man fix the wheel, in hopes that in gratitude the man might give him a few coins. As Brian got within a few yards of the horse, the horse flinched, startling the man. He stood up and turned towards Brian who was now just a few feet away. Brian noticed that he had a large iron wheel wrench in his hand.

"Not t'day Paddy!" He bellowed as without warning he swung the wrench at Brian's head. "I'll not be 'ad by yew nor any worthless Paddy, not t'day I won't ya bloody Mick!"

Brian instinctively ducked, turned, and threw his arms up to protect his head but it was too late. The wrench struck him hard on the upper left arm. The pain was incredible and the blow shook his entire body causing him to lose his balance and fall to the ground in front of the man.

He was lying on his right side holding his left arm trying to regain his wits. The man was standing over him now and was still screaming but Brian could not make out anything he was saying. Brian rolled over onto his back so that he could look up at the man.

Suddenly the man raised the wrench over his head and Brian realized that he meant to strike him with it again. Brian instinctively rolled to his left to avoid the blow. This caused him to roll right onto his injured arm which was now throbbing with pain.

When he completed his roll he was again lying on his back. He turned his head to his right just in time to see the large business end of the wrench slam into the ground exactly where his head had been only moments before. The man was still screaming and again raised the wrench. This man was trying to kill him!

Ignoring the pain in his arm Brian lifted his right leg and kicked the man as hard as he could in the side of his knee. He heard a sickening pop as the man screamed out in pain and collapsed to the ground dropping the wrench.

"Ya broke me fecking leg, ya broke me fecking leg ya son of a bitch!" He repeatedly screamed as he laid in the road next to Brian writhing in pain and holding his leg.

Brian grabbed the wrench with his left hand, quickly rolled to a kneeling position, stood up, grabbed the man by the collar at the back of his neck with his right hand, and lifted him off the ground and slammed him into the side of the cart. The man's chest hit the sideboards so hard that Brian heard him squeak as all the wind was forced out of his lungs. It was all he could do to support the man, who now had only the use of one leg, and keep himself upright as well as the excruciating pain returned to his left arm.

Then Brian realized that the man had reached into the bed of the cart for something. Fearing it was another wrench or a weapon, Brian tried to lift the wrench he was holding to strike the man first. He knew the wrench was in his hand but his arm hung limp and he found he could not move or feel it.

Brian felt as if all the rage over everything that had happened to him over the course of the last several months was at this very moment about to burst forth from his brain. He knew that if he did not get it under control he would kill this man with his bare hands. With the strength that comes from uncontrolled rage Brian spun him around, grabbed him by the front of his shirt and slammed him back into the side of the cart.

Their faces were only inches apart. The man had a cut on his chin from which blood was dripping down onto the front of his shirt and now onto Brian's fist where he gripped the shirt. The man's face was smeared with dirt and sweat and was flushed red and the visible blue and red veins in his face appeared ready to explode. He was still gasping for air and Brian could smell his rotting teeth and the stench of his unwashed body.

Brian looked into the man's eyes and saw that there was terror in them. This man was probably more afraid right now than he had ever been in his life. This man was expecting to die and at this moment Brian felt compelled to oblige him.

It pleased Brian that the man was so terrified and he began to consider exactly how he would kill this man. He was already having trouble breathing so it wouldn't take much to strangle him. He had also been crippled, so he could be thrown to the ground and stomped to death, and Brian's right arm still worked, so he could use the wrench to crush the man's skull.

"Please sir, I've a wife and children," pleaded the man as he brought his clenched hands up between them.

"Please sir?" Snarled Brian in a hoarse whisper. "Only minutes ago I was nuttin' more den a worthless Paddy. Ya tried ta kill me ya did. But now t'is you who are findin' death's door a frightenin' place ain't it friend."

The man was actually crying now and Brian's sense of smell told him that he had also lost control of both his bowels and his bladder.

"Please forgive me, please forgive me." He sobbed. "Here, here take dis, t'is all I got. Please spare me life, fer da love o' God please spare me. Here, here take it."

Brian noticed that clenched in the man's hands were two leather drawstring pouches each a little larger than his fist that were tied to opposite ends of a long leather strap. It was quite obvious that they were filled with coins. Brian let go of the front of the man's shirt and grabbed the strap and held the pouches up in front of him. They were heavier than he expected them to be. Without Brian to support him the man crumpled to the ground.

Brian's initial reaction was to throw the pouches into the road, but something stopped him and he looped the strap over his head so that the pouches were concealed inside the front of his shirt. He realized that he was still holding the wrench in his left hand and that the throbbing was returning as the feeling began to return to his arm.

Brian looked down at the man. He had his arms wrapped around his head and his good leg was drawn up into his midsection while the injured one lay useless.

He was trembling and whimpering. "Please spare me. Please spare me." Repeatedly.

Brian knelt down on one knee and grabbed the man by his hair and pulled his head up so he could look into his face. The man screamed out in terror.

"Ya stupid arse," Brian said as he shook the man's head. "I was gonna help ya fix yer wagon in da hopes dat maybe ya would be tossin' me a coin. Had ya denied me da coin, I woulda helped ya anyways. Yer ignorant English arrogance nearly got ya killed."

He let go of the man's hair and his head fell into the dirt. Brian stood up, tossed the wrench into the cart, and began walking down the road back the way he had come towards the banks of the Ballynaclough.

When he got to the river, he knelt down on the bank and thrust his head into the water face first. The water was ice cold. It felt like his face was being stuck with hundreds of razor sharp needles. He held his face under the water for as long as he could before he had to come up for air. When he did the cold November air made his skin burn. He bent over again and used his hands to scoop water onto the back of his neck. When he was done he removed his wool coat and dried himself on the inside of it. He put the coat back on and walked up the bank and sat down against a tree.

He could feel the leather pouches against his skin inside his shirt. He looked back in the direction of the road and considered going back and giving the man back his money. But, he decided against this, by now someone else may have come along and it would be awfully hard to explain how the man had ended up lying crippled in the road and why Brian had his money. He thought about tossing the pouches into the water. Ultimately he decided to take the pouches home so that he and Bridget could decide together what should be done.

The walk home should have taken a little over an hour, but it took Brian closer to three. Every time he thought he heard someone approaching or saw someone in the distance he would leave the road and hide, either in the woods, a ditch, or simply by lying down in a field. He was certain news of what had happened had spread and that right now everyone he saw was hunting him. The longer it took him to get home the more afraid he became.

Bridget, who was bringing a pot to boil over a small turf fire in the shed's small fireplace, looked up when he burst into the shed and was aghast at what she saw. Brian and his clothes were wet and filthy. His hair was muddy and matted. He was shivering and he looked as if the devil himself was after him.

He slammed the door behind him and leaned against it as if he expected someone to come crashing in behind him. He was breathing heavily and without turning to look at her he said, "*Ta me maraoidh beagnach fear.*"

"I've nearly killed a man."

"What are you talking about?" She asked in the Irish trying to look beyond him to see who or what might be in pursuit of her husband.

"They'll come for me, and I'll be hanged for sure," he said as he started to collapse against the door.

Bridget rushed to him and helped him into a chair at their small table. Once she had him seated she started to unbutton his coat and said, "I don't care if you've killed King George himself, we've got to get you out of these wet things before you catch your death."

He grabbed her hands to stop her and said, "I only wanted to help him, that's all, I only wanted to help." He let go of her hands and placed his hands in front of him on the table. "I was almost to Limerick..."

Bridget sat down in the chair next to him, put both of her hands on his, and listened as Brian relayed the whole story of his encounter with the man on the road. He told everything exactly as it had happened, except he told her that he had thrown the leather pouches into the Ballynaclough.

When he was done she reached up and put her hand on his cheek and said, "Brian, the man tried to kill you, you acted in self-defense, you did nothing wrong."

"He was an Englishman," Brian said. "Who do you think they'll believe?"

"It doesn't matter," she said. "You have no idea of who he is, nor does he know you, and the chances of either of you seeing each other again are extremely slim. Besides, there's nothing to tie you to the man."

She took his hands, pulled him to his feet, and walked him to in front of the fireplace. She again began to remove his clothing.

"Now, let's get you cleaned up and dried and get some hot food into you. No one's going to hang tonight," she said as she smiled at him and began to unbutton his shirt.

When she opened his shirt she saw the leather pouches. She looked at the pouches, then up at Brian, and then down at the pouches again.

"I thought you said..."

"I'm certain I did, I meant to, I thought I did," he said with a confused look on his face.

Bridget took the pouches from around his neck and placed them on the small mantel above the fireplace. She too was surprised at how heavy they were.

"We'll worry about those later," she said and returned to undressing him.

A few hours later, Brian washed and dried, was wrapped in a warm woolen blanket and sleeping peacefully on the straw that served as their bed in the small shed. Bridget had been able to get some hot soup into him and he had finally stopped trembling. She had never seen her husband in such a state before.

She had just finished cleaning up the mess that had been made in getting Brian cleaned up and clearing away the supper. She was sitting at the table sipping a cup of tea and wishing there was something more than laundry she could do to help her husband get the money they needed so they could go somewhere and start over. Then she remembered the leather pouches.

She looked up at the mantel and could just make out their shape in the light of the lone candle burning on the table in front of her. She glanced over at Brian and then stood and as quietly as she could she made her way over to the mantel, retrieved the pouches and brought them back to the table. She again noticed how heavy the pouches were.

She sat the pouches down in front of the candle. She sat down, placed her arms and hands flat on the table, and rested her chin on the back of her hands. The pouches were right in front of her eyes.

She moved her eyes to look at Brian. He hadn't stirred. Then she brought her eyes back to the pouches.

What was in there she wondered? Was it even money? Maybe it was buttons, or tokens, or even just stones. There was only one way to find out for sure. But, what would Brian say?

She stared at the pouches for a few more minutes and then reached out and untied the leather strap that held the pouches together. She slowly slid the strap off of the table and let it drop to the floor. She then sat bolt upright with her hands at her side and looked over at Brian. He hadn't moved.

She reached out and with one finger began toying with the leather cinch that held the top of one of the pouches closed. She ran her finger slowly down the side of the pouch poking at it every so often. Sure felt like coins. There was only one way to find out.

She sat up and placed her hands in her lap. She sat very still for a few minutes glancing at Brian several times to make sure he wasn't stirring. Then she placed her hands back on the table one on each side of the pouch.

With one final glance at Brian, she reached up, loosened the cinch, and opened the top of the pouch. She reached in. If this wasn't a coin, it was a very large button.

She pulled it out.

It was a coin. But, what was it? She could not tell in the dim light of the single candle. She quietly stood and walked over to the fireplace and got two more candles off of the mantel. When she returned to the table she lit the two candles from the flame on the first candle. She could see now.

She didn't look at the coin. Instead she was focused on her sleeping husband. Was he going to be angry that she had opened the pouch? If so, how angry would he be?

She didn't care. Her curiosity had the better of her now and she decided that, if it took her all night, she was going to find out what was in the pouches whether Brian liked it or not.

She looked down at the coin, it was a shilling. One shilling. She reached into the pouch and took out another coin. Another shilling.

One by one, very slowly, she removed every coin from the leather pouch. Every coin in the pouch was a shilling, and as she removed them she stacked them in groups of five.

When she had finished she found that she had 11 stacks of five shillings each and a stack of four. A total of 59 shillings. The pouch had contained just shy of three pounds.

Her heart was pounding as she stared at the stacks of coins. That was more than she and Brian could make in a month. Very slowly and very carefully she moved each stack of coins aside making sure to keep the stacks even and in neat rows. She then placed the empty pouch aside as well.

She sat very rigidly at the small table with her hands again in her lap, and turned to look at Brian. He still slept. It was late now, but there was no way she could sleep... yet.

She turned back to the table and looked at the remaining pouch. What were the chances that this contained a similar amount? That the two pouches together could contain over five pounds? But, even if it did, was it right to keep it? They had no legal or moral right to it. What should they do?

As she reached for the second pouch she very quietly whispered, "That's not something I'm going to decide now anyway. But, I am going to find out what is in this pouch."

She pulled the pouch over so that it was directly in front of her. Then she brought her hands up to cover her mouth, took a deep breath, slowly and quietly exhaled, and then reached out, loosened the cinch, and opened the pouch.

She placed both hands flat on the table one on either side of the pouch. A quick glance at Brian confirmed that he was still sleeping. With one hand she reached into the open pouch.

She could already tell without removing her hand that whatever she was holding was not a shilling. If this was a coin it was larger than a shilling. She slowly pulled her trembling hand out.

When she had the coin out she held it up to the light and gasped as she quickly brought her free hand up to her mouth to keep from screaming right out loud. She turned toward Brian and couldn't believe that he had not been awakened by her gasp which to her in the stillness of the small shed had sounded like a clap of thunder. She turned back to the coin.

It was a crown. A crown. A crown was worth five shillings. If you had four crowns, you had a pound. Her heart was racing as she set the coin on the table and reached back into the pouch. She kept her other hand at her mouth afraid that at some point she might indeed scream out.

The second coin was also a crown, as was the third, and the fourth, and all the others that followed. As with the shillings, she stacked them in groups of five.

After she had removed what she thought was the final coin she again reached into the pouch to make sure she hadn't missed any coins. There were no more coins, but she did feel a piece of parchment. It felt greasy, and she tried not to think of what it might have on it that would make it feel that way. It also felt as if something were wrapped in it.

She removed her hand, and with her other hand, which she had long ago removed from her mouth, she reached over, picked up the pouch, and tilted it so that the parchment dropped into her open hand. Having forgotten about the stacks of crowns for the moment, she laid the small parchment package in front of her. She wiped her hands on the front of her dress.

She leaned over and closely examined the small package. She noticed that it smelled of bacon. Whatever was wrapped in that paper now, it had at one time been wrapped around bacon.

She slowly began to unwrap the package, hoping that she was not about to discover the remnants of what had once been someone's meal. Once the parchment was peeled back, she could only stare in disbelief at what it had concealed. She could not breathe and tears were beginning to well up into her eyes.

There were three of them, and even in the not so bright candle light they shined. A farmer's wife didn't get the chance to see these very often, but there they were, three British Sovereigns. Each one of those coins was worth a pound all by itself. Three pounds wrapped in bacon paper. She suppressed a giggle as she got the joke.

She carefully picked up each of the coins individually and as thoroughly as she could wiped them clean on her apron, spitting or huffing on them as necessary as she tried to get the greasy feel off of them and make them shine even more. Then she neatly stacked them in front of the candles.

Bridget then turned her attention back to the stacks of crowns. She now noticed that she had seven stacks of five crowns each and one stack of three. A total of 38 crowns. There were four crowns to a pound, so she had nine and a half pounds worth of crowns.

Stacked in neat rows on the table in front of her were 100 coins. 59 shillings, 38 crowns, and three Sovereigns. It would take her awhile to figure out just how much money that actually was but she did know that never before in her life had she seen so much money in one place.

As she did with the shillings, she carefully slid the stacks of crowns aside keeping the stacks even and placing them in neat rows. The Sovereigns she picked up and held in her hands. Then she crossed her arms on the table in front of her and rested her head on them. Just for a minute she thought, I've got to rest my head just for a minute.

When she woke up she lifted her head and saw Brian sitting at the table across from her. He was wrapped in the same woolen blanket he had slept in, and daylight now filled the room. She felt stiff and as she stretched she felt the large coins she still had tightly grasped in her hands, which reminded her of the coins on the table.

She glanced down at the coins and then looked up at Brian. He was drinking a cup of tea. It was then she noticed that there was also a cup of tea in front of her.

"Thank you," she said in the Irish.

"You're welcome," he nodded and smiled.

"What time is it?" She asked.

"We're well into the morning," he answered, "but, being a woman of means," he continued, "I don't imagine there's any need for you to be getting up early to gather laundry."

She spread her arms over the stacks of coins. "Isn't this amazing?" She said as she looked down on the stacks.

"It's what the road to a hangman's noose is paved with that's what it is," he said, not angrily but calmly. He looked at his wife. "We have to get rid of it you know."

"Brian, do you have any idea how much is here?" She said

"Yes," he said. "I do. 12 pounds, 1 crown, and 4 shillings."

"You're wrong," she said, as she opened her hands to reveal the three Sovereigns she had been holding. "15 pounds, 1 crown, and 4 shillings."

Brian reached across and took one of the Sovereigns and examined it. He felt his heart begin to beat faster and tried to remember the last time he had held a Sovereign.

"Brian, we have gathered about 12 pounds on our own, with this we will have close to 28, that's more than halfway to what we said we need."

"Are you forgetting that this is stolen?" He asked.

"No, I'm not," she answered. "Are you forgetting that he was an Englishman and that he tried to kill you?"

"It doesn't matter," he said. "It's stolen and we have no right to it."

"Did we have a right to our farm?"

"What?"

"Our farm," she repeated. "Did we have a right to our farm? Because the Englishman who stole that certainly didn't seem to think so."

"That's different," he said.

"How about that road?"

"What road?" He asked.

"That road you were on yesterday," she said. "Did you have a right to be on that road? Because the Englishman who tried to kill you certainly didn't seem to think so."

"None of that matters," he said trying to keep the anger out of his voice. "This money is stolen." He got up and walked over and stood in front of the fireplace with his back to the table.

Bridget was getting angry too, but not at Brian.

"Brian," she began. "These people took our farm, our home, our dreams of a happy life on land that belonged to us, on land where we would raise our children, on land that would someday become our children's, and what marvelous things have they done with it? Nothing, they've done nothing with it. Why? Because some new pastime has grabbed their interest that temporarily replaces the joy they get from stealing our own country from us so they can build grand, over-sized, empty, lonely houses.

"And then," she stood and was shaking her finger at Brian as her voice got louder, "and then, they decide that we can't even walk the roads in our own country. My God, Brian, an Englishman was going to kill you because you had the gall to be an Irishman in Ireland.

"Wasn't our farm, wasn't our dreams, wasn't your life worth 15 pounds, 1 crown, and four shillings?"

"I nearly killed a man," he said softly hanging his head.

"Not for the money," she said. "You didn't even know he had any money."

"So, you think we should keep the money?"

"Yes, I do. Lord knows it's a small pittance of what we're owed."

"And, if we're found out?"

"We hang. But, keeping it gets us that much closer to getting out of here and starting all over."

"And, for that you're willing to chance being hanged?"

"Where thou hangest," she said with a smile.

"We're both daft," he said returning the smile.

They gathered up the coins and put them back in the pouches. Brian dug out a hole behind the small fireplace's stones and they hid the pouches there. Unless you knew what to look for when Brian was finished it was almost impossible to detect.

Chapter 7

The Rancocas
1858

They had been chopping wood all afternoon and the wagon was pretty well filled. A young Michael McBride climbed up onto the seat and looked down onto the backs of the two muscular mules who were stomping their feet and shaking their heads causing the harness that held them to the wagon to dance and rattle. They were trained well enough to know not to go anywhere until they were told, but it was obvious that they were anxious to head back to the barn so they could be released from their trappings and be turned out to graze on the cool fresh grass in the paddock. Despite their training they could be difficult and would take advantage of any opportunity to try and have their way. Their names were Queen Charlotte and Lord Northrup.

The owner of the mules, William McBride, the grandson of Brian McBride, enjoyed telling anyone who asked that his mules had been named after a couple of royal jackasses.

The fidgeting mules made Michael a little nervous and he checked to make sure that the reins were securely tied and that the wagon's brake was well set. He wasn't afraid of them but he did respect them. On more than one occasion he had seen for himself just how powerful they could be, and how willful and temperamental they could be if not handled firmly.

Michael had driven the team on occasion but always with his father seated beside him, and always on short trips from the barn to the house, or to the end of the lane. The mules seemed to know that although the master did not hold the reins he was still there so, they tended to behave themselves. He liked to think he could handle them on his own, but looking down on them from the seat of the wagon it seemed the more he thought he could, the larger and stronger they appeared to grow.

"Michael!" His father's voice interrupted his thoughts. "Michael, are you awake, son?"

"Yes Sir," Michael stammered.

"Hand me down the gun," his father said as he removed his leather gloves and tossed them onto the wagon seat.

Michael turned and lifted the heavy musket, powder horn, and the leather pouch which held the round shot from behind the seat and handed them down to his father.

His father turned and looked toward the Rancocas Creek, and said, "I'm going to walk down along the creek and check the traps." He laid the barrel of the musket across his shoulder and continued, "If the opportunity presents itself maybe I'll get us some fresh meat."

Michael started to climb down from the wagon.

"Where're you going?" His father asked.

"With you."

"No," his father said. "I'll walk up from the creek and meet you back at the house. You take the wagon back to the barn, unhook the Queen and his Lordship there and turn them out. You can start unloading the wood and I'll give you a hand with the rest of it after supper."

Michael just stared at his father.

"What's the matter?" He asked.

"Well, um... I mean..."

"You can do it. I wouldn't let you if I didn't think so."

"Yes sir."

"If you don't want to now's the time to say so."

"No sir," Michael said confidently. "I can do this."

His father looked up at him and smiled. "I know you can," he said. Then he turned and started to walk away. After a few steps he turned around and called to his son, "Michael."

"Yes sir."

"Three things."

"Yes sir?"

"One, make sure they know that you're in charge. Two, they'll know if you let your guard down so be careful, and three, use your head, I already have two jackasses hooked to the front of the wagon, I don't need a third sitting up on top." Then he laughed, turned, and walked away.

Michael stared after his father not sure how to take what he had said. Then he chuckled to himself, turned and sat back down on the wagon seat. With one hand on each side of him tightly gripping the front edge of the seat, he looked down on the mules again, this time from a whole new perspective.

These mules were valuable. Without them the work on the farm would grind almost to a complete halt. It would take nearly a year of the income the farm produced to replace them if something should happen to them. He was about to take on an awesome responsibility. He wiped his hands on the front of his shirt. As he was reaching for the reins he looked down and noticed his father's leather gloves lying on the seat next to him. Knowing that his father rarely went anywhere without the gloves he picked them up and turned to look in the direction his father had gone, but he had already disappeared into the trees that lead down to the creek.

He had his own gloves, they were worn out, dried out, stiff, too big, and were more hand sewn repairs than leather. They used to be his father's, but these were his father's. He slipped his father's gloves on. They were more than a little big but just having them on helped boost his confidence, these were man gloves. He untied the reins, took them in his gloved hands the way his father had taught him, and held them as he looked down along their length to where they connected him to the animals. He felt a strange sense of power.

He released the brake, slapped the reins across their backs, and in the deepest most commanding voice he could muster he repeated the words he had heard his father say so many times, "Let's go your highnesses, go on now!"

The mules turned their heads and looked back at him, and he thought to himself, they know.

They started to move, slowly at first, as the wagon full of wood must have been quite heavy. They soon settled down to a steady pace, and Michael said to no one in particular, "Well alright then, this is going to be good."

He took one hand off the reins and smugly pulled the brim of his tattered floppy slouch hat down further on his brow.

Then he noticed that Lord Northrup seemed to be walking faster than Queen Charlotte. At the same time she was trying to pull him to the right causing him to pull back and the wagon to weave back and forth on the narrow dirt road. The more he pulled on the reins trying to get them back under control the worse it got. They hadn't gone more than a couple of hundred yards and already there was trouble.

Finally, putting his feet against the foot board and taking a tight grip on the reins he used his legs and his arms, closed his eyes, and with a loud grunt pulled back on the reins as hard as he could almost lying down in the process. He heard the animals snort and felt the wagon come to a jarring halt. Had he been watching he would have seen that he actually caused Queen Charlotte to rear up onto her hind legs.

He opened his eyes and sat with the reins held taut while he caught his breath. The mules were standing perfectly still, and staring straight ahead. He set the brake, tied the reins to the brake handle, and jumped down from the wagon.

He paced back and forth alongside the wagon a few times while muttering to himself in an effort to slow his heartbeat, and settle his nerves. Then he walked around and stood in front of the animals with his hands on his hips. They eyed him suspiciously. He reached up and grabbed both of them by the bit and pulled their heads in toward each other so he could look both of them in the eyes at the same time.

He was angry but he did not speak loudly, instead he spoke slowly and firmly. "Listen," he said. "We are going to the barn and we are going to go there without all of this nonsense. We will stop every ten feet and have this conversation over, and over, and over again if necessary. So I'll let you decide whether or not we're going to make this trip as friends or not, and how long it's going to take."

He released the bits but neither mule lifted its head. He got back up on the wagon. He sat there for a minute and noticed that the mules had not moved a muscle or made a sound since he had pulled them to a stop. He was concerned that maybe he had pulled on the reins so hard that he had injured them.

He untied the reins, released the brake, but just sat there a minute.

"I'm not my father but he did put me in charge!" He hollered out to the mules. Then he sighed heavily and said in a voice that was strictly his own, "Alright my friends let's go home." Then he slapped the reins down across their backs.

At first nothing happened. Then slowly and steadily they began to pull. The single lane dirt road had a few twists and turns but it was just over a mile to the barn and a short time later they arrived without any further problems. After coming to a stop he sat there for a minute with a huge grin on his face trying not to let the overwhelming sense of pride he felt come spilling out of him.

His mother came out onto the back porch, wiping her hands on her apron, she called, "Where's your father?"

"He's checking our traps along the creek." Since he could now handle the mules, he thought it only natural that he also claim part ownership of the traps.

"Who brought the team up?"

"I did," he replied.

It didn't appear she'd heard him. She looked around the yard and repeated her original question, "Where's your father?"

"Down by the creek."

She said nothing but turned and went back into the house.

He called after her, "I brought the team up all by myself, all the way from Groves' woods!" But she was already gone and didn't hear him.

That she didn't hear him had no effect on his mood though, still grinning, he jumped down from the wagon, unhooked the team from the yoke, and led them into the barn to take the harness off of them. Queen Charlotte stood completely still and calmly allowed him to remove her trappings as he talked quietly to her about nothing in particular.

Lord Northrup did the same until he was removing the last leather strap. All of a sudden his Lordship turned and bit Michael, nipping him on the left shoulder. Then, when Michael jumped back the mule flipped his tail, sharply slapping Michael right across the face. The mule then calmly walked a short distance away. Michael laughed right out loud as he rubbed his sore shoulder and wiped his face. "I guess we're truly friends now," he said, and then turned them out into the paddock.

When he walked back into the barn rubbing his shoulder he noticed that his father was hanging up a freshly killed and gutted tom turkey. His father saw him rubbing his shoulder and said, "Let your guard down a little did ya?"

"Yes," he said, and chuckled. "I thought we were friends."

"Well, even a friend will bite you sometimes." His father laughed. "Come on let's go in and see what your mother is up to and then we'll unload that wagon."

They started towards the house. As they passed the wagon his father stopped and retrieved his leather gloves from the seat. He put his hand on his son's head and playfully pushed his hat down over his eyes as they continued across the yard.

As they entered the house through the squeaky backdoor, Joanna McBride, wife of William and Michael's mother, called out, "Remove your shoes! I'll not be sweeping this floor again today nor will I be picking up pieces of whatever animal's droppings the two of you have tramped through!"

The man and his son smiled at each other and did as they were told, neither one wanting to challenge this woman in her own kitchen. When they entered the kitchen she was dumping water from a bucket into the copper lined sink with her back to them. Brian McBride was nearly a foot taller than his wife. He walked up behind her and placed a kiss directly on top of her head. She smiled, swatted at him with a towel, and called him a fool.

"Now you two sit down and I'll get you some cider," she said. After pouring the drinks she sat down opposite her son and said, "So, anything different happen today?"

"Just chopping wood," her husband said as he sipped his cider. "Wood's wood, wanna get it in and give it a chance to season before the cold weather hits."

"I'll need some for the cooking too you know, whether it's cold or not, unless you prefer your meat raw," she said.

"There's plenty for the cooking," he said.

"So, nothing new?"

"No, just another day on the banks of the Rancocas," he answered. "After we cut what we need for the winter and for cooking," he said as he rolled his eyes in his wife's direction who playfully slapped him with her towel. "We'll use some of the wood from the east woods to build some fences and then take some to be milled for repairs to some of the out buildings in case we need it." He sighed, leaned back in his chair, and ran his hands through his thick dark hair as he glanced out the window at the setting sun. "Days are starting to get shorter too," he said.

Michael was about to burst. He wanted to scream out to his mother that he had brought the team up all by himself. But, it seemed no one but him considered it big news! He was 12-years old, nearly 13 really, and was poised on the brink of manhood. This just wasn't different, this just wasn't new, this was a milestone! He kept his eyes glued to his cider otherwise they might give away his anxiety.

"Oh," his father said. "Did I tell you what Michael did?"

Finally, here it comes. He raised his eyes and looked at his father, he felt his face begin to flush, and his chest begin to pound as he waited for his father to tell his mother what a great job he did of bringing the team up all by himself. That he was becoming a man.

"No," she answered. "What did Michael do?" As she smiled and looked expectedly at her son.

"Well," his father began. "As we were loading the wagon he went to kick this small branch aside, so he hauled off and gave it a real wail with his foot. Well, it turns out," and now he started to laugh, he caught his breath and started again, "it turns out it was actually a root!" Now he was really laughing, "Well, he wailed that ol' root and it did not budge! Well, he grabs his foot and begins yelping like a stepped on dog, and started hoppin' around like a one legged chicken! I near fell over from laughing so hard!"

Now, his mother joined in the laughter. She covered her mouth with her towel, reached across the table for his hand and said, "Oh, Michael darlin', you're not hurt are you? Do you want me to look at your foot? Does it need tending to?" She asked through her laughter.

"No," he said curtly. "It doesn't hurt, and it wasn't all that funny."

How humiliating! A stepped on dog, a one legged chicken? What should have been one of the proudest days of his young life was now nothing more than an embarrassment. He kept his eyes glued on the tabletop and wanted nothing more than to get away. How could they do this to him?

"Michael," his father said as he stood up and began to walk around the table. He had stopped laughing.

"Yes sir?" He said. He was confused, his father always walked around when he scolded him about something and his voice had that scolding tone. Was he about to be scolded? Did he do something wrong? Was the wagon damaged? Were the mules injured?

"Michael?" He asked as he laid his gloves on the table. "Did you use my gloves today?"

This was about the gloves, the gloves?! He looked down at the well-worn leather gloves that had felt so good on his hands a short time ago and couldn't believe this was happening, he was speechless, the gloves? He looked across the table at his mother but her face revealed nothing. He turned to his father who stood in front of the kitchen cupboard with his back to his son. Michael couldn't believe it, he really was in trouble.

"Well, did you?" His father asked again.

"Well, um…. I don't … I mean… yes sir I did, but…"

His father put his hand up, stopping Michael in mid-sentence as he tried to explain, as he tried to understand what was happening here.

"In the future I would prefer that you not use my gloves," he said.

All he could do was nod at his father, he was doing all he could to hold back the tears that were beginning to creep into his eyes, he did not want to cry, not today, not when he was this close to manhood.

"I would prefer that you use your own," he said and with that tossed a brown paper package onto the table in front of Michael.

Michael looked up at his father and then across at his mother, both of who were flashing great big smiles. His mother looked like she was about to cry. He looked back down at the package, and then back to his father.

"Go ahead," he said. "Open it."

The smile on Michael's face was so wide that his teeth hurt. His eyes were so big that he must have looked like an old hoot owl. It was all he could do to keep from just ripping into the package.

Instead, he very carefully untied the string and folded back the paper. There in front of him was a brand new pair of store bought leather gloves, and they were his, and no one had ever worn them before. He again looked up at his father and across at this mother.

"Go ahead, try them on," his father said. "It's important that leather gloves fit you well when you're handling a team. It gives you a better feel for what they're doing and protects your hands from getting burns and blisters from handling the reins."

Michael picked them up and rubbed them between his thumb and fingers. The leather was soft and pliable yet rugged and firm. He slipped them on, they fit, they fit good, they fit… well they fit, they fit like a glove he thought. He held his hand up to show both his parents his man's gloves, and they both applauded.

"I'm proud of you son, you did very well today," his father said.

He looked across at his mother who was nodding and crying, and holding the towel up to her face.

"My goodness woman," his father said. "Will you quit crying and get your men something to eat?"

"He's not my little boy anymore," she said between sobs.

"No, he's not," his father said as he sat down and reached across and rubbed his son's head. "We'll have to see how things go," he continued, "but come next spring when it's time to do the plowing I believe you may be ready to take a team. If you are it will make a big difference in what we can plant, grow, and harvest. You're not quite a man yet son, but you can be real proud of how much closer you are today. I know I am."

"Thank you," he said keeping his head down so his father wouldn't see that this almost man was struggling very hard to keep the tears that were welling up in his eyes from falling onto his face. However, had he looked up he would have seen that his father had his head down too.

His father cleared his throat with a not so real cough, yawned a not so real yawn, rubbed his eyes and said, "Now tell us Michael, how did everything go on your trip up from Groves' woods?"

Michael proudly relayed his story, about how the mules had not pulled properly at first, about how he yanked on the reins, and got down from the wagon and had a chat with the mules, and how his Lordship had nipped him and slapped him in the face, and they all laughed and talked as Michael told parts of his story over and over again. They talked through supper and right up to bedtime.

The wagon never got unloaded, and Michael never took his gloves off.

It had been a big day for Michael, a new stage of his life had begun, and from that day forward Michael always wore a good pair of leather gloves whenever he was working. In fact, when the running of the farm became his responsibility, he made sure that anyone who worked with or for him was also provided with a good pair of leather gloves, and every time he handed out a pair he was reminded of his father, and that day along the Rancocas.

Chapter 8

The Maigue
1789

A few weeks after Brian's encounter with the man on the road to Limerick, a story was circulating around the area that a local tea peddler, whose reputation for honesty was at best questionable, employed by an English tea merchant, reported that he had been accosted in broad daylight by a band of Whiteboys on a country road south of Limerick. He claimed that there had been at least five of them and that they had been armed. He also said that the leader was so arrogant that he did not even try to conceal his face beneath his white shirt.

According to the peddler, despite the fact that he had complied with their every demand, they not only stole his cargo of teas, and the few coins he had in his pocket, but they purposely disabled his wagon and that the leader was such a barbarian that just for fun he crippled the peddler and left him for dead. He couldn't understand why the authorities could not collect these outlaws and bring them to justice. He warned his fellow hucksters, if you travel the roads of Munster be particularly wary of this especially vicious band of rebels.

When Brian first heard the story there was no doubt in his mind that this tea peddler had been the man on the road to Limerick. When he relayed the story to Bridget he thought it interesting that he had become the leader of a band of armed Whiteboys, that he had stolen the man's cargo of tea, and that the man had only had a few coins in his pocket. Why had he reported the tea which had not been stolen, stolen, and why had he not reported the pouches full of coins stolen?

They decided that the peddler, being dishonest to begin with, probably was able to sell the tea to make back what had been in the pouches, but kept the money for himself thereby cheating his employer out of the tea and the money. As far as Brian being the leader of a band of vicious Whiteboys, he obviously did not want it to be known that he had been bested by a lone Irishman who had actually been trying to help him.

As the days past, Brian thought about his encounter on the road to Limerick and the story that had come of it. It seemed to him that it wasn't only the Irish who could conjure up a good fairy's tale, but it also occurred to him that there might be an opportunity here. He had been thinking about what Bridget had said about what was taken from them and what they were owed in return.

It was a day around the middle of November. Brian told Bridget that he was going to Limerick to see if there was any work on the docks. He bid her farewell and started walking northwest towards Limerick. But, as soon as he was sure he was well out of sight, he turned and giving a wide berth to the small shed, his cousin's farm, and anyone else around Mungret who might see him, he made his way to a narrow road that lead south, away from Limerick.

After walking about a half mile Brian came to an intersection where he turned west. He walked for almost another two miles before he came to another intersection with a road that ran north and south. He knew that this road was used by merchants travelling between the villages of Aldare and Clarina. He turned and walked north and after a short distance found himself in an area where the road was bordered on both sides by woods.

He left the road and walked into the woods just far enough so that he could still see the road but so that he could not easily be seen. He found a log and sat down. He reached into his coat and pulled out a white shirt that he had taken without Bridget's knowledge. He waited. As hour after hour, several travelers passed by. Most appeared to be farmers or other common folk just going from one place to another. One fine looking coach did pass by but the coachman appeared to be someone who was prepared to deal with delays, so Brian remained hidden.

It was about midafternoon, and Brian was cold and ready to give up when he thought he heard singing. He moved closer to the edge of the road and hid himself behind a large tree. Approaching from the south was a spring coach, not unlike the one that the tea peddler had been trying to repair. It was being pulled by a single horse, and the driver whose dress obviously identified him as a man of business, was singing and appeared to be intoxicated.

Brian took the white shirt and pulled it over his head so that his face was concealed but he had cut holes in it so that he could still see. As the horse drew even with Brian's tree, Brian stepped into the road and grabbed the horse's bridle bringing the horse and the coach to a stop. The startled horse tried to rear and it took Brian a few seconds to get the horse under control.

The man appeared surprised but was definitely more annoyed than frightened. Brian began to have second thoughts.

"Here, here," he said. "What is it yer about dere?"

Brian said nothing. He hadn't even thought about what he should say or was supposed to say while committing a robbery.

The man stood up and pointed at Brian. "Why are ya holdin' me 'orse?" He asked as he wobbled.

Brian got his wits about him. "Ya can proceed no further 'til yas 'ave paid da toll," he said.

"Dis ain't a toll road," the man said waving his arms around.

"T'is t'day," said Brian.

The man sat down hard, crossed his legs, put his elbow on his knee, rested his chin on his hand, and studied Brian.

He pointed and said, "You've a sack o'er yer 'ead." As if he had just made some important discovery. "Ya mus' be one o' dem white heads."

"Whiteboys," said Brian.

"Are ya da outlaw den what waylaid Jack Anderson up near Limerick and broke his leg?"

"Da tea peddler?" Brian asked.

"Dat be him."

"Yes," Brain said. "Dat be's us."

"Us?" Said the man as he belched. "Ya means to say dere are more o' ya den?"

This was not going as Brian had expected.

"Me companions are hidden in da woods on both sides o' da road."

"Hidden are dey?" He said looking around. "Well, I'll tank ya ta be takin' dat silly sack off yer head, and tell 'em ta come out, I'd like ta see 'em."

"I won't, and dey can't come out. T'is an ambush we're about," said Brian who was getting more and more frustrated. "Dey must remain hidden, and I warns ya, dey are heavily armed dey are."

"Oh, an ambush is it, and heavily armed? Well, I'll be makin' me apologies," he said. "T'was not me intention ta disrupt yer ambush. What do ya want o' me den?"

"Money."

"Ah yes, da day's toll. How much is it den?" He asked as he reached down and picked up a leather pouch off the floor of the coach nearly falling head first out of the coach in the process. The pouch was almost identical to those the tea peddler had carried.

"Jus' trow da pouch into da road," Brian said.

"My good man, I'll not be payin' anymore den da amount dat's due me I won't," said the man as he struggled to open the top of the pouch. His speech was becoming more and more slurred as their conversation went on.

"Da amount t'is all dat yer holdin'," said Brian who was tiring of trying to reason with this drunken fool.

"Dat hardly seems fair," he said not looking up as he still struggled with the pouch.

Brian released the horse and walked up and stood beside the coach and looked up at the man. "Listen ya drunken eejit," he said as menacingly as he could. "I broke yer friend's leg 'cause he was about pissing me off. Yer beginnin' to try me patience a bit as well. Now, ya toss dat pouch down into da road or I'll pull ya off dis coach, trow ya down into da dirt, and break both o' yer legs."

The man smiled. He looked at Brian as if he'd never seen him before. "Da pouch?" He asked. "In da road? Well o' course me good man, why didn't yas say so." With that he stood and unsteadily tossed the pouch into the road. "Now, if you'll be excusin' me." He turned, stumbled over the coach seat and fell headlong into the bed of the coach, and within seconds was snoring loudly.

Brian was dumbfounded as he stood looking into the coach at the sleeping man. He laughed, bent down picked up the pouch, removed the white shirt from over his head and shoved it back inside his coat, dropped the pouch down the front of his shirt, and began walking south on the road back the way he had come earlier that day. When he came to the intersection he turned toward the west instead of back towards the east, just in case someone was watching or following him. When he was well out of sight of the intersection he circled back around and eventually was headed east again, and then north towards home.

It was just after dark when Brian got home. He showed Bridget the white shirt and told her that he had decided that since he could only be hung once he might as well try and obtain as much money as he could while he could. If they're luck held they would get enough to leave before he had to face the gallows. So, today he had robbed a man on the Adare road.

Bridget was furious. What if he had gotten caught? What if this man had had a gun? Why didn't he talk to her about this before deciding to commit a second robbery?

Brian's answer to every question was the same. He did not want her to worry. Besides, the whole thing was kind of her idea, it was even her who had mentioned the Whiteboys.

Then he relayed what a comedy of errors the great robbery had been. They laughed themselves breathless as Brian told her of his loss for words once he got the horse and coach stopped. He had no idea what the script for a robbery was, and of how the poor man's drunkenness had infuriated and frustrated his attempts at being an intimidating highwayman. And, finally about how the man had finally just given up the money and fallen over into the coach and passed out.

As almost an afterthought Brian pulled the pouch out of his shirt. It wasn't as heavy as the tea peddler's pouches but it was quite full and its weight was promising.

"Anseo, go bhfuil tu ar n-bainceir."

"Here, you're our banker," Brian said as he handed the bag to Bridget.

Bridget set the pouch on the table in front of her and went through nearly the whole routine she had used the night she opened the tea peddler's pouches. Brian found it entertaining and amusing as he anxiously waited for her to discover what the pouch held. After finally opening the pouch, she very slowly and very deliberately started removing the coins. As before she stacked the coins in groups of five in neat rows.

The first four coins she pulled out were pennies. Then she pulled out five shillings, then a few more pennies, and then two crowns. When all was said and done they found that there had been 48 coins in the pouch. There were 24 pennies, 15 shillings, and nine crowns. The total proceeds from the robbery was two pounds, three crowns, and 2 shillings. The amount of their fortune was now 30 pounds, four crowns, and one shilling.

Brian had committed two robberies. The first of which had been a fight for his life with no expectation of ending up with any money, and the second was more like a minstrel show than a crime. Brian had already decided that he was going to do it again, if for no other reason than to try and get one right.

In the weeks that followed, Brian committed three additional robberies. One south of Adare, one south of Croom, and the most recent east of Limerick near Ballyneety. In each case Brian made sure that he was at least eight miles from the shed in Mungret.

These had gone much smoother than the first two. Brian, with the white shirt over his head, had simply burst from an area of concealment, shouted orders to hidden but nonexistent accomplices, and demanded money in return for life. He had also taken to holding a large stick under his shirt as if he were concealing a weapon. The money was generally surrendered without too much protest.

It seems, between the tea peddler with the broken leg, and the drunken man who must have split his head open when he fell into the bed of the coach, reporting that the injury was the result of him having been beaten into unconsciousness, Brian had become quite feared for the violence of his crimes. As part of his more recent crimes, after securing the money Brian would blindfold and bind the victim and leave them to be found. He would then disappear back into the woods or fields and slowly and circuitously make his way back to the small shed in Mungret.

As a result of Brian's additional crimes and their other labors they had acquired an additional 13 pounds. Their fortune now totaled 43 pounds, one crown, and two shillings. All safely hidden behind the stones in the shed's small fireplace.

Brian had just arrived home from a day at the mill and was enjoying a smoke while Bridget prepared supper when there were a series of raps on the door. The raps meant nothing to Bridget, but they were known to Brian and indicated that whoever was on the other side of the door may be familiar with the fraternity. Brian went to the door and gave a corresponding rap on the inside of the door. He received an answer confirming the affiliation.

When Brian opened the door there was a man, whose dress might have identified him as a clerk or bookkeeper, he was holding the reins of a fine looking saddle horse. Brian extended his hand and they shared a grip familiar to them both.

"Dearthair Brian McBride?"

"Brother Brian McBride?" The man asked.

Brian nodded.

"I am Brother Charles Kelly, Junior Deacon of Limerick #271. I bring a message from the Worshipful Master. May I come in?"

"Certainly Brother Kelly," Brian replied in the Irish. He started through the door and said, "Let me tend to your horse."

The man stopped him. "I'll just tether him out here," he said. "I won't be staying long."

"Very well," said Brian, "but, I'll have my wife prepare some tea."

"Thank you but that won't be necessary," said the messenger.

The man tethered the animal and entered the small one room shed.

"My wife Bridget," said Brian. He offered him a chair at the table but he politely refused.

"I've spent the good part of the day in the saddle," he said with a smile. "A pleasure to meet you Mrs. McBride," he added and bowed slightly in Bridget's direction. He then reached into an inside pocket and removed a sealed envelope. There was nothing written on the envelope. "I was directed to deliver this to you personally," he said. "Having done so, I shall take my leave."

"You sure you won't have something to drink or eat?" Bridget asked.

"No, thank you ma'am. It's best that I return to Limerick"

He and Brian shook hands at the door, and the messenger left, mounted his horse, and rode off in the direction of Limerick.

Brian returned to the table and sat down opposite Bridget. He held the envelope in front of him with two hands and kept turning it. "I wonder what's happening at the Lodge that warrants such a delivery."

"You won't know if you don't open it," said Bridget.

Brian opened the envelope, removed the letter inside, and began to read.

Friend,

I recently traveled to places east of the city. While in that area I observed a flier. The flier offered a reward for the capture of the man whose likeness appeared on the flier. I must admit I found it unsettling that there were more than a few similarities between the features of the man depicted and you. To avoid any unpleasantness as a result of this confusion I would suggest that you refrain from visiting the city or its immediate area until this matter is resolved. I wish you well.

A Friend

Brian handed the note to Bridget to read. This changed everything. Now they were afraid. Brian was a wanted man, and if he was found he would surely hang.

They decided that they could no longer stay in the small shed on Brian's cousin's farm. Not only did they not want to get anyone else involved, but they were ashamed of what they had been reduced to. They lied and told everyone they were going to Dublin to find work so no one they knew looked for them or expected to see them anywhere.

The poster the Worshipful Master had seen was hung on a wall outside a pub southeast of Limerick near Ballyneety. This was where the tea merchant, who employed the tea peddler, had his business. The pub was about six miles from a small clearing in the woods on the banks of the River Maigue south of Mungret. It was in this clearing a few days later that Brian built them a tiny one room hut from fieldstones, fallen trees, branches, and sod in which to hide. Their fortune was buried in a hole beneath the pile of grasses, leaves, and mosses that had become their bed.

The Maigue flowed northwest out of Ireland's central flatlands for nearly 40 miles until it joined with the great River Shannon about nine miles south of Limerick. The Maigue was well used by locals and turf boats but because of its tricky currents and shifting sandbars was never an important waterway.

They had sold most of their furniture and possessions when they had lost the farm. Most of what they had left Brian's cousin had agreed to store on the farm until they had found a place and gotten settled in Dublin. The only things they had with them in the hut were their clothes, two rickety wooden chairs Brian had found on the side of the road, some cookware, and a couple of tin plates and cups

It was January and although daytime temperatures were generally near 50 degrees, they were often below freezing at night. They would sometimes have a small turf fire, but were ever mindful of the smoke and the distinct odor of a turf fire, and the risk of being found. They were after all criminals in hiding.

The hut was about five miles from where their farm used to be. They had lost the farm the previous May and within days the house and barn had been destroyed, but nothing had been done in the eight months since. The ruined pile of rubble and ashes that had once been their home was just as it was when the walls had been toppled, and the fires had burned themselves out. Perhaps His Lordship, Lord Northrup, had changed his mind about building his grand house.

They had been living in the hut for about two weeks. Most everything they needed they had to scavenge for, including food. This was not going well, and they were getting hungry.

They decided that it was worth the risk for Bridget to walk the two miles into Clarina to visit the small mercantile there. She was not wanted, yet, and there was little chance of running into anyone who knew them. The shopping trip was a success, Bridget was able to get them some potatoes, tea, and some dried meats.

Brian waited for Bridget in a wooded area about a quarter mile from the hut just off the road from Clarina. When he saw her approaching he stepped out into the road and waved. She waved back.

Suddenly Bridget stopped, she dropped the packages she was carrying, fell to her knees, and brought her hands up to her face. Something she could see behind Brian had terrified her. Brian slowly turned.

Standing in the road behind him were three men. It was obvious that they were well armed. They must have been hiding in the same stand of woods that Brian had been in.

They began walking towards Brian. There was no place to run. Brian dropped his head in resignation and waited.

When the men got to where Brian was standing the one in the center, obviously the leader, spoke.

"Ta tu ag Brian McBride."

"You are Brian McBride." It was not a question it was a statement. These men knew who he was. Brian could only nod.

All three of the men were dressed as laborers would be. The one Brian assumed to be the leader might have been around 30, but the other two were closer to Brian's age. The leader was a few inches shorter than Brian but was stockier and of a muscular build. He wore a light colored tam that had shocks of hair that was almost blonde sticking out from underneath it. One of the other two was heavy but obviously powerful. He had a full dark beard and wore a bowler that came almost all the way down over his ears. The third man was closer to Brian's size, was clean shaven and hatless and wore his dark hair close cropped. These were not men to be challenged.

The leader looked around Brian towards where Bridget was still kneeling in the road and motioned for the clean shaven man to go to her. Brian started to move to confront the man. The leader reached out and put his hand on Brian's arm.

"No harm will come to her," he said in the Irish.

Brian looked at the leader and felt confident that he was telling the truth. He nodded and allowed the man to pass.

"We mean no harm to either of you," the leader said.

When the man who had gone to Bridget returned he was carrying the packages she had dropped, and had Bridget by the upper arm. She was quietly crying and was afraid, but had not been harmed.

"We'll be joining you for supper," the leader said. Then he nodded to the bearded man who turned and walked back up the road and into the woods where the trio had obviously been hiding. He then looked at Brian and Bridget and said, "At your place." He smiled and indicated to Brian that he and Bridget should lead the way.

No one spoke during the walk to the little hut in the clearing on the banks of the Maigue. When they arrived Brian turned to the two men, the bearded man had not returned, and said, "Home sweet home. Won't you come in?"

The leader turned to his companion and said, "Build us a good cook fire." He saw the look of concern on Brian's face and said, "Don't worry, we'll not be disturbed." Then he took the packages his companion was carrying and accompanied Brian and Bridget into the hut. "Quite a step down from the cottage on your farm isn't it," he said as he sat Bridget's packages on the dirt floor.

Brian and Bridget looked at each other. They were still afraid and uncertain as to where all of this was leading.

"Sir," Brian said. "For what purpose are you here?"

"That will be made clear enough Brian McBride," he answered. "For now, just rest assured that we mean you no harm. We're all Irish here." He then turned and went back outside.

"Who are they?" Asked Bridget when the man had left.

"I don't know. But, I believe him when he says they mean us no harm."

"What shall we do?"

"Wait and see what happens." They then went outside to join the men.

The clean shaven man had a good fire going and was gathering more wood from around the edge of the clearing. The leader was standing in front of the fire. The bearded man, who had left them on the road, entered the clearing carrying two bundles.

The first bundle he handed to the leader who laid it against the outside of the hut. The second bundle he laid on the ground near the fire and as he unrolled it Brian noticed that it contained several large portions of fresh venison, potatoes, several loaves of bread, and a medium sized keg. The bearded man lifted the keg, looked at Brian, smiled, and said, "Ale."

"I have a fondness for fresh venison," said the leader to Brian, "and nothing improves the taste of fresh venison like ale. Don't you agree?"

"I'm afraid we don't get venison very often, in fact, I don't remember the last time I had it, but I've always found that ale improves the taste of just about everything," answered Brian.

"Quite right," said the leader.

Brian and Bridget brought out the two rickety chairs and the utensils that they had and with the three strangers enjoyed a superb meal. Very little was said while the meal was being prepared or while it was eaten. Brian and Bridget shared the thought that if this was a last meal, then it was a very good one.

At one point Brian asked the leader if he and his men had names. The leader said that they did but that their names were not important. Brian accepted that he would just have to wait to see what these men wanted of them.

"Thank you," said Brian when they had finished. "We don't get to eat that well very often anymore."

"Yes," said the leader. "It does appear that there has been quite a change in your circumstances."

"You seem to know quite a bit about us," said Brian. "While I know nothing of you."

"Brian and Bridget McBride," the leader said turning to face them. "We," and he spread his arms to indicate he was including his two companions, "are members of a traveling band of performers. We do have names, but our names would mean nothing to you and are not important. We have come here to ask you, Brian, if you would be interested in joining our troupe."

"Me?" Said Brian with a confused smile. "I'm afraid I have no talent or experience that would make me suitable for such an offer."

"Haven't you?" The leader asked.

"I don't believe so," Brian answered.

"Let me see if I can explain," said the leader. "We perform for very select audiences. Almost exclusively English. Not only are the audiences select, but they are small, usually only one or two in attendance during a performance. We encourage, rather strongly actually, audience participation, and while we do not charge an admission fee, we do accept contributions at or near the end of the performance. Do you understand?"

"No," said Brian. "I'm afraid I don't."

"Our stage is often a lonely country road. Our audiences are not always willing participants and sometimes unfortunately, as the plot unfolds, an audience member may be injured."

Brian's heart rate began to increase and he was beginning to get an idea of what this man was trying to tell him.

"We wear one piece costumes but there is never any doubt of who our characters are or their intentions."

It hit Brian like a brick. These were Whiteboys. Real Whiteboys, not impostors like him. Now he understood, and now he was afraid again, for both of them.

"Since we know," continued the leader. "That you have been traveling here about portraying the same characters and performing the same show, we felt it only fair that we offer you the opportunity to join our band."

"Well, I...," began Brian.

The leader held up his hand to stop Brian. "Allow me to finish," he said. "In the hopes that you would turn us down."

Brian who was now completely confused just stared at the man.

"You see Brian McBride," the leader went on. "You aren't very good at it, and we cannot allow you, who our critics now believe are one of us, to be captured. If they think they have captured one of us they may begin to believe they can capture more of us. Since we know our cause to be a just political cause, despite our reputation as criminals, we cannot allow our enemies even the smallest of victories. Now do you understand Brian McBride?"

"I believe so," Brian said. "I'm to give no more performances, but I was already done with that anyway, but what happens now? I can't help but feel there's more to your visit than the delivery of this message."

"There is," the leader said with a smile. "You and your wife are leaving Ireland."

Bridget gasped and grabbed Brian's sleeve. It took a few seconds for the man's words to register. "We are?" Finally was the best he could do.

The leader nodded. "You are."

"Where?" Asked Brian.

"America."

"When?"

"Soon," said the leader.

"I'm not sure we've got enough money," Brian said.

The leader stood up and walked over to the bundle that he had leaned against the hut. He untied one of the bindings, reached inside the bundle and pulled out a leather pouch. Brian couldn't help but wonder if everyone in Ireland carried their money in a leather pouch.

He handed the pouch to Brian. "There are ten pounds in crowns in there," he said. "Add that to whatever you have and it will be enough. It's going to have to be, because there will be no more."

Brian looked at the pouch and then back at the man. "But..., he stammered.

"It's alright," said the man as he reached out and touched Brian's arm. "It's from a friend."

"A friend?" Brian asked.

"Yes," said the leader. "We performed for him just a few days ago. In fact he was so pleased with our performance that he insisted that I accept this as a token of his appreciation."

Brian stared speechless at the object the man reached over and pulled from the bundle. Then he began to laugh, then they all began to laugh. For the first time in months Brian felt as if an incredible burden had been lifted from his shoulders.

"May I?" Brian asked.

"Certainly," said the leader as he handed Brian the object.

Brian couldn't believe he was holding it. Even in the dim glow of the fire it glistened. He was certain that this exquisite ebony walking stick with its ornate gold knob was a sign that from here on things were going to be alright.

"Now," said the man. "Why don't you and Bridget go on in and get some sleep. Don't be afraid to build a fire if you're cold, we'll be nearby. No one will disturb you."

"Thank you," Brian and Bridget said almost in unison.

"You're welcome," said the man with a smile. "Now get some sleep, we're going to church tomorrow, and we'll talk more then." With that the men gathered up their belongings and disappeared from the clearing.

They did have a fire, but they didn't sleep. All they could think about and talk about was America. America, they had never even considered America. What a marvelous idea, and with Lord Northrup's generous "contribution" to their cause they were sure they now had enough money.

But why were they going to church? They finally did sleep, peacefully, and warmly, wrapped in each other's arms.

Chapter 9

The Catoctin
1859

Katherine Rosemary Calhoun sat staring across the creek and quietly watched as the afternoon mid-June sun began its decent over South Mountain to the west. She was wearing her new cotton dress. It was woven with a blue and yellow diamond pattern up the sides, white linen cording crisscrossed up the front of the bodice, and the three buttons on the front were also covered with white linen thread. Her grandmother had purchased the expensive dress for her in Baltimore.

It was quite beautiful, but she didn't like wearing dresses. She only had three besides this one. A cotton print that was reserved for mass and special occasions, and two plain homespun ones that she wore around the house when she had to. Otherwise she dressed like a boy.

She was sitting on a log with her bare feet dangling just above the waters of the creek. She had kicked the shoes off the minute she was out of everyone's sight. She knew that the log was dirty and that she was probably ruining the dress, but none of that seemed to matter. She was losing her best friend today.

Katherine was 11-years old. She tried to control her sobs as large tears fell from her emerald green eyes, ran down her face, and dripped onto her dress. It probably wasn't good for the dress either that every once in a while she was using the sleeve to wipe her nose. She had never felt so alone.

She remembered that it had been a little over a year ago that her brother Mark had gotten married and left the farm. She had been sad then too, but not like this. Mark and his wife Violet had bought a small farm just this side of Boonsboro. Though she still missed him, it was only about six miles away, and they visited each other often.

At first Katherine had not liked Violet. Everyone made such a fuss over her, she was such a girl. Violet was very pretty and she liked wearing dresses. It seemed she had a different one for every day of the week. She always said and did the ladylike thing. She had long beautiful hair, but most of the time she wore it wrapped up and pinned to the back of her head. It was never mussy.

Violet, unlike Katherine, didn't like getting dirty. But once, when Katherine was showing her around the farm, she had tripped and accidentally fallen into the pig pen. That had been a sight to behold. Now, Katherine knew, that Violet knew, that it had been Katherine that had tripped her, but to this day, Violet kept the secret. In fact she always laughed when anyone reminded her of the day she had wallowed with the pigs. Katherine did at least like that about Violet.

Since then, Katherine had come to love Violet very much. She was her big sister, even if she had stolen her big brother Mark. But not even Violet would be able to fill the void that would be left in her heart today. Besides, Violet was going to have a baby soon so she would have little if any time for Katherine.

Katherine's mother had died when she was born. Her father had never remarried but they had had an older woman from Middletown, Irene Lawson, live with them until just a few months ago. Auntie Irene, as they had all called her, did the cooking, the cleaning, and most of the child rearing, while Katherine's father, Brody, tended to the farm.

All of them, but especially Katherine, had loved Auntie Irene very much and were sad when she left to take care of her older sister, who was very ill, in Shepardstown. Now, Shepardstown was only about 16 miles away, and could easily be walked in a day if you had a mind to, but Katherine knew that at the age of 11, she wouldn't be walking the 16 miles to Shepardstown, as much as she knew that Auntie Irene wouldn't be walking the 16 miles to her. Except for her father, who despite how busy he was, always tried to make time for her, there was no one left for her.

With Auntie Irene gone the bulk of the cleaning and cooking had fallen to Katherine. It wasn't that she couldn't do it, but she'd rather be out in the fields. She hated being cooped up in the house, she didn't like doing girl things.

Matthew, was her other brother. He was the middle child of the three Calhoun children. He was two years younger than Mark who at 23, was the oldest, and at 21, he was ten years older than his little sister Katherine. Katherine loved both of her brothers very much but it was Matthew who she had always felt closest to. Matthew was her very best friend.

Matthew had gone and joined the army. He was leaving today to go somewhere very far away. To someplace in Pennsylvania where he would be taught how to be a soldier. Father had said that where Matthew was going was only a few days away by wagon and that maybe they could go and visit him sometime.

So, today they were having a party for him. To celebrate his leaving, to say goodbye. But why that was something to celebrate she didn't know.

Mark and Violet had come for the party. Grandma and Grandpa were here from Baltimore, father's brother Uncle Kevin, his wife Aunt Louise, and their three children had come up from Burkittsville, and there were a number of friends and neighbors from Middletown and the surrounding farms in attendance as well. Besides her cousins, there were a number of children at the party too, some of them her age, but she didn't know any of them very well, and was not in the mood for their silly games.

They were all there to celebrate what Katherine thought was a very sad occasion. When she woke up tomorrow she would be all alone, except for her father, who despite the presence of his children had always seemed kind of lonely himself.

She had left the party and come down to the creek because everyone seemed to be too happy about Matthew's leaving. The creek always made her feel better. The creek was her friend too, and the best part about it was that it would always be there, the creek would never leave her. She knew she could depend on the creek.

Without realizing it, and because he didn't know any better, Brody Calhoun had unintentionally done his daughter Katherine a great injustice. He had treated her just as he had treated her brothers. She could do just about everything around the farm a boy of her age could do, and most of it better than a boy of her age.

If it hadn't been for Auntie Irene she wouldn't have ever worn a dress or have known how to act like a girl when it was necessary that she do so. If Auntie Irene hadn't made her stay with her in the house on occasion instead of going with her father and the boys she wouldn't have learned how to cook or clean. Which was fortunate now that Auntie Irene was gone.

Her father and her two brothers had never given much thought to it. Katherine had always been there, she was always with them, and she was always treated as if she was one of them. They taught her to ride a horse, to fish, to swim, and to do everything they thought she was or might be capable of. She even participated in the practical jokes they all played on one another.

Katherine was allowed to listen, and at times to participate in the adult conversations that went on around the dinner table about what was happening not only in and around Middletown, but also what was happening around the country and the world. Katherine, who didn't like school but did very well at her studies and really enjoyed reading, was a very well informed little girl.

That was another reason why she had come down to the creek. The conversations didn't interest her. All the older women wanted to talk about was Violet's soon to be born baby, and the older girls just wanted to talk about how handsome Matthew would be in his soldier's uniform. She had no interest in what the other children wanted to talk about.

The men were talking about John Brown and Harper's Ferry. She knew about that, but it had happened months ago and she couldn't understand why everyone still found it so interesting. John Brown was an evil man they had said, so they hanged him. That meant he was dead, so why were people still talking about him?

They were saying that many people were afraid someone would pick up where John Brown left off. That someone else would lead slaves in an uprising. That's the part Katherine didn't understand, why would there be an uprising?

Katherine understood that slavery meant that one man could own another. That most slaves were black, and that most blacks were slaves. She did not know any slaves, nor did she know anyone who owned slaves. But, she had seen blacks on occasion when they would go to Middletown, and she assumed that because they were black, they must be slaves. They always seemed happy enough.

A lot of people, abolitionists they were called, wanted to end slavery. But it also seemed like there were a lot of people who wanted to keep slavery. She just thought everyone had a right to be happy.

The men had also been talking about another man named Lincoln. Mr. Lincoln wanted to be president. Why couldn't Mr. Buchanan still be president?

They were saying that if this Mr. Lincoln got to be president there would be a war. That America would be at war with itself that the free states in the north would fight against the slave states in the south. Katherine did not understand that at all.

Her father was concerned that Matthew, having joined the army, would find himself right in the thick of a war, if it was to come to that. That's why he had tried so hard to talk Matthew out of it. But, Matthew, who was an excellent horseman, had always wanted to be a soldier. He had his heart set on being selected for the cavalry, that's why he was going to Pennsylvania, there was a cavalry school there. Matthew wanted to be a horse soldier, war or no war.

Katherine knew a little bit about war from school. She knew that America had won its independence by fighting a war against England. She knew that America defended its independence by fighting another war with England in 1812, and that there had been a war with Mexico, just about the time she was born, over Texas. Why have a war with ourselves if there were other countries to fight? That's the part Katherine didn't understand.

To her mind, there were three kinds of men who went to war. Those who came home heroes, those who came home having done their duty and were forgotten, and those who never came home. If Matthew had to go to war, which would he turn out to be?

There were a lot of reasons for her to be sad today.

"I've been looking all over for you. Thought I'd find you here."

It was Matthew! She turned and there he was, standing there with his hands on his hips and that great big wonderful smile of his.

"How can we have a party if the most important person isn't there?"

She turned back to the creek, wiped her nose again with the sleeve of her dress, and said, "It's your goodbye party, nobody cares if I'm there or not."

"I care," he said.

"Why do you have to go?" She asked as the tears ran down her cheeks and she sobbed almost uncontrollably. "Why can't you stay here? Don't you like it here anymore?" She again wiped her nose with her sleeve.

Matthew came and sat on the log beside her. He put his arms around her and hugged her to him. Katherine could no longer control her sobs and she buried her face in his chest. Matthew could feel her tears soaking his shirt. Her little heart was broken, and he wanted so much to cry with her.

"I don't want to be a farmer," he said. "I never did. I want to see other places. I want to meet other people. I want the opportunity to have an adventure. I can't do that here"

"There's places around here we haven't seen, and people we don't know." She lifted her head and looked at him. "We could take a wagon and go down along the Potomac and have a real adventure, just the two of us!" She said.

"We could, yes," he said as he smiled down at her, "but when it was over we would be right back here, and I would be a farmer. An unhappy farmer. Don't you want me to be happy?"

"Not if it means you have to go away."

"You know," he said. "Someday, you'll leave here too."

"No I won't," she said and buried her face in his shirt again.

"In not too many years you're going to be a woman. Some man will come along and see what a beautiful person you are, and like Mark and Violet, you'll fall in love and get married and go off somewhere to start your own life and have your own family."

"No," she said and shook her head.

"Why not?"

"The only family I have and ever want to have is you, Mark, and Father. I don't care about anybody else, and I want us all to stay here alone with nobody else."

"Okay, but who's going to tell Violet that she and the baby she's about to have, have to go away? Who's going to tell Auntie Irene that she can't come back? What's going to happen to us when there are no children to grow up and take over the farm when we get too old to work it?" Matthew asked.

"I don't want Violet to go away. I don't want Auntie Irene not to come back."

"Katy, just like me and Mark did, you're growing up," he said. "Growing up means that you have to start understanding that nothing ever stays the same. That things and people change and that we can't stop those changes. That we have to make the best of them and hope the changes that affect the people we love are good ones."

"The creek never changes," she said.

"Maybe not, but do you understand that people do?"

"I don't want to."

"But do you?" Matthew asked.

"When I wake up tomorrow you'll be gone," she said. "Who will I go fishing with? Who will I go swimming with? Who will be my best friend?"

"You have to change too you know," he said. "You are going to have to take care of father and the house. You are going to have to be the woman of the house. You won't have as much time for fishing and swimming like you did when you were a little girl. And, you have to be there for father, don't you think he's sad that Mark is gone and that I will be too? You're going to be all he has left."

"Mark comes back a lot. Will you?" She asked.

"I'll come back as often as I can," he said.

"Promise?"

"I promise."

She wrapped her arms around her brother and squeezed him as hard as she could. "I love you Matthew," she said, "and I'm going to miss you a whole lot."

"I know," he said as he kissed the top of her head and tried to swallow the lump in his throat. "Me too. Me too."

"Am I interrupting?" It was Violet. Her hair was down and she was wearing a dark blue cotton dress that looked tight as a drum where it covered the large round bump that announced to the world how close she was to becoming a mother. "I followed you down Matthew, I hope you don't mind," she said.

"No," Matthew said, as he reached down and wiped the tears away from Katherine's emerald green eyes with his thumbs. "That's fine. We were just talking about growing up and how things change. Right Katy?"

"Yep," she said swallowing a sob. "We're coming back to the party now." She wiped her eyes and her nose with both sleeves of the dress.

"Before you do," Violet said. "Can I talk to Katy for a minute?"

"Sure," Matthew said. "I'll see both of you back up at the house." He stood up, stroked Katherine's cheek with the back of his hand, and said, "You're going to be fine." As he walked away.

"Thank you," Violet said as they passed one another. She walked over to where Katherine was still sitting on the log, smiled down at her, and said, "It's pretty here with the creek and all."

Katherine just nodded.

Violet noticed how dirty the log was and how soiled Katherine's dress was. Katherine looked away, embarrassed that she had gotten her new dress so dirty. She was old enough to know better.

Violet saw her embarrassment. Then Violet sat down next to her on the log. "Oh!" She exclaimed. "Little moist isn't it?" Then she laughed.

Katherine laughed too.

"I was talking to your father," Violet began, "and within a month this little rascal is going to get tired of being cooped up and is going to get born," she said as she laid her hands on the bump. "I already have a midwife lined up so I'll be fine there. But, I was thinking it would probably be a good idea for me to have someone I can count on around to take care of the house and help out with the cooking and all until I get used to being a mother."

She had Katherine's full attention.

"Now, I know it's a lot to ask," Violet went on. "Because I know you have a lot of responsibilities here, but I would like that person to be you, if you would want to. Like I said, I've already talked to your father and he said it would be alright."

"Me?" Asked Katherine surprised and a little more than shocked.

"Of course," said Violet with a smile. "Who better than my own sister and my baby's favorite aunt?"

Katherine threw her arms around Violet and exclaimed, "I would love to. Thank you!"

"Your father said he would bring you over to Boonsboro as soon as the baby's born and that you could stay for as long as I needed you."

"Thank you Violet, thank you so much!" She said as she gave Violet a squeeze.

"Easy," Violet said. "I don't want him popping out just yet."

They both laughed.

"Now, let's get back to the house, shall we?" Said Violet.

"What about my dress?' Said Katherine embarrassed by her appearance. "It's kind of a mess."

"Tell you what," said Violet thoughtfully surveying the dress. "We'll go around to the back, go up to your room, and you can change into your Sunday dress. If Grandmother O'Hara asks we'll tell her you changed out of it so it wouldn't get dirty. Then when Mark and I leave for Boonsboro tomorrow I'll take it with us, I'll clean it up and fix what needs fixing, and next time we see each other I'll give it back to you good as new. Alright?"

Katherine beaming a huge smile nodded enthusiastically.

"It'll be our little secret," said Violet.

"Like the pig pen?" Asked Katherine sheepishly.

"Yes," laughed Violet, "like the pig pen!" And she took Katherine by the hand as they started back to the house. It would also be a secret, at least for now, that Violet and her father-in-law conspired to help Katherine through this difficult time in her life. They both knew that Violet would not really need any help after the birth of her baby, but that right now, Katherine had a need to feel needed.

Matthew was right thought Katherine as she walked alongside Violet, she was going to be just fine.

The rest of the day went pretty well for Katherine. She actually spent some time playing with the other children and was sad to see them go as the party drew to a close. As the men left they shook hands with Matthew and many of them said they wished they could go with him. The ladies kissed him and wished him well. He got kissed so often that Katherine actually felt a little jealous.

It was getting late by the time all the guests were gone, and the cleaning up was done. Grandfather and Grandmother O'Hara said their goodbyes to Matthew and turned in. They would be leaving early in the morning for Frederick to catch a train to return to Baltimore.

Violet, at everyone's insistent had also gone to bed. Uncle Kevin, Aunt Louise, and the cousins also said their goodbyes and left for Burkittsville. A journey that, in the dark, would take a little more than two hours by wagon.

So there they sat, the four of them, all alone on the back porch, just like they had done so often on so many peaceful Maryland evenings before time and the world around them brought change to their lives. For Katherine this was the happiest part of her day, but it made her sad when she thought how terribly she missed the evenings like this they used to share, and when she thought that this may be the last time they would all be together on this porch for a long, long time. She couldn't know it, but her father and her two brothers were thinking the same thing, and feeling the exact same way.

Father started off by telling them stories about their mother, and it was plain to see that he still loved her very much and still missed her terribly. Then Mark and Matthew began to tell stories about some of the mischief they had gotten into when they were younger. The funniest stories were the ones about things they did that father didn't even know about. They cried, and they laughed, and then they laughed and they cried some more.

Eventually it had to end.

Mark and Matthew left the porch to go check on the barn, so they said. They were gone for quite a while, and when they returned it was obvious that they had said their goodbyes. Mark kissed Katherine on the cheek, patted Father lovingly on the shoulder, said he would see them all again in the morning and went off to bed.

Father was next. He too kissed Katherine on the cheek, and warmly embraced Matthew. Then he held Matthew at arm's length and said, "You know your mother would have been very proud."

Matthew could only nod.

"Don't you two stay up too late," father said as he entered the house wiping his eyes.

Matthew came and sat down next to Katherine. "I'll be gone in the morning before you get up," he said.

"I want to get up early so I can see you one more time," Katherine said as tears began to well up in her eyes again.

"I wish you wouldn't," he said. He had his elbows on the arms of the rocking chair he was sitting in and his hands were clasped together in front of him. He didn't look at her but just stared out into the night. "Leaving you is one of the hardest parts of this. I'd rather it was just father in the morning. I don't want to make you, or me, any sadder than we already are. I don't expect you to understand but that's how I would like it to be."

Katherine took her brother's hand and brought it up to her lips, and through her tears she said, "I do understand Matthew, and I don't want you to go away sad. So, I'll just say goodnight, and I'll see you when you come home again." Then Katherine got up out of her chair and went and stood in front of her brother. When he looked up she kissed him on the forehead and wiped the tears from his face with her hands. Without another word, she went into the house and went to bed.

Neither Katherine, nor her father, or Mark, or Matthew slept very well that night, all of them shed a lot of tears. The three who were staying behind prayed very hard that the Lord would watch over their beloved Matthew.

It was just after dawn when Matthew having said his final goodbyes to his father mounted his horse and set off for his new life. He didn't know it but as he forded the Catoctin about a quarter mile upstream from the house, a solitary figure stood on the bank, hidden in the early morning mist, and sadly waved goodbye.

She made a promise to herself that morning that she would never venture very far from these creek banks.

Chapter 10

The Deel
1790

In the morning Brian and Bridget awoke slowly, enjoying the warmth of each other's body, and the fact that they were not hungry or afraid. When they did get up they walked together down to the banks of the Maigue, washed up, and returned to the hut in the small clearing. Except for the ashes from the previous night's cook fire there was no evidence that anything had gone on here, but it did. Didn't it? They soon got their answer. Suddenly as if out of nowhere, without making a sound the three men, who had visited them last night, and who they now knew to be Whiteboys, almost magically appeared in the clearing. They exchanged greetings but nothing else was said as one of the men set about rekindling the cook fire.

"Ligean as a fhail as an tine ag dul aris, agus ta duinn roinnt tae agus fiafheola roimh ceann muid amach."

"Let's get the fire going again, and have us some tea and venison before we head out," said the leader, whose name they still did not know. "Well Brian and Bridget, I trust you slept well?"

"Better than we have in quite some time, thank you," said Brian in the Irish.

The leader smiled, nodded, and touched his well-worn tam.

They were sitting around the resurrected fire and the other two Whiteboys were preparing tea and cooking some of the remaining venison.

"You said we were going to church this morning?" Bridget asked.

"Aye that we are," he said with a grin, "that we are."

"Seems kind of peculiar," she said. "Going to church on a Wednesday."

"I don't doubt that there are those who could stand to go to church every day," he quipped. "Especially among this lot," he continued as he eyed his comrades.

In response several unkind remarks as well as a few clumps of dirt and small pieces of wood were tossed his way.

As the leader ducked he laughed and said, "There's the proof of it."

"Makes me wonder though," she said.

"Bridget darlin'," the leader began. "It will all be clear to you before long. In the meantime, after we've had a spot of breakfast, the two of you need to gather up everything that you intend to take with you. You'll not be coming back here anymore."

Brian and Bridget exchanged glances.

"We've family and friends in and around Limerick and Mungret," said Brian. "Will we at least be able to let them know we're alright?"

"You can write them when you get to America," said the leader.

"I don't know," said Bridget. "It seems so unfair to leave Ireland without even letting them know we're alive."

The leader was seated on a stump. He removed his tam, leaned forward with his arms on his knees, and while spinning the hat between his hands, he said, "We are not going to allow you to be caught and risk the lives of the rest of us or damage our cause. You must disappear, quickly and quietly. I don't mean to be harsh but the only other option would not be pleasant for any of us." He put his tam back on, stood up, walked around the fire, and said, "Now, that meat looks about ready to me."

After a few minutes of awkward silence, Brian said, "Thank you. All of you. We thank you very much." They all nodded to each other, smiled, and set about enjoying their breakfast.

"You aren't going to tell us your names though are you?" Said Bridget as she sipped her tea.

"No, we're not," said the leader. "We don't mean to appear unfriendly. There's good reason for it."

"I'm sure," she said, "and, I don't consider you unfriendly at all. Quite the contrary actually, but there should be some friendly way of addressing you."

The men just smiled.

"I know," she said after giving the matter some thought. "Since you're taking us to church, I shall call you Matthew, Mark, and Luke. Would that be agreeable?" She asked pointing to each of them in turn to signify which one would be which.

"If it pleases you, it pleases us," said the leader, who would from now on be referred to as Matthew, as he stood removed his tam, swept it in a grand arch in front of himself, and bowed deeply. They all laughed as the men kidded with each other about their new names.

After breakfast they put out the fire and cleaned up the clearing as best they could to eliminate any sign of their having been there. Brian and Bridget gathered up what belongings they could carry. Then the three men and Brian destroyed the hut. It reminded Brian of having watched his farm on the Ballynaclough be destroyed, and it saddened him that two places he and Bridget had once called home were now no more than piles of rubble. Then they left their little clearing on the banks of the Maigue.

When they got out near the road the leader, now called Matthew, had them wait just in the woods while one of the men, the clean shaven one now known as Mark, went out to the road and started walking south. After he had gone about a quarter of a mile Matthew, Brian, and Bridget started south on the road as well. Bridget turned and looked at the bearded man she had named Luke and silently wondered why he wasn't coming with them.

"Luke," Matthew said with a smile as if he had heard her unspoken thoughts, "will wait and walk some distance behind us." He lifted his head indicating Mark who was now well out in front of them. "We do what we can to avoid surprises."

"I don't suppose it would do any good to ask where we're going," said Bridget.

"No," said her Matthew. "It is a lovely morning for a walk though, isn't it?" As he began swinging his arms and whistling.

They walked south along the Maigue for nearly an hour. Then used small boats, that their guides pulled from concealment along the river's banks, to cross the river. Once on the other side they walked west for several more hours.

On occasion they would use the main road, but to avoid people and populated areas they primarily used the narrow country roads that crisscrossed this part of County

Limerick. They stopped twice to eat small portions of the cold venison with bread and ale, several other stops were made to rest, or attend to personal matters, and they did hide out in a small woodlot for nearly a half hour to avoid a caravan of merchants who were traveling east on the main road. Mark and Luke joined them for meals and breaks but, other than that the arrangement of one out front and one behind was maintained.

They walked for nearly nine hours and covered over 12 miles. It was nearly seven o'clock when they arrived at their destination. A stone church in the town of Askeaton on the banks of the River Deel.

The Deel was a muddy little tributary of the Shannon that flowed into the Shannon about two and a half miles north of Askeaton, and 15 miles west of Limerick. After Askeaton the Deel meandered for nearly 40 miles through the fertile farmlands of Limerick and Cork Counties, but it was only that small section from Askeaton to the Shannon that was really navigable to boats of any size. Brian knew of Askeaton, and the Deel, but had never traveled this far west before.

When they arrived at the church their leader, now used to being referred to as Matthew, took them around to the far side and through a door at the rear of the church. Their escorts, Mark and Luke, remained near the road. Once inside Brian and Bridget were placed in a small anteroom by themselves. The small damp windowless room contained one chair and a small table on which burned a single candle.

After about 20 minutes Matthew returned with another man who, from his dress, obviously was a member of the clergy. Brian guessed he was in his late 50's or early 60's. He had little hair on top of his head but around the edges it was quite thick and snow white. His face was pleasant enough but it was apparent from his bulk, and the discoloration of his nose, that he was a man who enjoyed food and drink.

"This is Reverend McCaghey," said Matthew once he had closed the door behind him.

"Failte a chur roimh Askeaton."

"Welcome to Askeaton," said the Reverend with a warm smile as he shook hands with both of them.

"Thank you," said Brian.

"Matthew said we'd be coming to church," said Bridget.

"Matthew?" Asked the Reverend with a confused look at the leader.

"It's the name Bridget here decided to call me by," he explained. "Mark and Luke are standing watch out on the road," he added with a smile.

"I see," said Reverend McCaghey with a chuckle.

"Anyway," Bridget continued. "I don't think we're here to attend a service."

"No, you're not," said the Reverend in a friendly voice that made the McBride's feel welcome. "You'll be spending the night and most of the day tomorrow here in this room. It's not ideal but I'm afraid it is necessary. We'll set up a couple of cots and see that you have food but I'm afraid that's the best we'll be able to do for now."

"Then I assume we have further to go?" Asked Brian.

"I'm afraid so," answered the Reverend.

"How far?" Bridget asked.

"Over 3,000 miles," answered the Reverend with a smile. "That's about how far it is to America."

Brian and Bridget just looked at each other and it was obvious that they were both a little overwhelmed by the reverend's answer. "We'll move you to a nearby location tomorrow evening," continued the Reverend, "where you'll have a little more freedom to move about until final arrangements are made to get you on board a ship."

Brian and Bridget joined hands. For the first time they actually started to believe that this was going to happen.

"I'll explain all the details of how everything will work over the next few days and answer any questions you may have, but in the meantime I'll get those cots. Is there anything else I can get for you to perhaps make you at least feel a little more comfortable and at ease?"

"Tea?" Said Bridget. "Is there any chance I could get a cup of tea, and perhaps some water to wash up?"

"Certainly," said the Reverend with an understanding smile. "Let me see to the cots and then I'll get you both some tea and perhaps something to eat, or at least a biscuit or two, and I'm pretty sure I can get you some hot water and towels too."

"Thank you," said Bridget. "Hot water would be heavenly."

"I suppose you'll be gone before I get back... Matthew was it?" Said the Reverend turning to their leader with a grin and extending his hand.

"I will be," he said as he took the Reverend's hand.

"Good job," said the Reverend. "Keep them coming."

"If I do," said the leader returning the grin. "It won't be long before you and I will be the only ones left in Ireland."

"Then our work will be done," said the Reverend as he patted the leader's shoulder and left the room.

After Reverend McCaghey had left the room Brian and Bridget, and the man they knew only as Matthew endured several moments of awkward silence until Matthew finally spoke.

"I need to be going," he said.

Bridget went to him, put her arms around his neck, embraced him, and standing on tiptoe kissed his cheek. "Thank you, and your two friends," she said as tears began to form in her eyes. "Whoever you are, thank you. I will never forget you. I believe you have probably saved our lives."

He returned the embrace and the kiss. "You're welcome Bridget darlin'. It has been a pleasure knowing the two of you and neither will we be forgetting you."

They separated and Matthew walked over to Brian and extended his hand. When Brian took it Matthew pulled Brian to him, put his arm around his back, and whispered into his ear. A Word. A Word that would mean nothing to those who did not know its origin, but a Word that spoke volumes to Brothers. At the same time he adjusted the way in which he gripped Brian's hand, confirming their bond.

"Good luck my Brother," said Matthew as they separated.

Brian was speechless. He stared at his hand as if he'd never seen it before. Then he looked up at Matthew with a knowing smile, "And to you my Brother," he said.

When Matthew got to the door he stopped. He turned and looked at Brian and Bridget and said, "Sean, my name is Sean. The man you call Luke. His name is Oliver, and believe it or not, the man you call Mark is in fact named Mark." He smiled, bowed, went through the door, and they never saw him again.

Several minutes later Reverend McCaghey returned with two other men. They brought with them two cots, two additional chairs, and some extra candles. The two men with the reverend wore the robes of Catholic friars.

Although they appeared friendly the two friars never spoke. Under the direction of the Reverend they set up the cots and placed the chairs next to the table and lit two more candles. When finished they politely bowed and left the room.

"Your tea, a small meal, and some hot water is being prepared and shall soon be ready," said the Reverend.

"Is this a Catholic church?" Asked Brian.

"No, it is not," answered the reverend matter-of-factly.

"I just thought," began Brian, "what with the friars."

"Other than that they are men of God, they are not associated with this church," he explained.

"I just don't want to mislead anyone," said Brian. "We are not Catholics."

"Nor am I," said Reverend McCaghey. "We know who you are, Brian and Bridget McBride," he continued with his warm smile. "We are all of us children of God, and God requires of all of us that we help those in need no matter what the color of our robes or theirs, or the manner in which we offer up our devotions to Him. It is not required that you be of any particular faith to escape tyranny."

"It's not that I'm lacking in faith or tolerance," said Brian. "It's just that I have not been as observant of the Sabbath as perhaps I should have been."

"God only asks of us what we can give."

The friars returned carrying two trays. On one of the trays was a large kettle and three mugs. On the other tray was a platter of fresh bread and some warmed mutton.

"I thought I'd join you for tea while you ate," said the reverend. "Then I can begin to explain to you what will be happening over the next several days. If that's alright?"

"Certainly," said Brian as Bridget poured the tea. "Absolutely, thank you."

"Incidentally," said Reverend McCaghey. "This is Brother Nicholas, and this is Brother Reginald." Pointing to each respectively.

Brian and Bridget rose from their chairs next to the small table. Brian bowed slightly and Bridget curtsied. "An honor," said Brian.

"Ta an-athas chun freastal ar deireadh an bheirt tu."

"It is a pleasure to finally meet the two of you," said Brother Nicholas with a smile as the friars returned the bow. "We have been looking forward to your arrival for the last few days."

"Ta suil agam go mbainfidh tu teach tar do fenacht le linn ceann taitneamhach."

"I hope you find your stay with us a pleasant one," added Brother Reginald. "If there's anything we can do, be sure and let us know."

"Thank you," said Bridget.

With that the friars bowed again and left the room.

"Brothers Nicholas and Reginald are part of a small group of friars that have been appointed guardians of a nearby friary that is no longer active," explained the reverend as he sat in the third chair, "but, I'll explain more about them later.

"Brian," he continued. "You have violated the seventh of God's ten commandments. Thou shalt not steal."

"Yes, I have," said Brian hanging his head.

"And you Bridget, his wife, by your actions, you have condoned his sin so are just as guilty of the offense as is he in the eyes of God."

"I am," she said, also hanging her head in shame.

"At some point you will each of you have to atone for your sins."

They nodded, their heads still hung in shame.

"As a man of the cloth, I cannot ignore your sins," the Reverend continued. "Look at me."

They raised their heads.

"But, as a man of the flesh, I can understand your motivation and how you may have felt that your actions were necessary. You see, I too am an Irishman who is being deprived of what I consider my God given right to live as I see fit in the country of my birth. God did not make all Englishmen bad. In fact, God makes no man bad. Men make a conscious choice to be bad, and any man can make that choice. There is no requirement that you be English. Many an Irishman has made that choice as well." He smiled. "You can, and will be forgiven your sins, but you must promise me now, that your days as Highwaymen are over."

"You have my solemn word," said Brian. "Not only was I not very good at it, but I have been ashamed and afraid from the very beginning." Bridget nodded in agreement.

"I believe you," said the Reverend. "It was your ineptness that brought you to our attention. While it is true that you were profiting from your crimes, it was only a matter of time before your luck was going to run out. By masquerading as a member of our organization you not only endangered yourself and those who were your victims, but our cause and its true members as well. Who as you have personally seen over the last several days are not evil criminals, but are truly Christian soldiers."

"They were wonderful," said Bridget quietly.

"What happens now?" Asked Brian

"Well," began the Reverend. "As I said before, you'll spend tonight and most of tomorrow here. Tomorrow night we'll move you to another location closer to the Deel. When the time comes you'll be placed on board a ship bound for America."

"Any idea when that will be?" Asked Bridget.

"With any luck you'll be celebrating Easter Sunday in America."

"Easter Sunday?" Said a surprised Bridget bringing her hand up to her mouth.

"That's in a little over two months," said Brian, equally as surprised.

"I know," said the Reverend, "and that includes about six weeks of sailing time."

Brian and Bridget joined hands and smiled at each other.

"Now," continued the Reverend, "I'll have my cup refilled, but I'll say nothing more unless the two of you agree to eat. The mutton's probably gone cold, and by now the bread could be stale." He laughed.

They smiled and after Bridget refilled the Reverend's mug, they eagerly turned their attention to the platters on the table.

"As a young man," the Reverend began. "I visited America, and while there spent nearly a year in Philadelphia before returning to Ireland. While in Philadelphia I struck up a friendship with a young carpenter by the name of William Powell. The friendship has continued and we correspond regularly.

"I wrote to him about a week ago, advised him of your plight, and asked for his help. He has graciously helped in the past with getting our friends started on new lives in America so I'm sure he'll be able to help the two of you as well. My letter should arrive a week or two ahead of you, so he'll have time to prepare.

"Mr. Powell also keeps me informed of what ships are sailing from ports along the Shannon to Philadelphia. That will be the next step, finding a ship willing to risk carrying fugitives as passengers. Now, you will be required to pay your own passage, and because of your circumstances it may be costly. How much money do you have?"

"Just over 53 pounds," answered Brian.

"53 pounds!" Exclaimed the Reverend. "You were a better sinner than I thought." He laughed. "I'm sure that will be more than enough."

"Ten of that came from the men who brought us here," said Brian sheepishly.

"Yes, I understand that came from someone with whom you are not unfamiliar," said the Reverend with a smile.

"Lord Northrup," explained Brian. "The man who stole our farm."

"The name Northrup is not pleasant to many Irishmen I'm afraid," the Reverend said shaking his head.

The door opened and the friars entered the room. Brother Nicholas was carrying a steaming bucket and Brother Reginald had towels.

"It is hot," said Brother Nicholas, "but, I'm afraid it won't stay so for very long." He sat the bucket in the corner opposite the door. Brother Reginald delivered the towels to Bridget.

"Thank you," she said.

"We'll leave you two to take advantage of the water before it cools too much and to get settled," said the Reverend as he stood. "We'll talk more again tomorrow. Incidentally, there's a bog out the door you came in and at the end of the wall to your right."

Then he and the friars left the room closing the door behind them.

Brian and Bridget immediately used the hot water to clean themselves up as best they could. Then they finished eating, slid the cots together, and finally, after talking and wondering about what was happening and what America was going to be like, they fell asleep.

Chapter 11

The Rancocas
1938

Katy and her grandfather had slowly made their way back to the house from the landing. He continued his story about the McBride family during their trip, but it was obvious that the walk had tired him. He needed her help in climbing the stairs to the back porch.

She helped him into the parlor and into his favorite chair. From this chair he could look out the front window and across the old mill lane that ran in front of the house. He could look north across the now barren fields that in the summertime would be thick with corn.

Unlike before their walk, he offered no resistance to her assistance, and in fact was asleep within minutes of settling into the chair. Before closing his eyes however, he had promised her that he would resume his story at supper. She kissed him lightly on the forehead and left him to his dreams and memories.

After getting her grandfather settled Katy set about the work of the house. She made her grandfather's bed, set out fresh towels and washcloths for him on the wash stand in his room, and laid out fresh pajamas. It was late in the afternoon by the time she finished.

As she was leaving her grandfather's room she heard the tractor pull into the yard. Mr. Davenport and his crew had finished in the fields for the day. But, their day was far from over.

Katy went downstairs and out onto the back .porch and sat down in the rocker. The two teams of four mules each entered the yard just as she was making herself comfortable. They were each pulling stalk cutters. The handlers waved as they drove the teams around and to the back of the barn.

The mule teams would cut the stalks left standing after the harvest. Mr. Davenport would then come along on the tractor pulling a grinder to grind up the stalks. Once this was done, a disc harrow would be used to further break down the debris left over from the stalks and mix it into the soil. Every effort would be made to have this done by the end of November before the ground froze.

Many of the other farmers in the area felt that cutting and grinding the stalks in this way was a waste of time and effort. However, it was something the McBride's had always done. From the very beginning they felt that this was an important step in preparing the soil for the next year's planting.

Not all the stalks would be ground up. About ten acres would be harvested. The dried harvested stalks would be mixed with the feed for the farm animals over the winter, and for starting and for building slow burning fires.

Katy wanted to talk with Mr. Davenport about how the stalk cutting was going but knew he would be busy now cleaning and preparing the equipment, including the tractor, for tomorrow. The mule handlers would also be busy cleaning the cutters, and caring for the mules. It would be at least an hour before Mr. Davenport would be available. She decided she would get supper started.

Katy went back into the kitchen and set about preparing the baked chicken that was the evening's main course. As she was doing so she remembered Evan's letter. She opened the cupboard where she had placed it before walking to the landing with her grandfather and was about to remove it when Mr. Davenport knocked on the back door.

"Come in, Mr. Davenport," she hollered.

The foreman entered the kitchen and removed his hat.

"Have a seat," she said, as she wiped her hands on a towel and gestured towards the table. "Would you like a glass of iced tea?"

"That would be nice Miss Kate. Thank you."

She removed a glass from the cupboard and as she was filling it asked, "So how is it going?"

"Well," he replied. "We still have about 20 acres to cut and grind before we can start harrowing."

"Do you think you'll finish before the frost?" Katy asked as she sat the glass in front of Davenport and sat down at the table across from him.

"We usually do," he said with a smile as he sipped his tea. "Would go a lot faster though if we had another tractor," he continued as he peered at her over the rim of his glass.

"Problem with the mules?"

"No, Ma'am," he said. "Mules are healthier and stronger than ever, and the handlers are doing a great job. But, they're not tractors."

"How many more tractors would you need?" She asked cradling her chin on the back of her hands as she rested her elbows on the table.

"Oh, one more would do it," he said with a grin.

"You're really trying to get me in trouble with Poppa aren't you?" She laughed.

"No, Miss Kate, but another tractor would be great," Davenport said with a smile as he lifted his glass in a mock toast to Katy.

"What do you think of the cutting and grinding Mr. Davenport?" She asked. "Is it a waste of time and energy like most of the other farmers say?"

"Miss Kate, I've been working for your grandfather since before you were born, and every year we cut and grind the stalks, then we harrow the fields, then in the spring we plow and plant. When it's time to harvest we always have the best corn and the most yield per acre. Is it because of the grinding? I don't know, but I'm sure it doesn't hurt, so I'll continue grinding until you or Mr. McBride tell me not to."

"Thank you," Katy said as she reached out and gave his forearm a squeeze. "More tea?"

"No thank you, Miss Kate. I'm going to check the tractor and the mules and head home. Roberta will be getting my supper ready." He stood and started for the back door.

"See you tomorrow?"

"Usually here before the sun." He laughed as he went out the door.

She followed him to the door. "Give Roberta my best," she called after him. "Yep," Katy whispered as she watched him cross the yard and enter the barn. "We're lucky to have a man like Davenport."

She went to the oven to check the chicken and then went to the cupboard and removed Evan's letter. She sat at the table and studied the envelope. It had taken over two weeks to come from San Francisco where it had been processed through the fleet post office.

Katy opened the envelope, removed the letter, and began to read. The first thing she noticed was the date on the letter. It had been written over two weeks prior to the date it was postmarked. Meaning, the letter had been written over a month ago.

Lieutenant Evan McBride sat at the small metal desk in the 8x10 foot stateroom he shared with two other lieutenants. With the exception of the small stainless steel washbasin alongside the desk and the white pillows and sheets on each of the bunks, the entire room was gray. There was a large air conditioning vent above the door and on rare occasions cool air could actually be felt coming out of it.

It was not a comfortable space, nor was it meant to be. Division officers aboard US Navy warships were kept extremely busy. They were not expected to spend much time in their staterooms.

Most days it was where they got to sleep, if they were not busy with their regular duties or standing a watch. On occasion, those same duties and watches required that they slept wherever they could. Their stateroom was where they kept their clothing and personal articles, and where they went when they had the opportunity, or it was required that they shower and put on a clean uniform.

Today had been a good day. Not only had Evan had an opportunity to shower and put on clean khakis, but for the first time in several days he had also been able to join some of the other officers for a meal in the wardroom. The meatloaf, mashed potatoes with gravy, and green beans, served with lemonade and fresh brewed coffee had been a feast to remember. Not to mention two scoops of chocolate ice cream for dessert!

Evan would have liked to have laid down on his bunk and enjoyed the nap that his full belly was urging him to take, but in an hour he would be going on watch on the bridge. Rather than risk over sleeping, he decided the time would be better spent writing a short letter to his sister Katy, and then going up to the bridge early. You never knew who you might pass on the way, or who might be up there, and it was never a bad idea to impress a senior officer by showing up early.

He had removed his uniform, partly because of the heat, but also because he wanted to avoid wrinkling it. Between the humidity on board the ship and the sweat it created, it never seemed to take long for a crisp khaki uniform to look like it had been slept in. So there he sat dressed only in his US Navy issued skivvies looking down at the blank piece of paper wondering what he should and could tell them about.

It was hot. He could tell them that. Evan smiled as he thought about the stuffiness of the tiny stateroom as compared to his memories of the cool days of autumn along the Rancocas.

It had been nearly ten years since Evan had left the farm. Though he had been back a number of times on leave since then, each time he returned it felt less and less like home. He had become a visitor to the place where he grew up, to the place that held his memories, and to the people he loved.

He supposed the Navy was his home now. Gray rooms on gray ships. Where you dressed based on what the Plan of the Day said, and your duties were determined by the Watch, Quarter, and Station Bill.

Evan knew that as a Lieutenant, on a US Navy aircraft carrier his thoughts and opinions mattered very little, if they were listened to at all. But, he also knew that as he advanced and gained knowledge about ships and men and how best to use them those thoughts and opinions would become more relevant, and would have more value, and would be listened to. However, in a peacetime Navy the opportunity for advancement would be slow, while the workload would remain the same.

He leaned back in the gray metal chair and sighed. Was he becoming frustrated? Maybe he was just tired. They were putting in some long days on these exercises and it had been weeks since they had been granted any shore leave.

"Tenn-Hutt!"

Startled Evan instinctively jumped to his feet and turned towards the hatch leading to the passageway snapping to attention as he did. There stood Lieutenant Baxter "Woody" Underwood, one of his roommates. He slumped back down into his chair.

"You son-of-a-bitch," Evan said with a chuckle. "You damned near gave me a heart attack."

"That's only about the five thousandth time I've got you with that," Woody said. "You're such an easy target you take all the fun out of it! Well, almost all the fun. Interesting choice of uniform you've got there Lieutenant Godiva. Planning something special for the Captain are you?"

"Why are you still here?" Evan asked with a sigh.

"Aw, you may be trying to hide it, but I can tell by your voice just how much you're going to miss me when I'm gone," Woody said.

"About as much as I'd miss a case of the clap," said Evan sarcastically.

"Now don't go getting all mushy on me," teased Woody.

Evan would miss his friend Woody. In the two years they had served together aboard the *Lexington* they had become close friends. Woody, who had been aboard for nearly three years, was being transferred.

Woody had been a year ahead of Evan at the Academy, and although they had known each other then, there had been very little interaction between them. Woody having been promoted to lieutenant a few months before Evan was senior to Evan. The seniority mattered little to the two friends except during the unending good natured jab sessions.

Woody was going to new construction. He would be reporting aboard the *USS Rhind*, a new destroyer that was being built at the Philadelphia Navy Yard. With travel time and leave Woody would be expected to report aboard his new ship in about 30 days.

"So, I repeat," Evan said. "Why are you still here?"

"Just waiting on the *Phelps* to come alongside, then I'll be on my way!" Said Woody as he walked over and sat on the middle bunk of the stack of three behind Evan's chair.

"What's the hold up?"

"Captain wants to finish recovering the patrols that were out and launch a new CAP first."

"Boatswain's chair to the *Phelps*?"

"It's either that or swim!" Laughed Woody.

"Swimming might be safer."

"Yeah," Woody said. "You'd think that in the most advanced Navy in the world they'd find a better way of transferring people ship to ship than by stringing a rope between them."

"Guarantee you'll get wet and, if I can get my hands on one of the lines dunked."

"You wouldn't!"

"Don't bet on it," laughed Evan.

"Yeah, but wet or dry, once I'm on the *Phelps* it'll be smooth sailing!" Quipped Woody.

"Now there's an original pun! How do you come up with them?"

"Sheer genius Mr. McBride, sheer genius."

"So, what's the plan for getting you to Philly?"

"The *Phelps* is being detached from the task force, why I don't know, and will be returning to Pearl. From Pearl I fly to San Diego aboard an Army transport, then I'll catch a commercial flight to Denver to see the folks. I'll take a train from Denver to Philly by way of Chicago."

"Got all of your stuff ready?"

"Yep, it's all up on the hangar deck. There's three other guys besides me going over to the *Phelps*."

"Did you remember the packages for my sister and grandfather?"

"Yeeeesss… and I will personally see to their delivery."

"You have the directions I gave you to the farm from Philly?"

"Yeeesss… anything else Aunty Evan?"

"Yeah," Evan said as he stood. "I am going to miss you, good luck on the *Rhind,* and I hope we sail together again some time."

"Me too Mac, me too." Woody stood and extended his hand which was taken by Evan and the two men shook hands. "You know, if the Vinson Act goes through, they're going to start building a lot of new ships, big ones. That means chances to move, and chances for promotion. Don't get too comfortable here."

"I won't, and I'll keep you posted."

"You do that. Besides, with what's going on in Europe and China, we may find ourselves in a war before too long."

"Really think it'll come to that? Asked Evan.

Woody shrugged. "Who knows," he said, "but at some point we're going to have to start getting ready for it."

As if on cue, a sailor in denims and a white hat appeared in the hatch. "Beg pardon Mr. Underwood," he said trying not to look at Evan who was standing there in his underwear. "Chief says it's time to come to the hangar deck."

"Thanks Reynolds," said Woody. "I'll be along shortly."

"I'm going on watch on the bridge soon, but I'll try to get to the hangar deck before they drown you," said Evan.

"Be nice to have a witness," said Woody. As he started through the hatch he pointed a finger and said, "Make sure you tell your sister I'm coming, and make sure she understands it's a quick visit. Hello, I'm Evan's friend, here's your package, and goodbye. No small talk, no meals, and definitely no bunking in!"

"I'll tell her, I'll tell her. Now get going before you piss the Chief off."

"Fair winds my friend," Woody said as he exited the stateroom and tossed Evan a casual salute. "Until we meet again."

Evan decided to dress and head to the hangar deck to see his friend off. He donned fresh well pressed khakis, buffed his highly polished black shoes, grabbed his khaki officer's cap, and after checking himself in the small mirror in the stateroom headed for the hangar deck. Evan's stateroom was on the same deck and just forward of the hangar deck so it took only a few minutes to get to the hangar deck and then out to the catwalk area along the starboard side. This was where the highline from the *Phelps* would be tied off and the transfers made.

The line was already secured and Woody, wearing a life vest and helmet, was waiting his turn to be strapped into the boatswain's chair when Evan got there. The *Phelps* was about 150 feet away keeping pace with the *Lexington*. The destroyer appeared much smaller than it actually was alongside the carrier and was bobbing around like a cork in the roughly churning waters the wakes of the two vessels created in the narrow channel between them.

There was also a heavy wind-blown spray being created by these churning waters that was intensified by the closeness of the ships as they held station alongside each other at a steady 12 knots. It was obvious that as expected Woody was going to get wet, but there was really very little chance of his getting dunked. If the two ships got close enough to create that much slack in the highline there would be much more to worry about than Woody's comfort. To avoid getting wet Evan decided to watch from the shelter of the hangar deck.

Along with Woody two enlisted men were being transferred from the *Lexington* and a Chief Petty Officer. The enlisted men had been injured in an engine room mishap and were being transferred to the hospital at Pearl. The Chief had been granted emergency leave.

The two enlisted men had been safely transferred when it was Woody's turn. As he was being strapped into the chair he saw Evan. Woody began waving to him. He wanted Evan to come out onto the catwalk. Despite Evan's reluctance to step out of the shelter of the hangar deck it was obvious his friend had something important to tell him.

As he started to step out into the wind an enlisted man shoved a life vest and helmet into his arms. "Here sir, you have to put these on if you're going out onto the catwalk," he yelled above the sound of the wind and the churning waters.

Evan nodded as he slipped on the vest, removed his cap, put the helmet on, handed his cap to the sailor, and said, "Hold onto that for me."

As soon as he stepped out onto the catwalk he fell victim to the cold spray and hammering winds. He knew immediately that the khakis he had on would no longer be suitable to stand a watch on the bridge and that he would have to change again before going on watch. He was also glad he had handed his cap to the enlisted man.

He made his way across the catwalk to its outer edge where Woody, securely strapped into the boatswain's chair, was pulling rank on the Chief in charge of the transfer detail to delay his departure until he could speak to Evan. The detail consisted of a Lieutenant (jg) from the Deck Division, who was obviously content to just stay out of the Chief's way, the Chief and about a dozen enlisted men, all of whom were anxious to get the transfers completed and go somewhere dry. He and Woody were not very popular right now.

Woody grabbed him by the upper arm as he got close to the chair. "Is she pretty?" He hollered over the wind.

"What?' Evan hollered in reply, not sure he had heard Woody correctly.

"Your sister, is she pretty?" Woody asked.

"Pretty?"

"Yes, pretty, is your sister pretty?"

"You called me out here for that?" Evan hollered in disbelief as he stood there in his now soaked khakis.

Woody grinning broadly gave an exaggerated nod, then asked again. "Well is she?"

Evan could not believe what was happening. "Is she what?"

"Pretty? Is your sister pretty?"

"I don't know dammit," Evan hollered. "She's my sister."

"Oh, for Christ sakes!" Bellowed the Chief who had stood there listening to the exchange between the two officers. "That's it. Shove off!" He yelled and the men on the catwalk began to take up the slack on the guide rope that would be used to pull the chair back to the catwalk if anything went wrong during the transfer.

As the chair started to move Evan shouted, "She has an amazing pair of eyes!"

Woody looked back as the chair left the catwalk and moved out over the water and shouted, "I'd rather she had an amazing pair of....!" The rest of what he said was lost to the spray and the wind.

"What? What did you say?" Hollered Evan.

"Ears, Sir."

"What?" Said Evan.

"Ears," repeated one of the enlisted men. "I think the lieutenant said he'd rather she had an amazing pair of ears." The man nodded as he looked at Evan without even cracking a smile while all the other men in the detail turned their heads in an effort to conceal their laughter.

Evan struggled to keep from laughing himself and said to the man, "Ears huh? Yeah, knowing Lieutenant Underwood as I do, I'm sure that's exactly what he said."

"Nothing like a woman with a nice set of ears Sir," the enlisted man continued, amazingly he was the only one within hearing distance who was still managing to keep a straight face.

"I couldn't agree more Lanetti," laughed Evan. "Carry on"

Evan turned and hurried back into the hangar deck, removed the life vest, and rushed back to his stateroom to change and get to the bridge in time for his watch. It didn't take long for the word to circulate about the conversation during the highline transfer in regards to a woman's ears. Not only was it a topic during Evan's watch but for weeks afterwards crew members could be heard discussing how large a woman's ears should be and whether or not large ears were preferable to smaller ones.

After his watch Evan returned to his stateroom and before turning in sat down at the small metal desk and finally wrote that letter to his sister Katy. There was not one word in the letter about ears, hers or anyone else's.

He asked about their health and how grandfather was holding up. About the weather, the farm, and some of the neighbors. What, if anything was going on in Rancocas or the surrounding communities.

He told her about Hawaii and the islands and places he had visited in Central and South America while aboard the *Lexington*, and especially about the people and the food. He knew she liked hearing about those things.

He told her about Lieutenant Baxter Underwood and that he would be visiting the farm to deliver gifts Evan had purchased for Katy and Poppa. He also explained that Woody would be very busy aboard the *Rhind* and would only have time for a short visit. He knew she would make Woody feel welcome and that like Woody she too would prefer a short visit.

He didn't tell her about Irene Northrup, a young lady in Honolulu he had been seeing for several months. There would be time to tell her about Irene in another letter. Besides, at this point he wasn't sure where the relationship with Irene was going.

Before he realized it he had filled up both sides of four pieces of paper. He closed the letter with love, sealed the envelope, and set it next to the wash basin so that in the morning he would be sure and remember to take it to the ship's post office. Then he wrote a letter to Irene, and before he turned in a short letter to Woody telling him all about the great debate aboard the *Lexington*, regarding the size of a woman's ears.

When Katy finished reading Evan's lengthy letter she stuffed it back in the envelope and decided that after dinner she would read it to her grandfather in its entirety. It contained no bad news, and though she wasn't thrilled about having a visitor she knew Poppa always enjoyed company.

She went to the sink and began to peel some potatoes and when she finished she decided to go into the parlor and check on Poppa. She was drying her hands on her apron as she entered the parlor.

"Looks like one of those fancy convertibles you like coming down the lane," Poppa said.

Katy went to the front door, opened it, and stood in the doorway watching as the car drew closer. It was a 1938 Plymouth. Katy could tell by the waterfall grille, and the bug-eyed headlamps.

It had been 43 days since Lieutenant Baxter Underwood had left the *USS Lexington*.

Chapter 12

The Shannon
1790

The sun was well up when they were awakened by a knock on the door. When Brian opened it there was Brother Nicholas with a platter with some bread, cheese, and fresh tea.

"Maidin mhaith."

"Good morning," he said as he entered the room. He handed the platter to Brian and walked over to the small table where he removed the platter from the evening before. He then nodded to Brian indicating that he should place the new platter on the table.

"Enjoy your breakfast," he said with a smile. "I'll return later with some more hot water." He took the previous night's bucket and left the room.

They had finished their breakfast and taken turns using the bog when Brother Nicholas returned with the hot water. He explained that Brother Reginald had returned to the friary the night before and that he too would be leaving to return to the friary shortly. He said that the church would be empty most of the day and that they should remain in the anteroom out of sight as much as possible. Brother Nicholas then left the room closing the door behind him.

They each made one additional trip to the bog, but other than that remained in the room as instructed. It was just after dark when Reverend McCaghey brought them more mutton, tea, and bread. He told them that they would be moving as soon as they finished eating, and left the room.

"Feicfidh tu a bheith ag caitheamh na."

"You'll be wearing these," Reverend McCaghey said when he returned carrying two sets of friar's robes. "It is not unusual for me to be seen walking through the town accompanied by friars. Just keep your hands clasped in front of you, keep up with me, and I'm sure we'll be just fine. Don't stop or talk to anyone."

"Is it really that dangerous?" Asked Bridget.

"No, I don't believe it is," answered the Reverend, "but neither am I willing to take the chance that it is."

Brian and Bridget nodded as they struggled to don the robes. "What about our things?" Asked Brian. "It's not much, but it is all we have."

"Leave it here, and I'll make arrangements to have it brought to you over the next couple of days."

Once they were ready Reverend McCaghey led them out the only door they were familiar with into the chilly January night and had them stop.

"When we get to the road we'll be turning left towards the river," he said quietly. "When we get to the river we'll turn right. We'll stay on that road until we get to where we're going. The whole trip should take us no more than 15 minutes. Remember, keep up, and don't stop or talk to anyone. Ready?"

They both nodded.

The town was dark and they did not see or hear another living person. They could not see the river but they could smell it and hear it lapping against its banks. As the reverend said the entire journey took no more than 15 minutes.

Their destination was surrounded by a wall. Behind the wall was the friary that was home to Brothers Nicholas and Reginald. Before they passed through an iron gate into the friary Reverend McCaghey had them remove their friar's robes.

"The friars' are uncomfortable with my choice of disguise," explained the Reverend. "While they understand that a disguise is necessary and that the robes are a practical disguise, they would rather that you not wear them in their presence or inside the friary."

"Perfectly understandable," said Brian as he and Bridget stepped out of the robes.

Inside the friary they were greeted by Brothers Nicholas and Reginald who introduced them to the three other friars who also served as guardians of the friary. They were shown to a sparse but comfortable bedroom, with separate beds. Brother Nicholas explained that they were free to roam the friary, with the exception of the friar's quarters, but should not venture beyond its walls.

"I'll allow you to get settled and learn your surroundings," said Reverend McCaghey. "I can assure you that you will be well cared for here. I'll have your things sent over in the morning. You will not see me again until I have news of a ship. How long that will be I cannot say. It may be a few days, it may be a few weeks. There is no way of knowing." He smiled that warm smile. "Any questions?"

"No, and thank you," said Brian.

"You're welcome," said the Reverend as he also bid farewell to the friars and left the friary.

As promised, during their stay the friars took good care of the McBride's, seeing to their every need and making them as comfortable as they could. It made no difference to the friars that the McBride's were not Catholic, nor was there any question or suggestion regarding their faith. Though they did join the friars for morning prayers. All in all, they were having a very pleasant stay.

On the afternoon of the sixth day they were visited by Reverend McCaghey. They joined him for a walk on the grounds.

"Ta ma nuacht loinge."

"I have news of a ship," he said.

Brian and Bridget held hands and their breath as they waited.

"In five days' time, Thursday, the fourth of February, the *Loving Union* will be setting sail from Limerick for Philadelphia. It will be getting underway with the morning tide, which should be around seven o'clock. It will take about three hours for it to reach the mouth of the Deel. When it does it will drop its sails and lay to on the pretext of making sure its rudder isn't fouled. It will wait no more than 15 minutes. That is when you will board."

"How?" Asked Brian

"How have you enjoyed the salmon you've been served during your stay?" Asked the Reverend with a grin. "The Deel is famous for its salmon."

"It's very good," said Bridget, "but what…?"

The Reverend held up his hand. "You've probably noticed that every other day or so two of the friars take a small currach out. The friars are well known for their skill at catching the Deel salmon.

"Before dawn on the morning of the fourth the two of you, and as many of your belongings as will fit, will be concealed in the bottom of the currach. At about seven o'clock, the same time the *Loving Union* is leaving Limerick, the friars will board the currach and head downstream. Since it is not uncommon for the friars to do so no one will suspect anything is amiss.

"It will take about an hour to reach the mouth of the Deel where it flows into the Shannon. They will fish those waters until the *Loving Union* arrives. Then they will sail out to the ship and you will board.

"The transfer from the currach to the ship will have to be done quickly, and it is dangerous. You will only be given one chance. If something goes wrong you will be left behind."

"Will we have to remain hidden the entire time?" Asked Bridget.

"Yes, there is no point in taking any chances at this point."

"Even when we reach the mouth of the river while the friars are fishing?"

"Yes. If anyone is watching they will expect the friars to return to Askeaton with a catch. It will only be suspicious if they come back empty handed," the Reverend explained. "Any questions?"

"Do we know what our passage will cost?" Asked Brian.

"The Captain of the *Loving Union* will tell you when you board and you will be expected to pay then. As I said, because of your circumstances it may be costly."

"What if it's more than we have?"

"I don't believe it will be, but if it is, and you cannot pay, you will be put ashore."

"So, what do we do now?"

"Enjoy the rest of your stay," said the Reverend with a smile, "and begin planning your new life in America. I will come by on Wednesday with more information. Now, let us join the friars for some of that delicious salmon."

"Thank you Reverend, for everything," said Brian.

Reverend McCaghey put his arm around Brian's shoulders and said, "Come on. Let's go eat."

Later that night Brian and Bridget laid in their separate beds in their room in the friary. They were both experiencing a myriad of emotions.

They were excited, anxious, a little afraid, and even a little sad. They were excited that they would soon be beginning a new life in a new world. They were anxious that they had very little personal control over what was happening. They were afraid that something could still go wrong, and they were sad that they were leaving Ireland, and in all likelihood would never see their homeland or those they were leaving behind again.

Despite these feelings, not once did they ever consider not leaving. They realized that they could no longer live here in Ireland. They also realized that they would not be permitted to.

On Wednesday after morning prayers and breakfast they again received a visit from Reverend McCaghey.

"Everything is going as planned with your departure," he said.

"What will happen when we arrive in Philadelphia?" Asked Brian.

"That's what I'm here to explain," answered the Reverend. "I have here a letter addressed to my friend William Powell," he continued as he handed a sealed envelope to Brian. "Do not open the letter, Mr. Powell expects to receive it with my seal attached. If my seal is not on it or is broken, he may not be willing to help, so please make sure you keep it in a safe place.

"Mr. Powell or his representative will meet you upon your arrival. As I said before I have already written to him asking for his help. Just present whoever meets you with the letter."

"How will we know for certain that it is Mr. Powell or someone he sent?" Asked Brian.

"The Captain of the *Loving Union* is aware of your circumstances and will make the introduction."

"Everything seems to have been so carefully planned," said Bridget.

"Surely you did not think you were the first to whom we have given our assistance did you?" Asked the Reverend with a smile.

"No," she answered. "I suppose not, but everyone seems to have gone to so much trouble."

"It was only trouble the first time," said the Reverend. "Now it has become routine."

"But why?" Asked Bridget. "Why do you do it?"

"In your case," began the Reverend. "There were two reasons. The first that you were unwittingly endangering our cause. We had to get rid of you, and this was the best option. Secondly, due to the tyranny of Lord Northrup, your chances of ever having a good life here in Ireland were slim. Until Ireland is returned to the Irish we'll keep helping people like you find opportunity elsewhere."

"How many have you helped?" She asked. "Too many," he answered sadly.

"Too many Irishmen are being driven from their homes, and not just by the English. By poverty, disease, and hunger as well."

"We'll never be able to repay your kindness," said Bridget.

"Write me a letter and tell me all about your wonderful new life in America," he said. "That will be payment enough."

"We won't be seeing you again will we," said Brian.

"No," answered the Reverend. "My role in assisting you in your journey has been completed. The only way we meet again is if you don't get on that ship. But, since that is not going to happen, I'm afraid that this is farewell."

Reverend reached out his hand, and it was taken by Brian.

"I do not know your grip," the Reverend said, "or any of the words or other signs or symbols by which members of your fraternity identify each other. But, I do know a good man when I meet one. You are a good man Brian McBride, and I will pray that God watches over you and your lovely wife as you continue your journey to the new promised-land. Don't ever forget that you're Irish, or that you have friends here on the banks of the Deel."

"We won't, thank you."

"I'm hoping I've earned a kiss Bridget darlin'." The Reverend laughed turning to Bridget.

"One for each cheek and the chin as well," she replied as she delivered them.

She was beginning to cry. The reverend held her at arms-length and said, "Those best be tears of joy, because your days of sadness are behind you." He beamed his wonderfully warm smile, turned, and left the friary.

On Thursday, the fourth. Brother Nicholas rapped on the door of their room in the pre-dawn darkness, and announced that it was time to go. Filled with excitement and apprehension, neither one of them had slept much. They were ready and joined the friar in the hall outside their room within a few minutes with two large cloth sacks that contained all their worldly possessions.

Their money was carried in four leather pouches. Brian wore two around his neck and Bridget the other two around her neck. They had spent nothing since they left the Maigue so still had over 53 pounds.

As he was leading them through the dark chilly halls of the friary Brother Nicholas explained that they would be placed under a canvas tarp in the currach, and that they would have to remain hidden and silent alone until he and Brother Reginald joined them at around seven o'clock. They would not be allowed to come out from under the canvas until they were alongside the *Loving Union*. Their possessions would be placed into the bottom of the currach with them.

They followed him out a door, through a small garden, and onto a small wooden dock. With very little conversation or wasted movement Brian and Bridget laid on a couple of blankets in the bottom of the small boat that Brother Nicholas had brought along to try and make them more comfortable. He then covered them with the canvas which was tented at the end towards the bow of the boat to allow at least some ventilation.

Brian and Bridget watched as the silent pre-dawn darkness slowly brightened and they began to hear the sounds of birds and barking dogs.

"I would have liked to see the sunrise," whispered Brian sadly. "I'll never see it rise again over Ireland."

Bridget squeezed his hand.

A short time later they heard someone approaching. Knowing in all likelihood that it was the friars they were still a little frightened until they heard Brother Nicholas whisper that they would soon be getting underway. After placing their equipment into the currach the friars kneeled on the dock and prayed. They then boarded the small boat, cast off, and headed out into the current.

Brian and Bridget felt the easy roll of the vessel as the friars hoisted the lone mast and small triangular sail. They could hear the light wind as it snapped the sail on occasion and hear the water of the Deel as it lapped against the boat's sides. The friars spoke very little and Brian and Bridget were too anxious about what was happening to be concerned about how uncomfortable it was in the bottom of the boat.

After what seemed like hours they felt a change in the action of the boat. The water had become rougher, and the wind stronger.

"I think we've reached the Shannon," whispered Brian.

"Ni mor duinn."

"We have," answered Brother Nicholas. "We'll be entering a small cove in just a few minutes where we'll be protected from the wind. We'll anchor there and fish. Remain hidden and quiet, it won't be much longer. We'll let you know when we see the ship approaching."

A few minutes later the action of the boat did settle, and Brian and Bridget were bumped about under the canvas as the friars, quietly apologizing the entire time, lowered the small boat's sail and dropped its anchor. They began to catch fish almost immediately and unfortunately, for Brian and Bridget, the only place to put the fish was in the bottom of the boat. The friars continued to apologize, but they also continued to catch fish.

Brian did not know how much time had passed, but did know that he and Bridget were sharing the bottom of the boat with at least six cold and wet fish, when Brother Nicholas whispered, "It approaches."

This was followed by the friars slowly and carefully pulling in the anchor and raising the sail. The small boat pitched and rolled as it caught the wind gaining speed as it started to race across the choppy waters of the Shannon. As the little boat picked up speed so too did the hearts of its hidden passengers.

"I'm going to roll back the canvas," said Brother Nicholas, "but, stay down until we get closer." With that the canvas was removed and for the first time in nearly six hours Brian and Bridget were exposed to the light.

The wind felt cold after having been covered up for so long and the spray off the river added to the discomfort. Brian and Bridget blinking as their eyes adjusted to the light could now see that Brother Reginald was handling the tiller in the stern of the boat. He looked down at Brian and Bridget and smiled.

"You should be on board in the next 15 to 20 minutes," he shouted to make himself heard.

The spray was causing all of them to get quite wet, but, Brian and Bridget didn't seem to notice as they sped towards the *Loving Union*.

"My God Brian!" A very wet Bridget shouted into Brian's face. "Can you believe this is really happening? Isn't it exciting?"

All he could do was nod and smile.

She took his face between both of her hands and kissed his wet lips. "We're going to America!" She screamed.

Brother Nicholas tapped Brian on the shoulder and pointed. Brian and Bridget raised their heads just enough so that they could see over the edge of the gunwale. About a half mile in front of them was the massive bulk of the three masted *Loving Union*. Her sails had been furled and she was barely moving.

It took about ten minutes but Brother Reginald was finally able to maneuver the currach around to the leeward side of the large ship and lie it alongside. Brian looked up and estimated that it was about ten feet from the currach to the deck of the *Loving Union*.

A man's head appeared over the rail for a few seconds and then disappeared almost as quickly. A few seconds later two more men looked over the rail and began lowering ropes.

There was a voice, a booming voice of authority from somewhere above. "Let's get these people on board quickly I don't like being out of the channel with no sails on!"

When the ropes reached the currach Brothers Nicholas and Reginald tied one off on each end of the small boat. While they were doing that more heads appeared at the rail and a narrow rope ladder was lowered.

"Step lively now folks!" One of the heads said. "Climb aboard quickly now!"

Brian grabbed Bridget by the arm.

"A theann tu ar dtus!"

"You go first!" He shouted.

Bridget nodded. As she lifted her leg to step onto the bottom most rung the bottom of her skirt got caught on the heel of her shoe. She pulled it loose and stepped onto the rope ladder but when she tried to step up with her other foot the same thing happened. She tried several times but with the same results. She was becoming frustrated and afraid that she might not be able to climb the ladder.

"Come aboard or cast off!" One of the heads shouted.

"Wait," shouted Brian in English as he again grabbed Bridget's arm. "I'll try and carry ya!"

Bridget, who was trying very hard not to cry, looked at Brian and shook her head no. She looked up at the faces of the men staring over the rail of the ship and turned to Brothers Nicholas and Reginald and said, "I'm sorry."

She reached down and loosened the waist band of her skirt and while holding onto the rope ladder with one hand carefully dropped her skirt and stepped out of it. She looked at Brian whose mouth was hanging open and said, "T'is no time fer modesty love. Carry dat," pointing to her skirt. "T'is much lighter den I."

As the men above cheered, she stepped onto the rope ladder wearing only her stockings and undergarments below her waist and slowly but determinedly climbed the ladder and within minutes disappeared over the railing above.

Brian who was still in shock at his wife's shocking behavior turned to look at the friars who were obviously more shocked and embarrassed than either Brian or Bridget.

"Come on Buck-o!" Someone yelled from above. "Or do you have to take your pants off first?" Brian could hear the laughter from above.

Brian looked at Brother Nicholas who pointed up towards the deck of the ship. "You'd best be goin'," he said with a smile.

Brian turned, shoved Bridget's skirt down the front of his shirt, grabbed the rope ladder, and started to climb. He looked up and saw Bridget smiling at him over the railing.

"Come on!" She shouted. "T'is fun!" He could hear the men applauding and couldn't help but worry about what the fun was and what they might be applauding with his half-naked wife on deck.

When he started to climb Brother Nicholas quickly untied the rope from the bow of the currach and tied the sacks containing their possessions to it. The sacks were also hauled aboard, passing Brian as he made his way up the rope ladder. In fact, before Brian climbed over the rail the currach had castoff and was headed back towards the mouth of the Deel, and the *Loving Union* was preparing to sail.

When Brian climbed over the rail Bridget threw her arms around his neck and squeezed him tightly. He had his eyes closed, afraid to open them, afraid he would see the ship's crew staring at his wife's nakedness. When he did open them, he saw that Bridget was wrapped in a blanket that hid more of her than her skirt would have.

"We only left Limerick this morning," a man standing behind Bridget, and noting Brian's concern said with a smile. "We're not quite mad yet."

"Mr. O'Donnell, get those people to my cabin, and let's get back out into the channel." It was the same booming voice of authority Brian had heard earlier and came from a man on the quarter deck.

"Aye Cap'n!" Answered the man behind Bridget as he turned towards the quarter deck. Turning back to Brian and Bridget he said, "If you'll follow me please." They were lead through a door and down a short passageway into the captain's cabin which though it appeared small would come to seem spacious in the coming weeks.

"Make yourselves comfortable," the man said. "My name's O'Donnell, I'm First Mate. I'll have some water and your things brought in and you can clean yourselves up and change. The Captain will be joining you once we're back on course in the channel. And, welcome aboard"

"Tank ya," Brian said.

O'Donnell touched his cap, nodded, and left the cabin.

"Anseo forgot tu seo."

"Here, you forgot this," Brian said to Bridget when they were alone as he reached into his shirt and pulled out her skirt. "Whatever possessed you...?"

She walked over and put her fingers to his lips. "Brian my love," she said. "I would have scaled the side of this ship completely naked if I had to."

"Obviously," he said with a chuckle. "The crew must have really enjoyed the show."

"Believe it or not, as I came over the rail Mr. O'Donnell wrapped me in this blanket, and I noticed that every man on the deck had turned and was facing away from me. They saw little if anything at all."

"Wish I could say the same for Nicholas and Reginald," laughed Brian.

"Oh my. Yes," said Bridget as she joined in the laughter.

There was a rap on the door. When Brian opened it there was a young sailor there with their sacks.

"Your things Sir," he said as he entered the cabin and sat them down in the center of the room. "Ma'am." He blushed as he touched his cap, turned and left the cabin.

As Brian was closing the door a second sailor appeared carrying a steaming bucket. This one was not nearly as young, had a dark unkempt beard, a weathered face, and what few teeth he had were discolored and crooked. He set the bucket next to a stand on which there was a pitcher and basin.

"I brung youse some hot water," he said. "I'm Otis, Cap'n Duckworth's Steward. I can get youse just about anything. All youse gotta do is ask." He wore no cap. He nodded, turned and left the room.

"Well, here we go," said Bridget in English as she dropped the blanket, walked across the cabin, poured some water into the basin, and started to wash.

Brian walked to the back of the cabin and stood looking out the large windows that ran across the entire beam at the stern of the ship. "Goodbye," he sadly whispered.

A short time later, after Brian and Bridget had cleaned themselves up and put on fresh clothes, there was another rap on the door. This one was louder, and was dome with more authority. They exchanged glances.

When Brian opened the door there stood a man who could not be mistaken as anyone other than the Captain of the *Loving Union*. He was well dressed in a suit that had no markings but for all intents and purposes was a uniform. As he entered the cabin he removed an elegant looking tri-corner hat with a large white plume along its left side walked over and placed it carefully on the table. Brian guessed he was a man of about 30 years old.

"My name is Alexander Duckworth," he said as he turned to face Brian and Bridget. "I am the Captain of the *Loving Union*."

Bridget, who had stood when he entered the room, curtsied, and Brian, who was still at the door, nodded and said, "I am Brian McBride, and dis is me wife Bridget."

"Yes, I know," he said with a smile. "Please be seated," he continued. "You've had a rough morning. Is there anything you would like, tea, or perhaps some brandy?"

"Tae would be nice," said Bridget.

"Yes, it would," agreed Brian. "Tank ya."

"Otis?" The Captain asked loudly. "If you're listening, he usually is," he said in an aside to the McBride's. "Bring tea please."

As if on cue, Otis entered the cabin with a tray with three cups and saucers, and a silver teapot on it. "Ain't listenin'," he grumbled, "but can't help but hear through these thin walls when a body speaks as loud as you do... Sir." He sat the tray on the table in front of the Captain, turned and left the cabin.

As Captain Duckworth began pouring the tea he shook his head and said with a smile, "I apologize for Otis, but he's been with me for more years than I care to count. I'm afraid I sometimes allow him excessive liberties."

Brian and Bridget just nodded and smiled, amused by Otis' demeanor, as they accepted their mugs of tea.

"Now, let's get the business of money out of the way so we can all relax. You were told you would have to pay your passage?" Said the Captain.

"Yes sir, but we've never been told da amount we're ta be payin'."

"It is usually eight pounds per person. However, in this case I'm afraid it will cost more," the Captain took a sip of his tea and continued. "Mrs. McBride's passage will be ten pounds, and yours, Mr. McBride, will be 15 pounds. I hope that is agreeable."

"T'is fine," said Brian as he reached inside his shirt and removed the two leather pouches from around his neck.

"You know you are a wanted man," said Captain Duckworth looking over the brim of his cup.

"We know dat someone who looks like Brian is wanted yes," said Bridget.

"No," said the Captain setting down his cup. "Brian McBride is wanted by name. You were identified as a member of the Whiteboys and as a violent highwayman. An order has been issued for you to be transported to Dublin upon your capture so that you might be hanged for crimes against the crown. You didn't know this?" Asked the Captain.

"No sir, I didn't," said Brian his voice quaking as Bridget gasped and brought her hand to her mouth.

"That is why your passage is so much. I'm taking quite a risk aiding a wanted criminal, already sentenced to hang, in leaving Ireland."

"We understand," said Brian, "and we tank ya. I cannot plead me innocence ta ya Captain. I did commit some robberies."

He opened the pouches and dumped their contents onto the table. He counted out 25 pounds and pushed them towards the Captain. "Our passage," he said with a smile.

"Paid in full," replied the Captain. "You've no need to explain to be Mr. McBride. I already know everything I need to know. But, I want you to understand that the risk continues for me even after you are safely delivered to America. I still must sail regularly to the ports of Ireland and England. If it is found out that I assisted you, my ship could be seized, and I could be imprisoned."

"We understand, and are fine wiff de amount, please don't trouble yerself over it," said Brian.

"I just don't want you to think I'm taking advantage."

"We don't. We appreciate yer explanin', but it wasn't necessary, and we are indebted ta yer courage."

"Your servant," he said with a smile. "Now," he continued. "This is my cabin so I'm afraid you won't be staying in here. I presently have duties to attend to but I'll have Mr. O'Donnell show you to your cabin. It is small, and perhaps not as private as you may like, but I trust you will find it comfortable. Once you're settled in your cabin he'll give you a tour of our ship and explain how things work so maybe you'll feel more at home. We're going to be living in close quarters for quite a while."

"About how long will it be takin' us ta reach America?" Asked Bridget.

"If the weather and winds are kind it should take about six weeks," replied Captain Duckworth. Now, Mrs. McBride, Mr. McBride, if you'll excuse me." And, he stood picked up his hat and started for the door.

"Excuse me, Captain Duckworth," said Bridget.

"Yes Ma'am?"

"Please, if you'll not be mindin', we're Brian and Bridget." And, she stood and curtsied.

He bowed in return, and said, "But, I'm afraid I do mind Mrs. McBride. You see, discipline, order, and proper behavior, are vital on board a ship on a long voyage. It helps keep everyone in line and prevents them from taking liberties. So, you shall be Mr. and Mrs. McBride, and I shall be Captain Duckworth. The crew too should be addressed by any title they may have. You may find it difficult at first, but you'll get used to it and you'll see that it really does serve a purpose."

"As you wish," she said with a smile. "After all, t'is your ship."

"You will join me for dinner here in my cabin?"

"T'will be an honor Captain Duckworth," she said and again curtsied.

"In my cabin however," he said with a grin, "I have my own rules. In here you shall be Brian and Bridget, and I shall be Alexander. Until dinner then… Bridget?" And, he bowed.

"Until dinner Alexander." And another curtsy, and a smile.

He placed his hat on his head and left the cabin.

Bridget turned towards Brian and found that he was again staring out the windows at the back of the cabin, and she realized that this was a lot harder for him than it was for her. She thought about going to him, but decided to let him alone with his thoughts. There would be plenty of time to comfort him over the course of the next six weeks.

It was about 6:00pm, Brian and Bridget had been settled in their small but relatively comfortable cabin and had been given a very informative tour of the ship and its workings, and had been introduced to most of the crew, all of whom seemed very friendly. Dinner with Captain Duckworth would be at eight bells on the dog watch, or as Mr. O'Donnell explained, 8:00pm to "landlubbers". Brian had joined Mr. O'Donnell, who had the watch on the quarter deck while Bridget rested in their cabin.

They had left the Shannon, and were now out in the bay. Brian noticed lights on the western horizon.

"What are dose?" He asked.

"Off to port there?" asked O'Donnell. "The lights of Ballybunion," he answered looking in that direction. "We'll be changing course soon to head more southwest. In about three hours' time we'll lose the sight and smell of land until we make Cape May at the mouth of the Delaware." He smiled at Brian. "America," he said and nodded. "Home."

Brian returned the smile and the nod but inside he was very sad. He was not going home. He was an Irishman, he belonged in Ireland. Ireland was, and always would be his home.

Chapter 13

The Rancocas
1938

Lieutenant Baxter "Woody" Underwood stepped off the train at the Reading Terminal in Philadelphia, with one day remaining on his leave. He had been granted the leave as a result of his transfer from the aircraft carrier *USS Lexington* in the Pacific to the destroyer *USS Rhind* which was nearing the completion of its construction at the Philadelphia Navy Yard. Having arranged for a porter to retrieve his bags and find him a cab, Woody was soon being driven south on Broad Street in route to "da Yard" as the talkative cabby referred to it as he skillfully maneuvered the cab through center city traffic.

After arriving at the Navy Yard, it took most of the rest of the day as Woody was shuffled from one office to another, but finally he found himself standing at attention in front of the desk of the lieutenant commander who had been assigned as the *Rhind's* executive officer. The XO's office was in a long three story brick building near the dock where the finishing touches were being put on the ship that would serve as Woody's new home. The building also served as the temporary barracks for the crew until they were able to move aboard their new ship. Woody had yet to see the ship, or its captain.

"Lieutenant Baxter Underwood, reporting aboard Sir!" Said Woody coming to attention.

The XO reached out his hand and Woody handed him the packet containing his orders and other transfer documents and records.

"Stand easy," said the XO as he opened the packet, removed the documents, and laid them in front of him on the desk that was already buried under mounds of paperwork.

"Lieutenant Baxter Underwood," sighed the XO without looking up. "All the way from the sunny south Pacific to the cold muddy shores of the Delaware River." Then he stood and smiled as he extended his hand to Woody and said, "Let me be the first to welcome you aboard. I'm Lieutenant Commander Henry Read, the XO. I'm going to assume that when not being referred to by rank you would prefer to be called something other than Baxter?"

"Woody, Sir," Woody replied as he took the XO's hand. "Thank you."

"Very good Woody. We'll get you checked in and then I'll have someone show you to your quarters. We're being housed in this building until the *Rhind* is ready for us to live aboard which should only be a few more weeks. You'll be sharing a room with two other lieutenants who have already checked in, and an ensign who should be arriving any day now. Any questions?"

"When will I get to see the *Rhind*, Sir?" Woody asked.

"After you're situated I'll take you to her and also introduce you to the Captain," the XO replied. "The Captain spends at least 16 hours a day on board working with the designers and yardbirds. Anything else?"

"No. Sir."

"Alright then, let's get you settled."

Woody was turned over to a Yeoman who gathered up his bags and led Woody up to the third floor.

"Officers' country," said the Yeoman. "You're down here on the end, Sir."

When they got to the end of the passageway Woody opened the door and looked into the room. It was about four times the size of the stateroom he had shared with Evan McBride onboard the *Lexington*. There were two sets of bunked beds, one set along each side wall, four small lockers on the wall behind the door, and a small table with two chairs in the center of the room. On the wall opposite the door was a large window below which was a radiator that rhythmically hissed and popped.

"Lieutenants Randall and Simons have already claimed the upper bunks Sir, so I'm afraid you'll have to choose one of the lowers," said the Yeoman.

"What?" Said Woody having not really been paying attention. "Oh, that's fine, that's fine," he said. "Either one will do, that's fine." Now noticing that both upper bunks were made up while the lowers were just bare mattresses.

"The officers' head and showers are back down the passageway on the right Sir."

"Did you say Randall?" Asked Woody.

"Sir?"

"Randall, did you say Lieutenant Randall?"

"Oh, yes Sir, Lieutenant Randall."

"Is that Lieutenant Edward Randall?"

"Yes Sir. I believe so Sir, Lieutenant Edward Randall."

"And which bunk is his?" Woody asked.

"It's the upper right there Sir," said the Yeoman pointing to the set of bunks on the right hand wall.

"Eddie Randall," said Woody as he slowly walked over to the set of bunks, "and which locker is his?"

"That one Sir," said the Yeoman pointing.

With a few quick moves Woody had the upper bunk completely stripped and the rumpled, balled up bedding tossed onto the lower bunk. Then he walked over and stood in front of the locker the Yeoman had pointed out.

"Hello Eddie Randall," he said with a smile as he slowly and meticulously began pulling the uniforms and other clothing and articles out of the locker and tossing them onto the bunk with the rumpled bedding.

"Lieutenant Randall a friend of yours Sir?" Asked the Yeoman standing there with a big grin on his face.

"A friend?" Replied Woody. "Yeah, I guess you could say that."

"What's your name sailor?"

"Edge, Sir," replied the Yeoman. "Yeoman third class Edge."

"Petty Officer Edge," Woody said. "Would you be kind enough to make up that upper bunk for me and stow my gear in that recently vacated locker right there?"

Woody then removed a sheet of paper from his satchel and in very large letters wrote, PROPERTY OF LT. BAXTER UNDERWOOD. He folded the paper into a tent shape and handed it to Edge. "When you're done with the bed put this on it," he said with a wink.

"Yes Sir," said Edge shaking his head and grinning. "I just hope Lieutenant Randall doesn't come back and catch me. There might be hell to pay."

"Well, then you'd better hurry," said Woody with a smile, "and if I know Eddie Randall, there will indeed be hell to pay." He chuckled, grabbed his cap, and as he headed out the door he turned and said, "I'm going down to see my new ship."

After a short jeep ride Woody and the XO arrived at the dock where the USS Rhind, with the numbers 404 painted on its bow, was moored awaiting her completion. Lines, hoses, cables, and scaffolding seemed to occupy every inch of space on her sloping decks. The sound of steel being hammered, power tools, and compressors was nearly deafening, and there was so much welding going on that the ship appeared to be infested with fireflies.

"Not quite the Lexington is she?" Shouted the XO as he leaned towards Woody.

"No Sir," said Woody. "How long is she?"

"341 feet," replied the XO.

Woody only nodded but did some quick figuring in his head and discovered that you could set two Rhind's on the Lexington's 866 foot long flight deck and still have plenty of room left over.

"Disappointed?" Shouted the XO.

"No Sir," Woody shouted back. "I think she's going to be perfect."

"Let's go aboard," shouted the XO and as if on cue most of the hammering and banging stopped.

Woody nodded as they shrugged at each other over the reduction in noise. The XO then led the way across the gangplank and onto the deck.

"She hasn't been commissioned yet so there's no ensign or quarter deck watch," explained the XO. "Let's see if we can find the Captain."

Woody soon found that the only way to tell the crew members from the yard workers was by their dress. Most of the crew members were dressed in the Navy's dungarees, while most of the yard workers wore blue overalls. After inquiring of several people, some of who were crew members and others who were yard workers, they learned that the Captain was on the bridge, so that's where they headed.

When they entered they found that the Captain was alone on the bridge bent over a set of blueprints that were spread out on a makeshift wooden table along the rear bulkhead. The bridge was completely enclosed so the noise level was drastically reduced. The Captain stood when the two men entered.

Woody noticed that the Captain was more than a few inches over six feet in height, and appeared to have an athletic build under his sweat stained rumpled khaki uniform. He was wearing a plain dark blue Navy ball cap, had an unlit cigarette tucked behind his right ear, and his pleasant enough looking face was in need of a shave. The insignia on his collar identified his rank as being the same as the XO's, lieutenant commander.

"Afternoon XO," the Captain said. "Guess you could tell we're getting closer to completion huh?"

"Afternoon Sir," the XO replied, "and to be perfectly honest Sir it doesn't look any different to me than it did two weeks ago."

"Yeah, me either," laughed the Captain, "but, they keep telling me we're getting close."

"How close Sir?" Asked the XO.

"We should be able to move the crew aboard inside of three weeks," replied the Captain. "New blood?" He asked as he nodded in Woody's direction.

"Yes Sir," said the XO. "Allow me to introduce Lieutenant Baxter "Woody" Underwood, who comes to us by way of the *USS Lexington*."

Woody snapped to attention and saluted.

"Stand easy," the Captain said as he returned the salute. "The *Lexington*? Impressive," said the Captain. "You're going to have to learn to live a lot closer to the waterline I'm afraid Lieutenant," he continued as he stepped towards Woody and stuck out his hand. "I'm Lieutenant Commander George Cooper, Commanding Officer *USS Rhind*. Welcome aboard."

"Thank you Sir," said Woody as he took the Captain's hand and was impressed by his firm grip. "It's an honor to meet you, and I'm looking forward to serving onboard the *Rhind*, Sir."

"Very well," said the Captain as he removed the cigarette from behind his ear placed it in his mouth and lit it. "You've been assigned as our Gunnery Officer, is that right?"

"Yes Sir."

"You were an Assistant Gunnery Officer aboard *Lexington*?"

"Yes Sir. An anti-aircraft division Sir."

"Isn't just about every gun aboard a carrier anti-aircraft?" Asked the Captain.

"Yes Sir. I suppose it is," replied Woody with a grin.

"I'm sure you'll do fine here," said the Captain. "In thirty days, I expect you to know everything there is to know about every weapon aboard this ship. How to load them, how to fire them, how to clean them, how to maintain them, and how to fix them when they're broke, and if they can't be fixed what contingencies you have for defending this ship. Understood?"

"Yes Sir."

"Questions?"

"No Sir."

"Good."

"What Class?" The Captain asked.

"'32, Sir," replied Woody.

"I'm '22 myself, and the XO is what '24, Hank?"

"Yes Sir, Class of '24," replied the XO.

"Don't we have another '32 aboard?" Asked the Captain.

"Yes Sir," said the XO. "Lieutenant Randall, Ed Randall, Supply Officer, Sir."

"You know Randall, Lieutenant Underwood?"

"Yes Sir," said Woody. "Lieutenant Randall and I are acquainted."

"Good," said the Captain. "Nothing like reconnecting with old friends when you report aboard a new duty station. Now, I've got work to do, and you've got a lot to learn about this lovely lady, so, we should both get busy."

"Yes Sir."

"XO, before you go, there's a couple of things I want to go over with you."

"That'll be all Mr. Underwood," said the XO turning to Woody.

"Yes Sir," said Woody as he saluted the Captain and XO and turned and left the bridge.

Woody spent the rest of the day trying to familiarize himself with the layout of the *Rhind* and the many spaces, ladders, passageways, and hatches that would make up his new home. The entire ship smelled of fresh paint and cordite, and you could hardly go anywhere without running into someone wearing a welder's mask. Overall Woody had thoroughly enjoyed the experience and was in a very happy frame of mind when he arrived back at the brick building that served as the crew's barracks several hours later. When he entered the lobby he found Yeoman Edge seated at the duty desk.

"Evening Edge," he said.

"Lieutenant," replied Edge with a nod and a smile. "Your friend's here," he continued as he pointed up the stairs.

"Randall?" Woody said. "Excellent. Can't wait to see him." And he started up the stairs taking them two at a time.

As Woody entered the third floor passageway he noticed a man walking towards him wearing a towel wrapped around his waist, and shower shoes, and carrying a ditty bag and shaving kit.

When he got close the man nodded and said, "You Underwood?"

"Yeah," replied Woody.

"I'm Simons," said the man sticking out his hand. "Rick Simons."

Woody took Simons' hand and said, "Glad to meet you. My name's Baxter, but everybody calls me Woody."

"Welcome aboard Woody," he said with a smile as he nodded back down the passageway towards their room. "Figured I'd give you two some time to get reacquainted. Randall's waiting for you, and he ain't happy." He was laughing and shaking his head as he turned to enter the head and repeated, "Nope, he ain't happy."

"Didn't expect he would be," said Woody with a smile as he continued down the passageway.

When he opened the door Lieutenant Edward Randall, dressed in a pair of khaki trousers and a white tee shirt, was sitting at the table in the center of the room with a cigarette in his mouth and a standard issue white Navy coffee mug in front of him.

"Hello Eddie!" Woody said with a big smile.

"You son of a bitch," Randall answered as he stood, picked up the mug, and drew back his arm ready to fire it at Woody.

Woody instinctively ducked, but the mug never came. Randall lowered his arm and tossed the mug underhand in Woody's direction.

"Whewww..." Woody whistled as he straightened up, and caught the mug. "You coulda killed me with this!" He said as he placed it on the table.

"And what's with this son of a bitch stuff?" He asked as he removed his cap and tossed it onto his bunk, the upper bunk. "You know, that's the last thing I was called when I left the *Lexington*, and now it's the first thing I'm called on the *Rhind*! If this keeps up I might just develop a complex."

Randall standing with his hands on his hips was smiling at Woody as he said, "Did you ever think that there might be a reason why so many people refer to you by that name?"

"Why no," Woody said placing his hand on his chest and giving Randall a less than convincing hurtful look. "Whatever reason could there be?"

"And what's this about?" Randall asked pointing to the bunks.

"Why Lieutenant Randall," Woody began, "I do believe my Date of Rank precedes yours by about ninety days."

"Thirty," said Randall. "Thirty days."

"Whatever," continued Woody, "thirty, ninety, two, it doesn't matter, the key word is precedes. As the senior officer," Woody said drawing out the word senior. "I was only exercising my right to take the bunk of my choice. Is there a problem with that lieutenant? And when you answer, please make sure the word Sir is included in your response." Smiling Woody sat down at the table in the chair opposite Randall who was still standing with his hands on his hips.

"You are precious," Randall said as he flopped down into his chair, put his elbows on the table, and lowered his head into his hands. "Absolutely precious..... Sir," he said as he lifted his head, looked across at Woody, and smiled.

Woody returned the smile. "How was your trip up from the Canal?" He asked.

"Alright. Definite change in the weather though."

"Yeah, me too," said Woody. "Did you get a chance to stop in St. Louis and see the folks?"

"I did," replied Randall. "How about you, stop in Denver?"

"Yep, spent most of the time arguing with Dad about the ranch and why I don't want to be a rancher, and assuring Mom that I, unlike every other sailor in the world, was not a frequenter of houses of ill repute." Woody laughed.

Randall laughed. "Well, when you write," he said. "Give Uncle Ron and Aunt Ursula my love."

"Will do cousin," said Woody. "Will do, and you do the same." Randall nodded.

"What's with the mug?" Woody asked picking it up and examining it. "Can't just be because of the bunk." Then he smiled and pointed at Randall, "You're still pissed about that girl in Baltimore aren't you?"

"Maybe a little," answered Randall sheepishly. "The mug was just because I didn't have anything bigger to throw. I would have thrown it too, but then I figured it wouldn't do any good, nothing was going to dent that skull of yours. And, she wasn't just some girl in Baltimore," he said leaning forward and raising his voice. "Her name was Linda, and before you came along with your endearing but, oh so fake, Colorado cowboy charm, we had something special. In fact, I was beginning to think that maybe she was, you know, the one."

"The one?"

"Yeah, well, maybe," Randall said with a shrug as he leaned back in his chair.

"And you've been so broken hearted over this Linda person that you've been chaste ever since? No other women, no dalliances, or encounters?"

"Well, no, of course not," replied Randall defensively. "There were a couple in Panama I was extremely fond of, but not like Linda, not special."

112

"You're full of shit, and you know it," laughed Woody accusingly. "Besides, she wasn't as good as she looked."

"I would have liked to have found out for myself if she was as good as she looked," said Randall beginning to get loud again, "but, after you spoiled her she wanted nothing to do with me!"

"Spoiled her?" Said Woody. "I don't know what she told you, but I can assure you I was far from the first trawler to fish those waters, and besides, you're about as serious about looking for the one as I am." He laughed.

"Yeah, well, maybe you're right about that," said Randall also with a laugh. "Don't think I'm ever going to let you get away with that again though," he continued shaking his finger at Woody. "And first chance I get I intend to get even!"

"Okay, okay," said Woody with a wave. "Now since I'm the new guy here. How about as a welcome aboard, you take me out on the town and treat me to a delicious dinner at one of Philadelphia's finest eateries?"

"How about as the richer cousin, you treat?"

"How about this?" Replied Woody. "You take care of the meal, and I'll pick up the bar bill?"

"Deal!" Laughed Randall. "Come on let's get dressed."

A short time later as they left the room, and Lieutenant Simons, who had denied their invitation to join them, Woody asked, "Shall we grab a cab?"

"A cab?" Exclaimed Randall. "Oh, no, no, no, come with me my fine fellow."

They exited the building and walked around to the parking lot in the rear where Randall led Woody to a brand new yellow Plymouth convertible.

"Ta-da!" Said Randall spreading his arms.

"Richer cousin my ass!" Exclaimed Woody with a laugh.

"Well, there wasn't a lot to spend my money on in Panama, so while I was home, I treated myself. Hop in. I love driving through this Philly traffic."

Later, as the two cousins shared a delicious but expensive seafood dinner at Philadelphia's famous Bookbinders, they brought each other up to date on their careers, exchanged sea stories, relived old memories, and ogled every female who came within eyesight, and as dashing as they were in their dress blues, were ogled in return. Woody told his cousin about his good friend Evan McBride and his promise to visit his sister and grandfather to deliver gifts from Evan. Woody did not try to hide the fact that it was not something he was looking forward to.

"Is she pretty?" Asked Randall.

"I don't' know."

"What did her brother say?"

"He didn't'"

"Did you ask him?"

"I did."

"And he said nothing?"

"That's right, nothing," Woody said shaking his head.

"And they live on a farm? A farm she's never left?"

"Yep."

"So, a girl who's never left the farm and whose own brother refused to describe as pretty is waiting for you across the river?"

"Yep."

Randall lifted what was the most recent of several scotches in a toast and said, "Cousin you are embarking on a very dangerous mission. My advice is to get in and get out at flank speed. Here's your gifts, your brother says hi, see ya. Then get your ass back to Philadelphia as quickly as possible where there are more enticing targets."

"Here, here," Woody said lifting his glass as well. "A sound and workable plan."

"I'll even let you use my car," said Randall. "Just don't get any ugly or homely on it that stuffs real hard to get out of the upholstery!" They both laughed so hard they nearly fell out of their chairs.

That night they left the Plymouth parked at Bookbinders and took a cab back to the Yard. Neither could come close to describing just how excruciatingly painful it was onboard the *Rhind* the next day as the hammering, banging, yelling, and welding continued in earnest.

Several days passed before Woody finally decided to get his visit to the McBride farm over with and borrowed his cousin's car. Following Evan's directions he only got lost about a half dozen times. Finally, in midafternoon, he found himself at the corner of Beverly-Rancocas Road and Bridge Street in the Village of Rancocas. There was an older gentleman sitting in front of what appeared to be a general store.

"Excuse me sir," said Woody.

The man looked up.

"Can you tell me how to get to the McBride farm?"

"Friend of Evan's are ya?" Asked the man noting that Woody was in uniform.

"Yes, yes I am." Smiled Woody. "And you don't know where he lives?"

"Well, I've never been here before," explained Woody.

"Doesn't matter," said the man. "I don't believe Evan's home."

"No sir," said Woody. "I know, he's still in the Pacific, I was with him."

"Why'd you leave?"

"I got transferred to Philadelphia," replied Woody beginning to get frustrated, "but I promised Evan I'd look in on his grandfather and sister."

"Oh," said the man. "Are they ill? Haven't heard any talk about any trouble at the McBride place."

"Oh, no," said Woody. "Nothing like that. Just a friendly visit."

"Good," said the man. "Would have expected to have heard something if there was trouble," he continued almost to himself as he turned his head and looked down the road in the direction of the McBride place.

"Can you give me directions?" Asked Woody sorry now that he had stopped to ask.

"What? Oh sure," said the man. "I've known the McBride's all my life, was just over to the house a week or so ago. They all seemed fine then."

"I'm sure they are," sighed Woody. "I just want to know how to get there."

The man looked at Woody as if he had won a prize. "Easy enough," he said with a smile. "Go straight down the Mt. Holly Road here," he continued pointing east. "You're gonna pass the Burlington Road on your left, don't turn there, after that you're next right will be Hilyard's Lane, it's a skinny little dirt thing, take that one. The house is just before the creek."

"Thank you," said Woody.

As Woody started to drive off the man said, "When you get back to the Pacific tell Evan I said hi." Woody waved and drove away laughing, fearing he might have just met the smartest man in Rancocas.

Within a few minutes Evan was on Hilyard's Lane with the McBride farm directly in front of him. He was impressed with the well laid out fields, the large solid barn, and the fine looking brick farmhouse that appeared to have been well built, and well cared for. He was dreading this but after all, he had promised his friend Evan, and you never broke a promise to a shipmate.

As he got closer to the house he saw the front door open and someone standing there on the porch watching him approach. He took a deep breath, "I really hope she's not as bad as I expect she's going to be." He said to himself.

Katy, equally dreading what was about to happen stepped out onto the porch and kept telling herself to try and look happy about meeting Evan's friend.

"Nice car," she thought admiring the approaching Plymouth.

Chapter 14

The Delaware
1790

It had been six weeks since Brian and Bridget McBride had boarded the *Loving Union* by climbing aboard from the little currach on the River Shannon. Two North Atlantic storms had required course changes that had slowed the crossing considerably and forced the ship off its intended course. While most of the crew seemed to take the screaming winds and massive waves that came with the storms in stride, Brian and Bridget had found them terrifying, and had serious doubts that this ship that had seemed so massive on the Shannon, and now seemed so tiny on the vastness of the ocean, could survive.

However, with the exception of those two storms, there was little else that threatened their floating sanctuary as it steadfastly continued on its journey. After the storms, the voyage became pretty much uneventful. Brian and Bridget had become friendly with most of the crew and while they took most of their dinners with Captain Duckworth in his cabin, they generally had breakfast and the noon meal with the junior officers or the crew. Even so, after six weeks at sea everyone was anxious for the journey to end.

In addition to its fugitive passengers, the *Loving Union* carried an assortment of cargoes bound for the port of Philadelphia. Included were teas and spices taken on board in Liverpool, and woolens, textiles, and trade goods such as fine china and pottery, and linens from the English merchants who ruled the ports of Limerick. Although some of what was in her hold was fragile, none of it was perishable so the delay caused by the storms would not adversely affect the cargo.

Almost from the outset Bridget had gotten involved in the ship's daily regimen. She helped out with preparing the evening meals whenever she could, or was permitted to by Otis, Captain Duckworth's steward. She mended clothing, if asked, discovering that many of the older hands preferred to do their own. She also did some barbering, and helped tend to the sick and injured. One of the younger members of the crew, who was probably Bridget's age, if not a year or two older, had told her that having Bridget on board was like having his mother along. At first Bridget had been flattered, but later laughed when she thought maybe she shouldn't have been.

Brian too helped out where he could and had even conquered his initial fear of the heights of the rigging. A few weeks into the voyage, with Captain Duckworth's permission and the encouragement and cheers of most of the crew and Bridget, Brian had climbed the ratlines as high as the main topgallant. While he continued to routinely help with setting the sails, he rarely climbed higher than the mainsail. He also on occasion helped the *Loving Union's* carpenter and other ratings as a runner, or just as an extra pair of hands. Under Mr. O'Donnell's tutelage he had also learned to use a sextant and take readings off of the sun and the North Star.

For the most part Bridget actually seemed to be enjoying the voyage and the friendships she had forged with the Captain and crew of the *Loving Union*. Although she was just as anxious to reach America as was everyone else she didn't seem as troubled by it all as Brian did. It was not unusual for Bridget to find Brian, especially in the evening, on the quarter deck looking out over the sea in the direction they had come. She knew that Brian missed Ireland very much, and hoped that eventually he would embrace the exciting new life they were embarking upon.

At Captain Duckworth's request Bridget kept her appearance as unfeminine as she could. She wore loose fitting clothing, kept her hair short and up, and did nothing that might be construed as flirtatious or suggestive.

She was permitted to bathe once every ten days. She bathed in a wooden tub in which she could barely fit that was filled with sea water. Captain Duckworth apologetically explained that they did not carry enough freshwater on board to allow for bathing. Their freshwater could only be used for drinking and preparing meals.

Although attempts were made to warm the sea water it was more often than not extremely cold which generally made for a quick bath. The tub was usually set up in Captain Duckworth's cabin, and while she was bathing no one, not even the Captain, was permitted below decks, and only the Captain and those who were actually on watch, were permitted aft of amidships. Most of the time, unbeknownst to the Captain and crew, Brian would bathe quickly after Bridget had finished before emptying the tub.

Brian and Bridget had always been accustomed to bathing at least once a week, and were somewhat surprised that the crew bathed rarely, if at all. Mr. O'Donnell had told Brian that Captain Duckworth shaved and washed thoroughly and regularly from a basin while at sea but only took a true bath when ashore. The rest of the crew washed from buckets periodically or as needed. Despite this, surprisingly the ship did not smell of unwashed men. Brian and Bridget surmised that it was because of the clean sea air that constantly moved across the decks, and through the spaces.

The hardest thing for Brian and Bridget to deal with was the lack of privacy. Their cabin was small, and the walls were thin. It was on the starboard side of the ship just forward of the captain's galley, just aft of Mr. O'Donnell's cabin which was similar in size to their own, and alongside the officer's mess.

The opportunity for any intimacy of any kind was almost nonexistent. In fact, what little they had shared on the voyage had consisted of stolen, hurried, fumbling moments that seemed more like acts of desperation than of affection. They both found it more frustrating than satisfying and longed for a time when they could truly enjoy the pleasure of one another and languish in each other's arms clothed only in their love.

It was a cold day in late March, but the early afternoon sun was bright and its warm rays made it comfortable. Brian was in the waist of the ship helping several other crewmen mend a sail and Bridget was aft helping Otis, the Captain's steward, scrub some pots when the cry rang out from above.

"Land ho'!"

It had been forty five days and over 3000 miles since they had last seen land. Everyone stopped and looked skyward into the riggings far above the main deck.

"Where away?" Hollered Mr. O'Donnell who was standing the watch on the quarter deck.

"Two points off the starboard bow," came the reply from 100 feet above the deck.

"Go aloft Mr. O'Donnell," said the Captain as he joined Mr. O'Donnell on the quarter deck, "and see if you can identify the location."

"Aye Cap'n," said O'Donnell as with the lanyard of a telescope around his neck, he leaped onto the rigging and scurried up the ratlines.

"I'm going forward," said the Captain to the coxswain. "Hold steady on this course." Before the coxswain could reply the Captain, with telescope in hand, had left the quarter deck and was making his way forward.

Almost the entire crew was now aware that land had been spotted and they too were making their way forward in hopes of getting a glimpse of it.

"Make way, make way, stand aside there!" Bellowed the Captain opening up a path as he made his way to the bow. He jumped up onto the railing and into the rigging. He looped one arm through and around a stay to steady himself and brought the telescope up to his eye as he carefully scanned the horizon.

"Can barely see the break at all," he said to no one in particular. "Who's in the rigging?" He asked still looking through the telescope.

"Ingling, Sir," someone from the crew replied.

"Man must have the eyes of an eagle," said the Captain lowering the telescope. He looked around at the crew. "Alright everyone, return to your duties, it'll be at least an hour or so before we'll be able to really see anything." He climbed down and looked up into the riggings. "Can you make anything out Mr. O'Donnell?" He called out.

"Not really, Sir," O'Donnell hollered down. "Appears to be a barrier island. Could be the Jersey coast."

"How far you figure?" The Captain cupped his hands around his mouth to project his voice.

"Maybe ten or twelve miles," O'Donnell shouted.

"Alright, come on down. We'll know more when we get a little closer," the Captain hollered back. "Tell Ingling to keep a close watch and let us know if he spots anything he can identify."

"Aye, Sir." From above.

Captain Duckworth made his way back to the quarter deck. When he got there he looked aloft and shook his head. "Eyes of an eagle," he repeated to no one in particular. "I had a telescope and I couldn't see a damned thing."

The Captain noticed Brian and Bridget standing at the railing amidships looking in the direction where land was supposed to be. They were holding hands, and were obviously anxious to get their first look at America, their new home.

"Mr. and Mrs. McBride," said the Captain. "Would you like to join me on the quarter deck?"

Brian and Bridget turned to look at the Captain.

"There's nothing to see yet, but when there is you might get a better look from here."

"Yes, tank ya," said Brian, and they climbed onto the quarter deck.

"Congratulations, Sir," said O'Donnell as he jumped down from the rigging and back onto the quarter deck.

"Don't congratulate me yet," replied the Captain. "We could be anywhere from Cape Cod to Cape Hatteras."

"I'd wager it's Jersey," said O'Donnell with a smile.

"First Mates can afford to wager," said the Captain with a grin.

After about a half hour, Mr. O'Donnell took a deep breath and said, "Ah, land. Can you smell it Mrs. McBride?"

Brian and Bridget both inhaled deeply. Looked at one another and then at Mr. O'Donnell, and shaking their heads in disappointment, said, "No."

"You will," Mr. O'Donnell said with a smile. "You will."

Another twenty minutes passed when Bridget suddenly pointed to a low dark line on the horizon and shouted out in excitement, "Look, look dere, I can see it! I can see land."

At almost the same time Ingling shouted down from above, "Breakers! Breakers dead ahead about five miles!"

"Mr. O'Donnell," said Captain Duckworth. "Steer south southwest. I'm going forward." Then looking at Brian and Bridget, he smiled and said, "Let's go you two."

When they got to the bow the Captain climbed up to the same spot he had occupied earlier. As he was putting the telescope to his eye Ingling yelled down from above, "It's the inlet, the inlet at Barnegat!" The Captain, now with the glass to his eye said, "Yes, so it is, so it is. The Barnegat inlet." He jumped down from his perch and looked aloft. "Good job!" He hollered up to Ingling. "Well done! Well done indeed!"

"Three cheers for Cap'n Duckworth!" One of the crew men shouted, which was followed by three loud and hearty "Huzzahs!"

"Would you like to have a look?" Asked the Captain offering the telescope to Bridget.

Bridget nodded eagerly and with Brian and the Captain's help climbed onto the railing and holding on to the rigging was finally able to get the telescope to her eye.

"What do you think?" Asked Captain Duckworth.

"T'is breath takin'," she replied.

"It's America," he replied with a smile.

Brian took a turn at the telescope as well but did not seem nearly as excited as Bridget did.

It was getting dark as they closed to within a few miles of the coast. Mr. O'Donnell told Brian that as long as the winds remained favorable they would probably stay within sight of the land until they entered the Delaware Bay. Then they would lose sight of it again until they actually entered the mouth of the Delaware River.

At dinner that evening, attended by the Captain, the McBride's, Mr. O'Donnell, and the junior officers, they celebrated their landfall with a fine meal and plenty of fine wine that had been reserved for this very occasion. During the meal, Captain Duckworth informed the McBride's that they could expect to reach Philadelphia within the next two days. This was followed by a hearty round of toasting.

Later, after dinner, as Brian and Bridget stood at the rail and peered off into the darkness where they knew a new land and life awaited them, Bridget turned to Brian and said, "I can smell it. Can yew Brian? Can yew smell America?"

Brian inhaled deeply and smiled down at the woman he loved more than he loved breathing and said, "Yes, I tink I can." Then with a sigh he said, "I'm jus' hopin' I won't be fergettin' da smell o' Ireland."

"Ya won't," she said turning to her husband she wrapped her arms around him and rested her head on his chest, "and I won't be a lettin' ya, neither will our children, or our children's children. T'will always be a part o' our family Ireland will, to be sure."

Brian, with his arms around his wife, kissed the top of her head, and after looking out across the water for several more minutes, they made their way to their cabin where each of them, lost in their owns thoughts, slept very little if at all.

At first light Bridget was up, quickly dressed, and rushed out on the deck to make sure that America was still there, that the events of the previous evening hadn't been a dream.

"It's still there," said a voice she immediately recognized as that of Captain Duckworth. He was on the quarter deck smiling down at Bridget as she stood at the rail.

"I wanted ta make sure it wasn't just a grand dream," said Bridget, a little embarrassed.

"Oh, it's real," said the Captain with a smile. "Why don't you wake Brian and join me in my cabin for breakfast? Say in about 45 minutes?"

"Dat would be wonderful," Bridget said with a smile and a curtsy. "We accept."

As they were enjoying a breakfast of coffee, tea, biscuits, bacon, and boiled potatoes Bridget turned to Captain Duckworth, and asked, "Alexander, T'is it my imagination, or are we getting' further away from da land?"

"We are," he replied. "I'm afraid that within the next hour or so we shall lose sight of it completely," he went on eating without looking up.

Bridget looked at Brian anxiously and then turned back towards the Captain. "Is everything alright?" She asked. "Is dere some problem dat requires we move back out ta sea?"

The Captain raised his head and laughed. "Forgive me my dear Bridget," he said, "for teasing you. There is no problem. We will lose sight of land because we will be entering the Delaware Bay. The Bay is some twenty miles wide in most areas so seeing land with the naked eye as we make our way across it to the mouth of the Delaware River is unlikely. I hope you'll forgive me my little joke."

"Certainly, but shame on ya Alexander." Blushed Bridget as Brian chuckled at his wife's embarrassment.

"The land will be visible again when we enter the river in about five or six hours. We'll continue up the river and anchor off of Salem tonight, where we'll pick up our pilot, before continuing on to Philadelphia tomorrow."

"Pilot?" Asked Brian

"Yes," explained Captain Duckworth. "The Delaware is quite a busy waterway. Its tides and currents make it quite treacherous for someone who is not intimately familiar with it. Our pilot will make sure that our next stop will be Philadelphia and not a submerged sandbar or similar hazard."

"What time will we be reachin' Philadelphia tomorrow?" Asked Bridget excitedly.

"Hopefully we'll catch the incoming tide at about first light, so, I would expect that our pilot will have us securely moored dockside in time for dinner," said the Captain with a smile.

"Brian, isn't dat wonderful!" Said Bridget.

"Yes, it t'is m'dear, it t'is," said Brian with a smile and was surprised that as they drew closer to their destination his level of excitement was also beginning to rise.

That evening, about a half hour before sunset, for the first time in nearly fifty days, the *Loving Union*, with her sails furled dropped her anchor and came to rest. She lay in the Delaware River about 1500 feet off the New Jersey bank, and perhaps a mile north of the mouth of the Salem River. She was only about 70 miles from Philadelphia, her final destination.

After dinner Brian and Bridget stood at the rail on the starboard side of the ship that had carried them from Ireland to America to begin a new life. In the darkness they could make out the dark line that marked where the water ended and the land began. They could make out shapes and could tell that heavy vegetation came almost to the water's edge.

"Eisteacht."

"Listen," whispered Brian. "Do you hear that?"

"Frogs," answered Bridget also in a whisper, and in the Irish.

"The bull's looking for a mate." Brian was still whispering.

"Wants to make some baby frogs."

"Better stay off of ships then," sighed Brian.

"Brian!" Bridget hoarsely whispered as she turned and struck her husband. "Please try to remember that a lady is present!"

"That's the problem," he whispered as he flinched and then turned towards his wife. "I can't forget that there is a lady present."

Bridget looked quickly around to ensure they were alone and then threw her arms around her husband's neck, pushed her body up tightly against his, and whispered in his ear, "Patience my darling, it can't be more than another day or so before we'll be able to find someplace to be alone."

Brian lifted his wife's chin and looked into her eyes. "I certainly hope so," he whispered then he passionately kissed her as his hands made their way down her back and pulled her even closer to him.

"Wheww," Bridget sighed as she leaned back and released herself from Brian's embrace. "I could use one of those cold saltwater baths about now," she said with a flirtatious smile.

Brian laughed softly and stroked her cheek with the back of his hand.

"I'm going to turn in," Bridget said. "Are you coming?"

"No," said Brian with a similar smile. "I think it best that I remain on deck a little while longer."

"Probably a wise decision," whispered Bridget as she rearranged her baggy clothing. "We wouldn't want to be rocking the boat." She flirtatiously flipped her head, took her leave and headed towards their tiny cabin, frustrated but delighted that the fire of their physical passion that had been smoldering for nearly two months could still so quickly be reignited.

Brian remained on deck for nearly two more hours before going below. When he entered the cabin he decided it best that he not disturb Bridget, so he took a blanket and made himself as comfortable as possible on the deck beside her bed.

They were awakened in the dark by a godawful sound and vibration that made the deck on which Brian had been sleeping tremble. It felt and sounded as if the *Loving Union* were being ripped apart. In a near panic they hurriedly dressed in the dark and rushed out onto the main deck hoping they would be able to get off of the ship before she floundered.

"Good morning," Captain Duckworth greeted them looking down from the quarter deck.

They turned and looked up at the Captain in the pre-dawn light, and the look of panic was clearly displayed on their faces.

"Is everything alright?" Asked the Captain with concern.

"Are we sinkin'?" Gasped Bridget.

"Sinking? Good heavens no!" Replied the Captain somewhat taken aback.

"Den what in God's name is dat horrible noise, and dis trembling?" Asked Brian trying to control the fear in his voice. Captain

Duckworth tilted his head and looked at them as if they were speaking a language unknown to him. Then, suddenly realizing what they were talking about he began to laugh. He laughed so hard and long that he had to remove his cap and bend over and rest his hands on his knees.

"What is it dat ya find so amusin' about our distress?" Asked Brian as anger began to replace his fear.

Captain Duckworth stood, wiped his eyes with the back of his hands, and replaced his cap on his head. "Forgive me my dear friends, but it is not your distress that amuses me, but it is the realization that after nearly two months aboard the *Loving Union*, you have never heard the sound of her anchor being raised!"

"Da anchor?" Asked Brian as he and Bridget turned to look towards the bow and then turned and looked back at the Captain.

"Yes, the anchor," the Captain said, still trying to catch his breath and still wiping his eyes. "The tide is favorable, our pilot is aboard, and we're getting underway for Philadelphia."

Bridget flopped right down onto her backside, dropped her head into her hands, then looked up at Brian and as she started to laugh said matter-of-factly, "da anchor."

"Da anchor," he repeated as he too began to laugh.

"If you two are feeling better," said the Captain. "I'll have Otis serve you breakfast in my cabin. However, I regret that I won't be able to join you as I must remain here on the quarter deck with our pilot."

"Tank ya, Captain," said Bridget as she started to stand. "Dat would be lovely."

Brian and Bridget spent the rest of the day going from port to starboard as they took in the sights of this new country. Most of the river bank was covered in thick vegetation or by large mature hardwood trees. There were countless small streams and creeks that flowed into the main river which seemed to promise that the land beyond the tress would be well irrigated and fertile.

Mr. O'Donnell pointed out some of the towns and villages they passed such as New Castle, Wilmington, and Chester. He pointed out the small shipyard at Marcus Hook, and told them that that was where his home was. He also identified many of the smaller craft that were plying the waters of the Delaware.

It was late in the afternoon when the steeples and taller buildings of Philadelphia finally came into view. Both sides of the river seemed to suddenly explode into life as they found themselves between the city of Philadelphia and the town of Camden across the river on the New Jersey shore. Brian and Bridget found the sights, sounds, and smells intoxicating.

Using only the topsails, the pilot barked out orders to the crewmen who were aloft in the rigging and slowly maneuvered the *Loving Union* until she was parallel to her dock. Under the pilot's direction the crew of the *Loving Union* adjusted the small uppermost sails so that they caught the slight but steady breeze to make way, or spilled it to take way off or even reverse it. The ship moved slowly to and fro like a falling leaf in autumn.

Finally, with a solid but practiced thump, the *Loving Union* was moored. For the next several weeks she would be part of the land no longer free to conjoin with the winds or dance with the waves. Like the souls she had carried her voyage was now ended. The *Loving Union* was home.

Brian and Bridget stood at the back of the quarter deck trying to stay out of the way as the officers and crew carried out their duties. The ship had been swung 180°. She was moored facing south, her starboard side against the dock at the base of Chestnut Street in the City of Philadelphia. The capital city of the United States of America.

"Tighten up all lines," yelled Mr. O'Donnell as he leaned over the railing on the starboard side of the quarter deck and watched the activity on the dock below. He stood and turned to Captain Duckworth. "Permission to lower the gangway, Sir?"

The Captain looked to the pilot who, standing just forward of the ship's wheel with his hands behind his back and little if any expression on his face, gave a simple nod.

"Permission granted," said the Captain.

Within seconds there was a heavy wooden bridge connecting the *Loving Union* to solid ground, and so connecting Brian and Bridget to America. The Captain escorted the pilot to the gangway where they exchanged a few words and shook hands before the pilot took his leave.

The Captain returned to the quarter deck. As he passed Mr. O'Donnell he patted him on the shoulder and said, "Well done Mr. O'Donnell, well done." Then he turned to his passengers and with a smile, removed his cap, bowed, and said, "Welcome to America and the City of Philadelphia."

Bridget began to cry and buried her face in her husband's chest. Brian nodded to Captain Duckworth and then turned his head and looked out across the waters of the Delaware at the scattered lights of Camden.

The sun was just about down by the time the work of securing the ship was complete. The Captain had Mr. O'Connell assemble the crew amidships so that he could address them.

"Men," he began. "I want to commend you for your service to me and the *Loving Union* during our crossing. As I expected each of you performed your duties well and brought us safely home again and are well deserved of the pay you shall receive on the morrow.

"I have received word from the company, and we will begin offloading our cargoes tomorrow morning after a hearty breakfast of fresh eggs, bacon, and potatoes which will be provided by our sponsors who are grateful for the safe arrival of their goods."

A cheer went up. The Captain held up his hands to quiet the men.

"After we are unloaded a paymaster will come aboard and you shall each be paid. It is also my understanding that there may be some bonuses paid as well for exceptional service."

Another cheer.

"The problem that we are now faced with, is that we find ourselves here in the City of Philadelphia after a voyage of nearly two months penniless, with no funds to go ashore and enjoy the amenities this fine city has to offer."

Murmuring and groaning.

"There is a tavern," the Captain continued, "just a few blocks north of here on Front Street by the name of The Nine Gulls. Men of the *Loving Union* may take food and drink there this evening at no charge thanks to the generosity of an anonymous benefactor."

Loud cheering, much back slapping, and raucous laughter.

"Mr. O'Donnell," said the Captain.

"Sir!"

"You are to go ashore within the hour and station yourself at The Nine Gulls. It will be your duty to see to it that the men of the *Loving Union* enjoy themselves. It will also be your duty to see to it that every man who leaves this ship is back aboard by midnight and is ready, willing, and able to turn to in the morning. Any man who is not will feel my wrath and will pay dearly for the food and drink he may partake of this evening. Understood?"

"Yes Sir!" Answered O'Donnell.

"Understood?" Asked the Captain looking out over the crew.

"Yes Sir!" Came the loud reply almost in unison.

"Good. Mr. O'Donnell, prior to your departure you will assign an officer to remain aboard with just enough men to ensure the security of the ship. The crew may begin going ashore fifteen minutes after your departure."

With that the Captain left the quarter deck and to the cheers of the crew proceeded aft to his cabin. Brian and Bridget who had watched all of this from behind the Captain found themselves caught up in the moment and joined in the cheering with the crew. A few minutes later as the crew began to work their way below decks to prepare to go ashore, Otis, the Captain's steward, approached Brian and Bridget and told them that the Captain requested that they join him in his cabin.

"Ya have a very happy crew about ta descend on Philadelphia, Alexander," said Bridget.

"Indeed I do," replied the Captain with a smile. "Indeed I do."

"We was wonderin'," said Brian. "If it t'is not too improper, if we might be allowed ta join da crew at Da Nine Gulls dis evening. At least fer a little bit o' a spell."

"I'm afraid I can't speak to the propriety of it, and I'm sure the crew would more than welcome your attendance, but are you sure that you want your first American experience to be in a sailors' tavern?"

"Da men o' da *Loving Union*, like its captain, are not just sailors Alexander. Dey 'ave become our friends, many o' dem, and especially da captain, are as dear ta us as family," said Bridget.

"I meant no offense," said the Captain with a smile, "and, I am flattered and humbled by the affection in which you hold me and assure you that the feelings are mutual.

"However, in a few minutes, a carriage will be waiting dockside to convey the both of you to The Indian Queen Inn. It is one of Philadelphia's finest eateries and lodging houses. Upon your arrival you will be shown to private rooms where you will each be afforded the opportunity to take a hot bath. Once you have freshened up and washed the sea off I was hoping you could join me for a fine dinner in the tavern's dining room. After which you may return to your room. In the morning, if you'd like, arrangements can be made for you to return here, or, once my duties are complete I will call on you at the inn."

"How, why...?" Brian and Bridget stood gaping at Captain Duckworth in disbelief.

"Consider it included in the cost of the passage." Smiled the Captain.

"But t'is not t'is it," said Brian.

"Then consider it a gift, a welcome to America gift, from the *Loving Union*."

Bridget ran sobbing and threw her arms around Captain Duckworth's neck. "Yas have all been so wonderful!" She sobbed. "How will we ever be able to leave ya?"

He peeled her arms from around his neck, held her by the shoulders and kissed her forehead. "That carriage will be here soon," he said. "You'd better gather your things."

Bridget ran crying from the room. Brian turned and extended his hand to the Captain. "I don't...."

"I know," said the Captain taking Brian's hand. Then the Captain adjusted his grip, smiled at Brian who instinctively adjusted his grip as well, and said to Brian, "Welcome home Brother."

Chapter 15

The Conodoguinet
1860

Trooper Matthew Calhoun, like most of the officers and men who had completed the training at the US Cavalry Training School in Carlisle, PA, in September of 1859, was expecting to be assigned to the 2nd US Cavalry Regiment in Texas. The mission of the 2nd Cavalry was to protect the homesteaders and new settlements along the Texas frontier from Indians and outlaws. It was an assignment that promised the newly trained horse soldiers plenty of action and adventure. However, with the civil unrest that was escalating with the approach of the 1860 Presidential elections it was decided to delay that transfer. So, instead of heading for Texas, Matthew and the rest of the troopers were held at Carlisle. Instead of action and adventure for the next several months the three troops of Carlisle cavalry marched in parades and passed in review in a number of large and small cities in the east including Harrisburg, Philadelphia, Trenton, New York, and Wilmington.

On November 6, 1860, as many expected, and perhaps just as many feared, Abraham Lincoln was elected President of the United States. Only 45 days later, on December 20th, South Carolina seceded from the Union. By the end of January, five more states, Mississippi, Florida, Alabama, Georgia, and Louisiana would follow suit.

Not only was the Union in danger, the life of the President-Elect had also been threatened. There were those who would see Abraham Lincoln dead rather than inaugurated. Civil unrest was quickly becoming anarchy and rebellion. Keeping the cavalry in Carlisle was perhaps turning out to be a wise decision.

Trooper Calhoun, the other members of B Troop, and their mounts waited in formation on the parade grounds along the banks of the Conodoguinet Creek. The creek served as the northern perimeter of the Carlisle post. Troops A and C were formed up on other parts of the parade ground. The three troops were a substantial distance from each other. The rumor was they were about to receive orders.

With the news of Texas' secession on February 1st, any hopes they had of leaving for Texas were gone. Now, all of them just wanted to go someplace warmer. Few of them actually believed that was about to happen.

The Captain of B Troop, Captain George Talbot, a West Point man, finally appeared on his mount with his aide at his side and took his place at the front of the formation. The aide removed a document from a satchel and handed it to the Captain. The Captain, removed a pair of spectacles from inside his coat and put them on.

Capt. Talbot scanned the document, cleared his throat and looked up at the men assembled before him. It did not escape his attention that the men and their mounts were in almost perfect alignment. He was proud of these men, and he was ready to lead them in battle, he just didn't know when or where that would be or who it would be against.

He returned his attention to the document and started to read; "From Colonel George Thomas, Commanding Officer, to the officers and men of Troops A, B, and C, of the 2nd US Cavalry Regiment;

"By order of Major General Winfield Scott, Commanding General of the Army of the United States, those detached Cavalry Troops of the 2nd US Cavalry currently garrisoned at Carlisle Barracks, Carlisle, PA, are to proceed to Baltimore, MD, planning their march so as to arrive no later than, 21 February. Col. George Thomas, Officer Commanding, upon arrival is to make contact with the Commanding Officer Fort McHenry who will be prepared to arrange for quartering for the troops and stabling for their mounts.

"The mission of the cavalry is to make their presence known to the citizens and civil authorities of the City of Baltimore and the surrounding areas, and to make it unquestionably clear that they are there to guarantee the safe passage of the train carrying Mr. Lincoln, his family, and others. The Officer Commanding is authorized to take whatever steps he deems necessary to fulfill this mission to include the arrest and detention of any person or persons whom he considers a threat to the safe passage of Mr. Lincoln's train, and the appropriate use of the troops at his command in the quelling of any such threat, civil disturbance, or breach of the peace. The Officer Commanding is reminded that he will be held accountable for any and all actions taken.

"Col. George Thomas, Officer Commanding, upon receipt of these orders is to prepare and forward to this office correspondence detailing the supplies, wants, and needs that will be required in carrying out this mission.

"Signed, Major General Winfield Scott, 7 February, 1861."   Captain Talbot folded the document and handed it back to the aide who returned it to the satchel. He removed his spectacles and put them back inside his coat. He then leaned slightly forward in his saddle and slowly turned his head scanning the formation.

"Men," he began. "Our country, our army, and each of us as individuals are fast approaching a serious crossroads. There are many of us who fear, myself included, that we are rushing headlong towards civil war. That we, as soldiers, sworn to protect this country from its enemies may find ourselves engaged in action against ourselves.

"I am sure that all of you, just as I do, pray very hard that war may be averted and that a peaceful resolution to the issues by which our country is confronted may be reached. However, as a member of this army, you have sworn to fulfill the missions to which you are assigned by our Commander-in-Chief. There is no passage in any part of the oath each of us has sworn that states that we agree only to do so if it is the Commander-in-Chief for whom we voted or of whom we approve. We march on the orders of our President, our Commander-in-Chief, he is no longer just a man.

"I do not know how we will be received in Baltimore or what we may be called upon to do, but of this I can assure you. B Troop will carry out its orders and fulfill its mission. If there be anyone among you who feels he can no longer live up to the oath to which he has sworn you will have until sunset tomorrow to present yourself before me. After that any dereliction of duty or hesitation in the carrying out of orders will be severely dealt with.

"We are at a crossroads gentlemen, it is time to choose which road you will follow."

Capt. Talbot turned his mount and, accompanied by his aide, galloped off in the direction of the cluster of large brick buildings that surrounded the parade ground at the center of the post. The four lieutenants, who served as the commanders of the four platoons that made up B Troop, spun their mounts so that they were facing the troops and almost in unison dismissed their charges. The men of B Troop could see that at just about the same time Troops A and C were also being dismissed. While they assumed that the orders that were read were the same, they wondered if the message that was delivered afterwards was.

The next morning Trooper Matthew Calhoun approached the platoon sergeant, Sergeant O'Neall, outside the troop's stable and asked for permission to speak with 2nd Platoon's commander, Lieutenant Nelson. Sergeant O'Neal was about five years older than Michael and had been in the cavalry for several years. He had been sent back from Texas to Carlisle to help train these new troopers and was none too happy that his return to Texas had been indefinitely postponed.

"What's it in regards to?" Asked the Sergeant without looking down from atop his horse. He was chewing on the stub of a cigar that had long ago gone out but that he kept moving from one side of his mouth to the other.

"It's a personal matter Sarge," answered Matthew who was not mounted but stood alongside the sergeant's horse looking up at the sergeant. Matthew had been working in the stable and smelled of horse, but that's how troopers were supposed to smell, and neither Matthew, nor the sergeant seemed to notice. It was however unusually warm for early February in central Pennsylvania, and neither Matthew or the sergeant wore a coat.

"How personal?"

"Personal enough for me to ask permission," Matthew answered with a grin.

"Calhoun," the Sergeant began. He removed the stub of the cigar from his mouth, leaned forward in the saddle and rested his arm on the saddle horn. He looked down at Matthew and continued, "You've always seemed to me to be not too much of a jackass, especially for a Mary-land plowboy." Making sure he pronounced the first part of the state's name in a less than manly manner. "Are you one of them there southern sympathizers?"

"What?" Asked Matthew.

"Are you gonna be asking the Lieutenant to speak to the Captain because you don't wanna go to Baltimore to protect the Lincoln train, or to carry out your duties like you swore you would?"

"What?" Matthew repeated. "No…, no, Sarge, it's nothing like that, nothing at all like that!"

"It better not be. I'll not have a man in my outfit turn traitor," Sergeant O'Neall said as he sat back up in the saddle. "You can see the Lieutenant, but if you're going traitor…" The Sergeant left the sentence unfinished, just shook his head and slowly started to turn the horse. "I'll let you know when the Lieutenant will see you," he said without looking back as he started to ride away.

Matthew just stood there for a moment staring after the sergeant before returning to the stable.

Shortly after the noon meal Matthew stood outside Lieutenant Nelson's quarters. He rapped three times on the door and waited.

"Come." Loudly from inside.

Matthew opened the door and stepped into the room, immediately coming to attention and snapping his right hand up in a salute. Lieutenant Nelson was seated at a table in front of a small stone fireplace in which a small fire was burning. He was wearing the white shirt officers normally wore, but it was opened at the neck, and the sleeves were rolled up. The lieutenant was leafing through a large book that looked like it contained maps.

"At ease," he said without returning the salute or looking up. "What can I do for you Calhoun?" He asked.

"Sir! Trooper Calhoun wishes to speak with the Lieutenant, Sir!" Matthew said bringing his hand back down to his side. He removed his cap and placed it under his left arm but remained at attention.

"So the Sergeant tells me. Stand easy and come on into the room, no point in us yelling at each other to be heard. Please excuse my appearance, I'm not usually so informal, but I've been in these books all morning."

Lieutenant Nelson like most of the officers Matthew knew was a West Point man. He was perhaps in his late twenties, tall and slim, was a good officer, and spoke and carried himself with confidence. He was well liked and respected by the men as well as the other officers. More importantly to Matthew however, he was one of the best horsemen Matthew had ever seen set a saddle, and Matthew trusted him.

Matthew walked over and stood in front of the table, his cap now in his hands and his hands behind his back. The Lieutenant leaned back in his chair, rested his left arm on the arm of the chair, and with his right hand rubbed the stubble on his chin as he looked up and seemed to study the young trooper standing before him. Matthew could feel the heat from the fire but he was sure it wasn't only the fire that was making him begin to sweat.

"Unlike Sergeant O'Neall, whose judgement I usually trust, I don't believe you've asked to see me to tell me that you want to leave us and head south," Lieutenant Nelson said. "Am I right?"

"Yes Sir you are," said Matthew with a smile. "I'm US Cavalry and a Union man all the way Sir."

"Yes, so I told the Sergeant," the Lieutenant said as he sat back up and rested his arms on the table. "This must be something non-Army related then. Am I right?"

"Yes Sir, well, sort of Sir."

"Well go ahead Calhoun, what's on your mind?"

"Well Sir," Matthew took a deep breath and let it out slowly before continuing. "As you may know Sir, I'm from Maryland. Near Middletown, Maryland, actually Sir, a little west of Frederick. About 15 miles west of it, Frederick that is Sir."

"Yes, I know, about Maryland that is. In fact I'm learning quite a bit about Maryland," said Lieutenant Nelson tapping the book of maps that was open in front of him on the table. "If this is a geography lesson Calhoun you're a little late."

"Sir?"

The Lieutenant waved his hand. "Never mind. Continue please, and please do come to a point soon."

"Yes Sir, well Sir, I was wondering Sir, if our march to Baltimore takes us anywhere near Frederick Sir, do you think I might be permitted to stop home for a few hours and see my father and sister? I didn't take the furlough at Christmas Sir, and it's been nearly eight months since I saw them and with the way things seem to be shaping up I don't know when I might get another chance."

"You didn't take your Christmas furlough?"

"No Sir."

"Why not?"

"Well Sir some of the married men with children would have had to cut their furloughs short so I stayed here and covered for them," Matthew explained.

"That was very admirable of you Trooper Calhoun," the Lieutenant said with a smile. "Very admirable."

"Thank you Sir."

"So let me see if I have this now," Lieutenant Nelson began. "As we're marching through Maryland on our way to Baltimore under orders from the Commanding General of the entire United States Army to protect the very life of our newly elected President and Commander-in-Chief, you want to just up and leave your troop and wander home to say howdy to pa and sis? Is that what you're asking of me?"

Matthew didn't know what to say. The way the Lieutenant put it made the request sound very silly. Matthew was embarrassed.

After swallowing the lump in his throat Matthew said, "I hadn't looked at it that way Sir. Sorry to have troubled you Sir." Matthew came to attention and was starting to salute.

"At ease Calhoun," said the Lieutenant. "Let me think on it and see if there isn't some way we can get you home for a couple of days. My apologies. I didn't mean to embarrass you or to make light of your request."

"Thank you Sir!" Matthew said with a smile.

"Don't thank me yet. I said I'd think on it. I can't make any promises."

"Yes Sir. Thank you Sir."

"Now go on, get out of here," said Lieutenant. Nelson with a smile. "I have more of the Old Line State to learn about."

Matthew came to attention, snapped off a salute, did a perfect about face, and marched out the door. As he exited out onto the wooden walkway he nearly collided with Sergeant O'Neall, who was standing near the door and may have been eavesdropping. The agile sergeant easily sidestepped the surprised Matthew, and as Matthew stumbled past, the sergeant gave him just enough of a shove to send him off the walkway and sprawling face first into the dirt.

"Well Calhoun," the Sergeant said looking down at Matthew with his hands on his hips. "If it's to Charleston you're headed, you'll have to walk, 'cause you'll not be taking any mount from this post."

Matthew rolled over onto his back, sat up, spit and wiped his mouth with his sleeve. Matthew peered up at the sergeant as he reached behind himself to retrieve his cap which had come off when he went sprawling into the dust.

"Sarge," he began shaking his head and slapping his dusty cap on his pant legs. "The only way I'll see Charleston is if I ride in under that flag," and he pointed to the stars and stripes waving from the flagpole in the middle of the square, "and in a blue uniform.

"Besides," he continued as he smiled up at the sergeant and started to stand. "How could I leave a place where I'm made to feel so welcomed and so loved?"

"My apologies Calhoun," the Sergeant said removing his cap and sweeping it in front of him as he bowed in Matthew's direction. "I was wrong about you."

"Well thank you Sarge," Matthew said as he placed his cap back on his head.

"You are a jackass!" With that the Sergeant burst into laughter and Matthew couldn't help but join in. "Come on trooper," the Sergeant continued as he stepped down off the walk and threw an arm around Matthew's shoulders. "I'll buy the first round and then you can buy all the rest."

They headed off towards the sutler's.

The next morning Colonel Thomas, his aide Captain Palmer, and his adjutant Major Stoneman, met with the commanding officers of the three troops under his command, as well as with the twelve lieutenants who commanded the platoons within those troops. The purpose of the meeting was to formulate a plan for moving the troops to Baltimore. The colonel had decided to have each of the troops take a different route, rendezvous just outside of Baltimore, and then enter the city as one unit once they had rejoined.

By taking different routes the colonel felt that their movement would not attract as much attention as moving all three troops together, and that if they did draw attention it would be more difficult to track the movement of each troop, or to interfere with their movement. It also would give them an opportunity to monitor the main roads that approached Baltimore from the west.

"Gentlemen," the Colonel, who was seated at his desk began. "I asked Captain Talbot of B Troop to develop routes and timelines by which we may move all three troops to Baltimore via different paths. I understand he has a plan he'd like to put before us."

"Sir?" Captain Ewing of A Troop interrupted.

Without looking up, the Colonel removed a cigar from one of the desk drawers. He did not light it or put it in his mouth but just laid it on the desk in front of him. He finally looked over at Captain Ewing, "Captain?"

"Sir," he began. "It is my understanding that Mr. Lincoln is scheduled to be in Harrisburg on the 22nd. Based on our proximity to Harrisburg would it not seem reasonable that one of the troops be dispatched to provide for Mr. Lincoln's safety while he is in that city?"

"Captain Ewing, I have not managed to attain my present rank and position by questioning the reasonableness of orders posted to me by my superior officers, and especially not by the Commanding General of our Army. Should you wish to continue to advance yourself in our Army, my advice to you would be that you follow suit. Besides, there is already a detachment of regular infantry in route to Harrisburg for that purpose.

"Gentlemen," he continued as he looked around the room at all of his officers. "There is no reason to believe that Mr. Lincoln will be in any danger while in Harrisburg. However, what was not revealed to you in the orders you received was that a plot to assassinate Mr. Lincoln while he is in Baltimore, as well as members of his family and entourage, was recently uncovered. That gentlemen is why we are going to Baltimore in force, with orders that have been specifically written to allow us the latitude to guarantee the safe passage of the man who is soon to be our Commander-in-Chief. Have no doubt that I intend to personally see to it that Mr. Lincoln departs Baltimore in the same, if not better, health than in which he arrives.

"Now, Captain Talbot, if you are ready, please share with us your plan for getting us to Baltimore," the Colonel said nodding in Captain Talbot's direction.

"Excuse me Sir," said Captain Talbot as he stepped forward and laid a large map on the Colonel's desk and unfolded it.

"Certainly," the Colonel said as he stood and picked up the cigar.

Depicted on the map were areas of central and southern Pennsylvania, as well as most of Maryland, showing many of the towns, roads, rivers, creeks, and other significant features. There were also three clearly marked routes which headed south out of Carlisle and ultimately converged west of Baltimore.

"First of all," said Captain Talbot. "Let me say that most of this plan was developed by Lieutenant Nelson of B Troop's 2nd Platoon, so if it is acceptable, the credit for the work should be placed appropriately."

"And if it fails also the blame," said Major Oakes who commanded C Troop. "Well done George."

All of the officers joined in the laughter the remark caused. Even Lieutenant Nelson, though not as heartily as the others.

"Yes, well perhaps," said Captain Talbot. "As you can see," he continued leaning over the map now and directing his attention, as well as the attention of the other officers to the marked routes. "Each of the troops leaves Carlisle on a different day. B Troop, under my command, will leave Carlisle on the 14th, taking the most western route. We will proceed to Chambersburg where we will bivouac and then continue on to Hagerstown the following day. We will bivouac in Hagerstown and then proceed east to Frederick, arriving on the 16th.

"C Troop under the command of Major Oakes, will leave Carlisle on the 15th. They will proceed to Emmitsburg via Gettysburg, where they will bivouac. On the 14th, they will continue on to Frederick where they will rejoin with B Troop.

"A Troop under the command on Captain Ewing, accompanied by the Colonel and his staff, taking the most eastern route, will leave Carlisle on the 17th, and proceed to Hanover where they will bivouac. On the 18th, they will continue onto Eldersburg.

"Also on the 18th, B and C Troops will depart Frederick and proceed to Eldersburg, where we will rejoin with A Troop. We will spend the 19th in Eldersburg on spit and polish in preparation for marching the final 20 miles into Baltimore on the 20th." Captain Talbot stood and looked at the colonel. "There you have it Sir," he said.

"Yes, very well done," said the Colonel. "My compliments to you and Lieutenant Nelson."

"Thank you, Sir," said the Captain. Lieutenant Nelson came to attention and nodded in the direction of the Colonel.

"Questions, comments, concerns, gentlemen?" Inquired the Colonel.

"Sir," said Major Oakes of C Troop, "would it not be prudent to dispatch a patrol at least a day ahead of each troop to insure that the towns in which we intend to bivouac are prepared for our arrival? There's no point in angering the good citizens by dropping hundreds of horses and men on their doorsteps unannounced."

"Sounds reasonable," the Colonel replied. "What about it Captain, Lieutenant. Nelson? Any problem with an advance patrol?" He asked.

Captain Talbot looked at the lieutenant who simply shook his head. "No Sir," said the Captain. "Sounds reasonable, very reasonable. Sorry we didn't think of it ourselves."

"Very well then," said the Colonel. "One day before their departure, each troop will send out an advance patrol consisting of a noncom and six troopers along each troop's route to prepare the communities for our visits. Anything else?"

"Excuse me Sir," said one of the lieutenants who commanded a platoon in B Troop.

"Yes, what is it Walters?" Asked the Colonel.

"The troopers know the purpose of our movement, what shall we tell the citizens the purpose of our movement is should they ask?"

"The truth," replied the Colonel. "It clearly states in our orders that we are to make our presence known and our purpose unquestionably clear. So tell them the truth and we'll see just how far the word spreads. Is that it?" No one spoke. "Good. Gentlemen prepare to carry out your assignments and we'll reconvene once we've all arrived in Eldersburg. Dismissed"

Each of the officers came to attention and saluted. The salute was returned by the Colonel, and the men began to leave the room and talk amongst themselves.

Chapter 16

The Delaware
1790

It took less than ten minutes for the carriage carrying Brian and Bridget to make the trip from the *Loving Union* docked at the foot of Chestnut Street, to The Indian Queen Inn on Fourth Street. It wasn't a very fine or elaborate coach, it was a carriage for hire, but it was the finest coach either of them had ever ridden in. Despite their efforts to display at least some level of etiquette and decorum, they giggled like school children and touched everything inside the coach.

It was when they arrived at the Inn that they were reminded that they were Brian and Bridget McBride, a poor Irish dirt farmer and his wife who had just spent nearly two months crossing the Atlantic. People who were not accustomed to or perhaps even entitled to expect to be welcomed at a place as fine as The Indian Queen Inn.

Bridget had not bathed for over a week, her hair was not clean and was piled on top of her head so that it looked more like a hastily built bird's nest than hair. She was wearing an oversized man's shirt with a baggy skirt both of which were well worn, to the point where the original color of the fabric could not easily be determined. Her undergarments could probably no longer even satisfy the definition of clothing they were so worn out.

Brian was in pretty much the same state. It had been longer between baths for him, his hair was ragged and dirty, and the shirt and britches he wore, if closely inspected, would be found to be on the verge of complete disintegration. As long as he stood still the shoes he was wearing appeared to be in one piece, but when he moved the soles, which were beginning to separate from the rest of the shoe flopped slightly up and down with each step he took.

When the carriage came to a stop they looked at each other and were embarrassed and ashamed. They knew, that despite the good intentions of those that had made these arrangements, that they were acting way above their station. In Ireland they could be severely punished for this. They were about to tell the coachman to return them to the *Loving Union*.

"Sir! Madam!" Rung out a cheerful voice as the door of the carriage was opened. "Welcome to the Indian Queen."

Bridget looked down and saw a white gloved hand extended in her direction. The hand was attached to a very dark man who was dressed in a very fine livery with a coat, waistcoat, ruffled shirt, well fitted britches, white stockings, and blackened shoes that nearly matched the gentleman's complexion. The man's eyes sparkled in his ebony face and his smile was broad and inviting.

"I'm not sure," Bridget said as she looked at herself and then at Brian. "Dat we belong."

"Ma'am," said the smiling man. "Here at da Queen we don't much cares what da package look like. Ain't it always mo' important what be's inside da package?

"Now, come on and step down, and come on inside. Ya ain't gonna find a finer place in da city, or anywhere else in 'Merica, I 'spects."

Bridget took the man's hand and with as much grace as she could, hoping desperately that she wouldn't trip or fall, she stepped down from the carriage followed by Brian. They stood on the sidewalk and looked up and down the busy street which looked almost surreal in the glow of the streetlights. They took in as many of the sights, sounds, and smells as they could, as if in an almost hypnotic state.

The Indian Queen Inn was a solid brick building of three stories with a large roof that sloped away from the street. The first two stories had large multi-paned square windows offset on the left and directly above and below each other. Brian thought it strange that only the lower window had shutters. The entrance, a large ornate wooden door, was on the right, and was just a step above street level. It was through this door that they were ushered into the inn.

They entered into a small foyer. On the left was a finely appointed dining room. There were several groups in the room seated at round tables covered in white linen who seemed to be enjoying themselves. Bridget hoped that perhaps this might be the room in which Captain Duckworth would be joining them for dinner.

On the right was a stair case leading up to the second floor, and beyond the foyer a narrow hallway ran straight back towards the rear of the building. Brian assumed that the bar and kitchens were back that way since there seemed to be a lot of activity, and he could hear the sounds of men talking and laughing coming from that direction. Brian was mesmerized, and the smell of whatever food it was that was being prepared made his mouth water.

"Good evening," said a woman who suddenly seemed to appear out of nowhere, "and welcome to The Indian Queen. My name is Mrs. House and I am the proprietor of this establishment and a very close friend of Captain Duckworth's."

Mrs. House was a woman in her early fifties. She was tall and slender and her figure would have been envied by a woman half her age. She was dressed in a blue floral print cotton dress with a rectangular lace trimmed bodice, and large billowing white cuffs. Her auburn hair sat high on her head and spiraled curls framed her face and fell at her shoulders. She was a very handsome woman.

"Tank ya," said Brian and Bridget their voices barely audible as both kept wondering when they would awaken from this dream.

Mrs. House turned and signaled to a black woman who was waiting further down the hall.

"Mrs. McBride," she said with a smile. "If you will accompany Tanya, she will see to it that you are properly pampered. Mr. McBride, I see that you have already met Oscar." Nodding to the man that had ushered them into the inn. "Oscar will be taking care of you. If there is anything you need please do not hesitate to ask. Otherwise, I shall see you later." With that she stepped aside, smiled, and nodded at Tanya.

Brian and Bridget, now completely speechless, nodded and followed Tanya towards the back of the building with Oscar bringing up the rear. They passed the bar which as Brian had suspected was further down the narrow hallway, and the kitchens. Just prior to going out the rear of the building there were two doors, one on each side of the hallway, Bridget was shown through the door on the right, and Brian through the door on the left.

The doors led into identical rooms. The rooms were small and had brick floors. On the back wall of each room was a large fireplace in which a fire was burning, over which hung a large pail of water which was just beginning to steam. The rooms were hot. In the center of each room was a large copper bathtub which was nearly filled with steaming water. On a small stand next to each tub was an assortment of soaps and oils.

Bridget who was nearly brought to tears turned to Tanya and jokingly asked, "Dat isn't seawater is it?"

Tanya who of course could not possibly have understood the joke, looked almost offended and said, "No Ma'am, I drawed dat water from da pump myself, and been heatin' it up fo' over a few hours now."

"I can't tank ya enough," said a smiling Bridget.

"Now," said Tanya softly, and returning the smile. "Let's get ya outta dose tings and get ya washed and oiled up all proper like."

Bridget offered no resistance as Tanya helped her undress, and assisted her into the tub. The water was very hot against her naked skin, and as Bridget slid down so that it covered almost her entire body it actually took her breath away. She could feel her face heat up and begin to sweat. Then Tanya brought the pail from the fireplace over and slowly poured that into the tub as well.

"Ahhhh," moaned Bridget. "I may never get out o' here."

"Would ya likes me ta help ya wash?" Asked Tanya.

"No, tank ya," said Bridget a little embarrassed, "but, do ya tink ya could be doin' anyting with me hair?"

"Ah," said Tanya with a smile. "That's my special."

Tanya went behind her and began to untangle her hair, pulling and yanking as necessary to get it as straightened out as possible. Bridget almost shrieked when without warning Tanya used a large cup to dump more hot water over her head. The hot water ran down her face and into her eyes and Bridget couldn't help but laugh right out loud. Bridget could not remember anything ever having felt so good.

Across the hall Brian was having a similar experience. Although he did not require any assistance in getting undressed or getting into the steaming tub, he did not refuse when Oscar offered to shave him and cut his hair. Oscar told him that he was an accomplished barber and serviced many of the gentlemen who frequented the Indian Queen.

After a thorough scrubbing and drying Oscar provided Brian with a clean cotton robe, and worn, but soft leather slippers, and led him up a back staircase to the third floor. There were only two doors leading off the hallway at the top of the stairs, both of them to the right. Brian followed Oscar to the door at the far end of the hallway.

Oscar opened the door and led Brian into a large bedroom. The large comfortable looking canopied bed was on the left, and there was a window on the far wall. On the wall on the right were two setting chairs and a small table which held a pitcher and basin. Brian noticed that there was a chamber pot strategically placed beneath one of the chairs. Oscar left but returned a few minutes later carrying a complete set of new clothes, including undergarments, stockings, and shoes.

"Where did dose come from?" Asked Brian. "Dose are not mine."

"I don't know Sir," said Oscar. "All I knows is dat I was tolt ta give ya dese and see dat you was properly dressed fo' dinner."

"But…," Brian started to protest.

Oscar politely interrupted, "It's time ta dress Sir. Your wife's gonna be needin' dis room shortly, and Captain Duckworth is downstairs in da bar and has asked dat you be joinin' him fo' a drink."

"Captain Duckworth, already? Very well," he said, "but I'll be damned if I understand any of dis."

"Don't gotta understands," said Oscar with a smile, "jus' gotta enjoy."

After he was dressed Brian was as presentable as any other Philadelphian who might be a guest at a place such as The Indian Queen.

"Ya know, Mr. McBride," said Oscar as he led Brian downstairs to the bar. "Dat room we was in is da room dat's been reserved fo' you and Mrs. McBride fo' tonight. Dere's only two rooms in dis part o' da inn, dat one, and da one next door to it. Da one next door's empty, and Mrs. House she says no one's ta be given dat room tonight. So," he continued with a smile. "Gonna be jus' da two o' you up here all night."

"Tank ya," said Brian a little embarrassed by Oscar's implication and at the same time thrilled at the thought of truly being alone with Bridget. "Tank ya very much."

At the bar, he was warmly greeted by a duly impressed Alexander Duckworth who, it appeared, had also had the opportunity to enjoy a bath.

Shortly after Brian and Oscar left the bedroom on the third floor Bridget and Tanya arrived. Almost the same scenario was played out. Tanya left and returned with a complete set of new clothes for Bridget. Included was the most beautiful dress Bridget had ever seen.

It was very much like the one Mrs. House had been wearing. It was a pink cotton print with a little bit higher rectangular neckline also trimmed in lace, and from the neckline down to the waistline the bodice was crisscrossed with white linen cording. Bridget almost started to cry.

"Now don't go getting' all weepy," laughed Tanya. "We jus' now got ya all fixed up. Lets' get ya dressed and downstairs. Dey's two men down dere can't wait ta see jus' how much beauty you was hidin' under dem sailor clothes."

After Bridget was dressed Tanya gave her a hug and escorted her downstairs to the dining room. She seated her at a table in the far corner in front of the large multi-paned window.

"Ya be's lookin' beautiful Miss Bridget," said Tanya. "I'll let da mistress know dat you are ready ta receive da Captain and yo' husband." She smiled and left the room. Bridget who was absolutely certain now that this was nothing more than a dream could only smile and nod as she tried to keep her hands from trembling.

Brian and Captain Duckworth were quietly talking at a corner table in the smoky bar. In front of each of them was a snifter of brandy. They looked up as Mrs. House entered the room and approached their table. They both started to stand.

"Please gentlemen," Mrs. House said with a smile, "keep your seats." She looked approvingly at Brian. "Mr. McBride," she said. "If I did not know any better

I'd say that it was not you who just a little more than an hour ago stepped out of a carriage in front of this inn."

"Tank ya Mrs. House," said Brian. "Oscar, and everyone has been so nice and so accommodatin'."

"That's what we do," she said with a smile, "but, you are none the less very welcome. I've come to tell you that Mrs. McBride is in the dining room and is prepared to receive you." She turned to go.

"Mary," said Captain Duckworth. "We'd be honored if you would join us for dinner."

"That's sweet of you Alexander," replied Mrs. House, "but, I'm afraid I have other things to attend to. Some other time however, I'm sure."

Taking their brandy Brian and the Captain left the bar and proceeded to the dining room. When they got there they stood in the doorway and scanned the room looking for Bridget. Twice they glanced at the table in the corner occupied by the beautiful young lady, and it was not until the third time that Brian realized that that beautiful young lady was Bridget. He nearly dropped his brandy.

He crossed the room with an enormous smile on his face and when he got to the table he looked down at his blushing wife and said, "Yer breathtakin', yer absolutely stunnin'. I've never seen anyone more beautiful."

She reached out and took his hand. She was unable to speak, all she could do was smile.

"Alexander?" Said Brian turning to face the Captain.

"Brian's right Bridget," he said. "I can't believe there is a more beautiful woman in the entire city this evening."

"Now just be stoppin' da two o' ya," she said having found her voice but still blushing brightly, "but tank ya just da same. Tank ya so very much, 'cause I really do feel beautiful dis evenin'."

"Ya are," said Brian. "Sit," she said as she kissed Brian's hand.

"Sit, da both o' ya, so's we can eat."

The three friends shared a fabulous meal of roast duck and pork, carrots, radishes, a variety of jams and jellies and small cakes, all accompanied by some of the finest wine The Indian Queen had to offer. Throughout the meal Brian and Bridget tried to pry out of the Captain who it was that had made the evening possible. The pampering, the new clothes, the fine meal, and the private room. All he would say was to consider it a gift from the *Loving Union*.

It had been nearly two hours since they had sat down to eat when Captain Duckworth raised his glass.

"To Brian and Bridget McBride." He toasted. "May you enjoy every blessing this life has to offer, and may any dream that you dream come true."

"Tank ya," they said as they too lifted their glasses and the three of them drank.

"Now," said the Captain as he stood. "It is time for me to take my leave."

"Really?" Said Bridget. "Already?"

"It is after ten o'clock," said the Captain. "My orders to the crew were that they were to be back aboard by midnight. As Captain, it is up to me to set a good example.

"Besides," he continued with a chuckle. "If I return now I can relieve the poor junior officer O'Connell left behind so that he can at least get to the Gulls and enjoy an ale or two."

"Tank ya, fer everything," said Brian as he stood and took the Captain's hand in their now familiar grip.

The Captain just nodded as he returned the grip.

"Will we be seein' ya tomorrow?" Asked Bridget.

"You can count on it my dear," said The Captain as he walked around the table took Bridget's hand, bent at the waist, and kissed it. "When you are ready to come to the ship let Mrs. House know and she will arrange it. Good night," he said as he bowed to them both, turned, and left the room.

"T'is been an incredible day it has," said Brian as he sat, reached across the table, and took Bridget by the hand. They were the only ones left in the dining room.

"T'is been amazin'," sighed Bridget. "I'm exhausted," she said and watched as Brian's whole face drooped. "Teasin'." She smiled as she squeezed his hand.

"Shall we go upstairs?" Asked Brian his voice squeaked and he could not believe that he felt and was acting like a nervous bridegroom.

"I taught mebee we'd give our legs a stretch and explore da neighborhood a little," said Bridget. "T'is a beautiful evenin'."

"Well," said Brian. "I suppose we could." The disappointment obvious in his voice.

"Den again, do ya tink it would be scandalous if I ran up the stairs?" Whispered Bridget smiling flirtatiously.

"No more scandalous den if I were to be chasin' ya," he replied.

At that moment Tanya entered the room carrying an oil lamp. "If ya's follow me," she smiled. "I'll show ya ta yer room."

The next morning when Brian awoke he found himself lying naked on top of the sheets in the comfortable canopied bed. Bridget was snuggled next to him. She had a sheet which barely covered her nakedness pulled up tight to her chin.

The night had been exhilarating. The first time they had been like a couple of animals, groping, and grabbing, as they rushed to couple, and afterwards somehow felt cheated. But, after that they took their time, and made love to one another. They explored each other's bodies and became reacquainted with their intimacy and their passion. When they finally slept they were both spent and entirely satisfied.

Brian lifted his head and kissed Bridget on top of hers. She moaned and stretched alongside him, and he found the touch of her skin against his extremely arousing.

"Ta gach duine awake?"

"Is everyone awake?" She asked looking up at her husband and blinking the sleep from her eyes.

"I believe so," he smiled as he answered in the Irish.

She took her hand and placed it on his stomach. She moved it down and slowly began to stroke him. Brian could not help but react.

"Well," she cooed as she began to nibble at his shoulder, "now it appears that not only is everyone awake, but their up too!"

They made love again.

Afterwards they washed and dressed in their new clothes and went down to the foyer. There to greet them was Mrs. House.

"I trust you passed the night well?" She asked with a knowing smile.

"Very well," said Brian returning the smile. Bridget turned her head and giggled.

"Well," said Mrs. House. "It's nearly lunch time but I'll have the kitchen prepare you some eggs and bacon. Now, you go on in the dining room and make yourselves comfortable and I'll have some coffee and teas brought in."

"Tank ya," said Brian and with Bridget on his arm, he entered the dining room.

Later as they were finishing their breakfast Mrs. House came to their table.

"I trust you enjoyed your breakfast?"

"Very much so Mrs. House, tank ya," said Brian. Then he continued, "Mrs. House, we 'ave money, and I'd like ta pay at least somethin' fer da baths, da barberin', da lodgin', and da meals dat we have been blessed ta receive here."

"Mr. McBride," said Mrs. House. "Your money is no good for anything you were provided with at this inn yesterday, last evening, or today. Everything has been taken care of. So, my advice to you is to just accept it graciously and enjoy it.

"However," she continued, "if at some future date you should find yourself in want of a fine meal and you should decide that the Indian Queen is the place to get that meal, well then," she said with a great smile, "I shall be more than happy to present you with a bill for that meal."

Brian stood and bowed to Mrs. House. "And I shall be honored ta pay it," he said, and the three of them laughed.

"Now, finish up," she said. "I've sent for a carriage to return you to the *Loving Union*, and it should be here soon."

"Tank ya," said Bridget. "Will we be returnin' here?"

"No, I don't believe so my dear," said Mrs. House with a smile, her hands clasped in front of her at her waist. "I believe other arrangements are being made. But, you'll always be welcome here."

"If everyone who comes tew America is welcomed in dis manner," said Bridget. "Den twon't be long afore every other country in da world will be empty o' people."

They shared a laugh and Mrs. House graciously bid them farewell when they left the inn, and climbed into the carriage to return to the *Loving Union*. Upon their arrival they had some difficulty in making their way through the numerous wagons and carts that lined the dock alongside the ship, and the men who were moving crates and boxes between them. What had appeared so serene the night before was now chaotic.

"May we be comin' on board?" Yelled Brian to Mr. O'Donnell when they finally reached the gangway. O'Donnell was standing at the head of the gangway with a journal making notations as crates and boxes went past.

"Certainly, certainly!" He answered with a smile. "The Captain's on the quarter deck," he said as they stepped off the gangway onto the deck and tried to stay out of the way.

When they climbed up onto the quarter deck they saw the Captain engaged in a conversation with two extremely well dressed older men. One was tall and thin and the other while not quite as tall was quite rotund. They did not appear to be happy with the Captain. When Captain Duckworth spotted them he smiled and waved them over to where he was talking with the two men.

"Gentlemen," the Captain said. "Allow me to introduce Mr. and Mrs. McBride." The two men mumbled something, doffed their hats, and bowed.

"This is Mr. Tillinghast," the Captain said nodding towards the taller man, "and this is Mr. Nixon. They are two of the merchants for whom we carried cargo on our voyage.

"Gentlemen," he continued. "Mr. and Mrs. McBride made the voyage with us from Liverpool," he said winking in Brian and Bridget's direction.

"Ah, Liverpool?" Said Mr. Nixon. "Very good. Very good. "Now Captain Duckworth, we must take our leave but I trust we will be able to resolve our differences?"

"I consider it already done my friends," said the Captain with a smile as he placed his hands on the backs of the two gentlemen and escorted them to the edge of the quarter deck. He watched as they climbed down to the main deck, crossed the gangway, and disappeared onto the crowded dock.

"Dey didn't look too happy." Said Bridget to the Captain when he returned.

"Those two?" He said. "They're never happy. They always seem to have difficulty remembering what the agreed upon price was for the goods delivered." He laughed. "After every voyage we have to negotiate to get to the price that was agreed upon to begin with!

"Look at you two!" He said with a big smile. "You look wonderful. You must have slept well."

"We did," said Brian with a slight chuckle. "We slept very well."

"Liverpool?" Asked Bridget.

"It is better," said the Captain, "that if someone seeking information about the arrival of someone from Limerick should ask, that those who might be asked believe our passengers were from Liverpool."

Bridget nodded. "Tank ya," she whispered.

"Have ya heard from Mr. Powell's man?" Asked Brian.

"I have," said the Captain. "We can expect him sometime this afternoon."

"T'is all so excitin'!" Said Bridget as she walked over, leaned on the rail, and watched the activity on the dock below.

Chapter 17

The Rancocas
1938

Lieutenant Baxter Underwood turned the Plymouth convertible off of Hilyard's Lane and into the narrow lane that ran past the front of the house. It wasn't until he brought the car to a stop that he realized just how dirty the car had gotten on his trip to the country. He laughed to himself when he thought about how angry his cousin, Lieutenant Edward Randall, who had loaned him the car, would be when he saw it.

He was here. No warning, no time to prepare, she must look a sight. She had only just now learned he was coming, what if Evan's letter had been delayed another day? They'd have no idea who this person was who was about to show up on their doorstep. It angered her that he should just show up like this, really angered her.

Why did he park there? Katy thought to herself as she stood on the porch watching. Can't he see that that's a road, not a place to park your car? Why didn't he keep coming down the lane and park in the yard like someone with any brains would have done?

Now, stop this. She said to herself. This is Evan's friend and no matter how you feel about his visit, you're doing this for Evan. But, Katy couldn't help herself.

"Go around to the back!" She yelled waving and pointing as he was stepping out of the car.

Woody, who had worn his dress blues, had stepped out of the car and was reaching into the back seat to get his uniform jacket, when he saw the woman on the porch waving and yelling. He smiled and waved back as he slipped on his jacket. What the devil is she yelling about?

Does she want me to go around to the back? What is this, dogs and sailors keep off the grass? Not allowed to enter by the front door?

"Oh well," he sighed.

He gave an exaggerated nod indicating he understood. Then he went to the rear of the car opened the trunk and retrieved the packages that Evan had sent. With the packages piled high in his arms he slowly began walking back down the narrow lane he had parked in towards the lane that lead around to the back of the house.

As he was walking he noticed that the road was very dusty and covered with tiny bits of corn stalks. The dust clung to his shoes and the bottom of his pants legs, and the little bits of corn stalks were already getting into his shoes and cuffs. All he could think about was how filthy his uniform and shoes were going to get.

Katy could not believe what she was seeing. Was this man really an officer in our Navy? If they were all this stupid why wasn't Evan an Admiral by now? She began waving and yelling again.

"No, the car. Around back, the car!"

Woody stopped and turned to look at the woman on the porch who he was now convinced was completely mad. She wants me to move the car around back? Doesn't want anyone to even see the car?

Woody turned around and started back towards the car. Fine with me lady, he thought, I don't particularly care to have anyone know I'm here either. Back door might even make for a faster get away.

When Woody got back to the car he carefully placed the packages on the ground, opened the trunk, put the packages back in the trunk, and walked around and got back in the car. He started the engine, put the transmission in reverse and backed up to where this narrow lane and the main lane intersected. He hesitated for a minute as he considered turning the wheel to the right and heading back out to the main road and back to the *Rhind*. But, Evan was a friend and a shipmate, so he turned the wheel to the left.

"What the devil's going on out there?" Asked Katy's grandfather, Michael McBride, as she came back into the house and passed through the parlor on her way to the back of the house.

"We have a visitor," she said exasperated and without stopping. "A friend of Evan's. I'm afraid he's a buffoon."

"He'll have news of Evan."

"Wouldn't count on it," replied an agitated Katy.

Woody turned the car into the yard and stopped. Where to now? Does she want me to hide it in the barn? Probably the first horseless carriage she's ever seen. He decided to stop right in the middle of the yard and await further instructions.

Katy came out onto the back porch. What is he doing now? Why is he parked right in the middle of the yard? She stood staring at the car with her arms crossed in front of her.

Woody stepped out of the car. "Is there somewhere specific you want me to put it?" He asked obviously annoyed.

Oh, yeah, there certainly is, she thought just as annoyed.

"Up here next to the porch would be fine," she said not doing a very good job of trying to sound friendly.

As he was pulling the car up Katy scolded herself. This was a friend of Evan's and no matter what she thought of him she was obligated to be nice to him for Evan's sake. After all, Evan had invited this man to visit their home, and no one was ever going to be able to say that they felt unwelcome in her house.

I'll park the car, he thought, get the packages, hand them off, give them a tilt of the old cap, Evan's fine, misses you and sends his love, and then I'll make some excuse to get the hell out of here, like I've got to get back because the ship struck an iceberg or something. Can't believe my old buddy conned me into visiting his crazy ugly sister. Pretty? Hell, I should have asked if she was crazy!

With the car parked Woody got out, no longer caring how dirty the car or his shoes and uniform were, and went around to the back of the car.

"Leave the packages until later," said Katy forcing a smile that appeared more grimace than smile. "Come in and have something to drink first, and we'll all get acquainted." Keep smiling, keep smiling she thought.

Woody sighed. Fine he thought. Let's just get this over with. He nodded and climbed the steps up onto the porch. He removed his cap and extended his hand.

"I'm Lieutenant Baxter Underwood," he said. "My friends call me Woody."

"Lieutenant Underwood," Katy said taking his hand. "Welcome to our home." Why did she call him Lieutenant Underwood? He said his friends call him Woody. Did she really mean to intentionally insult him like that? Stop this!

"I'm Katy McBride." She said, now she was embarrassed and was beginning to feel bad about how she was treating the lieutenant.

"Miss McBride," he said with a nod but no smile.

"Please come in," she said as she started to turn towards the door.

"Thank you, Miss McBride," he said, still no smile as he tugged his cap down on his head, "but I can't stay long. Besides, having moved the car so often, I'm afraid I might not have enough gas left to make it back to the ship."

Oh, she thought, as she turned back towards Woody, in addition to being stupid he's a smart aleck.

"Well, can't you at least stay long enough to tell us all the news about Evan? We'll try to get you out of here so you can begin your walk back to your ship before dark," she said sarcastically, "or perhaps we could saddle one of the mules for you? Then at least you would have someone to talk to on the trip."

"Yes, well perhaps I could tell the mule about Evan and then he could relay the information to you. That way it might be easier for you to understand."

"Exactly what is it that you are implying, Lieutenant Underwood?" Katy seethed, placing her hands on her hips.

"Implying?" He asked with a sarcastic smile. "Why nothing Miss McBride, it's just that I thought you might be more comfortable talking with your own kind."

"My own kind?" She exclaimed glaring at Woody. "You're the jackass that parked in the middle of the road."

"Road?" He asked. "That cow path? I have shoes that are not only wider than that "road", but are more heavily used."

"If it was all that bad, then why did you even park there?"

"My apologies," said Woody with an exaggerated bow. "I was not sure of the proper protocol, this is after all my first visit to Dogpatch!"

"Well!" Katy began trying to formulate a comeback. "You should have...." What did he say? "Dogpatch?" She asked unable to come up with anything else.

"Yes, Dogpatch," said Woody smiling and nodding as he started to laugh, "or is this just a suburb of Dogpatch?" He asked laughing even harder and spreading his arms as he looked around the yard.

Katy drew herself up to her full height, came to attention, threw her head back and with as much dignity as she could muster said, "My good man, I'll have you know, this is the capital of Dogpatch!" Then unable to control herself, she too broke into laughter.

Catching his breath Woody said, "Lady, you are nuts."

"I'm nuts?" She exclaimed.

Woody threw his hands up. "Please, please let's not go through that again," he said smiling at Katy. "Can we just start over?"

Katy glared at him, but then her look softened. "I suppose I can do that," she said almost smiling now.

Woody removed his cap, placed it under his left arm, bowed, extended his right hand, smiled, and said, "How do you do? My name is Lieutenant Baxter Underwood, but my friends call me Woody."

"Woody," said Katy curtsying and taking Woody's extended hand. "Welcome to our home. My name is Katy, Katy McBride."

"It is a pleasure to finally meet someone I have heard so much about."

"Likewise I'm sure," replied Katy demurely doing her best Betty Boop impersonation.

Several seconds passed before Woody realized he still hadn't released Katy's hand. Wait a minute, he thought, something's wrong. While she may be a little nuts, she wasn't ugly at all, and while she maybe couldn't be described as movie star beautiful, she was cute. No, cute wasn't it either. What she was, was, I don't know, lovely? Yes! That was it! Katy McBride was lovely. And, her eyes! She had the most beautiful emerald green eyes he had ever seen. Hadn't Evan said something about her eyes?

He hasn't let go of my hand, she thought. He must think I'm crazy carrying on the way I did. My God, he may be dumb as a mule, but he's got Robert Taylor looks!

"That's a very nice car," Katy said smiling and gently pulling her hand free.

"Thank you," said Woody, "but it's not mine. It belongs to a friend who was good enough to let me borrow it."

"Nice friend. Now let's get inside so you can meet Poppa."

Michael McBride was seated at the kitchen table when Katy and Woody finally entered the house.

"Poppa," said Katy, "why are you out here?"

"Well, the way you were shooing that young man and his car around the farm, I was afraid maybe I'd have to walk down to the landing to see him if I got to see him at all."

"Oh, Poppa," Katy said. She turned to Woody who was beginning to relax and wringing her hands said, "I know it may not look it, but the lane out front is often used by other farmers in the area and I didn't want to take the chance that your car might get damaged if they tried to go around it with a piece of machinery or a team of mules or something." Katy who was obviously flustered gave her grandfather her best be quiet or else look.

"Oh yeah, oh yeah, I remember now," her grandfather said. "I think I saw old Tom drive his truck down that lane not that long ago. When was that Katy Rose? June wasn't it? Yeah, I think it was back in June. We should check." He laughed. "The tire tracks may still be there."

Katy turned to Woody who was trying very hard to keep a straight face.

"I am sorry," she said. "It was just that, well, I didn't…"

"It's quite alright," said Woody seriously with a straight face. "This will all be a funny story we can tell our grandchildren someday."

"What?" Gasped Katy. "Our grandchildren?" She turned beet red and her mouth was going up and down but no words were coming out. She turned towards her grandfather.

He and Woody unable to control themselves any longer burst into laughter while Katy just got redder and redder.

"Yep!" Said grandfather. "He's a friend of Evan's alright. I like this young man. Come on lieutenant," he said. "We'll go into the parlor. By the way, my name is Michael McBride," he said extending his hand.

"I'm Woody," he replied as he took the offered hand.

"Katy Rose," grandfather said. "After you've composed yourself you can bring our friend Woody here something cold to drink. Grandchildren." He chuckled. "That was a good one."

Several minutes later when Katy came to the parlor she was more composed and brought with her a pitcher of fresh cider and the best fresh baked sugar cookies Woody had ever tasted. They talked until dinner time as he told them everything he could about Evan up until the time he had left the *Lexington.* He even told them about Irene Northrup, Evan's latest love interest.

Woody readily accepted Katy's invitation to join them for dinner. After dinner he offered to help Katy with the dishes but she chased Woody and her grandfather into the parlor. While she was doing the dishes she couldn't help but think how much like Evan Woody was. He was friendly, witty, easy to talk to, and, despite her first impression, intelligent. He was also charming, and not to mention box office gorgeous.

When she finished she joined her grandfather and Woody in the parlor. She was disappointed a few hours later, when it came time for him to leave.

"I'm sorry," he said. "I'm afraid I have to be going. Thank you for your hospitality, I really enjoyed myself, and Katy, the meal was absolutely delicious."

"Thank you," she said. "Are you sure you have to go?"

"Yes," he said. "It's well after dark, and I had enough trouble finding my way here in broad daylight. It may take me days to find my way back to the ship." He laughed.

"Evan give you directions?" Asked grandfather.

"Yes, he did."

"Come up the River Road?"

"Yes sir, passed through every quaint little town between here and Philadelphia."

"Evan's a boob when it comes to directions," he said. "Thinks everybody is from Rancocas."

"Poppa!" Said Katy.

"Well he is," said the grandfather. "Woody," he continued. "When you go out of here, at the end of the lane turn left. That's the Beverly-Mt. Holly Road. Take that out to Rt. 25, about four or five miles. Turn left onto 25, and watch for the signs for the Delaware River Bridge, that'll be about, I don't know, 10 or 12 miles. Once you cross the bridge you'll be back in Philadelphia. Find Broad Street and take it south until you run out of road. That'll be the Navy Yard."

"Thank you, Mr. McBride," said Woody as he crossed the room and shook the old man's hand. "Sounds simple enough."

"I'll walk you out," said Katy.

On the back porch Woody put his jacket on.

"I'm sorry your uniform and your friend's car got so dirty," she said.

"Car!" He said, smacking himself in the forehead. "The car. I never brought the packages in!" He looked at Katy and smiled. "Sorry. It'll only take me a minute, I'll get them now."

"No," she said as she reached out and took his arm. "Don't. If you don't bring them in now, that'll give you an excuse to come back." She smiled.

"I'd like that," he replied, "but I hope I wouldn't have needed an excuse."

"Me too. Think you can find your way back here to Dogpatch?"

"Delaware River Bridge, Rt. 25, Beverly-Mt. Holly Road, easy as crossing an ocean. Are there phones here in Dogpatch?"

"There are," she said feigning amazement. "We even have snap on lights, indoor plumbing, and automobiles now."

"I'll call you to let you know when I'm coming."

"Dudley 7-0404," she said. "You should write it down."

"No need."

"Oh, is your memory that good?"

"Not really," he said, "but 404, that's the *Rhind's* hull number." He smiled. "I really need to be going."

"I know."

They just stood looking at one another for a few awkward minutes before he finally turned walked down the steps, got into the car, and waved, as he drove away. Why didn't I kiss her, he thought as he was driving up the lane? I think she would have let me, and she has such kissable lips. Well maybe next time he said as he happily started to whistle the melody from the hit song "Nice Work if You Can Get it".

Katy walked out into the yard and watched until she could no longer see the tail lights of the car. Why didn't he try to kiss me she wondered? I think he wanted to. Would I have let him? I don't know, but I wish he would have tried.

Woody was not too gently awakened by his cousin, Lieutenant Ed Randall, shortly before 6am, the following morning.

"Meeting of all officers in the wardroom onboard the *Rhind* at 0700, cousin. You've barely got time to shit, shower, and shave," he said.

"Thanks," said Woody rubbing his eyes and sitting up in his bunk.

"What time did you get in?" Asked Randall.

"Well, I got back to the base about ten or so, but stopped in at the Officers' Club for a nightcap. Ran into a couple of the guys off one of the other cans, and had a couple more than I had planned to," said Woody. "Where were you?"

"I bunked out last night," replied Randall, who was completely dressed, with a grin and a wink.

"Anybody I know?"

"No, and no one you're going to know either," laughed Randall. "Where's my car?"

"Out back. Got a little dusty though."

"Well, you haven't been turned to stone, so at least she's no Medusa. How'd it go?"

"You know what, actually…" Woody stopped, did he really want Randall to know that the girl they had been making fun of was really quite attractive, and that he planned on visiting her as often as he could? "Actually, it wasn't as bad as I thought it was going to be. It was a nice ride, and Evan's grandfather is a really interesting old guy."

"She was rough though, huh?"

"I gotta get going here," said Woody as he jumped down from his bunk.

"Rough, or ruff, ruff?" Laughed the barking Randall as he headed out the door. "I'm going in search of coffee," he announced as he started down the passageway. "See you onboard."

Woody showered, shaved, and dressed quickly. Then he went in search of a pay phone. Calling to properly thank them for their hospitality and to let them know he had arrived safely back at the ship was simply the courteous thing to do. That's all it was, he was just being courteous.

He found a phone in the lounge. Whistling happily, he dialed the number she had given him. The phone was answered on the third ring.

"Hello?"

"Hello?" Answered Woody. This did not sound like Katy or Mr. McBride.

"Hello?" Said Woody again.

"Hello," said the voice.

"Who is this?" Asked Woody.

"I don't know," said the voice.

"You don't know who you are?"

"No Sir, I knows who I am, I don't knows who you are."

"This is Lieutenant Underwood, is this the McBride residence?"

"No Sir," said the voice. "It's a telephone."

"What? Oh," chuckled Woody. This sounds like a child's voice he thought.

"Is Miss McBride there?"

"Yes Sir."

Silence.

"Can I speak to her?"

"It's Lootin' Underman," said the voice still talking into the phone. "He wants to know can he speak to you."

Katy, who had been standing there the whole time listening to this delightful conversation and trying very hard not to burst out in laughter said, "Ask him how I can be sure it's him."

Mikey had to give this one some thought, so it took a minute. "Wants to know how I'm sure it's him."

Woody now understood that Katy McBride and her accomplice were having fun at his expense, and nobody appreciated a good joke more than Woody did. "Tell her I'm the Sheriff of Dogpatch," he said.

"Says he's Sheriff Dogpatch," the voice said.

He heard laughter in the background and then Katy's voice, "I'll take the phone now Mikey, thank you."

"Goodbye," said the voice.

"Goodbye," said Woody

"Hello Lieutenant," said Katy.

"Hello Miss McBride," said Woody happily. "Who was that?"

"That was Mikey," laughed Katy. "He's a little boy from up the road who helps out around the farm sometimes. I hope you didn't mind our little joke."

"No, not at all, actually, it was quite funny."

"I didn't' expect to hear from you so soon," said Katy.

"Well, I just wanted to call and thank you for a lovely time yesterday and to let you know I got back to the ship okay."

"Thank you. We enjoyed your visit very much, and I'm glad you got back okay."

A few moments of awkward silence.

"Listen, I've got to go," said Woody, "but, if it's alright I'd like to try and visit again this weekend, you know to deliver those packages."

"That would be very kind of you," said Katy.

"I can call later in the week to confirm," said Woody.

"That would be fine."

"I really did enjoy myself Katy."

"Me too," she said.

"Well, I've got to go, I'm late for a meeting, so, goodbye."

"Goodbye," said a blushing and smiling Katy as she hung up the phone before he could say anything else.

Now Katy girl, she said to herself as she looked down at the phone. Don't go getting all googly eyed over this guy. No one's really paid any serious attention to you since Nathaniel left. This guy's a sailor, and you know what they say about sailor's having a girl in every port. Yeah, she thought, but how many sailors have a girl in the port of Dogpatch? She giggled, a silly girly giggle, as she walked away from the phone.

She returned to the parlor to listen to her grandfather, Michael McBride, continue the story of his life and of how the McBride's came to America.

Chapter 18

The Delaware
1790

Brian and Bridget were visiting with Captain Duckworth in his cabin aboard the *Loving Union* when there was a rap on his door. "Yes?" Said the Captain.

"Permission to speak to the Cap'n?" Said a quaking voice from the other side.

"You may enter," said the Captain smiling at Brian and Bridget. "It may be vain," he said, "but I still do enjoy it a little when they're intimidated." He chuckled.

The door opened and there stood one of the younger members of the crew. A shy young man Brian and Bridget knew as Oliver. "Cap'n," he said with a bow. "Ma'am, Sir." he continued, looking at Brian and Bridget. He was obviously uncomfortable being in the Captain's cabin.

"Well, what is it?" Asked the Captain quietly. "A Mr. Powell," said the young sailor.

"A Mr. Powell is at the gangway and requests to see the Cap'n...Sir."

"Excellent!" Exclaimed the Captain turning and smiling at Brian and Bridget. "Bring him in. Bring him in," he said to Oliver.

"Yes Sir," Oliver replied as he bowed and backed out of the cabin closing the door behind him.

A few minutes later there was another rap on the door. When it opened there stood Oliver again, looking just as nervous. "Mr. Powell," he said, and then stepped aside.

William Powell was a man of about average height. He was thin and long limbed but did not appear weak or timid. In fact, he carried himself with a great deal of confidence and presence.

He was well dressed, but not overly dressed. He did not wear a wig but his light brown wavy hair was neatly trimmed and extended over his ears and laid on his collar at the back of his neck. He had a pleasant face with a large Romanesque nose that suited him.

"Welcome home Alexander!" He said with a beaming smile as he entered the cabin and extended his hand to the Captain.

"Thank you William," said the Captain as he stood and shook hands with the newcomer. "It is good to be home again, and in the presence of friends such as yourself."

"I see you have guests," said Mr. Powell glancing at Brian and Bridget. "I do hope I'm not interrupting. I can come back later, or even tomorrow, if you'd like."

"William," said the Captain with a laugh. "I don't think you could get out of here now if you wanted to." He turned to Brian and Bridget and said, "Allow me to introduce Brian McBride and his lovely wife Bridget. Mr. and Mrs. McBride, Mr. William Powell."

Brian nodded and Bridget curtsied. They both had such large smiles on their faces that they could not make their lips move to say anything.

Mr. Powell crossed the cabin and took Bridget's hand and kissed it and shook hands with Brian. "Welcome to Philadelphia, and America," he said.

Brian and Bridget could only nod, and squeaked out a barely audible, "Tank ya."

Mr. Powell turned to the Captain and they both laughed. "I seem to have had quite an effect on your passengers Alexander," he said.

"Indeed," replied the Captain with a smile.

"You have something for me Brian?" Asked Mr. Powell.

"I do Sir," said Brian regaining his composure. He opened his shirt and took out one of the leather pouches in which they kept their money. He opened it and took out the sealed envelope that was addressed to Mr. Powell that Reverend McCaghey had given him just before they left Ireland. He had folded it to fit into the pouch. It was now about an inch square with the seal folded to the inside to protect it.

While Brian was retrieving the envelope, Bridget, who had also regained her composure, said, "We've been waitin' a long time ta be meetin' ya Mr. Powell. I can't tell ya what a pleasure it t'is ta finally do so."

"Thank you Bridget, that's very kind of you."

Brian slowly and carefully unfolded the envelope under everyone's watchful eyes before handing it to Mr. Powell. He took it, looked at the seal and put it in his pocket.

"Aren't ya gonna open it?" Asked Brian.

"Hadn't planned on it," replied Mr. Powell with a smile.

"T'is just dat I've worried over keepin' it safe, and dry, and all together fer so long, I was sure it must say somethin' important."

Mr. Powell just looked at the young couple. Then with a smile he reached into his pocket took out the envelope and handed it to Brian. "Open it," he said.

Brian took it, looked at Bridget, and then back at Mr. Powell.

"Go ahead," said Mr. Powell turning and smiling at the Captain. "Open it."

Very slowly and very carefully while glancing at Mr. Powell, the Captain, and Bridget, Brian broke the seal and opened the envelope. Once it was completely unfolded and opened Brian just stared at it.

"What does it say?" Asked Mr. Powell.

"Nuttin'," answered Brian.

"What?" Said a surprised Bridget turning to look at the open envelope Brian was holding in front of him.

"Nuttin'," repeated Brian lifting his head to look at Mr. Powell. "I don't understand," he said.

Mr. Powell smiled and took the opened envelope from Brian. "My name on the envelope in Reverend McCaghey's hand with his seal affixed to it was just the way for me to confirm that you were who you claim to be. It is blank by design, so that if it should find its way into someone else's hands it reveals nothing but the name and address of a Philadelphia carpenter."

All Brian and Bridget could do was stare.

"Now," said Mr. Powell with a smile to Brian and Bridget. "My coach is waiting on the dock, so gather up any belongings you might have. You have spent your last night on the *Loving Union*, you're about to become residents of the City of Philadelphia."

Bridget turned to Captain Duckworth. "I do hope dat dis is not goodbye," she said. "We will be seein' ya again?"

"The *Loving Union* sets sail for Charleston, South Carolina, in two weeks' time," replied the Captain. "I will make it a point to call on you and Brian at least once before our departure."

"Promise?" Said Bridget.

"Promise," replied the Captain with a smile.

She crossed to him took hold of the front of his shirt, and pulled his face down to her level. She kissed his cheek, and said, "Just in case." Then she turned and left the cabin.

Brian shared a grip with the Captain who said, "I know where you will be and will call."

"I know," replied Brian. Then he turned to Mr. Powell. "We'll meet ya on da dock in five minutes?"

"That will be fine," he said.

When Brian entered their cabin he found Bridget sitting on the structure that had served as their bed during their time on the *Loving Union*. She seemed lost in thought.

"An bhfuil tu ceart go leor?"

"Are you alright?" He asked.

She looked up at him with a small almost sad smile. "You know," she answered in the Irish, "up to now this has seemed a grand adventure, but, there has always been someone there to guide us and to watch over us.

"Now," she continued. "I fear we are about to be left on our own, to fend for ourselves, strangers in a strange new world. It was easy to be brave when there was someone to turn to. Now I'm a little afraid."

He sat down next to her and took her hand. "There is nothing to fear as long as we have each other. You'll always have me to turn to."

"Oh, I know," she said. "I didn't mean to make it sound like I could ever doubt you. It's just that it's so, I don't know, frightening," she sighed.

He reached across and took her by the chin and turned her head so that they were facing each other. "Several months ago when we were told we had to leave Ireland for America it was you who were excited and confident, and I who was concerned and full of doubt. Now that we are here, suddenly it is you who have concerns and doubts." He smiled. "While I am convinced that not only is this right but that we are going to prosper here, as will our children, and our grandchildren. Now suddenly, it is I who am anxious and excited to begin this new life. We have changed sides," he said with a smile.

She reached up and with tears in her eyes she stroked her husband's face. "I love you," she said.

After nearly two months of calling the *Loving Union* home, Brian and Bridget were going ashore for good. They had a few changes of clothes, some personal possessions, and the balance of their ill-gotten gains. As forewarned, the fare had been costly. But, after paying the going rate for a fugitive's passage, they still had 28 pounds which would be over 100 dollars in this new nation's currency. It was a substantial amount for a young couple seeking a new life in a new nation.

Mr. Powell had indeed made arrangements. Brian and Bridget moved into two rooms on the second floor of a house on Pear Street, a short distance from the docks. They shared the house with two other families. A recently arrived German couple occupied the other two rooms on the second floor, and another Irish couple and their two young children occupied the rooms on the third floor. The clapboard house was small but it was sound and solid and the rent was more than reasonable. Mr. Powell owned the house and kept an office for his carpentry business on the first floor.

William Powell had also arranged for them to have jobs. Three days after moving into the Pear Street house Bridget began work as a maid's assistant in the home of Samuel Powell, a second cousin to William. Samuel Powell had been Mayor of Philadelphia and was now serving in the Pennsylvania Senate. The Powell house was on Third Street and was less than a ten minute walk from the house on Pear.

Brian went to work for William at a warehouse near the docks helping to build shipping crates and barrels for goods and materials that were leaving by ship, or had been unloaded from arriving ships and were being shipped over land to other destinations in an around the city. The warehouse was at the end of Walnut Street and was less than a fifteen minute walk from the house. They were both paid a fair wage and it was clear that Mr. William Powell expected nothing in return for his kindnesses except that the rent be paid when due and they give a fair day's work for the wage they were paid.

Brian's daily route to and from the warehouse took him past City Tavern which was on Second Street just off of Walnut. City Tavern had been built in 1773, and for the period leading up to, during, and following America's war for independence had served as a meeting and gathering place for the men whose vision, commitment, perseverance, and sacrifice had helped form this new democratic nation in a world of monarchies. Now, with independence won and the business of government more routine the tavern's proximity to the docks made it more a place for the owners and the masters of the nearby ships as well as the merchants with whom they did business.

That is not to say it was still not often visited by men of government or those with political sources, ties, or ambitions, and arguably it was still perhaps the best place in the city for the voices of political rhetoric. But, the voices were now those of the newer generation of politicos. Those who had been children during the war and were now preparing for the future of America, for when it would be their time. Now too, when one or more of the elder statesmen were in attendance they normally just sat back and listened and wondered if these well-intentioned new voices had any idea what it had cost to get them here.

Brian would on occasion visit City Tavern for he enjoyed drinking a few ales and listening to these political debates that seemed to go on and on. On one such visit he was invited to share a table and a pitcher with an elderly gentleman who introduced himself as Mr. Franklin, Benjamin Franklin. While Brian was aware that there was such a man who was quite famous, he did not immediately realize that this pleasant looking old gent was in fact that man.

What was more intriguing than the fame was that when he offered his hand, the old gentleman gripped it in a very particular way. Brian returned the grip with a smile, and with a brogue said, "Whereby one may know another in da dark as well as in da light."

Maintaining the grip the old man said, "I see that you are a traveling man."

"I am."

"Have you ever traveled?"

"I 'ave."

"Whence and wither?"

"From east ta west and from west ta east."

"What were you in search of?"

"A Brother, as I am da son of a widow."

"Let us sit my Brother and see what we can do to ease your journey," the statesman said as he released the young man's hand.

The old man was very easy to talk to and Brian found himself laying out the long sordid tale of how the English had stolen his farm, how he had turned to crime to flee the tyranny of the English in Ireland, and how he and his young wife now wished to take advantage of the promised freedoms of America. Mr. Franklin listened attentively only speaking when necessary to keep the young man talking, or to order more ale. When he was finally done Brian dropped his head and said, "I 'ave allowed da English ta make me a teef, I'm no better den dey are."

"And now you are here," said Mr. Franklin spreading his arms and looking around the room. After a bit of a pause he asked, "Were you a good farmer?"

"Yes, I was," replied Brian somewhat startled by the question. "Do you want to return to farming?"

"Yes, I do," he said sitting up and leaning forward.

"Can you grow corn?" The old man asked.

"What?"

"Corn... can you grow corn?" He formed the words very clearly and deliberately. "You see we have found that corn, which grows very well here, may be used for a variety of purposes and is quite a valuable commodity. So, I asked you, can you grow corn?"

"I've never tried, but with good soil, enough water and God's own sun I tink I can grow anyting you'd like," a somewhat confused Brian replied.

"And once you grew this corn, would you sell it at a fair and reasonable price to honest men? Men not unlike ourselves? Men who share our common bond," Mr. Franklin continued.

"I'm not sure I understand what yer about Mr. Franklin."

"What I'm about," said the old man as he leaned forward and with his forearms on the table tilted his head and smiled, "is, if a brother offered you a fair and reasonable price for your corn would you be more inclined to sell it to a brother as opposed to someone who were not? Even if the same price were offered?"

"Oh... yes! Well, I spose, I mean, I guess, yes, certainly I would." Now Brian was confused more than ever.

"Understand me my young friend," the gentleman continued. "I am not suggesting that you do anything that would go against your good judgment, or your conscience, or that you accept anything less than the true value of the fruits of your labors, I am only asking that when interacting with your newly adopted fellow countrymen you keep your obligations in mind.

154

"I am acquainted with and count among my many friends a number of Englishmen, both here and in England and even Ireland, who are members of our fraternity. Do not judge all Englishmen by those who have wronged you in a place you no longer call home. Do not let your pain cause you to judge men as anything other than men. Judge them based on their individual qualities not on their flag, and when the length of your cable-tow permits, reach out to a brother. In our new order you'll see we take very seriously our commitments to one another."

Brian slowly nodded and said, "Yes, Mr. Franklin, I will, and tank ya."

He returned the nod, laughed and said, "Never fails, a belly full of ale, an attentive ear, and a point to make, and any politician worth his salt will make a speech!"

Mr. Franklin called for another round, sat back in his chair, drew on a clay pipe that he had acquired and lit at some point without Brian even noticing, folded his arms across his chest, looked at Brian over a peculiar looking pair of spectacles, and said, "Prior to our independence my son William served as the Royal Governor of New Jersey. He had an estate there, Franklin Park, near Burlington. I have a friend who lives in that area. He is a man of property, and a brother as well, and he has a soft spot for young farmers who want to grow corn. If you would like perhaps I could speak to him about selling you some property which you could not only farm but on which you could build a home, and begin to raise a family. Would you be agreeable to that?"

Brian was dumbfounded, not only did he not know what to say, even if he had known, he wasn't sure he was even capable of speaking. Finally he blurted, "Yes, yes, o' course, o' course, dat would be wonderful Mr. Franklin, t'would be grand it would!"

He sat back in his chair and with his elbows on the arms of the chair and his fingers intertwined in front of him he slowly shook his head and as tears started to form in his eyes he said, "Tank ya. Tank ya so very much."

"Don't thank me yet," Mr. Franklin said with a smile. "We haven't contacted Jacob yet!"

Then Brian leaned forward and looked across the table at the smiling old man and said. "Why? Why, Mr. Franklin? Why would ya be doin' dis fer me? You've known me only a few hours, ya can't even be sure if anyting I've told ya is even da truth. So, why? Why do ya do dis?"

Mr. Franklin leaned forward in his chair and with his hands folded together on the table in front of him looked intently across the table and said, "And he pronounced the word Shibboleth, and the password was right." He paused and then continued, "My dear young friend Brian, do you think that the men who have helped you in your journeys do not know the caliber or the worth of the man in whom they have invested? Many of the men who came to your aid in Ireland, William and Samuel Powell, the master of the *Loving Union*, and even some of the men with whom you work at the docks have sworn an oath to assist a brother in need. Do you really think it just a coincidence that you and I are met here this evening? I, like the men I have mentioned, am simply a conductor, as will be some of the other men you encounter as your journey continues. You are not the first in whom we have made this investment, neither will you be the last."

With his hands flat on the table and as tears began to drop onto his cheeks he could only stare across the table at this amazing man and say, "I tank ya, all o' yas, fer yer charity."

"But that's the best part about it Brian, there is no charity," Mr. Franklin said with a smile. "You have paid for everything along your way. Your fares for the crossing, and you and your wife work each day to earn money to pay your rent and to purchase the things you need. And, if my friend decides to sell you property you will have to pay fair market value for it, it won't be given to you. We have given you nothing, nothing except opportunity which you have been wise enough to accept."

Brian was unable to speak. So he just nodded.

Mr. Franklin reached across the table and placed his hand over Brian's and said with a grin, "Besides, you didn't think we brought an Irish farmer all the way to Philadelphia just to build boxes did you? Now drink up and I'll get my coachman and we'll take you home. I'd like to meet your wife."

During the short ride Mr. Franklin explained that he and the men he had mentioned regularly assisted young men like Brian who they were made aware of by the far reaching influence of their fraternity. These men, from many different countries and circumstances, would, if found worthy, be assisted in making their way to America and in starting a new life in a new country that was full of nothing if not opportunity. These men understood that this new country needed men who were not afraid of risk, who understood and would take advantage of the freedom and opportunity not only to work and prosper but also to put forth and pursue new ideas and plans, and to help build this new nation. This would be a land where every man would have this freedom and opportunity, no matter his birthright or social status.

Later, as Mr. Franklin took his leave from the Pear Street house he warmly shook Brian's hand and said, "I don't know that we'll ever meet again, but if we do I will be pleased, if we do not, remember what has transpired between us this evening and when circumstances require, govern yourself accordingly. Goodbye Brian."

With that he climbed into his coach which then proceeded up Pear to Third and turned right towards the center of the city.

It had been nearly a month when in late May Brian received a letter addressed to him through Mr. William Powell, from a Mr. Jacob Hilyard. Mr. Hilyard explained that he had property available for sale which was suitable for farming along the Rancocas Creek in New Jersey near Burlington. He went on to say that Brian had been referred to him as a possible purchaser of the property by a mutual friend. Mr. Hilyard asked that Brian respond, if interested, with a suitable date when he could visit the area to view the property and if suitable discuss terms for its purchase.

Sadly, that mutual friend, died shortly after his visit with the McBride's. He was mourned on both sides of the Atlantic as well as by the McBride's, because not only had he helped to change the world, he had also changed their lives.

Chapter 19

The Rancocas
1860

The ninety two year old Michael McBride told his granddaughter Katy, as he continued his story, that as a 14-year old, he felt he was ready to handle a team of mules for the planting in the spring of 1860, but the winter of 1859 had been rough financially for the McBride's and they didn't have the money to purchase or even rent a second team. So, they made do with the one team and were able to get enough seed down to hopefully provide for their own needs and to market as well. By midsummer things were improving and William McBride had hopes that with a good crop he would be able to purchase an additional team before next spring, the spring of 1861.

But, in the summer of 1860, the talk around Rancocas, and in fact probably most of the towns and villages everywhere, was not about mules, the spring planting, or what the crop yield might be, it was about the upcoming presidential elections and the real possibility of war. No one seemed to be able to agree on anything. It almost seemed as if the plans for war had already been laid out, and that all that was needed was for someone to say, "Go!"

Michael, who, at 14, had completed his schooling at the Rancocas Friends School, enjoyed reading and tried to keep abreast of what was happening not only through the local newspapers but, when he had the opportunity, by walking the one and a half miles into the village's general store where one could always get the latest news. As he understood it, the economy of the southern states relied heavily on slave labor to get their cash crops of cotton, tobacco, and rice planted, raised, harvested, and marketed, and while there were still some slaves in the north, the north's economy, was based more on industry and manufacturing, so there was little if any dependency on slave labor. The abolition of slavery would be devastating to the southern economy while it would hardly be noticed in the North.

The South was afraid that if the Republican Abraham Lincoln were to be elected that he would not only oppose the expansion of slavery, but would work towards its abolition. While those in the North were afraid that if Democrat Stephen Douglas were elected his platform of allowing the individual states to decide the slavery issue themselves would not only allow expansion into the new territories to the west but perpetuate its existence in the southern slave states. Some of this was true and some of it was not, but getting people to listen or discuss either side of the argument calmly was difficult at best. Everyone seemed to have their own ideas about what the facts were, and anyone who did not have their own idea was eagerly supplied with someone else's.

In addition to Lincoln and Douglas there were other candidates as well. Incumbent Vice President John C. Breckenridge, nominee of the Southern Democrats was pro-slavery, and John Bell of the Constitutional Union Party was running on a platform of "moderation", that did not seem to address the issue of slavery at all. Throughout the summer and early fall representatives of the various parties held town meetings and rallies to promote their candidates and their platforms.

In September young Michael and his father William happened to be in Burlington when such a meeting was being held at the Belden House Hotel, which served as the local headquarters for Lincoln's Republican Party. The featured speaker at the event was Thomas H. Dudley, a Camden attorney who had been a delegate at the Republican Convention in Chicago in May, and had been instrumental in securing the nomination for Mr. Lincoln. Michael and his father curiously joined the crowd that had gathered in front of the Belden House's porch on High Street. The large gathering blocked the sidewalk on both sides of the street as well as a good portion of the street itself. Those in attendance did not just include white men of voting age, but children and young people like Michael, as well as women, and even several free blacks.

"I am a lawyer by profession," began Mr. Dudley when it was his turn to speak, "and was in the convention that nominated Abraham Lincoln."

Mr. Dudley was a well-dressed stern looking man. He appeared taller than the men around him, but Michael wasn't sure if this was because he was, or because of the way he carried himself. He wore his slightly greying hair stylishly, had a large bushy handlebar mustache, and a thick squared off goatee that was about four inches long and was also beginning to grey. He had a loud booming voice that exuded confidence.

"The delegates to the Chicago convention, which nominated Mr. Lincoln for the President, after much deliberation and negotiation, found themselves quite unexpectedly to be really for him. I came to believe, and continue to believe, that Mr. Lincoln was not only the right choice for our party, but is the right choice for our country.

"Mr. Lincoln is a constitutionalist and understands the rights and powers it gives and/or denies to individual state governments. Not only on the question of slavery but on other issues as well. He is prepared to hold the states accountable to this sacred document, especially those who are saber rattling in an effort to influence and disrupt this free election through intimidation.

"Mr. Lincoln is a Union man. He is prepared to do whatever is necessary, including a little saber rattling of his own if necessary, to hold this union together. He is the man for this time.

"Mr. Lincoln is a Christian man. He will look to God for his guidance, and he expects to answer to God for his actions. He is a man who is also prepared to answer to you.

"Some call him Honest Abe, some call him Rail Splitter. I know this man, he is without question an honest man, and he may have split a rail or two, but he is no backwoods buffoon, he is a learned man, an accomplished man, and like myself an attorney of some renown. But, with your help we shall soon call him by a new name, we shall call him President Abraham Lincoln.

"So when you vote, make it clear that you understand that it is time for a man who knows and will abide by our Constitution, that it is time for a man who is committed to preserving our Union, that it is time for a man of God, make it clear that you believe it is time for Abraham Lincoln!"

There was a hearty round of applause and a spattering of cheers when Mr. Dudley had finished speaking, but Michael couldn't help but notice that there were also some hissing and whistles of dissent.

"Mr. learned man," a voice cried out from near the front of the crowd. "Is there going to be a war?"

Mr. Dudley who had stepped back from the porch rail where he had delivered his speech stepped forward once again and raised his arms to quiet the rumblings as the crowd reacted to the man's question.

"My friends," began Mr. Dudley as he smiled down at the crowd. "Mr. Lincoln believes, as do I, that those states to the south of us who are flailing their arms, stomping their feet, yelling at the top of their voices, and threatening secession and war, are like little children upset that they are not getting their way. When the time comes it is highly unlikely that they will carry through on those threats."

Now there were further rumblings as some in the crowd seemed to agree with Mr. Dudley while others did not. There were those who were raising their voices to make it clear that they believed that war was not only inevitable but necessary. That the southern states who were making these threats had to be taught a lesson.

Mr. Dudley again raised his arms to quiet the crowd. "If in the event it becomes necessary to use force of arms to quell an insurrection or to preserve the Union, I can assure you that Mr. Lincoln will not shy from his duty. While the threat of war is not to be taken lightly, Mr. Lincoln will make every effort to avoid its eruption.

"War is an abyss that is a result of a society's failure. If we must fall into that abyss, then let us stand by Mr. Lincoln and pledge to climb out of that abyss the victors!"

The crowd loudly cheered and applauded as a smiling Mr. Dudley stepped back from the porch rail. There were a few more speakers, mostly local officials, before the meeting broke up, but it was clear that Mr. Dudley had been the star of the show and that if Burlington voted for Mr. Lincoln it would be in no small part thanks to Mr. Dudley.

Michael and his father visited a few of the city's shops before turning south onto High Street and heading out of town. They hadn't talked much about the meeting or Mr. Dudley's speech, but it was the topic of every conversation in the shops they had visited. It was hard to tell whether or not anyone was going to vote for Mr. Lincoln, but it was quite evident that Mr. Dudley was a very popular fellow.

As the wagon slowly made its way up the mile long gentle slope towards the road that would take them back to Rancocas, Michael turned to his father and asked, "Will there be a war?"

William didn't answer right away. It was not that he did not want to answer, or that his son was not deserving of an answer, it was just that he felt the question of war was something that required serious thought.

"Father?" Repeated Michael.

"I heard you son."

It was several more minutes before his father replied.

"I don't know," he said, and as he turned and looked at his son, he knew that his answer had been woefully inadequate. He turned and faced forward, and there were several more minutes of silence.

"I've never known war," William began. "During the Mexican War back in the forties I chose to stay at home and tend to the farm. There wasn't anyone else, and your grandfather wouldn't have been able to do it on his own.

"I know a man who fought in that war, a man from Beverly, Elias Abrams. Knew him before the war, and knew him afterwards too. It was like knowing two different men.

"Before the war he was a talkative good humored man who would walk a mile out of his way to share a word with someone. He was different when he came back. He was still friendly enough, but didn't talk or laugh as much, kept more to himself mostly, and always looked kind of sad.

"Never asked him what it was like, war, but it definitely changed him. I guess war changes most men. He wasn't wounded in any physical way that I knew of, but I believe his soul was wounded.

"For a time, I felt like a coward. Felt like I had let those who went to fight down by staying here. Now when I do think about it, I don't know if I did the right thing or not.

"I guess war affects even those who choose not to fight."

For several minutes no one spoke. William just stared out over the mules like he was somewhere besides in this wagon with his son. Michael looked at his father realizing that this man who had always seemed to be just a simple easy-going farmer who loved his wife and son was actually an intelligent and complicated man. Michael had never felt so proud to be his son.

Finally William turned and looked at his son with an almost embarrassed smile and said, "Will there be a war? I believe there will be. I don't see any way to avoid it now, too much strutting and pride at stake. No one will be the first to back down.

"I expect we'll be at war within the year. Probably last a year or two, and when it's all said and done the only thing that will be different is us. After America fights itself things will never be the same.

"The good thing is it won't be my war, I'm too old, and, thank God, it won't be your war, you're too young. But, maybe we can sell lots of corn to the army and make the money we need to buy them mules!" With that he reached over, slapped his son on the knee, and said with a smile, "Let's not talk of war anymore, it'll upset your mother. Besides it's depressing."

"Alright," Michael said, and as he settled in for the rest of the trip he couldn't help but wonder how he felt about the war that might be coming. He didn't know if he was glad or not that it would not be "his" war.

Less than two months later Abraham Lincoln, the honest plain spoken attorney from Illinois, was elected President of the United States. He had received less than 40% of the popular vote in what had been the largest voter turnout in history. Despite the fact that in ten of the thirty three states his name didn't even appear on the ballot. Christmas was white in Rancocas in 1860, and the cold temperatures caused a thin layer of ice to form on the creek. The McBride's had enjoyed their Christmas, Joanna's parents had joined them for dinner, as did her brother Thomas and his family who made the fifteen mile trip up from Newton Creek in time for Christmas dinner, returning home the following day.

"Well, it's done," said William McBride two days after Christmas, as he laid the latest edition of the Mt. Holly Herald on the table next to the Windsor chair he was seated in in the parlor of their farm house. The banner headline "South Carolina Secedes" only confirmed what had been suspected for days. Beneath the banner a smaller headline proclaimed "Other Southern States set to follow".

"Do you think other states will follow?" Said his wife Joanna, as she entered the room from the kitchen which was at the rear of the house.

"I don't believe South Carolina would have acted if there wasn't at least some sort of understanding that she wouldn't stand alone," he replied.

"Mr. Nagy said down at the store that Mississippi and a bunch of other states would be quitting the union soon too," said Michael who was seated in the other Windsor chair opposite his father in front of the room's fireplace.

"Oh, Mr. Nagy just likes to hear himself talk," said Joanna.

"This time he may be right," said William.

"Will there be a war?" Asked Joanna.

"Not right away," said her husband. "Buchanan won't do anything to provoke them, but once Lincoln is in he'll have to act. He's pledged to preserve the union."

"Well, we'll pray that it won't come to that," she said.

"Take more than that I'm afraid," said William. "It's going to take a miracle."

"Well, this is the season for it," said Joanna as she walked over to their Christmas tree that adorned the corner of the room farthest from the fireplace. "Another Christmas has come and gone," she continued, "and in a few days we'll have a new year.

"1861," she sighed as she fidgeted with the decorations on the tree. "I'm afraid it's not going to be a very good year." She turned and faced her husband and son, put her hands on her hips, and announced, "There will be no more talk of war or politics in this house today. What's left of our Christmas turkey is warming in the oven, I'm baking a fresh batch of biscuits, and roasting sweet potatoes in the coals. If you want to eat, you'll do as I say."

"Yes ma'am," said Michael and his father almost in unison.

"Now find something to do," she said as she left the room in route back to the kitchen.

Michael and his father looked at each other and shrugged. William picked up the paper and continued reading the news of the day.

Michael walked over to the Christmas tree and retrieved from beneath its branches what he considered to be the best Christmas presents he had ever received, a leather bound copy of Herman Melville's Moby Dick, and a soft cover copy of Edward Ellis' Seth Jones or Captives of the Frontier. He had overheard his father tell his mother that he had been able to purchase both books from Mr. Childs, the bookseller in Burlington, for fifty cents. Michael returned to the Windsor chair, settled in and began to read; "Call me Ishmael…"

William McBride, who was certain war was now inevitable, followed as closely as possible what was happening in the nation's capital. In early December, President James Buchanan, who couldn't wait to leave office, had delivered a message to Congress in which he stated that he believed secession to be illegal, but he also said that he did not believe the federal government had any right to take any action against a state that chose to secede. This message offended the Southern states who believed they had every right to secede, and perplexed the Northern states who could not believe that the federal government could not act. Buchanan's message only served to enflame the situation.

Then, about a week after South Carolina seceded, President Buchanan agreed to meet with a delegation from that state. From the outset, he made it quite clear that he considered them private citizens of the State of South Carolina and not representatives of some newly formed government. They in turn did not wish to discuss how the issues that led to their secession may be resolved, but focused instead on the federal garrison that had moved from Fort Moultrie to Fort Sumter in Charleston Harbor. Since their position was that the federal government no longer had any authority in South Carolina, they demanded that arrangements be made for the immediate withdrawal of the garrison. Buchanan refused to withdraw the garrison.

The New Year was sure to bring war, but on New Year's Eve, as was the family custom, William McBride brought forth a bottle of Laird's Applejack. Every year, William would purchase a bottle of the sweet liqueur from Mr. Mailin of Burlington, who was a brewer and distributor of fine spirits, for 75 cents, as a Christmas present to himself. William, Joanna, and even Michael, would then salute the ending of the old year and welcome the promise of the New Year with a toast.

Michael and his mother would each be poured about an ounce of the liquid for each toast, while William would pour himself about twice that, a little more if Joanna was not paying close attention. After the toasts the liqueur would be returned to the cupboard to reappear only for medicinal purposes or for special guests or occasions. Michael had always found that the first sip was difficult, but he enjoyed the way the velvety liquid warmed his body and made his face flush once he got it down.

Nine days into the new year, Mississippi joined South Carolina and seceded from the Union. Within the next two days, two more states seceded, Florida on the tenth, and Alabama on the eleventh. By the end of the month Georgia and Louisiana had seceded as well.

Despite the efforts of President Buchanan, prominent members of Congress, and others, there seemed to be no way of preventing the nation from being split wide open. Then came a last ditch proposal from a rather unlikely source. Governor John Letcher, of the State of Virginia, proposed that a Peace Convention be held to try and resolve the issues between North and South before the outbreak of war.

The convention began on February 4th, in Washington. None of the states that had already seceded sent delegates, and only 21 of the remaining states were represented. The convention lasted three weeks.

As a result of the convention compromises were arrived at and forwarded to Congress for their consideration and action. These compromises would have taken the form of new amendments to the Constitution. Sadly, in early March of 1861, just days before Abraham Lincoln was to be inaugurated as President, the compromises were defeated in the Senate by a vote of 28-7, the compromises never came to a vote in the House.

The 36th US Congress would adjourn having done very little to prevent further secession or worse yet, an American war.

On February 11th, Abraham Lincoln's train left Springfield, IL, in route to Washington, DC. The trip was scheduled to take twelve days with an arrival in Washington on the 23rd. Over seventy stops were planned in towns and cities both large and small as the newly elected President wound his way to the capital meeting and greeting thousands of his fellow citizens along the way.

He was scheduled to make a brief stop in Bristol, PA, on the 21st, as his train made its way from Trenton to Philadelphia. Bristol was directly across the Delaware River from Burlington.

"Is there any way we could go see him?" Asked Michael.

"See who?" Replied his father William.

"Mr. Lincoln…in Bristol."

William looked at his son as if he'd spoken a foreign language. "You do know that Bristol is in Pennsylvania on the other side of the Delaware, right?"

"Yes Sir."

"How would you propose crossing the river? It's about a mile wide at Burlington you know. It's not an easy swim, and I'm sure the water is pretty cold this time of year."

"We could take the ferry, or get someone to take us over in a boat."

"A boat?"

"Yes Sir."

"So, we should spend money to hire a boat to take us to Bristol in hopes that we might get a momentary glance of a man we don't know and will probably never see again?"

"We might be able to take the ferry, and yes Sir, we should."

"Why?"

"We may never get the opportunity to ever see a man that is to be President again."

William stared at his son, realizing he was probably right. "When is he supposed to be there?"

"Thursday, the 21st, sometime in the afternoon." Replied Michael.

"It is historical, that's for sure," said William as he considered his son's idea. "We'll go into Burlington early and see if we can get the ferry or find someone to take us over," he finally said. "If we can and the fare isn't too much, we'll see if we can get a look at this rail splitter from Illinois."

"Yippee!" Exclaimed Michael as he slapped his hands together and stomped his feet.

"What was that all about?" Asked his mother as she entered the room.

"We're going to Bristol to see if we can see the new President," William told his wife.

"All of us?"

"Yep, all of us."

"When?"

"Thursday."

"Yippee," she whispered as she turned around and returned to the kitchen.

On Thursday, February 21st, William, Joanna, and Michael McBride, having taken the ferry, and walked nearly a half mile to the Bristol train station, watched as Abraham Lincoln, the man who was on his way to Washington to become the new President of the United States spoke briefly from the back of a train. They were not close enough to clearly hear everything that he said, but were close enough to feel that they were a part of history. The visit was brief, less than fifteen minutes elapsed from the time the train stopped until it was once again underway.

Chapter 20

The Delaware
1790

It was late May, it had been nearly six weeks since Brian had spent an evening with Mr. Franklin when around mid-morning he boarded the *Sally*, a 45-foot single-masted cargo sloop, at the base of Walnut Street to journey to New Jersey. The sun shone brightly and it was a seasonably comfortable day for the time of year. The *Sally* routinely transported cargo from Philadelphia north to the landings along the Rancocas Creek. Particularly to Mt. Holly and Lumberton. She would make the outbound trip one day and return the following day. She sailed every day except Sunday.

Per Mr. Hilyard's directions, Brian was to take the *Sally* to the Rancocas landing on the Rancocas Creek. Since the *Sally* may, or may not, have to make several stops between Philadelphia and Rancocas it was not known how long the trip would take or exactly when Brian would arrive at Rancocas. However, upon his arrival he was to walk to the grist mill, which was just up the road from the landing, let someone know who he was and the purpose of his visit and they would notify Mr. Hilyard who would then meet him at the mill.

The *Sally* arrived at the landing in the early afternoon. Brian did as instructed and Mr. Hilyard soon arrived. He was driving a small open wagon being pulled by a large powerful looking mule. After their introductions, and a familiar grip, Mr. Hilyard advised that, since his home was in Burlington, they would be dining and spending the night here in Rancocas as guests of Samuel Wills and his family. Then in the morning they would visit the properties Mr. Hilyard was offering for sale.

The Wills' lived on the Mount Holly Turnpike about a mile distance from the landing and the two men arrived there in short order. During the trip Brian had noticed that the area appeared to be heavily wooded with only a few tracts of land that had been cleared. Everything was in full bloom, and the fields that he could see along the road and through the trees appeared to have been planted and in many cases were beginning to show yields.

The largest cleared area was near the mill. Here there were a number of plots on which Quakers had built small wooden cabins, and cleared land for gardens and small sheds and barns. They passed only two other houses along the road after the Quaker settlement.

Upon arriving at the intersection of the Turnpike and the landing road he did notice that there were about five well- built brick homes near the intersection as well as a brick meeting house. Most of the homes appeared to be of newer construction.

The Wills' house was a large two story brick house with large chimneys on each end and a covered portico on the front. There were two windows on each side of the large front door and five windows across the front on the second floor. It was directly across from the meeting house and seemed quite grand for a house located in an area that appeared to be mostly wilderness.

Mr. Hilyard and Brian were warmly greeted by Mr. Wills, whose grip was familiar, and his wife Sarah, and after a dinner that included a potato soup with a generous amount of onions, wild turkey with cornbread, mashed potatoes, cider, and a dessert of rice pudding with currant jelly, the men retired to a sitting room to talk and enjoy a smoke and some ale in front of a fire.

"Well, Mr. McBride what do you think of our budding burg?" Mr. Wills asked.

"Please sir, I would like fer ya ta be callin' me Brian," Brian answered, "and I tink t'is very nice it t'is. Doe to be honest Mr. Wills it seems ta be quite removed from everyting it does."

"Oh, but the potential for growth and prosperity in these fields and woods Brian," Mr. Wills said with a smile, "You can almost smell it. And, it will be my pleasure to call you Brian only if you agree to call me Samuel."

"Well I can't be arguin' with dat Samuel," Brian replied with a smile.

"It's not as removed as you may think Brian," said Mr. Hilyard. "There are three growing and thriving communities surrounding us, each of them less than five miles, from where we now stand. Burlington and Dunk's Ferry on the river, and Mt. Holly just up the Rancocas. We have the beginnings of a very good road and ferry system, and have a number of bridges in place with plans for many more to come."

"The turnpike," Samuel interjected, "that runs past the front of this house was surveyed and laid out by the English while we were still a colony. It wasn't completed until after the war. That road runs ten miles from the banks of the Delaware at Dunk's Ferry to the center of Mt. Holly. We are the midway point on that road. Just a quarter mile east of here," he continued as he pointed in that direction, "it intersects with the Burlington Road. Travel that road for five miles and you will arrive at the riverfront in Burlington. So you see Brian, we are the geographical hub for this developing region and there is no reason why we should not also become the agricultural and commercial hub."

"If that's not enough," interrupted Mr. Hilyard. "We have John Fitch running his steamship Perseverance back and forth between Burlington and Philadelphia now on a regular schedule. Despite the noise and the smell of the ugly contraption it is quite amazing!"

"Exciting to think you might be a part of something with so much potential isn't it Brian?" Said Samuel.

"Excitin'?" Brian asked. "Yes it t'is, but t'is also a bit of a fright," he continued. "Besides, we 'aven't looked at a square foot o' propity yet," he said laughingly as he lifted his mug in a toast to his two companions.

"Listen to us go on Jacob," said Samuel, "trying to influence this young man's future like a couple of traveling drummers selling cookware to a bunch of gossipy women," he laughed as he refilled their mugs.

"Yes, of course you're right Samuel," said Mr. Hilyard. "Please forgive a couple of overzealous visionaries as we try to see into the future. And please Brian. Call me Jacob."

"T'is nothing ta fergive sir. Yer both excellent salesmen. I'm feelin' I should purchase any land available I should, sight unseen jus' ta be a part o' yer grand vision. But, I tink dat I will control meself and wait and see it first anyway.

"And, as far as callin' ya Jacob, Mr. Hilyard, since we may soon be enterin' into negotiations and business dealin's dat are likely ta change me current circumstances, me life, and da life of me wife Bridget and da lives of all dose McBride's yet ta come, I'll be feelin' more comfortable continuin' ta call ya Mr. Hilyard 'til our business is concluded. Yew however must call me Brian." He paused. "Let's jus' say dat we 'ave entered into our negotiations and dat dese are da first o' me terms," Brian said with a smile.

"I agree to your terms my young friend," Mr. Hilyard replied, "though they seem somewhat one-sided." He raised his mug, winked at Brian, and said to Samuel, "Has anyone else's mug gone dry?"

Samuel laughed as he stood and went to retrieve the pitcher to refill their mugs. "Jacob," he said. "It looks like you may find our new friend quite a challenge."

"Indeed," laughed Mr. Hilyard.

With their mugs refilled Samuel turned to Brian and said, "Now Brian why don't you tell us a little bit about yourself?"

"I would sir, but I'm feelin' dere's not much I can be tellin' ya dat ya don't already know. I was forewarned dat I would be meetin' more," he paused, "how were dey described? Oh yes, conductors, in me journeys." He raised his mug in a salute to the two gentlemen.

Samuel looked at Mr. Hilyard who raised his mug as well and said, "To fraternity and brotherhood". And they all drank.

Brian commented on how fine the Wills' house was and Mr. Hilyard took the opportunity to discuss his plans for a house he was planning to build at the intersection in the village that would rival the Wills'. The two men teased each other about who would have the grander house and when the evening came to a close Brian retired to a very comfortable bedroom on the second floor.

They arose just after daylight and after a breakfast of bread, honey, cold turkey, and cider, Samuel provided a guided tour of his homestead and outbuildings as well as a tour of the village, pointing out locations where merchants and other men of business might eventually ply their trades. Mr. Hilyard then suggested it was time they visited the properties that were available for purchase. The *Sally* would be at the Rancocas landing early in the afternoon, so they were to hurry if Brian was to make the sloop.

Prior to parting company with Samuel, Brian thanked him for his kindness and hospitality. Samuel said that he hoped to see more of Brian in the future and kidded him about making sure he didn't let Mr. Hilyard cheat him too badly on any land purchase he might make.

The sun was again shining and it appeared as if it were going to be another comfortable day. As they left, Mr. Hilyard explained that he had two tracts that he thought Brian might be interested in. He suggested that they visit each tract and then talk price. The first was just a short walk, less than half a mile, south on the landing road.

It was a tract of nearly 15 acres. It was bordered on the north by the village, on the south by the cluster of Quaker homes and gardens adjacent to the mill, on the west by property owned by Daniel Wills, and on the east by property owned by Robert Hudson. There was no road frontage. Its western border was about 100 yards east of the landing road and they accessed the property by way of a narrow path.

Mr. Hilyard said that Daniel Wills had agreed to grant the buyer an easement so that a lane could be cut to provide access to the property from the landing road. Though it was possible that at some time the northern border of the property might actually front one of the village streets. However, at this time neither Daniel Wills nor Mr. Hudson had seemed interested in selling any of the property adjacent to this tract. He also advised that there was no flowing water on the property so the buyer would have to dig a well.

Walking the property Brian noted that on the southwest corner of the property there was a natural meadow about two acres in size. A narrow tree line separated the meadow from the Quaker settlement. There was an additional three to four acres on the northern side on which many of the trees had been cut but few of the stumps had been removed and not much of the other growth had actually been cleared. The manner in which the trees had been cut actually appeared as if they had been cut in preparation of laying out a narrow road or street.

Brian liked the size of the tract but was concerned that it was land locked, that there may not be an opportunity to acquire additional property in the future, and that there was no open water. In addition, because so little of the property had been cleared he would be at least one full season away from being able to plant enough crops to market. Satisfied that he had seen everything he needed to see at this location Brian and Mr. Hilyard returned to the Wills' house in the village and retrieved the wagon pulled by the large mule they had used the day before. Mr. Hilyard explained that the second tract was a little more than a mile southeast of the village.

They took the turnpike east out of the village. Mr. Hilyard pointed out the road that ran north to Burlington when they passed it. After proceeding about a half mile they turned south onto a narrow but well used wagon road. Mr. Hilyard explained that this road divided the property to the east, owned by Mr. George Haines, from the property to the west, which was owned by him. It was referred to locally as Hilyard's Lane.

They continued along this road for about another half mile where it intersected with another well used but narrow wagon road. This road, according to Mr. Hilyard, was known as the Old Mill Lane. If they were to travel east on this road for about a mile it would intersect with the Mount Holly Turnpike.

To the west about the same distance the road intersected with the landing road at the Wills Grist Mill. This used to be the main east-west road before the turnpike was laid out nearly twenty years ago. Now it was primarily used by farmers from the Mt. Holly area who were going to the mill or the landing.

Mr. Hilyard explained that the Old Mill Lane served as the northern border of the second tract of land. This tract was just over thirty acres in size. Hilyard's Lane continued south of the intersection, although it was less well-defined, for about three-tenths of a mile to the banks of the Rancocas Creek. About 100 yards to the east of Hilyards Lane was a small stream that flowed south into the Rancocas. The stream served as the eastern border of the property. The property line then fronted the creek, the southern border of the property, west for a little more than two-tenths of a mile, then turned north for about the same distance, west for about a tenth of a mile, then north again to the Old Mill Lane, the northern border of the property, then west about another three-tenths of a mile back to the intersection where they were sitting.

So, the property had frontage on two roads and nearly a quarter mile of creek frontage. In addition, as Brian could see, nearly fifteen acres here on the northeast corner was already cleared to the point of almost being ready for the plow, and the portion along the stream to the east of Hilyards Lane was a level grassy meadow which might serve as a good spot for a barn. The rest of the property appeared to be mostly pine and hardwood trees.

Mr. Hilyard said that since he also owned the property to the north he would perhaps consider selling additional property in the future, and that Mr. Haines, who owned the property to the east, might also be persuaded to make additional property available at a future date. They continued down the lane to the creek and then walked along the bank. They returned to the wagon and when they got back to the intersection they turned west onto the mill lane. They stopped along the way and walked several other areas of the property before continuing along the lane to the landing road and then on to the landing, arriving at about half past noon.

Along the way they ate a light lunch that Mrs. Wills had been kind enough to prepare, of cold turkey and bread which they washed down with cider.

The sloop was just coming into view upstream and would be at the landing in about half an hour. It was time to talk price.

Mr. Hilyard came right to the point. He told Brian that because the fifteen acre tract was land locked, had no open water, and was not sufficiently cleared, he would sell it for $22.00, which was less than one and a half dollars an acre. The second tract, because it had road and creek frontage, and was partially cleared would cost $90.00, about three dollars an acre. A fifty percent cash deposit would be required, for either property, at the time of transfer, and he would be willing to hold the mortgage on any unpaid balance. The terms of the mortgage could be worked out prior to the conclusion of the sale. He would also arrange for a survey of the property prior to the final agreement. He also presented Brian with a hand drawn map showing the two tracts and their proximate location to the village, landing, each other, and other significant landmarks.

Brian was awestruck. They had enough money to pay for the second tract in full, but that would leave them very little with which to set up housekeeping and purchase the equipment and supplies they would need to begin farming. However, if they went with the smaller tract they could still pay in full and have plenty left over for the other necessities. He could not make this decision without discussing it with Bridget.

The sloop was drawing closer. He would have to board soon. "Mr. Hilyard," he said. "I cannot tell ya how grateful I am fer yer kindness, consideration, and fairness. I'll not haggle with ya over a price dat I feel is much more den fair and perhaps even generous. But, I cannot make dis decision without talkin' it over with me wife first and havin' at least a few days ta consider it since it will change me life and da lives o' future generations o' me family. I'm sorry, and I do hope ya understand'."

"Brian," Mr. Hilyard answered with a smile. "I would not expect or even accept a decision at this time precisely for the reasons you have stated. You return to Philadelphia, discuss this with your wife, show her the maps, and be sure of what you both want to do. I will not solicit or entertain any offers on either property for thirty days. Will that be enough time for you?"

"More den enough Mr. Hilyard," Brian said with a huge grin. "Much more den enough, tank ya."

"You must satisfy my curiosity though, if you would, before you go. If you did have to pick right now which property would you take?"

"Da creek front," Brian replied without any hesitation.

"I had no doubt," Mr. Hilyard said with a smile.

Brian stepped down from the wagon, grabbed his satchel, and started walking toward the landing as Mr. Hilyard also exited the wagon. As Brian was walking past the large mule he stopped and admired him. He then walked to the front, stopped in front of the mule, and rubbed the animals muzzle.

"He's a fine lookin' crature he is," Brian said.

"That's Oliver. I purchased him and a molly, Annie, at an auction in Black Horse a few months ago."

"I'll be needin' a pair dat's fer sure." More to himself than anyone else. He looked at Mr. Hilyard and asked, "Once our business is complete would ya be willin' ta help me find a pair at a reasonable price?"

Mr. Hilyard crossed his arms in front of his chest, leaned back, tilted his head, and said, "I'll tell you what, buy the creek front property and for an additional $10.00 I'll throw in both mules and the wagon."

"Mr. Hilyard yer puttin' me in a position where I can't be sayin' no ta ya." Brian laughed.

"As we agreed," said Mr. Hilyard as he stuck out his hand. "You'll let me know within 30 days"

Brian gripped it and said, "30 days, as agreed. Tank ya."

"Now get aboard, and you're welcome."

Brian boarded the *Sally* which departed the landing just after one o'clock. Thanks to the outgoing tide, and steady wind out of the north, the sloop made the 18 mile trip back to the Walnut Street docks in just under four hours.

By the time Brian, who was anxious to share his exciting news with Bridget, made his way to the Pear Street house it was after six. When night came it brought with it a steady rain, and an unseasonably cold and bitter wind.

They sat up most of the night huddled in front of their small fireplace as Brian told Bridget of his trip to New Jersey. With great enthusiasm and in much detail he described the *Sally*, the river and what he saw along its banks. He talked affectionately about Mr. Hilyard and the Wills', and thrilled Bridget with the description of their fine house and of the growing village.

He showed her the map and told her about the properties he had walked, and of course about the offer of Oliver, Annie, and the wagon. As young couples do they discussed the financial aspects as well as the other pros and cons for purchasing one of these properties, or of making no purchase at all and maybe remaining in Philadelphia or perhaps traveling to some of the other states to see what they were like. They agreed that they would continue to discuss their options and would wait at least two weeks before they made any decision. It was turning out to be much more difficult than they thought.

It was a bright, warm, sunny Sunday morning in June. After attending church Brian and Bridget decided to go for a walk. It had been over three weeks since Brian had visited Rancocas. They owed Mr. Hilyard an answer.

They had packed a picnic lunch and started out walking along Dock Street towards the river. They arrived there in short order, turned, and walked south along the riverbank. They took the road when they could, but wanting to be close to the river they walked mostly the wooded trails and narrow paths that followed the riverbank.

As they walked, they talked. They talked about everything that had happened to them in the time since Lord Northrup's footman had knocked on the door of their cottage outside of Limerick in Ireland. Some of it was good, and some of it was bad. But, now that they were settled in their new country the bad didn't seem to matter as much as it once had.

After walking for about an hour and a half, they came to a small clearing overlooking Hollander's Creek where it flowed into the Delaware River. The creek was about 100 yards wide here. On the opposite shore of the creek were four young boys who couldn't seem to decide whether they were there to fish or swim. Three of them were as naked as the day they were born, and the fourth wore only a beat up old slouch hat that was way too big for such a small boy's head. He did take great delight however in using it as a bucket to douse his companions. They made no effort to cover themselves, so they either didn't notice Brian and Bridget, didn't care, or felt the distance protected their lack of modesty.

As Bridget spread out their blanket in the shade of a bent willow tree, Brian watched the frolicking boys and could not help but be reminded of the times he had spent doing the same thing along the banks of the Shannon and the Ballynaclough when he was their age. Those places were so far away now, and it saddened him that it would only be in his memories that he would ever visit them again.

"T'is a good spot fer a picnic," said Bridget bringing him back to the present.

"Yes, ta se."

"Yes, it is," he answered as he sat down alongside her.

"I've been tinkin'," she said. "We're Americans now, and I'm tinkin' we should be speakin' as Americans. After all, besides da two o' us, dere's no one ta be talkin' da Irish with anyway, is dere?" "

Ta muid Gaeilge agus is I an Ghaeilge at dteanga. Ba e an teanga ar sinsear, agus beidh se ar an teanga ar ar bpaist."

"We're Irish and Irish is our language. It was the language of our ancestors, and it will be the language of our children," Brian said as he turned and looked out over the river and tried to keep the anger and the hurt out of his voice.

"I'm sorry," she replied in the Irish. "I've upset you." She reached out and put her hand on his arm.

He didn't speak but kept looking out across the river. She removed her hand. Several minutes passed.

"No," he said softly in English. "Yer right. It t'is time fer me ta stop lookin' back and ta begin lookin' ferwerd." He turned to his wife, and she could see the sadness in his eyes. "We're on dis picnic ta decide how we will start dis new life o' ours. Me and you will always be Irish, but our children will be Americans with Irish parents, and with every generation of McBride's in America, Ireland will move farther away.

"So, let us begin t'day. From dis day forward we will speak da Irish only on Sundays' after worship. We will do it, and we will teach our children ta do it, who will teach our grandchildren ta do it. So's dat a hundred years from now if ya walks into a McBride house on a Sunday, ya will hear da Irish. No McBride should ever be allowed ta be fergettin' where da two people who are startin' all o' dis came from."

"I love ya Brian McBride," she said with tears in her eyes.

"Ta se an Domhnach agus taimid ag Bainim do adhradh, agus ni an oiread agus is brea liom tu Mrs. McBride."

"It's Sunday and we've been to worship, and not as much as I love you Mrs. McBride," said Brian with a smile

"And so it is, and so we have, and of the last I'm not so sure," she answered in the Irish.

On a hot steamy day in early August of 1790, Brian and Bridget McBride sat in the office of the Clerk of the County of Burlington on Broad Street, in Burlington, while it was recorded that they had purchased 30 acres of partially cleared land along the Rancocas Creek one mile east of the Village of Rancocas on the Mt. Holly Turnpike, from Jacob Hilyard of Burlington for the sum of $90.00. Brian made absolutely certain that there were no outstanding liens, levies, or taxes due on the property before it was transferred.

They had decided to pay for the property in full so that never again would anyone be in a position to take their land from them. Mr. Hilyard, as agreed, also sold them the wagon and the pair of mules for $10.00. Which they also paid in full, using the last of the money they had brought with them from Ireland to do so.

Mr. Hilyard then laughingly agreed to loan the $100.00, back to the McBride's. The collateral for this loan not being the property, but the two mules and the wagon that he had just sold to them for ten. They added the $100.00 to the money they had saved since arriving in Philadelphia, bringing the balance of their remaining funds to about $150.00.

Brian had calculated that it would cost about $75.00, to purchase the tools, supplies, and livestock they would need, which would include a plow, a bull, a cow, a boar, a sow, and a few sheep and chickens. The remaining $75.00, they would use to live off of until the next year's harvest. It would be tight, but Brian was confident they could do it.

With Bridget's help, and the two mules Brian figured he could plant about 20 acres come next spring. With good weather and God's blessing, the yield should be right around 300 bushels, and if corn stayed at or near its 1790 price, that would mean they could make as much as $150.00, their first year.

When the signings were done and the seals affixed Mr. Hilyard and Brian shook hands sharing a grip well known to both of them.

"Welcome home my Brother," said Mr. Hilyard.

And, Bridget wept.

Chapter 21

The Catoctin
1861

It was February 13, 1861. Sunrise was more than an hour away when the advance patrol from B Troop left the US Cavalry Post in Carlisle, PA, and started out for Chambersburg nearly 30 miles away. 2nd Platoon was given the assignment, and Trooper Matthew Calhoun was among those who had been selected for the mission. They were going to be in the saddle a long time, it would be getting dark by the time they reached their destination.

Counting Sergeant O'Neall, who was in command of the patrol, there were seven of them. Their mission was to act as an advance party preparing the communities along their route for the arrival of the larger force that would be following them the next day. Over the course of the next three days they would cover over 75 miles as they made their way to Frederick, Maryland.

Despite the cold hard ride ahead of them, Matthew was excited. Not only was the Troop proceeding on its first real meaningful mission, but the route they were taking would take them right past Matthew's home in Middletown, Maryland. He was hoping that he could convince Sergeant O'Neal to let him visit with his sister and father for a few hours. He hadn't seen them in nearly eight months.

Sergeant O'Neall's, "For'ard," was the only thing that was said as they headed west on the Newville Road out of Carlisle in the cold pre-dawn darkness. They wore their blue heavy wool great coats with capes, with the gold buttons and gold braid of the cavalry. Their forage caps were pulled down on their heads as they tried to protect their ears from the cold, and their leather gauntlets, though they covered their hands did little to keep the cold off.

Matthew, like most of the other troopers with the patrol had taken Sergeant O'Neall's advice and worn long johns and put on an extra pair of socks. Even so, the leather saddle was cold against his backside and other sensitive parts, and his feet were far from toasty. Matthew couldn't help but wonder if it was ever necessary for cavalry troopers in Texas to dress this way.

They had gone nearly five miles before the sun came up, and although it was a welcome sight, it had little if any effect on the cold. With the sun at their backs they continued to ride in silence. They had seen lights in the windows of a few of the farmhouses they had passed but had not seen anyone moving about on the farms or passed anyone on the road.

As the sun climbed in the eastern sky behind them, it slowly began to warm the backs of their heavy wool coats. As they began to thaw, they began to talk.

"You know, I could really go for a cup of hot coffee about now, what about you Sarge?" Hollered the trooper in line behind Matthew. The trooper's name was Trask, and he was from Ohio.

Sergeant O'Neall turned and looked over his shoulder in the trooper's direction, pulled his cap down tighter on his head, grumbled an oath, and just kept going.

"Come on Sarge, we gotta stop and rest the horses some time, besides, I gotta take a piss"

"Newville," said the sergeant without turning to look back at anyone. "We'll stop to rest the horses in Newville, and if I'm feeling really generous, I'll let you brew up some coffee, and maybe relieve yourselves. In the meantime, if you're thirsty... that's what you have canteens for."

"Mine's frozen," said Trooper Walters who was from New Jersey and was riding alongside Matthew.

"That's because you don't know how to protect the water in them," said the sergeant as he pulled his canteen out from beneath his coat, opened it, and took a healthy drink.

"How the hell do you protect water?" Asked Trask.

"By mixing it with something that doesn't freeze," said Matthew with a smile.

"Calhoun, you're probably gonna make Brigadier before your career in this man's army is over," said the sergeant. "Anybody else gotta piss?"

Most of the patrol responded in the affirmative.

"Alright, we'll dismount in that stand of trees ahead. You got five minutes, so do what you gotta do and get ready to get back in the saddle."

It was around eight thirty when they crossed the small wooden bridge that spanned Big Spring Creek on the east side of Newville. They continued down Main Street, to West Street, turned south and dismounted when they reached the fountain square at the center of town. It didn't take long for a curious crowd of onlookers to start to gather around the horse soldiers.

A well-dressed man of about forty wearing a wide brimmed black felt hat made his way through the crowd and approached Sergeant O'Neall.

"Excuse me sergeant," he said brusquely, "but are you in charge of these men."

"I am sir," replied the sergeant as he came to attention and bowed slightly in the man's direction. "Sergeant O'Neall, B Troop, United States Second Cavalry. At your service."

"I see," said the man in an officious almost offensive tone. "Why are you here, and when will you be leaving?"

"And who might you be sir?" Asked the sergeant with a bit of an edge in his voice.

The man, who was about the same height as Sergeant O'Neall, but nowhere near the same build, drew himself up to his full height, and announced, "I am Samuel Finley. I am the constable of Newville."

"I see," said the sergeant. "Trooper Calhoun," he said as he turned away from the man and towards the troopers, "go up to that inn," pointing up the street, "and see if they can provide a hot breakfast for us. Trooper Trask, you and Nelson find a place where you can get the saddles off the horses and get them some feed. Jump to it troopers, I want to be back in the saddle in an hour.

"In about 24 hours," said Sergeant O'Neall turning back to the constable with his hands on his hips and his best hard-assed cavalry sergeant look on his face, "about one hundred mounted cavalry troopers with their supply wagons, are going to be arriving here. Like us they will probably be staying only long enough to eat a meal and rest their horses. My assignment is to tell someone in authority that they are coming. Yours," he continued as he poked the constable in the chest with his finger, "is to make 'em feel welcome." Pause. "Questions?"

Constable Finley had more than met his match.

"No sir, sergeant…um sir… um that is," he said swallowing the lump in his throat. "Newville is proud to welcome you and your men, and will do all we can to see that the men who are arriving tomorrow feel just as welcome."

"That'll be lovely Constable Finley, just lovely," said Sergeant O'Neall as he put his arm around the constable's shoulders and started up the street towards the inn. "We would be most honored sir if you would join us for breakfast."

"Certainly sergeant, certainly, the honor will be all mine," the constable replied with just a hint of a stammer as he began to regain his composure.

During breakfast they were visited by the Mayor as well as several members of the town council as word spread of their presence, and their news. The town fathers were very gracious and after the initial shock it was apparent that they would do what they could to make B Troop feel welcome when they arrived the next day. The owner of the inn, a small framed rather nervous man, picked up the tab for breakfast for the troopers, but made it clear that he could not afford do it for the one hundred or so who would be arriving on the morrow. He seemed surprised, yet quite pleased with himself, when everyone had a good laugh at his unintentional joke.

Within the hour the well fed patrol was back in the saddle and riding west out of Newville. It was about eleven miles to Shippensburg, and Sergeant O'Neall intended to have his noon meal there.

"Sarge," asked Trooper Nelson, of Pennsylvania, when the sergeant told the men of his plan. "Why did we pack rations if we ain't gonna eat 'em?"

"Tell you what Nelson," answered the sergeant. "When we get to Shippensburg, you can stay with the horses and eat those wooden biscuits you're carrying in your saddlebags, while the rest of us enjoy some real food."

"I didn't mean to make you mad Sarge, I just don't wanna carry something if I ain't gonna use it."

"I'm not mad Nelson, sad is what am, I'm kinda sad."

"Sad Sarge?"

"Yep, sad that things has gotten so bad that the US Cavalry has to put jackasses like you on horseback!"

With the rest of the patrol laughing, Nelson decided it was best to just keep quiet.

It was about half past noon when the troopers reined in their mounts in front of Widow Piper's Tavern at the corner of King and Queen Streets in Shippensburg. It had warmed up considerably and most of them had removed their heavy great coats but were still wearing their wool capes. There were a number of people on the street, but only a few even gave them a second look. A young black boy of about 14 was huddled on the west side of the building out of the wind.

"Boy!" Hollered Sergeant O'Neall. "Where can I put these horses for about an hour so's they're outta the cold and can be fed?"

The boy came out to the edge of the street. "They's a big barn in the back," he said. "I can take 'em back there fo' ya if ya wishes, sir."

"These are cavalry mounts lad, do you know how to care for cavalry mounts?"

"No, sir."

"Nelson, Calhoun, go with this young fella and see that the horses are tended to."

"Sarge, I was only... I mean...," stammered Nelson.

"Fer Christ's sake Nelson," the sergeant said as he dismounted. "Once you two get the horses settled you can join us inside the tavern."

Sergeant O'Neall entered the tavern. No one was in the small lobby so the sergeant entered the large room on the right and walked across to the bar which was on the back wall. The room was warmed by the fire burning in the large fireplace on the far wall across from the door. The four troopers followed him into the building but stayed in the lobby.

There were several tables in the big room. There were three men sitting at one of the tables and two more men standing at the bar. The man on the other side of the bar, the bartender, was a large balding man with a greying beard that could best be described as disorganized. He wore a long apron over his plaid long sleeved shirt and until the sergeant entered the room had been leaning on the bar talking with the two men who were standing there.

"Afternoon Sergeant," he said with a smile as he walked over to Sergeant O'Neall. "What can I get for you?"

"What can you get for me?"

"Whatever you'd like."

"If only you could my friend, if only you could," said the sergeant as he wiped his mouth with the back of his hand.

"Sir?"

"My name is O'Neall, Sergeant O'Neall, B Troop, US Second Cavalry. I need to speak with your mayor, or some other civil authority."

"We about to be invaded?" Asked the bartender with a smile.

"Yeah, actually, kinda I guess," replied the sergeant returning the smile.

The bartender turned to the younger of the two men standing at the bar. "Samuel, run on over to the mayor's house and tell him the US Army is here to see him."

"What about my beer?" Samuel asked raising a half empty glass.

"I'll give you a fresh one on the house when you get back."

"Deal," he said as he guzzled what was left of his beer and headed for the door. "Damn," he said as he passed through the lobby. "Looks like the whole danged army is here."

"Not yet," laughed Matthew who had returned from the stables with Nelson. "Not yet."

"Now sir," said Sergeant O'Neall. "Would it be possible for me and my men to get a hot meal while we're waiting on the mayor?"

"How many are ya?"

"Seven."

"Sure, grab a couple of tables and I'll get the cook started. It's chicken and dumplin's today with boiled potatoes, and a leek soup."

"Sounds great, much obliged." He walked over to the door and looked out into the lobby. "Get your sorry asses in here and sit down, and try to conduct yourselves as gentlemen."

"Drinks?" Asked the bartender.

"Ciders all around," answered the sergeant.

About halfway through the meal the mayor arrived, and like the mayor of Newville, once he was over the initial shock he assured the sergeant that the town would be prepared to welcome B Troop as they passed through the next day. As the troopers were finishing their meal some of the local merchants, who had been summoned by the mayor, began to arrive. There was to be a meeting to prepare for the arrival of B Troop.

"We owe you anything for the grub friend?" Asked Sergeant O'Neall as the troopers prepared to leave.

"Let's see, 13 cents a meal, times seven meals, 91 cents oughta about cover it."

"91 cents?" Said the sergeant as he began to fumble around in his pockets.

"But, seeing as how I'll probably be makin' a lot more than that tomorrow, give me 50 cents, and we'll call it square."

"50 cents? Seems to be a serious lack of patriotism around here," said the sergeant as he shook his head, and turned towards the lobby. "Calhoun!"

"Yo!" Responded Matthew as he came back into the room.

"Give this "gentleman" 50 cents."

"Me Sarge?"

"Yes, you Calhoun, and make it snappy I wanna make Chambersburg before dark." With that the sergeant, muttering the entire time, and glaring at the bartender, stalked from the room.

"I gotta get it outta my saddlebags sir," Matthew said to the bartender. Matthew was not happy. Fifty cents was about a day's pay to a trooper of Matthew's rank, but he dug the money out of his saddlebag and went back into the inn and paid the bartender.

"Here Trooper," the bartender said as he gave half the money back to Matthew. "Don't tell your sergeant, let that cheap bastard think you paid his way. Might get you an edge someday."

Matthew looked down at the coins the bartender had placed in his hand and then back up at the bartender. "Thanks," he said.

"Had one just like him in Mexico," said the bartender as he turned and walked away.

It was nearing five o'clock when the troopers rode into Chambersburg's town square. The sun was nearly down and the cold had returned. The people who were on the streets were more concerned about getting home and out of the cold than they were about the squad of cavalry troopers that had shown up in the center of their town.

The Franklin Hotel was just south of the square on Main Street. Sergeant O'Neall, accompanied by Matthew, left the rest of the patrol in the town square and proceeded to the hotel. They dismounted, secured the horses to the post out front and started for the front door. Matthew reached out and grabbed the sergeant by the upper arm. The sergeant stopped and turned his head towards Matthew with a very menacing look on his face.

"You better have a damn good reason for puttin' your hands on me boy," he growled.

Matthew returned the stare and continued to hold the sergeant's arm. "I'm down a day's pay already because of you on this trip. I ain't paying for no more meals or for hotel rooms. So, if you're intending to stay here you better have some way, other than my pockets, of paying for it."

The sergeant reached up and none too gently peeled Matthew's hand off of his arm. Then he turned to Matthew and smiled.

"Calhoun, I'll see that you get your money back, with a little extra for your troubles. Did you really think your old sergeant was gonna leave you swingin'?"

"I don't know what I thought Sarge. I just know I ain't paying nobody's way but my own."

"You just let me handle this Calhoun and we'll be sleeping snug as bugs tonight in this here fine hotel, and nobody will have to pay nothin'." He smiled. Then he stepped up close to Matthew, so close that the brims of their caps were nearly touching. The sergeant's eyes narrowed, "and Calhoun," he hissed. "Don't you ever put them grubby paws of yours on me again... Questions? No? Good, now let's see a man about a bed." Then he turned and walked through the front door of the hotel.

Matthew found that although he was a little shaken by the sergeant's threatening manner, he was not afraid of him. He felt good about himself, he surely didn't want to tangle with the sergeant, but he wasn't going to be pushed around either. Matthew followed the sergeant into the hotel, once inside he positioned himself to the side of the door and stood at attention.

Sergeant O'Neall was standing before the desk clerk at attention with his cap under his left arm. If Matthew didn't know better he would have thought that the sergeant was standing before the Almighty himself. The man behind the counter was a slight bespectacled man, with a sunken face, heavily oiled dark hair, and a neat but ill-fitting suit that hung on him like an oversized sack. It was obvious that he was very much impressed with the sergeant.

"Sergeant O'Neall, B Troop, Second United States Cavalry, sir," said the Sergeant. "I am in command of a small detachment of US Cavalry troops who are an advance patrol for a much larger force. It is very important that I meet with some civil authority as soon as possible."

"Then why did you come in here?" The man squeaked.

"Well sir," began the sergeant with a smile. "As we were passing I was sure that whoever it was that was in charge of managing an establishment such as this would have to be a man of influence and prominence."

"I'm just a clerk, I am not the manager of this hotel."

"But you are in charge now, aren't you? Any decisions that would have to be made, would of course be made by you, seeing as how you are currently in command."

The clerk coughed, stood more erect, and placed his hand on his chest. "Well, I suppose that is true. Who is it you said you needed to see? A civil authority?"

"Yes sir."

"Well, I could give you directions to the Mayor's house."

"First sir," said Sergeant O'Neall raising his hand to stop the man in mid-sentence. "Allow me to get my men and mounts tended to. We have been in the saddle for many hours and are bone weary and need a meal. Can you direct me to a corral, stable, or perhaps a livery? It would be nice if we could find someplace to spend the night out of the weather."

"You mean you intend to sleep outside?"

"We're cavalry sir, that's what we do," said the Sergeant raising up on his toes, clicking his heels, and nodding at the clerk. "It's a very rare occasion indeed that we get to spend a night in a place as fine as this," he said with a smile.

"Well, there's the liv…"

"Excuse me sir," said the Sergeant stepping up to the counter. "I don't suppose me and my men could spend the night here? Wow," he continued turning around and admiring the lobby. "What a thrill it would be for the brave young men under my command to stay in such a fine place.

"Oh, I'm sorry," he went on as he turned back to face the clerk. "I had no right to suggest such a thing, besides, I wouldn't want to put you on the spot. You probably don't have the authority to permit such a thing."

The little man behind the counter tried to make himself appear as large as he could. "As you say sergeant, I am in command, er rather, in charge. So I suppose I may be…"

"Trooper Calhoun," the Sergeant said turning towards Matthew. "See if you can find someplace where we can get the men and horses out of the weather for the night."

"Yes sir, Sergeant Sir!" Matthew barked as he saluted smartly, he was catching on to what the sergeant was about, and it was taking quite a bit of will power to keep from laughing. "What about Trooper Nelson, sir?"

"Nelson?" Replied Sergeant O'Neall with a strange look on his face.

"Yes sir, Trooper Nelson, his illness has gotten much worse, sir," said Matthew with another snappy salute.

Sergeant O'Neall had his back to the clerk so the clerk couldn't see the big smile that spread across the sergeant's face. The sergeant winked at Matthew and quickly dispatched the smile as he dropped his chin on his chest.

"Ah yes, young Nelson," he sighed. "Well, we'll just have to do the best we can. We'll take turns sitting up with him and giving up our blankets. I just hope it doesn't get too cold for the lad."

"Yes sir, understood sir," said Matthew softly as he shook his head.

"Carry on trooper," said the Sergeant as he turned back to the clerk.

"Yes sir," replied Matthew, who after another salute executed a perfect about face and marched out of the hotel onto the wooden sidewalk. As he left he could hear the clerk making it quite clear to the sergeant that even though such a decision was normally outside the scope of his authority that he felt it his patriotic duty to make some provision for the troopers.

Matthew untied his mount and moved quickly away from the front of the hotel so that the clerk would not see him laughing. He rejoined his comrades who had dismounted and were gathered in the town square. They were huddled together and were stomping their feet in an effort to thwart the cold.

"What's going on in there?" Asked Trooper Walters.

Matthew looked over his shoulder back towards the hotel and said with a laugh, "Believe it or not, I think the sarge is about to get us all free hotel rooms." He turned to Trooper Nelson, "How you feeling Nelson?"

"I'm feeling fine why?" Asked Nelson suspiciously.

"Well," said Matthew, again looking back at the hotel. "When the sergeant gets here you best look like you're on death's door."

"Whatta you talking about Calhoun?"

"You'll see," laughed Matthew. "You'll see."

Before Nelson could say anything else Sergeant O'Neall exited the hotel untied his horse and began walking towards the troopers.

"Don't ever say your ol' sarge don't take good care of his boys." He began with a smile as he looked back over his shoulder towards the hotel. "I got us three rooms, one for me, and two for the six of you to share. Nelson and Calhoun will get one room, and you other four share the third room."

"There's seven of us," said Trooper Trask. "Why aren't we putting three in one room, and two in each of the other two rooms?"

"You think I should share my room? Do ya Trask?" Asked Sergeant O'Neall as he glared at the brazen trooper.

"Well, no, I guess not, but why do four of us have to share a room while Nelson and Calhoun get to have one to themselves?"

The Sergeant stepped up so close to Trask that the trooper leaned backwards to gain what little personal space he could. "Trask," he hissed. "Can you think of any reason on God's green earth why I would have to explain anything to you?"

"Um, no, Sarge, sorry Sarge," stammered the young trooper who stumbled backwards as the sergeant leaned in even closer.

"Alright Nelson," said the Sergeant turning to Trooper Nelson. "You're sick, real sick, so wrap your blanket around your head, and when you enter the hotel moan a little for effect."

"But Sarge, I feel…"

"Nelson, just shut up and do what you're told," said the Sergeant. "Calhoun, you and Walters help Nelson up to his room, and Nelson play the part, remember, you're damned near dead."

"Trask, there's a barn out back of the hotel. You and Taylor see to the mounts. Now, let's get settled."

The Mayor of Chambersburg, and several other local officials, summoned by the hotel clerk, met with Sergeant O'Neall over dinner that evening in the hotel's dining room. The mayor was quite excited about the arrival of B Troop and assured the sergeant that all would be in readiness. The mayor graciously paid for the sergeant's dinner as well as for those of the troopers who, except for Nelson who remained upstairs, were seated at a table nearby.

That night after arranging to have a meal prepared for poor Nelson, Matthew felt as though he had landed in the lap of luxury as he stretched out in the bed he was sharing with the not so ill trooper. The sheets were clean and fresh as were the pillows, and blankets. For ten cents Matthew had also gotten the opportunity to take a hot bath. At this moment, life was pretty good.

As he drifted off to sleep he couldn't help but think about home, and his father, his sister Katherine Rosemary, his brother Mark and his wife Violet, and their new baby. He missed them very much, and it made it worse when he thought about the fact that they were all less than 40 miles away.

Chapter 22

The Rancocas
1790

After signing the papers transferring the property form his name to theirs, Jacob Hilyard, the man from whom Brian and Bridget McBride had purchased their new property, welcomed them as guests in his home on Pearl Street in Burlington. Jacob's wife Martha, a slender woman with light brown hair, a narrow face, and dimpled chin, was a very gracious hostess. The McBride's were treated to a fine meal of baked ham, roasted potatoes, fresh asparagus, and cornbread. All of which was served with a delicious locally made red wine.

When they had finished their dinner, Bridget suggested that they take an evening stroll. There was still plenty of daylight left, and this was Bridget's first visit to Burlington, and so they did. They strolled along Pearl Street to Talbot, and then down to the river bank. They walked along the river bank on Green Bank, enjoying the evening breeze coming off the gently flowing waters of the Delaware River.

They passed many fine houses along the riverfront, but by far the most interesting was the Shippen house. The large brick house had three stories and an attic, with a grand front porch that offered an unobstructed view of the river and the Pennsylvania shore on the other side. The house had been built by Judge Edward Shippen, a wealthy Philadelphian who remained loyal to the Crown during America's fight for independence, as a summer home for his family.

It was Judge Shippen's daughter, Peggy, explained Mr. Hilyard, who had married the notorious traitor Benedict Arnold. In fact, there were those who believed that it was Peggy who had turned Arnold against his countrymen. Although no one seemed to know for sure if Arnold had ever stayed in the house or visited Burlington, the story made for some very interesting local gossip.

They walked back along Green Bank to Ellis Street, and then to Broad Street. They continued along Broad Street to Wood Street which took them back to Pearl Street and the Hilyard house. They had walked a little more than a mile.

Among the buildings they passed was the home of Congressman Elias Boudinot on Broad Street, and St. Mary's Episcopal Church on the corner of Broad and Wood Streets. They met and spoke with several people who were also taking advantage of the cool evening breeze. As they walked along Wood Street, on their way back to the Hilyard house Bridget commented on how lovely the town was, and how friendly the people of Burlington were.

In the morning, Brian was up well before Bridget or their hosts. The Hilyard's cook, a free black woman whose name was Odessa, but who everyone called Dessie, was up even before Brian. She cheerfully prepared biscuits and sausages, for him which she served with piping hot coffee.

Coffee was relatively new to Brian. He had first tasted it while on board the *Loving Union* during their passage from Ireland to Philadelphia. At first he had found its taste bitter and unpleasant, but it seemed that coffee was always there when he was working on the docks as a carpenter for Mr. William Powell during the time he and Bridget lived in Philadelphia.

The more coffee he drank, the more he developed a taste for it. Now he found that he actually enjoyed it, especially in the mornings. Bridget on the other hand had tried it once, said that it was worse than drinking sludge, and never took another sip.

When he had finished his breakfast Brian left the Hilyard house and walked to Mr. Vandergrift's blacksmith shop on East Broad Street. He had taken the two mules, he had purchased along with the property from Mr. Hilyard, to Mr. Vandergrift to be reshod. Brian's route took him up High Street, Burlington's main thoroughfare, to Broad Street, and as he walked he enjoyed the sights, sounds and aromas of the awakening city.

It took about fifteen minutes for Brian to walk to the blacksmith shop. When he got there Mr. Vandergrift and a young man of about 16, who Brian guessed was Mr. Vandergrift's apprentice, were just getting the fires in the large brick furnaces stoked. Even with the fires not yet up to temperature it was already uncomfortably hot in the small shop.

Mr. Vandergrift was a man of about 40 years old. He wore a brimless hat pulled down over his large round head, he had a round weathered face with bright blue eyes, a crooked nose, and thin lips that almost disappeared when he smiled, which he did a lot. As would also be expected, the large friendly man had a thick neck, barrel chest, well defined muscular arms, massive hands, and a large round belly, all supported by short skinny legs that made it look like his upper body had been placed on the wrong lower body.

When Brian entered Mr. Vandergrift acknowledged him with a nod, and a friendly smile. He pointed to a tin pot which was sitting on an anvil just a few feet from the intensifying fires.

"Help yourself," he called out in order to be heard.

Brian nodded, returned the smile, found a cup on a nearby workbench and had another cup of coffee. He immediately discovered that the blacksmith's coffee was easily the thickest, and strongest he had ever had, and it took everything he had to keep from spitting it onto the shop's dirt floor. So, he smiled, lifted his cup in a mock toast to Mr. Vandergrift, and pretended to drink the thick bitter liquid it contained.

Once Mr. Vandergrift was satisfied that the fires were good he left them in charge of the young man and joined Brian who had stepped through the large doors at the front of the shop and out onto the street to escape the rapidly increasing heat inside the shop. It was cooler outside but the sun, which was just up over the eastern horizon, was already burning brightly, and it promised to be another typically hot and humid August day.

"The heat takes some getting used to," said Mr. Vandergrift as he too stepped out into the street. "I guess I been smithin' too long, I don't even seem to notice it no more."

"Never had heat like dis back in Ireland," said Brian.

"It'll bring out the sweat in you, that's for sure."

"Don't know dat da Devil himself might be findin' it a bit warm here."

"I don't know about that," laughed the blacksmith. "Feels a little cool to me out here on the street."

"Well den, either yew've no reason ta be fearin' da Devil, or yer completely daft," said Brian as he smiled at the large man.

They both laughed.

"Your mules are done," said the blacksmith wiping his hands on a rag that was attached to his belt, "and I gotta tell you, you've got a couple of real fine animals there. Not only are they strong and healthy, but they have good tempers, which is strange with the sort. Your wagon's been loaded with the tools and other supplies that were on your list, and as soon as we settle up I'll have young Nicholas hitch the mules to it and bring it around."

"Tank ya, Mr. Vandergrift. What is it I'll be owin' ya den?"

"Well, Mr. Chaikin over at the hardware says you've already settled up with him, so, replacing the shoes on both animals, their board, and tending to the wagon and supplies? I figure fifty cents oughta about cover it, and if you want to throw a little something extra to the boy I'm sure he'd appreciate it."

Brian reached into his pocket and took out the leather pouch that he had acquired long ago on a lonely road south of Limerick, Ireland. He opened it, took out what he owed Mr. Vandergrift and paid him. Brian also took out an extra five cents to give to Nicholas when he brought the wagon around.

"Thank you, Mr. McBride. A pleasure doing business with you." He turned back towards the inside of the shop. "Nicholas," he hollered. "Hitch those two mules to Mr. McBride's wagon and bring it around."

"Right away sir!" Came the reply from in the shop.

"Word is you're setting up to farm some land over in Rancocas," said the blacksmith.

"Dat we are sir. Me and me wife Bridget 'ave purchased tirty acres o' good ground from Mr. Hilyard."

"Jacob's a good man, and fair."

"Dat he is sir, dat he is."

"Rancocas?" Said the blacksmith as he rubbed the stubble on his chin. "Walter Fish has a shop over there. He's a good smith, and I'm sure you'll be happy with his work. But, if you're not, you come on back here to Burlington. William Vandergrift will take right good care of you." With that the large man stuck out his massive hand.

Brian took Mr. Vandergrift's hand and noticed that his hand, which he had always felt was of good size, completely disappeared when the blacksmith closed his hand around it.

"Well, I'd best get to work," he said with a smile. "Nicholas won't be but a minute more, the stables are around the back." With that he turned and walked back into the heat of the shop.

"Tanks again," said Brian as the two mules being led by the young apprentice and pulling the wagon came around the corner.

"Here you are sir," said Nicholas. "They've been fed and just had a drink from the trough."

"Tank ya," said Brian as he climbed up onto the wagon and took the reins while the young apprentice held the lead. Once Brian was settled Nicholas hooked the lead to the harness on the back of one of the mules.

"Here ya are," said Brian as he handed the five pennies down to the young man. "Fer yer troubles."

"Thank you sir! But, was no trouble at all. Thank you very much!"

Brian nodded, slapped the reins across the backs of the two mules and started back to the Hilyard's house. When he got there he tied the wagon up out front, walked around to the back of the house, and entered through the back door. He passed through the kitchen and joined Bridget and the Hilyard's who were in the dining room having breakfast.

"Well, you were up and out early," said Jacob with a smile.

"Good morning Jacob, Martha, Bridget darlin'," said Brian nodding at each in turn as he took a seat at the table next to his wife. "I wanted ta get an early start. I'm anxious ta gets ta Rancocas."

"I don't know why," Martha said with a grin. "There's nothing there yet. You should stay on for a couple of days and let Bridget get to know Burlington."

Brian and Bridget exchanged glances. "Well I suppose...," began Brian.

"I'm teasing my dear boy!" Chuckled Martha as she wiped her mouth with her napkin. "I know how excited the two of you are to get started."

"Would you like something to eat Brian"? Asked Jacob.

"No sir, tank ya, I've already eaten, but I would like a cup o' coffee, I just had a cup o' Mr. Vandergrift's and I'm hopin' I am dat it hasn't killed off me tongue."

Everyone laughed.

"Vandergrift is famous, or maybe I should say notorious, for his coffee," said Jacob. "Rumor is that he's never dumped what's in it, or ever cleaned what it's in."

Everyone again shared a laugh.

After breakfast Brian and Bridget gathered up their belongings from the room they had spent the night in, bid farewell to the Hilyard's, climbed onto the wagon, and headed out for Rancocas to begin their new life. Their route took them up High Street, and now, unlike earlier when Brian had walked along this street, the people and merchants of Burlington were awake and open and going about their business in earnest. There were a number of wagons and carriages on the street and Brian had to stop several times, but everyone was friendly and courteous, making the delays just a minor inconvenience.

The road was relatively flat for the first mile or so, but then it was uphill to the cut off for Rancocas. Brian held the reins loosely and just let the mules travel at their own pace. The Rancocas Road flattened out after they crossed the Cooperstown Road and from that point it was only about another four miles to Rancocas.

"Da way home," said Bridget with a smile when they made the turn onto the Rancocas Road. She reached across and squeezed her husband's forearm.

He leaned over and kissed his wife on the cheek.

"Does it seem real ta ya yet?" He asked returning the smile.

"No," she replied with a slight shake of her head as she stared straight ahead. "I keeps waitin' ta wakes up and find meself in da Limerick gaol, or still bobbin' about on da *Loving Union*."

Brian slipped the glove off of his right hand and put his arm around Bridget's shoulders. He pulled her to him.

"T'is time ta stop worryin' about da past, and start dreamin' about da future. We owns land, in a land dat's free. Never again can somebody take someting from us just because dey wants ta."

"We owned land in Ireland too."

"Yes, but Ireland was not free."

"Dat's quite a lot o' stuff ya gots back dere," said Bridget as she turned and looked back into the bed of the wagon. "Er ya sure ya got everyting?"

"Takes a lot ta start a new life," Brian answered with a smile, "and, no, I'm not sure I got everyting, but I got yew, I got land, and I got tew good mules, and dat's as good a start as any man can ask fer."

She nestled her head into her husband's muscular shoulder and asked, "How much longer?"

"An hour at least, and mebbe a half more. We should be at da Wills' before half twelve," he answered looking up at the sun.

Brian had met Samuel Wills and his wife Sarah on his first visit to Rancocas when he had met with Mr. Hilyard to look at properties Mr. Hilyard was offering for sale. Brian had stayed with the Wills' during that visit, and when they heard that Brian had purchased property near Rancocas they had insisted that Brian and Bridget spend their first night in Rancocas as their guests. Bridget had met the Wills' when Brian had brought her to Rancocas to see the property before making the final determination to purchase it.

It was just not quite twelve thirty when Brian turned the wagon off the Rancocas Road and onto the Mt. Holly Turnpike, which served as the main street for the Village of Rancocas. The Wills house was about a quarter mile down on the left, and they arrived there in just a couple of minutes. Brian pulled the wagon around to the back of the house and stopped in front of the carriage house.

"Brian, Bridget, welcome!" Said Samuel Wills as he exited the back door of the house, stepped off the rear porch, and started for the wagon.

"Hello Samuel!" Said the McBride's almost in unison, as Brian jumped down from the wagon and turned to help Bridget.

"It's so good to see you again my dear!" Said Samuel with a wide smile as he reached out and took Bridget's hand. "Sarah is anxious to see you again too, why don't you go on inside while I help Brian with the mules."

"Tank yew, Samuel, I tink I will," said Bridget with a curtsy and a smile.

"Bridget, how lovely to see you again!" Said Sarah Wills who had come out onto the rear porch. "Come in, come in, and we'll get you freshened up."

Bridget waved to Sarah and started towards the house. "Brian," she said turning back to her husband. "Yew won't be fergettin' da satchel now will ya?"

"I won't love," he answered with a smile. "I'll be bringin' it along when I come."

She turned and continued on towards the house and her friend Sarah Wills.

"You're a lucky man my friend," said Samuel as he watched Bridget climb onto the porch where she was greeted by Sarah.

"Don't be forgettin' I'm Irish," said Brian with a smile. "I'm sposed ta be lucky." He laughed, as did Samuel.

"Let's get the mules unhitched and settled," said Samuel. "I've put two of my horses down to the blacksmith's for a day or two, so there are two open stalls for the mules."

"Tank yew, Samuel, but dat wasn't necessary. Da mules woulda been just fine outside in da paddock."

"They needed shoeing anyway, and besides," he laughed. "Who knows when these poor animals may finally get a roof over their heads!"

"Well, I guess I can't be arguin' witcha dere," answered a laughing Brian.

They got the mules settled, and as they finished covering the wagon, which would have to be left outside, with a canvas tarp to protect its cargo, Samuel asked Brian if he had everything he needed to build a place for him and Bridget to live in.

"Well," began Brian, crossing his arms in front of him and leaning on the side of the wagon. "I've got a couple o' good sharp axes o' various sizes ta cut down trees and notch dem so's ta fit dem together, ropes, blocks, and pulleys, ta lift dem and position dem, and several heavy hammers and pry bars ta coax dem into place wit. So, I'll be guessing I gots what I needs ta get started at least."

"How big a cabin you plan on building?"

"Tirty foot by ten foot, a ten by ten sleepin' room, and a twenty by ten room wit a stone fireplace fer cookin', eatin', and settin'."

"Quite an undertaking."

"A spot'll have ta be cleared fer ta build it on, and dat'll take more than a day, then I figger it'll take me at least a day or tew ta cut da trees I'll be a needin', anudder ta cut dem to size and notch dem, four or five days ta get dem stacked, a couple days ta chink dem, a couple o' days fer da roof, a couple ta gather da stone fer da chimney and fireplace, and a few more ta builds it. Figger anudder day or two for da finishin' touches, and it'll be ready."

"How many trees you figure you'll need to cut?"

"I'm guessin' sixty to seventy."

"Yes, that's about what we figured too."

"What?" Asked Brian. "Who figgered?"

"Oh, nothing, nothing, never mind," answered Samuel with a wave of his hand. "So, you figure you can build this cabin of yours on your own in about a month?"

"I tink a little less den dat, but yes, I dew."

"You know there's an area large enough that is already mostly cleared where Hilyard's lane and the old mill lane intersect. It's only about a quarter mile to the creek. It's well above creek level, and pretty flat. Not to mention it's a lovely spot for a house."

"Dat's de exact spot Bridget and me picked when we walked da propity," said Brian with a smile. He slapped his friend on the back and said, "Talkin' about work almost makes a man as tirsty as the doin' o' it does. Let's go on up ta da house and drink some o' yer ale."

"Yes, let's," said Samuel.

The next morning Brian was up before dawn. He quietly made his way downstairs to the kitchen intent on finding himself something to eat and perhaps a cup of coffee. When he got there he was more than surprised to find Samuel already seated at the table having a cup of coffee.

"Care to join me?' Asked Samuel.

"Sure," answered Brian as he sat down across from Samuel as Samuel poured him a cup of steaming hot coffee from a black tin pot.

"I'm afraid we're on our own. I can fry us up some bacon but I'm afraid that's the limit of my culinary talents," he said with a smile.

"Dat would be fine," said Brian, "but, why er yew up at dis hour?"

"Why shouldn't I be?"

Brian just looked at Samuel.

Samuel leaned on the table and looked at his friend. "You're my friend, and neighbor. You are going to be building a house for you and your wife to live in so that you can become a part of this community. I'm going to help you, just as I expect you would help me if the tables were reversed. That's what friends and neighbors do. So, I ask you again, why shouldn't I be up?"

"Tank yew." That was all that Brian was able to get out, mostly because of the lump in his throat.

"I should wake Bridget," said Brian as Samuel threw several strips of bacon in a black pan and placed it on the fire.

"Let her sleep," said Samuel. "Sarah will bring her over later."

Brian nodded and couldn't help but think how nice it was going to be to live in a community where they had such wonderful friends. Once they had finished the bacon, that was more than a little too well done, and had another cup of the coffee, which was actually quite good, they headed out to the yard to get the mules hitched to the wagon and get started on their day.

After hitching the mules to Brian's wagon, Samuel went back into the carriage house and came out leading one of his horses which was also in harness. Brian watched as he hitched the horse to a smaller wagon that was backed into an open shed. Samuel climbed up onto the wagon and pulled it up alongside Brian's wagon.

"You can never have too many tools," he said with a smile as he pointed over his shoulder with his thumb to the bed of the wagon which contained axes, saws, hammers, and a variety of other tools and implements which might be of use in the raising of a cabin. "Now," he continued. "Should we head on over to the McBride farm?"

"Yes, by God!" Said Brian happily. "Yes, let's head on over tew da McBride farm!" He slapped the reins down across the backs of the mules who effortlessly began pulling the wagon out of the Wills yard an out onto the Mt. Holly turnpike.

"Huzzah!" Hollered Samuel as he too guided his wagon out onto the turnpike.

It took a little more than ten minutes for them to travel the just over half a mile to Hilyard's Lane. They turned right to continue the additional half mile to where the old mill lane crossed Hilyard's Lane. They had gone about halfway, when Brian noticed what appeared to be several wagons and a number of people milling about at about where the intersection was.

Brian could not believe his eyes when he brought his wagon to a halt at the intersection. There were seven wagons, all loaded down with logs of about fifteen feet in length. The men, of whom there were about a dozen, were off loading one of the wagons, and each wagon appeared to have ten or eleven logs in it.

A large area had already been cleared and staked out, there were several stacks of milled lumber nearby, and a large pile of river rocks. Two tripods rigged with pulleys and ropes were set up, and it looked as if there were more ladders than men. Brian knew what his eyes were seeing, it was just that his brain was having trouble believing it.

Where had all of this come from? Brian turned and looked back at Samuel.

"Can't build a log cabin without logs!" He said with a large smile.

When Brian jumped down from his wagon the men stopped working and walked over to him. By this time Samuel had also gotten down and walked over and stood beside Brian. There was an awkward silence as the men just stood there.

"Brian," said Samuel. "These men, who seem to have lost the ability to speak, like me, are now your neighbors. They're here to help you build your cabin, because, as I said, that's what friends and neighbors do. So, tell them who you are Brian."

Brian looked at Samuel and then back at the men. "My name is Brian McBride," Brian began. "Me and me wife Bridget were come ta America from Ireland last April. We've been livin' in Philadelphia. Ta be sure, we've been meeting some wonderful people who've helped us and welcomed us ta dis amazin' country. Now it looks like we er about ta be helped and welcomed by s'more wonderful people."

"Well gentlemen," said Samuel. "You know who he is, so why don't you all just step forward and introduce yourselves."

The man right in front of Brian stepped forward and stuck out his hand. "I'm John Leeds, and this is my son Harland, I run the store right down the road from Samuel's house in the village. Welcome." Brian shook hands with John Leeds and his son.

They all stepped forward in turn, shook Brian's hand, and welcomed him. There was; Philip Keen, Simon Tait, Silas Haines, who owned a farm on the Mt. Holly Turnpike, and brought two of his hands, a man named Israel and a man named Norman, Edgar Tomlinson, William Fish, the blacksmith's son, who brought along their apprentice, a young Indian boy named Peter, Jacob Groves who owned a large farm on the Burlington Road was there with his son Nathaniel, and two of their hands, Edward, and a man named Wick. Brian was overwhelmed by their warm welcome and generosity.

Once the introductions were all done, Jacob Groves, who obviously was a man who was used to giving orders, said, "Well, I ain't yet seen a cabin build itself, so unless one of you is gonna work a miracle, we best get started."

"Wait!" Said Brian. "I won't be startin' off under a lie's cloud. Dere's someting yas has da right ta know if yer gonna welcome me into yer town."

They all stopped and looked at Brian. "Well what is it son?" Asked Groves.

"I left Ireland 'cause I was a wanted man. If I had stayed da English woulda hunted me down and hanged me."

Jacob Groves walked a few steps closer to Brian, tilted his head, looked hard at Brian, and said, "Did you kill anybody?"

"No, I was a highwayman and robbed ta get da money ta come here."

"And you never killed anyone?"

"No."

"Ever hurt anyone?"

"Well, no...not seriously anyway."

"Well that's somethin', ain't it? But, you got the money, and you're here now?"

"Yes."

"Will you be robbing anybody here?"

"No."

"Have you asked God for forgiveness?"

"Yes."

"Well, then there's nothing more to be said." Jacob turned and faced the other men. "Let he who is without sin cast the first stone. Now let's go, I'll buy the whiskey if we have the roof on by sundown tomorrow."

"Jacob Groves buy?" Exclaimed Simon Tait. "I'll work all night long just to see that happen!" The men all laughed as Jacob glared at Tait.

Jacob started to walk toward the wagons and then stopped and turned back to Brian. "Come on Brian," he said reaching out his hand. "Show us how you want your house laid out."

Chapter 23

The Rancocas
1938

"There must be more to the story," said Katy entering the parlor carrying two cups of coffee.

"What?" Asked her grandfather

"The McBride story," said Katy, handing a cup to her grandfather. "There must be more to it. You just stopped and haven't said a thing about it for days."

"I told you that I would tell you how it was that the McBride's came to America, and I did."

"Yes, but that can't be it. What happens after that? What happens to Nana's brother Matthew Calhoun, and Brian and Bridget, and you, and what about Nana?"

"You mean I haven't been boring you?"

"My God no! In fact, I've been writing everything down so that I can share it with Evan and any future McBride's that may come along."

"Well, let me see," began Michael McBride with a wistful smile. "I believe Matthew and his cavalry detail were in Chambersburg weren't they?"

The telephone rang. Katy sighed, looked at her grandfather, smiled, and went to the kitchen to answer the phone.

"Hello?"

"Katy? Hello, it's Woody, Woody Underwood."

"Oh, hello Woody," Katy said trying to keep the excitement out of her voice and happy that Woody wasn't there to see her blushing.

"Is this a bad time?"

"No, Poppa and I were just having a cup of coffee."

"Good…" Just hearing her voice had made Woody lose his train of thought.

"Is that why you're calling? To approve our coffee break?"

"What? No, no, of course not. I thought I would, that is if it's okay, I thought I would come out to the farm either Saturday or Sunday, you know, um, to deliver those packages from Evan."

"You'll have the weekend off?"

"Yes, the shipyard workers are testing some of the electrical systems or something this weekend and there's not much we can do, so the Captain is giving most everyone liberty. He says it could be the last time before we start preparing for sea trials."

"The last time?" Katy didn't even try to hide the disappointment in her voice.

"Could be."

"Then why don't you come for the weekend?" Oh my God! She thought, what did I just do? Did I just invite a man I barely know to spend the weekend here?

What will Poppa say? How do I take it back? Katy was so concerned about her invitation that she did not hear Woody's answer.

"Katy, are you there?"

"What? Yes, I'm sorry. What?"

"Did you hear me?"

"Yes, um, I'm sorry no, I'm sorry, no I didn't. What?"

"Do you think me coming for the weekend is a good idea? Shouldn't you check with your grandfather? Aren't you concerned about how it may look to people?"

Silence.

"Maybe," began Woody.

"No," said Katy interrupting him. "No, I meant it. Poppa would love to spend some time with you, and what could people say about us being kind to a friend of Evan's who is far from home and serving his country?"

"Well," said Woody. "When you put it like that it makes me feel like it would be unpatriotic not to come."

"Yes, doesn't it though," laughed Katy. "Besides, I'd like to see you too."

"You would?"

"Yes, I would."

"Good, because seeing you again has been all I've been able to think about."

Katy's heart was racing. "Are you trying to make me blush?"

"I'm not trying, but if you are I'm glad," said Woody. "I should be able to get there by noon on Saturday if that's okay?"

"Get here earlier if you can," said Katy no longer concerned about trying to be coy.

"I'd be on the road tonight if I could."

"I can wait until Saturday."

"I don't know that I can, but I'll try."

"I'll see you on Saturday?"

"I guarantee it."

"Goodbye," whispered Katy as she slowly hung up the phone.

"Goodbye," said Woody as he heard the click on the other end of the line.

Katy marched back into the parlor, and announced, probably too loudly and with too much authority, that she had invited Lieutenant Baxter Underwood to spend the weekend.

Her grandfather gave her a puzzled look, "Fine," he said. "I really liked that young man, it'll be nice to see him again."

"You don't mind? Really?" Asked a very relieved Katy. "I like him Poppa. A lot. Do you think that's okay?"

"First of all Katy Rose," he said with a knowing smile. "You don't need my permission to invite anyone into this house. Secondly, I knew right away that you liked him, and thirdly, okay? Not only do I think it's, okay, I think it's wonderful."

"I don't know Poppa, I just don't know," sighed Katy as she took a seat on the sofa opposite her grandfather. She picked up her coffee cup and as she held it on her lap, she looked down into the milky brown liquid. "I'm kind of old to have a school girl crush on someone."

"Maybe it's more than that," said her grandfather lifting his cup to his lips and sneaking a look at his granddaughter across its rim.

Katy looked up at her grandfather, and said, "How could it be? I only met him once, and we spent what, maybe three hours together?"

"How many meetings, and how much time does it take to be something more?"

Katy shrugged, and her grandfather could see that she was really struggling with how she felt about this young naval officer.

"You know," he said. "I knew the minute I looked into your grandmother's eyes that she was who I wanted to spend the rest of my life with. I knew nothing about her, not her name, where she was from, how old she was. All I knew was that she was there, and I was in love with her."

"Was it really that simple?" She asked with a smile. "Or, have the years and what the two of you had made it what you wanted it to be?"

"No," he said looking off into the distance. "It was that simple. It was the years, and the wonderfulness of it that confirmed it was a miracle, and that it was what we thought it was from the very start."

"If only I could be so lucky."

"Maybe you have been."

Katy shrugged, placed her cup on the side table, stood up, walked to the front door, and stared out across the fields. "I don't believe I'm in love with him. I don't know if I've ever been in love with anybody really," she sighed. "I thought I was in love with Nathaniel, but I let him walk out of my life. I'm not sure I know, or even would know, what love is."

Michael McBride wanted so badly to stand and walk across the room to his granddaughter and put his arms around her to comfort her, but it was late in the day, and it seemed anymore that the later in the day it got the less reliable his 93 year old legs became. It saddened him that, although she always appeared happy and fulfilled, that she was missing the one thing that truly mattered, another's love. He had never been convinced that Nathaniel was the one, but there was something about this lieutenant.

"I believe that love is different for everyone," he said. "I don't believe anyone can tell someone else what to expect when it happens, or how it feels. Everyone feels it differently.

"The only thing I am sure of, is when it happens, the person it happens to is changed forever. Even if it is a love that is not returned, or ends badly, life is never the same again."

"How do you tell the difference between love and desperation?" Katy asked still staring out the door.

"I don't know," Michael answered, "but I would think that love would feel more natural, while desperation would feel like something that was being forced."

Katy turned towards her grandfather, crossed her arms in front of her, and leaned against the frame of the door. She looked across the room at the man whose love had always filled this house, and who had taught her everything she knew about life.

"I felt good when he was here," she said, "or when I hear his voice on the phone, or think about him, which I do all the time, and it does feel natural to feel this way about him. It's like he has always been there, just out of reach, waiting for the right moment to show himself. Is that love, or just a woman who is terrified of growing old alone?"

"Only you can know that."

"Maybe I've made a terrible mistake, maybe I should call him and tell him not to come, maybe…. Oh, I don't know," she said turning to look out across the fields again. "What if he doesn't feel the same? Do I really want to make a fool of myself?"

"What if he does feel the same? What if he's fallen in love with you? Whose heart are you afraid of, Katy Rose, yours, or his?"

"Mine I think, I'm afraid it'll get broke, and there won't be anyone here to fix it." She continued staring out across the fields everything seemed to be so far away, especially the *USS Rhind.*

It was Tuesday, and Lieutenant Baxter Underwood was still reeling about Katy's invitation when he realized he had a very serious problem. He had no way to get to Rancocas for the weekend. The car he usually borrowed from his cousin, Lieutenant Edward Randall, was not going to be available.

"I already told you about this friend I have," said Lieutenant Randall.

"Not much you haven't, not even a name," chided Woody.

"Alright, her name's Nancy, but that's all your getting. You have a history of interfering with my navigation if you get too much information."

"Nancy?" Said Woody as he smiled at his cousin. "Cute name."

"That's it, no more, that's all you get," Randall said putting up his hands. "Anyway, like I said, Nancy, wants to go to Atlantic City for the weekend. Gene Krupa has a new band and they're playing at the Steel Pier."

"I thought everything was still closed down there because of the hurricane in September?"

"I'm sure there's still a lot of damage, but the clubs are open, and the entertainers are showing up to entertain," answered Randall. "What did you want the car for anyway?"

"Well," began Woody. "When I was at Evan's grandfather's farm, I got distracted talking to the old guy, and I never left the packages Evan sent. They're still in the trunk of your car."

"You already did your duty didn't you? You're saying you want to go back to the dog pound? Just mail 'em."

"Nah, that wouldn't seem right. I promised Evan I would personally deliver the packages."

"Well, if you want to be exposed to the ugly germ again, and risk coming down with a big bad ugly old case of it yourself, I guess that's up to you."

Woody had to restrain himself to keep from telling his cousin that there was no ugly in Rancocas. That Evan's sister was really very attractive, and that Woody even though he had only spent a few hours with her, thought he might be falling in love with her. He didn't really know why he was so hesitant about telling him. He supposed it was because he had done his cousin a bad turn with that girl in Baltimore, and he was afraid his cousin might take the opportunity to get even.

"So what am I going to do?" Asked Woody.

"Take the train."

"What?"

"The train, take the train. You know, runs on a track, whole bunch of cars hooked together, has a little whistle, toot...toot," teased Randall as he mimicked pulling a whistle cord with his right arm.

"Yeah, I could, but then I couldn't take the packages."

"Why not?"

"There's quite a few of them and I'm not sure I could handle them all on a train," said a frustrated Woody.

"What is so important about the damned packages?"

"Evan was a shipmate, and a friend, and he asked me to deliver them, so that's what I'm going to do."

"You're a pain in my ass," said his cousin as he stood and went to his locker. He reached in and pulled out a roadmap of New Jersey and spread it out on the table in front of Woody and himself. "I got this so I wouldn't get lost going to Atlantic City," he said.

"Don't you just go east until you hit ocean?" Asked a smirking Woody.

"This is no time to be a smartass," said Randall. "I'm trying to help you out here... although I have no idea why."

"I appreciate that," said Woody. "So I'll just sit here quietly and let you come up with something."

Ed Randall gave his cousin a sidelong look and chuckled. "Look," he said. "How about if we do this? You can ride with us and I'll drop you and your packages here," he said pointing to a place on the map. "How will that be? It doesn't look like it's too far out of the way."

"That's Mt. Holly," said Woody. "That's only about five miles from the McBride farm. That would be perfect. I could even take a cab or something from there."

"They have cabs out there?"

"I don't know," chuckled Woody, "but I'll find some way to get out to the farm from there."

"You know," said the cousin inquisitively. "I'm beginning to get the feeling that there's more to this than a stack of packages and an interesting old man. Is there something you're not telling me?"

"What? Of course not," said Woody breaking eye contact and looking down at the map.

Lieutenant Randall eyed his cousin suspiciously. "Alright then, here's the plan," he said. "I figure that, with the side trip to drop you, Atlantic City is at least a three to four hour drive. So, I'll let Nancy know that I'll pick her up at 0800 hours sharp. Then we'll head for Mt. Podunk, or whatever you said it is, drop you off, and then head for Atlantic City. We should be there in time for me to make it up to her by buying her lunch at a nice place."

"A weekend away with a single lady," said Woody with a soft whistle. "Is this serious, or are you just playing the cad?"

"Are you being a smartass again?" Asked his cousin. "I'd be careful if I was you."

"My apologies," said Woody feigning a bow. "I shall shut my yap."

"Besides," said Randall with a sheepish grin. "I think it just might be kind of a serious thing."

"Ah," said Woody just nodding and smiling at his cousin. That makes two of us he thought to himself.

"How you going to get back to Philly?" Asked his cousin.

"I'll figure that out once I get there," said Woody. "Besides, once I lose the packages I can do the train."

"True," said Randall as he folded up the map and put it back in his locker. "Want to go get a drink?"

"Let me go call Kat....um...I mean...um...the McBride's first and let them know I'm coming."

"Something is going on isn't..."

"You know," interrupted Woody. "By 0900 hours Saturday, I'll not only have met the mysterious Nancy, but I'll know exactly where she lives." He winked at his cousin.

Lieutenant Randall just stared. "You know what?" He finally said. "I don't care. Because this one is much too smart to fall for your phony cowboy charm. Besides, once we start sea trials, do you want to try to go to sleep every night wondering when it is that I'm going to throw your interfering Colorado ass overboard?"

"Well," laughed Woody. "Since you put it that way, I give you my word, as an officer and a gentleman that I will be on my very best behavior."

"Wow, can't tell you how reassuring that is," laughed his cousin. "Now go make that phone call, and then let's go get us that drink."

It was after eight o'clock, and Woody wondered as he dialed the number if maybe it was too late to be calling the McBride farm. Katy answered on the second ring.

"Hello?"

"Hi, it's me?"

She had been sitting at the kitchen table thinking about the man who was now on the telephone. "I know," she said.

"You do? Did you know I was going to call?"

"No," she said, trying to figure out why she was beginning to feel annoyed. "I recognize your voice."

"I like that you recognize my voice, unless it means that I've been calling too much."

"No," she sighed. "You haven't been."

"You sound annoyed, did I wake you?"

"No, I've just had a lot on my mind lately."

"Anything I can help with?"

"No, I'll get it sorted out." Katy didn't have the nerve to tell him that it was him that was occupying her thoughts. "But, thanks for the offer."

"Listen, about the weekend."

"You're still coming aren't you?" Katy asked hurriedly, but she wasn't sure what she wanted the answer to that question to be.

"Oh yeah, but I've had to do some finagling to get there, I won't be able to borrow my friend's car because he'll be using it to go to Atlantic City. He can get me to Mt. Holly but I'll have to find my own way from there, are there cabs in Mt. Holly?"

"Um... I'm sure there probably are...maybe... I guess."

"Good then I'll grab a cab when I get there and have them bring me out to the farm."

"No, wait," interrupted Katy. "Why don't I just come get you?" Just hearing Woody's voice was brightening her mood considerably.

"I don't want to cause you any more trouble, you're already putting me up."

"It's no trouble, I'll bring the truck. It's maybe a fifteen minute drive."

"If you're sure," said Woody

"I am. It won't be a comfortable ride, but it'll beat walking. Just tell your friend to drop you in the middle of town by the fountain and that's where I'll pick you up. What time will you get there?"

"We're picking his date up at zero eight hundred here in Philly, so around oh nine hundred I guess?"

"Oookay," Katy lightheartedly inquired, "and what time would that be here in Dogpatch?"

"Oh, I'm sorry," chuckled Woody, "9:00am."

"Very good, I'll be there."

"That'll be great," said Woody. "'Til Saturday then?"

"Until Saturday then." Katy did not want to hang up.

"Saturday."

Neither did Woody. Neither of them knew how long the silence lasted, but it was probably nowhere near as long as it felt.

"Good night," said Katy finally as she slowly lowered the receiver into the cradle.

"Good night," said Woody who continued to hold the phone against his ear until he heard the click and was sure she was gone.

Katy, with her heart and head more mixed up than ever, headed off to bed, and Woody headed out the door to join his cousin, Lieutenant Ed Randall, for a drink at the Officer's Club. Katy and Woody were very happy that they had saved the weekend, and both were very happy that they were going to get to spend some time together, but neither of them knew why they felt the way they did.

Chapter 24

The Conococheague
1861

When Sergeant O'Neall, B Troop, 2nd US Cavalry, came down to the lobby of Chambersburg's Franklin Hotel just after sunrise the next morning, he was greeted by a well-dressed man the sergeant guessed was perhaps in his early fifties. The white hair on top of the man's head barely covered most of his scalp and it was so thin that it appeared to be moving even though the air inside the lobby was perfectly still. He was a large man, but was not obese, and it was obvious he carried some sort of authority.

"May I speak to you Sergeant O'Neall?"

"And who might you be, sir?" Asked the Sergeant.

"Privately?" The smiling man placed his left hand on the sergeant's right shoulder and with his right hand gestured towards an office that was just off the lobby. He increased the pressure on the sergeant's shoulder with his left hand to encourage him to move in the direction of the office.

The sergeant, feeling he wasn't going to be given much of a choice, allowed himself to be guided to the office. He didn't know what this was about, but was sure he could talk his way out of it, or blame it on someone else. His soldiering instincts however told him to allow his adversary to make the first move before going on the offensive.

The man closed the door behind them when they entered the office and gestured the sergeant towards a chair in front of a large wooden desk behind which the man took a seat. The man intertwined his fingers and placed his hands, which the sergeant now noticed were quite large, on the top of the desk. He was still smiling but the sergeant didn't think it was the kind of smile that meant they were going to become friends.

"I trust you passed a pleasant night?" The man asked.

"I did," replied the Sergeant who noted that the man had a slight southern drawl.

"Sergeant O'Neall," began the man as he looked down at a journal which was open on the desk, and which the sergeant recognized as the register he had signed the previous evening. "My name is Norman, Edward Norman, and I am the proprietor of the Franklin Hotel."

"And right proud you should be of it," said the Sergeant as he casually leaned back in his chair. "It is indeed a fine place."

"Sergeant," began Mr. Norman. "I don't know if I'm more shocked by your obvious skills as a grifter, or by the fact that someone like you has a position of authority and leadership in the military which allows you to influence the attitudes of the brave young men placed in your charge."

"Why Mr. Norman," replied the Sergeant with a smile. "I'm afraid I have no idea what you're talking about."

"This is my business," Mr. Norman began. "It is how I make my living, and support my family. Last night," he continued. "You used your talent as a fast talking swindler to steal from me."

"Begging your pardon Mr. Norman," said Sergeant O'Neall leaning forward in his chair and glaring at the man behind the desk, "but I didn't steal nothin', and I ain't gonna sit here and listen to you accuse me of it!"

"Did you pay for the rooms in which you and your men stayed last night?"

"No sir, we didn't, but you're clerk, who seemed like a gentleman and a patriot, offered us those rooms. There was no stealing involved."

"Do you deny that you fast talked him and confused him?"

"I do, and before you go making any more accusations against a decorated US cavalryman, you might want to speak with your clerk about what happened. Now," continued the Sergeant as he stood, placed both his hands on the front of the desk, leaned over, and brought his face as close to Mr. Norman's as he could. "I am going to leave, and if you tell any more of these damned lies about me to my men, or my superiors, I'm afraid I'll just have to demand satisfaction."

"A duel Sergeant, really?" Said the man behind the desk with a smug smile as he leaned back increasing the space between himself and the sergeant.

"No, Mr. Norman, not a duel actually," said the Sergeant leaning in still further. "I will simply drag your sorry ass out into the street and pound you into road dust. Questions? No? Good."

Sergeant O'Neall turned towards the door and as he opened the door to leave Mr. Norman said, "I understand you're on your way to protect that sorry excuse of a man Lincoln. Well, I'm no more afraid of him than I am of you."

Sergeant O'Neall stopped and turned back towards the man. "Well I'll be damned," said the Sergeant with a knowing smile. "I gotta tell you, I'm a little surprised to find a southern sympathizer this far north."

"I was born and raised in Winchester, Virginia," said Mr. Norman proudly.

"So," said the Sergeant walking back to the desk and glaring down at the man seated behind it. "This wasn't about your business or your livelihood at all was it? This was about politics." Sergeant O'Neall walked around the desk, sat down on it right in front of and facing Mr. Norman, crossed his arms in front of him and looked down at the man. The Army Colt he wore holstered on his right hip laid on the desktop with the barrel pointed directly at the man behind the desk.

"Like I said," said Mr. Norman. "I'm not afraid of you or your man Lincoln."

"Well, you see, here's the thing," began Sergeant O'Neall. "Lincoln, President Lincoln, that is, well, he's a politician, and so, he's probably gonna break some of the promises he's made, 'cause that's what politicians do, they break promises. While me, I'm a horse soldier, and a horse soldier, well, he never breaks a promise." He could see that he was beginning to get to the man seated in front of him because beads of sweat started to form on the man's brow, he swallowed, was blinking a little more rapidly than was normal, and had pushed his chair back some so that there was a little more room between him and the sergeant. "And I promise you," he continued. "That the next time I see you, no matter where, no matter why, and without any more of this here friendly small talk, I'm going to turn you into a pile of horse shit. I promise," he said as he raised his right hand, as if he were testifying, and smiled down at Mr. Norman who feeling a little uncomfortable, just stared at the sergeant.

Sergeant O'Neall then lifted his right leg placed the bottom of his cavalry boot right in the middle of Mr. Norman's chest and as the man's eyes opened unnaturally wide, pushed him and his chair over backwards. The Sergeant then stood and left the office. As he went through the door, without looking back, he said, "Questions? No? Good."

In the lobby Sergeant O'Neal found four of the troopers from his patrol waiting for him.

"Where's Calhoun and Trask?" He asked.

"They went to get the mounts," said Trooper Nelson.

"Good," said the Sergeant looking back towards the office. "I want to get out of this damned town as soon as possible."

"What about breakfast?" Asked Trooper Walters. "Can't ride without breakfast and a cup of coffee," he said with a smile as he turned to the other troopers who lightheartedly murmured their agreement.

The Sergeant turned towards the troopers and said with a snarl, "You'll ride when I tell you to ride, and today it'll be without either. Now, get your shit together, get out in the street, and as soon as the horses get here get your asses up in the saddle. We're leaving."

The troopers, knowing better than to challenge their sergeant when he was in this type of mood, nearly fell over each other as they hurriedly gathered up their gear and rushed out into the street. Troopers Calhoun and Trask arrived a few minutes later leading the saddled horses. It wasn't as cold as it had been the day before, but the frozen ground crunched under the troopers' boots and the horses' hooves.

"Where we having breakfast?" Asked Trask as they reined their mounts to a stop in front of the hotel.

"We ain't," said Trooper Nelson as he stowed his gear behind his saddle and mounted his horse. He nodded towards the sergeant who had already secured his gear behind his saddle, mounted his horse, and without a word started riding south on Main Street. By the time all six troopers were in the saddle the sergeant had a several blocks head start on them.

Sergeant O'Neall was angry. Not particularly at anyone other than himself. He knew that that man, Norman, was just trying to get to him by accusing him of tricking the clerk into giving the troopers those rooms for free. What angered the sergeant was that he had let him do it. Sergeant O'Neall didn't have a problem with his threats to turn the man into road dust, or a pile of horseshit. Those were just words.

What he was angry about was that he had gotten physical with the man. The sergeant hadn't waited around to see if the man was injured or if the chair or anything else was broken. An injury or damages, well, that would be hard to explain if Norman reported him to Lieutenant Nelson, or worse yet, Captain Talbot when the rest of B Troop passed through Chambersburg the next day.

Damn! Why had he let that man get to him? He had a feeling that it wasn't going to be too long before he would have plenty of opportunities to fight with men from Virginia. Why did he have to jump the gun like that?

The patrol covered the eleven miles to Greencastle in just under four hours. The sergeant stayed in a foul mood and there was very little conversation among the troopers during the ride. They didn't know what had set the sergeant off, nor were any of them brave enough to ask. When they stopped in front of the Hays Hotel on the southwest corner of the town square, the troopers hoped that perhaps they would be staying for a hot meal, but soon discovered that they were to be disappointed.

"Calhoun!" Barked Sergeant O'Neall.

"Yo!" Replied Matthew.

"Continue south out of town on this road and find a place where we can rest the horses, boil some coffee, and have a bite. I'll be along shortly."

"Alright Sarge. Let's go boys," said Matthew as he turned his horse south on Carlisle Street followed by the other members of the patrol.

About a mile south of the town square there was a large barn and farmhouse. There was a weather-worn painted old sign that hung on the side of the barn that said "Johnson". A man, probably in his forties, was standing on the porch watching as the troopers stopped in the road in front of the house.

"Excuse me sir, but are you Mr. Johnson?" Asked Matthew nodding towards the sign.

"I am."

"Would you have any objection sir to us resting in your barn for a spell? We'd like to get our horses and ourselves out of the weather and maybe boil up some coffee and have a bite."

"You're welcome to put your horses in the barn. You're also welcome to feed them from the oats bin as long as you don't take advantage. I don't want no fires near my barn so get your horses settled and come on inside and we'll see that you have coffee and something to eat."

"Thank you sir, that's very kind of you."

"Lost a brother in Mexico," he said and turned and went into the house. "He was a horse soldier too."

Matthew and the other troopers exchanged glances as they dismounted and lead the horses into the barn. The clean well cared for barn smelled of alfalfa. There were two large draft horses in stalls at the back of the barn that snorted when the troopers lead their mounts into the barn, but after that paid little attention to the troopers or their horses. They tied their horses to some cross members, unsaddled them, and gave each of them a small amount of feed from the farmer's oats bin, and water they got from a pump in the yard. Matthew then led the troopers back to the house, up onto the porch, and to the door the farmer had entered.

"Make sure you got nothing on the bottom of your boots," Matthew said as he lifted each of his and inspected the bottoms. The other troopers followed suit and two stepped off the porch to wipe theirs off. Matthew knocked on the door.

"Come in boys, come in!" Sang a woman's voice from inside.

"Nelson, you stay out here and flag down O'Neall when he comes by," directed Matthew. When the troopers entered the house they snapped off their caps and bunched up behind Matthew. "We really appreciate this ma'am. It is far more than we expected," he said bowing to the lady he assumed was the farmer's wife.

She was a short round woman and was wearing a ruffled cap that covered almost her entire head, and what appeared to be a faded old blue house dress under a full length clean but worn apron. Her plump round face was lit by a pair of bright blue eyes and a wide happy smile. "Nonsense!" She said in her sing song voice. "Come and sit down, all of you, there should be enough room, and if not we'll make room," she said with a chuckle. "I've got a fresh venison stew and some just baked bread, and there's plenty to share with you soldier boys."

"There's another one of us outside waiting for our sergeant who had some business in town. He should be along shortly...if that's okay," said Matthew as he and the other troopers took seats at the large wooden table. The large fireplace, on which the stew was bubbling, was on the far wall, and even though the fire was small the room was quite warm.

"Of course!" Said their hostess still beaming that great smile as she began filling up bowls she had removed from a cupboard.

Each of the troopers was given a more than healthy portion of the stew, two thick slices of the warm bread, and a mug of cool cider. Matthew was enjoying his meal and was just starting to relax when Nelson opened the door and poked his head inside. "Sergeant O'Neall wants to see you in the barn," he said to Matthew.

Matthew looked up at Nelson then glanced back at their hostess. "Excuse me ma'am," he said as he stood and went to the door. "Go ahead in and get yourself something to eat," he said to Nelson as he passed him on the porch.

When Matthew entered the barn he found Sergeant O'Neall standing next to his horse with his hands on the horn of his saddle, and his head buried in his arms. Matthew could understand if the sergeant was feeling a little tired, they had spent a lot of time in the saddle the last couple of days, but it struck Matthew that the sergeant also looked troubled, which was unusual for a man who always seemed to be so in control of himself and everything around him.

"You alright Sarge?" Asked Matthew.

"Couldn't be better," grumbled the Sergeant seeming to pull himself together as he took a deep breath and straightened himself up. "Give me a hand with this nag will ya?"

Matthew helped the sergeant get the saddle and blankets off the horse, and saw to it that the horse had some oats and water. They didn't speak during the few minutes that it took them to complete these routine and often performed tasks, even though Matthew told him about how they had stopped at this farm and how the rest of the patrol was inside right now enjoying a hot venison stew.

When they were finished Matthew turned and started towards the door. "I say we eat," he said.

"You go ahead," said Sergeant O'Neall. "I'll be along in a minute."

Matthew stopped and turned back towards the sergeant. "You gonna tell me what's wrong, or are you just gonna stay pissed off for the rest of the trip?"

The sergeant glared at Matthew. Matthew shrugged, and turned back towards the door.

"I did something stupid back there in Chambersburg," Sergeant O'Neall blurted. Matthew stopped and turned back again. "I got physical with the owner of that hotel we stayed in. He pissed me off and so I roughed him up a little."

"So what?" Said Matthew. "He probably had it coming. Besides, you're always knocking us upside the head for doing stupid stuff."

"That's different, you guys are my troopers, I'm expected to knock you around once in a while to keep you in line, but not a civilian. A trooper can never put his hands on a civilian! I can't believe I let that asshole get to me!" He shouted as he kicked the bucket they had used to carry the water across the barn. "Damnit!"

"Anybody see you?" Asked Matthew.

"No," replied the Sergeant, "but if he tells Talbot when the rest of the Troop shows up there tomorrow, I could be in some deep shit."

"How deep?"

"Could cost me my stripes and land me in jail," said Sergeant O'Neall slapping his gauntlets across his thighs and shaking his head.

"Listen," said Matthew. "You can dig yourself out of shit better than any man I've ever met, so instead of being all pissed off, why don't you just start figuring out how you're going to explain what happened to the Captain so that it all looks like it was the other guy's fault?"

The Sergeant just stared at Matthew. "Maybe you're right Matthew, but if that idiot says he's been injured or that something was damaged, it'll be tough to explain."

"Trust me Sarge, you're an artist when it comes to explaining that kind of stuff." It did not go unnoticed that Sergeant O'Neall had for the first time ever called Matthew by his first name.

"Yeah, I usually am," said the Sergeant nodding. "Well," he sighed shaking his head, "nothing to be done about it now. So," he continued. "If you're done running your mouth, would you mind getting your sorry ass moving so we can get something to eat before the sun goes down?"

"Sure Sarge, sure," replied Matthew as he turned and headed out of the barn and back towards the house with the sergeant, who was maybe feeling a little better, at his side.

After having their fill of venison stew, and visiting with Mr. Johnson and his wife, each of them chipped in so that they could leave their smiling and oh so grateful hostess a dollar for her troubles. Then with Sergeant O'Neall, who seemed in a better frame of mind, out in front, the patrol was back in the saddle headed south to Hagerstown, Maryland, some ten miles away. The bright afternoon sun was warm which, with the improved mood of their sergeant, made for a much more pleasant ride.

It was just after dark when they arrived in the center of Hagerstown at the intersection of Washington and Potomac Streets. The Washington House was on Washington Street just east of the intersection and it was here that Sergeant O'Neall made arrangements for them to have a dinner of boiled ham and potatoes while he waited to meet with the constable, a Mr. King. To the amazement of the troopers, the sergeant paid for the meal out of his own pocket without even trying to haggle over the price.

After speaking with the clerk at the hotel, Sergeant O'Neall directed Matthew to take the patrol to Marrs' Blacksmith and Livery on Mulberry Street near Franklin, the sergeant would join them there after meeting with Mr. King. The clerk had informed the sergeant that William Marrs, who owned the livery, had a large barn on the property with plenty of room for the horses, and a large bunkroom above the barn where the men could sleep. To the surprise of all the troopers, except Matthew, the sergeant made no attempt to get rooms for the troopers in the hotel.

The horses had been tended to, and the troopers were in the process of spreading fresh straw they had brought up from the barn onto the pallets that would serve as their beds in the bunkroom when Sergeant O'Neall arrived at the barn. Though not quite as bad as it had been earlier, his mood was somber. Matthew, who was taking more and more of a leadership role with the other troopers had Troopers Trask and Nelson tend to the sergeant's horse while he helped the sergeant prepare his pallet.

When they had finished, Matthew turned to the sergeant, "Want to go outside for a smoke?"

"You smoke?"

"No, but you do," answered Matthew.

The sergeant shrugged and followed Matthew out onto the street that ran by the front of the barn.

"What now? I thought you were feeling better about whatever it was that happened in Chambersburg," said Matthew.

Sergeant O'Neill reached into his shirt and withdrew an envelope. "Got this, came in over the telegraph," he said.

"What's it say?" Asked Matthew.

"Don't know, ain't opened it."

"Who's it from?"

The sergeant just stared at Matthew.

"Right, you haven't opened it," he said. Matthew sighed, "You know you're going to have to open it don't you?"

"If that piss ant in Chambersburg told the captain what I did, and this is from him, it is probably telling me that I'm relieved of my post and to place myself under arrest."

"Or it could have nothing to do with whatever happened in Chambersburg."

"Here," said Sergeant O'Neill. "You open it." As he held the envelope out to Matthew.

"Me?" Exclaimed Matthew. "I can't open an official dispatch. I don't have the authority for that, I haven't even been in the cavalry a year yet!"

"You can if I say you can," he said still holding the envelope out.

"Oh for...," said Matthew snatching the envelope. He tore open the envelope, unfolded it, and began reading.

Chapter 25

The Rancocas
1790

It had only been a few hours and already the McBride cabin was beginning to take shape. Brian, who had gone to the wagon to get a small hand axe, leaned back against the wagon and watched as his new friends and neighbors worked diligently in the construction of the cabin that would serve as his and Bridget's home. Though satisfied, Brian was not really happy, and it must have showed.

"Something troubling you friend?" Asked Samuel Wills who had followed Brian to the wagon.

"T'is nothin'," replied Brian shaking his head.

"Tell me," said Samuel. "What is it?"

"Well," began Brian lowering his head. "I can't begin to be tellin' ya how grateful it is I am for da help o' yew and dese fine gentlemen, but..." He stopped talking and looked away.

"Go on, but what?"

"Da cabins in da wrong place," sighed Brian as he looked sheepishly at his friend. "Bridget and me, we wanted it over dere," he continued pointing across the old mill lane to the clearing on the opposite corner. "Dis spot here along da stream where we're buildin' da cabin was where we figgered on puttin' da barn."

"We know," said Samuel with a smile.

"Yew know?"

"Yes."

"Den why is it we're building a cabin in da wrong place?"

"But, we're not."

Brian just stared at Samuel.

"Look, my friend," said Samuel. "Every one of us agreed that the best place for a house was that spot across the lane. We also agreed that a spot as perfect as that deserved a proper house, not a rough-hewn log cabin thrown up in a few days, but a house of brick and mortar, a solid structure in which to raise a family and make memories. The kind of house you and Bridget really deserve. And, when the time comes, we'll be here to help you build that one too."

Brian turned to his friend, swallowed the lump in his throat, and said, "O' course yer right. T'is the perfect place for a proper house, and it will be, because McBride's are gonna be a livin' in it fer the next hundred years and more."

"Hey! Are you two done playing patty fingers?" Yelled Jacob Groves. "If so, I'm sure we can find something to occupy your time over here."

"We're a comin' Jacob me friend, we're a comin'," answered Brian as he put his arm around Samuel's shoulders and together they walked back over to the cabin that was quickly being raised.

About midday Bridget, Sarah Wills, and several of the other wives arrived at the site with enough food and drink to feed a small army. Makeshift tables and benches were thrown together using the lumber that was being used to build the cabin. John Leeds, the storekeeper, blessed the food, and as they shared a meal Brian and Bridget McBride became better acquainted with the people who were to be their new neighbors.

Bridget had also noticed that the cabin was in the wrong place, but when Brian explained to her why their new friends had done so all she could do was smile and wipe the tears from her eyes. "Isn't America wonderful?" She whispered.

Prior to leaving, after cleaning up after their small feast, the ladies were reminded that their help would be required the next day. For, in addition to again providing a meal, the ladies would be responsible for bringing the clayey mud from the banks of the Rancocas up to the cabin site. The men would then mix the mud with straw and it would be used as chinking between the logs, and as a mortar for the chimney stones. The ladies were also welcome to assist with the chinking.

The men worked until just before sundown, and might have worked longer had Walter Fish, the blacksmith, not showed up with a keg of ale. Even still, by the time they called it a day they had stacked enough logs so that all the walls, the four exterior and the one interior, were nearly three quarters of the way done. Where there had been nothing but grass and dirt when the sun came up, there now stood a structure that could be easily recognized as a house.

It was as Brian had planned, thirty foot by ten foot, with space left on one end for a fireplace and chimney. The sole interior wall was ten feet from the end opposite where the fireplace would be and not only served as a divider between the living space and bedroom but also as a support for the peaked roof. There was a door in the middle of the front wall which faced north towards the Mt. Holly Turnpike. There was a window, evenly spaced, on each side of the front door, with three more windows evenly spaced across the back wall.

The work began again the next day just after sunrise, and by the time they quit the walls were up and the roof, constructed with the milled lumber, was on. The chimney was not yet done, neither were the doors, windows, or shutters, and only about half the chinking was completed. Inside the floor, which was being constructed of split logs laid tightly together with their flat sides up, needed to be finished, and the fireplace and hearth built.

But, Jacob Groves had promised to buy the whiskey if the roof was on by the end of the second day. He had not mentioned that the cabin needed to be completed, only that the roof be on.

"You pirates know exactly what I meant," said Jacob Groves in pleading his case. "I meant that the cabin be finished. All it is right now is a wooden box with a lid on it. No one could live in it yet."

"That's not what you said," Silas Haines reminded him. "You said, that you would buy the whiskey if the roof was on by the end of today…and, it gives me great pleasure to point out, that the roof is indeed on." He laughed.

"You scallywags tricked me. Philip and I were left on our own with the chimney, while Norman was the only one chinking. Everyone else was working on the roof! You weren't interested in finishing the cabin! You only wanted the whiskey! You're scallywags I tell ya, the whole bunch of ya!"

"Do you have a dollar Jacob?" Asked John Leeds the storekeeper.

"What?"

"A dollar, do you have a dollar?"

"Why?"

"Well it so happens, that I have a small keg of fine Maryland whiskey in my wagon that I am willing to sell to you, this evening only, for the rock bottom price of one dollar," said Leeds with a laugh as he slapped his friend Jacob on the back.

"Scallywag even brought it with him." Jacob laughed. "Go ahead and add it to the ledger!" He said. "But I get the first drink!"

"Of course my friend, of course! To the wagon gentlemen, and bring your thirsts!" Said Leeds as with his arm around Jacob's shoulders he started for the wagon.

At the wagon John Leeds pulled a small wooden keg and a sack out from under the wagon seat. The sack contained tin cups which were passed around. Then Leeds jumped up onto the back of the wagon and began pouring the golden elixir.

"Step right up friends, and enjoy some fine Maryland whiskey!" He exclaimed. "Courtesy of Mr. Jacob Groves."

Everyone laughed. Including Jacob who was first in line and just kept muttering, "Scallywags."

It took about another week, with Brian doing most of the work, before the cabin was done. The solid front door and the shutters on the five windows were made of the same milled lumber that was used on the roof. The windows could be swung open, and the four panes on each of them were covered with paper treated with animal fat so they were translucent and waterproof.

The fireplace and hearth were constructed of stone, and the mantel was a log that had been squared off. Brian had built a counter along the back wall near the fireplace into which he had built a tin lined dry sink. He had also built a large cupboard in which Bridget could store her cooking utensils, and dry goods.

Over the bedroom Brian had also constructed a loft. He told Bridget that for now it could be used for storage, but that at some future time it could also serve as a child's bedroom. Bridget blushed but, like her husband, was concerned that their marriage had not yet produced a pregnancy.

The only thing missing was furniture. What they didn't already have, or could afford to buy, Brian built. They had purchased a bed and a small chest from a merchant in Mt. Holly, and the Hilyard's and Willis' had given them two ladder-back arm chairs as a welcoming gift.

It was late September, the McBride's had been living in their cabin for a little more than a month. During that time Brian had, with the occasional help of neighbors, dug a well, built a small barn behind the cabin as well as a smoke house, and privy. He had just started to clear and prepare the fields for next year's spring planting. Brian was as happy as he had ever been.

He had finished his noon meal and was heading out the door of the cabin. He looked north towards the Mt. Holly Pike, about a half mile away, and watched as in the distance two wagons made the turn onto Hilyard's Lane and started towards the cabin. As they got closer he noticed that one was a finely appointed open coach being pulled by a matching pair of greys, and that the other was an open wagon with a tarp over the bed.

"Who is it dat comes a callin' dis time o' day?" Asked Brian.

"I'm sure I don't know," answered Bridget as she walked over and stood beside her husband in the doorway of their cabin.

Brian could not help but be reminded of another time, not that very long ago, when he had received a visit from a man in an open coach. That visit had resulted in the loss of their farm, a stint as a thieving highwayman, and the need for him to flee Ireland. Brian turned and looked at Bridget and could see that she too was remembering that awful day.

Could it be happening again? Here in this land of the free? In this land of opportunity where no man bowed to another? Could it be?

"Fetch me da gun," said Brian to his wife still watching the approaching wagons. "I'll not be losin' another farm."

She put her hand on his arm. "Wait," she said.

As the wagons drew closer they could see that the man seated in the open coach was well dressed but was not near as elegantly attired as Lord Northrup had been. There were no footmen, and the driver, though a well-dressed one, appeared to be just that, a driver. They had all but forgotten about the second wagon.

The coach turned off of Hilyard's Lane and pulled up in front of the cabin only a dozen yards or so from the door. The gentleman seated in the coach turned and looked at the McBride's with a huge smile on his face. The driver got down and opened the door as the man, who looked very familiar, stood in preparation for stepping down.

Bridget brought her hand up to her mouth, lifted her head and looked at her husband with tears in her eyes.

"Brian!" She exclaimed. "T'is Alexander! T'is our own Alexander!" With that she burst through the door and ran towards the coach and into the arms of Alexander Duckworth, Captain of the *Loving Union.*

"So it t'is," said Brian as he too started across the yard. "So it t'is indeed."

"What a very special surprise dis is," said Bridget as she stepped aside to allow Brian the opportunity to greet their old friend. "Whatever 'er ya doin' here?"

"I've brought gifts!" Replied Alexander.

"Gifts? What sort o' gifts?" Asked Bridget.

"Well," began Alexander. "I recently returned from another trip to Ireland, and while in Limerick I happened to make the acquaintance of a man who, as it turns out, like me counts among his many friends Brian and Bridget McBride."

"And who is it dat was such a person?" Asked Brian.

"Brother Thomas Goodwin," responded Alexander with a smile, "of Limerick Lodge #271."

"Mr. Goodwin?" Exclaimed Bridget. "How wonderful! I do hope he's doin' well."

"He is, he is indeed," said Alexander. "Any way, when I learned that he was a friend, and that he was concerned that the two of you had simply disappeared into thin air, I called upon his Masonic obligation of secrecy and in confidence relayed to him the story of your travels to America. He was very happy for you and wanted me to convey to you that he wishes you the very best."

"Why, and what sort o' gifts would Mr. Goodwin send?" Inquired Brian.

"Oh, well, Mr. Goodwin didn't send any gifts exactly," said Alexander, "but Mrs. House did. You remember Mrs. House?" He continued as he turned and reached into the coach and removed a sack. "O' course," said Bridget. "Mrs. House from da Indian Queen!" Alexander reached into the sack and removed two bottles of wine. "She recalled how much you enjoyed this label during your stay."

"How wonderful!" Exclaimed Bridget

"May I presume," continued Alexander, "that I may spend a few days in your company as your guest?"

"Certainly…certainly ya may, and welcome ya are too!" Exclaimed Brian.

"Good," he said as he handed the bottles to Bridget. "My journey has left me with a powerful thirst and hunger that I'm hoping you may resolve."

"O' course Alexander," said Bridget. "I'll go and prepare someting right away."

"In the meantime, I'll take care of these gentlemen and join you and Brian inside your lovely home in just a few minutes."

Bridget turned and went into the cabin while Brian stood and listened while Alexander Duckworth paid the men who had driven the wagons and instructed them on what they were to do. As it turns out, they were from Burlington. They were instructed to return together to Burlington with the coach and to leave the wagon with the tarp at the McBride's. Alexander told them that he would return the wagon upon his return to Burlington in a few days on his way back to Philadelphia.

The two drivers left in the open coach and Alexander pulled the remaining wagon into the McBride's yard. With Brian's help he unhitched the horses and staked them out in the field adjacent to the barn. When Brian asked what was under the tarp Alexander just smiled and told him to wait, that he would find out in due time. Then he and Brian went into the house to join Bridget.

Bridget had set out a plate of smoked ham and cheeses and had poured everyone a cup of cider. "We'll have the wine with our supper." She said when the two men entered.

"Will ya ever be tellin' us what's in da wagon?" Asked Brian as he took a seat at the table.

"Well," said Alexander, as he too took a seat. "Mr. Goodwin told me about a man in Mungret who had contacted him and told him that he was holding some things of yours and wanted to know what Mr. Goodwin thought he should do with them. Mr. Goodwin told him that he would see what he could find out about your whereabouts, everyone thought you were in Dublin, and that he should hold on to the items until he heard back from Mr. Goodwin. So, I asked Mr. Goodwin if he could take me to see this gentleman and he said that he could. The following day myself, Mr. Goodwin, and Mr. O'Donnell, you remember Mr. O'Donnell, our first mate?"

"O' course we do!" Said Bridget. "I trust he's well?"

"Very well."

"Please tell him we asked after him."

"I will."

"Da story, could we be getting' back to da story please?" Injected Brian with a chuckle and a shake of his head.

"Oh, certainly, of course," said Alexander. "Well, myself, Mr. Goodwin, and Mr. O'Donnell, traveled to Mungret the following day and met with an Everett McBride, who, I learned was a cousin of yours Brian."

"And so he is," said Brian with a smile, "but, I'll not be askin' after him until you've done yer story."

"Well," continued Alexander. "He showed us the possessions you had left behind, and with help from Mr. Goodwin we were able to persuade him to sell them to me." He smiled at Bridget. "I have brought them with me, and they are under the tarp on the wagon in your yard."

Bridget reached out and grabbed Brian's hand and squeezed it. "My God," she whispered as tears began to form in her eyes. "Could it be?"

"Would you like to see what I have brought?" Asked Alexander.

Bridget squealed, jumped up from the table and ran out the door. By the time Brian and Alexander had gotten outside she was already standing next to the wagon. She had her apron balled up in her hands and was holding it up to her mouth.

"T'is like a grand Christmas it t'is," she said.

With Brian's help Alexander pulled back the tarp to reveal two large crates, and one smaller crate. Brian retrieved a hammer and pry bar while Bridget stood off to the side trembling in anticipation. The two men teasingly took their time chatting about the weather and such while Bridget tried to contain herself.

"For da love o' God open dem already!" She finally screamed.

They laughed and without further delay opened the first crate. Brian reached in and pulled out a chair. It was one of the four chairs that went with the dining table that their parents had given them as a wedding present. With the captain's help the remaining chairs and the table were removed from the crate and carried into the cabin.

Bridget danced ahead of them as they were carrying them and then directed where they should be placed. The table and chairs that had been left behind when they fled Ireland were not fancy but they were well made, highly polished, and had value beyond what they might have cost monetarily. The roughhewn table and chairs that Brian had built for them were unceremoniously removed from the house and placed in the yard.

When they returned to the wagon and opened the second crate Bridget became so overwhelmed that she fell crying to her knees right there in the yard. In the crate was the sideboard that had been a part of her dowry. It was something that she had thought she'd never see again. With tears of joy cascading down her face she also directed where the sideboard should be placed in the cabin.

The smaller and final crate was removed from the wagon and carried into the cabin. It was placed on the floor and opened, and when it was Bridget got down onto the floor, placed her arms around the crate, and wept. In the crate, carefully packed in straw, was Bridget's china, the balance of her dowry.

"I don't know how we can ever be tankin' ya," said Brian swallowing the lump in his throat.

"Consider it payment in advance for room and board for future visits," said Alexander.

"Whenever yew want, and fer as long as you'd like," replied Brian.

"Come on," said Alexander placing his hand on his friend's shoulder. "Let's leave Bridget to properly enjoy the reunion. Besides, I also have something for you."

The two men went back out into the yard leaving Bridget alone in her unbridled happiness at the return of the possessions that she had thought she would never see again.

Alexander Duckworth stayed with the McBride's for three days. During that time he helped out around the farm with the animals, in the clearing of the fields, and other tasks. He told Brian that when the time came for him to give up the sea that he wanted to find a place just like this in which to live out his life. Brian assured him he would always be welcome along the banks of the Rancocas.

During his stay he had also mentioned that Brian should consider building a landing at the end of Hilyard's Lane as a stop for the many ships that plied the waters of the Rancocas. The banks of the creek were steep there and the water deep enough to allow ships to come alongside a dock if one were to be built. Such a landing would make it much easier for Brian to ship and receive the goods he would need to work the farm as the farm grew, and by charging other farmers a small fee to use it, it could serve as a source of income as well. Brian didn't give it much thought at the time, but did eventually take his friend's advice and build a dock and small warehouse. By 1795, Hilyard's Landing was a busy and well-known stop along the Rancocas.

Near the end of October of 1792, Bridget informed Brian that she was with child. She gave birth to Colin McBride the following June. Brian had a son.

In March of 1795, a second son would be born to the McBride's, after Bridget endured a difficult pregnancy. Sadly, the child, who was not strong, would not survive the summer. On Christmas Day of 1797, a strong healthy daughter, Colleen, would become the newest member of the McBride family. There would be no more children after Colleen.

Colin and Colleen would be raised in the log cabin their father had built with the help of their neighbors. A room was added in 1800, but it wouldn't be until 1814, that work on the proper house that Brian and his friend Samuel Willis had talked about would begin. In fact, it would be Colin, with the help of his father, who was now approaching fifty years of age, and some of the same men who had helped build the cabin, who would build that proper house of brick and mortar, and it would take them nearly two years to do it.

By the time the house was complete Colleen McBride had met and married a shopkeeper from Philadelphia. She kept in touch with her family, but her visits to Rancocas were infrequent. Brian and Bridget would, on occasion, use their daughter as an excuse to travel to Philadelphia, and when there they always made it a point to stop in and visit their friends at the Indian Queen Inn.

Colin McBride, with the support of family, friends, and neighbors, finally convinced William Hannon, the father of Margaret "Peggy" Hannon of Charles Town, that he was good enough for his daughter. They were married in 1817. Colin and Peggy would raise five children in their "proper" house, one of those would be a son, William, who years later would become Michael McBride's father.

Brian and Bridget would never live in the "proper" house. They found they preferred the cabin, and happily lived out their lives there. Brian died in 1839, followed five years later by his beloved Bridget. They were buried side by side overlooking the banks of the Rancocas.

Before he died Brian had said that there were only two things he regretted about his life. The first was that he had never gotten to see Ireland again, and the second that he had never gotten the opportunity to say, "Thank you," to Mr. Benjamin Franklin.

Chapter 26

The Catoctin
1861

Matthew's eyes were immediately drawn to the large black fancy script centered across the top of the handwritten telegraph message; "The Western Union Telegraph Company", below that in the same script was printed "Hagerstown, Maryland", and below and to the right of that in a smaller script was "date". Handwritten next to "date" was, "14 Feb 61 12pm".

The operator who had received it was not blessed with good penmanship, and it took Matthew a few minutes to decipher the scribbled message. In addition, it was hand stamped with the official Western Union seal signifying it as an official telegraph message. It had been stamped over the written message, and then someone had scrawled their initials over the stamp. It occurred to Matthew that had Western Union actually tried, they could not have made the message more difficult to read.

"It's from Lieutenant Nelson," said Matthew without looking up. "It was sent from Shippensburg earlier today."

"Then before Chambersburg," said Sergeant O'Neall with a sigh, "so, before anyone could have talked to that blubber butted hotel owner."

"That's right," said Matthew. "So, I was right. This telegram's got nothing to do with that."

"Spared for now anyway," said the Sergeant. "Go on then, as long as you're holding it you might as well read it."

"Let's see," said Matthew struggling with the writing. "Seems there's been a change in plans."

"For Christ's sake, will you just read what it says!"

"It says," began Matthew not trying to hide the annoyance in his voice. "Sergeant E. O'Neall, 2nd US Cavalry, from Lieutenant J. Nelson, 2nd US Cavalry at Shippensburg, Pennsylvania. Proceed to Middletown on 15 February. Find suitable bivouac for B Troop and await our arrival. Do not proceed to Frederick. Repeat do not proceed to Frederick."

"Damn," said Sergeant O'Neall. "Now what do you make of that?"

"Beats me," said Matthew with a smile and a shrug as it occurred to him that this change in orders would probably make it possible for him to visit his father and sister at the family farm outside of Middletown. However, before he could say anything the sergeant walked past him, went back into the barn, and climbed the narrow stairs up to the bunkroom. Matthew quickly followed.

"Listen up troopers!" Barked the Sergeant as he reached the top of the stairs. "Change in plans. We ain't going to Frederick tomorrow. We'll be stopping in Middletown to find someplace where all of B Troop can join us for a jolly old campout. I want to be in the saddle at first light, so it'll be coffee and hardtack for breakfast. Questions? No? Good."

"Hey Calhoun?" Asked Trooper Walters. "Ain't you from somewheres around Frederick?"

"Middletown," answered Matthew with a smile. "My family's farm is just west of Middletown."

"There you go Sarge," Walters continued. "We got us a guide."

"Middletown, Calhoun? Really?" Asked O'Neall turning to face Matthew.

"Yep."

"You know of any place that all of B troop could bivouac?"

"Sure do," said Matthew turning away from the sergeant and rearranging the straw on his pallet.

"Well, are you going to tell us, or do I have to put my boot in your ass to loosen your tongue?"

Matthew, still smiling, turned and faced the sergeant. "Our farm is a mile west of Middletown just off the National Road along the Catoctin Creek. There's a meadow, probably about four acres, along the creek that should work."

"Your people will be alright with it"?

"I could probably talk them into it." Matthew brought his hand up and began rubbing his chin. "I could probably be more persuasive though if there was an understanding that I could get to sleep in my own bed for a night or two," said Matthew eyeing the sergeant.

"Hey Calhoun, you sound just like the Sarge trying to work a deal!" Laughed Trooper Trask.

"Shut up Trask!" Growled Sergeant O'Neall. "Where you sleep Calhoun will be up to the lieutenant," he said in a mocking tone to Matthew, "but whether or not you even get see Middletown? Well, I guess that's kinda up to me, ain't it?" The Sergeant grinned as he rearranged the straw on his pallet and turned away from Matthew.

"I'm sure the meadow won't be a problem," said Matthew with a sigh, as everyone, including the sergeant, shared a laugh.

The blacksmith who worked for Mr. Marrs was a large black man who went by the name of Bricks. Bricks always started his day well before sunup. In addition to being an accomplished blacksmith, Bricks considered himself quite the cook. He knew the troopers were staying at the livery so he thought it would be nice if he had a breakfast ready for them before they left Hagerstown.

It was still dark when Matthew was awakened by the smell of coffee brewing. It wasn't long before the other troopers were awakened too.

"You smell that?" Asked a voice in the dark.

"Sure do," answered Matthew.

"Mmmm... smells good," continued the voice. "I say we go find out where it's coming from."

"Just hold your horses." Sergeant O'Neall's voice boomed from the darkness. "One of you see if you can find a lantern and get it lit without burning the whole place down, and we'll all go. Time to get cracking anyway."

A lantern was lit and in the dancing shadows it created the troopers got up, got dressed and began gathering their gear. It wasn't long before the troopers had descended the narrow stairs and were standing in the street in front of the barn in the subdued light of dawn. The blacksmith shop was to the right of the barn and was separated from the barn by a narrow alley.

The coffee smell was coming from the shop and now there was also the smell of meat cooking. The large double doors on the front of the shop were swung wide open and as the troopers approached the entrance they could also hear singing. The deep booming voice was singing with enthusiasm but no one could make out the words, or recognize the tune.

As they stood in the doorway, peering into the shop, they discovered the source of not only the smells, but of the singing as well. The large man, who was standing over a fire, turned and smiled. In the darkness of the shop he was just a silhouette with large sparkling eyes, and a toothy friendly smile.

"C'mon in!" He said with a laugh and a wave. "I's biled ya's up some coffee and is fryin' ya's up some ham steaks too," he continued as he turned back to the fire. "Was gwanna have ya some eggs, but dem chickens din't hold up dey part o' da bargin!" He laughed, a contagious laugh that the troopers couldn't help but share. "Git out ya cups, po' ya some coffee, and find yas a place to squat. Da ham jus' 'bout done."

"This is mighty nice of you friend," said Sergeant O'Neall.

"Bricks, dey calls me Bricks, and I's happy to do it fo' you sojer boys. Heared a man say oncte dat a army marches on its stomachs. Guessin' it wouldn't hurt to have some coffee and ham in it den."

While the troopers enjoyed their unexpected breakfast Bricks sat and talked with them about things that were being talked about and going on in and around Hagerstown. Many of the townspeople and local farmers did business with Mr. Marrs' blacksmith shop. While they were waiting for work to be completed, or for their turn, they often talked among themselves with little regard for Bricks who was always nearby listening

Bricks said that it seemed as if the town was just as divided as the country was. Some people were pro-Lincoln and felt that everything that could be done should be done to hold the Union together. While it seemed just as many felt it was time for the North and South to go their separate ways.

"Is dey gwanna be a war Cap'n?" Asked Bricks.

"I'm just a sergeant Bricks, and I think there is gonna be one yeah."

"You tink dey gwanna let colored folk jine up and fight?"

"Don't know," answered the Sergeant, "hard to say."

"I sho' hopes so," said Bricks. "'Cuz you cain't spects people to let you be part o' sometin' werf havin', if'n you ain'ts willin' to stan' up nex' to 'em and fights for it."

Sergeant O'Neall smiled at the big man and stuck out his hand which almost disappeared in the grip of the large blacksmith. "We gotta get going," the Sergeant said, "and Bricks," he continued still grasping the black man's hand, "if they let you in, you come look me up. I'll stand a post with you."

"I'll do dat Cap'n," Bricks said with a great smile. "I'll do dat."

Despite Bricks' protests, the troopers chipped in and gave the man a dollar. Mr. Marrs had said there was no charge for the stabling and boarding of the horses, or the use of the bunkroom. It was a pretty happy bunch that headed south on Mulberry Street and turned left onto the National Road.

The morning sun was just about full up when they had covered the three miles into Funkstown. The bright sun quickly burned the frost off the ground and it felt as if it was going to be a pleasant day, weatherly speaking. The town was just waking up, and the few people who were out and about waved but other than that paid little attention to the troopers. Their next stop on the National Road would be Boonsboro, a little more than two hours further down the road.

The troopers rode in a column of twos, with Sergeant O'Neall out front. Matthew was in the first rank alongside Trooper Nelson. They encountered the occasional rider or wagon, but other than that they more or less had the road to themselves.

"Sarge, permission to come up?" Asked Matthew.

The Sergeant stuck out his hand and almost begrudgingly waved him forward. "What's on your mind Calhoun?" He asked when Matthew's horse fell in alongside his.

"I got a brother, Mark," Matthew said. "Has a farm on the other side of Boonsboro, not quite a mile out of town."

"So?"

"I'm sure we'd be able to rest, care for the horses, and get a hot meal there."

"What's in it for you?" Asked O'Neall turning his head and eyeing Matthew.

"A chance to visit for an hour or two. Talk with my brother and sister-in-law, catch up on the family news, and meet my nephew. He's nearly nine months old, and I've never even seen him."

The Sergeant sighed and looked away. "Alright we'll stop," he said. "Can't guarantee how long we'll stay though, now get back in formation."

"Alright, and thanks Sarge."

Sergeant O'Neall just grunted and waved his hand dismissing Matthew as if her were swatting at a pesky mosquito.

Matthew fell back in alongside Trooper Nelson. "Going to get to see my brother," he said with a smile.

Nelson just nodded.

When they arrived at the center of Boonsboro there was a group of men gathered at the intersection of Potomac and Main Streets. Sergeant O'Neall brought the patrol to a stop in front of the men.

One of the men, an older rotund man, dressed in a suit and wearing a felt top hat, addressed the sergeant. "Figured we'd be seeing some of you fellows sooner or later."

"Why's that, sir?" Asked the sergeant.

"Because of that trouble over in Frederick. Is it true?"

"Well sir," said the sergeant looking back at the troopers. "I'm afraid I'm not really authorized to discuss the Frederick situation with civilians."

"I suppose I can understand that," said the man. "Just seems as so the whole country's going crazy though."

"So it does sir. So it does. But just what side of the craziness are you on? If you don't mind my asking that is?" Asked Sergeant O'Neall with a grin.

"Not at all Sergeant," answered the man touching the brim of his hat. "Name's Harrison, and I'm as pro-union a man as you're likely to meet."

"Well, I'll tell you what, Mr. Harrison," Sergeant O'Neall said, with a glance back at the troopers. "You being a union man and all. You tell me what you know about what happened over in Frederick, and I'll let you know just how accurate your information is."

"Well," began the man. "There was a rider through here yesterday said that there was a bunch of anti-Lincoln folks over in Frederick who had gotten word that the US Army had already gotten orders to march south into Virginia, so's to be ready to attack into the deeper south the minute Lincoln got inaugurated. He said there was over 5,000 of you cavalry types coming down out of Pennsylvania that was gonna be passing through Frederick."

"5,000?" Said the Sergeant.

"Yes sir, 5,000 he said. Anyway, these anti-Lincoln folks got a lot of people all stirred up carrying on that Lincoln ain't got no right to move the army anywhere just yet, and that Lincoln was gonna make things worse, and that the army would be recruiting the men and boys out of the towns they passed through on their way south and Frederick was gonna be their first stop, they had them all riled up. How am I doing?" Asked the man eyeing the sergeant.

"You're doing good so far," answered Sergeant O'Neall. "Keep going, what is supposed to have happened next?"

"Well," he continued, taking a breath. "Them folks in Frederick decided they wasn't going to let the army in! So, they set up road blocks at all of the roads leading into town from the north. They had some of their finer citizens stationed at the road blocks to explain to the army that they would have to by-pass Frederick. They wasn't going be allowed into town! Now I ask you, ain't that something?" He shook his head and looked up at Sergeant O'Neall.

"Was there any plan on using force to stop the army?" Asked the Sergeant.

"Can't say for sure, the fellow who brought the news said nothing about that."

"Well friend," said the Sergeant reaching up and pushing his cap back further on his head. "I'll tell you, there is a force headed south out of Pennsylvania for Frederick. I'm afraid I'm not at liberty to discuss its strength, but I can tell you this, its mission is not to continue south, but to turn east and head for Baltimore."

"Baltimore, really?" Said the surprised Mr. Harrison. "Expecting trouble there are they?"

"No sir, at least we hope not," continued Sergeant O'Neall. "Its mission is to meet Mr. Lincoln's train and escort him into Washington City."

"Rather a large force for an escort, wouldn't you say?"

"As I said sir, I'm not at liberty to discuss its strength."

"Ah, yes, of course not, of course not," he harrumphed. "There you have it gentlemen," he continued turning to the small group of men who were standing on the corner with him. "The information which I obtained and relayed to you has been confirmed."

The men murmured and nodded at each other.

"While we're at it sir, could you tell me where I might find someone in authority?" Asked the Sergeant.

The man removed his hat and looked up at the sergeant. "Well, that's easy enough," he said. "That'd be me, William Harrison. So happens I'm the Mayor of Boonsboro. Allow me to welcome you and your men to our town."

"Thank you Your Honor," said Sergeant O'Neall. "My name's O'Neall, Sergeant O'Neall, B Troop, US 2nd Cavalry. We're an advance patrol for a larger force which is about a day's march behind us. I expect that they'll be arriving here at just about this same time tomorrow."

"A larger force you say? Just how large a force?" The sergeant stared down at the man with a grin. "Of course, you're not at liberty to say," he sighed, "but, I can assume that they too are in route to Baltimore?"

"They may need some provisions, but they mean you no harm and will not take more than you can afford to offer. You will be paid for anything they take. My advice is that you let them in. Don't let anyone block any roads or try to delay them. They will not take kindly to it and it will only cause you grief."

"As I said Sergeant, this is a Union town. Your comrades will be welcomed with open arms and we will do our best to see to their needs."

"I appreciate that Sir," said the Sergeant. "Now, we must continue on our way."

"If there is nothing more we can do for you, then I will bid you farewell and a safe journey," said Mayor Harrison doffing his hat to the sergeant.

The Sergeant started to leave, but then stopped suddenly. "There is something you can do for me Mr. Mayor," said Sergeant O'Neall.

"What would that be Sergeant?"

"When the column arrives here, would you be good enough to let the commanding officer know how I conducted myself?"

"I should say that we should be proud to have you in our service Sergeant."

"Thank you Mr. Mayor, thank you," Sergeant O'Neall lifted his right arm, and with a wave and a "For'ard" led the patrol east out of town.

"Calhoun!" Barked the Sergeant. "How far to your brother's place?"

"Not even a mile," answered Matthew. "Get up here, and show me where."

It took them a little less than fifteen minutes to reach the intersection with the Rohrersville Road. Just beyond the intersection there was a lane on the left. Matthew turned his mount into the lane followed by Sergeant O"Neall and the rest of the troopers.

The house was not grand, but it was typical of the farmhouses of the period and area. It was a two-story four up and four down whitewashed wood framed house with a large covered porch, and a brick chimney on each end. It was about 100 feet off the main road and faced east.

Beyond the house was a large wooden barn, and some other out buildings. Matthew remembered that on his last visit the barn was still under construction. It was obvious that his brother, Mark Calhoun, took a great deal of pride in his farm, as the buildings and yard were clean and well cared for.

As they approached the house a young girl came around the far end of the house carrying a basket of laundry. She stopped when she saw the troopers and put her hand up to shield her eyes from the afternoon sun. She appeared to be in her early teens, and was wearing a brown knitted shawl over a blue cotton house dress.

"Can I help you gentlemen?" She asked.

Matthew couldn't believe his eyes. "Hello Katherine," he said matter of factly.

"Matthew!" She screamed. Katherine Rosemary Calhoun, Matthew's 12-year old sister dropped the basket spilling the laundry all over the ground. She brought her hand up to her throat, let out a scream, and came running towards him, losing her shawl in the process.

Matthew jumped from the saddle just before she got there and was nearly knocked off his feet when she threw her arms around his neck and jumped into his arms. She was already sobbing as she buried her face into his neck. Katherine clung desperately to her brother as she repeatedly whispered his name.

"You two know each other?" Chuckled Sergeant O'Neall.

Matthew swung around and faced the sergeant with Katherine still clinging to him. Red-faced, he released Katherine and raised his arms with a shrug, though she continued to hold on to the brother she had not seen for nearly eight months. He put his arms around her again and whispered in her ear, "It's alright Katherine, I told you I'd come see you, didn't I."

Katherine finally released her brother and as she wiped the tears from her eyes she turned to face the sergeant. "I'm sorry," she said sheepishly. "I haven't seen my brother Matthew in a very long time, and I did miss him desperately." She glanced back at Matthew and smiled.

Sergeant O'Neall removed his cap and bowed. "No need to apologize young lady," he said with a smile. "It's good to know that Matthew has family that cares for him almost as much as the US Cavalry does."

Several of the troopers started to laugh but stopped short when the sergeant turned and glared at them.

Katherine turned back to Matthew. "Mark and Violet aren't here," she said. "Uncle Kevin broke his leg in a fall so they've gone to Burkittsville. I expect them back today some time."

"Why are you here?" Asked Matthew.

"Violet didn't want baby Mark to have to make the trip so I came up from home to take care of Marky and watch over the place."

"Are you here alone?" Asked Matthew.

"Oh no," answered Katherine. "Mr. Adams, who works for Mark, is here too. He and his wife Bonnie have a cabin down back by the stream. Bonnie's been doing the cooking so we eat our meals together. Then in the evening they go back to the cabin and Marky and I stay here at the house."

"Alone?"

"Matthew!" She said. "I'm nearly 13 years old. Besides, I always lock up good, and I'm a much better shot with a shotgun and pistol than I used to be."

Matthew just stared at her, but Sergeant O'Neall and the rest of the patrol couldn't help but burst into laughter.

"I'll bet you are little lady," said the Sergeant. "I'll just bet you are."

Matthew just shook his head.

"It's a good thing you and your friends showed up now instead of after dark," Katherine said, "or else you might have found out just how much better I've gotten."

"Well Miss," said Sergeant O'Neall. "Since it seems your brother is not going to ask, then I will. We'd like to rest our horses in your barn and have ourselves something to eat out of the weather if that's okay?"

"Of course," said Katherine. "How long will you be staying?"

"An hour or two is all," replied the Sergeant. "We have to make Middletown by nightfall."

Katherine turned to Matthew. "Only an hour or two?"

"Sorry," said Matthew, "but we do have to get to the farm."

"Our farm?" She asked. "Yes."

"Well, I'll be there tomorrow and we can visit again then, can't we?"

"For a bit we can. Yes"

"Sir," she said, turning her attention to Sergeant O'Neall. "I have some ham and bean soup with bread that I can share. There should be plenty for everyone, but I don't think we'll all fit in the kitchen."

"That's very nice of you young lady. You just get it ready while we tend to our horses, and then we'll come up to the house and take whatever you can spare out to the barn with us. We'll be more than comfortable. Trooper Calhoun can eat in the kitchen with you so you two can have some time alone together to get caught up."

"Thanks Sarge," said Matthew smiling up at the sergeant, who almost smiled back at Matthew.

"Come on the rest of you," the Sergeant said to the other troopers. "Let's get the horses settled. Trask, take care of Calhoun's mount." Matthew handed Trooper Trask the reins to his horse as he passed.

As Sergeant O'Neall and the troopers approached the barn, a man, who Matthew assumed would be Mr. Adams, came from around the back of the barn and approached the sergeant. They spoke briefly, then Mr. Adams reached up and shook hands with the sergeant. He then opened the large barn doors and led the troopers inside.

Matthew helped Katherine pick up the spilled laundry, and then followed her into the house. The house was warm, and not just because of the fires burning in the fireplaces, but because it was like coming home. Matthew had helped build this house, and had spent many hours in this house with family and friends.

A baby cried.

"Come meet little Mark," said Katherine.

Chapter 27

The Catoctin
1861

It had been Sergeant O'Neall's intention to have his contingent of troopers back in the saddle and on their way to the Calhoun farm west of Middletown by one o'clock. They were just beginning to prepare to depart when Matthew's brother, Mark and his wife Violet returned home from Burkittsville. Mark and Violet had gone to Burkittsville to help Matthew and Mark's Uncle Kevin who had been injured in a fall.

Mark dropped Violet off at the house and was surprised when he pulled up in front of the barn to find it full of people, many of whom were soldiers. He spotted his sister Katherine among them and asked, "Well, what's going on here?"

"Matthew's come to visit!" She said getting up off of the wooden box she had been seated on.

"Did he bring the whole US Army with him?" Mark asked with a smile.

"No, I didn't," said Matthew as he stepped away from his comrades and walked toward the wagon. "Just the best part of it."

"If you ain't a sight," said Mark as he jumped down from the wagon and embraced his brother. "Look at you!" He exclaimed holding his brother at arm's length. "A proper soldier. Did you make General yet?"

"No," laughed Matthew. "Probably take another couple of months or so."

"Mark?" Hailed Violet as she came around the open barn door. "Katy and the baby aren't in the house, are they out here with you?"

"No," he said turning to his wife with a huge smile. "They're out here with Matthew!"

"Matthew?" She asked as it took a moment for her to comprehend what she had been told. Then she saw him. "Matthew," she almost whispered as she tilted her head and smiled. "Well get over here and give me a kiss you dashing young crusader!" She squealed as she held out her arms.

Trooper Nelson who was known for his antics, jumped up, extended his arms, and started across the barn towards Violet.

"Where are you going?" Bellowed Sergeant O'Neall.

"She wants a kiss from a dashing young crusader," said Nelson as he stopped and turned towards the sergeant. "That's me isn't it?"

"No, you're a bumbling young embarrassment," said the Sergeant. "There's a difference."

"Oh, my mistake." Shrugged Nelson as he turned and started back to his seat. Sergeant O'Neall just stared, but everyone else in the barn laughed heartily, as Nelson stood and bowed.

It was after three by the time the sergeant and his detail were ready to leave the farm of Matthew Calhoun's brother. This meant that they wouldn't make the farm of Matthew Calhoun's father until after dark. Sergeant O'Neall would never admit it, but he had enjoyed the visit with Matthew's brother and his family just as much as the rest of the detail had, but now he was angry that they had been delayed as long as they had been.

It had gotten cold again, and they hadn't gone very far along the National Road before they were all bundled up in their wool great coats and capes. In less than a mile they started up the western slope of South Mountain. Despite the temptation to get out of the cold, they pushed on and did not stop at the South Mountain Inn when they passed through the little crossroads settlement at Zittlestown.

The setting sun was disappearing behind the mountain as they passed through Turner's Gap and started down the mountain's eastern slope. It would take almost two more hours before they would reach the turnoff for the Calhoun farm in Middletown, and they rode in silence as the darkness and the cold descended upon them. The troopers huddled down into their great coats, the flaps turned up against their ears, with their hats pulled down tight over their heads, while their breath and the breath of their horses formed little clouds of icy fog each time they exhaled.

"How much further?" Bellowed Sergeant O'Neall who was barely visible in the darkness at the head of the formation.

Matthew lifted his head which had been pulled down between his shoulders and looked around for a familiar landmark. "Not much further," he answered. "A half mile or so maybe to the lane, and then another half mile to the house."

"Get up here and point it out. Don't want to miss it. It's too damned cold to go wandering around in the dark."

"If we come to the creek we'll know we missed it," said Matthew as he pulled up alongside Sergeant O'Neall.

"If we miss it and come to the creek, I'll be tossing your sorry ass into it," threatened the sergeant.

About fifteen minutes later Matthew pointed to a well-used lane on the right. "This is it," he said. "Home sweet home." He was beginning to get excited about not only being home but of seeing his father again.

"This your family's land here?" Asked the sergeant nodding to the left after they had made the turn.

"Both sides actually," said Mathew proudly. "It's about 135 acres all told, with nearly a quarter mile of frontage on the National Road, and over a half mile of creek frontage".

"And you left this to ride around on a smelly horse in the dark and the cold? Didn't think you were quite that stupid."

"Didn't want to be a farmer," said Matthew. "Wanted to see more of the world than just what's in this little valley between South Mountain and the Catoctins. Besides," he chuckled as he leaned forward and patted his horse on the side of its muscular neck. "Rooster's not all that smelly."

"I don't think you knew how good you had it," said Sergeant O'Neall wistfully.

"How about you though Sarge, where'd you grow up?" Asked Matthew.

"Saratoga," answered the Sergeant.

"You're one hell of a horseman, so I figured you were from horse country somewhere. What made you leave home to become a horse soldier?"

Sergeant O'Neall turned his head and glared at Matthew. "Just get us somewhere where we can get out of the damned cold Calhoun," he grumbled.

About ten minutes after leaving the National Road, the candles burning in the windows of the Calhoun house came into view. Matthew's heart began to beat a little faster. He turned towards the sergeant with a huge smile on his face.

The Sergeant just looked at him, then waved his hand as if dismissing a child. "Go ahead," he said. "Go tell 'em we're here."

Matthew kicked his horse into a gallop as he quickly covered the last couple of hundred yards. He reined up in front of the house, dismounted, and walked up onto the porch. There was a candle burning in the parlor window to the left of the door, and another one burning in a window on the second floor. Matthew knew that that would be the window in his father's bedroom.

He peered in the parlor window and saw that there appeared to be several candles burning in the kitchen, and he was sure there was a fire burning in the kitchen's fireplace. As he looked in this window he couldn't help but remember the day of his mother's funeral, he was nine at the time, when he and his brother Mark had stood in this same spot looking through this same window watching as their broken hearted father sat in a chair and wept. It was also the day their sister had gotten her name, Katherine Rosemary.

He walked back over to the door, removed his gauntlets and hat, and knocked. Matthew was pretty sure that the door would be unlocked, but he didn't think it would be a good idea to go bursting in on a man, even if he was your father, who was not expecting company. He could hear someone coming.

"Who is it?" Demanded a voice on the other side of the door.

"It's Matthew." He felt a lump form in his throat when he recognized his father's voice.

"Matthew who?"

"For crying out loud Pa, how many Matthew's could you possibly be expecting?"

Matthew hadn't finished his sentence before the door swung open and Brody Calhoun, having recognized his son's voice, came bursting out of the house and threw his arms around his son in a loving embrace. After their embrace they held each other at arm's length and studied each other.

"You look well Pa," said Matthew.

"Thanks," said the elder Calhoun. "I'm keeping myself together," he chuckled. "You look cold and tired though," he said with concern.

"I am," answered Matthew. "We left Mark's place about three, been sitting in that saddle nearly four hours."

It was then that they noticed that the rest of the detail had arrived at the house.

"Pa," said Matthew. "This is my sergeant, Sergeant O'Neall, Sarge, this is my father, Brody Calhoun."

"A pleasure Mr. Calhoun," said the Sergeant as he brought his hand up to the brim of his hat.

"Please, call me Brody," he answered.

"And these are the rest of the boys," said Matthew pointing to the troopers who were lined up behind the sergeant.

222

Brody Calhoun smiled and nodded, and the troopers all touched the brims of their hats as well. "You all look cold and tired," he said. They all murmured in agreement. He turned and hollered through the open door. "Dave! Come out here, we got us some company!" He turned to face Matthew. "Dave's my hired hand."

Matthew nodded. "Oh?"

"Well, what'd you expect?" He laughed as he slapped Matthew on the shoulder. "Both my sons abandoned me, and I couldn't work this place on my own."

A few minutes later a tall, well-built black man arrived at the door. Matthew guessed the man was maybe in his mid-thirties. His head was shaved, and Matthew noticed that he had a crescent shaped scar on the left side of his face along his jaw.

"This is my son Matthew, and his army," Brody Calhoun said to the man with a smile. "Matthew, this is Dave, Dave Stokes."

Dave nodded in the direction of the soldiers aligned in front of the house, and then turned and shook hands with Matthew. "I've heard a lot about you Sir," he said. "It's a pleasure to finally meet you." He had a strong grip, and it was obvious that he was not your typical uneducated farm laborer.

"Dave," said Brody Calhoun. "Would you show these men to the barn so they can get their horses settled?"

"Certainly," answered Dave.

"After you've seen to your mounts Sergeant, you and your men come on back to the house. Dave's missus has cooked up a very tasty sausage soup, and there's plenty to go around."

"Thank you Mr. Cal… Brody," said Sergeant O'Neall with a smile. "That's mighty nice of you."

"Barn's around the back," said Dave as he started off the porch. "If you'll just follow me." Matthew started to follow, but the hired hand turned and said, "I'll take care of your horse, you go on in and get reacquainted with your father."

Matthew looked at the sergeant who nodded his approval. "Thanks," he said to Dave. "That's very nice of you." Dave picked up the reins of Matthew's horse and with the troopers following disappeared around the corner of the house.

Brody Calhoun turned to his son, he reached up and put his right hand on the back of his son's neck and pulled his head down so that their foreheads were touching. When he released Matthew and looked up he had tears in his eyes. "I can't tell you how happy I am to see you," he said.

"Me too Pa," said Matthew. "Me too."

They went into the house and Brody Calhoun introduced his son to Olivia Stokes, Dave's wife. She was an attractive light skinned woman who Matthew guessed was several years younger than her husband. Olivia, his father explained, had been hired to take care of the house and do the cooking.

When Matthew asked why those jobs weren't being done by Katherine, Brody Calhoun laughed and said that while Katherine was an adequate housekeeper, when she did the cooking it was only the pigs and dogs who would gain any weight. He laughingly said Olivia was hired when it got to the point where his pants would no longer stay up. In addition to her regular duties, Olivia was now charged with teaching Katherine to cook.

If the delicious aromas that filled the kitchen were any indication, Matthew did not have to be convinced of Olivia's abilities. After their introduction, Olivia had turned her attention back to the large pot suspended over the hot coals in the fireplace that contained the sausage soup. Matthew also noticed that there were several loaves of fresh baked bread under a towel on the counter.

By the time Dave and the troopers returned to the house, Olivia had set the table to accommodate everyone, and Matthew and his father had gathered enough chairs for everyone. The ten of them, Matthew and his father, the other troopers, and Dave and Olivia, shared a fine meal and enjoyable conversation. Although, Matthew was sure that some of the stories his father told would come back to haunt him.

"So, why is the US Cavalry seated around my table?" Asked the elder Calhoun when the meal was done. "Is it because of the trouble over in Frederick?"

"No," began Sergeant O'Neall. "It's got nothing to do with Frederick, not yet anyway. We only learned about that ourselves earlier today when we passed through Boonsboro. We're an advance patrol for B Troop of the US 2nd Cavalry," he continued. "Tomorrow afternoon sometime the rest of B Troop is going to be arriving here."

"Here?" Asked Brody Calhoun. "You mean in Middletown?"

"No Sir," answered Sergeant O'Neall with a smile. "I mean here." As he tapped the top of the table with his index finger. "Here, on your farm, and they'll be looking for a place to bivouac."

"Bivouac… How many….?"

"About one hundred and twenty five men and horses, maybe three or four supply wagons, and one or two pieces of light artillery."

"Tomorrow afternoon?"

"Yes Sir."

"Matthew, did you know about this?" Asked his father.

Matthew looked at the sergeant and then back at his father. "Well," he began. "It was kind of my idea. I thought if I volunteered the farm as the bivouac area it would give me a better chance to visit with you and Katherine."

"Your idea? Hmmm… well how about that. Well Sergeant," Brody Calhoun said. "Tomorrow morning I'll show you around and we'll see if we can find a place to put your army."

"Thank you," said the Sergeant. "I appreciate that, and I'm sure our Commanding Officer, Captain Talbot, and the rest of B Troop will too."

"Seems a small price to pay to have my son back for a day or two," he said with a smile. "Now," he continued. "I won't have my son's comrades in arms sleeping out in the barn. Matthew can stay in my room with me, and we have two extra rooms upstairs that you're welcome to. Three men should fit in each room comfortably, but there's only one bed in each room and the beds won't fit any more than two men, so somebody's going to have to sack out on the floor."

"That's awfully kind of you Brody," said the Sergeant. "We'll put three men in each room and I'll sack out here in front of the fireplace if it's not too much trouble."

"Sergeant," interrupted Dave. "Our house is just back down the lane a few hundred yards, and we've got an extra room. You're more than welcome, and you'll have a bed all to yourself."

The Sergeant just stared at Dave, and for a few moments there seemed to be some tension building. Then, the Sergeant smiled and said, "Thank you Dave. I wouldn't mind a night away from these young varmints. I'd be honored." Nobody sighed out loud, but it wouldn't have been a surprise if someone had.

Brody Calhoun had Dave bring up a keg of hard cider from the cellar and they all sat around sharing stories and cider for another hour or so before they called it a night. Matthew and his father retired to his room but sat up until well after midnight catching up and just enjoying each other's company. That night for the first time since he was a little boy, Matthew dreamed about his mother.

The next morning after breakfast, Sergeant O'Neall assigned all of the troopers except Matthew to Dave as a working party. Dave was told that he could use them to perform or help with any job or task he needed done. Not a single one of them complained, they seemed to welcome the change to their routine.

Then, Matthew, his father, and Sergeant O'Neall, rode out to find the best place among the 135 acres to bivouac the men of B Troop. It had to be large enough to accommodate the entire Troop and be easily accessible to water. Brody Calhoun had a couple of sites that he thought Sergeant O'Neall should consider.

The first one was a six acre area right behind the barn that would give easy access to the house and barn, but had no creek frontage. There was also a seven acre tract that had frontage on both the National Road as well as the Catoctin Creek. Sergeant O'Neall decided that the seven acre area would be the best spot. Not only would it accommodate all of B Troop, but there would be easy access to the main road and creek, and this site was about a quarter of a mile from the house, so there would be less likelihood that the activity in and around the camp would disturb their host.

When they had finished their noon meal Sergeant O'Neall assigned Troopers Nelson and Walters to ride back along the National Road to the eastern side of Fox Gap, a distance of about three miles. They were to wait there for B Troop. As soon as B Troop came into sight one of them was to gallop back to the farm to advise the sergeant. The other trooper was to wait and guide B Troop to the Bivouac area.

Shortly after three o'clock, Trooper Walters came galloping up to the back of the house. He dismounted, climbed the porch and burst through the back door into the kitchen. Brody Calhoun and Sergeant O'Neall were seated at the table drinking coffee.

"They coming?" Asked the Sergeant eyeing the young trooper.

"Yes Sergeant," he said a little out of breath.

"How far behind you are they?"

"I don't know," he said shaking his head. "I came on pretty good, half an hour, maybe a little more."

"Okay," said the Sergeant. "Good job Walters. Now go out back and stick your head in the trough before you pass out."

Walters nodded and went out the back door. He had no intention of sticking his head in the trough, but he was wearing a huge smile because this was the first time the sergeant had ever told him he'd done something right.

When Captain Talbot and his aide, escorted by Trooper Nelson, and accompanied by Lieutenant Nelson, turned off of the National Road just short of an hour later, Sergeant O'Neall was there to meet them. The troopers under Sergeant O'Neall's command were in line abreast just behind the sergeant with their sabers drawn and being held upright in their right hands while the blades rested in the hollow of their right shoulders. Brody Calhoun was also mounted and was alongside the sergeant. Sergeant O'Nealls' cavalry salute was returned by the Captain.

"Welcome to Middletown, Sir," said the Sergeant.

"Thank you Sergeant O'Neall," said the Captain. "I hope you've found a suitable place for the Troop to bivouac."

"I think you'll find that this area directly behind us here will do nicely," answered the Sergeant turning in his saddle and indicating the seven acre meadow just off the highway and running alongside the creek.

"Yes, that does look like it will do just fine."

"Sir, if I may," said the Sergeant. "This is Mr. Calhoun, Brody Calhoun, this is his farm."

"How do you do Mr. Calhoun?" Said the Captain touching the brim of his hat and nodding in Mr. Calhoun's direction. "I hope you won't find our presence too much of a distraction."

"It's an honor to be of service," said Calhoun.

"We'll only be staying a night or two," said the Captain. "Calhoun? Don't we have a Trooper Calhoun?" The Captain asked turning to Lieutenant Nelson.

"Yes Sir," answered the Lieutenant. "Trooper Matthew Calhoun."

"This is Trooper Calhoun's family's farm," added Sergeant O'Neall. "Brody...uh, Mr. Calhoun here is Trooper Calhoun's father."

"Ah, very nice," said the Captain. "Lieutenant Nelson," he continued again turning to the Lieutenant. "Bring the rest of the Troop up and let's try to get settled before the darkness overtakes us."

"Yes Sir," said the Lieutenant as he snapped off a salute swung his mount around and started back along the National Road.

"Captain," said Brody Calhoun. "I'd like to offer my house to you and your officers. There's three bedrooms so you could have a room to yourself and your officers could share the other two rooms. My son and I will move in with my hired man during your stay."

"Well, that is very gracious of you," answered the Captain. "We normally require our troopers to remain with their units, but in light of your generosity, not only with your land, but with your home as well, I think we can make an exception in this case. Don't you agree Sergeant?"

"Yes Sir Captain. Absolutely," answered O'Neall.

"Good that's settled then. Now," said the Captain with a smile. "If you'll be good enough to show me the way, I'd really like to get down off this blasted horse."

"Certainly Sir," the Sergeant said as he turned towards the mounted troopers who were still in line abreast behind him. "Calhoun," he barked. "Take charge of the detachment and see that they get settled, then report back to me."

"Yes Sergeant!" Answered Matthew.

"If you'll follow me Sir," said Sergeant O'Neall as he turned his mount and started back up the lane towards the Calhoun house. Brody Calhoun fell in alongside the captain with his aide following behind.

B Troop had just cleared the National Road when Katherine Calhoun finally turned into the lane in a small wagon being pulled by a single horse. She stopped and watched in awe as the army she had been stuck behind for most of the trip from Boonsboro, with practiced routine; set up its camp. She was also covered in this army's road dust, and was feeling none too kindly towards them.

When she got to the house she learned from her father, who was in the parlor with Captain Talbot, that there were going to be two lieutenants, two men, staying the night in her room. This only served to increase her dislike of the mounted intruders who suddenly seemed to be everywhere. She had to keep reminding herself, that if they weren't here, Matthew wouldn't be here either.

"If it's quite alright," she said to the Captain after having been introduced, and perhaps not in as friendly a tone as her father might have wished. "May I be permitted to use my room to cleanse myself of your army's road dust, and put on clean clothes?"

"Certainly Miss Calhoun," answered the Captain with a smile and a bow, "and, if you would rather that we not utilize your room that would be perfectly understandable."

"No," answered Katherine. "My father has already made the offer, and I do not wish to appear unpatriotic. However," she said shaking a finger in the Captain's direction. "You make sure that whoever uses my room doesn't put their dirty boots on my bed or any of my furniture. Also, I do not want to come back to it and find the floors full of mud and manure."

"I will see to it personally," the Captain answered with a smile.

"Very good then," Katherine said. "I will trust you to do so."

"My lady," said the Captain bowing once more. "You may indeed trust me, for I am an officer by an act of Congress, and a gentleman by birth and conduct."

Katherine couldn't help but smile as she curtsied, turned and started up the stairs to her room.

Katherine and Matthew, and their father had a very nice meal prepared by Olivia Stokes in the Stokes house that evening. After preparing the meal David and Olivia returned to the main house to see to Captain Talbot and his officers. It had been a long time since the three of them had been together.

It was well after dark. The three of them were sitting out on the porch of the house sharing stories about what had been happening in their lives in the months they had been apart. They heard the horse and rider coming long before they saw him.

"Captain Talbot?" He asked breathlessly as he reined his horse up in front of the porch. It was obvious that the man and the horse were at the end of a hard ride and that both were nearly played out.

"Farmhouse at the end of the lane," said Matthew pointing up the lane. "Little more than a tenth of a mile"

The trooper just nodded turned his mount, and spurred him into a gallop.

"Courier," said Matthew watching as the rider disappeared into the darkness. "Something must be up."

"You're going to be leaving aren't you?" Said Katherine.

"Yes," said Matthew. "If not tomorrow than definitely the next day."

"When will you be back?" She asked.

"Don't know." He shrugged. "I guess it all depends on what happens over the next couple of months."

"War?" Said Brody Calhoun. "You really think it's going to come to that?"

"Yes I do," said Matthew. "I wish I didn't think so, and I certainly hope it doesn't happen, but I think it's going to."

"You'll be careful? No matter what happens won't you?" Katherine asked.

"I promise," answered Matthew. "Now, isn't there something more cheerful we can talk about?"

The three of them remained on the porch for a couple of more hours. Matthew and his father had just turned in when there was a knock on the bedroom door. When Mathew opened it he found Sergeant O'Neall standing in front of him.

"Wanted to let you know," he said. "Reveille is at five. We're to be in the saddle by seven. Make sure you're with the platoon by six."

"Saw the courier," said Matthew with a nod. "I'll be there, and thanks Sarge."

O'Neall nodded and left.

It was a little before six when Matthew said his goodbyes to Katherine and his father. Matthew promised that he would return for another, perhaps even a longer, visit as soon as he could. It took all Matthew had to keep from shedding a tear as he stepped down off the porch and walked towards the area where 2nd platoon was preparing to break camp and get underway with the rest of B Troop.

A few tents still needed to be struck, and smoke from a number of smoldering fires still rose into the cold gray sky when the Troop formed up and prepared to move out onto the National Road. In double column, the formation of B Troop's four platoons, totaling just over 100 men on horseback, was nearly a quarter of a mile in length. It was just after 7:00am when the column started to move.

Second Platoon was assigned the third position in line. Once the formation started to move it took about ten minutes for 2nd platoon to get out onto the National Road and reach the bridge that crossed the Catoctin Creek. Matthew didn't know it but as he crossed that bridge, a solitary figure stood on the banks of the Catoctin Creek, about a quarter mile downstream, hidden in the early morning mist, and sadly waved goodbye…again.

Chapter 28

The Rancocas
1938

It was just after 9:00am, when Lieutenant Edward Randall brought the yellow Plymouth convertible to a stop at the intersection of High and Mill Streets in Mt. Holly. It was a pleasant autumn day, but not quite warm enough to have the top down. He was accompanied by his girlfriend Nancy, who sat between him and his cousin and shipmate, Lieutenant Baxter "Woody" Underwood on the Plymouth's front bench seat. Both men were in their dress blues.

"Okay, this is great right here," said Woody as he started to exit the car. "I'll just get my bag and the packages out of the back, and you can be on your way. It was very nice meeting you Nancy," he said with a smile. "Thanks for the lift Ed, and I'll see you back in Philly on Monday."

"Don't you want us to wait to make sure your ride shows up?" Asked a smiling Randall.

"No, that's alright I'll be fine. Besides, I don't want to hold you guys up."

"No problem. Besides, I'd like to get a look at your friend's sister."

"She might not be coming. It might be the grandfather who's picking me up," said Woody with maybe a little too much urgency in his voice. He was not too keen on having his cousin meet the very attractive Katy, after he had allowed him to believe that she was just the opposite.

"Didn't you say he was in his nineties?"

"Well maybe, but they could send a hired hand or something."

"That's okay, we'll wait. We aren't in any hurry, are we Nance?"

"No, not now. I'm curious now to see who, or what, shows up," laughed Nancy. "Are you two always like this?"

"Like what?" They asked almost in unison.

Nancy shook her head. "Never mind," she said.

"I believe your chariot's arrived," said Randall with a smile as he reached up and adjusted the Plymouth's rear view mirror.

Woody, who was standing on the sidewalk on the passenger side of the vehicle turned and watched as the well worked 1932 Ford farm truck squeaked to a stop behind the luxurious Plymouth. Katy waved from behind the steering wheel when she saw him and started to slide across the seat to exit the truck on the passenger side.

"Here we go." Woody thought to himself.

"Got a front end like a tug," chuckled Randall still peering at the mirror.

"Get out, and let's introduce ourselves," said Nancy as she elbowed him in the ribs, and started to slide out the passenger side of the car.

"What? Oh, sure," said the Lieutenant, as he opened the driver's side door.

Katy was standing on the sidewalk next to the truck. She had tried very hard to make herself look nice, and just as hard not to overdo it. She was wearing a dark green dress with an oversized collar that, in the fashion of the day, fell just below her knees. It had a white V design running from the neckline to the waist that was inverted below the waist. It was a pleasant day, so she wasn't wearing a coat.

She wore her auburn hair off her forehead, but down so that it framed her face. It had some curl to it, but not a lot. She did not like makeup, but she was wearing just a hint of lipstick. Katy did not want to look like a farmer or a housekeeper today, it was important to her that Woody see her as a woman.

Katy smiled at Woody when he turned towards her as she stood on the sidewalk. Then she began to have doubts. Something was wrong. Woody didn't look like he was happy to see her at all, in fact, he looked like he didn't even want to be here.

A very attractive blonde girl, about Katy's age, slid out of the car and stood on the sidewalk next to Woody. As Woody walked towards Katy he smiled, a sheepish kind of smile, and he shrugged. It was the same kind of smile and shrug Mikey, the little boy who hung around the farm, would give her whenever he knew he was in trouble and was seeking forgiveness. Did he need forgiving? What did the blonde have to do with it? Katy was confused.

"Hello!" A booming voice interrupted her thoughts. She turned towards the voice and saw a man, a man almost as tall as Woody, and almost as handsome, walking towards her from the driver's side of the Plymouth. Katy could tell from his uniform, that like Woody, he was a naval lieutenant. He had a friendly smile, and as he approached Katy he stuck out his hand, and in the same booming voice said, "I'm Ed, Ed Randall."

"Hello, I'm Katy." Katy hoped she had said it out loud, but she wasn't sure. She also hoped she was returning his smile, as she made the conscious effort to extend her hand.

She realized that a less than steady Woody was now standing at her side. "Katy," he said awkwardly. "This is my cousin, Ed Randall, Lieutenant Ed Randall. He's also assigned to the *Rhind*. He owns the car."

"That's nice." She heard herself say as she quickly looked from one lieutenant to the other.

"Hello." A woman's voice, the blonde. "I'm Nancy."

"Hello Nancy," answered Katy. "I'm Katy, it's so nice to meet you," she said as she turned her attention to the blonde who was now standing next to Woody's cousin. "I didn't know you were cousins," she said looking at Woody.

"Yes, we are," said Woody. "Now, you two better get going," he said to his cousin. "They're going to Atlantic City," he continued, turning back towards Katy.

"In a minute, in a minute," said Ed Randall smiling at Woody. He turned his attention to Katy. "Katy," he said. "It is so good to finally meet you. Woody talks of nothing but you."

"How flattering," said Katy blushing and looking at Woody who appeared to be terribly uncomfortable.

"It's curious though," continued Lieutenant Randall. "His description of you does not do you justice."

"Really? How nice of you to say so." Katy too was beginning to feel a little uncomfortable.

"In fact his description was woefully short of your true appearance. He described you as, let me see how can I put this delicately, without embarrassing anyone?" He looked over at Woody and was happy to see that his cousin looked like he was about to have some sort of seizure. He drug the moment out for as long as he could before he spoke. "Pretty I think he said. Yes, that's it. He said you were pretty. Why, when any fool can see that you are in fact so much more than just pretty."

"How sweet, thank you Lieutenant Randall," Katy said glancing quickly over at Woody and then back at the cousin.

"Ed please," he said. "Call me Ed." As he looked over at Woody who looked like he was about to hyperventilate.

"Alright," said an embarrassed and brightly blushing Katy as she looked down at her hands.

"Let me ask you something Katy," said Lieutenant Randall with a side glance at his cousin. "Who do you think are more honest? People from Colorado, or people from St. Louis?"

"Well, I don't know," said a confused Katy looking back and forth between Woody and his cousin. "The only person I know from Colorado is Woody, and I don't know anyone from St. Louis."

"Now you do," said the Lieutenant as he took Katy by both her hands, stepped towards her, and lightly kissed her on the lips.

"Oh my!" Said a surprised Katy.

Nancy slapped Lieutenant Randall on the back of the head as he released Katy's hands, and Woody still looked like his feet were glued to the sidewalk.

"My apologies," said the cousin smiling at Katy. "Now, we have to be going, but when your boyfriend starts breathing again, you can tell him for me, that I consider us even. It has been a pleasure meeting you," he said with a bow. He turned towards Woody, who looked like he was about to be ill, and said with a smile, "The cowboy wins again."

"What the devil are you talking about?" Asked Nancy who was now almost as confused as Katy was.

"Nothing my love, nothing," answered Lieutenant Randall as he took Nancy by the hand and led her back to the car. Woody and Katy never moved but just stood and watched as they got into the car and pulled away from the curb. Lieutenant Ed Randall honked the horn and waved as the car headed east on Mill Street.

"Your cousin's quite the character," said Katy still looking down Mill Street. "He seems nice though," she continued as she turned towards Woody. Woody's face was beet red and he was bent over with his hands on his knees. "Are you alright?" She asked.

Woody turned his head and looked up at Katy. Suddenly he broke out in laughter. An almost uncontrolled laughter. He straightened up, stepped over to Katy, took her in his arms, lifted her off the ground, and spun her around several times, laughing the entire time.

When he finally set her down and released her, Katy smoothed and straightened her dress. She was once again beginning to have doubts about Woody's sanity.

"Alright?" He said with a great smile on his face. "My dear Katy I have never been better in my life!" He said. "Is there somewhere in this town we can get a cup of coffee?" He asked as he picked up the packages and the duffel bag he had removed from the back of his cousin's car and put them in the rear of the truck.

"There's a restaurant in the Washington House up on High Street," she said.

"The Washington House it is," he said as he opened the passenger door of the truck, took her hand, and helped her in. "It's alright if I drive isn't it?" He asked. Then before she could answer he walked around to the driver's side, jumped behind the wheel, started the engine, coaxed the transmission into gear, and pulled away from the curb, then immediately applied the squeaking brakes bringing the tired old truck to a stop. He looked over at Katy. "Where is the Washington House?" He asked sheepishly.

Now it was her turn to laugh. "We'll have to go around the block," she said. "Go up here and make a left, and I do hope you're going to explain to me what is going on!"

"I am," he said. "I am."

Over coffee and fresh pastries Woody told Katy the whole story from beginning to end. From how he had wronged his cousin in Baltimore by stealing his girl, up to and including the terrible misconception Evan, her brother, had created about Katy's looks, and how Woody had let his cousin continue to believe that Katy was less than attractive so that the cousin would not try to get even with Woody by stealing her away.

As the story unfolded Katy couldn't believe that Woody would think that she would find it funny, or be okay with having been the butt of what she considered such a cruel joke. Not only was she hurt, but she was angry as well.

"So your cousin was lying?" She said not even trying to hide the anger in her voice.

"What do you mean?" Asked a surprised Woody.

"You never told him I was pretty, did you?"

"No, I'm sorry, I didn't," said Woody. "I couldn't."

"You don't think I'm pretty?" He could hear the anger, and the hurt.

"Pretty? My God Katy, I think you're beautiful, you're lovelier than any woman I've ever met!"

"Then why did you let everyone think I was ugly? Who knows how many people you and your cousin have told, or they have since told, about Evan's ugly sister? How could you think I would think this was okay?"

"What? I've told no one, and I don't know if Ed's told anyone or not, but the important thing is that you're not ugly." Woody immediately knew from the look on Katy's face that that had not come out right. "I mean, that I don't think you're ugly, and now Ed knows just how attractive you are too."

"But, why? Why did you do it?"

"Because I was afraid of losing you. I was afraid that if Ed knew just how lovely you were that he would want to meet you and that you would like him, everybody likes Ed, and that to get even, for what happened in Baltimore, he would steal you away from me, whether he really liked you or not."

"How can you lose something you don't have?" She asked almost coldly. Now it was Woody's turn to be hurt, and Katy could see from the look on his face that she had hurt him, but what concerned her more was the unpleasant realization that she had wanted to hurt him.

"You're right," Woody whispered as his head dropped and he looked down at the table. "I was way out of line and far too presumptuous. I had no right. I guess I was just sort of hoping..." He lifted his head and looked at Katy. "I'm sorry," he said.

Katy just looked across the table at him. She knew she liked him, but she couldn't stop being afraid of liking him too much to figure out just how much she really did like him. She also knew that her hurt and anger no longer mattered. That now she was sorry that she had hurt him.

"Listen," he said with a hint of a smile. "Is there any chance we can just start over?"

"We already did that once," she said testily. "Remember, on the back porch? How many times do you think we should start over?"

Woody reached across the table and took her hand, and she let him. "As many times as it takes," he said. "I think that we can have something special, and I think that you think so too."

"Maybe," she said, "but if something does happen, if we do.... is it always going to be this hard?"

"I hope so," he said.

"What do you mean?" She asked surprised by his answer.

"It should be hard, or at least a little bit hard," he said shaking his head. "Because if it gets too easy we might begin to take it for granted, and I would never want to take you, or us, or my feelings for you for granted."

"Is there an us?"

"I want there to be."

"You can't possibly have any feelings for me, we hardly know each other," she said quietly. "Do you?" She asked. "Have feelings for me?" Not really sure that she wanted to know the answer.

"I'm not sure," he said with a slight smile, squeezing her hand. "I know that nothing makes me happier than hearing your voice or being with you, and that I can't seem to stop thinking about you."

"You feel this way after spending only what, five hours with me, and speaking to me on the phone a couple of times?"

"Yes," he said. "You know, I could ask you the same question." Katy just looked at him, knowing what was coming. "How do you feel about me?"

She sighed, and looked away. She had to be careful, this was where the road to heartbreak could begin, and that was what she was most afraid of. "I don't know," she said, making eye contact with him once again, "and I don't know that I'm ready to try to put it into words."

"But you did invite me here," he said with a smile.

"It was your idea to get something to eat."

"I mean here," he chuckled tapping the top of the table with his finger, then he paused and looked up at her. "Where are we?"

"Dogpatch," she answered. She tried to keep a straight face but couldn't. She laughed and he joined her. Still holding her hand. "Poppa's fond of you," she continued. "I only invited you here for him."

"Really? Then maybe it's his hand I should be holding, but I don't think I'd enjoy seeing him blush as much."

Katy pulled her hand away, smiled, and said, "You're an idiot."

"Shall we go?" He asked returning her smile.

"Yes," she said, "but I'm still mad at you about the "ugly" thing, so you better be on your best behavior."

"I have two days to make it up to you."

"Yeah, well, we'll see. By the way, I'm driving," she said as she stood and boldly walked out the door. Woody was still shaking his head and chuckling as he paid the check and followed her out to the truck.

The drive from Mt. Holly to the McBride farm on the banks of the Rancocas only took about fifteen minutes. Katy was right about the old farm truck not being a smooth ride, but the road was paved, so it was not severely uncomfortable. The trees alongside the road that bordered the many farms they passed were just beginning to burst out in their fall colors. After spending the week smelling fresh paint, acetylene, and fuel oil, Woody gulped in the fresh fragrant air of autumn in the country.

As they rode, Katy pointed out the farms and houses of friends and neighbors, and seemed to have a little story about every one of them. It was obvious to Woody that Katy loved her life along the Rancocas and that it was where she belonged. He envied Katy's seemingly uncomplicated world and wondered if he could ever become a part of it, because he knew he could never ask her to give this up to become a part of his world.

They weren't far from the village when Katy Turned to Woody, and said, "Want to take the scenic route?"

"More scenic than this?" He answered.

"Hold on!" She laughed, as without barely slowing down she turned the truck about 45 degrees to the left onto a very narrow rutted dirt road. The road was bordered on both sides by wire fencing with a clearance on each side of the truck of maybe a foot. "It's the old mill road!" Katy hollered as the truck bounced and bucked in the ruts of the seldom used lane.

Despite Woody's best efforts to remain on the seat, he was bouncing all over the inside of the truck. Twice he hit his head on the roof, almost went out the window on another occasion, and came close to kissing the windshield when the truck bottomed out in a dried up mud puddle. Not only was he beginning to have some real concerns about his safety, but he was sure the old truck would be nothing but a chassis and a steering wheel by the time they got back to the farm. Finally Katy slowed the truck down, and although far from smooth, the ride did improve to almost tolerable.

"Was getting worried," said Katy.

"About me I hope!" Said Woody.

"No," laughed Katy. "The truck, I can't afford to have to buy a new one right now."

"Thanks!" Laughed Woody as he continued to try and stay on the seat of the truck.

"It's only about another half a mile," said Katy. "I'll try not to do any permanent damage to you or the truck."

"Appreciate it," said Woody.

The truck, Woody, and Katy survived. When they finally arrived in the yard behind the house Woody found it difficult to let go of his grip on the dashboard. He was certain that the old truck was going to continue to bounce for several minutes, even after coming to a stop.

"Are you okay?" Asked Katy as she looked over at Woody whose face was completely void of color.

"I don't think I have a single organ that is still where it is supposed to be," he said.

"I thought you were a cowboy?" She said teasingly. "Haven't you ever broke a wild mustang, or rode a bucking bull?" She asked in an exaggerated childlike awe.

"A mustang and a bull have a heart and soul. This demonic truck has neither," he said as he started to relax his grip on the dashboard.

"Hmmm... maybe I brought the wrong cousin home," Katy said coyly as she exited the truck.

"Now that was just mean," replied Woody as he opened the passenger side door. He slid out of the cab and steadied himself by hanging on to the wooden sideboards that enclosed the truck bed. "Hmmm," he said as he looked over the sideboard into the truck bed.

The boxes that held the gifts Evan had sent for his sister and grandfather were scattered all over the truck bed. Some of the boxes were dented, and the brown wrapping paper on many of them was torn. Woody also noticed that his satchel had come open and some of its contents had spilled.

He looked up and saw Katy looking into the bed from the other side. "Oh my," she said. "I hope nothing's broken. Are those your clothes?"

"Yes, it's a little embarrassing."

"I'm sorry," Katy said. "I didn't even think about what was back here. I really am sorry."

"I'll just climb up in there and gather up the boxes and …. Stuff," laughed Woody sheepishly.

"Are those blue jeans?" Asked Katy.

"They are," said Woody as he climbed into the bed from the rear of the truck and started to gather up the clothing that had spilled from the satchel.

"I'm impressed," she said. "I never thought of you as a blue jeans kind of guy."

"Born and raised on a ranch in Colorado," he answered with a smile. "Rarely wore anything else."

"Do you do your own laundry?" She asked. "Because those white umm, things, are really white." Woody looked up and saw that Katy was trying very hard not to laugh.

"No," he answered trying just as hard not to laugh as he gathered up some of the more embarrassing items. "The ship has a laundry."

"Don't be embarrassed," said Katy. "Everyone wears them."

"Do they?" He said as he stood with his hands on his hips, and grinned down at Katy. "Do you wear white US government issued boxers with your name stenciled across the butt?"

"Well…no, I guess not, but…"

"Then what do you wear? You know... under all of that?" Woody asked waving his hands to indicate Katy's clothing.

Now it was Katy's turn to be embarrassed. "I...I...I...," she stammered. "I don't think I feel comfortable discussing such things with a man, or perhaps anyone, thank you very much."

"Then there's very little chance that I'll get to see them?"

"Certainly not!" Shrieked Katy. "You should be ashamed. Why would you even think such a thing?"

"I was just wondering if I'd enjoy seeing your skivvies as much as you've enjoyed seeing mine," Woody said with a grin as he finished stuffing the loose clothing back in the satchel. "Of course, if and when the time finally does come, I'm quite sure that I will enjoy it very much."

Katy's face was now beyond crimson, her mouth was opening and closing and her lips were moving but no intelligible sounds were coming out. She wasn't even sure that she wanted the words she was forming in her mind to come out of her mouth. Finally, embarrassed and exasperated, she just growled, shook her head, turned and walked away. She smiled just a little though as she walked away because some of the embarrassment she was feeling was due to the fact that she found what Woody had suggested flattering, and maybe even a little exciting.

"Hypocrite!" Woody hollered after her laughingly as he gathered the packages and began checking them for damage.

About an hour later, after Woody had backed the old truck into the wagon shed, stowed his gear in Evan's old room, which is where he would be sleeping, and been greeted by and relayed the story of the exciting drive home to Katy's grandfather, Michael McBride, the three of them, Woody, Katy, and her grandfather, sat around the kitchen table staring at the pile of mangled packages that Woody had brought all the way from Evan and the *USS Lexington* in the South Pacific.

"You know," he said wistfully. "They were high-lined over open ocean water from the *Lexington* to the *Phelps*, rode in the cargo bay of an Army transport from Hickam to San Diego, then travelled over the Rockies to Denver on TWA, from Denver to Philly by train, changing trains in both St. Louis, and Chicago, and two trips from the Philadelphia Navy Yard to the banks of the Rancocas in the back of a Plymouth, and survived intact. But, they couldn't survive a one mile ride in the back of a farm truck driven by Katy McBride." Woody sat upright in his chair, brought his right hand up in a salute, and began humming Taps. Michael McBride followed suit.

Katy dropped her head into her hands with her elbows on the table and said, "This is going to be impossible." When she looked up they all burst into laughter.

There were seven packages. Three each for Katy and her grandfather, and one that was for both.

"Well, I'm not bashful!" Said Katy as she picked up one of the packages. The package was partially crushed, and the brown wrapping paper was torn on one of the corners. "It doesn't sound like it's anything that's broken," she said after shaking it as she began to peel away the paper.

When all the packages had been opened Katy had received a bright red Hawaiian silk robe with a large tropical flower print, a polished coconut shell bracelet with hibiscus flowers of carved coral, and a china plate in the center of which was painted an image of the Lolani Palace surrounded by other scenes from around the

Hawaiian islands. Her grandfather had received a lauhala weaved straw hat with a bright blue band, a coffee mug with the *USS Lexington's* minuteman logo on it, and a book of photos depicting scenes, ships, and planes from Pearl Harbor, Hickam Field, and Schofield Barracks. The package that was for both of them contained a framed 8x10 color photograph of Evan on the bridge of the *USS Lexington*.

Two of the items had been damaged. The china plate had a ½ inch chip along the rim, and the glass over Evan's photograph was broken. Katy said that she thought she could fix the chip, and her grandfather said that he would get a new glass for the frame. Woody promised that if Evan ever asked he would be told that everything had arrived intact.

Katy spent the rest of the afternoon showing Woody around the farm. They explored the barn where he was introduced to each of the 12 mules, and shown the secret places where Evan and Katy had hidden themselves, behind half walls and loose boards, carved their initials, and hidden treasure. They walked to the landing and sat on the dock, watched the Rancocas flow by, and for the first time got to talk and learn about each other.

Woody got to meet Mr. Davenport and they discussed the difference between running a farm where the emphasis was on raising corn, and running a ranch where the emphasis was on raising cattle. It somehow pleased Katy that Davenport seemed to approve of her young naval officer. He also got to meet Davenport's nephew, Mikey.

"Are you Lootin' Underman?" Asked Mikey when they were introduced.

"Underwood," said Woody. "Lieutenant Underwood, but my friends call me Woody." He stuck out his hand. "I'd like it if we could be friends," he said.

Mikey just stared at his hand. "I's already Miss Kate's friend," he said.

Woody left his hand out there. "Well, you know what they say," he said with a grin, "any friend of Kate's…"

Mikey tilted his head back and looked up at the tall stranger. "Who said dat?" He asked.

An exasperated Woody dropped his hand back down to his side. He looked up at Davenport and Katy who were standing there with one hand over their mouths to keep from laughing. Both of them were familiar with the difficulties of trying to reason with young Mikey. "Umm, I don't know," said Woody. "It's just, you know, a saying."

Mikey looked at Katy and then back at the lieutenant. "Whatta you gonna do with Miss Kate?" He asked.

"Do with her?' He asked. Woody couldn't believe he was losing a battle of wits to this little fellow. "Nothing," he finally said. "I'm not going to do anything with her."

"Den, why's you here?"

"I'm going to take her away on my boat," said Woody changing strategies as he crossed his arms in front of his chest. He winked in Katy and Davenport's direction and stared down at Mikey.

"You got a boat?"

"I do."

"At da landin'?"

"Nope, it's too big won't fit at the landing or in the Rancocas."

"You gotta boat bigger den da 'Cocas?"

"Yep."

"What kinda boat is bigger den da 'Cocas?'"

"A US Navy Destroyer," answered Woody still staring down at his challenger. "It's got four 5" guns, four .50 caliber machine guns, four torpedo tubes, and two depth charge racks, and I'm in charge of all of it."

Woody could see he was on the verge of victory. The very impressed Mikey was wearing a huge smile. "Like in da pitcher shows?" He asked.

Woody gave an exaggerated nod. "Just like in the pictures," he answered. He brought one hand up and began rubbing his chin. "In fact," he continued. "A lot of times, when I make a new friend, I send them a picture of my boat."

Mikey glanced up at Katy who was still covering her mouth with her hand. She nodded at Mikey, smiled, and whispered, "Go ahead."

Mikey looked up at Woody, smiled, and stuck out his hand. "A real naby destryer Mr. Woody?" He asked.

Woody took his hand, shook it, smiled, and nodded. "A real naby destryer Mr. Mikey," he answered.

When they eventually walked away Katy thanked him for being so sweet to Mikey.

"He's a tough little character," laughed Woody, "and, he's got a huge crush on you."

Katy blushed, and smacked Woody on the arm. "You will send him, the picture though won't you?"

"I'll put it in the mail on Monday," he answered. "I'll address it directly to him in care of Katherine McBride."

"Oh, he'll like that," she said.

A dinner of baked ham, boiled potatoes, and asparagus, was followed by healthy portions of a chocolate cake with a vanilla frosting. After dinner Katy, leaving the dishes for later, served coffee in the parlor and Woody entertained them with stories of what it was like growing up on a cattle ranch in Colorado. Katy's grandfather retired early, but Katy and Woody retired to the kitchen where Woody helped with the dishes and then they sat talking at the table long into the night.

Woody had agreed to wear his dress blues when he accompanied the McBride's to church on Sunday morning. He made sure that he looked especially sharp, that all the creases were razor sharp and that everything that could shine glistened, including his shoes, and the bill of his cap. Katy had said that the Sunday schedule would be church, then home for a big Sunday breakfast, and then they would have an early dinner, because Woody had to be in Beverly to catch the 6:00pm train to Philadelphia.

When the resplendent Woody came downstairs and into the kitchen he found Katy and her grandfather seated at the table. They both looked up, smiled and said, *"Maidin mhaith."* Which was, "Good morning", in the Irish. It was Sunday in the McBride house, and as Brian and Bridget had decreed nearly 150 years ago while on the banks of the Delaware River, the Irish was to be spoken.

"What?" Asked Woody.

"I guess we should have told you," laughed Katy. "That was good morning in the language of the Irish. It has been a McBride tradition for over a hundred years to speak Irish on Sundays."

"Really? That was Gaelic?"

"Yes. *Ta a fhios agat ar an garlacha*?"

Woody just looked at her and shrugged.

"I asked if you knew of the Gaelic?"

"I know that Gaelic is the language of the ancient Irish, but I'm afraid I don't speak a word of it. My ancestors were English."

"Béarla? Is rud maith mé tar éis fás cheana Fond de tú nó eile gur mhaith liom a toss tú amach ar do chlua."

"English? It's a good thing I've already grown fond of you or else I'd toss you out on your ear," said the elderly Michael McBride with a smile.

"Now what was that?" Asked Woody as he turned to face Michael.

"Poppa," scolded Katy. "Behave yourself." Then she turned to Woody and fibbed. "He thinks it's interesting that you're English."

"Is that what you said?" Asked Woody.

"Gar go leor," answered Michael. "That means close enough." He laughed.

They went to church in a horse drawn carriage with Michael on the reins. Woody was surprised that there were only a few cars parked at the church. Most of the congregation had also arrived by carriage or walked.

Woody enjoyed the service and meeting the warm and friendly people Katy introduced him to. He knew, and he was quite sure Katy did as well, that the two of them would be a popular topic of conversation around kitchen tables and in the parlors of Rancocas this day. He also thought that it looked like Katy was enjoying knowing that she was cultivating gossip.

Woody was also glad that he had made the effort to look especially sharp in his uniform. It was obvious that the men were duly impressed, and that the ladies, though not quite swooning, noticed as well. The best part though was that Katy and her grandfather appeared to be proud to be with him, and that Katy liked that some of the other young ladies were jealous of her and her handsome young naval officer.

The leisurely ride home took only about twenty minutes, and during the trip Katy and her grandfather tried to teach Woody some basic Gaelic phrases. He struggled with the pronunciation and there was probably a lot more laughter than there was educating. None the less, by the time they arrived home Brian knew that a horse was "*copal*", and a carriage was "*iompar*".

The Sunday breakfast that Katy prepared was not only delicious, but the amount of food was overwhelming. Afterwards Michael McBride retired to the parlor where he announced that he was going to pretend to listen to the radio while he napped. Katy wanted to go looking for some bittersweet vines to make a wreath and convinced Woody to walk the old mill lane to the Centerton Bridge with her in search of the bright orange berries.

They walked and talked and thoroughly enjoyed being together. They found a cluster of bittersweet vines near where the old mill used to be. Using his pocket knife Woody cut enough of the vines for Katy to make her wreath. Then they started for home. Katy had to hurry and get dinner cooked and served if Woody was going to make the six o'clock train from Beverly to Philadelphia.

They were not far from the house when Woody stopped, took Katy by the hand, turned her so that she was facing him, put his arms around her, and kissed her.

Katy did nothing, she stood flat-footed, her arms remained at her side, and although her lips responded, there was no emotion.

"I'm sorry," said an embarrassed Woody as he released her and stepped back. "I guess I shouldn't have done that."

"No, no," responded Katy as she brought her hand up and rubbed her forehead. "You surprised me that's all, I wasn't ready, I, I, oh… I don't know."

"It's just that, well, I've wanted to do that for such a long time, and I thought, you know, that you, that we, I don't know, I thought…" Woody sighed and looked away.

There was silence, for what seemed like an eternity but was no more than a few seconds. Then, Katy reached out and took his hand. "Just shut up and kiss me will ya," she said as she looked up at him with a smile and dropped the bittersweet on the ground so she could put her arms around his neck.

It could not be described as a passionate kiss. It was a kiss between two people who were trying to come to grips with how they felt about each other. It was a comfortable kiss. A kiss so comfortable that they both knew instantly, that it was only the first of many kisses to come.

They held hands as they walked the rest of the way to the house, and stopped to kiss again before climbing the steps to the back porch. When they went in Katy happily set about preparing dinner, while a beaming Woody joined her grandfather in the parlor. They both knew that things were different now, but were either of them really ready for what that meant?

Shortly after dinner Woody said his goodbyes to Michael and he and Katy climbed into the same old truck that had brought him to the farm from Mt. Holly, to head for Beverly and the train that would take him back to his ship. He had made Katy promise that she would stay on paved roads and not try to rearrange his insides again. She laughingly agreed as she coaxed the reliable old truck into gear and headed up Hilyard's Lane towards the Beverly Mt. Holly Road.

The train depot was a little over six miles from the McBride farm, and they made the trip in just a little over fifteen minutes. They arrived at the depot at the corner of Cooper Street and Railroad Avenue about twenty minutes before the train was due. They had tried to keep the conversation light during the drive, both of them avoiding the things that perhaps they knew now needed to be said.

It was just getting dark, and despite the chill in the air, the small cab of the truck was uncomfortably hot. Woody turned to Katy, and took her hand. She could see that he was nervous and was trying to say something, which only made her more nervous and begin to wish that he wouldn't.

Finally, he took a deep breath, exhaled and very slowly and deliberately said, "*I mo thuairimse, is breá liom tú.*"

"Wha… what?"

"Maybe I didn't say it right," Woody said sheepishly. "I'll try it again." He took another deep breath exhaled and said it again. "*I mo thuairimse, is breá liom tú.*"

"No, no, you said it right… I think, I mean, if that's what you meant to say. Do you know what you said?" Katy asked as she turned in the seat to face him. She could feel her heart begin to pound in her chest.

"Yes, I said, *I mo…*"

"No," she said looking down where their hands were joined. "In English this time."

"But it's Sunday," he said smiling, as with his other hand he lifted her chin so that their eyes met.

"Please," she whispered.

"I think I love you," he said as he caressed her cheek with the back of his hand. "I said, I think I love you."

Katy was aware that three things were beginning to happen. Her eyes were beginning to fill with tears, and any second now they would spill over onto her cheeks, the same cheeks that were now on fire where he had touched them, her heart was beating so loudly that it could probably be heard outside the truck, and the hand he was holding was sweating so profusely that he was probably going to need a towel. Woody had only said it twice, but she kept hearing it over and over again in her mind.

"Did I say it right?" He asked. "I can repeat it in the Irish again if you'd like."

"No, no," she said as she began to cry and laugh at the same time. "It sounded just as beautiful in both languages."

He looked at her inquisitively.

"Well of course!" She said through a sob. "I must love you... I do love you. I keep dragging you out here to the boonies don't I?" Katy wiped her eyes with her free hand. They just stared at each other. Finally Katy said, "Do you remember what I told you earlier?"

Woody shook his head. "No, what?"

"Just shut up and kiss me will ya," she squeaked as she threw her arms around his neck. After their kiss was ended Katy asked, "How did you know how to say it?"

"Your grandfather taught me while you were preparing dinner."

"You told Poppa you were in love with me?"

"I didn't have to tell him," Woody said with a laugh. "He already knew. He said that it seemed to him that everybody knew. Everybody except us that is. He's a pretty clever fellow."

"Yes, he is at that," said Katy. "Remember..."

"Just shut up and kiss me will ya," Woody interrupted with a smile.

Their euphoria was short lived. The bright light that was approaching from the north meant that their parting was at hand. They got out of the truck and slowly walked to the platform, hand in hand.

She kissed him goodbye on the platform and held his hand as long as she could until the train began to move. He promised her that he would call and come back to see her as soon as he could. Then she stood and watched until she could no longer see the red marker lights on the rear of the train.

"I'm in love with a silly Colorado cowboy turned sailor named Baxter Underwood," she whispered as the lights of the train disappeared into the darkness. As she started back to the truck she decided that she should write her brother Evan a letter thanking him for sending Woody to her.

The *USS Rhind* was commissioned in November and left on an extended shake-down cruise to Brazil. There had only been one more opportunity for Woody to visit Katy, but before the *Rhind* set sail, he made sure that he called her every chance he got. While Woody was away Katy wrote to him every day, and Woody wrote as

241

often as he could, but sometimes weeks would go by before their letters would be delivered.

Woody wrote that in February the *Rhind* would be returning to Philadelphia for repairs and adjustments to the equipment and machinery that had been tested on the cruise. The estimate was that they would be in Philadelphia for about 90 days. After that Woody had no idea where they would be sent.

Unbeknownst to Katy, Woody had written to Michael McBride, Katy's grandfather, and asked permission to propose to Katy when he was next able to visit the farm. Michael of course was thrilled and wrote back giving his full support and blessing. At the same time, Katy, unbeknownst to Woody or her grandfather, had begun to think how beautiful a May wedding might be.

Chapter 29

The Patapsco
1861

As they moved east along the National Road, the word that filtered down through the Troop was that B Troop was to avoid Frederick by passing south of the city, while C Troop, which was coming down through Gettysburg, was to avoid the city by passing north of it. In the original plans, B and C Troops were supposed to have joined forces in Frederick. Colonel Thomas, who commanded A, B, and C Troops of the 2nd US Cavalry, felt it would be best to avoid any entanglements in Frederick that might delay their arrival in Baltimore, so rerouted B and C Troops around the city.

Per the new orders, received by courier from the Colonel the previous evening, B Troop was to proceed to New Market, Maryland, on the 17th of February, bivouac somewhere in that area, and then move on to Eldersburg to join with A Troop on the 18th. Likewise, C Troop was to bivouac somewhere along their northern route on the 17th, and also move onto Eldersburg on the 18th to join with A and B Troops. The three Troops would then move in mass into Baltimore on the 20th.

B Troop bivouacked on the Tate farm about a mile east of New Market. Matthew had just finished his evening meal and was going to go check on his horse, Rooster, when he received word that Lieutenant Nelson, the platoon commander wished to see him. Matthew hurried to the Lieutenant's tent, which was alongside the farm house up near the road.

"Over here trooper." Heard Matthew as he approached the front of the tent. He looked to his left and saw the Lieutenant and Sergeant O'Neall standing beneath a large tree right next to where the farm's lane intersected with the National Road.

Sergeant O'Neall was standing at attention in front of the Lieutenant who was facing the Sergeant, and had his hands behind his back. Neither man looked happy. Matthew hurriedly fell in alongside the Sergeant, came to attention, and saluted the Lieutenant.

"Stand easy Calhoun," said the Lieutenant as he returned the salute. "You too Sergeant," he continued as he tilted his head back and looked up at the darkening starless winter sky.

As the Sergeant and Matthew assumed the at ease position, Matthew stole a glance at the Sergeant, his jaw was set, and his unblinking eyes were staring straight ahead. The Lieutenant turned to his right and walked a few steps towards the National Road away from Matthew and the Sergeant. Then he turned around, walked back, stopped in front of the sergeant, and turned to face him. Although it had been no longer than a minute or two since Matthew had arrived, he felt like he had been standing there for hours.

"A few nights ago," began the Lieutenant. "I was enjoying a glass of reasonably good whiskey on the porch of the Franklin Hotel in Chambersburg, when Lieutenant Walters, of fourth platoon, approached me accompanied by a civilian. Lieutenant Walters said that this civilian had asked to speak with whoever it was that was in charge of the advance detail that had passed through Chambersburg the previous day.

"I amicably greeted this civilian who introduced himself to me as a Mr. Norman, Edward Norman. Mr. Norman, as it turns out, was in fact the proprietor of the very hotel which was attached to the porch I was standing on while enjoying this glass of reasonably good whiskey. I offered to buy Mr. Norman a drink. He refused. I offered him a seat. He refused."

It was not a warm evening, but Matthew was beginning to sweat... a lot.

"Mr. Norman," continued the Lieutenant. "Then related to me a story in which he accused a sergeant, under my command, of extorting rooms for himself and the troopers in his charge from the clerk on duty at the hotel the night prior to our arrival. He claimed that at no time did this sergeant make any offer or attempt to pay for these rooms.

"He then claimed that the following day when he invited this sergeant into his office in an effort to resolve the matter satisfactorily, that this sergeant became offensive and rude, and finally, losing control of his temper, assaulted and injured Mr. Norman, and caused damage to Mr. Norman's personal property!" The longer he talked the louder and angrier the Lieutenant became. He also appeared, to the frightened Matthew, to be getting larger.

"Now," the Lieutenant said, taking a deep breath, and lowering his voice. "There was only one sergeant assigned to lead that advance detail, and that sergeant was indeed under my command, and Sergeant O'Neall, that sergeant was you."

"Yes Sir!" Barked Sergeant O'Neall in a clear and controlled voice.

"I'd like to hear your side of the story now," said the Lieutenant, "and Sergeant," he continued. "If you value your rank and your career, it better be the truth, the whole truth."

"Yes Sir," said the Sergeant, "but, before I do Sir," he continued. "You need to know that Trooper Calhoun here had nothing to do with anything that happened in Chambersburg. I don't know why you've sent for him Sir, but he's not involved."

"Trooper Calhoun," said the Lieutenant turning his attention towards Matthew. "Were you present in the lobby of the hotel when Sergeant O'Neall procured rooms for himself and the detail?"

"Yes Sir," said Matthew trying to keep the quaking out of his voice as he again stole a glance at Sergeant O'Neall who continued to stare straight ahead.

"That's why he's here, and that's why he is staying," said the Lieutenant to Sergeant O'Neall. "Whenever you're ready Sergeant."

The Sergeant then proceeded, in more detail than even Matthew recalled, to describe for the Lieutenant exactly how he had procured rooms for himself and the detail at the Franklin Hotel. He described how he had played on the clerk's ego, and may have done a little fast talking, but did nothing he considered to be extortion. The only thing he said that was not true was when he said that it had been his idea to pretend that one of the troopers was seriously ill.

When the Sergeant had finished the Lieutenant turned to Matthew. "Is that how it happened?" He asked.

"Yes Sir," said Matthew confidently. "Except, it was my idea to claim that Trooper Nelson was ill, not the Sergeant's. He must've forgot."

"I see," said the Lieutenant, "and what happened the next morning in the office?" Asked the Lieutenant turning back to the Sergeant.

Again, the Sergeant described in detail his meeting with Mr. Norman, including his pushing him over in his chair with his boot, and his threats to pummel him.

"According to Mr. Norman," began the Lieutenant. "He received an injury to the back of his head when it slammed into the floor when this sergeant kicked him to the ground, then this sergeant placed a boot on his chest, took out his sidearm, pointed it at Mr. Norman's head, and made a number of very serious threats.

"Mr. Norman permitted me to examine the back of his head, and also invited me into his office to see his damaged property. I saw no evidence of any real injury or any real damage. Yet, you have admitted that you pushed him over while he was seated in a chair. Why do you think that is Sergeant?"

"I don't know Sir."

"Well, I think that the reason there was no evidence of an injury or damage is because Mr. Norman is greatly exaggerating the seriousness of this encounter."

"You do?" Said the Sergeant who seemed to relax a little as he stole a glance at Matthew and then looked back to the Lieutenant.

"I do," said the Lieutenant. "I certainly don't believe you would have pulled your sidearm on him. I did not like Mr. Norman. He ruined my enjoyment of that glass of reasonably good whiskey, made serious accusations against a decorated non-commissioned officer under my command, and by the time we parted company I wanted nothing more than to give him a good thrashing myself.

"Do either of you have anything further to say?"

"No Sir," said Matthew and the Sergeant almost in unison.

"Your admissions do you credit Sergeant, and in a different time I may have felt more obligated to take other action, but since I saw no evidence of injury or damage, and since I do believe that you were provoked, I see no need to take any formal action. However, as your commanding officer, allow me to thank you in advance for contributing at least half of your next pay to the widows and orphans fund. Thank you." The Lieutenant paused and stared at the Sergeant.

Sergeant O'Neall coughed. "Certainly Sir, my pleasure Sir, glad to do it Sir, thank you Sir."

"And finally Sergeant," said the Lieutenant. "I had lunch at the Widow Piper's Tavern in Shippensburg. Had a nice conversation with the barman." Pause, silence. "Sergeant?"

"Sir?"

"Did you have lunch at the Widow Piper's?"

"Yes Sir?"

"And?"

Sergeant O'Neall glanced at Matthew and then turned back to the Lieutenant. "After I've made my contribution to the widow and orphans fund Sir, I'll repay

Trooper Calhoun the fifty cents he's owed for buying lunch for the detail at the Widow Piper's."

"Plus an additional fifty cents for the delay?"

Sergeant O'Neall hesitated.

"Sergeant?"

"That's really not necess..." Matthew started to speak but the Lieutenant silenced him with a look.

"An extra fifty cents Sir. Yes Sir. Sounds perfectly reasonable Sir," said Sergeant O'Neall.

"Sergeant," said the Lieutenant. "I did not like having this conversation with you and I would like never having to do it again. Is that clear?"

"Yes Sir. Thank you Sir."

"Good. You are dismissed Sergeant. Calhoun, you stand fast." After the Sergeant had saluted and left the Lieutenant turned his attention to Matthew. "Sergeant O'Neall is a good man, and a damned fine soldier," he said. "He got a little out of line and had to be reined in. This was not an official action, but I think it will have the desired effect. You were here because you were present and had knowledge of the incidents that were discussed. Everything that was said here is confidential, and once you leave here is not to be discussed with anyone. Is that clear?"

"Yes Sir," said Matthew.

"Sergeant O'Neall trusts you, and so do I. Listen to him and learn from him, but be careful not to blindly emulate him."

"Yes Sir. Thank you Sir."

"Rejoin your outfit."

Matthew saluted, turned and walked away. With a sigh of relief and a smile on his face he headed towards where the horses were staked to check on Rooster.

Shortly after 7:00am, the following morning the Troop was again formed up and headed out onto the National Road towards Eldersburg some twenty miles away. They passed through Mt. Airy late in the morning, and stopped for their noon meal about eight miles east of Eldersburg on the Liberty Road. B Troop arrived in Eldersburg late in the afternoon of the 18th of February, followed just about an hour later by the arrival of C Troop from Creagerstown.

A Troop under the command of Captain Ewing, accompanied by Colonel Thomas, had arrived in the area earlier in the day, and had chosen an area about three miles east of the town along the Patapsco River where all three Troops would bivouac. Once established, it was a very large camp, and drew curious visitors and onlookers from Eldersburg, Randallstown, and the surrounding countryside.

The three Troops spent the next day, the 19th, preparing for their arrival in Baltimore. The Colonel had made it very clear that when they entered the city he wanted them looking their very best. Everything that could shine was expected to glimmer, every uniform was to be spotless and creased, the horses were to be brushed, and the saddles and tack to be cleaned and polished. They were to appear as if on parade when they made their grand entry into the city.

There was a large meadow at the top of a hill about a mile east of the bivouac area. The three Troops were to form up in that meadow to be inspected by the Colonel at 7:00am, on the 20th. The Colonel did not leave his tent until 7:00am, and was very pleased to learn that the Troops had been in formation and ready for him well ahead of schedule.

As he crested the hill accompanied by his adjutant Major Stoneman, and his aide Captain Palmer, the troops came into view. Despite the number of times in his military career that he had seen a cavalry formation, it never failed to impress him, or fill him with pride. On this particular morning, he was even more impressed, and more proud, because these were his troopers.

The Colonel tried very hard not to let his pride show as he rode up and down between the columns of mounted men, but they knew, as did their sergeants, as did their lieutenants, and as did their captains and majors, that they looked good. It took nearly half an hour for the Colonel to complete his review.

When he was finished he called the troop commanders together. "Captain Ewing, you'll ride out front with the Major and me."

"Thank you Sir," said the Captain and nodded.

"Color guard behind us," he continued. "We'll keep the colors cased until we enter the city. I want columns of twos, A Troop, B Troop, and C Troop at the rear. That'll make the column its longest. I don't want to only impress, I want to intimidate. We'll move smartly, but not too quickly, I don't want to be kicking up a lot of dust. Questions?" None of the commanders spoke.

"Alright gentlemen," said the Colonel as he pulled down on the brim of his hat. "Let's take them to Baltimore."

Once the entire column was formed up and out on Liberty Road headed east towards Baltimore, it was over a half mile long. They passed through Randallstown about midmorning, and judging from the amount of people who lined the sides of the road, and their reaction, the long column of mounted troops was having just the effect the Colonel was looking for. The same thing happened when they passed through Rockdale, and every other little crossroads and hamlet along their route.

Just after crossing the tracks at the Highland Park Station, the column left the road. They dismounted, along a small creek, fed and watered their horses, and had their noon meal. They were about a mile outside the city limits of Baltimore, and about six miles from their final destination of Fort McHenry.

Matthew had had little contact with Sergeant O'Neall since their meeting with Lieutenant Nelson. After seeing to his horse and gulping down a hard biscuit and a piece of salt pork he went in search of him. The Sergeant was seated around a small fire with two other sergeants. He was holding a cup of coffee in his hands, and did not even look up when Matthew approached.

"What do you want Calhoun?" He asked in an annoyed voice.

"You got a minute Sarge?" Asked Matthew. "I'd like to ask you something?"

"Is there some other relative you want to visit now?" Said the Sergeant mockingly causing the other two sergeants to laugh.

"Well," said Matthew figuring he'd play along. "My grandparents do live in Baltimore, but I got something else I'd like to ask you," he said. "If you have the time that is."

The Sergeant shook his head, and set his cup down next to the fire. As he stood up he sighed and said, "Sure, why not, why should I be allowed to enjoy a little peace and quiet and some hot coffee."

They walked far enough away that Matthew didn't think they could be overheard. "Listen Sarge," he said. "I just wanted to let you know that if anything I said or did got you in trouble with the Lieutenant, then I'm really sorry."

Sergeant O'Neall shook his head, turned and looked away, and then turned back towards Matthew. "Any trouble I got into with the Lieutenant was of my own doing. You didn't do nothing wrong, in fact I appreciate you speaking up the way you did about Nelson's illness and all. You got the makings of a good horse soldier Calhoun. You're alright, I kinda don't even dislike you too much," the Sergeant said almost smiling, "but, we can't be pals, so you're going to have to find someone else to have these little chats with."

"Lieutenant Nelson says I should watch and learn from you."

"Did he?" Asked the Sergeant shaking his head. "The Lieutenant's a good man, damned shame he's an officer though. Listen, I know I'm a damned good soldier, and I ain't ashamed to say so, so if you're going to watch and learn, watch and learn from the soldier, not from the man, 'cause sometimes I ain't as good a man as maybe I should be." The two men just stood looking at one another. "Anything else?"

"No Sarge. Thanks."

"Then if it's alright with you," the Sergeant said as he turned and started walking away. "I'll go and finish what is now my cold cup of coffee."

"I think you're a good man," Matthew said to his back.

"We're going to be moving out soon," said Sergeant O'Neall without looking back. "Go rejoin your unit, and don't worry, you'll get your damned dollar."

The three Troops were soon reformed and once again on the march. By the time the end of the column was back on Liberty Road, the front of the column was turning onto Pennsylvania Avenue. Within half an hour the entire column, headed southeast on Pennsylvania Avenue, was within the city limits of Baltimore.

"I don't know what kind of reception we can expect," said Colonel Thomas turning to Captain Ewing who was behind. "Pass the word back. I want the formation kept tight. No matter what happens we maintain ranks. We stop for nothing or no one until we reach Fort McHenry."

"Yes Sir," said the Captain.

"Oh, and Captain," said the Colonel before the Captain could turn his mount. "Sir?"

"Uncase the colors."

"Yes Sir!" Said the Captain snapping off a salute as he turned and started back along the column to deliver the Colonel's orders.

The column continued down Pennsylvania Avenue to Franklin Street. They crossed Franklin Street onto Green Street, and then turned east onto Baltimore Street. They continued east on Baltimore Street to Hanover Street where they turned south.

Although the column began to attract attention almost as soon as it entered the city, there was generally nothing more than an idle curiosity exhibited by those who began lining the streets. However, as they drew closer to the inner city, and once they were on Baltimore Street, and then Hanover Street, they began to receive mixed reviews from the gathering crowds. Not all of it was good.

A majority of the onlookers just stood in silence watching, others waved, and there was even some cheering. This was after all an American city, and these were

American troops, not the invading army of some foreign power. This was the type of welcome they should expect.

However, America was a country in turmoil, and at this moment, the City of Baltimore was the epicenter of that turmoil. There were those who did indeed look upon these soldiers as an invading army, and they made their opposition to their presence known. Verbally as well as physically.

The crowds continued to grow as they moved steadily along Baltimore Street. There were small groups among the crowds that jeered at the troopers, and yelled threats and obscenities at them. Some rocks and bottles were thrown, as was dung that was picked up out of the streets and thrown.

In one instance a young man darted from the crowd and tried to grab the halter of one of the sergeants' horses. The sergeant, without even looking at the young man, and while maintaining his place in the column, used the reins as a whip and expertly lashed the young man across his face. The young man fell into the street holding the side of his face, and blood could be seen seeping through his fingers. No one else tried to physically interfere with the column.

The column continued south on Hanover Street to Fort Street where they turned east and proceeded the last two miles to Fort McHenry. About a mile from the fort there was a railroad crossing. The commanding officer of Fort McHenry, had dispatched a platoon of infantry to this location to meet the cavalry column.

When Colonel Thomas saw the waiting infantry ahead of his column, he turned to his aide Captain Palmer, and said, "Ride ahead and instruct the officer in command of that detail to split his troops on each side of the road so that we may pass between them. I have no intention of stopping now. Once we are through, his detachment is to form at our rear and follow us into the fort. He will then deploy his troops across the road at the entrance of the fort to act as a rear guard until I've had an opportunity to meet with the fort's commanding officer."

"Yes Sir!" Answered the Captain as he spurred his horse and galloped ahead of the column to relay the Colonel's orders to the infantry detachment.

As the column approached the Colonel noted with satisfaction that the infantry detail was split. As he drew even with the lieutenant who was in command of the detachment the lieutenant saluted and gave the order, "Present Arms," and the infantry soldiers who lined both sides of the street smartly brought their rifles up in front of them. After the colors had passed the lieutenant gave the order, "Order Arms," and the soldiers smartly brought their rifles down to their sides.

It took nearly fifteen minutes for the entire column to pass by, and once they had the infantry platoon fell in behind them and followed them down Fort Street to the entrance to the fort. There were a few civilian stragglers following the cavalry column, but they seemed to lose interest when they saw the infantry. As directed, when they got to the fort, the infantry fell into a line of two ranks facing back up Fort Street.

Once on the grounds of the fort, the column broke down into Troop formations. The troopers dismounted and were put at ease to await further instructions. The Colonel, his aide, Major Stoneman, and Major Oakes of C Troop went to meet with the fort's commanding officer.

The entrance was on the east side of the star shaped brick and earthen fort. To gain entry, it was necessary for the Colonel and his entourage to cross a bridge, spanning the dry moat which surrounded the fort, guarded by a pair of sentries, they passed through a brick and earthen triangular ravelin which guarded the entrance, then crossed a drawbridge which lead to the fort's sallyport, also guarded by two sentries. At the entrance to the sallyport, one of the sentries directed them to a large two-story brick building on the right just inside the main portion of the fort. A captain was waiting for them as they reined in their mounts in front of the building.

"Good afternoon," said the captain as he came to attention and saluted. "My name is Captain Larrimore. Welcome to Fort McHenry."

"Thank you Captain," said Colonel Thomas returning the salute as he, his aide, and the two majors stepped down off their horses. Two enlisted men appeared, took the reins, and, led the horses away.

"If you'll follow me," said Captain Larrimore. "Major Morris is expecting you."

"Certainly," said the Colonel.

They entered the building and went into a room on the right just off the porch. This was an outer office where a sergeant, who had been sitting behind a desk, stood and came to attention when they entered. They passed through this office and entered the office of the commanding officer.

Major William Morris stood up from behind his desk and came to attention as did two other captains who were seated in chairs along a wall to the left, when the Colonel, accompanied by Majors Stoneman and Oakes, and Captains Palmer and Larrimore, entered the room.

"As you were," said the Colonel as he approached Major Morris, removed his gauntlets, and stuck out his hand. "Gentlemen," he said with a nod to the two captains who had also come to attention.

"Welcome to Fort McHenry," said the Major as he took the Colonel's hand.

"Thank you Major," said the Colonel, "and thank you for the infantry escort, they were a welcome sight."

"I hope you didn't encounter too much unpleasantness," said the Major after the introductions were made. He pointed to a chair positioned in front of his desk. "Please Sir, be seated."

"Thank you Major," the Colonel said as he sat. "Gentlemen, everyone, please be seated." The Colonel said nodding to the other officers in the room as he sat and placed his hat and gauntlets in his lap. "There was some unpleasantness," the Colonel continued. "The worst of it was the rocks, bottles, and dung that was thrown at us, but we managed to maintain ranks and no one was injured, except for a civilian who attempted to grab the halter of one of our horses. He received a cut from a well-placed rein in return for his transgression."

There was some additional conversation regarding what was happening in Baltimore and the surrounding area, the trouble in Frederick, the secession of some of the southern states, the likelihood of war, and finally the upcoming arrival of President-elect Lincoln.

"What about the provisions I requested Major? Were you able to get most of them?" Asked the Colonel.

"Actually Sir, yes. We were able to get just about everything," answered the Major. "The last fifty bales of hay arrived yesterday and are stored in the stables just inside the main gate with the other 150 bales you requested. I'll tell you though Sir, getting 350, fifty pound bags of feed corn this time of year was just a little bit of a challenge."

"Yes, I can imagine it would be," said the Colonel.

"We were able to procure two hundred bags from a warehouse at Skinner's Dock just back up the peninsula here, and that's been delivered and is in the stables as well. The other 150 bags are coming from a warehouse in Wetheredville, and we were promised delivery of those on the 23rd."

"Thank you Major," said the Colonel. "Very, very well done. My compliments to you and your staff for you diligence."

"Thank you, Sir."

"Now, what about the men? I'm hoping we can get them out of the weather."

"Yes Sir," said Major Morris. "Accommodations have been made for you and your officers to stay on the second floor of this building. There is a room across the hall from the outer office here that I believe you'll find suitable as an office."

"Excellent," said the Colonel.

"There is an old two story barracks building outside the walls of the fort opposite the ravelin. That building has bunks and will house about 150 men. We've also put pallets down in the old artillery shed, which is just inside the main gate. This too should house about 150 men. It may not be as comfortable as one would like, but the men will be warm and dry.

"Also, we've erected a temporary shelter behind the old barracks building where the men can take their meals."

"Very good, very good indeed Major. Now, what about our mounts."

"Well, as I said Sir, the hay and feed corn is here and is in the stables which are next to the artillery shed at the main gate. There is a fence which runs along the fort's boundary from the main gate to the water's edge at the harbor, but there is no fencing to keep the horses from wandering the grounds. I apologize that I do not have the stable space for over three hundred horses Sir."

"Nonsense Major," said Colonel Thomas. "You have done extremely well, and I shall make special mention of how well prepared you were for our arrival when I file my reports. Thank you again."

"Glad to be of service," answered the Major.

The Colonel turned to Major Oakes. "Major, return to the formation and see to your Troop. Also, pass along to the other Troop commanders the information regarding the housing of the troops and their mounts so that they may do likewise."

"Yes Sir," said the Major as he stood and came to attention.

"I will meet with all officers in one hour's time in the office across the hall. Thank you, and carry on."

The Major turned smartly and left the office.

Chapter 30

The Patapsco
1861

Having gotten their individual Troops settled, Major Oakes, Captains Ewing and Talbot, and the twelve lieutenants under Colonel Thomas' command were gathered in the first floor office of the headquarters building just inside Fort McHenry. The only furniture in the room, that the Fort's Commanding Officer Major Morris, had graciously made available to them, was a couple of tables, and eight wooden chairs. The Colonel was seated behind one of the tables flanked by Major Stoneman and Captain Palmer. The troop commanders were seated in chairs, while the lieutenants stood along the walls of the now crowded room.

"Gentlemen," began the Colonel as he stood to face them. "The latest information I have indicates that Mr. Lincoln's schedule is unchanged. We can expect him to arrive here at the Calvert Street Station at around 12:30pm on the 23rd, and depart from the Camden Street Station that same day at about 3:00pm. Understandably, those two and a half hours will be the most critical of our mission.

"In the meantime, beginning at 8:00am tomorrow morning we will station a platoon at the Calvert Street Station, a platoon at the Camden Street Station, and a platoon at the President Street Station. A fourth platoon will be assigned to patrol the area around City Hall, and the business areas. The four platoons of C Troop will have the first duty.

"The Troops will rotate every eight hours. So, A Troop will relieve C Troop at 4:00pm, and B Troop will relieve A Troop at midnight. Questions?"

"Sir," said Captain Ewing of A Troop. "Why the President Street Station? It is my understanding that neither Mr. Lincoln, nor any of his group are scheduled to arrive or depart from there."

"Captain," answered the Colonel. "Not only do I want anyone who may be contemplating foul play to know that we are watching, I also want them to know that we are keeping an eye on who is arriving and leaving the city as well. Anything else? Good.

"Gentlemen," he continued addressing the troop commanders. "I want you on station at the appointed hour, so plan accordingly. The Calvert Street and President Street Stations are about an hour's ride from here. Thank you, that is all."

Over the course of the next two days, the elements of the US 2nd Cavalry that had been deployed to Baltimore carried out their assignments. There was the occasional run in with local anti-Lincoln rabble rousers, and a few arrests were made, but no one seemed eager to tangle with the intimidating horse soldiers. However, the tension did seem to grow as the time for Mr. Lincoln's arrival drew closer.

Every night, B Troop was assigned the overnight midnight to 8:00am detail. Captain Talbot did not know why his Troop had gotten the least desirable of the assignments, but neither was he prepared to inquire of the Colonel as to why. To help break up the monotony of the long nights, the platoons rotated between the assigned locations.

The 2nd Platoon of B Troop was assigned to the President Street Station for the midnight to 8:00am detail on the 23rd. Everyone considered this the worst assignment Not only was it not really part of Lincoln's route, but its location was not central to the city, and most of the activity occurred only when trains were either arriving or departing. There was usually very little, if any, activity overnight.

Lieutenant Nelson and the sergeants under his command were provided with a schedule of arrivals and departures. The three squads took turns standing a watch inside the station. With one squad inside the station, the other two squads patrolled the area around the station unless a train was coming or going. Then everyone would be at the station.

It was a little after 3:00am, and Sergeant O'Neall and Trooper Matthew Calhoun, of 2nd Platoon's First Squad, were standing on the platform on the Canton Avenue side of the station looking east. There was no one else on the platform. It had been an unusually slow night.

Lieutenant Nelson was with 1st Squad patrolling the city docks along Block Street, and 3rd Squad had been sent to check on a boisterous gathering of revelers outside a tavern on Grant Street a few blocks north of the station. It was a clear night, and not uncomfortably cold. Sunrise was still over four hours away.

Matthew pointed out that there were two men with a team of horses, in harness, just off Canton Avenue on Central Avenue near where the switches were that allowed trains to enter the station.

"We should check that out," said the Sergeant, and started to walk down the platform in that direction.

Suddenly, about a mile away, there appeared a single bright light. It took only a few seconds for the Sergeant to realize what it was…a train. He didn't remember any train being scheduled to arrive at this hour. He quickly reached into his pocket and removed the schedule the Lieutenant had given him. He stepped under a gaslight and confirmed that there was not supposed to be a train approaching the station at this hour.

He quickly went to the door of the station, jerked it open and yelled inside, "Trask! Get your sorry butt out here!" Then walked back out onto the platform. He turned to Matthew and said, "Get our horses." Matthew just stared. "Go! Damn it! Get our horses!" Matthew turned and ran back up the platform towards President Street where their horses were tethered.

Within seconds Trooper Trask came busting through the door. "What's up Sarge?" He asked in a confused voice.

Sergeant O'Neall grabbed him by the front of his uniform shirt and pointed towards the light. "You see that?" He asked. "It's a train. It's a train that is not supposed to be there. I don't know what's going on, but I don't like it.

"Send a rider to the docks to find the Lieutenant and get him back here with 1st Squad. Get the rest of 2nd squad and get down to where the tracks turn onto President Street. Do whatever it takes but unless you hear from me, that train does not turn onto President Street. Understand?"

"Yes Sergeant!" Answered Trask turning to go back into the station.

"Calhoun and I are going to go meet that train and see what we can find out," Sergeant O'Neall yelled as he turned and looked back at the approaching train. It worried him that the train, which appeared to be made up of only two or three cars, seemed to be moving very slowly, and that except for the headlight, the train was completely blacked out.

When Matthew arrived with the horses, they set off at a gallop to attempt to intercept the train. The men who were with the horses on Central Avenue were nearly run down when they stepped out onto Canton Avenue and tried to wave the galloping horse soldiers down. They met the train, which had slowed even more, at Caroline Street.

Sergeant O'Neall spun his horse around, as did Matthew, and they fell in alongside the locomotive. Sergeant O'Neall peered into the cab at the engineer.

"Where you going?" He hollered over the noise of the big steam engine.

"President Street Station," the engineer yelled back.

"You ain't on the schedule."

"Special train."

"What's special about it?"

The engineer shrugged. "I just drive 'em," he hollered.

"Bring it to a stop," hollered the Sergeant.

"He can't do that," said a small wiry bearded man in a dark suit who stepped out of the shadows at the back of the locomotive's cab.

The Sergeant pulled out his sidearm and aimed it at the two men. "Yes he can," he hollered, "or this train is going to get to the station without either of you knowing about it."

The bearded man nodded to the engineer and then leaned out of the cab and hollered, "Alright, but I hope that switch is pulled because by the time we get his thing stopped we'll need to be on the siding to the station."

When the train finally did come to a stop, the engine, tender, and the first car, a passenger car, were on the siding leading into the President Street Station. The second car, a sleeper car, was still on the tracks which ran along Canton Avenue. The bearded man jumped down from the engine and started walking back towards the passenger car.

"Hold on there friend," said Sergeant O'Neall still brandishing his sidearm. "Before you go anywhere, I need to know just what is going on here."

"I'm afraid I can't tell you that," the man said as he stopped and turned towards the Sergeant.

"Then I'm afraid I'll have to detain you, your engineer, and stoker, until I can check this train out and find out what's so special about it."

The men who had been standing with the team of horses on Central Avenue started towards the second car with the horses.

"Sarge," said Matthew nodding towards the men.

"That's far enough gentlemen," said the Sergeant looking over his shoulder in their direction. "Calhoun," he said loud enough to be heard by the men. "If either one of them touch this train, shoot them, but spare the horses."

Matthew drew his Sharp's Carbine out of its boot alongside his saddle and leveled it at the two men. The men raised their arms and stepped back away from the train.

"Calhoun, me and... what is your name Sir?" Asked Sergeant O'Neall addressing the bearded man.

"My name is not important, and it would mean nothing to you," said the man.

"You're beginning to piss me off," said the Sergeant.

"Sergeant," said the bearded man. "You and your companion are making a very serious mistake. Is there a superior officer I could talk to?"

Sergeant O'Neall looked back up the tracks towards President Street and saw Lieutenant Nelson and several men from 1st Squad approaching.

"Yes," said the Sergeant. "It looks like there is."

"What's going on O'Neall?" Asked the Lieutenant as he reined up next to the Sergeant.

Sergeant O'Neall then explained about the approach of the mysterious train, the men with the horses, and the bearded man's reluctance to answer questions related to the train.

"Sir," said the Lieutenant turning towards the bearded man. "You are within seconds of being placed under arrest. Now, you'd better tell me about your train."

"Lieutenant," said the man. "If you will dismount so that we can talk privately, I believe you will understand."

The Lieutenant looked at O'Neall and then back at the man. "Very well," he said and handed his reins to the Sergeant as he stepped down off of his horse. The bearded man led the Lieutenant around behind the tender where they would be out of the troopers' sight.

"If he comes back alone," said Sergeant O'Neall to Matthew. "Drop him."

Matthew nodded. His throat was so dry he couldn't speak. It had been less than fifteen minutes since Sergeant O'Neall had first spotted the train, and things were getting extremely tense.

"O'Neall, Calhoun," hollered the Lieutenant as he emerged from the darkness with the bearded man and began hurriedly walking towards the second car. "Dismount and come with me."

The two men exchanged glances.

"You heard the man," said the Sergeant grabbing his Sharp's out if its boot as he dismounted.

They handed their reins to a trooper from 1st Squad, and trotted to catch up with Lieutenant Nelson and the bearded man. When they got to the back of the car the Lieutenant and the bearded man climbed up onto the landing while the Sergeant and Matthew remained on the ground. The bearded man lifted his arm to knock on the door of the railroad car.

Lieutenant Nelson reached out and grabbed the man's arm to stop him. "Men," he said staring at the bearded man and without looking at Sergeant O'Neall or Matthew. "If this goes wrong, you shoot this man first and then anyone who comes out this door. Understood?"

"Yes Sir!" Answered the Sergeant.

"Alright Sir," said the Lieutenant nodding to the bearded man as he released his arm. "Go ahead."

The man, looked uneasily at the Lieutenant, swallowed, then raised his arm and made several rhythmic knocks on the door. These were answered by a similar series of knocks from inside.

"Plums," said the bearded man loud enough to be heard through the door. The door opened. "I have a lieutenant and two armed troopers with me," he said to whoever was behind the door. "We're coming in. Follow me," he said turning to the Lieutenant.

"Let's go," said Lieutenant Nelson waving to Sergeant O'Neall and Matthew.

The inside of the car was dimly lit. Matthew noticed that each of the windows were covered on the inside by heavy black curtains. There were only two other men in the car.

The man who had opened the door, a tall stocky man, had moved towards the front of the car and was standing next to a man who was seated in a chair. Matthew noted that the man in the chair looked very uncomfortable. It was obvious that the man was very tall and did not fit well in the chair. His hair was disheveled, his clothes were rumpled, and he had a shawl draped around his shoulders. The man also appeared to be very tired. He also looked strangely familiar.

"Well Mr. Pinkerton," the man in the chair said in a raspy voice as he yawned and stretched his long legs out in front of him. "Have we arrived in Washington?"

"No Sir," answered the bearded man, who everyone now knew was the famous detective Allan Pinkerton. "Baltimore Sir, we've just arrived in Baltimore."

"And why have members of the military come calling?"

"These Sir," said Mr. Pinkerton gesturing towards Lieutenant Nelson. "Are members of the US 2nd Cavalry. Apparently they were dispatched here by General Scott to guarantee your safe passage. They found the arrival of our unscheduled train suspicious, and now have refused to allow us to proceed until Lieutenant Nelson here, it is Nelson isn't it?" Asked Pinkerton turning towards the Lieutenant.

"Yes Sir, it is."

"Thank you. Until Lieutenant Nelson here is able to confirm that, as I told him, this train is carrying the President elect, and that we are trying to slip through Baltimore undetected."

Matthew suddenly realized that he was standing only a few feet from Abraham Lincoln. The man who, in ten days' time, would be inaugurated as President of the United States.

"Well," said the tall man as he slowly lifted himself out of the chair. "My name is Lincoln, and for better or worse, I am on my way to our nation's capital to assume the Presidency." He removed the shawl and tossed it onto a nearby chair. "I'm sorry Lieutenant, but our government does not issue its President-elect a carte de visit or any document that would allow me to prove that I am who I say I am. I am told though, that I have a very distinctive, if unpleasant appearance." He laughed. "However, should that not be sufficient, this is Mr. Ward Lamon," he continued pointing to the man who had opened the door. "Mr. Lamon is a very well-known and respected attorney in Springfield, Illinois, and one of the most honest men I have ever known. I'm quite sure he'll vouch for my identity.

"Of course, I would think that my words would be supported simply by the fact that I have prominence enough to warrant having a train to myself," he said with a smile. "Despite how suspicious that might seem."

"Welcome to Baltimore Mr. Lincoln," said Lieutenant Nelson nervously. He turned to Mr. Pinkerton. "You may proceed with your plans," he said. The Lieutenant then turned to Sergeant O'Neall. "O'Neall you and Calhoun will remain in here with

Mr. Lincoln and Mr. Lamon. No one comes through that door except Mr. Pinkerton or myself. Understand?"

"Yes Sir," answered the Sergeant.

"Lieutenant?" Asked Mr. Lincoln. "Do you really think it necessary to keep me under armed guard?"

"I don't know Sir. However, what I do know is that if I do nothing, I'll have a captain and a colonel who will want to know why."

"Very well," said the President-elect, "and, thank you for your diligence."

Lieutenant Nelson nodded and left the car.

"Alright Calhoun," said the Sergeant. "You take the front of the car, and I'll take the back. That way we're in position to cover each other if anything does happen."

"Got it Sarge," said Matthew as he moved towards the front of the car.

"Well Mr. Lamon," said Mr. Lincoln with a laugh. "It appears we've become an occupied territory."

Mr. Lamon walked over to one of the windows and peered out around the edge of the curtain.

"Please don't do that Sir," said Sergeant O'Neall.

Mr. Lamon sighed and sat down in one of the several chairs that lined the side of the car. "So what happens now?" He asked.

"Well," said Mr. Lincoln taking a seat across from his friend. "There is a strictly enforced city ordinance which prohibits trains from moving through the center of the city at night. So, a team of horses is being hitched to the front of this car and will be pulling us to the Camden Street Station. Once there we will be attached to another train and proceed to Washington."

"Won't it arouse suspicion if anyone sees a team of horses pulling a train car through the city?"

"It is my understanding that though not a frequent occurrence, the practice is not uncommon."

Lamon just nodded. "How long will it take?" He asked.

"Mr. Pinkerton said that we should be hooked up and on our way to Washington within an hour."

"Lincoln my friend," said Lamon with a smile. "This is the strangest damned train ride I've ever been on!" The two men laughed together, the kind of laugh that friends share.

Shortly after they arrived at the Camden Street Station Mr. Pinkerton, accompanied by Captain Talbot and Lieutenant Nelson entered the car. The men had agreed that notifying Colonel Thomas at this time would not only cause an unnecessary delay, but also arouse suspicion.

"There's a problem," said Mr. Pinkerton after the introductions had been made.

"What sort of a problem?" Asked Mr. Lamon.

"The Baltimore and Ohio train this car is to be hooked to has been delayed."

"When will it get here?" Asked the President-elect.

"I don't know," answered Mr. Pinkerton.

"How long can we wait?"

"If we're still here at dawn your safety could very well depend on the Captain's cavalry," said Mr. Pinkerton nodding at the Captain.

"If necessary," said Captain Talbot, "we'll put Mr. Lincoln on a horse and make a run for Fort McHenry."

"Let's hope it doesn't come to that!" Said Mr. Lamon.

"I have great faith in the American railroad system," said Mr. Lincoln with a smile. "I'm confident our delay will not be excessive."

"Lieutenant Nelson," said Captain Talbot. "You will remain here at the station with your 1st and 2nd Squads. I will take 1st Platoon and your 3rd Squad, and take up a position at the Hill Street School. In the event of trouble I can be here within minutes."

"Yes Sir," said the Lieutenant.

"I will also send riders to the 3rd and 4th platoons with instructions that they form up and begin to move in this direction. If worst comes to worst, we'll have nearly one hundred men readily available."

"What about the Colonel, Sir?"

"I'll send a courier to the Colonel to inform him of what is going on."

"My dear Captain," said Mr. Lincoln in an almost exasperated tone. "Is all of this really necessary?"

"With all due respect Mr. Lincoln," answered the Captain with a smile. "Colonel Thomas said that you would leave Baltimore in as good as, if not better health, than what you arrived in. I'll not disappoint him."

"Very well, Captain," said the President-elect raising his hands over his head with a smile. "I surrender."

"If that train gets here in time Sir," said Mr. Pinkerton. "We'll have no need of the cavalry."

"And if it doesn't Mr. Pinkerton?" Asked Mr. Lincoln fixing the detective with a stare. Mr. Pinkerton looked away and said nothing.

"Let's get to it then," said the Captain as he turned, bowed in Mr. Lincoln's direction, and left the car.

"O'Neall," said Lieutenant Nelson to the Sergeant. "You and Calhoun will remain here at your posts until President-elect Lincoln is delivered safely to Washington."

"Yes Sir," said the Sergeant.

"I got a feeling we're all going to be headed that way before this is over anyway. Questions?"

"No Sir."

"Then we'll see you in Washington," said the Lieutenant as he turned towards Mr. Lincoln. "It has been an honor Sir," he said as he too then turned and left the car.

"Lamon," said the President-elect to his friend once the Lieutenant was gone. "If this is the caliber of the men who would be called upon to quash a rebellion, then I have no doubt that our union is secure."

"So it would seem Lincoln," replied his friend, "so, it would seem."

Time passed, and the train did not come. As the sky in the east was beginning to lighten, the decision was made to try and secret Mr. Lincoln off the train, onto a horse, and get him to Fort McHenry where he would be safe. That plan was being set into motion when something banged into the front of the President-elect's car.

"The train is here," said Mr. Pinkerton as he came bursting through the door of the car. "We're hooking up now."

Within minutes the train was pulling out of the Camden Street Station and heading south towards Washington. Mr. Lamon and Mr. Lincoln tried to sleep on the way to Washington, but found that the berths on the sleeper car were too small to accommodate their large frames. They eventually gave up and spent the last part of the trip nodding off in the chairs in the sitting area at the rear of the car.

At 6:00am, on February 23rd, the train from Baltimore pulled into the Baltimore and Ohio Depot in Washington. No one paid much attention to the three stragglers, one of whom was tall and lanky, wrapped in a thick traveling shawl, and wearing a soft low-crowned hat, who exited the sleeper car at the back of the train Neither did they notice the two cavalry troopers armed with Sharp's carbines, who were left standing on the platform when the train departed.

On the morning of Monday, March 4th, 1861, Trooper Matthew Calhoun proudly rode with the rest of his cavalry comrades, in the procession that escorted President James Buchanan, and his successor President-elect Abraham Lincoln, from Willard's Hotel on 14th Street, to the Capital building for the inauguration. Matthew watched from a distance as Mr. Lincoln was inaugurated, and although he heard very little of what was said, it was one of the most exciting moments of his life.

Six weeks later, Confederate forces in Charleston, South Carolina opened fire on Fort Sumter in Charleston Harbor. President Lincoln called for the raising of 75,000 troops to quash the rebellion. America was at war with itself.

On July 21st, Matthew Calhoun would experience the bitter taste of battle for the first time at Bull Run near Manassas Junction, Virginia. He would fight in every major battle in the eastern theater over the next two years. He would be wounded, and on Christmas Eve of 1862, following the battle of Fredericksburg, and be promoted to the rank of sergeant for his actions during that battle.

Chapter 31

The Rancocas
1940

Christmas had come and gone, and the New Year, 1940, was not as full of promise for a world at peace as one would hope. In Europe, Germany, under the rule of their dictator Adolph Hitler, had already annexed Austria, and as part of a tenuous treaty with France and Britain, had agreed that if also allowed to annex parts of Czechoslovakia, they would not seek further expansion. The entire world knew however, that it was only a matter of time before Hitler broke that treaty and Europe was thrust headlong into war.

In the Pacific, Japan had invaded China and was skirmishing with Russian forces along the Manchurian and Mongolian borders. World opinion was that it would not be long before Japan moved into Southeast Asia. If war broke out in Europe, and Japan continued its aggression in the east, it would not be long before America would be drawn into a world war.

This worried Katherine Rosemary McBride. Two of the most important men in her life, her brother Evan McBride, and the man she thought might become her husband, Baxter "Woody" Underwood, were lieutenants in the US Navy. If war came, in either place, they would no doubt be in the thick of it.

Despite the troubles in the world, Katy and her grandfather, Michael McBride, had enjoyed a merry enough Christmas. They had attended a local pageant put on by the village children at the church, and been visited by a number of friends and neighbors. They had had their foreman, Mr. Davenport, and his family for Christmas dinner, including his young nephew Mikey, and his family.

Neither Evan nor Woody had been able to get home for the holidays. Katy had sent gifts, and received gifts in return, which did not make up for their absence, but perhaps helped ease the pain. Woody had sent a beautiful necklace of aquamarine and morganite with matching earrings that he had purchased in Rio de Janeiro, and Evan a Hawaiian handwoven dyed reed rug.

The greatest gift however had been the telephone call. Evan had called from Honolulu. He said that he had started trying to call at 8:00am his time, and had finally been able to get through at 1:00pm his time. Katy had just finished serving dessert to everyone when the phone rang. It was 6:00pm in Rancocas.

It had taken her a few minutes to understand what the long distance operator was saying, but when she finally realized that the voice she was hearing over the staticky connection was Evan's she got so excited she nearly dropped Mrs. Davenport's pumpkin pie. The call lasted less than five minutes, but that was long enough for her and her grandfather to wish Evan a Merry Christmas and to tell him how much they missed him and loved him. It was the perfect way to end the day.

Katy McBride now spent most of her evenings recording in a journal the stories her grandfather Michael was telling her about the history of the McBride family. What was supposed to have been a story that would be told in an afternoon, had turned into a detailed history of the McBride family that was now taking weeks and weeks to be told and recorded. Whenever it seemed to her that her grandfather felt well enough, or was inclined to do so, she would ask him to reveal more about the McBride family history.

Katy forced herself to write everything down in as much detail as she could recall, and often went back to her grandfather and asked him questions, or asked him to repeat a certain part of the story. It was important to her that she get this right, not only for herself and her older brother Evan, but for her grandfather, and for future generations as well.

She was enjoying the stories about her Great Uncle Matthew Calhoun, whom she imagined as a handsome and dashing young cavalier. Katy wondered why she did not know more about her relatives from Maryland. From what her grandfather was saying these people had been very important to her grandmother, and he seemed to know quite a lot about them. Why had they never met, and why did she know so little about them?

Katy stopped to wonder what it must be like for her grandfather. There had been so many changes in the last eighty odd years. He had been there when the horse was still the primary mode of transportation, when ships were powered by sail and made of wood, when the only things that flew were birds, and the only way to communicate over distance was by mail that also moved primarily by horse.

Now there were paved roads choked with automobiles and trucks of every shape and size, there were huge iron ships the size of small cities powered by huge engines that could cross oceans not in weeks, but in a matter of days. There were airplanes made of steel that could not only get off the ground, but cross those same oceans in a matter of hours. You could talk to someone half a world away by telephone, and sit in your parlor in front of a radio, and listen to your favorite entertainer live from places such as New York City, and Hollywood, California. Most feature films not only talked, but were now in color, and it was said that in a few years people would be able to have televisions in their homes and watch the shows they could now only listen to on radio.

Katy couldn't help but smile as she thought what a wonderful time it was to be alive. The world was a huge mysterious place, but it had been made significantly smaller and more accessible thanks to modern technology. She hoped that someday, like her brother Evan, she would have an opportunity to see more of it for herself. What would the world be like in eighty years she wondered, what would life along the Rancocas be like in 2018?

Once Katy had completed writing about the McBride family in her journal, she decided to pen a letter to her brother Evan. He had told them during the Christmas telephone call that the *USS Lexington* had returned to Pearl Harbor, and that his life, at least for the time being, had returned to what could be considered normal, at least for a lieutenant in the US Navy. He had also briefly mentioned the young lady that he was keeping company with, Miss Irene Northrup, and it sounded as if the relationship might be getting serious.

In a previous letter Evan had mentioned that Irene's father, Johnathan Northrup, was the President of a shipping company based in Honolulu. Mr. Northrup had brought his family from Ireland to Hawaii in 1920, to rebuild after his family's company had been almost wiped out as a result of the First World War. The name of the company was Meadow Hill Shipping. Irene Northrup claimed that her family was descended from British royalty, though she didn't know how.

Katy wanted to know more about her brother's love interest. There were some very intriguing coincidences in the limited amount of information she had. Wouldn't it be something, if Irene Northrup was a descendent of a certain Lord Northrup? This definitely required further investigation.

In her letter, she shared the news and gossip of people in and around the Village of Rancocas. Talked about their grandfather and how well he was doing. Gave Evan bits and pieces of the stories grandfather was telling, and of how things were going on the farm.

She told him the latest news from Woody, who was serving aboard the *USS Rhind* in the South Atlantic, and asked that he share any news Woody may have shared with him. She wrote about her concerns about the possibility of war and her fears about what war would mean, not only to the men who would be called upon to fight in it, but also the families who would be at home waiting for their return. Hopefully, everyone would come to their senses before things got too out of hand. Katy told her brother how excited she was that Woody would be back in Philadelphia in a few weeks. The *Rhind* was returning to the Navy Yard to repair and make adjustments to the equipment and systems that had been tested during their extended shakedown cruise. The work was expected to take up to three months.

When she had finished the letter to her brother she wrote one to Woody. She tried to write to Woody every day. Sometimes the letters were long and maybe just a little sappy, and other days they were perhaps only a few lines to say good morning and have a nice day.

The weather the next day was supposed to be unseasonably pleasant for late January, so Katy decided that she would take her letters and any other mail that was going out tomorrow to the post office in the village on horseback. She hadn't ridden for several months, mostly because of the weather, but also because the increased car and truck traffic on the main roads in and around Rancocas made the horses jittery and took a lot of the fun out of riding. Tomorrow she would go cross country through the unplanted fields. This would allow her to avoid most of the roads and traffic.

The McBride's had two saddle horses. Indigo, a gentle 12-year old mare, who had been given to her as a gift by her grandfather on her 14th birthday. Then there was Jester, an 8-year old gelding that Evan had purchased on his graduation from the Naval Academy in 1933, but it was anybody's guess why.

Jester was mischievous. He loved to run, and could be unpredictable. Katy decided that she would take Jester to the post office, and if the weather was nice enough perhaps go for a ride along the creek and visit some of the other farms.

With temperatures getting into the fifties the following day, Katy and Jester extended their ride and ended up galloping across the fields and through the woods until they found themselves almost to Burlington. By the time they returned to the farm it was getting late in the afternoon. By the time she had unsaddled, cooled, and brushed Jester, she barely had enough time for a bath before it would be time to prepare dinner for herself and her grandfather.

"I'm home!" She hollered into the parlor as she prepared to climb the stairs to her second floor bedroom.

"Patrick from down to the post office stopped by to see you," her grandfather announced in response.

Patrick? She thought, now what would he want. Patrick Oldman was a part-time clerk at the post office, and had been on duty when Katy dropped off the mail earlier in the day. Patrick was in his early twenties, and Katy thought he might have a crush on her.

"What did he want?" She asked still standing at the bottom of the stairs, the annoyance evident in her voice.

"He brought you something."

Oh no. She thought, I don't really need this complication now. Patrick was a decent enough fellow, he wasn't the best looking guy in the world, and he was too book wormy, and nowhere near outdoorsy enough to suit Katy.

However, a gentleman caller had brought her a mysterious package, and despite what Katy might think about him, was there really any woman in the world who would not be flattered or curious by such a gesture? She glanced up the stairs, sighed, turned, and entered the parlor. Might as well see what it is, she thought.

When she entered the parlor her grandfather pointed to a table just inside the front door and said, "He said he was sorry, but he forgot to give them to you when you were in this morning."

On the table was a stack of envelopes about six inches in height bound together with string. Katy's heart began to race as she approached the table. She picked up the stack and began to thumb through them.

"They're all from Woody!" She exclaimed as she swung around and faced her grandfather with a huge smile on her face.

"Are they?" He said. "And wasn't it nice of Patrick to bring them all the way out here. I'll tell you," he continued, smiling at Katy. "That Patrick is a pretty nice fellow."

"Uh huh," she muttered absently as she started back for the stairs still thumbing through the packet of letters. When she got to the stairs she stopped, turned around and sat down. She placed the letters on her lap and began working on the knot in the string that was holding them together.

"Probably be easier to cut it," said her grandfather who was now standing in the doorway to the parlor smiling down at her. Katy had been so intent on the knot that her grandfather's voice startled her.

"What?" She said as she jumped.

"Cut it," he said with a knowing chuckle.

She laughed as she stood up and handed the letters to her grandfather. "Here," she said with a smile. "Put these somewhere until I've cleaned myself up and made dinner, or else we'll both go to bed hungry, and I'll still be smelling of horse!"

"Good idea," he said as he leaned over and kissed Katy on the forehead. Then he turned and went back into the parlor as she bounded up the stairs singing "Nice Work if You Can Get It", Woody's favorite song.

They had finished dinner, and Katy had finished the dishes and gotten her grandfather settled in front of the radio in the parlor. She reached across and picked up the stack of bound letters from the side table next to his chair. "I'll take those," she said smiling down at her grandfather.

"Not going to listen to Robert Trout tonight?" He asked with a smile.

"I don't think so," she said returning his smile and pointing at the letters. "I'll be in the kitchen."

"Well try not to make too much noise swooning." He laughed. "I have enough trouble hearing as it is."

"I don't swoon," she said slapping him on the shoulder with the packet of letters. As she turned to leave the parlor she stopped and turned and said, "Well, maybe just a little." Then she giggled and hurriedly walked to the kitchen.

Sitting at the kitchen table, Katy took a paring knife and with probably way too much care, slowly cut the string binding the letters together. She took the stack and separated the envelopes and placed them in order by postmark, from the oldest to the most recent. There were 28 of them, and some of them were nearly a month old. She sat back and congratulated herself on her solution in determining how to make sure she read the letters in the order in which they were written.

Then she had a thought, what if some of the letters had not been sent on the day they were written but at later dates? Could it be possible that though the postmarks were now in chronological order that the letters were not? Best to open each of the envelopes and go by the dates the letters were written she decided.

So, with meticulous care she began to open the envelopes. She removed the first letter from the envelope with the oldest postmark. Unable to help herself, she began to read;

> *My Dearest Katy,*
>
> *I can't begin to tell you how much I miss you, and though there are so many miles between us I know that ...*

Stop! It took everything she had to do it, but she was committed to reading the letters in order, and although it was very likely that this was the first, she would not read until she was certain.

Exercising every ounce of willpower she had, Katy very carefully opened each envelope and lovingly placed each letter in chronological order by the date written at the top of the first page in Woody's handwriting. She found that only one or two of the letters had been out of order based on the postmarks. She also noticed that the salutations sometimes differed. Sometimes the letters began with; *My Dearest Katy,* sometimes just; *Dear Katy*, others began *My Beloved Katy,* these were her favorite, and others said; *Dear Queen of Dogpatch.* She was anxious to see if the contents of the letters gave any clue as to why the salutations differed.

Some of the letters were only a page or two in length, some were as long as eight or nine pages, but most of them were three to four pages. They were all wonderful, and Katy took her time with each one of them, consuming them with as much delight as if she were enjoying a fine meal. As the pile grew smaller she even began to read slower.

It had taken Katy over two and a half hours to read the letters. She had stopped only to check on her grandfather and to take him his evening tea. As she opened the last letter she had already decided that when finished she would start over again with the very first letter.

Havana is an amazing city. The food, the music, the people, are all so colorful. Not to mention spicy. You'd love it here, and I'd love to show it to you someday. What a perfect place it would be for a honeymoon!

I do not wish to stay any longer than necessary though because nothing could be more amazing than being able to look into your eyes and hold you in my arms. It's hard to believe, that after all this time, we will be back in Philadelphia in less than two weeks.

Katy paused in her reading, Cuba, how exciting. "A honeymoon?" She whispered with a smile, maybe dreams really do come true she thought.

Wait! She sat bolt upright, stared down at the letter, and read again, back in Philadelphia in less than two weeks. Two weeks, they were coming back earlier than expected!

Katy shuffled through the pile of papers looking for the envelope that had contained the last of the letters. She found it and stared at the postmark. It had been stamped 12 days ago. Woody could be back any day now. My God, she thought, he could be in Philadelphia already!

The telephone rang. Katy sat paralyzed. It was after ten o'clock. No one called at this hour unless it was with bad news. Unless…

She heard her grandfather cough, the phone had awakened him. "Katy?" He called. "What's going on?"

"It's the telephone Poppa," she said the nervousness evident in her voice. "I'll get it."

"Who the devil calls at this hour?" He asked.

Katy stood and walked over to the telephone. She stood staring down at it as it continued to ring. She didn't know how many times it rung, but she did know that if she didn't answer it soon, it would stop.

Very slowly she reached out and lifted the receiver from the cradle, and brought it up to her ear. "Hello," she said her barely audible voice quaking.

"Would you say that again?" The voice on the other end said. "It's the most beautiful thing I've ever heard."

"Woody," she whispered as she began to cry and laugh at the same time.

"Hello my darling," he said. "I've come home."

During the ensuing conversation Woody told her that he had some time coming and wanted to know if he could come to the farm on Thursday and stay until Sunday. Katy and her grandfather were of course thrilled. Woody would be coming by train, and Katy would pick him up at the station in Beverly. The place where he had told her for the first time that he thought he was in love with her.

On Friday Woody told Katy that he wanted to take her on a real date into Philadelphia on Saturday. It took some convincing but eventually Katy agreed. They would visit the Museum of Art during the day, have dinner at Bookbinder's, then see "Angels With Dirty Faces" starring James Cagney and Patrick O'Brien at the Fox, a nightcap at McGillin's Ale House on Drury, and finally catch the midnight train for New York City from the 30th Street Station that stopped in Burlington. He promised her it would be a day she would never forget.

They had spent hours at the museum, and were now sitting in the bar at Bookbinder's, sipping champagne, waiting while their table was being prepared. Woody reached across the small round table and took her hand. "Are you having a good time?" He asked with a smile.

She finished sipping from her glass, and as she set her glass down, she hiccupped. Embarrassed, she quietly giggled, and brought her free hand up to her mouth. "Oh my," she said with a smile. "I could learn to enjoy this."

"Maybe you should take it a little easy there with the bubbly," laughed Woody squeezing her hand.

"I'm having the time of my life," she said, "but, not because of the museum, or the champagne, or dinner, or anything, but because I'm with you. Because I love you Baxter Underwood." She smiled. "Despite your fake Colorado cowboy charm."

Woody laughed. "You sure that's not the champagne talking?" He asked.

"Nope," she replied. "It's just me."

"Well, I love you too Katherine Rosemary McBride, even if you are the Queen of Dogpatch."

"Just shut up and kiss me will ya," she whispered, and he leaned across the table and did.

The meal was expensive but exquisite and worth every penny of it. They both enjoyed the movie, although Woody probably more so. They were both tired, and decided to skip the drinks and try to catch an earlier train home.

They had a hot dog and Coke at the 30th Street Station while they waited for their train, not because they were hungry, but because they could not resist the smell of the boiling hot dogs as it wafted through the cavernous edifice that was the 30th Street Station. Katy fell asleep with her head on Woody's shoulder on the train ride home. They arrived back in Burlington on time, at 12:05am.

With Woody driving the old farm truck, it took them not quite half an hour to get back to the farm. He parked the truck at the back porch, went around and opened the passenger door and helped Katy out of the truck. They kissed lightly and walked up the stairs to the porch holding hands.

Woody stopped on the porch and they turned to face each other. "You know," he said with a smile. "This is the spot where we first met."

Returning the smile, Katy said, "I thought you were rude and stupid."

Woody chuckled and said, "That's okay, because I thought you were crazy."

Katy reached up and stroked his cheek. "And now here we are," she said. "The both of us crazy."

"We were standing here when we said goodbye that night," he said, "and I think that that is when I began to think that maybe I was falling in love with you."

Katy started to speak but Woody brought his free hand up and placed his finger against her lips, and said, "Shhhh…" silencing her. Then, as Katy began to tremble, and tears began to well up in her eyes, Woody, still holding her hand, began to drop to one knee. While he was doing so he reached into the pocket of his dress blue uniform jacket and removed a small box.

"Katherine Rosemary McBride," he said looking up at her while kneeling on one knee in front of her. "Would you do me the honor of becoming my wife?"

Katy was trembling and tears were spilling out onto her cheeks. She wanted to scream "Yes!", but she was afraid she was not going to be able to speak at all. She took a deep breath, swallowed, and with as much control as she could muster, she looked down at him, and through her tears said, "Lieutenant Baxter Underwood, I would be honored to call you my husband."

Woody stood up opened the small box and removed a beautiful diamond ring. He took Katy's left hand and slid the ring onto her ring finger. Woody took her in his arms looked down at his fiancé, who was now beginning to sob, and said, "Just shut up and kiss me will ya." And they kissed, a long loving kiss, a commitment kiss.

"We have to tell Poppa," Katy said excitedly.

"Now? It's almost one o'clock in the morning."

"Yes, now!" She said laughing, taking him by the hand, and bursting through the back door into the kitchen. As they got to the base of the stairs and started to climb them, they were stopped in their tracks by a voice from the parlor.

"Well, did you say yes?" It was her grandfather.

She turned and looked at Woody. "Did you tell him?" She asked.

"No," he replied.

They went into the parlor and found her grandfather, Michael McBride, seated in his favorite chair. He smiled up at the happy couple and asked again, "Well, did ya?"

"Did I what?" Asked Katy.

"For God's sake girl!" He said slowly coming to his feet. "Are you going to marry the boy or not?"

"Oh!" She said laughing as she started nodding her head up and down repeatedly. "Yes, yes I did, I mean I am!" She stuck out her hand to show her grandfather her ring. "Isn't it beautiful?" She said.

"Yes," he said as he reached out and took his granddaughter into his arms. "It certainly is." When he released Katy he turned to Woody and stuck out his hand. "Congratulations son," he said as Woody eagerly took his hand. Then Michael McBride pulled Woody toward him and the two men embraced as well. "You know," he said. "I knew all along that this was going to happen."

"Did you?" Asked Katy.

"I did," he said with a smile. "Because I knew that our young lieutenant here was serious that first night when he said that how you two met would be a funny story you could someday tell your grandchildren."

They all laughed.

"But how did you know he was going to ask me tonight?" Katy asked her grandfather.

"Well," he answered with a smile. "When I man tells a woman she's going to have a day she's never going to forget only one of two things are probably going to happen, and one of them is a proposal."

"What's the other?" She asked.

"Well," he answered again, with a bigger smile. "If it was the other, I'd be getting down the shotgun!"

It took Katy a minute. "Poppa!" She exclaimed as her grandfather and Woody laughed, although the nervousness in Woody's laugh was evident.

Later, after Michael McBride had gone off to bed, Woody and Katy decided that they were not going to be able to sleep. Eventually they found themselves sitting on the bench on the back porch under a blanket watching as the slowly rising sun, still below the horizon, began to chase the stars away. Katy, with her bare feet and legs tucked up under her, was nestled against Woody with her head resting on his chest. Woody had his arm around her holding her close.

He gently kissed her on the top of her head, and began to gently and lovingly caress her arm. "I think your ears are the perfect size," He said.

She lifted her head and looked up at him not sure she heard him right. "What?"

"Oh, nothing," he chuckled. "You know what I can't wait to do once we're married though?" Woody whispered huskily.

"Woody!" She exclaimed blushing brightly.

Woody pointed out into the yard laughed, and said, "Get rid of that demonic truck and buy you a car with a comfortable ride." He looked down at Katy with a mischievous smile and said, "What did you think I meant?"

Katy was bright red and stuttering.

"Just shut up and kiss me will ya?" He said rescuing her from her embarrassment.

And she did.

Chapter 32

The Delaware
1864

It was early January, 1864, Michael McBride and his father, bundled up against the cold on the seat of the open wagon, were returning from Burlington, to the family farm along the banks of the Rancocas Creek. They had gone to Burlington to drop off a plow blade that needed to be repaired in time for spring. While there they had picked up some sacks of flour and other dried goods.

"Pa," Michael said. "You remember a few years ago, before the war, when we were in Burlington and listened to that lawyer from Camden talk about President Lincoln?"

"Yeah?" Said William McBride as he looked over at his son who was looking straight ahead as the two mules pulled the wagon along the Burlington Road.

"You remember on the way home we talked about whether or not there was going to be a war, and about how wars affected people? People who didn't even fight in them? You said that you felt like you might have let the people down who went off to fight in Mexico, because you didn't go, and that you wondered, even now, if you'd done the right thing. Do you remember?"

William sighed, "What's on your mind son?"

"You said that if war did come it wouldn't be my war, because I was too young. Well," Michael continued. "The war has lasted a lot longer than everybody thought it would, and it doesn't look like it's going to be over any time soon."

"Do we have to talk about this now?" Interrupted William who did not like where this conversation was going.

"Yeah, Pa, we do," said Michael turning to face his father. "I'll be turning 18 next month, so as it turns out, this is going to be my war. I intend to enlist, and I'd like your permission and blessing."

"And if I don't give it?"

"I'll be disappointed, but I intend to enlist anyway."

"Without my permission?"

"Yes Sir."

"It's that important to you?"

"Yes Sir."

"Why?" Asked William McBride.

"Because I know that you believe you made the wrong decision back then, and that for over twenty years you have been saddened and tormented by it. Well, twenty years from now I would rather not have that torment."

"And what if you're making the wrong decision about this war? About your war? Just like I made the wrong decision about my war."

"Well then, I suppose it'll be just something else I have in common with my father," answered Michael grinning at his father.

"And if you get wounded or killed? What then?"

"I believe that if I don't go I'll have a wound that will never heal, and if I do go? Well, I'll hope that the almighty will be watching over me."

William McBride turned and looked out across the fields away from his son. "Someday," he said. "You're going to be a father, and I hope that, should you have a son, that he'll make you as proud of him, as I am of you right now." Then he wiped his nose on the sleeve of his heavy coat, looked at his son, smiled, and said, "This wind is making my eyes tear up and my nose run."

"Yeah, me too," said Michael McBride taking his gloves off and wiping his eyes.

"You'll have my permission," said William, "but, not my blessing."

"Fair enough," said Michael. "Thank you."

"You can tell your mother tomorrow evening after dinner."

"Me?"

"Well, you didn't think I was going to did you?" Laughed William. "Besides, if you're going to be a soldier you might as well start working on your courage now. Be a good way of preparing yourself for battle."

Matthew tried to tell his mother as gently as he could about his decision to enlist when he turned 18 in March. Her immediate response was a tearful promise to do all in her power to prevent it. When she learned that her husband had given his permission, the roof came off.

It took most of the evening, and it was not pretty, or easy, but finally, realizing that she was fighting a losing battle, Joanna McBride accepted that her son, Michael J. McBride, was going to war. She made it quite clear that she did not like it, and that she was not giving her permission, only that she saw no way to stop it. Everything she ever knew about being a mother changed that night.

"If something happens to our son." She said to her husband later that night as they laid side by side neither one able to sleep. "I will never forgive you, and worst of all, I will never forgive myself." She rolled onto her side, away from her husband, and quietly wept.

On March 22nd, the day after Michael McBride turned 18, he rode a mule from Rancocas to Beverly, formerly Dunk's Ferry, and enlisted in the United States Army at the recruiting office just outside the gates of Camp Cadwallader. He was told to return on April 1st, and report to the mustering officer inside the camp to be formally inducted and to begin his training. To both Michael and his parents, those ten days were both the longest and the shortest they had ever known.

With the clothes on his back, and a small satchel holding a single change of clothes, Michael reported to Camp Cadwallader. He was accompanied by his mother Joanna and his father William. They had insisted on seeing him off.

Joanna McBride, though her mother's heart was broken, shed only a few tears when she hugged her only son and bid him farewell. She had promised herself that she would be brave and not let her son's memory of her be that of a blubbering hysterical woman. She proudly kept that promise, but only on the outside.

William McBride helped his wife back onto the wagon and then turned to say goodbye to his son. Father and son stood looking at each other, neither one speaking, until they finally reached out and embraced. When they broke the embrace William held his son at arm's length and clearing his throat said, "I was going to tell you to be a good boy, but you're not a boy anymore are you, so be the man I know you to be, and come home to us safe and sound." Then he climbed up onto the wagon nodded to his son, slapped the reins across the backs of the two mules, and drove off, leaving Michael standing alone in front of the entrance to the camp on Broad Street. It was just after noon on a Friday.

"Well, you coming in boy, or you just gonna stand there whimpering after your mammy and pappy?" Came a voice.

Michael turned and for the first time noticed that there was a sentry at the camp's gate. The sentry did not look that much older than he was, and it was obvious that the uniform, that was a little on the large side, was new. The sentry was trying to look tough, but he wasn't pulling it off very well.

"I guess I'm coming in," said Michael as he walked towards the gate.

"Halt!" Said the sentry bringing the rifle, which looked too big for him, up to the position of port arms and stepping in front of Michael. "State your business."

"You just asked me if I was coming in," said a confused Michael. "So other than coming in, what other business could I state?" The sentry maintained his position. "I'm supposed to report to the mustering officer," said an agitated Michael. "Is that business enough?"

"You got any papers?" Asked the sentry with as much authority as he could muster.

"I got the letter they gave me when I enlisted that says I'm to report back here today. You want to see it?"

Michael could see that the sentry was thinking about what his answer should be. "No," he said. "Long as you got the letter." He brought the rifle back down to his side. "You may pass," he said.

"Where do I go?" Michael asked.

"Go into the barracks," said the sentry tilting his head and rolling his eyes to indicate it was the large three-story brick building directly behind him, "and ask for Sergeant Prettyman."

"Alright," said Michael, then he stuck out his hand and with a smile said. "My name's Michael, Michael McBride."

The sentry just sighed and gave him a disparaging look. "Don't you know nothin'?" He said. "Sentries ain't allowed to engage in idle chit-chat. I said you could pass, so pass."

"Sorry," said Michael dropping his hand. "Well, here I go," he said giving the sentry a final nod and starting up the steps to the front door of what he now knew to be the barracks building. Michael thought he remembered that before the war the building had been some sort of factory.

Sergeant Prettyman was not a friendly man, but he did not seem like a bad sort. Michael was taken into a large room with two rows of long tables with chairs. He was told to have a seat and wait. The sergeant left.

Several minutes later a young officer entered the room and sat down across from Michael. He had a number of papers with him that he began sorting and laying out in front of him. He said something, but Michael didn't hear him. Michael's attention was drawn to the officer's left sleeve. It was empty and pinned up to his shoulder.

Michael tried very hard not to stare but didn't seem to be able to help himself. The officer who was a lieutenant, noticed. "Gettysburg," he said without looking up. "With the 13th New Jersey. Cemetery Ridge. Ball ricocheted off a rock in a stone wall, hit me in the upper arm and shattered the bone."

"Does it hurt?" Michael felt like an idiot the instant the words left his mouth, but it was too late. "I...I...I'm sorry," he muttered as he dropped his head in embarrassment and shame.

"That's alright," said the lieutenant looking up and smiling. "No, it doesn't hurt. Thing is though, sometimes it itches like hell, but," and he reached over with his right hand and lifted the empty sleeve, "there's nothing there to scratch."

Michael could only nod.

"Now," he said turning his attention back to the papers. "Private Michael J. McBride, let's get you inducted so I can get back to my juggling."

"I thought there'd be a lot more people," said Michael.

"There will be. You're just a little early. This place will be nearly full by the end of the day."

When the paperwork was done Sergeant Prettyman reappeared and led Michael up to the third floor of the building and into a wide open room with large drafty windows all along each wall. There was a wood burning stove at each end of the room for heat, but the room was still cold. The room was filled with three rows of two-tier wooden bunk beds that looked more like shelving than beds. There was about three feet on each side of the beds, and about ten feet between each row.

Michael guessed that the room would hold upwards of 100 men. Most of the beds along the back wall were already made up. As they passed, Michael could see that there was a sheet, pillow, and blanket on each bed. There were also knapsacks and haversacks hanging from pegs at the end of most of the made up bunks.

Michael followed Sergeant Prettyman to almost the end of the middle row. He pointed to a lower bunk and told him that that would be his home until he left Camp Cadwallader. The platform was made of wood. The mattress was rolled up at the head of the bed and when Michael unrolled it he found that it was thin and well-used, as was the pillow, which was rolled up in the mattress, along with a worn but clean sheet. There was a heavy woolen blanket on the bed that appeared to be new.

"The blanket is yours," said the sergeant. "Everything else stays here when you leave. First thing you do every morning is make up your bunk. If you want to know how, ask one of the recruits who have been here a while. If you do it wrong I'll rip it apart, and I'll keep ripping it apart until you get it right.

"The bugler will sound mess call for supper at five o'clock. The mess is the one story building across the parade ground. If you don't know what mess call sounds like you'll learn or go hungry. Otherwise just follow someone who knows.

"Some of your mates are already here, and the rest should be coming in today. Reveille is at 5:30, tomorrow. There are water barrels, and pumps in front of the mess, and the latrines are to the left of the mess along the railroad tracks. Assembly will sound at seven o'clock. You will have washed, dressed, fed, and will be standing in formation on the parade ground before the bugler is finished blowing it. You will not be late.

"You and the other new recruits will get issued your kit tomorrow, then you'll join the rest of the recruits to begin your training. Until tomorrow you're on your own, but don't leave camp." The sergeant pointed to a slate board that was hanging on one of the bed posts. "Write your last name in chalk on the slate. If you can't write find somebody who can.

"Also, this is an induction and training center, so the place is crawling with officers. You don't approach 'em, you don't talk to 'em, you don't even look at 'em. Got it? Good.

"I'm your sergeant, not your friend. If you're dying, or you see someone else dying, let me know. Otherwise stay out of my way and don't talk to me." With that the sergeant turned and left.

Michael studied how the bunks that were already done were made, and after several tries was satisfied with how his turned out. As he was finishing other recruits, escorted by Sergeant Prettyman began arriving. Some were alone, others were in groups. It didn't matter, everyone got the exact same speech from Sergeant Prettyman that Michael did.

Michael walked around introducing himself and helping out with the beds or just getting acquainted. Most of them were about his age and seemed friendly enough. Although there were a few who Michael felt uneasy around.

A little after four o'clock the recruits who were coming off duty and had already been in camp, at least for a few days, began to arrive in the barracks. Michael watched as the sentry, minus his gun, who had been manning the gate when he arrived came into the barracks and sat down on the bunk directly across the aisle from his. As he suspected, the sentry, like him, was just a recruit.

"Is idle chit-chat allowed now?" Asked Michael. The sentry, a little embarrassed, glanced quickly at Michael and then turned away. "If so I'll offer my hand again," said Michael with a smile crossing the aisle.

The sentry did not look at Michael, but he did reach out and take Michael's hand. "As I said before," said Michael. "My name's Michael, Michael McBride."

The sentry looked up and nodded. "Name's Frank," he said. "Frank Jefferson."

"I'm from Rancocas," said Michael. "Where you from?"

"Kingston," he said. "Ain't never heard of Rancocas."

"It's only about six miles from here, my family's got a farm there. Where's Kingston?"

"Up north, near Princeton."

"How'd you end up down here?" Asked Michael.

"Kinda nosy ain't ya?"

"We're going to be together for a while, figured we might as well get to know each other.

Frank sighed, smiled up at Michael and nodded. "Guess you're right," he said. "Pa works the railroad, ain't never home, and ma passed just after the New Year. Didn't have nobody else. So, I figured I'd make my way to Philadelphia, lots of building going on there. I'm a pretty good carpenter. Thought maybe I could get me an apprenticeship or something.

"Got waylaid by a couple of ugly brutes in Bordentown who took most everything I had, money, food, clothes. By the time I got here I was too cold, hungry, and tired, to keep going, so I joined up," said Frank. "Been warm, fed, and rested ever since." He laughed. "Probably end up being the best damned decision I ever made, long as I don't get myself killed."

"When did you get here?"

"About four days ago. There was about 20 of us come in that day. They issued us our kits the second day, taught me how to properly hold a rifle and stand a guard yesterday, and put me on sentry duty today. I'm a regular ol' veteran already!" He laughed, and Michael joined in.

"You certainly did look fearsome out there, that's for sure," teased Michael.

"You probably couldn't tell," Frank said with a smile, "but, I had no idea what I was doing. The rifle wasn't even loaded! Hellfire!" He continued. "I didn't have any cartridges or caps, or nothin', not even a bayonet! If old Bobby Lee himself had tried to come through that gate the only thing I coulda done to stop him was bite him!" The two recruits nearly fell over from laughing.

Frank showed Michael around the camp. The barracks building they were in was in the southeast corner of the camp. There were a number of single story wooden barracks buildings on the north side of the camp, but these appeared to be empty. The word was that the camp was soon to be converted into a hospital and would no longer be a mustering in or training site.

Frank showed Michael where the mess, and the latrines were. Taught him how to recognize some of the bugle calls, and told him to make sure he got his water from the pumps, and not to use the stale water in the barrels. Sometimes people would spit, or worse, in the barrels.

Frank was nearly a year older than Michael. He had a good sense of humor, laughed easily, and didn't seem to take life too seriously. Michael McBride was glad that he had met Frank Jefferson and was convinced that he and Frank were going to become good friends.

By nightfall, just as the one armed lieutenant had said, the barracks was pretty much full. The next morning, at 7:00am, Michael and the rest of the new recruits, Michael figured they numbered about 200, were on the parade ground. Frank, and the recruits who had been in camp for a few days were carrying out duties elsewhere.

The new recruits aligned themselves in what they considered a proper formation. However, it was quickly obvious when Sergeant Prettyman showed up, that he did not agree. With the help of two other sergeants, and four enthusiastic corporals, they were pushed, prodded, and kicked until the formation was to his satisfaction.

It couldn't be considered marching, it wasn't very pretty, and didn't look very military, but they were all moved across the compound to one of the warehouses which were on the west side of the camp. Here they were placed in single file and one by one sent through a door on the end of the building. They were about to be issued their kit.

When Michael, like everyone else, came out the far side of the building he was carrying a large cotton sack, and a sheet of paper on which there was a list of everything the sack contained. He had put an "x" next to every item on the list when it was dropped into his sack. He had, drawers, socks, shoes, a uniform shirt and trousers, sack coat, forage cap, and belt, all one of each. Also in the sack was a knapsack, and a haversack containing a lice comb, sewing kit, mucket, tin plate, and cup. He also received a canteen, cartridge box with a musket tool, a cap box, and a bayonet with scabbard.

It took over two hours for everyone to pass through the building. When they came out they were jostled back into formation in front of a raised platform. Standing on the platform was Sergeant Prettyman.

"Ladies," the Sergeant began when they were formed up. "With the exception of a musket, and ammunition, you have just been provided with everything you need to go to war. You are responsible for it, but you don't own it. The Army owns it, just like it now owns you. You will now be marched back to the barracks. You will go inside and change into your newly issued uniform. You will wear nothing you were not issued today. You will put on your Army drawers, socks, shirt, trousers, belt, shoes, cap, and coat. Do not put on your canteen, knapsack, haversack, cartridge box, cap box, or bayonet scabbard. You will neatly place these things and everything else, including your list of issued items, in your knapsack and haversack, and neatly hang these on the pegs at the end of your bunks. The sacks in which you are carrying everything, once empty, will be placed in the barrels at the end of each floor." With his hands on his hips he looked the recruits over then shook his head from side to side. "What a sorry lot," he said, then he turned to his assistants. "Move 'em out," he said and with a barrage of obscenities, constant pushing, and an occasional kick, the sergeants and corporals began herding the formation back towards their barracks.

When they arrived at the barracks Sergeant Prettyman, who always seemed to be one step ahead of them, appeared in front of them again. "In 45 minutes," he said. "Assembly will sound. You will be in uniform, and in formation on the parade ground before the bugler is finished blowing it. You will not be late. Now, when I say dismissed, you will fall out in an orderly manner and enter the barracks in single file," he sighed, looked over the formation, and quietly said, "Dismissed."

When Michael got to his bunk, he noticed that his mattress and all of his bedding had been pulled off the bunk and tossed into the middle of the aisle, along with just about everybody else's. He was really disappointed, he had thought that he had done a good job of making up his bunk. Frank's had not been tossed and Michael actually thought that his bunk was better made than Frank's.

Michael had set his sack down and was preparing to pick up his bedding when Sergeant Prettyman appeared. As he was walking by, he kicked Michael's bedding out of his way, and said, "Nobody's supposed to get it right the first time."

Michael couldn't help but laugh to himself as he hurried to get his uniform on and the rest of his gear put away.

When they reformed on the parade ground Michael noticed that they were joined by Frank and the other recruits. There were several recruits whose uniforms were obviously either exceedingly too large or too small. These individuals were turned over to one of the corporals and taken back to the quartermaster to be issued better fitting attire.

They were organized into two companies, Company A, and Company B. There were 92 recruits in each company. Michael and Frank were in Company A. Sergeant Prettyman was in overall command. Each company was assigned one of the other sergeants and two corporals.

There were a variety of other officers, sergeants, and soldiers around the camp, who occassionally spoke with Sergeant Prettyman, or stood and observed as the recruits were indoctrinated into military life, but other than that had little if anything to do with them. It seemed there were always groups of soldiers and civilians coming and going but no one knew why. The world of Company A, and Company B, was ordained over by Sergeant Prettyman.

For the rest of the morning, they were given a crash course in military protocol. How to tell the difference between officers and non-commissioned officers, how and when to salute and address them, how to respond when they were addressed, and how to come to attention whenever an officer entered a room. Michael reckoned the safest thing to do until he figured it all out was to salute, and call everybody "Sir". However, he soon learned that Sergeant Prettyman, the sergeants, and corporals did not take kindly to being saluted and addressed as "Sir".

That afternoon, and the entire next day the companies were drilled individually in basic marching techniques. They endlessly practiced getting into and out of formation and dressing their lines. Staying in step by marching "left-right", "left-right", and moving as a unit.

On Sunday, there was a non-denominational church service held in the mess which every recruit was required to attend. There would be no drilling on Sunday, but they were expected to wash their uniforms and other laundry, clean the barracks, and see to the latrines. Though not ordered to do so, they were strongly encouraged to write letters home, and tell family and friends how well the Army was taking care of them.

On Monday morning they were told to wear their cartridge boxes, cap boxes, and bayonet scabbards with bayonet. They were lined up and told that they were going to be receiving muskets. As they excitedly walked past the door of the armory by company, one of A Company's two corporals, whose names they knew now to be Kendricks and Vincent, handed each of them a wooden plank. Each plank was 56 inches long and shaped like an elongated triangle. The "stock" end was about 6 inches wide, while the "muzzle" end was about 2 inches wide. They were cut from oak and it was made very clear that they were to be treated with the same care and respect as an actual weapon.

After spending all day Monday and Tuesday on the same basic marching drills, now armed with their wooden weapons, on Wednesday, they began to get into more complicated maneuvers, not only individually, but with the two companies drilling together. Moving from columns to line of battle, wheeling right and left, marching to the rear, deploying skirmishers and flankers. They also began working on the manual of arms, learning how to handle their wooden weapons so they would be prepared to handle the real ones when they got them. When they had finished drilling on Saturday, they lined up in front of the same large shed and turned in their wooden weapons. Michael thought this was unusual since for the entire week they had been keeping them in the racks in the barracks. The joke was that they had to turn them in because the Army was afraid they might shoot splinters into each other if they got to keep them.

On Monday morning they were again marched to the armory and lined up outside the door. They were all expecting to have their wooden rifles returned to them. This time however, as they passed by, Corporal Kendricks handed each of them a brand new Springfield Model 1861 rifle. They were ordered to take the weapon and fall back into their formations with the weapon in the Parade Rest position. Since they had learned and practiced this with their wooden weapons, they knew exactly what to do.

Once all the weapons had been issued they were marched to one of the empty wooden barracks buildings. Inside they were taught about their weapons. They were taught to clean them, which they did for the first time that morning. They were taught the proper nomenclature for each section and part, how to care for them, and how to repair them if they should fail.

After the noon meal it was back to the drilling. This time while carrying real weapons. The weapons they would carry into battle. The weapons they would use, to kill other men.

On Tuesday, Michael's twelfth day in camp, they were broken into four groups of 48 men each. Each group was assigned a sergeant as an instructor. These were new sergeants who worked under the guidance of Sergeant Prettyman and were assisted by the two regular sergeants. These new sergeants were responsible for teaching them how to load and fire their rifles. Although no actual rounds would be loaded or fired.

While standing at attention, with their weapons at their side, they repeated out loud the step-by-step procedures for loading and firing their weapons as told to them by their instructors;

"One... Rifle in the left hand, butt on the ground, barrel pointed up.
"Two... Remove cartridge from cartridge box.
"Three... Tear off top of cartridge with front teeth.
"Four... Pour powder from cartridge into barrel.
"Five... Put ball in barrel push down with thumb, discard paper cartridge.
"Six... Draw rammer.
"Seven... Ram ball down into barrel until seated.
"Eight... Withdraw rammer and return to its proper location.
"Nine... Bring rifle up in front of body at angle with barrel   pointed up.
"Ten... Half cock rifle.
"Eleven... Remove cap from cap box.
"Twelve... Place cap on nipple.
"Rifle is ready to fire!
When given command...Ready...Aim...Fire!"

They spent the entire morning repeating this procedure over and over again with their weapons at their side. As the morning went by they were expected to do it faster and faster, not only committing the procedure to memory, but instilling it in themselves so that it would be as natural as breathing or walking. Periodically the instructor would single someone out and have them recite the procedure individually. Those who were unable to do so, were subject to extreme verbal abuse.

By the time they broke for the noon meal, they were verbally repeating the entire procedure in unison in about 20 seconds. The instructors said that that wasn't too bad for saying it, but 20 seconds was also how long it should take them to actually do it. A well trained infantryman should be able to load and fire three aimed shots every minute.

After the noon meal they began practicing the loading procedures with their weapons, but without cartridges or caps. They recited each step out loud as they performed it with their rifles. They started out very slowly, increasing their speed as the procedure became more familiar to them.

For the next two days, the routine was the same, marching drills in the morning, loading drills in the afternoon. It was not uncommon for Sergeant Prettyman or one of the instructors, sergeants, or corporals to walk up to a recruit at any time, and anywhere, and have him repeat the loading procedures as quickly as he could, and God help the recruit who faltered. Michael was finding that repeating the procedure in his head was chasing any other thoughts he might have out of it.

On Friday morning, Company A, began their marching drills, while Company B, lined up in front of the armory. Michael couldn't see what was going on, but after passing by the armory, Company B, formed up, and led by Sergeant Prettymen marched out the gate onto Broad Street, and turned north towards the center of Beverly. Were they on their way to the war already?

About an hour later there was the sound of a ragged volley being fired in the distance. "They killed the sons-a-bitches." Whispered someone behind Michael. It was all he could do to keep from laughing right out loud.

About ten minutes later another volley was heard, then another, and another, there were six volleys heard in all, each spaced about ten minutes apart. An hour later, Company B, returned to the camp. At the noon meal the recruits of Company A, learned that Company B, had been marched to the river bank and had fired six live rounds out across the Delaware River.

That afternoon, it was Company A's turn. The march from Camp Cadwallader to the Beverly riverfront was just under a mile. Michael was quite familiar with Beverly and enjoyed the familiar sites as Company B, proudly marched through the town.

There were some citizens on the street, and some waved and smiled, but mostly they were ignored. Apparently the good citizens of Beverly were becoming use to having soldiers in their midst.

On Saturday morning both companies were ordered to fall out in their Sunday uniforms. Which meant no rifle, no cartridge box, no cap box, and no bayonet scabbard. Just the uniform.

After forming up they were marched, quite smartly Michael thought, to the end of the parade ground where the raised platform was. They were put at Parade Rest, and waited. Sergeant Prettyman was on the platform, and he too was at Parade Rest.

"Attention!" Barked Sergeant Prettyman loudly as he too snapped to attention. Michael could see out of the corner of his eye a half a dozen men approaching on horseback. One he recognized as the one-armed lieutenant. There was a sergeant with large gold stripes on his sleeve going in both directions, several officers whose ranks Michael was not sure of, and an older officer with plenty of gold on his uniform, and gold stars on his shoulder. Even though he had never seen one before, Michael knew, this man was a general.

The general climbed the platform followed by the lieutenant, the sergeant, and the other officers. When he stepped onto the platform Sergeant Prettyman saluted and held the salute until it was returned by the general. The general walked over to the sergeant spoke with him and shook his hand.

The general walked to the front of the platform and turned and said something to the lieutenant who was alongside, and just behind him. The other sergeant and officers fell in alongside Sergeant Prettyman. "Companies…Parade Rest!" Shouted the lieutenant. And they did so, smartly.

"Good morning men." Began the General. "I am Brigadier General George Robeson. I am the Commanding Officer of Camp Cadwallader. I congratulate you on your enlistment, and on your commitment to our Union, and to our President.

"It is not the mission of Camp Cadwallader to fully train you as soldiers, but to instill in you a pride in yourselves, and in your service, and introduce you to military life. The training you receive here in marching and weaponry is very limited. Your real training will begin when you arrive at your individual units.

"You are replacements. When you leave here you will be sent to New Jersey units that have suffered losses due to battlefield casualties, illness, injuries, expiration of enlistments, or desertions. You will be separated and sent where ever needed.

"You mark the end of an era here at Camp Cadwallader. You are among the last troops who will ever be inducted and trained here. In a few short months Camp Cadwallader will become a military hospital.

"You will be departing Camp Cadwallader within the week. You will not be informed of the specific day until that day arrives. Therefore, when we are finished here you will be returned to your barracks where you will carry out the tasks and duties usually performed on Sundays.

"Tomorrow morning, immediately following church services, provided those tasks and duties have been carried out to Sergeant Prettyman's satisfaction, Sergeant Prettyman will issue each of you a pass which will permit you to leave Camp Cadwallader temporarily. That pass will expire at 6:00pm, tomorrow evening. If you fail to return at that time, you will be hunted down, arrested, and charged with desertion.

"While away from Camp Cadwallader you will conduct yourselves in a military manner so as not to bring embarrassment or shame upon yourself, your service, or your country. If upon your return you are found to be inebriated, or to have been brawling, or to have been engaging in immoral acts, or frequenting places where such acts are tolerated, you will be severely dealt with.

"You have embarked on an honorable crusade, do not tarnish it before it has even begun."

"Companies… Attention!" Ordered the lieutenant loudly as the general stepped back and executed a perfect about face.

Sergeant Prettyman saluted, and held the salute until the general had returned the salute, and the General, and his entourage had left the platform. They moved smartly to their horses, mounted, and rode off back towards the other end of the camp. This would be the one and only time the recruits would see Brigadier General Robeson.

While they were cleaning the barracks, some of the recruits jokingly complained that since the general had pretty much forbidden them to do anything that would have been worth doing, that the passes were worthless. Others wondered if there was even any place nearby where one could get a drink, or seek comfort from a fallen angel. Everyone seemed to be in a pretty good mood, and anxious about leaving Camp Cadwallader.

Michael convinced Frank to accompany him to the McBride farm in Rancocas the next day when they received their passes. He was certain that they could walk the six miles or so in two and a half to three hours, then after visiting for a few hours, his father could bring them back to the camp long before the passes expired. Frank was not too keen on the walk, but could not say no after Michael described what Sunday dinner was like in the McBride house.

The next morning, in their new uniforms, minus rifle, cartridge box, cap box, and bayonet scabbard, and with their passes in hand, Privates Michael McBride and Frank Jefferson set out for Rancocas. They had only walked about a mile and a half when they were picked up by a man and his wife from Beverly who were on their way to Mt. Holly to visit family. Their route would take them right past Hilyard's Lane, and the McBride farm.

It was not yet noon when they were dropped off at the head of Hilyard's Lane. The half mile walk to the house took less than fifteen minutes. Michael's father, William, was just coming out of the barn when they entered the yard.

"Cad a iontas iontach!"

"What a wonderful surprise!" Exclaimed William in the Irish upon seeing his son. "Your mother will be so happy!" He continued. "As am I! As am I!" Father and son embraced as Frank Jefferson tried to figure out exactly what was happening.

"This is my friend Frank," said Michael in the Irish when they broke their embrace.

"Welcome," said William as he extended his hand. "It's a pleasure to meet you."

Frank just stood there with a confused look on his face. He had no idea what anyone had said since they arrived at the farm.

William and Michael looked at each other and laughed. "I'm sorry," said Michael in English. "It has always been a tradition in our house to speak the Irish, the language of our ancestors, on Sundays."

"Oh," said Frank with a smile as he reached out and shook William's hand. "For a minute there I thought maybe I had fallen into a den of code speaking rebel spies."

"No, just a proud Irish family," said William as they shook hands, "but we'll suspend the tradition for today, in honor of your visit. Come on, let's go into the house."

With William leading they walked up onto the porch and into the kitchen. Joanna, the lady of the house, was at the fireplace, her back to the door, tending to a large kettle, and a Dutch oven.

"Look who's come to visit," said William as he entered the kitchen.

"San Irish de tu le do thoil."

"In the Irish if you please," answered his wife as she turned towards her husband. Upon seeing her son she gave a happy squeal and rushed to take him in her arms. "What are you doing here?" She continued in the Irish. "How long can you stay, and who is this?" She asked still clutching her son.

"We have a pass," answered her son in English. "We have to be back by six tonight, this is Frank Jefferson, and Pa said we could speak English so that Frank knows what's going on."

"Of course we can," she said finally releasing her son and turning towards their visitor. "Welcome Frank," she said with a smile as she reached out and squeezed his upper arm. "As you can see, we're very happy to see our son."

"Yes Ma'am," answered Frank with a smile, sadly being reminded of how much he missed his mother.

"Don't you both look so smart and handsome in your uniforms?" Said Mrs. McBride. "At least we'll have time to feed both of you properly and fill them uniforms out a little bit before we take you back."

At about four o'clock, after having a lovely visit, and eating until they were about to burst, Michael and Frank were driven back to Camp Cadwallader by Michael's father William. His mother had decided to say her goodbyes at the house, and having learned that Frank had recently lost his mother, she gave Frank the same goodbye hug and kiss that she gave to her own son. No one tried to hide their tears.

All the recruits were back by the six o'clock deadline, though a few of them cut it awfully close. Many of them had attended church services and suppers at one of the churches in Beverly, some had taken the train up to Burlington to explore that city, while others had just explored Beverly and the surrounding area. There were a few who bragged about getting away with some of the forbidden activities, but Michael had his doubts about the truth of those stories.

Reveille was at 5:30 the following morning, and the routine began all over again. Marching and formation drills in the morning, weapons drills in the afternoon. On Tuesday and Thursday the companies were marched individually to the banks of the Delaware where they again fired live rounds out across the water. This time however, instead of only six, each recruit got to load and fire thirty rounds.

At breakfast on Friday morning, Sergeant Prettyman told the recruits that when they fell out for assembly they were to bring everything they had been issued, including their blankets. They would not be returning to the barracks, nor would they be spending another night at Camp Cadwallader. Michael joined in as the men cheered, but he was sure, that just like him, many of them had mixed feelings about their departure.

At 7:00am, on the dot, they were perfectly formed up in front of Sergeant Prettyman who wore the same expression as he did the first day of their training when they had resembled more of a herd than a military unit. They had everything they would need to go to war, from their army issued underwear, to their Springfield rifles. Everything that is except ammunition.

Sergeant Prettyman called them to attention. "When you walk out that gate, you will no longer be recruits. You will be soldiers in the Union Army, and may God have mercy upon those who find themselves depending on your sorry butts."

With that Sergeant Prettyman, the two sergeants, and the two corporals marched Michael and the other soldiers out the gate and onto Broad Street, where they turned left and headed for the river. Just as they made the turn they all heard the sound of a steamship whistle, one long blast, two short blasts, and another long one.

"Hear that boys?" Said Sergeant Prettyman. "Sounds like our ride's here."

As the formation crossed Third Street, a quarter mile from the river, they could begin to see the large steam ship tied to the town wharf at the base of Broad Street. The smoke from its seventy foot high stack dissipated in the still morning air high above the waiting vessel. Michael, like most of his comrades, had never ridden on a steamship before.

Chapter 33

The Delaware
1864

The iron hulled *John A. Warner* was 220 feet in length, and had a beam of 28 feet. It was powered by a vertical beam engine that drove two 50 foot paddle wheels. The *Warner,* under the command of Captain Jonathan A. Cone, was the swiftest steamer on the Delaware and could make the trip from Beverly to the Chestnut Street Piers in Philadelphia in under one and a half hours.

The *Warner* had two main decks, both of which were mostly under cover. There was an uncovered area on the first deck that extended about fifty feet back from the bow. The wheelhouse was perched on the front of the second deck. Immediately below the wheelhouse on the main deck were several cabins. The area behind the cabins on the main deck was enclosed but was an open common area, the massive paddle wheels were outboard on each side of this area. Beyond the paddle wheels the main deck was covered, but open, as was most of the second deck.

The two companies of new soldiers boarded the ship in single file, and as they did their corporals were there to take their rifles and place them in racks along the bulkhead at the front of the enclosed portion of the main deck. After giving up their weapons they were directed to the second deck where they would remain during their voyage to Philadelphia. Sergeant Prettyman assigned six soldiers from each company to guard the weapons. Two at a time for a half hour each during the hour and half trip.

At 9:00am, with three short blasts of her whistle, the *John A. Warner* slowly pulled away from the Beverly wharf. The ship had been tied up facing north, so, as she slowly pulled out into the main channel she made a wide sweeping turn to port until she had swung entirely around and was facing south. Once in the channel she began to gather speed.

It was early March, and though the weather was relatively mild for the time of year, the speed of the ship was soon generating a chilling wind off of the open river. Though they were wearing their sack coats, the soldiers huddled together in the small area of the second deck that was partially enclosed, in an effort to stay warm. There wasn't much of an opportunity for sightseeing. The main deck would have been more comfortable, but that was reserved for the civilians who were onboard. It was just past 10:30, when the *Warner* signaled its arrival at the Chestnut Street piers with one long, two short, and one long blast of its whistle. Captain Cone brought the ship smartly alongside the pier and in what seemed like a few short minutes the ship was securely tied to the pier, and the passengers ready to disembark. The soldiers remained on the second deck until all of the civilians had gone ashore.

As they disembarked their weapons were returned to them and they were formed up into their two companies on the pier alongside the ship. Private Michael McBride was awestruck by the number of ships that lined the piers along the waterfront, and by the sight of building after building which seemed to go on forever as he tried to see what lay beyond the water's edge. The noise of the city was deafening and the smells though unpleasant, were somehow at the same time intoxicating.

They were met on the pier by a captain and two lieutenants. The captain spoke briefly with Sergeant Prettyman.

"Alright ladies!" Boomed Sergeant Prettyman's voice over all the other noises on the pier as he stood in front of the formation. "We're going to march about a mile to the Refreshment Saloon.

"People are going to be watching, so make sure you look sharp! Don't embarrass me. You won't like me if I get embarrassed. Let's move 'em out," he said turning to the two corporals. The captain took a position at the head of the formation, and each of the lieutenants fell in alongside one of the companies. As far as Michael could tell, other than the brief conversation the captain had had with Sergeant Prettyman, the captain and lieutenants spoke to no none.

It was only a short distance from the pier to Front Street. At Front Street they turned left and headed south. As the sergeant had said, there were people along the sides of the street, and they were smiling, cheering, and waving small American flags. Private Michael McBride marched proudly, as did the rest of the newly arrived soldiers from Fort Cadwallader.

Michael could see that there were other formations of blue uniformed soldiers also marching south several blocks ahead of them. When they passed the pier at Walnut Street he saw that there were more soldiers disembarking from a ferry. He was beginning to realize just how insignificant a part he was of this grand Union Army.

The Union Volunteer Refreshment Saloon of Philadelphia was located at the intersection of Swanson and Washington Streets. The column was brought to a halt, and placed at ease, at the intersection of Front and Washington Streets. As they waited their mouths began to water as the smells from the saloon filled the air.

Before long an older man slight in stature but well-dressed, approached the formation and spoke with the captain and Sergeant Prettyman. After speaking with the man Sergeant Prettyman called them to attention. The captain then turned and nodded to the man.

"Good day men," began the man. "My name is John Wilson, I am a volunteer here at the saloon, and it is an honor to have you brave soldiers here with us today. Soon you will be marched down to the food pavilions where you will be served a hot meal.

"Please feel free to eat and drink as much as you'd like. Mrs. Mary Lee, and Mrs. Hannah Baily, will be your hostesses so if there is anything you need just let them know. After you've had your fill, you may proceed to the commissary where you may fill your haversacks and knapsacks with a variety of fruits, baked goods, smoked meats, and personal supplies. Again, you may take as much as you'd like, but only if it fits into your haversack or knapsack. We ask that you not fill your pockets or carry anything out in your hands. Also, I don't believe your sergeant would appreciate it if you were to empty your haversack or knapsack of what has been issued to you by the Army, to make room for what you may find in the commissary.

"When you are done at the commissary, there are warehouses along the waterfront that have been converted to barracks. Your unit has been assigned a specific area within the barracks, and that information is being provided to your sergeant. Several units will be assigned to each building.

"While you are here we ask that you refrain from the use of intoxicating spirits, that you not smoke inside the barracks, and that you conduct yourselves as the gentlemen your uniforms and your bravery have shown you to be. There will be a church service on the green in front of the food pavilion at seven o'clock this evening, all are invited to attend.

"By tomorrow evening most of you will be on your way to your next destination. Please know that wherever your duties take you that you go there with our prayers for your safety and the hope that you may return to your homes and loved ones as soon as possible. Thank you." Mr. Wilson spoke briefly with the captain and Sergeant Prettyman again before turning and walking towards another formation that had just arrived on Washington Street.

"Listen up!" Barked Sergeant Prettyman. "We're assigned to barracks number two, section one. We're going down there now and you will stack arms outside the barracks. Then we will reform, and march back up here to the food pavilion.

"We will go through in single file, me first followed by A Company, then Corporal Kendricks followed by B Company, and Corporal Vincent will bring up the rear. Any of you misbehaves you'll have me to answer to. When you've finished eating and visiting the commissary see me in the barracks, I have your assignments for where you'll be headed from here. Alright, let's move 'em out," he said turning to the corporals. The captain and the two lieutenants disappeared, and they never saw them again. "Window dressing," is how Sergeant Prettyman would refer to them when asked about them later.

Private Michael McBride gorged himself on baked ham, boiled potatoes, and mashed carrots. He had several glasses of the deliciously sour lemonade, and several small sweet cakes. It reminded him of Christmas on the Rancocas, which was the last time he had eaten so much.

He could barely move as he made his way to the commissary. In addition to some more of the small sweet cakes, he stuffed his haversack with a good supply of dried beef jerky, and coffee. He also took a couple of bars of soap, a shaving brush, a razor, a bone toothbrush, and some tooth powder. As he was exiting the commissary there was a young girl handing out small Bibles. He took one of those as well. When he got back to the barracks, he went in search of his friend Frank Jefferson. The three warehouses turned barracks were huge two-story brick buildings on the east side of Swanson Street. The stacked wooden bunks inside the barracks were not unlike those that had been in the barracks at Camp Cadwallader in Beverly. Only here they were stacked four high instead of two. Michael estimated that each floor could probably accommodate 1,000 men.

Frank Jefferson had staked them out two lower bunks in their assigned area near a window. Frank was seated on one of the bunks rearranging the supplies he had picked up in the Commissary in his knapsack. He looked up and smiled at Michael as he approached.

"I think if I can move some things around I can get a few more treats in this thing," he said.

"I've got all I'm going to need," answered Michael. "Besides, anything you stuff in there, you're going to have to carry for who knows how far."

"I've got it on good authority," said Frank, "that when we leave here we'll be travelling by train, so if I can fit it on the train, the train will carry it for me."

"Okay," said Michael shaking his head, "but, we're foot soldiers, which means that at some point we're going to be walking."

"I guess you're right," said Frank, "but, I maybe can get a few more of them little cakes in here. They ain't heavy, and besides by the time we get off the train I'll probably have eaten them."

"Suit yourself," said Michael tossing his bulging knapsack and haversack onto his bunk. "What say we go in search of the sergeant and see if we can find out where we're headed?"

"You really want to know?"

"Yeah, don't you?"

"I suppose," answered Frank closing up his knapsack and getting up off the bunk.

They found Sergeant Prettyman seated outside at an open fire enjoying a cup of coffee, and a cigar. The two corporals were with him as well as another sergeant they had not seen before. He looked up as the two men approached.

"Jefferson and McBride," he said shaking his head. "I suppose you want to know where you're off to, to become heroes."

"Sure do," said Frank. "Somebody's gotta win this war."

"Yeah? Well, somebody's gotta lose it too," said the Sergeant eyeing the two young soldiers. "Tomorrow morning at five thirty, you'll be forming up out here on Swanson Street. You'll be marched into the city to the Philadelphia and Reading Railroad Terminal where you will board a train bound for Pottsville, Pennsylvania."

The two men looked at each other. "Then where?" Asked Michael.

"Well, that's when your adventure will really begin," answered the Sergeant sarcastically. "Next morning your train will continue on to beautiful Mauch Chunk."

"What the hell's in Mauch Chunk?" Asked Frank.

"The 10th NJ Infantry Regiment. You'll be joining up with them there."

"Where is Mauch Chunk?" Asked Michael.

"It's north of here," said the Sergeant. "So, turns out you two heroes are going to end up further north than you would have been if you'd stayed on the farm."

"Why Muck Chuck?" Asked Frank.

"Mauch Chunk," corrected Sergeant Prettyman. "Well, it seems several months ago some of those coal mining fellows decided they didn't want to be part of Mr. Lincoln's Army. So, a bunch of them got together and decided they wasn't going to be drafted, neither was they going to allow anybody else to be drafted.

"Couple of civilians got killed over it, there was some rioting, and the 10th New Jersey was sent in to keep the peace. That was in November. Couple of them miners were convicted and hanged. Trials are about over I would think, so who knows what's going to happen to the 10th now."

"Muck Chuck," said an obviously disappointed Frank. "There ain't no Rebs in Pottsville."

"Well, I wouldn't be too sure about that," said the Sergeant sarcastically. "If one of them Rebs gets lost down there in Virginia, he could wander the two hundred and fifty miles up north here where he could join up with them southern sympathizers up in good ol' Mauch Chunk and cause quite a little dust up."

"Shit," said Frank kicking at the dirt.

"Cheer up," said Sergeant Prettyman. "I haven't given you the best news yet."

The two men looked at the sergeant hoping for a reprieve from their disappointing news.

"I'm going with you," he said as he stood up and dumped what was left of his coffee onto the ground. "Yep, Mauch Chunk, Pennsylvania. On our way to save the Union," he grumbled and kicked over the stool he had been sitting on.

The next morning, having marched two and a half miles from the barracks on Swanson Street, Private Michael McBride along with Private Frank Jefferson, Sergeant Prettyman, and twenty other soldiers from Camp Cadwallader, arrived at the Philadelphia and Reading Railroad Terminal, at the corner of North Broad and Cherry Streets. Just before seven thirty, they climbed into a boxcar for the three and a half hour trip to Pottsville. The boxcar had sliding doors on each side, and a large bucket at each end which was supposed to serve as the necessary for the twenty-five soldiers on board. They kept the doors closed in an effort to keep out as much of the soot and smoke from the engine as possible, and Sergeant Prettyman promised to bodily throw from the train any man who tried to make use of the buckets.

When they arrived in Pottsville their boxcar was put on a siding. They were told that the next morning they would be hooked up to another train that would take them the rest of the way to Mauch Chunk, and the 10th New Jersey. The trip of nearly sixty miles would take about two and a half hours.

Less than a half mile from the siding was a camp that had been built by the 10th New Jersey Regiment for their stay in Pottsville. The camp was laid out in a grid, and consisted of about 75 rustic 12x12 clapboard huts with small stone fireplaces. It was on an eight acre tract of land between Greenwood and Jefferson streets that the Army had leased from the Yuengling family who owned and operated a brewery in the area. With temperatures dropping into the twenties overnight, Michael and the others were happy to have a place to get out of the weather where they could at least have a small fire.

Sergeant Prettyman reported their arrival to Captain Charles McChesney of the 10th New Jersey's G Company. The nearly 200 men of Captain Chesney's G Company, and Captain George Scott's E Company, had been left in Pottsville to guard the railways, bridges, mines, and other sites and concerns important to the production and transportation of coal against southern sympathizers and saboteurs. In addition, they learned that Company A from the regiment was over in Cumberland County rounding up deserters and evaders who had failed to report for conscription.

Colonel Ryerson had taken the other three companies that formed the regiment and moved to Mauch Chunk to quell the riots and provide security during the trials of the men who had incited the riots and killed some of those who refused to support them. With the trials over the regiment had remained in Mauch Chunk to protect the citizens from further violence, and the interests of the coal mining companies. Captain McChesney told the Sergeant, that unfortunately he and his replacements would have to continue onto Mauch Chunk since that was where the regiment was now officially based.

At ten o'clock the next morning, they returned to their boxcar, and were hooked to the rear of a coal train headed for Mauch Chunk, and the 10th New Jersey Infantry Regiment. Again the sliding doors were closed this time to keep out the cold as well as the soot and smoke, and Sergeant Prettyman made it clear that the same rules applied regarding the buckets. A little after noon, they arrived at the Lehigh and Susquehanna Railroad Depot along the banks of the Lehigh River in Mauch Chunk.

Sergeant Prettyman had the twenty two soldiers in his command form up on the platform once they exited the boxcar. Once in formation, Michael noticed that there was a sergeant peering at them out of one of the depot's windows. There also seemed to be an unusually large number of soldiers in uniform wandering the streets of the town.

The sergeant who had been looking out the window came out onto the platform and approached Sergeant Prettyman. "Name's Johnson," he said extending his hand.

"Prettyman," said the Sergeant taking the man's hand.

"You must be the replacements come up from Philadelphia."

"That's us."

"Captain Evans of D Company said you'd be coming. I'll send someone to get him. Just have your guys stand at ease 'til he gets here."

"Appreciate it," said Sergeant Prettyman. "You heard the man," he said turning towards the troops. "Stand at ease while we see what's what."

Sergeant Johnson went back to the depot door and yelled to someone inside. Then he rejoined Sergeant Prettyman and the two men walked to the far edge of the platform to smoke and talk. They were just finishing their smoke when a captain, accompanied by another sergeant, arrived at the station on horseback.

The two sergeants came to attention and saluted. The captain returned the salute and dismounted. "Well, I see our replacements have finally arrived," he said glancing towards the formation on the platform. "Although there doesn't appear to be near enough of them."

"Yes Sir," said Sergeant Johnson. "This here is Sergeant Prettyman. He's with 'em."

"Welcome to the 10th NJ Prettyman," said the captain as he removed his gauntlets.

"Thank you Sir," said Sergeant Prettyman as he handed the Captain the packet that contained their orders and other documents.

"I'm Captain Evans. I've got D Company," said the Captain as he took the packet. "You're being assigned to me along with some of these other men. The others have been assigned to other companies and I have a list of the assignments here for you." The Captain removed a document from inside his heavy uniform coat and handed it to Sergeant Prettyman. "Break them down by company and Sergeant Johnson here will have someone take each group to where they need to be. After you're settled come to see me. I'm in the American Hotel right up the street there on Broadway. Sergeant Johnson will know where to find me."

"Yes Sir. Thank you Sir," said Sergeant Prettyman. Salutes were again exchanged and Captain Evans returned to his horse and, with the sergeant who had accompanied him, rode off back towards the center of the town of Mauch Chunk.

When Sergeant Prettyman returned to the troops and read the names off the list Captain Evans had given him, Michael McBride found out that he along with Frank Jefferson, Philip Anson, Ira Corey, and Martin Stafford, were being assigned to H Company. Sergeant Johnson told them that H Company was part of the 2nd Battalion, and was commanded by Captain John Cunningham. A private, who looked none too happy about being out in the cold, walked up onto the platform and approached Sergeant Johnson.

"This is Private Kemble," said Sergeant Johnson. "Of H Company. You five go with him. He'll take you to where you need to be."

"Follow me," muttered Kemble who was barely audible from inside his heavy coat with the collars pulled up so tight that they almost completely concealed his face.

They walked a short distance north on the street the train depot was on to a large three story wooden building. Michael estimated the building was about 120' long by about 50' wide. They entered through a door on the southeast corner of the building and found themselves inside a large dark barracks with rows and rows of two-tiered bunks. The wooden floors and the wooden bunks appeared to be of recent construction, but the walls were black and oily, and there was a strange smell that though familiar, Michael could not quite identify.

"H Company's on the far end of the third floor," said their escort Kemble as he started to climb a set of stairs that also appeared to be of recent construction. When they got to H Company's area Kemble told them to find empty bunks and let him know where they were. When they were done he would take them to see H Company's First Sergeant, Sergeant Hoffman.

Sergeant Hoffman, and all the other non-coms were housed on the first floor. There were three companies of the 10th NJ in Mauch Chunk, and each company had a First Sergeant. All the First Sergeants, by virtue of their rank, had small private rooms. Private Kemble knocked on the door that had a large H painted in the center of it.

"Yo!" Boomed a voice from behind the door.

"Private Kemble, First Sergeant. I've got the new replacements with me."

"Be right out."

Sergeant Hoffman was a tall powerfully built man with dark hair he wore brushed straight back, and a full but well-trimmed dark beard. He had frighteningly intense grey eyes that looked out from under dark bushy eyebrows. His voice was not loud, but it was a voice of authority, a voice that demanded attention, and compliance.

"Who you got here Kemble?" Asked Sergeant Hoffman as he stood in the doorway of the small room.

"Anson, Corey, Jefferson, McBride, and Stafford, First Sergeant," said Kemble pointing to each man as he announced their names.

"Alright," said the Sergeant visually appraising each of them in turn. "Listen up, because I'm only going to go through this once. You are now in the 10th New Jersey Infantry Regiment. Our current strength is about 618, including officers and non-coms. Your Commanding Officer is Colonel Henry Ryerson. The Regiment consists of two battalions. You are in H Company which is part of the 2nd Battalion which is commanded by Major James McNeely. H Company is commanded by Captain John Cunningham.

"Now, let me make one thing perfectly clear. Those officers I have just named? You have zero contact with unless you come through me first. Even if you only want to kiss their asses, your lips better still be warm from kissing mine first. Clear? Good.

"Anson, Corey, you're being assigned to Lieutenant Herring's 2nd Platoon. Jefferson, McBride, you'll be with Lt. Ryan's 3rd Platoon, and Stafford you're 4th Platoon with Lt. Baldwin.

"Get settled in, I'll let your Lieutenants know you're here and they'll have your squad sergeants run you down. That's all." With that Sergeant Hoffman went back inside his room and closed the door.

"Hoff's tough, but he's fair," said Private Kemble as they started back towards the third floor. "I'm in Third Platoon too," he said turning his attention to Michael and Frank. "Wonder what squad they'll put you in? I'm in Second Squad. We only got six guys, so we sure could use a couple."

Private William Kemble, who seemed to be warming to the new arrivals, helped Michael and Frank get settled. He showed them where the mess was, the latrines, and introduced them to other members of H Company. Kemble, who was a few years older than Michael, was from Beverly, and although he did not recall ever having met Michael personally, he did know some of the same people from Rancocas and Beverly that Michael knew.

They also learned that their barracks used to be a coal shed and that although the floors had been replaced, the exterior walls, which had been whitewashed, were original. This explained the number of areas where black oily residue could still be seen, and the smell. Smoking was not permitted in the building, and what little bit of heat there was, was provided by three coal burning stoves on each floor that were tended 24-hours a day. So, that odor Michael had smelled when he first entered the building was coal dust. He decided it would be best to get out of the barracks whenever possible.

Michael and Frank did get assigned to William Kemble's Second Squad, and got to meet their sergeant, Sergeant Cheeseman during breakfast the next morning. Where Sergeant Hoffman was what you would expect an Army Sergeant to look like, Sergeant Cheeseman was what you would expect your favorite uncle to look like. He was lean, of average height, well groomed, and had a voice better suited for a preacher than a sergeant.

"Cheesey's good people," said Kemble. "Just do what you're told and keep your nose clean and you'll never have any trouble from him, and oh yeah, don't ever let him hear you call him Cheesey." He laughed.

After breakfast, the twenty seven men who made up the three squads that were the Third Platoon under Lieutenant John Ryan formed up in front of the train depot. They had been assigned to walk the three and a half miles of track from Mauch Chunk south to Lehighton along the Lehigh River to insure that the tracks hadn't been tampered with. They would ride a local work train back from Lehighton to Mauch Chunk.

For the next couple of weeks Michael McBride, spent his days doing marching drills, shooting drills, inspecting tracks, guarding mine shafts, coal sheds, coal trains, bridges, road intersections, and business offices. He eventually became familiar, if not friendly, with most of the other members of H Company, and some of the other companies as well. He wrote home often, and regularly received letters in return. Frank Jefferson, who had no family to write to him, enjoyed Michael's letters from home almost as much as Michael did. Michael decided that provost duty was boring, and though it had not been what Michael was looking for when he joined the Army, he was content.

Then, on April 5, 1864, things began to change. The three companies of the 10th New Jersey Regiment, over 300 strong, boarded trains and headed back to Pottsville. Their days of provost duty were over. In Pottsville they would rejoin with Companies E and G, and gather up A Company when they passed through Harrisburg, PA, on the 6th.

The 10th New Jersey, now at its full strength of 618, was to make its way south, by rail, to Washington, DC, arriving on April 7th. They were to become part of Major General John Sedgwick's VI Corps. The Regiment was to be assigned to the VI Corps' First Division as part of the First New Jersey Brigade.

On April 18th, the Regiment marched from Washington to Centreville, VA. On the 20th, it was on to Warrenton. It was not lost on Michael, or many of the others in the Regiment, that during their march they crossed the fields on which some of the heaviest fighting in the early days of the war had been waged. Fields on which many a good man, blue and gray, had died in pursuit of a cause in which they believed. Though it was sad, Michael also thought it served as a reminder of the reasons why they must continue this crusade of freedom, so that the men who fell on these fields shall not have died in vain. The mood of the Regiment was different after they crossed those fields, and for the rest of their lives, it never went back to what it had been before they did so.

On April 22, 1864, the 10th NJ Regiment arrived at Brandy Station and reported for duty with the Union VI Corps. The VI Corps was now a fighting force of nearly 34,000 men. The rumor was that it would not be long before they would be on the move south towards the Confederate capital at Richmond.

Chapter 34

The Rancocas
1940

It almost seemed to Katy as if her grandfather was getting younger instead of older. They had recently celebrated his 94th birthday, it was pretty much the same crowd as they had had at Christmas. There was cake, and of course ice cream, and gifts. The foreman, Mr. Davenport had also built a platform that allowed Michael McBride to climb up onto the tractor and take it for a ride up and down Hilyard's Lane.

Her grandfather was in great spirits, seemed to be able to move around better than he had a year or so ago, and was eager for the warmer weather to arrive so that he could spend more time outdoors. Katy was happy that he was doing so well, but at the same time was worried that maybe he was trying to do too much. What could it be that had resulted in this rejuvenation?

Katy was seated at the kitchen table having just finished making her latest entries in the journal she was keeping about the McBride's and her grandfather's life along the Rancocas. As she closed the book in front of her she couldn't help but wonder who, besides herself and her brother Evan, she was writing it for, future generations of McBride's, if there were to be any? Katy was engaged to be married to Lieutenant Baxter Underwood, but they hadn't set a date yet, and neither an engagement nor a marriage was a guarantee that they would have children.

"Wonder if I could get a cup of tea?" Michael McBride asked from the doorway interrupting Katy's wandering thoughts.

"Certainly," she said with a sigh as she lifted her head and lovingly smiled at her grandfather. "How are you feeling Poppa?" She asked as she went about filling the kettle.

"Wonderful," he replied taking a seat at the table.

Having lit the stove she turned and looked at him. "I don't want this to sound like the dumbest question that was ever asked," she said almost with an embarrassed smile, "but."

"Go on," he said smiling up at his beloved granddaughter. "Even if it is, I'll do my best to give the dumbest answer that was ever given."

"Alright then," she said with a sigh. "Why? Why do you feel wonderful? Why do you seem to be so much better than you were even six months ago?"

"It's true," he said. "I feel good, and as amazing as it may sound, I keep feeling better every day. I don't know why, at least, I'm not sure why."

"But, you have an idea why?" Asked Katy.

"Yes, I do," he said with a grin, then silence. The silence lasted too long for Katy.

"And…" She impatiently urged with a smile. "Care to share?"

"I suppose," her grandfather said with a chuckle. "I, that is we, lost your grandmother nearly a year ago. For most of this past year I wanted to be dead more than I wanted to be alive. Without your grandmother, I felt I had no reason to be alive."

"Well, there was me," Katy said, "and Evan."

"Yes, yes, there was," he said, "and, please don't be hurt or offended, but, as much as I love you, and as important as you are to me, you still aren't my Katherine. When your grandmother died she took half my heart with her, and then the other half had nothing to live for. I was just a lonely old man who was waiting to die."

"That's so sad," said Katy as she sat down across from her grandfather and reached out and took his hand.

"More like pathetic wouldn't you say?" He replied with a smile. "But, I knew I couldn't die, because there were too many things unsettled. What would become of you and Evan? What would become of the farm? When I join your grandmother I want my soul to be at peace, not tormented."

"And your soul is at peace now?"

"Yes," her grandfather answered confidently. "I believe it is."

"What's changed?" She asked.

"I was given a glimpse of the future," he said, "and I saw that all was going to be well in it. So," he continued, "content with that knowledge, I can now die peacefully. Only trouble is, that I'm so content and at peace now, that I don't seem to be dying anymore," he said with a laugh.

"And just what was it that you saw in this vision?" Asked Katy as she stood and turned to the stove to pour her grandfather's tea. "That has brought you such peace."

"The farm for one thing," he said. "Since god created the heaven and the earth, only two people have ever lived on this land. The Lenni-Lenape Indians, and the McBride's. Who knows how long the Indians lived here, but it's been ours for the last 150 years.

"Well, that's coming to an end. You will be the last of the McBride's to ever live on this land. I understand that, I accept it, and I thank God for the time we've had here."

"You don't know that," said Katy. "While it's true that if Woody and I have children that their name won't be McBride, McBride blood will be in their veins, and in their hearts."

"Katy Rose my darlin', once you and your young man are married you won't want to stay here, and I don't think a life along the Rancocas will be all that appealing to your children. Don't get me wrong, I know how much you love this muddy creek and the land along its banks, and the little village that for far too long has been the center of your world. But, you've always talked about wanting to see what's beyond the Rancocas and the Delaware.

"Well, once I'm gone you'll have your chance. There's a great big world out there, and if anyone deserves to explore it you do. And, it'll mean so much more if you explore it with someone you love."

Katy, having served the tea, sat back down, and looked across at her grandfather with a tear in her eye. "That's just it though Poppa," she said. "You will never be gone from here. Even after you die, you will still be here."

"In some ways perhaps," he replied.

"No," she said. "In every way. This dirt, this dust, that this house and barn stands on, and from which the corn grows, and beneath which our ancestors lie, is what you are made of, it is what I am made of, and what every McBride for the last 150 years has been made of.

"When we are laid to rest and they say, ashes to ashes and dust to dust, this is the dust they're talking about. This dust, the dust right out in that yard that gets on our shoes, and gets blown into our eyes, and mixes with our sweat. That is the dust we come from, and that is the dust we will return to.

"So you see, as long as this land is here you will be here too, as will I, as will Evan, and grandmother, and my father and my mother, and Brian and Bridget McBride, and Colin, and Colleen, and all the rest of them. So, don't talk about when you are gone from here because you never will be, nor will I."

In the quiet that followed they both understood, maybe for the first time, that Katy was right. They did not just live on this piece of land alongside the waters of the Rancocas, they were a part of it. As much as they lived on the land, the land lived within them. No matter what happened, they would forever be a part of each other.

"Quite a legacy, isn't it," said her grandfather quietly as he reached across the table and took her hand.

"I may go away from here from time to time," said Katy, "but, I will always come back. This will always be my home. I will hold onto this farm forever. That I promise you."

"What about Woody?"

"Woody knows how much this place means to me, he knows it is part of me, and that he can't have one without the other."

"He's quite a fella, this Baxter Underwood of yours."

"Yes," she said with a prideful smile. "He is isn't he?"

"Well anyway," her grandfather said. "That's why I think I'm feeling so darned good. Because now I can die peacefully. Thanks in no small part it appears to Woody, even though he is an Englishman!" They laughed and talked as Michael McBride enjoyed a second cup of tea before going off to bed. Katy went into the parlor, tuned the radio to a classical music station, and drifted off to sleep thinking about the wonderful men in her life, her grandfather, her brother, and her fiancé.

"Woody called this morning," Katy told her grandfather as she was preparing his lunch the next day. "He's coming for the weekend and wants to bring a friend. I told him it was okay, I hope you don't mind."

"No, not at all. Is it his cousin Ed?" He asked. "That Ed is quite a character, had me in stitches the whole time he was here."

"No," she answered. "I don't think its Ed. He just said it was a shipmate. He said they would probably get here about ten o'clock on Saturday morning."

Lieutenant Ed Randall, Woody's cousin, and a shipmate aboard the *Rhind*, had visited the McBride's for a weekend with Woody at Katy's insistence several weeks ago. She wanted to make sure that Ed knew that there were no hard feelings over the secret Woody had kept about Katy's appearance. It had worked out and they had all become very good friends.

"Isn't the church social this weekend?" Asked her grandfather.

"Yes," she answered. "I believe it is."

"Why don't you call Woody back and see what he thinks about you getting a partner for his friend for the social? I'm sure you would all have a good time. They're going to have a live four-piece orchestra with a singer from Trenton."

"That's a great idea!" Said Katy. "I'll do that. Why don't you come with us?"

"I just might. I wouldn't mind drinking a little punch and doing some flirting," he said with a wink causing them both to laugh.

The next morning over breakfast Katy told her grandfather that she had finally been able to get in touch with Woody. "He said that it wouldn't be necessary to make any arrangements for his friend. I also told him to invite Ed and Nancy along too, I think they might enjoy themselves as well."

"Good idea! What did Woody think?"

"Well," said Katy. "It was kind of strange. He really didn't seem all that keen on inviting them. In fact, I almost had to insist."

"I would think that having Ed along might help this other fellow feel more at ease," offered her grandfather.

"That's what I thought too," she said, "but he said he was sure that this fellow was not going to be the least bit uncomfortable."

"Must be quite the ladies' man. Maybe I can pick up some pointers," said Michael McBride. "Well, in any event, I'm glad Ed is coming."

"It all seems very strange to me though," said Katy with just a hint of concern in her voice. "Maybe having this other fellow here isn't such a good idea." Then fixing her grandfather with a stare and shaking her finger she sternly admonished him. "And, you had better behave yourself." Then she laughed.

Katy spent all day Friday preparing the house for the arrival of their guests. She couldn't remember the last time she had had to make sleeping arrangements for so many people. She giggled when she thought about what her grandfather might say if she suggested they sew Woody into a bundling sack and let him share her bed. She halfheartedly scolded herself for her less than virginal thoughts when she considered the possibilities of such an arrangement.

In the end it was decided that Nancy would share her room with her, Woody would stay in Evan's room as usual, and Ed and the new fellow could share the downstairs bedroom. It would be a little crowded, but it would only be for the two nights. Fresh linens on the beds, and fresh towels on the washstands and in the bathroom, and all was in readiness.

It was just after ten o'clock on Saturday morning when the yellow 1939 Plymouth convertible pulled into the yard behind the McBride house. A tooting horn and a cloud of dust signaled their arrival. Katy and her grandfather came out onto the porch to greet their guests.

When the car came to a stop, Ed Randall was the first one out of the car exiting on the passenger's side. Woody must be driving surmised Katy as she smiled at Ed and waved. Ed waved back and then turned back to the car and helped his girlfriend, Nancy, out of the rear passenger seat.

Katy was surprised when she saw Woody exit the rear door on the passenger side. He turned, smiled, waved, and blew her a kiss as he threw his arms over his head and stretched. Obviously, the new guy was driving she thought.

To Katy's astonishment the next person out of the car, also from the driver's side rear, was an attractive woman about Katy's age. She was tall, had light brown hair, and an unusual complexion. She waved and smiled, it was a genuinely friendly smile.

Great, thought Katy. No one had told her there was going to be another female. Now she would have to rethink the sleeping arrangements. She blushed a little as she thought to herself that maybe the bundling sack idea was back in the running.

The driver seemed to be taking his own sweet time getting out of the car, not only that, but none of the other passengers seemed to want to leave the car. Was this new fellow someone of importance? Someone they had to wait for? Had Woody brought the captain of their ship to spend the weekend?

Finally, the driver got out of the car. He was wearing his dress blues including his cap. He exited the car and stood looking at the barn with his back to the house. Which Katy thought was a little rude.

As he slowly turned Katy could see that he was wearing sunglasses. Completing his turn, he dropped his head, removed his cap and placed it upside down on the roof of the car. Then he removed his sunglasses and tossed them into his cap.

Then he lifted his head, looked up at Katy, smiled, and said, "Hi sis."

It was Evan! Evan was home!

For the rest of her life Katy was unable to remember how she had done it, but she somehow had gotten off the porch to Evan and had him locked in an embrace. She knew she was crying but was not the least bit embarrassed or concerned. She had not seen her brother for nearly two years.

"Okay Katy, okay," said Evan happily as he tried to peel his sister's arms from around his neck. When he had done so, he held her at arm's length, smiled, and said, "You look great, I've really missed you." Then he leaned over and kissed her on the forehead. "Now, let me get on over to the porch and say hi to Poppa."

Katy was still crying, unable to speak. She turned Evan loose, wiped her eyes with her hands, smiled, and nodded her head. Then she stepped back so that Evan could get to the porch.

It had taken every bit of strength Michael McBride had to keep from collapsing when he had seen his grandson. With everyone watching Katy, he was able to stagger unobserved to the bench on the porch and sit down. Like Katy, he too was crying, and also like Katy he was not the least bit embarrassed or concerned.

When Evan bounded up onto the porch Michael McBride stood. He was unsteady and did not know how long he would be able to remain standing, but he wanted to greet his grandson standing up. When Evan got to him, he looked at his grandson through his tears, and said, "I was afraid I'd never see you again. My God, how good you look to me."

"I'm so sorry I couldn't be here for Nana's funeral," said Evan.

"But you were here," answered his grandfather softly. "I felt you holding my hand."

That was when Evan's emotions overtook him. As he started to cry he threw his arms around his grandfather and buried his face against his neck. Michael McBride did not have to worry any longer about falling over, he was perfectly safe in the strong loving arms of his grandson.

Woody had made his way to Katy's side and now held her as she tearfully watched the reunion taking place on the porch. As she looked around, she noticed that Ed was holding Nancy, but that the young woman who had exited the rear of the car was standing all alone. Every one of them were wiping tears from their eyes.

Katy, feeling sorry for her, freed herself from Woody's embrace and walked over to the young woman. She decided that two and two would make four, so stuck out her hand and said, "Hi, I'm Katy McBride. Welcome to our home. You must be Miss Northrup."

The young lady smiled warmly, took Katy's hand and said, "Thank you, but I'm afraid I'm not Miss Northrup."

Now Katy was embarrassed. Two and two had turned out to be zero. There was no rock big enough to hide under. Not knowing what else to do Katy turned and looked towards Evan who was sitting on the bench on the porch with their grandfather. He was looking in the young lady's direction with a huge smile on his face.

"I, I, I'm sorry…," stammered Katy. "I thought, that is…"

"That's okay," said the woman still holding Katy's hand and still smiling. "My name is Irene. I used to be Miss Northrup. Now I'm Mrs. McBride."

Katy knew that her chin had dropped probably somewhere down around her waist, and that her eyes were probably the size of dinner plates. "Oh." Was all she could get out as she tried to deal with another unexpected and fantastic surprise.

Irene McBride held her left hand up so that Katy could see the diamond ring and wedding band on her finger, and with a huge smile said, "I married your brother, we're sisters."

Katy knew she was crying again, as she threw her arms around Irene's neck, she squealed, "Oh my goodness! How wonderful! I've never had a sister before!"

"Hey!" Yelled Evan from the porch. "Don't break the bride!"

Katy turned her new sister-in-law loose and turned toward he brother. "Why are we all standing around out here?" She asked as she wiped her eyes with the back of her hands. "Let's go in the house where we can get something to drink and be more comfortable. Besides," she continued with a laugh. "I'm in desperate need of a tissue." Looking around she said, "I think maybe we all are!"

Inside, Katy took over and, as the luggage made its way through the door, assigned the rooms. Evan and his new bride Irene were given the downstairs bedroom, partially because it was the biggest, and partially because it would provide them the most privacy. Woody and Ed would share Evan's old room, and Nancy would share Katy's room with her.

Once everyone was settled Katy offered iced tea, coffee, or Coke, with freshly made sugar cookies, but the ever reliable Ed, produced a bottle of champagne with which to toast the newlyweds. Besides, he said, it had always been his experience that nothing enhanced the taste of a well-made sugar cookie like a glass of champagne. As she sipped her champagne, and took another bite of her cookie, Katy decided that Ed Randall was a genius.

When the toasting was over Michael McBride made his way into the parlor, collapsed into his favorite chair, and was soon napping peacefully. Woody took Irene, Nancy, and Ed on a walk to the landing. This gave Katy and Evan an opportunity to be alone.

"So," said Katy with a smile as they sat together on the bench on the back porch. "You're an old married man."

"Yeah," answered her brother. "I suppose I am."

"When did all of this happen?" She asked.

"I don't know," replied Evan. "I just kind of realized that I was head over heels in love with Irene, and that I wanted to spend the rest of my life with her. I was pretty sure she was kind of in love with me too, but I didn't know if she was enough in love to consider a proposal of marriage." He paused and looked at his sister. "She's beautiful though isn't she?"

"Uh huh," said Katy smiling and softly nodding at her brother.

"Well, that was part of the problem too," Evan continued. "She was very popular, and very sought after. I was afraid if I waited she might think I wasn't as serious as I knew I was, and then somebody else might swoop in, and I would lose her, and I just couldn't risk that."

"So, you took the risk of proposing?"

"I did," he said with a smile. "Then she said yes, almost before I finished asking her. Then I was really terrified!" He laughed.

"So, when was the wedding, and why didn't you tell us?"

"Well, her father, who is a great guy, gave us his blessing, and the Navy approved my request to get married, so we had a small intimate wedding in a little chapel on Ewa Beach outside of Honolulu, two weeks ago today."

"Happy anniversary." said Katy with a smile.

"Thank you," answered a beaming Evan. "We kept it a secret because I knew I wanted to bring her here to meet you and Poppa, and I thought it would be inappropriate to ask her to come all this way as anything but my wife, so we got married and then made the trip. Besides, made for a great surprise, didn't it?"

"You were surprise enough! Then to find out there was a Mrs. McBride! Holy cow!" Katy playfully punched her big brother on the arm. "So, what happens now?" She asked.

"Well," he answered. "We plan on staying here until next Friday, then we'll have to leave and make our way back to Pearl, so I can rejoin the ship."

"I hope she's prepared to be fussed over."

"I think she's looking forward to it," said Evan with a smile. "She's an only child. Her mother died when she was very young, and though her father denies her nothing, she's never really had anyone to fuss over her."

"Good," said Katy. "Because I've wanted a sister to fuss over my whole life!" They laughed, that special brother sister laugh that had gone unshared for far too long.

"Well," said Evan. "What about you and Woody?"

"Woody?" She sighed wistfully. "Where to begin."

"I heard it was love at first fight," he teased.

"Yeah," laughed Katy. "I guess it kind of was. I thought he was an idiot, and he thought I was nuts. Turns out after getting to know each other better, that maybe we were both a little bit right."

"No date yet?"

"No, I think we both are ready and want to take the next step, but… whew… I don't know, I just don't know. It's kind of scary."

"Yes, it is scary," said Evan, "but, once it's done, there's not a feeling like it in the world. Marriage is love's ultimate commitment. You need to set a date," he continued. "For two reasons, Poppa, and me."

"I know," she sighed and looked away.

"Poppa's 94-years old, it would break your heart, and his, if you waited and then he wasn't here to give you away or be a part of it. And, Irene and I want to be a part of it too, and there's no telling when we'll be able to get back here."

Katy turned and stared at her brother. She was trying to comprehend what he was proposing. Was he really suggesting that...? "Are you saying that we should get married now?"

Evan smiled at his sister. "Poppa's here, we're here," he said with a shrug. "Kind of makes sense if you ask me."

"Now!" She exclaimed as she jumped to her feet and began pacing on the porch. "You're saying that Woody and I should get married by next Friday? Not only is it crazy, I don't even think it's possible."

"All you need is a license and a preacher," said Evan with a smile. "Believe me I know."

Katy flopped down on the bench next to her brother. "I don't know," she said shaking her head. "I just don't know."

Evan turned to her and took her hand. "Look," he said. "Just think about it, and if you think you might want to, talk it over with Woody."

Katy turned to him and nodded. "Okay," she whispered.

"They're back," he said, nodding in the direction of Hilyard's Lane.

Katy turned, and noticed that Ed was carrying a second bottle of champagne, and that they all had glasses containing various amounts of the bubbly liquid. They were laughing and talking, and thoroughly enjoying themselves. Woody waved and blew her a kiss. She smiled and waved.

"Married by next Friday," she whispered, "and a few hours ago, a bundling sack seemed like a crazy idea."

That evening they all attended the church social in the village. However, it turned out to be more of a homecoming and wedding reception for Evan and Irene, and an engagement party for Katy and Woody than a social. So that they could all go together, they decided to hitch two of the mules to a wagon, and with Evan handling the reins, arrive at the church in style.

The evening was a huge success, and everyone had had a wonderful time. Woody and Katy, with the other couples, were snuggled up in the back of the wagon as they started on their way back to the farm.

"Did you have a good time?" He whispered.

"Uh huh."

"You sure?"

"Yes. Why, didn't you?" She asked looking up at her fiancé.

"I did yes, but, I don't know, you seemed kind of preoccupied most of the evening."

She had decided that she did want to discuss Evan's suggestion with Woody, but didn't think the back of the wagon with everyone around was the right place. She had talked to the pastor at the social, and although he wasn't thrilled with the idea, he confirmed that it could be done.

Woody squeezed her. "You okay?" He asked.

"What?" She said, trying to bring her mind back to the wagon. "Yes," she said. "Yes, it's just been quite a day, Evan coming home, Irene, the social, I'm just tired I guess."

"You certainly have had quite a day," he said kissing the top of her head and holding her closer.

After breakfast the next day, Ed and Nancy left to return to Philadelphia, Woody would take the train after dinner. Evan saddled Indigo and Jester, and took Irene for a ride along the banks of the Rancocas. Katy and Woody walked down to the landing. Katy drew comfort from the muddy waters of the creek, and she wanted to be comfortable when she discussed Evan's suggestion with Woody.

Woody listened carefully to Katy as she told him about her conversation with her brother. When she had finished he reached out and took both of her hands in his. They were clammy, she was nervous, and maybe a little scared.

"What do you think of this idea?" He asked.

"It does seem to make sense," she answered turning her head and looking out across the creek.

"Katy," he said. "I love you and want you to be happy more than anything else in this world. I want to marry you so badly I ache."

"But?" Katy whispered looking up at the man she loved.

"But," Woody said with a smile. "We are only going to do this once, and I want it to be everything both of us ever dreamed it should be. I want to see you walk down the aisle dressed in a beautiful wedding gown in that little church in the village surrounded by your friends and neighbors, and the people that care for you.

"I want your grandfather there to give you away, I want Evan and Irene there, but I also want my parents there, and I want my friends there. And, when it is all over I want to have the greatest wedding reception this little village has ever seen in that little church where we danced last night. Then, I want to whisk you away on a honeymoon that we will both remember for the rest of our lives.

"That Katy, is what I want, not a hastily arranged shotgun wedding, and I think it is what you really want too. Am I wrong?"

"No," she said shaking her head as tears began to flow down her cheeks. "I love you Lieutenant Baxter Underwood."

"I know," he said as he pulled her to him and kissed her.

"So, we agree that getting married by next Friday is not what we want?"

"Yes," she said. "So what now?"

"We just learned this week that the *Rhind* is going to be in Philly until at least the middle of June," he said as he removed his wallet and took a small card out of it. He held it up for Katy to see and she saw that it was a calendar. "Got any plans for Saturday, May 11th?" He asked studying the card. "If not, I'd like you to marry me on that day." She crossed her arms in front of her, and resting her chin on her right hand, appeared to be deep in thought. "I may have to move some things around," she said with a smile, "but, I think I can work it out." With that she squealed and jumped into Woody's arms. He spun her around, as they both laughed, until they almost collapsed from their dizziness.

"I'll tell Evan," she said. "He's going to be disappointed."

"We'll tell him together," he said.

"Okay," she sighed.

Hand in hand they started back up the lane to the house. As they walked, Woody began to formulate a plan that might get Evan back to Rancocas in May.

Chapter 35

The Rapidan
1864

The New Jersey Brigade was camped on a low ridge northwest of Brandy Station. They had been in camp for over a week now. From their position Michael could look in all directions, and everywhere for as far as he could see, he could see the twinkling fires of the VI Corps of the Union Army. How could anyone stand against such a formidable force he wondered?

"If not tomorrow the next day," said Frank Jefferson who had come up behind him.

"What?" Asked a startled Michael.

"If not tomorrow the next day."

Michael met Frank's pronouncement with a blank stare, his mind still on the overwhelming number of men encamped around Brandy Station.

"We'll be on the move," Frank said sounding slightly annoyed. "If not tomorrow the next day. At least that's what they're saying."

"Oh yeah," said Michael shaking his head and bringing himself back from his mental wanderings. "Wonder if we'll run into any Rebs?"

"Hope so," answered Frank.

"Hope what?" Asked Bill Kemble who now joined them on the ridge.

"Hope we run into some Rebs when we leave here in the next day or so," said Frank

"Oh," said Bill picking a stick up off the ground and throwing it into the brush.

"You ever seen any Rebs?" Michael asked.

"Yep," answered Bill, "back in '63, April of '63. Down outside of Suffolk. We had us a dust up with Longstreet's Corps."

"Was you in it? Really?" Asked Frank. Bill Kemble certainly had their attention now.

"You mean did I see the elephant?" Bill responded with chuckle. Frank and Mike nodded. "Sure did," he continued. "We was sent out along the Edenton Road with some cavalry and artillery to see if there was any Rebs about. We had only gone a couple of miles when we ran smack into a whole bunch of Longstreet's boys. They was already deployed in a line of trees, and when they opened up on us things got really dicey. We didn't even have time to form a line we just took cover in some woods and waited for the cavalry.

"When the cavalry came up they pitched right into 'em, but they was a whole bunch of Rebs in them trees and they drove the cavalry back too. Well, the cavalry just kept pecking away at them boys. They'd attack and then back off, then attack again, and back off. They was making them boys real uncomfortable.

"Finally, a part of the Reb line broke, and when we seen that we jumped up and took out after them. Them Rebs must've thought there was a whole lot more of us than there was 'cause when they seen us coming the whole line started to crumble.

"We pushed 'em right on back through the trees and all the way back through their own camp. Our officers knew we was more than a little bit outnumbered so they stopped us on the far side of the Rebs' camp. Half of us formed a line in case they turned and came back while the rest set to destroying everything in the camp. Once we destroyed the camp we formed up and headed back to Suffolk."

Michael and Frank were mesmerized, they had hung on every word.

"How'd you know it was Longstreet?" Asked Michael.

"We captured a young boy who was left to guard the camp, and he told us they were the 17th Virginia, a part of Longstreet's Corps."

"Did you do any shootin'?" Asked Frank.

Bill looked at Frank like he had just asked him if he had ever been to the moon. "Shoot?" He answered with a grin. "Oh no, I just kept waving my hanky at 'em and hollering at 'em to shoo!" He laughed as he pranced and waved his hands in the air. "Of course I shot my gun you idiot! I don't know, three, four, maybe five times."

"Kill anybody?" Asked Michael.

"Don't know," said Bill a serious and somber tone to his voice now. "Was a lot of smoke, people running everywhere, and a whole bunch of screaming and hollering, and I don't know that I ever want to know either."

Michael just nodded, and felt he understood what Bill meant about not wanting to know. It must be a terrible burden to know you've killed someone, even if it was in a war.

"Did anybody get killed?" Asked Frank.

"I know we lost a couple, and the cavalry did too. Must've been near twenty horses down too. Saw some Rebs on the ground. Don't know if they was dead or just wounded, and didn't bother to stop and ask."

"Seen any action since?" Asked Michael.

"Nope, joined up in '62, and except for the Edenton Road, all I been doing is marching, drilling and guarding." He laughed.

The next morning, May 2nd, the Second and Third Divisions of Sedgewick's VI Corps, left Brandy Station and moved six miles west to Culpepper Courthouse. That night Sergeant Cheeseman told the men of Second Squad that they would be moving out early the next day. Four additional Corps were to the east and were on the move south as well, and if all went as planned the Army of the Potomac, nearly 120,000 strong, would assemble somewhere in the area of Chancellorsville.

In the chilly early morning hours of May 4th, the 10th New Jersey Regiment fell in as the last regiment in line with the 1st New Jersey Brigade. The Brigade was the last in line in the First Division, so as it turns out, with the exception of the supply wagons, ambulances, and herds of horse and cattle, the 10th New Jersey was at the very end of the line. Once on the road, the distance from the lead elements of the Division, to where the 10th New Jersey was bringing up the rear was nearly two miles.

The Division would march nearly eleven miles to the banks of the Rapidan River at the Germanna Ford where they would cross the river and march an additional five miles before encamping in the area of the Wilderness Tavern. The Second and

Third Divisions, marching from Culpepper, would follow the same route but would be a few hours behind the First Division. The entire Army of the Potomac would be arriving in that area over the next couple of days.

It was a little after 1:00pm, when the 10th New Jersey covered in the dust kicked up by the thousands of pairs of feet that marched ahead of them, halted and was directed to fall out on a small rise on the east side of the Germanna Plank Road. They were to grab something to eat, fill their canteens and be ready to move out again within the hour. The 10th New Jersey, was still a half mile from the ford and the river and could see neither from where they rested.

Lieutenant Ryan, Third Platoon's Commanding Officer, called the platoon together near the crest of the small rise. "The Corps will be forming up and moving out in about twenty minutes," the Lieutenant said. "H Company, which includes the Third Platoon, will not be going with them."

The unexpected announcement caused some men to grumble, others swore in protest, while still others remained silent. It appeared that not everyone was anxious to cross the Rapidan. Michael who had remained silent did not really know how he felt.

"Once the Division is across the river," continued the Lieutenant. "H Company will cross the river and take up a position to defend the pontoon bridges and the ford against any advance by the enemy. The ford has to remain open so that Second and Third Divisions, which will be along in a couple of hours, can cross."

"We gonna move up once they cross?" Asked one of the men from First Squad.

"I don't know," said the Lieutenant. "I guess we'll stay here until the generals feel it's no longer necessary for us to guard the ford."

"We came a long way to do the same thing we was doing in Mauch Chunk," someone from behind Michael said.

"Those are our orders," said Lieutenant Ryan. "Now, we'll move down to the ford once the Division is done crossing."

As Michael sat on the small rise watching the Division begin the process of crossing the Rapidan, he began to wonder if he was glad that they would not be moving forward with them, and if being glad about it meant that he was a coward. He supposed he was no more of a coward than the next man who had never been in a battle and didn't know what to expect. Was it possible that he might never get to be in a battle, and may never find out whether or not he was a coward?

It was after four o'clock by the time First Division was across the Rapidan. The supply wagons, the extra horses, and beef cattle were the last to cross. The dust they kicked up had barely settled when Third Platoon and the rest of H Company, led by Captain Cunningham, fell in, moved forward, and crossed the ford.

Once across the river, Third Platoon was assigned to move forward and establish a picket line at Spotswood Crossing not quite a half mile east of the ford. The other platoons were deployed around a blacksmith's shop on the south side of the Germanna Plank Road, and at the ford itself. Except for the birds and insects, and an occasional squirrel, they heard or saw nothing, until just before six o'clock.

That was when Sergeant Cheeseman told them that a runner had just come forward to report that the Second and Third Divisions of the VI Corps had arrived at the ford and were preparing to cross. Of course, Michael and the rest of the platoon did not really need to be told this. An army of over 24,000 men did not move silently.

They had heard the Divisions at least fifteen minutes before the runner brought the news of their approach.

As the Second and Third Divisions passed through their picket line they taunted the men of Third Platoon who were not moving forward towards the enemy.

"Hey, shouldn't you boys who are just here to watch the parade be waving little flags and handing out sweet cakes or something?"

"Anything you Jersey boys want us to tell the Rebs that are up ahead for ya? Like, Hey Mr. Greyback, please don't bring your scary self this way!"

"Hey! Is it true you Jersey boys have tomatoes growing behind your ears, and corn cobs sticking out your ass?"

Third Platoon returned the taunts and insults, and everyone laughed and enjoyed the exchange, but Michael and the rest of the platoon knew, that their being left behind to guard the ford while the rest of the Corps moved to meet the enemy would be a stain on them that would not be easily washed off.

It was nearly three hours before the last elements of the Second and Third Divisions had passed Spotswood Crossing. The sun was down and in the growing darkness it was all but impossible to see any distance up the Germanna Plank Road, or into the surrounding woods. Sergeant Cheeseman assigned sentry duties, and the men took turns sleeping and standing watch through the night.

The next morning, May 5th, having received no orders to move up, H Company maintained its position on the Rapidan. They felt forgotten as they just sat and watched the empty road, and wondered what if anything was happening up ahead around its bends. If this was what they had come to Virginia for, then they might as well have stayed in Mauch Chunk.

At about ten o'clock Bill Kemble spotted a group of troops coming their way. There were not many of them, at first, and they didn't seem to be in any type of formation. Lieutenant Ryan who had the men deployed on each side of the road passed the word to be ready to fire on his command. He also sent a runner back to Captain Cunningham to let him know that he had troops approaching his position.

"You ready?" Michael, who was knelt down behind a boulder, asked Frank.

"I think so," Frank answered. "Besides, ready or not, looks like we're going to be in it."

"Hold your fire!" Hollered Bill suddenly as he jumped up and began waving his arm in the air. "Lieutenant, I think they're our boys!"

They waited until the approaching troops were within 200 yards of their position. Then, they could tell that the approaching troops were indeed Union soldiers. They were also wounded. Wounded men who had received preliminary care at field dressing stations and field hospitals, and were now making their way to the rear.

"Let's get out there and give 'em a hand boys," shouted Lieutenant Ryan. The men of the Third Platoon left their positions and moved forward to help the approaching wounded soldiers.

Most of the wounds were through wounds, meaning that a bullet had passed through a part of the body without hitting an organ or breaking a bone. There were also several soldiers who had wounds to their arms that had broken or shattered bones. These wounds were the most painful and in many cases would, at some point, probably require amputation.

One of the more gruesome had had a bullet pass through his face. The bullet had struck him in one cheek, rattled around inside his mouth, and passed out the other cheek. He had a bandage stuffed in the hole in each cheek, and then wrapped around his head, but was continually spitting teeth, pieces of bone, and blood.

"How far away's the fighting?" Asked Frank as he helped one of the soldiers.

"About five miles back up this road," the soldier said. "They came at us at first light. We pitched into them along the Fredericksburg Pike, but they was a lot more of them than we figured. They messed us up something awful. We're only the beginning, you're gonna see a lot more wounded come limping down this road."

"What outfit you with?" Asked Frank.

"119th Pennsylvania, Third Brigade, if there's anything left of it."

The soldier was right, within the hour the flow of wounded became a steady stream. Ambulances also began to pass through, transporting the more seriously wounded from the field hospitals near the front to larger and better prepared hospitals around Brandy Station and Culpepper. Each ambulance carried six to eight men, and for many of them the rough ride in the rear of the ambulance only intensified the pain they were already in. The moaning and the screaming, and the other unearthly sounds they made could not be ignored, or forgotten.

Private Michael McBride, Second Squad, Third Platoon, and the rest of the men of H Company, Second Battalion, 10th New Jersey Regiment, spent that day, and all of the next day, May 6th, assisting the wounded who were making their way to the rear via the pontoon bridges at the Germanna ford. The wounded, who unlike them, were engaged in a great battle, gaining glory for themselves, their units, and their country, while H Company did nothing.

On the morning of May 7th, shortly after ten o'clock, a courier arrived with a message for Captain Cunningham. H Company was to move forward and rejoin the Regiment at Chancellorsville. They were to take the more northerly route by way of Herndon's Mill to avoid contact with the enemy. They were on the march by eleven o'clock. They expected to arrive in Chancellorsville before sunset.

The courier had also brought sad news. In intense fighting on the evening of the sixth, their commanding officer, Colonel Ryerson, had been mortally wounded and taken prisoner. Lieutenant Colonel Charles H. Tay was now in command of the 10th New Jersey.

The 10th New Jersey had borne the brunt of the Confederate attack on the VI Corps' right flank. In addition to losing their colonel, nearly forty men had been killed or wounded, and an additional eighty captured. The total strength of the devastated regiment now stood at less than five hundred.

All while H Company sat at the Germanna Ford.

Michael and the rest of H Company arrived at Chancellorsville as expected just before sunset. While on the march, they could smell the smoke from the raging fires caused by musket flashes in the dense foliage of the Wilderness. Upon their arrival, it came as no surprise to them that they were not warmly greeted by those who had been subjected to the blood bath in the Wilderness. They hoped that in the coming days they could redeem themselves.

General Ulysses S. Grant, not wanting to get into a prolonged battle in the thick undergrowth of the Wilderness, decided to disengage, sidestep the Confederate lines and continue south towards his intended target of Richmond. General Robert E.

Lee, realizing Grant's intentions, quickly moved his army south to block the Union advance. The two armies would meet again at Spotsylvania Courthouse.

The First Division of the VI Corps, with the First New Jersey Brigade, and the nearly spent 10th New Jersey attached, moved forward on the 8th, of May. They marched six miles to Todd's Tavern on the Brock Road, before continuing on to the crossroads at Gordon Road, about three miles northwest of Spotsylvania Courthouse. Throughout the day both armies brought up reinforcements and prepared to do battle once again.

The Second and 10th New Jersey Regiments were detached from the Brigade and placed in reserve at the Red Field Farm along the Brock Road to try and recover from the fighting in the Wilderness. They were perhaps a mile back from the Confederate lines. Michael and the rest of the Regiment could clearly hear the musket fire as the armies exchanged fire.

It was just after noon when Frank Jefferson, who had gone to fill their canteens at a nearby spring, returned to where they were seated along what was left of a post rail fence.

"Have you guys heard the news?" He asked.

"What, that we're the most hated company in the Army of the Potomac?" Answered Bill Kemble.

"No," whispered Frank. "I just heard a courier tell some boys out on the road that General Sedgwick's been killed."

"What?" Exclaimed Michael sitting straight up and leaning towards Frank.

"General Sedgwick's been killed," he repeated. "Shot by a sniper."

"Who's in command now?" Asked Michael.

"Don't know."

"My God," said Michael. "First Ryerson, and now Sedgwick. With the way they beat up on the Regiment back in the Wilderness and now this, you've got to think that we must be cursed or something."

"Don't know about that," said Frank, "but, I do know that Sedgwick is dead."

Later that day their Company Commander, Captain Cunningham, confirmed the news that General John Sedgwick had indeed been killed. General Horatio G. Wright, formerly of the First Division, was now in command of the VI Corps. General David A. Russell, formerly of the Third Brigade assumed command of the First Division.

Over the course of the next two days, the 10th New Jersey remained in reserve, but well within earshot of the fighting. It took everything Michael had in his power to keep from curling up into a ball and screaming, for much to his shame, he found the noise of battle terrifying. Whenever he heard the distant sound of muskets or cannons, he would begin to sweat and tremble. The louder and more prolonged the noise the worse the terror would become.

Boom, Boom, Boom, the noise of the cannon would shake the ground, cause his brain to scream out in pain, and his insides to tremble with each and every discharge. The almost rhythmic cacophony of the musket fire would keep ringing in his ears even long after it had stopped, and it turned his bowels to jelly. Boom, Boom, Boom, even when the cannon were silent, they continued to pound in his brain. They never stopped, and neither did the headaches or the trembling.

Although no one said anything, he was certain those around him could see his fear. He tried to get away by himself whenever he could so he could cover his ears and close his eyes and try to picture scenes along the Rancocas at home to calm himself, but this was not always possible. When it came time for him to "see the elephant", how would he ever be able to stand and fight, if he could not even face the sound the elephant made?

"You know," said Frank that night as they lay in their shelter tent. "Being afraid first time you go into battle ain't nothing to be ashamed of. They tell me everybody's afraid the first time."

"I ain't afraid," said Michael in a little more than a whisper.

"Good," said Frank. "'Cause I'm damned near pissing myself just listening to it and thinking about it."

"Really?"

"Yep."

"Well," said Michael. "I ain't afraid, I'm terrified. If it's this bad just sitting here, how bad will it be when we get there?"

"Don't know," said Frank, "but, I guess we're going to find out, 'cause I sure don't see any way out of it that don't involve a firing squad."

Michael just nodded. Just knowing he wasn't alone in his fear, did help a little.

Around 7:30, on the night of the 13th, the Second and 10th New Jersey, now attached to Colonel Emory Upton's Third Brigade, formed up and fell in. They spent the next seven hours marching around the eastern side of the Confederate lines. The night time march was made in a pouring rain over treacherously muddy roads.

Their destination was a small farm on a hill less than a half mile east of the crossroads at Spotsylvania Courthouse, and opposite the extreme right of the Confederate lines. When they arrived they immediately began building breastworks, and digging trenches, which was made more difficult by the darkness, and the rain, and the mud. It was getting light when the men were finally able to rest, and the rain was still falling.

The farm belonged to the Myers family, and the hill the Brigade now occupied was known as Myers Hill. Michael and the 10th New Jersey were positioned north of the farm house. The ground was higher here and maybe even a little bit drier. Using boards from fencing and out buildings, and by felling small trees they had built a suitable barrier from which to defend their position against an assault.

He had not slept much, even though he was exhausted, and even though he had tried. The fear of not knowing what was going to happen, and how he was going to react gnawed at him like a hungry predator. He trembled almost uncontrollably, and it was not only because of the cold rain.

"Hey!" Said Frank as he shook Michael. "Get you a look at this."

Michael looked up at Frank who was peering over the top of their fortification. As he stood up he realized how wet, cold, and miserable he was. "What am I looking at?" He asked grumpily as he peered over the wall.

"The whole Reb Army," said Frank, pointing down the hill.

He was right. From their position on this hill they were overlooking the entire Confederate line. From its extreme right flank just south of the crossroads in their front, north to the intersection of the Courthouse and Brock Roads. The line was over a mile long.

"Them boys ain't gonna like us lookin' down on 'em," said Bill who had now joined them. "Look," he said, pointing down the hill. "Looks like they're forming up. I believe they intend to try and push us off this hill. Better get ready," he said as he turned his attention to his musket.

Michael nodded, but his throat had gone incredibly dry. He stared unblinking down the hill at the gray figures in the distance who were getting into line, and were going to be coming up this hill, with the sole intent of doing him harm.

"Looks like we're going to have some company!" Boomed the voice of Sergeant Cheeseman. "Load and prepare to fire, on my command, and not before. Let's let them get in close."

Michael prepared his musket and took a position along the barricade between Frank and Bill. He could see the gray troops. They hadn't even started to move yet, but his breathing was labored, tears burned his eyes, and he was sweating so profusely that he did not know whether or not he'd be able to hold onto his musket if he did fire it. He silently prayed that the first shot fired in this engagement would pierce his heart, mercifully ending his suffering.

Michael didn't know how long it took, but before long the gray line started to move. It moved en masse, the entire Confederate line was coming, and they were all coming directly at him. It was an amazingly terrifying sight, and thought.

The Confederate line closed to within about 150 yards of the union position, at which point they stopped, reformed their lines and prepared to fire. However, the blue troops were already prepared to fire. When the Confederates came to a stop, Sergeant Cheeseman gave the order.

"Fire!"

The entire Union line erupted as deadly tongues of fire leapt from their rifled barrels and sent a barrage of lead down the hill and into the wall of gray. Michael didn't fire. He was frozen, petrified by fear. Some of the gray men fell, others screamed or cried out, but not because of anything Michael did.

"Oh Jesus, oh Jesus, oh Jesus," being repeated constantly was all he could hear from Frank who was on his left firing and reloading. On his right Bill, silently and methodically did the same. Michael did nothing.

The gray wall returned fire, and Michael heard it as it slammed into their barricade. The impact on the outside caused dirt and small pieces of wood to fly off of the inside. Some of the balls were actually penetrating their shield.

The two lines exchanged a number of volleys, and still Michael, with his musket resting on top of the barricade aimed down the hill, did nothing. The noise was deafening, the smoke blinding, and the acrid smell of the burning powder nauseating. This was never going to end, he had arrived in Hell.

"Damn it!" Yelled a voice to his right. It was Bill. He was clutching his upper right leg, and there was blood oozing out between his fingers. "I'm hit!" He yelled. "I'm hit!"

Sergeant Cheeseman suddenly appeared behind Bill. "A dressing station's been set up in the barn," he hollered in Bill's ear. "Think you can make it back there?" Bill nodded. "Come on, I'll give you a hand getting started," hollered the Sergeant.

With the Sergeant's help, and using his musket as a support, Bill moved away from the line and back towards the barn. In the space where Bill had been was a pile of empty cartridge papers, and a puddle of blood.

"Oh Jesus, oh Jesus, oh Jesus." Was still coming from his left.

He turned and looked out over the barricade. Suddenly there was a flash! A ball struck near the top of the barricade and although it missed Michael completely, it threw dirt, debris, and wood splinters into Michael's face and eyes.

He screamed, dropped his musket, and brought his hands up to his eyes, sure he was either blinded or dead. He fell over onto his back, he was kicking his legs and screaming, his hands still covering his eyes. He had also lost control of his bladder. So, not only was he a coward, he was a coward who had pissed his pants.

Michael jumped to his feet, turned, and rushed towards the rear, away from the wall, away from the killing and dying. Suddenly someone grabbed him stopping his attempt to outrun death.

"McBride!" It was Sergeant Cheeseman. "Get to the barn," he yelled, and then he released him.

But, Michael did not go to the barn. As he ran away from the Sergeant he spread his fingers. He could see, everything was hazy, and his eyes burned something fierce, but he could see.

And, what he saw was an open field, and beyond that field was a line of trees, and in those trees, there was no shooting, there was no killing, and there was no dying. He needed to be in those trees. He started running as hard as he could, with the sound of battle behind him, and the sound of spent balls whizzing overhead, he ran for the trees.

Michael didn't know how long he had been running, but suddenly, he crashed into the tree line. He kept going, briars and bushes tore at his skin and uniform, he crashed headlong into trees, but he kept going, trying to get as far away as possible from the terrifying elephant.

As he pulled himself free from a patch of briars he fell head first down an embankment and into a stream. The water was about four feet deep, and it was ice cold. He screamed out in frustration and pain as he regained his footing and stood up in the middle of the stream. He was gagging and choking as he spit out the brown gritty water, and struggled to catch his breath.

Then he realized there was silence. The only sound was the gentle swishing of the flowing water. There were no guns, or screams, just water.

He stood shivering, chest deep, in the icy water. Then, taking a deep breath, he slowly lowered himself until he was completely underwater. He held his breath for as long as he could, then he surfaced, and then he did it again, and again, and again, and again.

He lost track of how many times he submerged himself, but when he was done he made his way to the opposite bank, he found a small patch of grass, he laid down, curled himself into a ball, and shivering from the cold, and his state of mind, he started to cry, and he cried for a long time. He cried until he fell asleep, and when he awoke it was dark, and although he was lost, he also knew that he was found.

As Michael laid there in the darkness he realized, that he wasn't really a coward, he was just a boy, a boy who had placed himself in a situation that now required he be a man. He listened to the softly flowing stream, and he thought of all the times he had lain along the banks of the Rancocas as a young boy, wondering when the time would come that he would no longer be a boy, but a man. And, in the quiet darkness along this little stream, hundreds of miles from the banks of his beloved Rancocas, he realized that that time was now.

Michael was about a mile and a half from where the 10th New Jersey had been engaged with the Confederates on Myers Hill. He figured that when he ran he had run east. So, when the sun came up, he put it at his back, and headed west, back towards Myers Hill, in search of the Regiment.

He hadn't gone very far when he came across the Fredericksburg Road. He encountered couriers, and various sized groups of troops on the road, but he continued west, until he found the road that would lead him back to Myers Hill and the 10th New Jersey.

When he reached the farm at the top of the hill, he found that the house had been burned, and what was left of it was still smoldering. The smell of the smoke hung heavy in the air, and mixed with the smoke of the numerous cook fires that were burning in the yard and fields surrounding the farm. He suddenly realized how hungry he was, not having had anything to eat for nearly two days.

Although he could see that there were troops stationed at the breastworks, there were no shots being fired in either direction. The Regiment had obviously secured the high ground. He was glad to be back, but he was also concerned about what was going to happen now, he had deserted his post, he had run from battle. But, he also knew, that whatever happened, he was now better prepared to face it.

It didn't take him long to find Frank Jefferson, and the other members of Second Squad who were gathered around a fire cooking fatback, and boiling coffee.

"Praise Jesus!" Exclaimed Frank when he saw Michael, as he jumped up and grabbed him in an embrace. "I was certain you was dead or captured!"

"Nope. Here I am," said Michael sheepishly.

"I saw you go down," continued Frank. "Looked like you took a head shot. Scared the bejesus outta me!" Then holding Michael at arms' length he took a good look at him. "Did you get attacked by a bear or something?" He asked with a laugh. "You're tore to pieces."

Michael then took a look at himself and saw the cuts and scratches all over his arms, face, and legs the briars and brush had caused, as well as the rips and tears in what was left of his uniform. "Guess I'm a sight, ain't I," he said with a grin.

"You are at that, and a damned fine one too," said Frank. "I got your stuff. Your haversack and knapsack, your gun, and even your cap. I fired your gun, 'cause it was loaded, and when they pushed us back yesterday, they was coming so fast there at the end, I didn't have time to reload mine. So, after I fired your gun I just grabbed up everything and took off along with everybody else."

"Wait, they pushed you back yesterday?"

"Sure did!" Said Frank with a smile. "Came up over the top of this hill like a herd of wild monkeys. But, we regrouped, and before it was dark we took it right back, and ain't heard shot one from 'em since."

"McBride you're back," said a voice from behind Michael. When he turned he came face to face with Sergeant Cheeseman. "Guess you must have got out of the barn before the attack. When they overran us most everybody in the barn got left behind."

Michael took a deep breath. "I never went to the barn Sarge," he said. "I was…"

"No, of course you didn't," said the Sergeant. "I remember, you couldn't see. How could you be expected to find the barn? I should have had someone take you there."

"No Sarge," Michael began again. "That wasn't it."

"Of course it was," said Sergeant Cheeseman softly as he looked Michael directly in the eye. "You were having trouble seeing. Your vision was blurred. But, it looks like your vision is good now, isn't it? How about it Michael?" He asked as he reached out and put his hand on Michael's shoulder. "Can you see things more clearly now?"

"Yes," Michael answered trying to swallow the lump that had come up in his throat. "Very clear. I'm fine now, and anxious to do my part."

"Good," said the Sergeant as he slapped Michael on the upper arm. "Glad to hear it, because I won't be able to help you next time, I mean if there ever comes another time when you lose sight of things. Understand?"

Michael just nodded.

"Now, get something to eat and get yourself cleaned up, you look like hell. Who knows when we'll be on the move again."

When the Sergeant had left, Michael turned to Frank. "What happened to Bill?"

"Took a ball in the thigh. Didn't hit no bone or anything. Should be fine. After we retook the hill, they put him in an ambulance and shipped him to a hospital in the rear."

"Good," said Michael. "Good."

As he looked around he noticed that it appeared as if there were a lot of familiar faces missing. When the Regiment left Spotsylvania five days later on the 20th of May, they had less than 400 in the ranks. They had crossed the Rapidan sixteen days earlier with over 600. In the following weeks, the Regiment would be engaged in battles along the North Anna River, at Hanover Court House, and Cold Harbor. The heaviest fighting they would encounter would be at Cold Harbor. Through it all, Private Michael J. McBride, would carry out his duties.

He may not have been considered the most gallant, but he was reliable and steady. He saw men die, both Union and Confederate, both friend and stranger. He saw the fear and terror in the faces of the men in the lines of gray he would fire into as they would crumple and fall.

Often he would wear their blood as a result of close quarters fighting, or by trying to help the wounded, from both sides. He could wash the blood off, but not the memories or the nightmares they spawned. His father had been right, war changed men, even those who were not wounded physically, because war wounded men's souls, and those wounds did not easily heal.

Chapter 36

The Shenandoah
1864

On June 12th, the 10th New Jersey, their strength now at less than 200, along with the First New Jersey Brigade, and the rest of VI Corps, once again disengaged from General Lee's Army of Northern Virginia, and moved south towards Richmond. The VI Corps, crossed the Appomattox River, and on June 14th, encamped at Hopewell, eight miles northeast of Petersburg. Here they would remain in reserve, as General Grant laid siege to Petersburg.

On the morning of July 9th, shortly after breakfast, Michael, Frank, and other members of the Second Squad were preparing to form up and head out to the docks at City Point to help with the loading of wagons headed to the front. They had been assigned to this duty for the last couple of weeks. It was not very exciting work, but as Frank pointed out, neither was anyone shooting at them.

"Look sharp!" Said Sergeant Cheeseman as he hurriedly approached. "Grab your weapons and follow me, we're falling in with the rest of the Regiment."

"What's up Sarge?" Asked Frank.

"Company's coming."

"Company? What sort of company?"

"Grant," answered the Sergeant. "General Grant himself is on his way to inspect the Regiment. So, shut up and try not to do anything too stupid."

The Regiment quickly fell in and formed up on a small parade ground outside their camp area. As they waited Michael glanced around at the formation. They were nowhere near regimental strength.

There were now only five companies; A, D, E, G, and H. A, D, and E Companies made up the First Battalion, and G, and H Companies were all that was left of Second Battalion. H Company was now the largest with about fifty men, E Company the smallest, at about 35. With officers and enlisted, they were right around 200. A regiment was generally supposed to consist of around 1,000 enlisted men and officers. General Grant, accompanied by General Wright of VI Corps, General Penrose of the First New Jersey Brigade, and about eight other officers of various rank approached the Regiment on horseback. It was immediately obvious that here was a man who was comfortable on a horse. Colonel Tay called the Regiment to attention, and all the officers drew their swords and saluted. The Commanding General returned the salutes.

From his faded battered slouch hat, which displayed no insignia of any kind, to his well-worn mud-caked boots, Ulysses S. Grant, was an ordinary scrubby looking man. He wore a private's coat with the insignia of his rank sewn onto the shoulders. His aversion to fancy uniforms and the other trappings of rank were well known.

After speaking briefly with the Colonel he surveyed the ranks. His eyes, peering out from beneath his hat and above his dark beard, were measuring them. An unlit cigar was clenched in his teeth. Despite his appearance there was no doubt that the man before them was a leader, and that he would accept no less than victory.

"Colonel," said the General not taking his eyes off the troops. "Please put your men at ease. I'd like to speak to them informally."

"Y-y-yes Sir," stammered the Colonel as he turned to Majors McNeely and Berriman. "Have the Regiment stand at ease," he said.

"Yes Sir," answered the Majors as they saluted. They then turned to their respective Battalions and in unison gave the order. "Battalion, stand at ease."

In unison the company commanders passed the order on, and the Regiment sharply complied with the order.

General Grant smiled and nodded. "Well done," he said. "Good morning men. I don't think there's any need for me to introduce myself to you. This is nothing formal, I just thought I'd come down and visit with the men of the 10th New Jersey." He dismounted, and with Colonel Tay at his side began to walk up and down the ranks.

"I understand that many of you are from around Burlington, back in New Jersey, along the Delaware. Is that right?" Many of the men nodded or responded with a yes sir, or other confirmation. "I have been told that Burlington is a fine town. In fact it has been recommended that I move my own family there until this conflict is resolved, and it is very likely that I shall do so. So, it is possible that we may have more in common than our blue uniforms, and our love of the Union, we may actually become neighbors." He stopped in front of Michael. "What is your name soldier?" He asked.

"Michael," stammered Michael. "Um, Private McBride that is Sir, um, Private Michael McBride Sir."

"Are you from Burlington Private McBride?" The General asked with a smile.

"No Sir, Rancocas, Sir."

"Are you familiar with Burlington?"

"Yes Sir, very much so," answered Michael with a smile.

"So," said General Grant. "Should we become neighbors, are you someone I could count on?"

"Yes Sir!" Exclaimed Michael.

"Good, because I believe that neighbors should always be able to count on one another." The General walked back up to the front of the formation and turned to face them. "Just as I did not need to be introduced to you," he continued. "Neither did you need to be introduced to me. I am well aware of what this Regiment has accomplished and endured the last couple of months. Your gallantry, your courage, and your sacrifices have been an inspiration to this entire Army.

"I had hoped that I would be able to let you rest and recover here in Hopewell while we laid siege to Petersburg, but I'm afraid I must call upon you to return to action. We have received word that General Early's Second Corps has left the Shenandoah Valley, and is moving on Washington. It is necessary therefore that Washington be reinforced.

"Later today you and the rest of VI Corps, along with XIX Corps, will be boarded onto steamers that will then set out for Washington at the best possible speed.

I have every confidence that this action will insure the safety and security of our capital. I know I can count on you men to do what is necessary, as my soldiers, and as my neighbors. Carry on."

With that General Grant mounted his horse, saluted the Regiment, spun his horse, and started back up the road towards City Point, with his entourage in pursuit, as the 10th New Jersey Regiment let loose with a deafening cheer.

They arrived in Washington on the 11th. That same day General Early attacked Fort Stevens on the northern edge of the city's defenses, but when he learned of the arrival of the VI and XIX Corps, he disengaged and fell back into Virginia. The VI and XIX pursued General Early, and on July 18th, fought him at Snicker's Ford east of Winchester. The Confederates were defeated and retreated south.

Generals Wright and Emory satisfied that the threat to Washington had passed, put the VI and XIX Corps on the march back towards Petersburg. However, when General Early learned of their departure, he took full advantage and on July 23rd, attacked and routed Union forces at Kernstown, in the Shenandoah Valley. Then he sent his cavalry north and on July 30th, they burned the town of Chambersburg, PA, before crossing back into Virginia on August 3rd.

General Grant had had enough. On August 5th, the VI, VIII, and XIX Corps were formed into the Army of the Shenandoah and placed under the command of General Philip H. Sheridan. General Grant's orders to General Sheridan were to completely rid the Shenandoah Valley of General Early and his Corps once and for all. On August 10th, The Army of the Shenandoah started south from the area of Harper's Ferry, West Virginia, to engage General Early.

The First New Jersey Brigade, with Private Michael McBride, and the 10th New Jersey fought with elements of General Early's Corps on the 17th, outside of Winchester, Virginia. The Brigade was assigned to hold the Front Royal Road, and when initially attacked they drove the enemy back. However, General Early countered and sent a large portion of his Army forward to take the road. It was just after six in the morning.

"We can't stay here!" Michael heard Sergeant Cheeseman loudly exclaim to Lieutenant Ryan, Third Platoon Commander, as the overwhelming numbers of Confederate infantrymen continued to advance on their position.

The 10th, was deployed in a defensive position on Guard Hill on the east side of the road. The rest of the Brigade was deployed on their right in the open fields on the west side of the road. Despite holding the high ground, it was obvious, even to Michael that it was only going to be a matter of minutes before the Confederates would be in their flanks.

"We're falling back!" Yelled Lieutenant Ryan.

"Fall back!" Hollered the Sergeant. "Maintain your lines, but fall back!"

Michael looked to his right and could see from the top of the hill that the 4th and 15th New Jersey Regiments, had broken and were beating a hasty retreat up the Front Royal Road. Although it was straggly and full of gaps, the 10th did maintain some semblance of order as it tried to escape the Confederate onslaught. They had opened up the gap between themselves and the Confederates to about 300 yards when, unable to stand the pressure any longer, they too broke.

Despite the fact that the rest of the Brigade continued their retreat north towards Ninevah, Colonel Tay rallied the 10th at the Kenner Farm about a mile north of their original position. With no support, they formed a line with the intent of slowing the Confederate advance long enough to allow reinforcements to arrive. What they did not know was that a large force of Confederates had beaten them to this location and were about to strike the left flank of their vastly outnumbered regiment.

With the blood curdling Rebel yell the Confederates on their left burst from the trees, and while the line of Confederates to their front continued to pour lead into them, attacked. In seconds they were on them. They were in front of them, behind them, and among them.

Quickly the fighting became hand to hand. Men on both sides were being bayoneted, muskets were being used as clubs anything men could get their hands on was being used as a weapon. It was the bloodiest and most violent fight Michael had ever seen.

Using his musket to block the blows, Michael was defending himself against a man who was swinging his musket at him. The butt of the man's musket struck the end of Michael's with such force that it snapped off Michael's bayonet, and knocked his musket from his hands leaving him defenseless. The man drew back his musket as he prepared to strike the blow that Michael knew would be his end.

Suddenly, a shot rang out from somewhere behind Michael. Where the man's face had been there was now a bloody hole. The faceless man stood there for what seemed like several seconds before collapsing in a heap, the musket still firmly in his grasp. Michael turned to look, but did not see where the shot had come from, who fired the shot, or even from what side it came.

What he did know was that if they did not flee, the entire regiment would be destroyed. He looked around and saw Frank Jefferson a few yards away lying in a pool of blood. While the fight continued to rage around him he rushed to Frank and knelt down at his side.

The right side of Frank's shirt was covered in blood, and there was a bloody gash across his forehead, but he was still breathing. Grabbing him by his left arm, Michael pulled him up, threw him over his shoulder, and with his head down ran. Somehow he managed to escape the melee, gasping for air, and with his legs about to give out at any minute, he ran north until he collapsed.

He continued in this fashion, running with Frank on his back and stopping to rest when he had to. They had covered about two miles when Frank regained consciousness. However, he was disoriented and very weak. Sometimes helping, but mostly carrying Frank, it took Michael nearly five hours to travel the three and a half miles and get them to the Union lines at Ninevah.

Thankfully, Frank's wounds were not serious. The wound in his side was from a bayonet, but was not very deep, and only required cleaning and bandaging. The gash on his forehead required stitching, and would result in a headache that would last for days, and a scar that would last forever.

After a few days' rest, Frank was able to return to duty. However, it would be several more days before he could comfortably wear a hat. Michael considered them both very lucky to have survived the fight on the Front Royal Road.

Many had not survived. The Regiment lost nearly eighty men, either killed or captured. Among them was their Commander Colonel Tay and several of the other officers including Third Platoon's Lieutenant Ryan. Sergeant Cheeseman had been lost as well. The Regiment's strength was now at less than 150.

Over the next couple of days the First New Jersey Brigade moved north to Charles Town, where they would remain until September 2nd. On that day, with Major Lambert Boeman now in command of the company sized regiment, the Army of the Shenandoah marched south to Berryville. General Sheridan vowed he would continue moving south through the Valley until General Early's Second Corps ceased to exist.

The 10th New Jersey, and the rest of the Brigade were held in reserve when General Early attempted to block General Sheridan's movement by striking VIII Corps' left flank at Berryville. After his initial success, General Early realized how vastly outnumbered he was and withdrew west towards Winchester. He established a defensive line along the Opequan Creek.

For the next several days the two Armies repeatedly skirmished. General Sheridan probed and tested the Confederate lines looking to exploit any weakness he might find. Meanwhile, the New Jersey Regiments remained encamped east of the creek, away from the fighting.

General Early mistook General Sheridan's probing for a reluctance to engage and so spread his Army out, sending units as far away as Martinsburg some twenty miles to the north. General Sheridan learning that General Early had divided his forces, realized his opportunity had arrived. On September 19th, just before noon, he struck, and he struck hard.

Michael, and the New Jersey Regiments were called into action. They moved forward with the rest of VI Corps, and engaged with General Rodes' Confederate Division in the center of the Union line. They advanced very little as the rebels put up a stiff resistance against the depleted brigade.

Throughout the day, General Early desperately tried to concentrate his Army around Winchester. As his troops arrived he was able to hold against the heavy frontal assaults for several hours, but when late in the afternoon, Union cavalry north of Winchester crushed his left flank he had no choice but to withdraw.

When the left flank collapsed Michael and the New Jersey Regiments rushed forward, driving the Confederate troops before them. General Rodes' Division along with the rest of General Early's Army was in full retreat. They fled, whirling through the streets of Winchester in confusion and panic.

General Early was able to get control of his troops at Kernstown five miles south of Winchester. He continued moving them south an additional fifteen miles taking a defensive position on the formidable heights south of Strasburg known as Fisher's Hill. Here he dug in and waited for Sheridan.

General Sheridan arrived in Strasburg with his Army of the Shenandoah in the afternoon of September 20th. The 10th New Jersey Regiment, with the rest of VI Corps, was positioned west of the town.

"We going up that?" Frank Jefferson asked no one in particular as Fisher's Hill came into view of the Regiment. The imposing mound towered nearly 300 feet above the valley floor, and from where they stood it appeared to go straight up.

"I hope not," Michael answered. "Be suicide to even try."

They slept in the shadow of Fisher's Hill that night, and in the early afternoon the following day, they formed into line of battle and advanced on the Confederate positions on the high ground to their front. They had advanced less than a mile when they encountered a picket line deployed on the smaller hills near the base of Fisher's Hill. They quickly disposed of the pickets and for the rest of the day held this position.

Captain George Adams and his First Rhode Island Artillery took up a position to their right and began shelling the Confederate positions nearer the crest of Fisher's Hill. There was some minor skirmishing to their right and left during the day and into the night, but no major engagements. The 10th New Jersey spent the night alongside Captain Adams' artillery in the trenches and breastworks that their predecessors had been driven from.

The next morning, Michael and the few remaining men who made up Second Squad were sitting around a small fire boiling a pot of coffee. The cannons to their right were silent, and there was only sporadic musket fire coming from their left.

As Michael sipped his coffee, he looked up at the face of Fisher's Hill, and said, "They're not going to let us just sit here while the Rebs hold the high ground."

"So, you think they're going to send us up it?" Asked Frank.

"I don't see any other way," answered Michael. "We can't move around them. The valley is only about four miles wide here, and from up there they could cause us some serious damage if we tried."

"Maybe he'll leave," said Frank wistfully as he glanced up at the hill.

"If he does he may as well go all the way to the Carolinas, because that hill is the key to this entire valley," said Michael. "The Rebs need this valley, it's just about the only place left where they can get food. No, he's not going anywhere, at least, not without a fight."

"Thanks for brightenin' my day," said Frank with a smile.

"My pleasure," answered Michael as he lifted his cup in a toast to his friend.

It was after three o'clock that afternoon, when they received orders to prepare to move forward. Their new regimental commander, Major Boeman, with an excessive amount of fanfare, maneuvering, and parading around, eventually got them into line of battle, prepared to advance. It took so long, and involved so much unnecessary movement, that the men of the Regiment began to doubt the competency of their new commander.

They advanced slowly as did other regiments to their left and right. The entire line would advance a couple of hundred yards, occasionally taking ineffective fire from the heights, then stop while the officers adjusted or straightened the line.

"We're not going up this hill," said Michael softly to Frank, who was on his right.

"What?" Asked Frank.

"We're not going up this hill, at least not like this. Something is going on," he continued. "We're a diversion, that's why we're making such a spectacle of ourselves."

"What the devil are you talking about?"

"Look out there to the left," said Michael nodding in that direction as they were once again stopped. "See, beyond our lines are the fellows from the Nineteenth Corps, but if you look to our right, there's only the Sixth Corps, our fellows. General Crook and his Eighth Corps is missing."

"So, what does that mean?" Asked Frank.

"They're up to some mischief somewhere."

"Well," said Frank. "Whatever they're up to, I wish they would get on with it. I'm beginning to develop a real fear of heights."

By four o'clock they had reached the base of the hill and were preparing to begin their assault. The fire from the top of the hill was still sporadic and not very effective. However, once the Union troops started up the hill and closed on the Confederate positions, they would be much easier targets. Successful or not, the assault would be a bloodbath.

"Looks to me like we're going up," said Frank.

"I don't know," said Michael glancing back and forth along the line. "Where's Crook?"

"Back in Strasburg, drinking whiskey, and being held in reserve," said Frank nervously.

"No," said Michael. "He's here somewhere."

Then the order came to advance, and the 10th New Jersey, and the entire Union line started up the steep face of Fisher's Hill. They hadn't gone far when they heard the sound of heavy musket fire coming from in front of their far right. Something was happening on the Confederate left flank.

At first, they advanced up the hill rather slowly. They began to notice, that the troops on their right were moving quicker, and Michael and the rest of the Regiment and VI Corps, were having trouble keeping up with them. Then, the word came down the line.

General Crook and his VIII Corps had struck the Confederate left. They had caught them completely by surprise, were in their rear, and were rolling up the entire Confederate line. The right flank of the VI Corps had linked up with the left flank of the VIII Corps, and the whole Union line was now quickly advancing towards the summit. Michael and the other troops who were ascending the face of the hill were struggling up the steep rocky slope. They would advance, stop to fire a volley, and then advance again. In this manner they slowly worked their way to the top.

Darkness was beginning to descend on the valley when Michael, Frank, and the rest of the Regiment, finally made the top of the hill. Exhausted, they stood and watched as on the valley floor below, the defeated Confederate II Corps beat a hasty retreat south. For the second time in four days, they had routed the enemy.

In the weeks that followed General Sheridan continued to push General Early south. Union cavalry constantly harassed his rearguard, and advance units would sometimes skirmish with the rearguard, but General Early continued his retreat. The pursuit continued until they reached Staunton, some seventy miles south of Fisher's Hill.

General Sheridan was convinced that General Early and his II Corps, were no longer a threat to the valley. Abandoning their pursuit they turned around and marched back up the valley systematically burning farms, crops, and mills as they marched. No longer could the Confederacy rely on the Shenandoah Valley to feed their Armies.

Chapter 37

The Delaware
1940

"Your dad still have that friend in Washington?" Lieutenant Baxter "Woody" Underwood asked his shipmate, and cousin, Lieutenant Edward Randall. They were seated at a table in the Officers' Club at the Philadelphia Navy Yard.

"You mean the Senator?" Answered Ed. "Yeah, I think so. They're Lodge buddies." There was a pause. "You ever think of joining up?"

"I did join up," answered Woody. "That's why I'm here."

"No," said his cousin, "not the Navy, the Masons. Dad never came right out and asked me to join, but he was always dropping these little hints. I figured if he would have really wanted me to join, he'd just come right out and say so, instead of beating around the bush, so I just kept blowing him off."

"They're not allowed to," said Woody.

"Who?"

"Masons, they're not allowed to ask anybody to join, you have to ask them."

"How do you know that?"

"Evan, he's a Mason," answered Woody. "So is his grandfather, his great-grandfather, his great-great-grandfather, and so on, and so on, and so on, for as far back as he knows."

"No kidding? Ain't that something?"

"My dad came right out and asked me, but I turned him down. We weren't really on good terms at the time."

"Was that when you told him you didn't want anything to do with the ranch?" Asked Ed.

"Yeah, it was right in there, along with some other issues. I thought he kind of accepted that I wasn't cut out for a life on the range once he realized I was serious about the Navy, and wasn't just being rebellious or anything. He seemed proud enough about my appointment to the Academy, but I don't know, maybe he was a little bit angry. I think he was hurt too, and he had every right to be I guess."

"Next time I write," said Ed. "I'm going to ask my dad about joining. Why don't you, maybe we can do whatever it is you have to do together."

"I'll think about it," said Woody. "I really will think about it."

"Yeah, well anyway," said Ed, "Uncle Harry, yeah, he's still in Washington. In fact, he's the Chairman of the Committee on Military Affairs. Why?"

"Because we have to get Evan back to Rancocas by May 11th," said Woody, "and, we're going to need some real horsepower to get it done."

"Why May 11th?"

"Because that's the day Katy and I have picked for the wedding."

"You old sea dog!" Exclaimed Ed. "Congratulations, it's about time you two settled on a date."

"I want you to be my best man," said Woody, smiling at his cousin.

Ed just stared at him. Woody couldn't believe it, but it seemed possible that this request had really touched Ed. If nothing else it left him speechless.

"It would be an honor," Ed said finally. "I'm not sure I'm deserving or worthy, but if you want me, I will be there for you. You know, I love the both of you very much."

"I know you do Ed, and I never considered anyone else," said Woody. "We've known each other since we were kids, we're cousins, we're shipmates, but more importantly, we're friends." Woody stuck out his hand.

Ed grabbed Woody's hand, stood up, pulled Woody to his feet, and threw his arms around Woody in an embrace. "I love this guy!" He announced to everyone in the club as he rocked Woody back and forth.

An embarrassed Woody finally managed to break himself free, and they sat down. "Scotch!" Said Ed, flagging down a waitress, and pointing to Woody and himself. "Doubles, and keep them coming."

They had finished eating, and the flow of Scotch had slowed considerably. "As groom," said Ed, with just a hint of a slur. "You are the Captain of this wedding. As best man, I am the XO. My first assignment, as I see it, Captain, is to get the target, Lieutenant Evan McBride, from the *USS Lexington*, in Pearl Harbor, Hawaii, to Rancocas, New Jersey, for the wedding on 11 May, 1940. Is this correct?"

"It is," answered Woody sipping from his glass. "You have less than two months to complete your mission."

"Well then, consider it done, Sir," said Ed. "Evan McBride is as good as here. Even if I have to fly to Pearl myself, shanghai his sorry ass, and carry him back here strapped across my back. My mission will be accomplished!" He barked as he jumped to his feet, came to attention, and saluted Woody.

"Very well!" Said Woody, jumping up and returning the salute. "Carry on, Mr. Randall."

"Aye aye, Sir!"

Then they both collapsed back into their chairs, laughing. They decided that they had had enough. They paid their tab, and headed back to the *Rhind*.

For the next several weeks, numerous telephone calls were made back and forth from the Philadelphia Navy Yard to the Randall residence on Demenil Street, in St. Louis, and to the office of Senator Harry S. Truman, in Washington, DC. Lieutenant Ed Randall was convinced that it was going to get worked out, and that Lieutenant Evan McBride would be in Rancocas for his sister's wedding. Woody was not so sure.

In the meantime, in Rancocas, Katy was busy planning her wedding. Ed's girlfriend Nancy had agreed to serve as her Maid of Honor, and was taking the train every weekend out to the McBride farm to help get everything ready. Clara Jacobs, of Burlington, a baker of local renown, had been commissioned to create the wedding cake, while Mary Meredith, and Louisa Laws, from the village would be preparing the bulk of the food. Ed had hired a photographer from Moorestown, as part of his wedding present to the couple.

Katy had decided to wear her mother's wedding gown. She had brought it down from the attic, and found that while it was in need of some repair, and alterations, there was nothing that could not be fixed. With Nancy at her side, they paid a visit to Susan Carter, Mt. Holly's leading dress maker, who confirmed that not only could the dress be saved, but that it could indeed be restored to its former glory.

Katy McBride had never been much for fashion. She had a few nicer stylish outfits, but nothing extravagant. Most of her clothes were plain and practical. When she was going through her closet, she looked at everything and chuckled to herself, "No wonder I'm 24 and single."

On the other hand, her Maid of Honor, Nancy, did know a thing or two about fashion. With Katy in tow, they caught the train into Philadelphia, and by the time they were finished, Katy had a wardrobe fitting of a young attractive woman of the times. Katy initially felt guilty about the purchases she had made, but felt better after Nancy explained how important it was for the wife of an up and coming young naval officer to look the part, and to be "squared away".

On April 6, 1940, Lieutenant Evan McBride, and his wife Irene, were enjoying a Saturday evening dinner with her father at his estate overlooking Fort Shafter in the hills north of Honolulu. The *USS Lexington* was in port for the weekend, but would be leaving to return to sea early Monday morning. Johnathan Northrup was a gracious host, and thought very highly of his daughter's choice in husbands.

"Seems I'm to go to Washington," announced Mr. Northrup.

"Washington?" Asked his daughter in surprise. "When, why?"

"May," answered her father. "I'm to appear before the Military Affairs Committee. I received a letter this morning from the Committee Chairman, Senator Harry S. Truman. Seems they want to discuss improving the ability of the Navy to utilize, repair, and service civilian merchant vessels at naval facilities in times of crisis or war."

"I'm impressed," said his daughter.

"Congratulations, Sir," said Evan. "Testifying before a Senate Committee is quite an honor."

"Yes," said Mr. Northrup. "I suppose it is. We are expected to arrive in Washington, no later than May 6th. The hearing will be held on the 7th, and 8th, and then on the 9th, we will be given a tour of the service and repair facilities at the Philadelphia Navy Yard."

"We?" Asked Irene. "Is someone going with you?"

"Yes," answered her father with a smile. "Your husband, and you too I would imagine." Evan and Irene just stared. "There was a handwritten note from the Senator in with the official document. It said that my son-in-law, Lieutenant Evan McBride, would soon be receiving orders temporarily detaching him from his current duties, and assigning him to me as my naval liaison. The orders would cover the period from May 3rd, to May 17th.

"There was a postscript from the Senator, it said, and I quote, "Enjoy the wedding, compliments of George Randall, of St. Louis, Missouri, Senator Harry S. Truman, of Washington, DC, and Lieutenant Ed Randall, of the *USS Rhind*, best man."

"Well, I'll be damned," exclaimed Evan. "They actually pulled it off."

"Am I to understand," said Mr. Northrup, with a chuckle, "that my great honor is no more than a scheme to get you two home for your sister's wedding?"

"No, I'm sure there really is going to be a hearing," chuckled Evan. "I'm just not sure how important it was that you have a junior officer off of an aircraft carrier, assigned to you as a "naval liaison"."

"Well, in any event," said Johnathan Northrup, with a smile. "Looks like we're going to a wedding."

On April 8, 1940, Lieutenant Baxter Underwood, and Katherine Rosemary McBride, went to Mt. Holly, where they applied for and were issued a marriage license. That same day, they met with Pastor Whitall, at the church to confirm the date of the wedding, and to reserve the Grange Hall, at the end of 2nd Street for the reception. All was in readiness, well, almost.

On Thursday, Katy, dressed to go out, took the old farm truck and drove the mile and half to the small one story white washed clapboard cabin on the Burlington Road. This was the home of the Simmons family, Marcus, his wife Olive, and there young son Mikey.

Katy knocked, and the door was opened by Mrs. Simmons. "Well, Miss Kate," she said with a smile. "Don't you look nice? Come in, come in. Please make yourself to home, take a seat."

"Thank you, Mrs. Simmons," said Katy, stepping into the center room of the house which served as the main living area. She was carrying a small sack. The furnishings in the house were old and worn, but the house was clean, and several vases of fresh spring flowers brightened the room. "I wonder if I might speak with Mikey," asked Katy, as she took a seat.

"Of course," said Mrs. Simmons. "He's in the kitchen waiting to lick a cornbread bowl. Mikey!" She hollered. "A young lady has come to call on you."

Within seconds, Mikey burst into the room. His eyes got big as saucers when he saw Katy. "Hello, Miss Kate," he said blushing. "You sure look pretty."

"Thank you Mikey," she said.

"You still gwanna marry dat Lootin' Underman?"

"Yes," she said with a smile. "I hope you'll be happy for me."

"Hmmph." Was the best Mikey could do, crossing his arms in front of him. He had always believed that once he was grown, it would be him that would marry Miss Kate.

"I thought you liked Lieutenant Underwood?"

"I do, I 'pose, just not as the marryin' man for you."

"He makes me happy," she said with a smile. "Don't you want me to be happy?"

"Course I do," he sighed rolling his head around and avoiding eye contact with Katy.

"Well, I've come to talk to you about the day we're going to get married, the wedding," she had Mikey's full attention now. "We need someone reliable, honest, dependable, and strong to help us out, and naturally, I immediately thought that this could be a job for you."

Mikey walked over and sat down beside Katy. "What kinda job is it?" He asked.

"Ring bearer."

"What's a ring brearer?"

"Oh, it's a very important job," she said. "You would walk down the aisle of the church ahead of me. Kind of as my guard, making sure everyone got out of my way, and that I was safe."

"Uh huh," he said, now completely mesmerized.

"You would be carrying a small pillow, and on that pillow will be the rings that Lieutenant Underwood and I will give to each other when we become husband and wife. It is very important that those rings arrive safely at the altar, because if they don't, there can be no marriage, and if that happened, I would be so sad, that probably nothing would ever make me feel happy again. So, you can see how important a job this is can't you?"

Mikey, his eyes wide, just nodded. His mother was standing across the room, smiling and watching as Katy hooked Mikey, and carefully began to reel him in.

"Would you like to see the pillow you'll be carrying?" Katy reached into the sack she had brought with her and removed a small specially designed and made navy blue silk pillow. Embroidered in gold into the center of the pillow was the logo of the *USS Rhind*, on the reverse side were the names of the bride and groom, and the date." She handed Mikey the pillow. He held it like he was holding a priceless artifact.

"Lootin' Underman gibbed me a pitcher of the USS Rhyme," he said.

"I know he did," she said.

"What happens to the pillow when the marryin's over?" He asked.

"Why?" She asked.

"Seems," he said holding the pillow at arms' length and studying it, "dat da person 'sponsible for it durin' the marryin', should be 'sponsible for it afterwards. Seein' how importin it is an everything."

Katy thought about it. "Okay," she said, "but, under one condition. You've got to promise me that you'll take good care of it forever, that you'll never lose it, or let anything happen to it. Can you promise me that?"

Mikey nodded.

"Then it's a deal," she said sticking out her hand. Mikey took her hand, and they shook on it. "Now," she said turning her attention to Mrs. Simmons. "If it's alright, I'd like to take my ring bearer into Mt. Holly for lunch at the Washington House. Then we'll do some shopping and get him a new suit of clothes for the wedding."

"Certainly, Miss Kate," said Mrs. Simmons. "Thank you so much, but you let me know how much those clothes are, and me and Marcus, we'll pay you back for them."

"Nonsense," said Katy. "It's a gift. Besides," she said stroking Mikey's cheek. "When you break a young man's heart, you should let him down easy."

Katy and Mikey piled into the truck, and headed out for Mt. Holly. They spent the rest of the day thoroughly enjoying themselves. Katy thought that maybe this was what being a mother felt like.

All was now truly in readiness.

Saturday, May 11, 1940, began as a cloudy dreary day, but by ten o'clock, the clouds began to break up, and there was a hope that the sun would shine. The wedding would begin at two, and Katy, to her surprise, felt completely in control. She could not have known it of course, but Woody on the other hand, having barely survived his bachelor party, was a complete mess!

There were two cars parked in the yard. Ed Randall's washed and waxed shimmering yellow 1939 Buick convertible, and a second 1939 Buick convertible identical in almost every way, except for the color. The second car was green.

Woody's parents, Ron and Ursula Underwood, and his younger brother Ted, had arrived in Rancocas in the green car from the airport in Camden, on Thursday. On Friday, Ted had used the car to pick up George and Peggy Randall at the airport, and bring them to Rancocas. The Underwood's and the Randall's were staying at the Washington House Hotel in Mt. Holly.

Katy and her soon to be in-laws had hit it off immediately. They insisted that she call them Mom and Dad, which made Katy cry, because she had never had anyone to call Dad before, and had had no one to call Mom, since her mother's death when she was ten years old. The Randall's, were to be known as Uncle George and Aunt Peggy.

Ted gave everyone a laugh when he apologized and announced that the only name he could go by was Ted. That was, until his mother pointed out that Katy could always call him Teddy, a name he absolutely abhorred. Ted earned himself a kiss from Katy, and a promise that to her, he would always be just Ted. Unless he angered her, then he would be Teddy.

Throughout her life, the only family Katy had ever known was her grandfather, her grandmother, and her brother Evan. Now, she was on the verge of having a mother and a father, an aunt and an uncle, a cousin, and another brother. Family had always meant so much to Katy, now there were going to be so many others to share it with.

By one o'clock, Katy, along with everyone else, was dressed and ready to go to the church. Nancy and Irene were absolutely stunning in emerald green chiffon gowns with matching hats, and white gloves. Her grandfather, who had refused to wear a tuxedo or tails, had agreed to a new very fashionable double breasted suit, in which he looked very dashing.

Katy, presented herself, dressed in her mother's restored wedding gown, to her grandfather in the parlor of their home. "Katy Rose," he said. "I've only ever seen one bride more beautiful, and that would be your grandmother, my Katherine Rosemary. How much I wish she were here to see this."

They both cried, as did Nancy and Irene, which delayed their departure for the church while everyone's makeup was repaired. Mikey, handsome in his new suit, was embarrassed, even more so when all the ladies insisted on planting kisses on his puffy little cheeks.

Nancy and Irene rode in Ed Randall's yellow Buick driven by Lieutenant Rick Simons, a shipmate of Ed and Woody's off of the *Rhind*. Katy, her grandfather, and Mikey rode in the green Buick, with Ted Underwood at the wheel. The trip to the church took less than five minutes, and all along the way friends and neighbors from the village lined the streets and waved. Katy felt like a princess in a fairytale.

With her grandfather at her side, and Mikey bravely leading the way, Katy walked down the aisle to give herself in marriage to a man she had known less than a year, but felt like she had known her entire life. There was no doubt in her mind this was right. There was no doubt in her mind that she was going to be very happy.

Most of the ceremony was a blur. Katy knew that there were statements and responses, and was sure that she had said and done the right thing just like in the rehearsal, but the only thing that she could clearly remember when it was over, was when Reverend Whitall said, "I now pronounce you man and wife. You may kiss the bride." What a kiss, their first as husband and wife.

They exited the church beneath a shower of flower pedals, and an arch of crossed naval swords held aloft by eight US Navy officers decked out in their dress blues. It had turned out to be such a lovely day that they decided to walk the short distance to the Grange Hall. The other part of Ed Randall's wedding present, a five piece dance band, was set up and ready to go when they got there.

The newlyweds enjoyed a fine dinner, and tried to meet and greet all of their guests. Katy danced with her grandfather, which resulted in there not being a dry eye in the house. Then she danced with Evan, then her new father-in-law, then Uncle George Randall, Ed Randall, brother-in-law Ted, Mikey, which lead to another round of tears, Johnathan Northrup, Lieutenant Simons, a host of other naval officers decked out in their dress blues, then friends from the village and surrounding towns and farms, the bandleader, and finally, her husband. Their first dance as husband and wife was to the band's very nice rendition of Bing Crosby's "Only Forever".

They were finally able to break free from the reception and taking the green Buick, they returned to the farm to change and gather their luggage. Katy insisted that they change in separate rooms and that there be no "funny business", until they arrived at the Warrick Hotel in Philadelphia. They would be spending their wedding night in the bridal suite.

The following day they would catch the train to Niagara Falls, where after spending three days and nights exploring this natural wonder, they would continue on to Denver, by air, arriving there on the 16th. The Underwood Ranch, the R Bar U, was about a three hour drive northeast of Denver. Woody's parents and brother would be home by then, and Katy was more excited than she could describe about seeing Colorado and the ranch.

"How will the car get back?" Asked Katy as they were driving to the Warrick Hotel following the wedding.

"Ed will drive Ted over sometime tomorrow and take it back to the farm," answered her husband.

"Good," said Katy, thinking aloud. "Because they're probably going to need it to get everyone where they've got to be to get home."

"Ed's got it all worked out as usual," said Woody. "When all is said and done, the car will be back at the farm when we get back."

"Back at the farm?" Asked Katy. "Why back at the farm?"

"Oh," Woody said turning to smile at his wife, "didn't I tell you?" He tapped the wheel and said, "This beauty is a wedding present from the folks."

"What? This is my car?"

"No," said her husband with a chuckle. "This is our car."

Katy squealed and began looking everywhere in the car, in the glove box, over the visors, under the seats, suddenly more interested in exploring every square inch of it, now that she knew it was theirs. Woody, concerned that she had never driven in the city before, wouldn't let her drive, but promised her she could take it for as long as she wanted when they returned to Rancocas from their honeymoon. Even so, when they arrived at the hotel, Katy jumped into the driver's seat and tried out the all the buttons and pedals.

Niagara Falls was breathtaking, as they explored the area in and around the falls on both sides of the border. They dined at the finer restaurants, danced at the most popular clubs, and every night became more and more knowledgeable of each other as husband and wife. On the 15th, they took the short train ride from Niagara Falls to Buffalo where they would board a plane to Cleveland, stop in Chicago overnight, and then fly on to Denver on the 16th.

Ted met them at the Denver Municipal Airport in a 1935 Ford Station Wagon with wood sides. It wasn't quite as bad as the McBride's farm truck, but one look at it and you knew that it was a work vehicle, and not meant for luxury. With Ted at the wheel, and Katy taking in every site she could while Woody slept, the 140 mile drive over primarily dirt roads took just over three hours. They were still over ten miles from the house when Ted announced, to Katy's amazement, that they were on R Bar U property. It was well after dark by the time they arrived at the house.

The next morning after a hearty breakfast prepared and served by the Underwood's cook, Heidi, Katy's father-in-law asked what she would like to do. "I want to see where the buffalo roam, and the deer and the antelope play!" She announced.

"I'm not so sure we can arrange for any buffalo," he said with a smile, "but, chances are pretty good you'll get to see some deer and antelope."

"Once we're through," said Woody. "We'll saddle up a couple of horses, and if Ted isn't too busy, maybe we can get him to take us on a tour."

"Forgot your way around already?" Asked his father trying to keep the sarcasm out of his voice.

"No," answered Woody, "but, Ted knows this place like the back of his hand. If anybody can show Katy where the deer and the antelope play, it'll be him. What do you say Ted?"

"Sure," said Ted. "I've got something out in the barn I want to show Katy anyway."

About an hour later, Katy and Woody entered the huge barn. Katy was wearing jeans, a checkered linen shirt, boots, and a stylish western hat. Woody looked like a cowboy.

It smelled of horse and alfalfa, and there were at least thirty stalls along the main passage, and another ten in the center of the barn where another passage intersected with the main one. There were three young boys who appeared to be in their teens cleaning the stalls and caring for the horses. They nodded and tipped their hats, but didn't have much to say.

Woody explained that this was where all the hands who worked at the ranch started. They employed 45-50 hands full time to care for the over 3,000 head of cattle that roamed the 17,587 acre ranch, but that number could triple during round up season. There was also miles and miles of fencing that had to be maintained.

"Well here it is," said Ted as he came from the side passage. He was leading a beautiful red and white spotted pinto. "My wedding present to you Katy," he said with a smile and a bow. "Along with the saddle. Anytime you come to the R Bar U, he'll be here waiting for you."

Katy, absolutely caught off guard and speechless, carefully approached the horse. Ted handed her the reins, and Katy rubbed the horse's muzzle, and stroked its forelock. The horse nuzzled Katy in return.

She handed Woody the reins and walked over to Ted and threw her arms around his neck and planted a huge kiss on his cheek. "Thank you so much!" She said. "What's his name?"

"That's up to you," said Ted with a smile. "He's your horse."

Katy turned and looked at her horse. "Rusty," she said. "His name should be Rusty." Then she examined the saddle. It was a fine leather western style saddle, adorned with fringes, and oversized polished wood stirrups. Engraved on each fender in green was "Katy". "It's beautiful," she said, wiping a tear from her eye.

"Well?" Asked Woody. "Are we going to ride, or not?"

Ted had already saddled his horse, as well as Woody's horse, a fine looking Appaloosa named Yankee. As the sun continued to rise in the eastern sky, they rode the bluffs, ravines, stream beds, and open range that surrounded the home ranch. Katy did see deer and antelope, and hundreds of head of cattle, but not one buffalo. After stopping back at the house for lunch the Underwood's joined them, and they rode down to one of the two lakes on the property. This one had been formed by damming the largest of the streams that flowed through the property. The other lake, a natural lake, was three times the size of this one, and was four miles to the south, closer to the southern border of the property.

"We can get some pretty long dry spells out here," explained Woody's father. "So, it's important that we control the water as best we can, so that during those spells we still have access to water, even though we may have to ration it. Not only that," he laughed, "but, this makes a great place to skinny dip when it gets really hot." Everyone laughed, but it also earned him a slap from Ursula. "She slaps me in front of company, but she knows what I'm talking about," he said with a laugh as he distanced himself from his wife who was swatting at him again.

The two days at the ranch flew by, and Katy was sad when the time came for them to leave to return to Denver to catch their flight back to Chicago. Katy promised that they would visit the ranch whenever they could, and the Underwood's promised to consider joining them for Christmas in Rancocas. As her last act before leaving she made Ted swear an oath to personally care for Rusty.

They spent the night in Chicago, and the following day caught the morning flight all the way into Central Airport in Camden. As usual, Ed Randall was there to greet them, but this time he was driving the new green Buick. Katy was not going to be denied this time.

"Hand them over," said Katy as soon as the greetings were over.

"What?" Asked Ed, trying to play the innocent.

"The keys," she said. "The keys to my..., that is," she said with a sidelong glance and smile at Woody, "our car."

"Go ahead," chuckled Woody. "There's no way we're going to stop her."

Katy maneuvered the powerful beauty out onto Route 25, and with the top down, and the wind in her hair, sped north. Though probably not technically in violation of any traffic laws, she made sure that any vehicle she spotted ahead of her, was soon behind her. She was having a wonderful time, while Woody and Ed tried to remain calm.

After a joyful reunion with her grandfather, Katy and Woody moved their luggage and other belongings into the larger bedroom on the first floor of the house. They had decided that not only was this room larger and more comfortable for two than the smaller bedrooms on the second floor, but it also offered the most privacy, and easier access to the bathroom. They had also decided, that in the coming weeks, that they would completely remodel the room, and buy new furniture, making the space exclusively theirs.

Two days after their return, Woody had to report back aboard the *Rhind*. He also went back on the duty schedule. So, at least several times a week, and once every three to four weekends, he would have to remain on board the ship. It was an adjustment for the newlyweds, having to spend so much time apart, but Katy took it in stride.

Besides, if she really wanted to see Woody, she just climbed into her Buick and drove down to the Navy Yard. She was becoming very popular with the officers and crew of the *USS Rhind*.

Chapter 38
Cedar Creek
1864

On October 10th, The Army of the Shenandoah encamped south of Middletown along Cedar Creek. The previous day, General Sheridan had turned his cavalry loose against General Thomas Rosser's Confederate cavalry division. The Union cavalry completely routed the Confederates. With the victory, the Confederate cavalry ceased to be a factor in further operations in the Shenandoah Valley.

The 10th New Jersey, as part of the VI Corps, was encamped west of Middletown, and just north of the Belle Grove Plantation, General Sheridan's Headquarters. The XIX Corps was along the east bank of Cedar Creek just below the plantation, and VIII Corps was just east of and along the Valley Pike. The cavalry was camped north of VI Corps.

For several days, the Army rested. They were refitted, were able to bathe, relax, and receive mail. They were convinced that General Early and his II Corps were no longer a threat to them.

Michael McBride had received a number of letters from his parents and others from friends and neighbors back in New Jersey. Frank Jefferson, who had no family, also received a number of letters, many of them from the same people who had written to Michael. Michael's mother had enlisted letter writers for many of the boys in the 10th New Jersey who had no family, or no one to write to them. They were both extremely happy to have received mail, but there was one letter in particular that really excited them.

It was from their old squad mate, Bill Kemble. Bill had been wounded at Myers Hill during the battle of Spotsylvania back in May, and sent to a hospital in Fredericksburg. They had heard nothing from him since.

"Open it already, will ya!" Urged Frank reaching out trying to assist and hurry Michael as he tore at the envelope,

"I am, I am!" Answered Michael. "But, I don't want to tear the thing into little pieces trying to open it. Then we'll never know what it says." He finally got it open, and looked at Frank with a smile.

"Well go ahead," said Frank. "Read it!"

The letter, which had been written in September, said that Bill had recovered from his wound, but while in the hospital in Fredericksburg, had contracted typhoid fever. Eventually, he was sent home to Beverly to convalesce. He was now back with the Army, but, despite efforts to get back to the Regiment, was being held in City Point. He wished them both well and hoped to see them soon.

General Sheridan, confident that there was no threat to his Army, left the Shenandoah Valley to attend a war conference in Washington. Morale was high, but conditions were perhaps a little lax. For despite what everyone thought, General Early was not yet done.

Moving his reinforced Army throughout the night of October 19th, General Early took up positions on both flanks of the unsuspecting Union Army. In a pre-dawn fog he launched his attack. Within an hour he had driven both the VIII and XIX Corps from their camps and overrun their lines.

The VI Corps, and the 10th New Jersey, warned by the sound of battle and the number of Union troops who were retreating through their camp quickly prepared for the attack they knew was coming. The Confederates hit them like a runaway train. They held for a short time, but like the VIII and XIX Corps, were driven from their camp and forced to retreat.

The VI Corps fell back to the town cemetery and there rallied, and prepared to meet the Confederate onslaught. Union cavalry took up a position on their right, but their left flank was exposed to Confederate forces that were already moving through the town. The fighting was desperate, but the VI Corps held.

The 10th New Jersey was on the right of the line where it linked up with the cavalry. The troopers were from the 2nd US Cavalry. Most were dismounted, but some remained mounted so that they could exploit any Union success, or Confederate weakness.

Michael looked to his right and was glad to see Frank in his usual position. They were lying down, using headstones as breastworks. It was not yet light out, and even if it was, a thick fog hugged the ground, add to this the thick smoke of battle created by muskets and cannons, and it was almost impossible to see anything more than a few feet away.

Minie balls began striking the ground in front of them, and ricocheting off of the headstones. Some of them were striking the men. It was like being attacked by spirits flinging death at you from somewhere behind the curtain of smoke and fog.

Thus it continued, for over an hour, the enemy firing out of the curtain, and the VI Corps firing into it. Neither knowing if they were having an effect, or even if anyone was there. Then the fog began to lift, and there they were.

Perhaps 200 yards to their front was a solid line of gray. Some were standing, some were kneeling, but all were in the process of either firing or reloading their weapons, and now they could see their targets. At first the sudden ability to see what was in their front startled both sides. There was a brief moment when the firing stopped, and they just looked across that deadly space at each other, maybe a little bit shocked, that someone was actually there.

The firing on both sides resumed in earnest. More men were falling now that targets could be seen. It appeared that more gray uniforms were dropping than were blue, and Michael began to hope that maybe they could drive them off.

Michael was kneeling and continually firing from behind a headstone that had the name Charles Dugan inscribed on it. Every time a ball would strike the headstone pieces and chips of it would fly off stinging Michael's face, hands, and arms. He wondered how long it would take for the balls to chip away enough of the headstone to completely expose him.

He looked to his right. Frank was lying with his back to him. Michael assumed he was reloading.

"Frank!" Michael called out to him above the din of battle. There was no answer. "Frank!" He yelled again. "Frank! Goddammit, answer me!" He yelled.

Frank did not answer, or move. Michael's heart began to race, his mouth was dry, and his eyes burned, but not only because of the fighting. Why did Frank not answer?

"Frank!" He half yelled and half sobbed. Then he laid down and low crawled the few feet between them to get to Frank's side.

Michael grabbed Frank by the shoulder and shook him, nothing. He kept whispering Frank's name as he continued to shake him. Minie balls were striking the headstone and the ground all around him.

It was then that he noticed that there was a puddle of blood under Frank's head. Michael rolled Frank onto his back. Frank's eyes were open, but there was no life in them. A ball had passed through the top of his Kepi, and into his skull, killing him instantly.

Oblivious to what was going on around him Michael put his arm around his friend, held him close, and wept. It seemed like he laid there for hours, but in actuality it was only a few seconds.

Michael lifted his head and looked to his left, the line in that direction appeared to be holding. He looked to his right, there was no one there, at least no one who was not wounded or dead. He suddenly realized, that he was the extreme right of the Union line.

He patted Frank's cheek, kissed him on the forehead, and with tears in his eyes, crawled back to his headstone. Michael raised up and was prepared to fire into the gray line, when he suddenly saw someone coming out of the mist to his right. Certain he was being flanked, he quickly turned, and started to squeeze the trigger on his musket.

"Hold on!" Yelled a soldier in blue. "We're on your side. I've got over a dozen men!" The man yelled. "We're going to fall in here on your right."

Michael could tell from their uniforms that they were cavalry. He just nodded. He watched as the trooper, who he now noticed was wearing sergeant's stripes, looked down at Frank as he tried to position himself behind the headstone where Frank was lying.

"He was my friend!" Yelled Michael more menacingly than he intended to. The cavalry sergeant looked at Michael, nodded, and moved to the next headstone. "I'm not leaving here without him!" Michael hollered almost threateningly in the cavalryman's direction.

The sergeant, who was still less than ten feet away, nodded. "If we have to leave!" He hollered back at Michael. "I'll help you carry him."

Michael nodded, and tried to smile, then they both turned their attention to the gray line. They fired and received several more volleys. Then, renting the air with their cursed Rebel yell, the gray line charged.

"Here they come!" Yelled the cavalry sergeant then turned and looked at Michael. They both looked down at Frank's lifeless body. They both knew he was dead. "Get him under an arm!" Yelled the trooper as he jumped up and hooked his right arm under Frank's.

Michael hooked his left arm under Frank's, and hunched over, dragging Frank between them, they began to run. They had gone perhaps 150 yards when the trooper cried out, dropped Frank, grabbed his left arm, and fell to the ground. When the trooper dropped Frank, Michael tripped and fell face first onto his musket, almost knocking himself unconscious, and opening up a nasty gash on his chin.

Then, the Rebels were on them. Most of them ran past them. One stopped, raised his musket, and as Michael watched in horror, plunged his bayonet into the middle of Frank's body.

The Rebel then turned his attention to the cavalry sergeant and, again thrust his bayonet down towards his victim. The trooper rolled, causing the Rebel to miss and instead of striking him in the chest, the bayonet was driven into his wounded left shoulder. The trooper screamed. The Rebel cursed, raised his weapon, and was about to strike again.

Michael knew that if he did not stop this man he would finish off the cavalry sergeant, and then turn his attention to him. In one swift motion, Michael withdrew his bayonet from its scabbard, jumped to his feet, and plunged it into the Rebel's chest. He struck with such force that the blade of the bayonet passed through the man's heart, through his spine, and out his back. Michael's hand, tightly grasping the base of the bayonet was right against the man's chest, and the man's warm blood was running between his fingers.

Their faces were only inches apart, and Michael watched as the light of life in the man's eyes faded and was gone. Michael had never taken the killing in this war personal, but this one he did. This man might not have been the man who had killed Frank, but he was the one who desecrated his body.

"You son of a bitch!" Hissed Michael with a sneer full of hate as he twisted the blade hard before pulling it free and allowing the man to crumple to the ground. He stood over the man, hating him more and more, and wishing so very much that he was home, or anywhere, besides here.

Suddenly, something slammed into Michael. He felt himself flying backwards through the air. His insides were on fire. It felt like he had swallowed hot coals. Everything was moving in slow motion.

He heard a gunshot, loud and close. He looked at the trooper and saw a smoking pistol in his hand. Why would the trooper shoot him he wondered as he slammed into the ground and everything went black. Michael did not know how long he laid there. He slowly opened his eyes, his vision was clouded, but he could tell the sun was down. His insides were still on fire, breathing was difficult, and there was no feeling in his arms or legs.

"The one in the middle is dead." He heard someone say. "But, these two are still alive. Get some stretcher bearers and an ambulance over here, and we'll get 'em outta here."

Michael could not see who it was, but someone was leaning over him. "You sure you want to take this one?" The leaning man asked. "Don't look like he's gonna last much longer."

"What're you a doctor now?" Grumbled the original voice. "Get him on an ambulance. If he dies we'll just turn him over to the graves detail."

Michael tried to speak. He could make no noise. He wasn't even sure he could move his mouth. Michael was certain he was being taken prisoner. He felt himself sinking back into the bottomless black pit.

Someone grabbed him and lifted him. The pain was incredible. Michael tried to scream, but nothing came out. He knew he wasn't dead, but oh how he prayed for death so that the pain would stop. He was on a stretcher and being carried. With every bounce the pain increased. When they slid the stretcher into the ambulance, the wooden legs of the stretcher grinding across the wooden floor of the ambulance caused every nerve in his body to scream out in pain. Michael needed to scream, but he couldn't.

"They're cavalry," the original voice said. "Take them to Merritt's hospital in Newtown."

"That's five miles," a new voice said. "Half of them will be dead before we get there. The dressing station at Miller's is less than a mile."

"General Merritt wants his boys brought to the hospital at Newtown. So, just shut up and do it, will ya?"

I'm not cavalry thought Michael. I'm infantry, 10th New... 10th New... 10th New... the empty blackness overtook him again.

Michael McBride did not regain consciousness for five days. When he did it was only briefly. The pain was not as bad, it was dull, and seemed to be lingering in the background. However, it was still very difficult to breath.

"I'm thirsty," he heard himself croak.

Almost immediately there was a man there with a cup of cool water. He held the cup to Michael's lips. "Slowly," he said. "You don't want to choke, or cough it all back out."

Michael drank slowly. He couldn't recall ever having tasted anything as good as the water that flowed over his dry, cracked, bloody lips, and down the back of his parched throat.

"Where am I?" He rasped.

"We're at the Union hospital in Winchester," the man said. "They brought us here a couple of days ago.

"You been out a long time," he continued. "What's your name anyway? We haven't been able to find out who you are."

Michael just stared at the man. "I don't know," he answered finding it difficult to talk or remember anything.

The man nodded and smiled. "That's alright," he said. "You've been through a lot. It'll probably come back to you."

"Am I going to die?" Asked Michael, his voice still scratchy, but louder.

"No," said the man. "At least, they don't think so. You took one in the chest, but miraculously nothing vital got hit, the surgeon said that you probably have a lot of internal bruising because of the impact. You were pretty lucky. That Reb was standing right on top of you when he fired. They got you pumped full of laudanum to help with the pain. It's going to take a long time, but they think you're going to be alright."

"Thanks," said Michael. "Are you the doctor?"

"No," said the man with a smile. "I'm the guy whose life you saved. My name is....."

Michael, a man who did not know who he was, once again succumbed to the quiet peacefulness of the inky blackness.

"You're worthless to me with one arm Sergeant," said Captain Robert Smith of the US 2nd Cavalry. "The surgeons managed to save your arm, but there's no guarantee you'll ever be able to use it again. Only time will tell that.

"At least two months they said, it'll be at least two months before they know if you'll regain its use. You're a good soldier, and I hate to lose you, but you need to understand that your career in the Army may just be over."

"I won't accept that Sir."

"No, I didn't expect you would," said the Captain with a smile.

"There must be something I can do here, Sir."

"There's not, we'll eventually be moving south to Petersburg to rejoin Grant. In the meantime, you are going on convalescence leave, and you're leaving tomorrow. Is that clear?" Asked the Captain. "If necessary, I can make it an order."

"No Sir, I'll go."

"Very well."

"Sir?" Asked the Sergeant. "What's going to happen to the rest of the men who are in the hospital here?"

"They'll be sent to larger hospitals up north."

"What about the man who saved my life? Have we been able to learn who he is yet?"

"No," sighed the Captain. "We've been in touch with the VI Corps since it was they who were deployed there at the cemetery with us, but they haven't sent anyone over to try to identify him."

"A request Sir?" Said the Sergeant.

The Captain sighed, and suspiciously eyed the young sergeant.

"Let me take him with me."

"What!"

"He saved my life Sir, and I intend to do everything I can to do the same for him."

"You want me to let you take a soldier whose name, unit, and everything else is unknown to us home with you?"

"Yes Sir."

"Sergeant, this man is not a stray puppy, he is a very seriously wounded man who is going to need a lot of care."

"I know that Sir, and I also know that when my family learns what he did, that they will welcome him and care for him. If he goes somewhere else, he'll probably get lost in the shuffle and die. I've already talked to the Medical Officer, and he says there's nothing else they can do for him here. He thinks me taking him home might just be his best chance."

The Captain dropped his head and shook it, then looked up at the Sergeant. "I can't believe I'm even considering this."

"Captain, I can't let him die," said Matthew.

"How long will it take you to get home from here?"

"Two days."

"I'll give you 24-hours to make travel arrangements for yourself and your savior. If you don't have it worked out by then, he stays, but you go. If you manage to work it out make sure you speak with the surgeons. I don't want him suffering on the trip, and you wire me as soon as you find out who he is and what unit he belongs to."

"Yes Sir. Thank you Sir," said the Sergeant as he saluted, turned, and left the Captain's tent.

The Sergeant went straight from the Captain's tent to the Quartermaster. If anyone knew how to get something from one point to another, it would be the Quartermaster. Besides, there were always teamsters hanging out around the Quartermaster's looking for work. After speaking with a fellow sergeant in the Quartermaster's office, he approached a man sleeping in a wagon alongside the stables on Fairfax Street. He had been told that this man had lost his farm in the fighting around Winchester the previous summer. The man had done some work for the Army, but wasn't under contract.

"Hello friend," said the young sergeant as he approached the man.

The man lifted his head and looked over the side of the wagon. He studied the sergeant whose upper body was almost entirely wrapped in bandages. The sergeant's right arm was free, but his left was in a sling tightly secured to his chest.

"What happened to you?" Asked the man who appeared to be in his late thirties.

"Stumbled into a war," answered the sergeant with a smile. The man just looked at him. "A bayonet, and a gunshot, nearly ripped off my arm." The man just nodded. "I'm looking to hire a teamster," the sergeant said.

"What's the cargo?" He asked.

"Myself and another man, and our personal possessions."

"Is he wounded too?"

"He is, and a lot worse than I am."

"Where we going?"

"North into Maryland, should take us about two days."

"Eight dollars, and I get paid even if one or both of you die on the way."

"Five in gold, and I pay expenses. If you stick with eight it's in greenbacks, you pay your own expenses, and yes, you're paid no matter what."

"Make it six, and you've got yourself a teamster."

"Done," said the sergeant. "Three now, and three when we get to Maryland."

The man jumped down out of the wagon and stuck out his hand. "Name's Tanner, Ira Tanner."

The sergeant shook his hand. "We'll leave tomorrow morning around ten, it'll probably take that long for me to get my friend released from the hospital. In the meantime," he said handing Mr. Tanner four gold coins. "Fill the back of this wagon up with straw. I don't want my friend bounced around."

"I'll be outside the hospital at ten," said Mr. Tanner.

The sergeant nodded and headed off to the hospital to see the surgeon about how best to make his anonymous friend comfortable. Then he would go back to the Captain to let him know plans had been made.

Chapter 39

The Rancocas
1864

Joanna McBride did not care to read about the war. Since her son Michael had left she had not read the Gazette, or the Harper's Weekly, her husband William would bring home when he went into Burlington, Beverly, or Mt. Holly. Her only news of the war came from her son's letters, and the letters of his friend Frank Jefferson.

They didn't talk of battle or hardship, but described the farms, cities, and people they would encounter. She was sure their letters were sugar-coated, but she didn't mind, the less she really knew the easier it was for her to cope with what her son and his friend must really be going through. However, it had been nearly a month since she'd heard from either one of them, and that worried her some.

On the other hand, William stayed as up to date on the war as he could. Through the papers, and the rumors, and tales that got shared in the shops and businesses in and around Rancocas. He kept track of where the VI Corps was, figuring that wherever the VI Corps was the New Jersey Brigade, and the 10th New Jersey Regiment would be nearby.

Also, his son wrote him letters too. Not sugar-coated letters, but letters that described in detail what war was like and how he was dealing with it. William knew that his son had run from his first battle in terror, but that since then, he had done his duty and performed bravely. He was very proud of the soldier his son had become.

Michael would describe the noise and violence of battle. The feeling one got when a shot he fired would fell an enemy soldier, or someone with whom he had shared a cup of coffee, a piece of hardtack, or a canteen, was felled by an enemy bullet.

After every battle the Gazette would print up a casualty list. William checked every one very closely looking for the name McBride, or Jefferson. Finding neither name listed, it was not unusual for him to shed a tear or two.

On October 17th, William McBride came home from the Rancocas Post Office carrying a stack of letters. Six of them were for Joanna, four from Michael, and two from Frank. There were two for William from Michael. Nothing else in the stack mattered.

They read their letters and were very glad to see that their son and his friend were well. Joanna's letters were sugar-coated, as Michael described the lush fields, and gently rolling hills, of the Shenandoah Valley. In William's letters, Michael described the fighting.

Michael described the Battle of Winchester and how the Union cavalry had collapsed the Confederate left flank, and how the 10th New Jersey had driven General Rodes' Division in panic through the streets of the town. He also described the battle of Fisher's Hill, and how only three days later they again collapsed the Confederate left flank, driving them down the Valley.

William looked at his wife who was sitting at their kitchen table reading her son's letters for perhaps the third time. He said nothing of his letters, they had agreed, when Michael had left, that he would only tell her what was in his letters if she asked. He could not recall a single time that she had asked.

"Frank is such a nice boy," said Joanna as she laid the stack of letters on the table in front of her.

"I'm not sure it's fair to refer to him as a boy anymore," answered her husband.

"Oh, you know what I mean," she said, "and, I've been thinking."

"Ut-oh," said William as he stood and walked over to the table and sat down across from her.

"He has no family, and when this dreadful war is over, he'll have no home to return to."

"He'll always be welcome here," said her husband.

"Yes, I know," she said, "but, I want to do more."

"Go on," he said.

"If he is willing, why don't we sell him some of our acreage? He's told me in his letters, that he has nearly a hundred dollars saved up."

"Why don't we just hire him?" Asked William. "He can live here for free, and at the same time be earning money so that he can at some point but his own place nearby."

"I like that idea better," said Joanna reaching across the table and taking her husband's hand. "I'll write to him and carefully plant the seed, and see what he says." Five days later, October 22nd, Joanna McBride walked into the village, and posted letters to her son and Frank.

On October 26th, William McBride was in Burlington to have a blade repaired on a scythe that would be used to cut down the cornstalks on his farm, now that the harvest was over. While waiting for the repairs to be made, he decided to walk over to Allison's Drug Store, on High and Union Streets, to see if the latest edition of the Gazette was out. It was, and he purchased a copy. A banner on the front of the paper said that the issue contained the casualty list for the Battle of Cedar Creek.

He paid for the paper, tucked it under his arm, and turned to leave the store. When he did so, he had a momentary feeling of doom. William tried to excuse the feeling, but all the way back to the blacksmith shop, the feeling stayed with him.

When he got back to the shop, he climbed up on to his wagon, and laid the paper on the seat next to him. He really didn't want to read it. Convincing himself that he was just being silly, William picked up the paper and opened it to the Casualty List.

First New Jersey Brigade
Known Casualties
Battle of Cedar Creek, VA
October 19, 1864

He ran his finger down the page.

10th New Jersey Regiment

He continued down the page, A Company, D Company, E Company, and G Company. Every company was listed, and every company had suffered grievous losses. Then he came to H Company, and tears began to form in his eyes, because he knew that a nightmare was about to become a reality.

H Company

William continued running his finger down the list. His heart was racing, his mouth was dry, and his eyes burned, as he stopped and read each name, even though he did not know anyone who appeared on the list. Then he got to the 16th, name on the list, and his finger began to shake.

Pvt. Frank Jefferson – Killed

He lifted his head and looked into the blacksmith shop, no one was there. William looked down the street towards the creek. There were wagons coming and going, and people walking.

The tears were flowing now, and he did nothing to try and stop them. He raised his head and looked to the heavens, afraid to go down the list any further. But, he knew he had to, and he was all but convinced about what he would find.

There it was, six lines below Frank's name.

Pvt. Michael J. McBride – Missing

William knew that he had to get home. Joanna could hear this from no one but him. He picked up the reins, released the brake, and slapped the reins across the back of the two mules.

"William!" Hollered the blacksmith as he came out of the shop. "Where are you going? The scythe is not quite ready." He stood and watched as William guided the team to the center of town, turned left, and headed for Rancocas.

It generally took him about two hours to make the trip from Burlington to Rancocas, but today was different, he had to get home quickly. As he crossed the wooden bridge over the little stream known as London Ditch, William considered driving the mules hard to get him home. It took every fiber of his being not to.

These animals were valuable, and critical to the operation of his farm. Without them they could not farm. Without them they could not survive. So, he would not push them.

When they finally got to the Groves' place on the Burlington Road, they were less than a mile and a half from the house. It was a cool October day, the road was flat and straight, nor were the mules winded. It didn't take William long to decide it was time to push them. When they finally reached the yard behind the house, the mules were lathered and winded.

Joanna stood at the backdoor and watched, more than a little concerned. She hadn't expected to see William coming down the lane for at least another three hours. Nor, was it like her husband to drive the mules that hard.

William did not park the wagon in the shed. He pulled the wagon up to the trough so that the mules could drink, but did not unhook them from the wagon. He jumped down from the wagon grabbed a paper off the seat, quickly walked to the house, and entered the backdoor. When he passed Joanna she could see the redness in his eyes, and tell that he was distressed.

"What's wrong?" She asked quietly, not certain she wanted to know the answer to that question.

"We should sit," he said quietly, as he went to the cupboard removed two glasses, and the bottle of Laird's Applejack that was reserved for holidays and special occasions.

"What's wrong?" She asked again as she sat down at the table.

He sat down across from her, took both of her hands in his, looked into her eyes, and with as much control as he could muster said, "Michael is missing." Nothing, there was no reaction at all, she just looked at him. "Did you hear me?" He asked quietly. "Our Michael is missing."

Still nothing. He poured them each a drink and set hers in front of her. "Drink that," he said. "It will help."

"No," she said pushing it aside. "What you said," she said looking at her husband, "was that Michael is alive."

"What I said, is that he is missing," said William. "They don't know where he is. He could have been captured, he may even be dead."

"He is not dead," she said emphatically, staring at her husband. "If he was dead I would know it, because I am his mother, and if he was dead, part of me would have died too. He is not dead," she repeated shaking her head back and forth. "He is not dead."

"Very well," said her husband. "Then he is just missing."

"He's not missing!" She said jumping up from her chair. "He's a soldier in the Union Army!" She yelled. "No one can be missing in an Army of half a million men. Someone knows where he is. Michael may not know who he is or where he is right now, the people around him may not know who he is, but dammit, somebody in that Army knows where our son is!" She sat back down at the table and buried her face in her hands, she wasn't crying, she was thinking.

William stared across the table at his wife. He had known this woman as a girl, and as a woman, and in all that time, he had never heard her swear.

Joanna lifted her head and looked at her husband. "We have to get in touch with Frank," she said. "Frank may know where he is."

"Frank is dead," whispered her husband, sliding the paper, open to the casualty list, across the table towards her.

She looked at her husband for a moment and then tears filled her eyes. "That poor boy," she said quietly. Then she reached out and picked up the glass of liquor and took a sip. "He deserved so much more from life," she said.

There was silence in the McBride kitchen for the next several minutes. "Alright," said Joanna, taking another sip of the liquor, and looking across at her husband. "We're going to Virginia."

"What?" Asked an astonished William.

"We're going to Virginia. Michael was at the Battle of Cedar Creek, we know that that is in the Shenandoah Valley in Western Virginia, so that is where we will start. Someone who is there, or was there, knows where he is.

"We are going to find that person, then we are going to find our son and bring him home, and we are going to find Frank Jefferson too, and bring him home as well so that he can be laid to rest near the people who loved him."

"Have you lost your mind? Asked William.

"No," answered Joanna, "and I haven't lost my son either. Not yet! I'm bringing him home William," she said as she started to cry. "I'm going to find my son, and dead or alive, I'm bringing him home." She sobbed.

William, now crying as well, stood and went to his wife, kneeled down alongside her and put his arms around her. "Then we'll go to Virginia my love," he whispered to her. "That's what we'll do. Tomorrow we'll go into Burlington and find out how we go about getting to the Shenandoah Valley."

By eight o'clock the following morning William and Joanna were on their way into Burlington. Along the way they discussed making arrangements for the care of the farm and the house while they were away, and for making sure someone knew how to contact them in the event Michael showed up in Rancocas, or there was word of his whereabouts. They figured they would be gone at least a month, maybe more, depending on how their search went.

William thought that it would be best for them to take a steamer to Philadelphia, head west to Harrisburg by rail, and finally south into the Shenandoah Valley, also by rail, if possible. They could make Harrisburg in a day, after that their travel time would depend on their means of travel. He also thought that they should plan on leaving by the end of the following week.

"We'll go down to the wharf, look over the steamers' schedules, and decide which tickets to buy," said Michael as they entered the town.

"Take me to Wood Street," said Joanna matter-of-factly.

"Wood Street?" Asked William turning to look at his wife. "What's on Wood Street?"

"I'm going to call on someone," she said.

"On who?"

"Mrs. Grant," answered Joanna with a sidelong glance and a smile.

"Mrs. Ulysses S. Grant? Is that so? Why in heaven's name..."

Joanna turned towards her husband. "Her husband is our son's Commanding Officer. She lives here, she is our neighbor. General Grant spoke to our son one time, and he told him that neighbors should be able to count on each other. Michael wrote to me about it," she said as she held up one of the letters she had received earlier. "Who better to be able to count on for help at a time like this than General Grant, and who better to get us a meeting with General Grant than Mrs. Grant? Besides, she is also a mother, she has three sons, who, if this war continues a few more years will be of enlistment age. I'm sure she will be able to understand a mother's despair. So, take me to Wood Street," she said insistently.

William just looked at his wife. He had always known that Joanna was a resourceful intelligent woman, but he had never really understood just how much until now. He leaned across and kissed her on the cheek.

"That makes more sense than anything I could have ever come up with," he said with a smile. "Wood Street it is." She returned his smile and nodded.

The residence on Wood Street was a large two story stuccoed house with a flat roof. There was also a flat roofed porch that ran across almost the entire front of the house supported by four columns. The front door was in the center of the house and on each side of the door were two very large and impressive floor to ceiling walk out windows. Across the second floor directly above the door and each of the windows were three more large, walk out windows. The door and windows were most impressive and announced to the world that this was the house of someone of importance.

"You go on to the wharf and get us those steamer schedules," Joanna said looking at the house. "It's best if I go in to see Mrs. Grant alone."

William nodded. "I'll be in front of St. Mary's up there on Broad when you're through."

His wife smiled, reached out and touched his arm, and then climbed down from the wagon. She stood on the sidewalk and watched as the wagon pulled away and continued down Wood Street towards the river. Joanna brushed off the front of her dress, tucked some strands of loose hair up under her hat, adjusted her hat, and then let herself through the small gate in the fence that surrounded the Grant house. She confidently walked up onto the porch, and knocked at the front door. The door was opened by a dark haired woman Joanna guessed was in her early thirties, wearing a black dress under a full length white apron. "May I help you?" She asked politely.

"Yes, good morning," said Joanna trying very hard to keep the anxiety and nervousness out of her voice. "I'm Mrs. McBride, Mrs. Joanna McBride, I wonder if I might have a word with Mrs. Grant?" She asked with a smile.

"Is Mrs. Grant expecting you Mrs. McBride?"

"No, she's not," answered Joanna shaking her head. "I thought I might catch her at home."

"I'm sorry," said the woman, "but, Mrs. Grant sees no one without a previous arrangement."

Joanna started to panic, maybe this wasn't such a good idea, but she couldn't give up now. "My son Michael is a soldier," she began. "He is missing, in Virginia, the Shenandoah Valley," she continued, holding up the casualty list she had brought with her. "I know he may be dead." Now the tears were flowing and Joanna was trying desperately not to fall completely apart. "But, even if he is, I have to find him." She sobbed.

"Who is it Marie?" Asked a woman's voice from inside the house.

"A Mrs. McBride, Ma'am, her son is missing."

"A child, from the neighborhood?" Asked the voice. A woman came out of a room on the right of the center hallway.

"No, he was…that is he…he is, a soldier, Ma'am."

"I see," said the woman arriving at the front door. Joanna recognized the woman as Julia Grant. Mrs. Grant took one look at the weeping Joanna and reached out and took her by the hand. "We can't leave you out here like this now, can we?" She said with a smile. "Come, let's go into the parlor. Marie, would you be kind enough to get us some tea?"

"Certainly Ma'am," said Marie as she headed for the rear of the house.

"Isn't this better?" Said Mrs. Grant guiding Joanna to a settee.

Mrs. Grant sat down in a chair facing Joanna and said, "You take a moment and get yourself together, then we'll talk about why you've come to call." Mrs. Grant was about five and a half feet tall, she was a dark haired, full figured woman, but she was not overly heavy. She had a plain but not unattractive face, and Joanna noticed that her eyes did not seem to align properly. She was wearing a dark blue dress with a white collar, and white piping along the sleeves, and at the waist.

"I'm so embarrassed," said Joanna sheepishly, dabbing her eyes as she began to gather herself.

"Don't be dear," said a smiling Mrs. Grant as Marie entered the room with the tea. "How would you like your tea?" She asked.

"Just milk?" Answered Joanna.

"Marie?" Said Mrs. Grant, smiling at the young woman. "I'll have some as well please," she said. "Thank you." Marie served the tea and left the room, closing the door behind her. "Better?" Asked Mrs. Grant once Marie was gone.

Joanna, sipping the tea as graciously as she could, nodded and smiled.

"Now," said Mrs. Grant. "Why don't you tell me why you are here?"

Joanna told her about Michael, told her a lot more than she had intended to. She told Mrs. Grant about Michael from the time he was a little boy, up until the time they had found him listed as missing on the casualty list for the Battle of Cedar Creek. She also told her about Frank Jefferson, and about his death.

Through it all Mrs. Grant listened. She nodded, commented, or asked a question when appropriate or necessary, and never made Joanna feel like she was unwelcomed. Mrs. Grant was a special kind of lady.

"I came up with the idea that we, my husband and I, should go to the site of the battle," explained Joanna. "I thought there must be someone there who would know something, or give us an idea about where to begin our search, but then I thought we may be one of thousands looking for sons who are dead or missing, just how cooperative would, or could, the Army be? Then, I thought I would come to you, and ask for your help."

"You're convinced your son is alive, aren't you?"

"I am."

"Why?"

"Because, like I told my husband, if Michael were dead, a part of me would have died as well."

Mrs. Grant reached across and squeezed Joanna's hand. "I know," she said with a knowing smile.

"Your husband, the General, spoke with Michael the day they left City Point for the Shenandoah Valley," said Joanna, removing Michael's letter from her purse. "He wrote me about it. The General told them that he was considering moving you and the children here, to Burlington. He told them that that would make them neighbors, and that he felt that neighbors should always be able to count on each other. I thought that maybe you could tell me who to see, once we got to the Shenandoah Valley, someone who might be able to help."

"No one," said Mrs. Grant with a smile.

"Excuse me?" Said Joanna a bit taken aback.

"No one," repeated Mrs. Grant. "You're not going to the Shenandoah Valley."

"I don't understand," said Joanna thinking that maybe Mrs. Grant had just listened to be nice, and now was going to try and stop them from looking for Michael.

"You're going to City Point," said Mrs. Grant. "With a letter I will write to the General asking that he do everything possible to assist you in your attempts to locate your son and his friend and bring them home."

Joanna just stared, then she started to cry.

342

"Where is your husband?" Asked Mrs. Grant.

"Waiting for me in front of St. Mary's Church."

"You finish your tea, then we'll walk up and meet him."

Joanna was only able to nod. A few minutes later, Joanna, accompanied by Mrs. Ulysses S. Grant, walked the short distance from the Grant house to the front of the Church. William was sitting in the back of the wagon examining the scythe he had left at the blacksmith's the previous day when he saw the two women approaching. He immediately jumped off the wagon and removed his hat.

"William," said Joanna. "This is Mrs. Grant." Then turning to Mrs. Grant she said, "My husband, William McBride."

Mrs. Grant offered her hand, and William took it, he couldn't believe that Joanna's plan had worked, and that he too was getting to meet the wife of General U.S. Grant. "Mrs. Grant, it is an honor," stammered William.

"A pleasure to meet you Mr. McBride," said Mrs. Grant with a smile. "Your wife has told me about the terrible news you have received, and your plans. She and I have discussed those plans, and I'll allow her to tell you how we plan to go forward from here.

"In the meantime, I would like to invite the two of you to join me for lunch at my house, on Monday, at one." She held up her hands and smiled. "Now," she continued, "before you protest, I travel routinely to where you are going, and at lunch will assist you in making the plans for your trip. So, it is really in your best interests to be there, isn't it?"

"Thank you," said Joanna, starting to cry again. "We'd be honored."

Mrs. Grant walked over and put her arms around Joanna, and then held her at arms' length. "Save those tears, my Dear," she said. "You may need them for a happier time." Then she bid them goodbye, and started back to her home. Then, she stopped and turned. "And oh," she said, "don't dress. I will be dressed similar to this, and what you are wearing now will be more than appropriate for a neighbors' lunch." Then she turned and resumed walking.

William helped Joanna up onto the wagon, and climbed up next to her. "I didn't know what to expect," said Joanna. "I didn't expect that she would be mean or unkind, but I never expected that she would be so kind and gracious. William," she said, turning to her husband. "I am now convinced more than ever, that Michael is alive, and that we are going to find him."

William put his arms around his wife, and held her. On the way home Joanna told him the entire story of her visit with Mrs. Grant, and Mrs. Grant's offer to help get them to City Point, and giving them a letter to take to the General asking him to assist them. He didn't know how, or why, but when his wife had finished, he, like her, was absolutely convinced that Michael was alive.

Chapter 40

The Catoctin
1864

On the morning of October 28th, a barely conscious Michael McBride, whose identity was still unknown, was loaded onto the back of teamster Ira Tanner's wagon by two hospital orderlies. The doctors, had loaded him up with laudanum to keep the severe pain he would still be feeling in check. They had also given Sergeant Matthew Calhoun, of the 2nd US Cavalry, a small amount to administer to Michael should the current dose wear off, or the pain get worse.

The back of the wagon was covered in at least two feet of hay to help cushion the ride. In addition, Tanner was told by Sergeant Calhoun to take his time and avoid the holes and ruts in the road as much as possible. Sergeant Calhoun did not care how long it took to get home, he was more concerned that his unknown friend survive the trip.

"I know you said we were going to Maryland, Sergeant," said the teamster as they headed east out of Winchester on the Berryville Road, "but, you never said where, and Maryland's a pretty big place."

"Middletown," said Matthew. "It's about ten miles west of Frederick."

"Frederick's probably better than forty miles," said Tanner. "At this rate, it's probably going to be a good three days to get where you're going."

"That's alright, long as my friend here doesn't get jostled too much. I'll make sure you're well paid for the extra day."

"Just sayin'." Nodded Tanner, his back to his passengers, as he loosely held the reins to the two walking horses that were pulling the wagon.

"What time you figure we'll make Berryville?" Asked Matthew.

"About two," answered the teamster.

"We'll stop there to eat and rest the horses." The teamster just nodded. "There's a small spring about ten miles north of Berryville. I figure on spending the night there."

"I know the spot," said Tanner. "Should be able to make it by dark."

They pulled off into a grassy meadow about a mile north of Berryville. Tanner unhitched the two horses and staked them out so that they could graze. When he returned to the wagon, the Sergeant had built a small fire, and was feeding his friend from a cup that had a spout on it.

"It's an invalid cup," said Matthew when he saw the teamster looking. "It's the only way I can get anything into him, his insides don't seem to be working right yet."

"What happened to him?" Asked the teamster as he removed a couple of pieces of fatback from a sack, put them in a small frypan, and set it next to the fire.

"Took a pistol round to the chest at point blank range at Cedar Creek. Blew right through him, didn't hit anything vital, but the doctors said his insides were probably badly bruised. They think he'll recover, but it's going to take a lot of care, and a lot of time."

"What's in the cup?"

"Warm chicken broth. Probably tastes like hell, but it seems to be the only thing he can keep down. He gets a cup in the morning, two this time of day, and he'll get another one this evening. I'm hoping it keeps him alive until he can eat something. He's nothing but a bag of bones, and he doesn't have much more weight to lose. I give him water all day long too."

"What about, you know…?" Asked Tanner.

"You mean the necessities of nature?" Asked Matthew with a grin. The teamster just nodded, perhaps a little embarrassed. "I clean him up a couple of times a day. He's not eating much, so there's not much doing on that end, and even though he's getting a lot of liquids, he must be absorbing them or something, because that's not a major issue either."

"Must be hard, seeing your brother like this."

"Oh," said Matthew. "He's not my brother. In fact, I have no idea who he is, and neither does he. He doesn't seem to be able to remember anything."

"Then why?" Asked Tanner.

"He saved my life. He came up off of the ground, his face covered in blood, a bayonet in his hand, and stabbed the Reb who did this to me right through the heart, before he could finish me off. I just laid there and watched.

"There was another Reb who pulled out a pistol and shot this man lying here. I just watched that too. When I finally got my wits about me I did pull my pistol and kill that Reb, but not in time to stop this." He said nodding at Michael. "He saved my life, now I intend to do the same for him."

The teamster nodded. They finished their meal and were back on the road in a little over and hour. They stopped along the spring as they had planned, and the next morning continued on towards Charles Town.

Michael was not unconscious, or unaware of what was happening around him. He had heard everything the cavalry Sergeant, whose name he now knew to be Matthew Calhoun, and the teamster, whose name he did not know, had talked about. Michael's problem was his memory, and that he did not seem to be able to talk. He felt like he was in a constant fog that he did not seem to be able to get out of. At the same time, he felt like there was something terrifying hiding in the fog that made him want to stay hidden.

The Sergeant's description of the events that had led to him getting shot helped restore some of his lost memory, and he was glad to know that it was not the Sergeant who had shot him. He was confused as to why the Sergeant felt guilty for not having acted sooner to keep the Reb from shooting Michael. Michael, vaguely remembering these events after hearing the Sergeant describe them, felt that maybe there was something he had failed to do too, but he could not remember what.

"What happened to your farm?" Matthew asked the teamster.

"A war stumbled into it," answered Tanner with a laugh. After a short silence he continued, "Me, my wife, and two boys, had a small farm, about three miles east of Winchester. The Yankees got beat up, and were leaving Winchester in a hurry. They

345

were retreating by passing right through our place. The last one hadn't been gone long before the Rebs started showing up.

"They set up a battery of cannons right along our lane, no more than fifty yards or so from the house and barn. I went out and talked to the Reb officer and tried to explain to him that if he moved his cannons another two or three hundred yards to the east he'd be on higher ground and have a better view of the roads the Yankees were on. He didn't care.

"They started firing, and the Yankees who had cannons on a ridge about a mile to the east, started answering. The Yanks were pretty good shots, it wasn't long before they knocked out a couple of the Reb cannons. But, they were missing every now and then too, and the misses were hitting our barn and our house.

"By the time it was over, the barn and the house were pretty much destroyed. The Rebs just hooked up what was left of their cannons and went on their way. If they had moved that couple of hundred yards, my house and barn might have been spared."

"What about your wife and children?" Asked Matthew.

"Sent them north to stay with family in Hagerstown. Ain't going to rebuild until I'm sure this war is over. I won't have two houses destroyed."

Matthew just nodded and they continued on in silence.   .

"Frank," he muttered, his voice cracking, and barely audible.

"What?" Asked Matthew taken completely by surprise. "What, did you say something?"

Michael opened his eyes, and looked up at the Sergeant. He tried to smile and nod. He tried again. "Frank," he croaked, then closed his eyes and drifted away.

"Did you hear what he said?" Matthew asked Tanner. "He said something, did you hear what it was?"

"No," said the teamster. "It really didn't sound like much of a word."

"I don't know," said Matthew. "I just don't know."

They made Charles Town by eight o'clock the next morning, and Matthew had Tanner take them to the Union Hospital on Samuel Street. There, Matthew presented the documents authorizing him to transport the wounded soldier in his care, and letters from the doctors in Winchester, asking that the doctors in Charles Town change the bandages on both of them, and administer more laudanum to the unidentified soldier, if necessary. The doctors were skeptical about the wisdom of releasing a wounded soldier into the care of a cavalry sergeant, and of transporting him in the back of a wagon along country roads, but they complied with the requests of the Winchester doctors, and by ten, they were on the road towards Harper's Ferry.

Michael was aware that his bandages had been removed. He found that without the bandages it was much easier for him to breath. He also found that breathing was painful, but the ease of breathing made the pain bearable.

He tried to speak to relay this to whoever it was that was replacing the bandages, but again, nothing would come out. When replaced the bandages were just as tight, and breathing was again difficult. The vile tasting liquid he had been receiving occasionally, was again poured down his throat. It was not long after that, that he was again overcome by the inky blackness.

They had lunch along the Potomac River in Harpers Ferry. Michael was conscious, but cloudy by then, and was able to swallow the two cups of broth the Sergeant fed him. He enjoyed the broth, but longed for something more substantial.

Michael thought that maybe, if he could eat something his strength would begin to come back, and he could talk, and let people know he was in here, and wanted desperately to get out.

"I have family in Burkittsville," Matthew told the teamster Tanner. "I'd like to make it there today. I'm sure my aunt will fix us a real meal, and that they'll put us up in real beds for the night." It was two o'clock, they had just crossed the Potomac, and Burkittsville, and the farm of Kevin Calhoun, was still a good ten miles away.

"Sounds good to me," said Tanner. "Shouldn't be no problem making it by nightfall."

When right around sunset Matthew knocked on the door of the Calhoun farmhouse, his Uncle Kevin answered with a loaded and fully charged pistol. It took him a few minutes to recognize, that the soldier in blue, whose entire left side seemed to be wrapped in bandages was his nephew Matthew. Looking at the bandages, he resisted the urge to take his nephew into his arms.

"Matthew," he whispered with a smile. Then turning his head, he called for his wife. "Louise," he said. "Come here, we have company."

With everyone's help they managed to get Michael into a bed on the first floor of the two story farmhouse. Then with Aunt Louise's assistance Matthew got him cleaned up, and fed him his evening broth. After making sure Michael was settled and comfortable, Matthew joined Ira Tanner, and his Aunt and Uncle in the kitchen for dinner.

As promised, Aunt Louise prepared a wonderful meal of baked ham, boiled potatoes, radishes, and raspberry preserves with fresh baked bread. They had a fresh cider with their meal, but after the table had been cleared, Uncle Kevin produced a small keg of ale. While they enjoyed their ale, Matthew relayed the story of what had happened at Cedar Creek, and how this wounded stranger had come to be in his care.

Michael awoke long before dawn. He knew he was in a bed, was quite comfortable, and feeling better than he had in days. The room was dark and cool.

"Frank," said Michael in a clear voice. He swallowed, it did not hurt, but his breathing was still labored. "Frank," he repeated, again in a clear voice, and a little louder. "Frank," he said again.

Who was Frank he wondered? Was he Frank? He wasn't sure. Frank seemed like a name that should be important to him, but he didn't think that it was his name. He drifted off to sleep, but it wasn't that clouded, empty sleep, it was a restful sleep.

In the morning Matthew's Uncle Kevin took him on a tour of the farm. Two years ago, in September of 1862, the farm had been an eyewitness to war. Part of the battle for Crampton's Gap was fought only a few hundred yards from the house. Kevin and Louise had hid in the basement until the roar of the cannon, and the banging of the muskets had moved further west.

When they did come out it was like stepping into Hell itself. In the yard and in the fields around the house there were wounded, dying, and dead men. Most of them were wearing the Union blue, and the pleadings and cries of the wounded were not only heart breaking, but terrifying.

The barn was used as a hospital, and the rooms on the first floor of the house as operating rooms. When the Army left nearly a week later, there was a stack of amputated limbs alongside the house almost three feet tall. Kevin Calhoun had gathered these rotting fly and maggot infested remnants of what had once been whole men together, dragged them out into the fields, and burned them. The stench lingered in the area for months.

It was over a year before they could use the rooms in the house again. They stripped and scrubbed the floors and walls, and still the smell of the dying remained as did the blood that had soaked into the floors. The smell eventually went away, and they used floor coverings to hide the blood stains, but the memories and the nightmares remained, and now they were considering selling the farm and moving somewhere, anywhere, where war would not arrive on their doorstep.

"Where are the children?" Asked Matthew. "I noticed last night, that they weren't around."

"When we heard the Rebs were in Middletown just before the battle, we sent them off to stay with your mother's parents in Baltimore. They been gone two years now. We think by this Christmas we'll be ready to have them come home."

"That was nice of them, to take them in like that," said Matthew.

"It was," answered his Uncle Kevin. "They're really nothing to us, but they do love the kids, and the kids consider them their grandparents, since they've never known any others. So, yes, it was really very nice of them."

"Have you seen the kids?"

"We have, we've been up to Baltimore probably half a dozen times since the battle. Couldn't bring ourselves to bring them home though. We just hate the thought of our kids being in a place where there was so much violence and death."

Matthew just nodded and stared out across the fields.

"Your father fared much better," his Uncle said as he turned and started walking back towards the house.

It was nearly ten o'clock in the morning when Matthew entered the room to check on Michael. He found Michael awake and looking at the ceiling. He turned his head and looked at Matthew. "I'm hungry," he said in a voice that was hoarse and a little cracked, but loud and clear enough to be heard.

Matthew just stared at Michael for a minute, then a big smile crossed his face. "Welcome back," he said. "Do you really think you could eat something?"

"I'd like to try," answered Michael, his voice still hoarse, but a little clearer.

"I'll see what I can do," said Matthew as he left the room to find his Aunt and see what she thought about what might be best for their patient. He returned to the room a few minutes later and told Michael that his Aunt was going to be bringing something up.

"I'd like to try and sit up a little," he croaked.

"When my aunt gets here we'll see what we can do," said Matthew. "I don't think I could help you on my own," he said raising his one good arm.

Michael nodded. "Is my name Frank?" He asked his voice cracking.

"I don't know," said Matthew, "but I guess it could be, you still don't know?"

Michael just shook his head.

Kevin and Louise Calhoun entered the room, and with their help, Michael was raised into a semi-upright position. Almost immediately his breathing became more labored, but when they tried to lay him down again, he waved them away. He wanted to eat, and it would be impossible to do so lying down.

Matthew's Aunt Louise had soaked a few slices of bread in a bowl of warm milk. Michael choked on the first couple of attempts to swallow the bread, but he persevered, and was soon able to get the small spoonful's Louise fed to him down. He couldn't remember ever eating anything that had tasted so good.

"Do you think your name is Frank?" Asked Matthew when Michael had finished eating.

"I don't know," Michael answered hoarsely. "I don't think so, but it's a name that I think should mean something to me."

Matthew nodded. "We're going to lay you back down," he said. "You rest, we're going to be leaving for Middletown in a bit."

Michael drifted off to sleep, his stomach was unsettled, but for the first time in a long time, it had food in it. For the first time in weeks he dreamt. He dreamt about a man. Could this man have been Frank? The man kept calling his name, but he couldn't hear what the man was saying.

When they went to lift Michael off of the bed and onto the stretcher to take him out to the wagon, his bowels released. Everything that he had eaten, and more, now soaked him, and the bed he was lying on. He was overcome with embarrassment and shame. He cried.

"Don't you worry darlin'," said Aunt Louise as she stroked his cheek. "We'll get you all cleaned up and on that wagon in no time. I probably shouldn't have fed you so much for the first time. This is my fault, not yours, you have nothing to be sorry about."

Within the hour, Michael had been loaded on the wagon, the goodbyes had been said, and with teamster Ira Tanner handling the team, they were once again on their way. It was obvious to Matthew that his wounded friend was in pain, probably as a result of being moved about. He offered him some of the laudanum, but Michael refused. He wanted to be awake, and he thought he could bear the pain. Besides, he was finding that he was perhaps looking a little too forward to getting to the place the drug took him, and this frightened him.

The last leg of their trip would take about three hours. They had been on the road for about two of that, when they stopped along the Catoctin Creek to rest. Matthew wanted to see if he could get some broth into his wounded friend.

Michael was in a great deal of pain, and it was getting harder and harder to breathe. He needed the laudanum, and he hoped that his need for it was greater than his desire for it. He wanted to be behind that swirling inky black wall that held the pain at bay.

"I need the laudanum," Michael said softly when Matthew tried to put the cup with the broth to his lips.

"You should drink this first," Matthew said.

"No!" Demanded Michael hoarsely. "I need the laudanum!" Matthew just looked at his friend, worried. "The laudanum dammit!" Croaked Michael. "I need the laudanum."

Matthew nodded. He retrieved the vial from his satchel, and carefully poured the small but adequate amount that was left into Michael's mouth. Then he turned and angrily threw the vial into the creek.

Within minutes, Michael could feel the black wall approaching. Soon the pain would be on the other side of the wall, it would not be gone, but it would not be able to touch him. He smiled, as the drug began to take effect.

Matthew had last seen his home in September of 1862, during the battle of South Mountain. At that time, both the Union and Confederate Armies had passed within a half mile of the house and barns. Except for a few missing fence posts, and the theft of some pigs, and chickens, the farm had not been touched. The nearest fighting had occurred three miles to the west, and although a number of houses, churches, and other buildings in and around Middletown, had been used as hospitals, the farm had not.

During the battle, Matthew's Second US Cavalry had been assigned Provost Guard to General McClellan's Headquarters. During the battle General McClellan had made his headquarters at the Koogle Farm on the National Road, less than two miles from the Calhoun Farm. Matthew had had several opportunities to visit with his father, and his sister Katherine, during their stay.

After South Mountain the armies moved on to Sharpsburg, the site of a bloody twelve hour battle on September 17th. The 2nd US Cavalry was still assigned as Provost Guard, and played little, if any, part in the battle. General Robert E. Lee and his Army retreated south after the battle, with the Union Army in cautious pursuit. That had been over two years ago, and Matthew had not been home since.

As they drove down the lane, Matthew noticed that the house that had been occupied by his father's hired hand, and his wife, was still empty. Dave and Olivia Stokes, a free black couple, had fled north into Pennsylvania prior to the battle of South Mountain, when they heard that the Confederate Army was approaching the valley. That had been two years ago, and they had yet to return.

The first thing that Matthew noticed when they pulled up to the house, was that the house, barn, out buildings, and the farm in general was not as well maintained as it had been in the past. He imagined that it was difficult for his father with only his sixteen-year-old daughter to help. Most of the men in the area who were available to be taken on as hands were either too young, too old, or recovering from illnesses or wounds.

His sister Katherine came out the front door onto the porch and waved. The first thing that Matthew noticed was that in the two years since he had last seen her, his little sister had blossomed into a very attractive young lady. Ira Tanner, the teamster, yanked off his hat, brushed back his hair, and spat out the large wad of chewing tobacco he had stuffed in his cheek when he saw Katherine.

Matthew, after checking his wounded friend, climbed out of the back of the wagon, and walked up onto the porch. By the time he got there his father had come out onto the porch as well. His father and sister just stood and looked at his bandaged left side.

"It's not as bad as it looks," he said. "You can hug my right side, and my face wouldn't mind a kiss or two."

"Welcome home," said Katherine with a huge smile as she lightly took him into her arms and planted kisses on his forehead, both cheeks, and lips.

When Katherine released him, his father did the same, but gave everyone a good laugh when he planted a loud kiss right on the end of Matthew's nose. Then they walked down to the wagon. Matthew introduced them to Ira Tanner, and then took them around to the rear of the wagon to meet his nameless friend.

"He looks awful," whispered Katherine. "Are you sure he's going to be alright?"

"He's in a lot of pain, and has trouble breathing," answered Matthew. "I gave him a big dose of laudanum, so he'll be out of it for a while. The doctors say he just needs time to heal, that other than internal bruising, there's no serious damage to his insides."

"We set up a bed for him in the parlor," said Matthew's father Brody Calhoun. "Let's get him settled before the drug wears off. Then you can tell us all about how we've ended up with an unknown, unconscious soldier in our house."

"He saved my life," said Matthew.

With everyone's help they soon had Michael in the house. He needed to be cleaned again, and Katherine insisted on helping despite the protests of Matthew, her father, and even Ira Tanner. Afterwards, he was placed into the bed, and left to sleep.

It was late by the time both Matthew and Ira, had told their stories, and they were through reminiscing. Everyone slept well in the house that seemed so full again, everyone that is except Michael. Demons had come calling.

In the morning, Matthew settled up with Ira, paying him an extra days wage in addition to what he was owed. Ira tried to refuse the extra money, but Matthew wouldn't hear of it. They shook hands, and Ira said that he was going to head up to Hagerstown to see his family.

Chapter 41

The Appomattox
1864

Despite how gracious and unassuming their hostess was, it was still a bit intimidating sharing a table with the wife of the man who was in command of the entire Union Army. The lunch of boiled chicken with rice, squash, and fresh bread was very good, and she was excellent at making small talk. However, she was after all the wife of General Ulysses S. Grant.

When the meal was done, they retired into the parlor to discuss the McBride's trip to Virginia to try and find their missing son Michael. Mrs. Grant had persuaded them not to go to the scene of the battle at Cedar Creek in the Shenandoah Valley, but to go to City Point and meet with her husband. She would give them a letter to take with them, requesting that he do whatever he could to assist them.

"I think it would be best," Mrs. Grant began, "for you to take the steamer from here to Philadelphia, then to continue on to Washington by train. You can board a steamer in Washington that will take you to City Point outside of Petersburg which is where the General is currently headquartered."

"Won't it be difficult for us to get passage on a steamer out of Washington?" Asked William McBride, Michael's father. "Won't most of the ships be on government or Army business?"

"Yes," she said, "but I've also written a letter to a dear friend at the War Department, asking him to help you gain passage. You can carry the letter with you and place it directly into his hands."

"How will we find him?" Asked Joanna McBride.

"His name is Colonel Baker. He's at the War Department, and he is a good friend to me as well as to the General. I'm confident he'll do what he can to get you to City Point. Can you leave on Thursday?"

"Yes. I believe so," said William.

"Good," said Mrs. Grant. "I've spoken to the agent at the wharf and he is holding two tickets for you for Thursday morning's 8:00 o'clock departure on the *John Warner*. You can pay the fare when you pick up the tickets.

"You should arrive in Philadelphia by ten. That'll give you plenty of time to get to the train station on Market Street to make the noon train for Washington."

Mrs. Grant had everything written down on a piece of paper along with steamer and train schedules. If her husband was this good at planning battles, the war was as good as won, thought William. But, would there be anyone who could tell them where Michael was?

"Your train will get into Washington around three," Mrs. Grant continued. "It will be too late to meet with Colonel Baker, so hire a carriage to take you to the Willard Hotel. I've also written a letter for you to present to Henry Willard, one of the proprietors. The rooms are about three dollars a night, but that includes a very nice meal. In the morning it will be a short walk from the hotel to the War Department.

"From there it will be up to Colonel Baker to get you to the General, and the General to get you to who you need to see about finding your son."

"I don't know how we'll ever be able to repay your kindness," said Joanna.

"By keeping me informed," said Mrs. Grant with a smile. "Write to me once a week and let me know how your quest is going. Then when you have found your young man and brought him home, bring him around so that we may meet him, and welcome him home properly."

"You have done so much more than we could ever have the right to ask of you," said William.

"Thousands upon thousands of young men have died in this war," said Mrs. Grant. "We must do everything we can when there is an opportunity to save even one." They parted with tears, handshakes, hugs, and promises.

On Thursday morning the McBride's, in possession of the three letters written by Mrs. Grant, boarded the *John A. Warner* at the foot of the wharf in Burlington. They hoped it was a good sign that they were taking the same boat that had taken Michael. Maybe it was the beginning of the trail that would lead them to their son.

They met with Colonel Baker at the War Department on Friday morning after being treated like royalty at the Willard Hotel the night before. Colonel Baker told them that he would not be able to get them onboard a ship for City Point until Tuesday. That would mean four additional nights at the Willard.

They had brought everything they had with them, just short of one hundred dollars. They had already paid for the steamer fare to Philadelphia, train fare to Washington, and their meals. They would be travelling on an Army cargo vessel to City Point, and would not be charged for that part of the trip. Even so, at three dollars a night, they could not afford to stay more than the one night at the Willard.

When they returned to the Willard, William asked to speak with Henry Willard, the gentleman they had given Mrs. Grant's letter to. William sat in the lobby and waited, and watched what he assumed were probably some of the most powerful men in the country pass by. He was lost in thought, and was startled when Mr. Willard spoke. "Mr. McBride isn't it?" He asked.

"Yes, yes it is, Mr. Willard," stammered William. "Thank you for seeing me."

"It is my pleasure Mr. McBride," he said. "Is everything satisfactory? I hope that you are enjoying your stay with us? At least as much as you can under the circumstances."

"Everything is perfect Mr. Willard," said William. "It's just that well, I was wondering if maybe you could recommend another hotel, perhaps something a little less expensive?"

"You do not like it here?"

"Oh no, Mr. Willard, it's nothing like that, it's just that we cannot get a boat out of Washington to City Point until Tuesday, and I'm afraid we cannot afford to stay that long in such luxury as this magnificent hotel."

Mr. Willard studied William, and thought for a minute. "What is it that you can afford to pay Mr. McBride?" He asked.

"Some place that isn't much more than a dollar or so a night," answered William sheepishly not being able to hide the embarrassment in his voice.

"I will not have the parents of a hero staying in squalor," he said with a smile. "You have paid three dollars for your stay with us. That is all you will pay, there will be no additional charges. You may stay as long as is necessary. It is our honor to have you with us." Mr. Willard offered his hand.

"Thank you," croaked William as he took Mr. Willard's hand. "Thank you so very much."

"It is our pleasure," said Mr. Willard, and with a bow he turned and left William staring after him in the lobby.

On Tuesday morning at seven o'clock, the *Excelsior*, loaded down with goods and supplies for the Army of the Potomac, set sail for City Point, Virginia, from the Navy Yard docks on the Anacostia River in Washington, DC. On board were William and Joanna McBride. The Captain of the *Excelsior,* Commander Timothy Hanratty, was told only that his passengers were to be escorted to General Grant's headquarters immediately upon their arrival at City Point.

The McBride's were given a small cabin near the stern of the ship. It had a small porthole, a curtain for a door, and upper and lower wooden bunks with mattresses that were mattresses in name only. There was a small bucket that would serve Mrs. McBride's needs, but Mr. McBride was expected to use the head at the bow of the ship just as the crew members did.

They had dinner with the Captain in the evening, but their two other meals, lunch on the first day, and breakfast on the second, were taken with the crew. The Captain and the crew were civil, but not very friendly. They both found it nearly impossible to sleep between the sounds of the engine, and the water rushing against the side of the ship.

They arrived off of City Point Wednesday morning just after ten o'clock. The journey of over 250 miles had taken a little over 26-hours. When they came up on to the main deck, what they saw took their breath away.

The sights and the sounds they beheld were amazing. A vast fleet of ships stretched as far as the eye could see. Many of them were waiting to be summoned to one of the wharfs to unload their cargo, others were preparing to get underway to their next port. As the *Excelsior* wound its way through this fleet William could see that there were a number of wharfs with ships tied up to them two and three deep.

There also appeared to be a city of warehouses and other buildings on the shore beyond the wharfs. Everywhere there were men in motion, loading, unloading, directing, and engaged in every phase of moving the never ending arrival of cargo. The thundering sound from the huge number of trains that were on the wharfs awaiting cargo to be transferred, going up towards the warehouses, or disappearing beyond the warehouses was so deafening that it nearly caused them to cover their ears.

The *Excelsior* tied up at the wharf that was the furthest upstream. The activity on this wharf did not seem as chaotic as it was on the others. The other ships that were tied up here appeared to be more for the transportation of passengers, than for cargo.

As soon as the ship was secure, the Captain went on to the dock and spoke with a Union officer. The officer wrote something and handed it to a soldier who immediately left. The Captain came back aboard and summoned the McBride's.

"I have asked the Harbor Master to notify the Provost that I have two passengers who, per the War Department, are to be taken to General Grant's headquarters immediately upon our arrival. He has sent a message to the Provost so advising him. I expect that your escort will be arriving shortly."

"Thank you Captain Hanratty," said William.

"At your service Sir," replied the Captain, tipping his cap. "I hope that your trip was not too uncomfortable."

"Not at all Sir," said William, "and, we thank you and your crew for your hospitality."

The Captain tipped his cap again. "Now," he said, motioning in that direction. "If you'll remain aboard in the area of the gangway until your escort arrives. Once you are delivered I will have to move back out into the channel and await wharf space. We will not be unloading our holds here."

"Yes Sir," said William as he and Joanna gathered up their belongings and made their way to the gangway.

Less than an hour later a carriage pulled up to the end of the gangway. The carriage was being driven by a Union soldier, sitting alongside the soldier was a young officer. He jumped down from the carriage, approached the ship, addressed the Officer of the Deck, and was granted permission to board.

"Are you the civilians who are to be taken to General Grant's headquarters?" He asked.

"Yes," answered William.

"My name is Lieutenant Yates, and I'll be escorting you there," he said. "If you'll climb into the carriage, we'll be on our way." Gathering their belongings, again, they climbed into the carriage. Once they were settled the carriage began making its way up the wharf, away from the river. As they slowly progressed through what to the unknowing eye appeared to be mass confusion and chaos, William could see that what he had been able to observe from the deck of the *Excelsior*, and what he could now see from this carriage, was but a fraction of this depot's expanse.

It went on forever, and was magnificent to behold. It had to be one of man's greatest achievements. What troubled William though was the fact that such a place had been created for the sole purpose of waging war.

As they made their way up the hill away from the wharfs, a fine house came into view. It sat on the highest point above the river, and commanded a breathtaking view of the confluence of the James and Appomattox Rivers. William and Joanna were sure this was the house where General Grant would make his headquarters. The carriage came to a stop in front of a somewhat rustic cabin about 100 yards south of the big house.

Lieutenant Yates jumped down from the carriage. "Wait here," he said. "I'll let Colonel Rawlins know that you're here." The Lieutenant returned a few minutes later followed by a man who was not in a proper uniform, but obviously was someone in authority.

"I'm Colonel Rawlins," the man said. "I'm General Grant's adjutant. May I inquire as to why the War Department has sent you to see the General?"

"I'm William McBride, and this is my wife Joanna. We have this letter from Mrs. Grant," said William, producing the envelope. "Our instructions are to deliver it to the General personally."

"May I see the letter?" Asked the Colonel.

William handed it to him and said, "I would prefer that you not open it."

The Colonel nodded, and examined the envelope. "It does appear to be Mrs. Grant's hand," he said, "but, I can't help but think that there's more to your visit than the delivery of a letter."

"Our son is missing," said Joanna.

"Missing?" Asked the Colonel.

"He was at the battle of Cedar Creek," she continued. "After the battle he was listed on the casualty report as missing. We've come to Virginia to find him."

"I see," said the Colonel, "and, you think that there's something that the General can do to help you find your son? Do you have any idea how many sons are listed as missing in this war?"

"No," said Joanna. "I only know that mine is, and I know that Mrs. Grant, who is a neighbor, wrote that letter to her husband on our behalf, and told us to place it into his hands. Now, are we to return home, and tell Mrs. Grant that we were not permitted to do as she asked? Or, will you let the General know we wish to see him at his convenience?"

"Madam," said the Colonel with a smile. "I would much rather cross the General and suffer his wrath, than even contemplate crossing his lady and risking hers. Unfortunately, the General is on an inspection tour, and is not expected back until later this evening.

"Lieutenant Yates," said the Colonel turning his attention to their escort. "See to it that Mr. and Mrs. McBride are properly quartered, and make arrangements for them to take their meals in the officers' mess. See to it that they are back here at ten o'clock tomorrow morning. Understood?"

"Yes Sir!" Said the Lieutenant.

The Colonel then turned his attention to the McBride's. "Return here in the morning and I will see to it that the General makes time to meet with you. Will that be satisfactory?" He asked handing the letter back to William.

"Yes Colonel," said Joanna McBride with a smile. "Thank you."

The Colonel offered his hand to William who took it, and the two men, who had never before met, immediately realized that they shared a common bond.

"Mt. Holly #18," said William.

"Miners #273, Galena, Illinois," said the Colonel with a smile. "I promise, my Brother, that all that can be done shall be done."

"Thank you Brother," said William with a nod as they released their grip.

The McBride's passed the night in a cabin that was much smaller, but not altogether unlike the one that Colonel Rawlins occupied. It was a one room cabin with two bunks that were reasonably comfortable. It was a cool night, but the blankets the Army provided were warm enough so there was no need to have a fire in the small fireplace.

As promised, the next morning, Lieutenant Yates came calling at eight-thirty. He escorted them to the officers' mess where they enjoyed a breakfast of eggs, bacon, biscuits, and coffee. The Lieutenant was friendly enough, but was unwilling to answer any questions about the depot and its workings. At about a quarter to ten, Lieutenant Yates delivered them to Colonel Rawlins' cabin.

"Aren't we going to meet with the General at his headquarters?" Asked Joanna.

The Lieutenant looked at her inquisitively. "This is his headquarters, and his quarters," said the Lieutenant.

"This isn't Colonel Rawlins' quarters?"

"No, ma'am. The Colonel's quarters is just a few doors from where you stayed last night. He has a one room cabin just like yours," answered the Lieutenant.

"I would have thought the General would have been staying in the big house," she said.

"Not this general," he said proudly. "General Grant likes to keep things simple."

They were lead into the cabin and took seats in two of several chairs that lined the front wall of the cabin. Lieutenant Yates then left the cabin. There were two field desks jammed into the small room that had a fireplace on the back wall and a single window opposite the fireplace. The room smelled of cigars and men. There was a closed door to the right of the fireplace that obviously lead into another room.

They had only been waiting a few minutes when that door opened and Colonel Rawlins, now in a proper uniform, entered followed by a man William and Joanna recognized as General Ulysses S. Grant. They immediately jumped to their feet. He was not an imposing man. His hair was disheveled, and he looked very tired. If not for his dark beard, he would have appeared very ordinary. There was no pomp and circumstance about him, if not for the rank insignias on his shoulders he could have been mistaken for a blacksmith.

Colonel Rawlins smiled and nodded, and indicated to the McBride's that they should retake their seats. Then he walked over and took a seat behind one of the desks. The General walked over to the other desk opened a box on top of the desk and removed a cigar. He stuck the cigar in his mouth, but did not light it.

"Good morning," he said as he turned towards the McBride's with a smile, and removed the cigar from his mouth. "I assume that you are Mr. and Mrs. McBride?"

"William and Joanna," answered William nervously. "Yes Sir. We are."

"You have something for me from Mrs. Grant?" He asked as he walked over to them and pulled one of the chairs away from the wall turned it around and sat down facing them.

"Yes Sir," said William reaching into a pocket and producing the letter. He handed the envelope to the General.

"It's always good to get a letter from home," said the General with a smile. "Excuse me while I read this one."

"Mrs. Grant seems to have taken quite an interest in your misfortune," said the General after reading the letter. "It says in here that I spoke with your son? Your son was Private McBride?"

"Yes Sir," said Joanna, producing the letter she had received from Michael. "Just before they left Hopewell for the Shenandoah Valley."

General Grant took the letter and read the part Joanna pointed to. "Ah yes," he said. "The 10th New Jersey, part of the First New Jersey Brigade. They were pretty well used up. I had hoped to be able to let them remain here and rest, but unfortunately

I had to send them north to reinforce Washington. They ended up chasing Jubal Early up and down the Shenandoah Valley.

"I do in fact remember having this conversation with the members of your son's regiment. I did tell them that neighbors should be able to count on each other. So, let me see then what I can do for this neighbor," he said with a smile tapping the letter as he stood, put the cigar back in his mouth, and walked over to the desk where Colonel Rawlins was seated.

"Lieutenant Yates!" Colonel Rawlins called out after he and the General had had a short conversation. Almost immediately the Lieutenant was standing inside the cabin door at attention and saluting. "Find Major Hudson, and have him report here to General Grant."

"Yes Sir!" Replied the Lieutenant as he dropped the salute and exited the cabin.

The General walked back over and sat down opposite the McBride's. "Here's the problem," the General began, once again removing the cigar from his mouth. "The VI Corps, the 1st New Jersey Brigade, and your son's regiment, are all still in Winchester. Those are the people that you need to talk to in order to find your son, and the body of his friend. It can't be done from here."

"So," said Joanna. "We've come all this way for nothing?"

"No, no you haven't," answered the General reassuringly. "Colonel Rawlins here tells me that he is fraternally obligated to do everything in his power to assist you," he continued with a smile and a glance in the Colonel's direction, "and I wouldn't want to violate such an ancient bond. Therefore, I am going to assign Major Hudson from my staff to accompany you back to Washington, where you will board a train to Winchester. When you arrive in Winchester you will meet with VI Corps Commander, General Horatio Wright. Major Hudson will have in his possession a message from me directing the General to do whatever is necessary to try and locate your son.

"In addition, I will send a wire to General Wright advising him that you are on your way to see him. I'm afraid there's not much more I can do than that."

"Thank you General," said William. "We are very grateful for everything you and your staff has done for us already, and especially for Mrs. Grant."

The General smiled and nodded. "I pray that it is not so, but you know one of the outcomes of this will be discovering that your son is dead."

"He's not dead General," said Joanna with a smile. "I know this because I am his mother, just as Mrs. Grant, or any mother would know, were it their son."

"Of course," said the General with a sympathetic nod.

Lieutenant Yates, accompanied by a Major entered the cabin. Both men came to attention and saluted the General. The General returned the salute. "You are dismissed Lieutenant," he said to Yates.

"Sir," said Yates as he saluted, turned, and left the cabin.

"Major Hudson," said the General. "This is Mr. and Mrs. McBride. I am assigning you to escort them back to Washington by steamer, and then onto Winchester by rail. Where you will meet with General Wright, and whoever else is necessary in an effort to locate their missing son."

The Major looked confused as he glanced back and forth between the McBride's and the General.

"Questions, Major?" Asked Colonel Rawlins.

"No Sir," answered the Major a hint of confusion in his voice. "When will we be departing?"

"You will arrange transportation for yourself and the McBride's on the very next vessel departing for Washington," said the Colonel. "So, I suggest you get down to the harbor master's office and find out when that will be. Report back to me when you have that information, and I'll get you to the McBride's."

"Yes Sir," said the Major as he saluted, turned, and left the cabin.

The General stood and offered his hand. "I'm afraid I have matters I must attend to," he said. "I wish you the very best on your crusade and hope everything works out with the best possible outcome."

"Thank you General," said William and Joanna as they stood and shook hands with the General.

"Colonel, I'm going down to the stables," said General Grant as he put the cigar back in his mouth. Then he stopped, turned back towards the McBride's, removed the cigar, and with a smile said, "When you write to Julia, be sure and tell her that I was able to refrain from smoking in your presence, at times I'm afraid I tend to forget myself where this habit is concerned. You can also tell her that I wasn't tired and in the best of health. She won't believe you, but I'd appreciate it if you told her anyway."

"Certainly General," said Joanna with a smile.

"Goodbye," he said as he exited the cabin.

About an hour after they had returned to their cabin, Lieutenant Yates stopped by to tell them that they would be on a ship that would be leaving City Point for Washington at two o'clock that afternoon. He and Major Hudson would be by to pick them up within the hour. The McBride's were impressed with how quickly General Grant was able to make things happen.

To their surprise they were to be aboard the *Excelsior,* which was now unloaded, and returning to Washington. They boarded with Major Hudson, and when the Captain learned that the Major was from General Grant's staff they found it interesting that the Captain was so much friendlier than he had been on their first voyage, and that their accommodations were so much nicer than before. They were back in Washington by late in the afternoon of the next day.

Major Hudson, who they learned was General Grant's nephew, turned out to be a very personable young man once he let his guard down. He had wanted to find quarters at the Navy Yard, but William and Joanna convinced him to allow them to treat him to a night at the Willard. When they arrived at the Willard they ran into the proprietor Henry Willard who was anxious to know how their quest was going. He invited the McBride's and the Major into his office, where over a few glasses of sherry they described in detail what had happened at City Point. Mr. Willard then arranged for them to have two rooms for the night, along with supper that evening, and breakfast the next morning, for five dollars. The McBride's, who were very grateful, were more than happy to pay.

There was a train leaving for Pittsburgh that would be stopping in Winchester, the following morning, which was a Saturday. That train would have them in Winchester before two o'clock in the afternoon. The Major had arranged for them to be on that train. Over the course of the last ten days, the McBride's had travelled nearly seven hundred miles, and they were not done yet.

They hired a carriage upon their arrival in Winchester which took them to General Horatio Wright's headquarters at Hollingsworth House south of the town. When they arrived at Hollingsworth House an aide, also a Major, told them that General Wright was not seeing anyone else today, would not be seeing anyone tomorrow, which was the Sabbath, but would see them at ten o'clock on Monday morning.

"Is General Wright aware that I have a message with me from General Grant directing him to attend to this matter immediately?" Asked Major Hudson.

"He has received a dispatch from General Grant regarding this matter but is afraid Monday morning is as immediate as he can make it," answered the aide as he started herding them towards the door. "If there's nothing else then, we look forward to seeing you on Monday morning."

"We should go to General Sheridan," said Major Hudson when they were back outside and in the carriage. "He could order General Wright to see us now."

"Wouldn't that tweak General Wright's nose though?" Asked Joanna. "Which might make him a little less enthusiastic to our cause?"

"Perhaps," said the Major.

"Then let's just find a place to stay, and come back on Monday morning," said Joanna.

They took a room at the Taylor Hotel on Loudon Street. There was only one room available, and its cost, without meals, was two dollars per night. It was exorbitant, but the McBride's had little if any choice. The young Major said that he had friends in the area, and would make arrangements to stay with them.

The Taylor Hotel had served as a hospital during the battles in and around Winchester, and still smelled and looked like a hospital. Many of the beds and furnishings were broken or otherwise damaged. Only a few of the window curtains and other decorative pieces were still present, and many of the wounded who had been treated here were still here.

Joanna asked around and learned that many of the wounded who had been treated at the Taylor had been transferred to hospitals in Harrisburg, and Frederick. She also learned that many of the more seriously wounded who could not travel were moved to the hospital at White Sulphur out on the Jordan Springs Road. Joanna had decided that she wanted to visit that hospital.

"I don't think that's such a good idea," said Major Hudson when Joanna told him on Sunday morning about her desire to visit the hospital. "With all due respect Mrs. McBride, you've never been in an Army hospital. The men in that place have suffered grievous wounds, many of them have had arms and legs amputated, many are unrecognizable, not only as individuals, but as men. No, I think it best that we stay away from White Sulphur."

"One of those unrecognizable men may be our son," she said.

"It is unlikely, but even so, how could even you recognize a man who has no face, because that's what you will encounter there."

"A mother will always know her son," she said with a smile. "If you don't believe me ask your own mother."

The Major turned to Mr. McBride. "Is there any chance that we can avoid this?"

"I don't believe so," said William with a knowing chuckle.

"Alright," sighed the Major, "but, don't say I didn't warn you."

The Major had been able to procure an Army carriage and horse from the local quartermaster. The ride out to the hospital at White Sulphur took about an hour and a half. They arrived shortly before noon.

They met with the senior medical officer who told them that they did have a number of men who were unidentified. Some because they had never regained consciousness, others did not seem to be known by anyone, and in many cases it was not even known what unit they were with. Others were unidentified because there was no way to physically identify them.

"I'd like to see them all," said Joanna. She was terrified about what she might see, but steeled herself to the task. She prayed that Michael wasn't here, but if he was, she would find him.

"Major, I...," began the Doctor.

"Doctor," said the Major holding up his hand. "I have done my best to dissuade her, and have warned her of what she might encounter, but I'm afraid she is intent on seeing this through."

"As the senior medical officer, I can deny her entry," said the Doctor.

"If you wish to do so Doctor, you may. But, my instructions from General Grant are to do whatever is necessary in assisting the McBride's in finding their son."

"General Grant?"

"Yes Sir."

"Very well," sighed the Doctor. "Follow me."

They spent the next hour visiting the bedsides of the unidentified wounded. There were nearly one hundred of them. It was the most heartbreaking thing the McBride's had ever been exposed to.

Many of them were blind, could not speak, or constantly mumbled incoherently, or wailed, or screamed, or just cried. Others looked perfectly fine, but had suffered head wounds that had shut down their brains. Then there were those who were disfigured, and as the Major and the Doctor had said, no longer even looked like men. Joanna looked at every one of them. Michael was not among them.

They spent a few additional hours visiting with some of the other wounded. The Doctor explained that most of the men here had received mortal wounds and were beyond hope. They were being kept as comfortable as possible until it was their time. Then they would be buried in the fields around the hospital with the others who had not been able to make the trip to Frederick or Harrisburg.

When they were done Joanna asked the doctor if any of the unidentified had been moved to Harrisburg or Frederick. He told her that there had been a number of them. Then he told them a strange story about an unidentified soldier, and a cavalry sergeant.

"I was assigned to the field hospital out by Hollingsworth shortly after the battle at Cedar Creek. They were bringing the wounded from General Merritt's Cavalry there from the hospital in Newtown. One of the men they brought in with the cavalry had a tag on him that said he was unidentified infantry. He was the only infantryman we received that day.

"He was in really bad shape. Took a round to the chest at point blank range. Was lucky though, nothing vital was hit. He had lost a lot of blood and had some very serious internal trauma. He had difficulty breathing, could barely talk, and had no memory. Had no idea even who he was. It was bad, but if he could survive the first couple of days, we believed he had a good chance of pulling through. Though it would take a long time, and he would need a lot of rest and care. The kind of care he might not be able to get as an unidentified in an Army hospital.

"Anyway, he was brought in with this cavalry sergeant, the sergeant's arm had been nearly severed, and had to be reattached. I still have doubts about it healing properly, and believe that at some point that arm is going to have to come off.

"But, this cavalry sergeant never let this infantry soldier out of his sight. Said the soldier had saved his life, and he was going to do the same for him. Did everything for him, made sure he got water and broth into him, cleaned him up when he soiled himself, and all with one arm. I never saw anything like it before."

"What happened to them?" Asked Joanna.

"The cavalry sergeant was placed on convalescence leave. The infantry soldier was scheduled to be transferred to the Union hospital in Harrisburg."

"Is that where he is now?" Asked Joanna.

"No," said the Doctor. "That cavalry sergeant managed to get that soldier released into his custody, and he took him home with him! Extremely unusual, and not in keeping with regulations at all."

"Where was home?" Asked Joanna.

"I don't know," answered the Doctor, "but I'm sure someone in the cavalry would."

Major Hudson and the McBride's thanked the doctor, and returned to Winchester. They dined at the Red Lion tavern on Loudon Street before returning to their lodgings. They ate, but none of them had much of an appetite. Joanna cried herself to sleep that night, unable to get the White Sulphur wounded out of her mind. It would be a vision that would haunt her during sleepless nights for the rest of her life.

At ten o'clock Monday morning, they arrived at Hollingsworth House and were escorted into a room to meet with VI Corps Commander, General Horatio Wright. They waited nearly a half hour before the General, accompanied by several other officers entered the room. Some of the officers were carrying portfolios.

When the introductions were made, William and Joanna learned that besides members of General's Wright's staff, present were Colonel William Penrose, Commanding Officer of the First New Jersey Brigade, Major James W. McNeely, Commanding Officer of the Tenth New Jersey Regiment, and Captain John Cunningham, H Company's Commanding Officer. They were all seated around a large oval table. The Major, who had denied them entry on Saturday, stood behind General Wright.

"Let me begin," said General Wright, "by offering my apologies to you for not being able to meet with you sooner. But, you see, it would not have been possible to get the men seated here all together at one time and place, before now, and these are the men who are probably the best prepared to answer your questions. I hope you understand."

The McBride's, who were more than just a little intimidated by the power and authority of the men in the room, could just nod and smile.

"I understand from the limited information in General Grant's dispatch," the General said, "that you are searching for your son, who was listed as missing, at Cedar Creek."

"Yes Sir," said William. "That's correct, and we also want to find the body of Frank Jefferson, who was reported killed at Cedar Creek and take him home to be buried amongst his friends and loved ones."

"I see," said the General. "Well, why don't we start with something that we may be able to resolve rather quickly? Captain Cunningham?"

"Sir?"

"I believe that Private Jefferson was assigned to H Company?"

"Yes Sir, he was Sir," replied the Captain who pulled some papers out of the portfolio he had brought to the table. "I can confirm that Private Frank Jefferson was killed on the morning of 19 October, during fighting in the cemetery west of Middletown. He was identified by his lieutenant, and several members of his squad. Private Jefferson was interred in the Union cemetery on the Valley Pike, north of Middletown.

"By all reports, Private Frank Jefferson was a fine soldier, who was well liked by his fellow soldiers, and superiors. I'm sorry for your loss."

"Thank you," said William quietly. Joanna removed a handkerchief from her purse and dabbed at her eyes. She smiled and nodded at the Captain.

"Major," said the General to the officer standing behind him. "Please make arrangements to have Private Jefferson's body exhumed, prepared for shipment, and shipped to wherever the McBride's wish as soon as possible. All at the Army's expense."

"Yes Sir," said the Major who then turned and left the room.

"Now," said the General. "On to our missing private. Major McNeely, Private McBride was in your Regiment, why don't you explain for us what happened the morning of the battle, and perhaps we can discover at what point our private went missing."

"Yes Sir," said Major McNeely. He rolled out a map showing the area in and around Middletown where the battle had been fought. "The Tenth, was encamped with the rest of VI Corps, here north of the Belle Grove plantation house." As he spoke he marked the locations on the map with a pencil. "In the pre-dawn darkness we were attacked by Confederate forces. We held for a while, but eventually were forced to withdraw. We fell back almost a mile to here." Marked the map. "And established a line that ran from the town here, west through the cemetery here.

"The Tenth occupied that portion of the line that covered the southeast corner of this wood lot, here." Marked the map. "Then west to the western edge of the cemetery, here. H Company was the end of the line, the right flank, at the edge of the cemetery."

"There was no one on the right beyond H Company?" Asked the General.

"No Sir," answered Major McNeely.

"Sir, if I may?" Said Captain Cunningham.

"You have something to add, Captain?" Asked the General.

"Yes Sir, later, just before sunrise, the right flank was extended by dismounted cavalry from General Merritt's Division. They stayed with us, even when we were forced to withdraw again."

The hair on the back of Joanna's neck stood up, and her heart began to race. She was finding it hard to breathe as tears began to well up in her eyes. She reached out and squeezed William's hand.

General Wright observed that Joanna seemed to be in distress. "Excuse me Mrs. McBride," he said. "I know this must be difficult for you. If you would like to stop for now and continue later that would be perfectly acceptable."

"No, no General," she said. "I'm really quite alright, but let me ask a question. Is it possible that some of the infantrymen became mixed in with the cavalry, and if so, and if they were wounded, is it possible the infantrymen would have been sent to a cavalry hospital?"

"Yes, I suppose that is possible," said the General, "but, usually the wounded are removed to the nearest field hospital, despite what unit they are with, or whether or not their cavalry or infantry. Colonel Penrose, can you add anything."

"Well Sir," began the Colonel. "General Merritt did have the cavalry wounded removed to a hospital in Newtown, on the 19th, and not to the hospital at Miller's, even though it was considerably closer."

"So," said Joanna. "A wounded infantryman could have been removed to the cavalry hospital by mistake?"

"Yes," answered the Colonel. "That is possible, but as soon as they discovered who he was, they would have sent him to one of the other hospitals."

"What if they didn't know who he was, or who he belonged to?" She asked.

There was silence. All of the officers exchanged glances. "Then he could still be mixed in amongst the cavalry wounded," said Captain Cunningham.

"Gentlemen," said Joanna with a smile. "I can't thank you enough for your assistance, but I am now convinced that my son is alive, and I do believe that I know where to find him."

"Please Mrs. McBride." Patronized the General. "I urge restraint in this matter. While it is possible that your son is listed as an unidentified cavalryman in a Union hospital somewhere, it will take weeks, perhaps months, to check them all, and even then, you may find yourself still disappointed. So, please let's not jump to any hasty conclusions."

"My son is not in a Union hospital General," said Joanna. "He is convalescing with a cavalry sergeant at his home somewhere, and I need to speak to someone from the cavalry as soon as possible."

"Mrs. McBride," said Colonel Penrose. "What you're suggesting is extremely unlikely. Forgive me for saying so, but it seems an act of desperation."

"You are forgiven Colonel," said Joanna, "but I know I am right, and desperation has nothing to do with it."

"Where can we find the cavalry?" Asked William.

"General Merritt's cavalry division is encamped at the Hackwood Farm about four miles north of here," said General Wright. Then intently eyeing the McBride's he asked, "Are you absolutely sure you want to do this?"

"Yes Sir," answered William.

"Very well," said the General. "Colonel Penrose, Captain Cunningham, you will accompany the McBride's and Major Hudson to General Merritt's headquarters, along with my adjutant Major Eagan. Please make sure you make it very clear to General Merritt, that he is to do whatever he can to assist the McBride's, and make sure that he understands that that comes not only from this headquarters but General Grant's as well."

"Yes Sir," said Colonel Penrose.

The officers all rose, walked around the table to William and Joanna and shook their hands and wished them well. Within twenty minutes, William and Joanna were in the carriage, being driven by Major Hudson, following Colonel Penrose, Major Eagan, and Captain Cunningham north towards Hackwood Farm. They arrived at the farm in a little over an hour.

General Merritt at first showed very little interest in meeting with the McBride's or listening to why the officer's from General Wright's VI Corps were at his headquarters. However, when he was advised that this was something that General Grant was taking a very particular and personal interest in, he became a little more receptive. They were all invited to join him in the parlor of the farmhouse that was serving as his headquarters.

"This all seems to be grasping at straws," said an obviously disinterested General Merritt after listening to the explanations of what had occurred at the White Sulphur Hospital, and Hollingsworth House. "So, I presume what you would like to determine," he said, "is which cavalry unit was put into the line on the right flank of the VI Corps at the Middletown Cemetery?"

"Yes Sir," said Colonel Penrose. "I believe that is the best place to start."

"Sergeant Randolph!" Hollered General Merritt.

A large man in an immaculate cavalry uniform with numerous gold stripes, pointing up and down on the sleeves, stepped into the room, snapped to attention, and barked, "Sir!"

"Sergeant, I need to know what Brigade was dismounted and deployed on the right flank of VI Corps in the Middletown Cemetery on October 19th, during Cedar Creek, and I need to know that now."

"I'll get right on it Sir," replied the Sergeant as he smartly about faced and left the room. During his absence there were short periods of small talk accompanied by longer periods of awkward silence. The Sergeant returned to the room about twenty minutes later.

"Ah, Sergeant, there you are," said General Merritt. "I was beginning to think that maybe you had taken your retirement, or been taken prisoner."

"No Sir," said the Sergeant smiling but obviously not seeing the humor in the General's remarks. "The First and Second US Cavalry Regiments from Colonel Lowell's Brigade were deployed in the Middletown Cemetery on the morning of the 19th," said the Sergeant. "I've sent for Captains Baker and Smith. Sir," he said.

"Well done Sergeant," said the General with a smile.

"Sir," said the Sergeant as he again about faced, and left the room.

It wasn't long before the Sergeant reentered the room and came to attention. "Sir," he said. "Captain Baker of the First US Cavalry, and Captain Smith of the Second US Cavalry."

"Thank you Sergeant," said General Merritt. The Sergeant, executing another perfect about face, left the room. "Captain Baker, Captain Smith, do come in and join us. Please, sit down."

The Captains entered nervously and took seats in wooden chairs along the back wall of the room. General Merritt, with the help of Colonel Penrose, and Joanna

McBride, explained as best they could, why the Captains had been called to headquarters. Captain Baker had no idea what they were talking about, but Captain Smith did.

"Sergeant Calhoun," said Captain Smith.

"Excuse me?" Said General Merritt.

"Sergeant Calhoun, Sir," continued the Captain. "Sergeant Matthew Calhoun. His left arm was nearly severed at Cedar Creek. He was sent home on convalescence leave. An unidentified infantryman, who Sergeant Calhoun said had saved his life, was released into his custody, and left Winchester with Sergeant Calhoun."

"And who authorized this?" Asked the General, staring directly at the young Captain.

"The Senior Medical Officer. He said that there was nothing further they could do for the infantryman in the hospital here or any hospital he might be sent to. That what he really needed was plenty of rest and care, preferably someplace safe and quiet. As Calhoun's Commanding Officer, I concurred and also signed the release," nervously answered Captain Smith.

"So, an unidentified seriously wounded infantry soldier was sent on convalescence leave with a cavalry sergeant who did not even know his name?"

The other officers in the room looked at their boots, the ceiling, out the window, or anywhere rather than make eye contact with the General, or the Captain who was now in the General's cross hairs. The McBride's however, hung on every word.

"Yes Sir." Managed Captain Smith trying to swallow the lump in his throat.

"Do we know where the sergeant took the infantryman to convalesce?" Asked the General sarcastically.

"Sergeant Calhoun indicated he was going home, Sir. I believe his home is in Maryland."

"Maryland?" Asked the General, nodding. "Anyplace in particular, or were they simply going on a tour?"

"I can get our regimental clerk, Sir," answered Captain Smith. "I'm sure he has that information."

"WE have that information, Captain!" Snapped the General, who was obviously annoyed. "This is after all headquarters, is it not? Sergeant Randolph?" He hollered. Sergeant Randolph entered the room.

"Calhoun," said the General before the Sergeant could even speak. "Sergeant Matthew Calhoun, Second US Cavalry, currently on convalescent leave, I want to know where he calls home." Sergeant Randolph simply nodded, and turned and left the room, this time there was no smart about face, the Sergeant was growing weary of whatever it was that was going on in the parlor.

The Sergeant was gone about ten minutes while a dark cloud hung over the room. No one wanted to speak in fear of making what had become an uncomfortable situation, into a disaster. The McBride's just waited, trying to keep their excitement in check.

When Sergeant Randolph returned he was carrying a paper which he walked over and handed directly to General Merritt. "Calhoun, Matthew K., Sergeant, US 2nd

Cavalry," he stated while walking towards the General. "Middletown, Maryland."

"Middletown?" Asked the General as he took the paper.

"A farm, owned by his father, Brody Calhoun, a mile west of the town on the National Road where it crosses the Catoctin Creek," said the Sergeant with a smirk on his face, which he followed with a patronizing, "Sir."

The General just stared at the Sergeant. "Sometimes Randolph," he said with a bit of a laugh. "You amaze even me."

"Was with B Troop back in '61, before the war, when we rode from Carlisle to Baltimore to escort Lincoln," said the Sergeant. "Bivouacked on the Calhoun farm along the way."

"So, you know Calhoun do you?" Asked General Merritt.

"No Sir," answered the Sergeant. "Wouldn't say I know him. Might have seen him in passing a few times, but wouldn't say I knew him, No Sir. Calhoun rode with Eric O'Neall's squad back then. Sergeant Eric O'Neall, good trooper, got killed at Gettysburg, but I remember he thought a lot of Calhoun. If O'Neall liked you, you had to be doing something right."

"Thank you for that ringing endorsement of Sergeant Calhoun," said the General sarcastically. "You say his farm is a mile west of Middletown on the National Road?"

"Yes Sir."

"Very well. Captain Smith!" Barked the General.

"Yes Sir!" Said the Captain jumping to his feet and coming to attention.

"Tomorrow morning you will take a squad from your command and personally escort Mr. and Mrs. McBride, along with Major Hudson, from here to the Calhoun Farm, one mile west of Middletown, on the National Road, where it crosses the Catoctin Creek." The General cast a smile towards Sergeant Randolph. "You will remain with the McBride's until they determine that your services are no longer required, you will then return here. If the soldier in Middletown turns out to be our missing infantryman, you may expect to be received favorably on your return. If the soldier in Middletown remains unidentified, it may be necessary for you, and I, to further discuss the wisdom in your decision regarding his convalescence."

"Yes Sir!" Gulped the Captain.

"Captain Baker, Captain Smith, you are dismissed," said the General, as the Captains saluted and hurried from the room. "Colonel Penrose, Major Eagan, Captain Cunningham, I thank you for your assistance in this matter, you are dismissed, and may return to General Wright's headquarters. Please report to him what has transpired here today. If he needs anything further, advise him that I am at his service."

"Yes Sir," said Colonel Penrose, as the officers stood. Saluted the General, bid farewell and good luck to the McBride's, and left the room.

"Now Randolph," said the General to the Sergeant who had this time remained in the room. "Please find a place for Mr. and Mrs. McBride to spend the night here within my headquarters, and accommodations for Major Hudson. Mr. and Mrs. McBride will be dining with me this evening," he said smiling at the McBride's. "I've a feeling we should be celebrating."

"Yes Sir," said Sergeant Randolph as with a smile on his leathery face he started for the door.

The next morning, shortly after breakfast, the McBride's, in a carriage being driven by Major Hudson, and with a cavalry escort, left Hackwood Farm, and turned east on to the Redbud Road to begin their trip to Middletown, Maryland. It had been three weeks since the Battle of Cedar Creek had been fought.

Chapter 42

The Catoctin
1864

He still did not know who he was, or who any of the people around him were. He knew their names from hearing them, but they weren't family or close friends, if they were they would know him and be able to tell him not only who he was, but where he came from, and the other things about himself, that he no longer knew.

They were taking care of him, very good care of him. He was feeling better every day. The pain was just a dull shadow of what it had been, and did not require anything to cut or control it. He was breathing easier, and sleeping much better.

It was morning, and he was floating, suspended in that dark safe place through which you must pass as you go from being asleep to awake. This had become one of his favorite places. It hadn't always been, at one time it was a place that terrified him. It had been a place filled with demons, the spawn of that vile elixir, who reached out with ice cold black tentacles and tried to drag him into that empty black pit where there was no pain, but neither was there life. But, that had changed when it became a better place, the place where she came to visit him.

As he floated he took advantage of this magical place, and avoided the real world that waited just beyond. The real world wasn't a bad place, it was just that there did not seem to be a place for him in it anymore. He could not yet feed himself, he could only sit up for short periods of time to take water or nourishment, nor could he even take care of his very personal needs. He liked it here away from the real world, where it didn't matter that he didn't know who he was.

He knew she would come to him just before he awoke, and as he floated and waited he smiled. He knew that she was somebody very special in his life, but he didn't know why, or even who she was. She had warm brown eyes, and soft brown hair that always smelled like sunshine. Her touch was loving, and her smile was both forgiving and encouraging. She was looking for something, but he didn't know what.

That she came to him here was a secret that he would never share with anyone. These fleeting moments were his and his alone and were more precious to him than life itself. For he knew, if she gave up on him, or stopped coming, that he would die.

She had quietly crept into the room trying very hard not to wake him. The knifelike rays of the mid-morning, autumn sun seemed to search desperately for a break in the plain woolen curtains so that their light could explode into the room. The heavy well-worn woolens had been hung for the express purpose of delaying this intrusion for as long as possible.

She peered around the edge of the curtain and out the window towards the National Road to the north. She gave thanks almost every day, that although both Armies had marched and fought nearby, their home had been spared. There were many in the area who had not been so fortunate. Now the war was here again. Two soldiers, both wounded, one a beloved family member, the other unknown, even to himself.

Katherine Rosemary Calhoun turned from the window, and looked over at this unknown soldier who had come into their lives nearly two weeks ago. He had been asleep most of the time. He was only awakened so that they could give him water and warm broth. He didn't even wake up when they cleaned him, but she thought that sometimes he pretended to be asleep to avoid the embarrassment.

Matthew said that he believed that the sleep was his body's way of dealing with what was happening to it. The doctors had said that he would need a lot of sleep as his body healed. No one mentioned whether or not his mind would heal though.

Katherine didn't mind doing her part. Matthew had described how this man had saved his life, and Matthew had pledged to do whatever it took to save this man in return. She visited their hero several times every day, talked to him like he was awake and able to converse, and for the last week or so had begun reading to him in the evenings.

He had good features, and she was quite certain that once well and on his feet again, he would turn out to be quite handsome. Katherine thought about him all the time, who was he, how old was he, where was he from? She wanted to know more about this man, who war had brought to sleep in her mother's parlor.

Katherine turned and looked out the window again. Through the trees she could just make out the waters of the creek shimmering in the early morning sunlight less than a hundred yards away. It was fall. In another week or so most of the leaves would be down. Then she would have a much better view of the creek from this room.

The Catoctin twisted and wound its way south through Maryland's rolling countryside and flowed into the Potomac River about 10 miles south of the farm. In most places it was less than a hundred feet wide, but it was the lifeblood of the farmers who lived along its banks. Katherine loved the Catoctin, and as a young girl had made a promise to herself that she would never wander far from its banks.

She smiled as she recalled the countless hours she had spent with her brothers, Mark and Matthew, playing, fishing, and swimming along the creek's banks. Katherine used to see it as her moat, keeping at bay the things that might hurt her or those she loved. At other times it seemed an ocean that hid from her the wonders of the world beyond. But, it had let her down, it had not protected her, or her family, from war, and the wonders that it had kept hidden, had turned out to be horrors.

Katherine's older brother Mark, was married and had a farm in Boonsboro. He had had his leg broken at Sharpsburg, and would walk with a pronounced limp the rest of his life. Matthew had nearly lost an arm at Cedar Creek, and could still lose it.

Katherine envied her brother Matthew. He was like the mounted knights and cavaliers she read about in books and stories. He had always been the adventurous one. His letters were always full of new places he had seen, and the exciting things he had done riding around the country with the US Cavalry. Until the war, then his letters became less frequent and darker. She still looked forward to them but mostly as a confirmation that he was alive and well. The truth was, he had seen and done more in the four years that he had been gone than she could ever hope to see or do.

It was said, that she was the picture of her mother, but she had no memory of her mother. Her mother had died giving her life. Her name was Colleen, and she was resting in a beautifully maintained grave, under a giant maple tree, halfway between the creek and the house. Her father visited the site every morning and every evening, and to the best of her knowledge had missed only a handful of days since the day she died. Katherine visited the grave as well, but perhaps not as often as she should have.

Like her mother, she could best be described as having a pleasing appearance. She was a little more than average height and working around the farm for most of her life had kept her trim. She had an attractive figure that was proportionate, but not voluptuous.

With Katherine it was her eyes. Like her mother's they were a deep almost hypnotizing emerald green. They could radiate with joy and almost be heard to laugh, or they could flash with an anger that those who knew her knew it was best to avoid.

Her shoulder length auburn hair she kept tied up in a bun on the back of her head. Katherine considered herself pretty, though at times she thought her nose was a little too large. She had a great sense of humor, loved to laugh, and could hold her own with anyone in a battle of wits.

As she watched an oh so familiar smile formed upon her patient's lips, she couldn't help but smile herself, because she knew he was visiting with someone who made him happy. Katherine wondered if perhaps it was a sweetheart, or a wife, or someone else from his past, or maybe even someone that existed only in his mind. She didn't know why it would, but it bothered her that it might be a sweetheart or a wife.

Katherine had noticed that often, just before he awoke, he would sigh and there would be a troubled look of sadness on his face. She thought that maybe this was when he was trying to figure out who he was, or perhaps, who his visitor was. Then the smile would return. Katherine figured that that was when whoever his visitor was had promised to visit his dreams again. She often would smile herself, happy that this poor young man had at least a little happiness in a world in which he was lost.

Sometimes at this point he would wake up, but on most days he would just continue to sleep. His body was struggling as it slowly continued to recover from its wounds. She had no doubt that he would recover, and that at some point he would be well enough to leave them.

Katherine didn't want that to happen, the leaving part, not the getting well part. She didn't know why, he was after all, a stranger. Why should it matter to her where he might go?

"Why?" Katherine heard herself whisper. "Why would you go? I don't want you to go." She shook her head, what was wrong with her? This is crazy she thought. He doesn't even know who he is let alone who I am.

Katherine waited, but as she suspected, he did not wake up. She noticed though that the smile was gone, replaced by a look of longing, and as she watched she saw that tears were flowing down the once strong and handsome face that had been hardened by war, loss, and pain. Without even thinking, Katherine reached out and took his hand in hers and with her other hand lovingly wiped away the tears.

Then, he opened his eyes releasing still more tears. He looked deep into Katherine's eyes, and asked, his voice a little hoarse, "Are you an angel?"

"No," said Katherine quietly, a lump forming in her throat.

"You're beautiful enough to be an angel," he said.

"Thank you," she said smiling as her eyes began to fill with tears.

"I wish you were an angel," he sighed. "So that you could take me away from here."

"Don't you like it here?" She asked. "I would be very sad if you were to leave."

"It's not that," he said. "It's just..."

"You're going to get better," Katherine said with a smile. "I promise, you just have to be patient."

She looked into his eyes, and it was almost as if she was looking through them and directly into his wounded soul where she could see, and almost feel the depth of his pain, his sadness, his fear, and his loneliness. Katherine had never felt so helpless before, this poor man needed something to bring him back to the world that had abandoned him. What was it? Was it something she had? Was it something she could give him?

Tears were beginning to fall onto her face now as well as she realized that what he was missing, and that what he needed, was love. That was where the void was, he didn't know if there was anyone anywhere that he loved, and even worse, he didn't know if there was anyone in the whole world that loved him. How terribly, terribly awful that must be she thought.

"I'm Katherine," she said as she squeezed his hand, "and I'm not ready to give up on you just yet. So, I'm afraid you'll just have to stay here with me."

"Katherine," he said. "It's a name suited for an angel."

He closed his eyes and then slowly reopened them. They were focused now and Katherine noticed that they were brighter than they had been since his arrival at the Calhoun farm.

"You know what would be worse than me never being able to remember who I am, or anything about my past?" He asked.

"What?"

"Waking up one morning and not being able to remember you. I want you to always be my most beautiful memory. I never want to forget you Katherine."

"Do you think I'm ever going to let that happen?" She asked, as still holding his hand she reached up with her free hand and brushed his hair back off of his forehead.

He smiled, and looked down at where their hands were joined. "This is something we can tell our grandchildren about one day," he said, and then drifted off to sleep.

Katherine, still holding his hand, sat and watched him for a while trying to figure out what it was that she was feeling, and why. She didn't have time for this, she had other things to do. She shook her head to clear it, sighed, and left the room.

She returned to the room just before noon to check on her patient. She found him sitting up in bed pulling at the bandage that was wrapped around most of his upper body. Katherine stopped dead in her tracks, and just stared.

"Hello Katherine," he said, his voice still hoarse. "Can we take this bandage off, or at least loosen it? I think if we could it would be a lot easier for me to breathe. Oh, and I'm starving," he said with a smile. "Do you think that I could have something to eat other than broth?"

Katherine was wearing a smile that went from ear to ear, and lit up her whole face. "I have to get Matthew!" She gasped, and turned and ran from the room.

Michael McBride, still unknown to himself and everyone around him, had cleared a giant hurdle. His body had almost recovered from its internal trauma.

However, he was still very weak. He had weighed over 140 pounds when he was wounded, and now was probably at or less than 100 pounds. It would take time to put that weight back on and to build his strength back up.

With Katherine, and his father's help, Matthew removed the bandage from around Michael's body. It was immediately evident that without the bandage, he breathed much easier. He told them that there was very little pain, even when he took a deep breath.

Katherine and Matthew carefully examined the wound itself. The actual spot where the round had entered his body, and the corresponding spot on his back, where the round had exited. There was no sign of infection or seepage, and when they touched it, it was not hot, nor did it cause Michael any undue pain. Just to be on the safe side however, they placed a small bandage over the two spots.

Michael seemed in good spirits, it was a little bit of a struggle, but he chatted with Matthew, Mr. Calhoun, and Katherine. He had a lot of questions about the battle and how exactly he had saved Matthews' life and gotten wounded, but Matthew thought it best that those topics be discussed at a later time. Everyone noticed that he paid much more attention to Katherine than he did anyone else, as did she to him.

"What shall we call you?" Asked Katherine. Everyone stopped what they were doing and just stared at her. "Well," she continued. "We can't just call you him or the soldier, or the mystery man in the parlor, can we?"

"I don't know," chuckled Matthew. "I kind of like the mystery man in the parlor thing."

"No," said Brody Calhoun. "Katherine is right, we have to give him a name, or something, at least temporarily until his memory comes back."

"Call me Frank," said Michael. "I don't believe it's my name, but it's the only thing I remember, although I don't know why."

Katherine, Matthew, and Brody all looked at each other and nodded.

"Then Frank you shall be," said Katherine with a smile. "Until we discover your real name."

"Frank," said Michael with a nod.

As the days passed, Michael continued to improve. His voice became clearer, his breathing was almost normal, and he slowly grew stronger. With Matthew and Brody Calhoun's help he was even able to get out of bed and use the chamber pot. He was beginning to feel like a human being again.

Katherine spent every free moment she had with him. She told him about growing up along the banks of the Catoctin with her brothers Mark and Matthew, about her grandparents who lived in Baltimore, and her aunt and uncle in Burkittsville. She read to him, from the Bible, from Charles Dickens, and other books from the family library. Katherine changed the subject whenever he asked about the war. He had had enough of war, and she was intent on keeping him from it.

It was early evening, Michael had gone to sleep. Katherine came into the kitchen to fix herself a cup of tea. Her brother Matthew was waiting for her.

"Feel like talking?" He asked.

"What's on your mind?"

"Frank," he answered, "or whoever the mystery man is in the parlor."

"Isn't it wonderful?" She said taking a seat across from her brother. "He's getting so much better."

"Yes," said Matthew. "It's great, but at some point he's going to have to go back."

"Back? Back where?"

"To the army," said Matthew.

"Oh no," said Katherine shaking her head. "He's not going back there. I won't allow it. He's done his share, he's staying right here."

"For how long?"

"What?"

"For how long Katherine? For how long are you going to keep him here? In another few weeks he should be able to travel. Don't you see, I have to take him back to the army?"

"Why?"

"So he can find out who he is. He had to have been part of VI Corps. They are probably still at Winchester. I have to take him back there because there must be someone in VI Corps who knows him. We have to do all we can to help him find out who he is. We can't keep that away from him. "

"You mean me," she said, her eyes starting to tear. "You mean I can't keep that away from him."

"Look," he said. "I know you've grown very fond of him, and you've done a marvelous job of taking care of him, but it can't last forever."

"But that's just it Matthew," she said. "It has to last forever, because I think I've fallen in love with him."

Matthew could only stare as Katherine got up and left the room. She went upstairs to her bedroom where she fell onto her bed and cried herself to sleep, because she knew that her brother was right. She was going to lose him, without even finding out who he was.

Matthew spent most of the next morning with Michael. He brought him up to date on the siege at Petersburg, and other news about the war. He answered the many questions he had about the battle of Cedar Creek, their stay in the hospital, and how Michael had ended up at the Calhoun farm.

"You said we were dragging someone when you first got shot?" Asked Michael.

"Yes, that's right. He was already dead. You said he was a friend of yours, and you were not leaving without him. So, I helped you drag him."

"His name was Frank," said Michael.

"What?"

"The soldier we were dragging, I'm almost certain that was Frank."

"That was Frank? You remember that? Do you remember anything else? His last name? My God, your own name?"

"No," said Michael. "I just know that that was Frank."

"Well, that's a start I guess," said Matthew reaching out and patting his friend on the arm.

"If you hadn't been helping me drag him, you wouldn't have gotten shot."

"No way of knowing that," said Matthew, "but, what I do know, is that you saved my life."

Matthew then told Michael of his plans to take him to VI Corps at Winchester, in an effort to discover who he was. Matthew was pretty certain that someone there was sure to recognize him now that he was looking more like his old self. However, Matthew was concerned that Michael did not seem as excited about going to Winchester as he thought he would be.

"What happens after that?" Asked Michael.

"I don't know," said Matthew. "Once we find out who you are, I'm sure we'll be able to find out where your home is. So, I would imagine that you would be going home."

"Couldn't I come back here?" Asked Michael.

"Here?" Asked Matthew. "Why would you want to come back here? Wouldn't you want to go home? To where your family is?"

"I'd rather come back here," said Michael.

"Here? Why in the world....." Silence. "Katherine." Sighed Matthew.

"Katherine," said Michael with a smile.

Matthew just looked at his friend and smiled. "Look," he said. "Let's just see if we can find out who you are. After that, you tell me where you want to go, and I'll see that you get there. Even if it means coming back here."

"Thanks," said Michael. "You may have just done what you set out to do from the very beginning."

"What's that?" Asked Matthew.

"Saved my life," said Michael with a smile.

The next afternoon Matthew and his father were sitting on the porch enjoying the warm autumn sun when Matthew spotted men on horseback coming up the lane. He immediately recognized them as a squad of cavalry troopers. There was a carriage with them.

"What do you suppose this is about?" Asked Brody Calhoun.

"I have no idea," said Matthew as he stood and watched them approach.

When they reined up in front of the house Matthew recognized the officer in charge as his commanding officer, Captain Robert Smith, of the 2nd US Cavalry.

"Captain Smith," said Matthew. "Welcome Sir."

"Sergeant," said the Captain removing his hat and smacking it against his leg. "How's the arm?"

"It's improving Sir," he said. "Slowly, but it is improving." Matthew's arm was now in just a sling, full feeling had returned to the arm and his fingers, but he still was not able to use it or move it very much.

"Good," said the Captain.

"Is that why you're here Sir?" Asked Matthew. "To check on my arm?"

"No," said the Captain. "If we may dismount, I think I have some people here you may want to talk to."

"Certainly Sir, please come in."

"You other fellows follow me," said Brody Calhoun coming down off of the porch. "I'll take you to the barn so you can tend to your horses. Not the first time we've accommodated cavalry."

A man and a woman exited the carriage, along with a major. Captain Smith waited until they had passed, and then followed them onto the porch. Matthew led them into the house, and then to the kitchen.

"Please, be seated," he said, as they all took a seat.

"Sergeant," said Captain Smith. "This is Major Hudson, from General Grant's staff. Major, this is Sergeant Matthew Calhoun, 2nd US Cavalry."

"Sir," said Matthew nodding in the Major's direction.

"Sergeant," said the Major. "This is Mr. and Mrs. William McBride, from Rancocas, New Jersey. They believe that the unidentified soldier you brought home with you to convalesce, is their son, Private Michael McBride."

"My God! Really!" Exclaimed Matthew. "That would be wonderful."

"How is he?" Asked Joanna McBride.

"Well, ma'am," began Matthew, "a week or so ago, not so good. However, in the last several days he's gotten much much better. He can set up by himself, his breathing has almost returned to normal, as has his voice, he's eating and sleeping much better, and with help can get out of bed and use the chamber pot. The wound itself is healing nicely, and he says he has little to no pain."

"I'd like to see him," she said.

Matthew hesitated. "Ma'am," he said. "The man in the other room has absolutely no memory. He doesn't even know who he is. If he is your son, seeing you may bring back his memory, or it may not. It may even be too much for him to handle, and make things worse. I wouldn't want that to happen, and I'm sure you wouldn't either."

Joanna just stared at Matthew, contemplating what he had said.

"You say he has no memory at all?" Asked William.

"The only thing he remembers," answered Matthew, "is the name of the soldier whose body we were dragging between us when we were wounded, he refused to leave him behind, he said he was his friend, and his name was Frank."

Joanna inhaled sharply, brought her hand up to her mouth, and reached out and grabbed her husband's arm. "Frank Jefferson," she said, tears beginning to roll down her cheeks. "His name was Frank Jefferson, and he was our son Michael's very best friend. So," she continued. "The man you have here must be Michael."

The deafening silence in the room was broken by the entrance of Brody Calhoun. "Your boys are tending to their horses Captain, and picking out places in the barn to bed down for the night."

"Thank you Mr. Calhoun," said Captain Smith. "That's very kind of you."

Brody Calhoun suddenly realized that he had walked into the middle of something, but he didn't know what. He turned and looked at his son.

"This is Mr. and Mrs. McBride," Matthew said to his father. "They're from New Jersey, and it seems that the mystery man in our parlor, is their son Michael."

"Halleluiah!" Exclaimed Brody. "Isn't that marvelous!"

"Sergeant," said Joanna. "What you said earlier about not wanting to make things worse for Michael, I completely understand, and I agree. I suggest that we enter the room, you, William, and me, and if Michael recognizes us go forward from there. If he does not, we'll leave the room and decide between us what we should do, and what would be best for Michael. Agreed?"

"Yes, Mrs. McBride," said Matthew. "I think that may be the best way to proceed." There was a period of silence. "So, whenever you're ready."

William and Joanna McBride looked at each other. Their hearts were pounding. Joanna's tears had already spilled onto her cheeks, and William's were just beginning to fill his eyes. They took each other by the hand, smiled at each other, and stood.

William turned to Matthew. "Lead the way," he said.

Matthew led them to the door to the parlor. He opened the door, and the three of them stepped into the room. Michael was sitting up in bed.

Katherine was seated next to the bed reading to him. He hung on every word she spoke. When Matthew entered the room Katherine stopped reading, lifted her head, and looked at Matthew and the man and woman who were with him, as did Michael.

Michael studied the woman for a moment, as the wheels in his troubled brain slowly began to turn. He knew that she was somebody very special in his life. She had warm brown eyes, and soft brown hair that always smelled like sunshine. Her touch was loving, and her smile was both forgiving and encouraging. She was looking for something.

There was a period of silence.

Then, "You're the woman in my dreams," he said quietly, trying to figure out what was happening. The wheels in his brain were picking up speed, and lights were beginning to come on in the areas that had been darkened by pain and loss. Katherine without even thinking reached out and took his hand.

"Am I?" Asked Joanna, trying to control the flood of emotions that were rushing through her.

"Yes," he said. There was another period of silence, then he said, "You've been looking for me."

"Yes, I have," she said.

He closed his eyes and started to cry, and the only sound in the room was his crying for what seemed like hours, but in reality was only a few minutes. Matthew was worried that perhaps they had done more harm than good. Joanna too felt that perhaps they should step out of the room, but wasn't sure now that she had seen her son, that she could.

Michael opened his eyes. The fog that had clouded his brain was dissipating rapidly. He turned and looked at Katherine, and then turned back to the woman.

"You're my mother," he sobbed, "and my name is Michael."

"That's right my darling!" Sobbed Joanna as she rushed to his side, and threw her arms around her son. William, tears streaming down his face as well, was right behind her.

Katherine, with tears dropping onto her cheeks, let go of Michael's hand, stood up, and walked over to where Matthew, wiping tears from his eyes as well, was standing. "Let's leave them," she whispered, as they left the room and quietly closed the door behind them.

No one was happier that the soldier in the Calhoun's parlor turned out to be Private Michael McBride, than Captain Robert Smith. The next day, with the McBride's blessing and thanks, the Captain, his cavalry squad, and Major Hudson left to return to Winchester. Major Hudson would return to Petersburg, but the 2nd US Cavalry would remain in Winchester until December, when along with VI Corps, they too would join Grant at Petersburg.

As Michael's memory continued to improve he told anyone who would listen about his life growing up along the banks of the Rancocas Creek. His most frequent and attentive listener being Katherine. He would stumble sometimes as he told his stories, but William and Joanna, who rarely left his side, were always there to help him fill in the blanks.

The McBride's had been gone for over three weeks. It was November now, and it was decided that William would return home to Rancocas to see to the farm. Joanna would remain with Michael at the Calhoun's, who graciously insisted that she do so, until he was ready to make the long trip home. The goal was to have Michael home for Christmas.

On Thursday, November 24th, 1864, only the second time Thanksgiving would be celebrated as a national holiday, Michael J. McBride, asked Katherine Rosemary Calhoun, to become his wife. She said yes, which of course pleased everyone, and it was decided that Michael and his parents would return to the Calhoun farm sometime in May, and that they would be married in Colleen Calhoun's parlor.

"On December 11th, 1864, under my own power, with my mother at my side, I stepped off of the *John Warner* onto the wharf at the end of High Street in Burlington. My father, your great-grandfather, was there to greet me, as was Julia Grant, and a number of the city's residents. Seems, despite myself, I had left a boy, but returned a hero." 94-year-old Michael J. McBride smiled at his granddaughter. "So, Katy Rose, there you have it. Now you know the full story, and the truth about how I met your grandmother."

Chapter 43

The Rancocas
1974

Katherine Rosemary Underwood, now almost sixty years old, stood looking out across the swirling muddy waters of the Rancocas Creek. The lane that had once led to this spot was overgrown, and now almost nonexistent, and the dock and small warehouse that had once been Hilyard's Landing had rotted away. She wistfully sighed as the memories of what this place had once meant to her and those she loved filled her mind.

She turned and looked up what was once Hilyard's Lane back towards where the house stood. Oddly enough, the house was still there, but you couldn't see it, or even get to it from here anymore. The New Jersey Turnpike saw to that.

In 1950, they had lost their fight to stop the Turnpike from crossing their land. As a result, they had lost over half the farm. They were left with only the forty acres that lay to the west of the house.

They had managed for a while, even with the traffic on the Turnpike passing less than two hundred yards from the back porch. Then they lost the barn. Between the rumblings of the heavy equipment that had built the Turnpike, and the passing traffic once it opened, the 150-year-old structure began to crumble, and finally had to be taken down.

The foundation's original cornerstone, had the date it was laid, and the Masonic G, and square and compasses engraved on it when it was put into place on April 14, 1818. She had had the stone removed, and placed on her grandfather's grave as his headstone. They had had his name, and the dates of his birth and death inscribed on it; Michael J. McBride, born March 21, 1846, died November 30, 1941. That was all he had wanted, so she had complied with his wishes.

Her grandfather had died one week before America entered World War II. He was laid to rest in the family plot alongside his beloved Katherine overlooking the Rancocas.

"Tell Evan that I am sorry I did not get to see him one more time," he had said to her in the Irish, as was the McBride custom on a Sunday. "There's a war coming, tell him to guard his soul, and to never look at the faces."

"I will," she answered tearfully.

Then he squeezed her hand and whispered, "Katy Rose, I have loved you with all of my heart from your first breath, and now to my last, and I will miss you so very much, but your grandmother is calling me, and it is time for me to go to her."

Then he closed his eyes and slept, and a few hours later was gone.

Her husband Woody, her brother Evan, and cousin-in-law Ed Randall, all naval officers, survived the war, and for that she was thankful. She knew however that they had not come through it completely unscathed. Her grandfather had once told her that war changed men, even those who were not wounded physically, because war wounded men's souls, and those wounds did not easily heal. The effects were subtle, but she saw them in each of them.

The end for the farm came in 1958, when they again lost a fight with the government. This time to keep Interstate 295 from taking what was left of the farm. When I-295 was completed in 1972, the house would be sandwiched between two major highways that were less than 300 yards apart.

They decided to leave the farm in 1965, the year her husband, Admiral Baxter "Woody" Underwood, retired from the Navy after more than 32 years of service. They moved to Virginia Beach, where Woody took a job as a consultant to a group of defense contractors.

Katy's brother, Evan resigned his commission after the war, and became his father-in-law's right hand man in running his shipping business. Through a series of investments, and purchases, Meadow Hill Shipping, had become a major international concern. Johnathan Northrup retired in 1960, at which time Evan took over as CEO. He, his wife Irene, and their three children now lived in Los Angeles, where the company was based.

The fun loving Ed Randall married Nancy Curtis, of Philadelphia, just before the war. He too, like Evan, resigned his commission after the war. Ed took over his father's beverage distributorship in St. Louis, and he and Nancy still lived there with their twin girls.

Her grandmother's beloved brother Matthew had died in 1904, at the age of 65. His arm never healed well enough for him to return to the cavalry which he loved so much. He became very bitter, and remained on the farm in Middletown until his death. He never married, rarely left the farm, corresponded with no one, and discouraged visitors. Katy's grandparents had made numerous, but futile attempts to include him in their lives, including several trips to Maryland. When the property sold, his body along with his father Brody's, and his mother Colleen's, was moved to a cemetery in Middletown. Michael and Katherine McBride travelled to Maryland to attend the funeral.

Among his belongings was a letter addressed to Michael. In it he recounted the events of the day in the cemetery at Cedar Creek. He begged for Michael's forgiveness, because there had never been a second confederate soldier, it had been Matthew trying desperately to kill his assailant who had fired the shot that struck Michael. Michael had the letter placed in Matthew's coffin. On the outside of the envelope he had simply written, "Forgiven".

Mark Calhoun of Boonsboro, and Uncle Kevin of Burkittsville, sold their Maryland farms, and in 1870, uprooted their families and moved west to the newly opened Oklahoma Territory. They tried to convince Matthew to join them, but he turned them down. Katy could find no record of where they ended up, or where their descendants may now be.

Katy still owned the land the house was on, as well as several small pieces of ground that were separated by the highways. The most important of these was the family cemetery that overlooked the Rancocas from a small hill just west of where the landing had been. The cemetery, that was south of the turnpike, was surrounded by a white iron fence, and the fence, and the ground and the graves within it were meticulously cared for. A gravel road, just about a mile in length, ran alongside the turnpike from the Beverly –Rancocas Road to the cemetery.

A monument had been erected in the cemetery to the memory of her father, he had died in France during World War I, but his body had never been recovered, other than that, nearly every McBride who had ever lived on this property was buried here. Among the twenty-one graves were those of Brian and Bridget McBride, who had been the first to inhabit this land. Interred here as well was the body of Frank Jefferson, the man who her grandfather had served with during the Civil War, and the man who had died at her grandfather's side at the Battle of Cedar Creek.

Katy returned at least once a year to visit the cemetery and check on what was left of the property. The house was beginning to deteriorate, and she knew that the time was rapidly approaching when the remaining property, except for the cemetery, would have to be sold. It broke her heart to even think about it.

"Are you about ready, Miss Kate?" Asked a voice from behind her.

"Yes," she said. "I suppose I am."

Katy turned and looked at the man behind her. He was not only one of her oldest and dearest friends, but her attorney, and the man who saw to it that the cemetery and the gravel road were maintained to her exacting standards. Many of her memories of her life on this farm included this man.

"I have something for you," he said when they had walked back from the landing to the car. He was holding a beat up old cardboard hatbox. As she walked towards him he laid it on the hood of the car. "Go ahead open it," he said with a grin when she got to the car.

"I don't believe it," she said, as she looked down into the box after removing the lid. "I thought this was lost forever."

"I promised you I would take good care of it," he said, "and you know I've never broken a promise to you."

She reached in and lifted the navy blue satin pillow, which was carefully wrapped in tissue paper, out of the box. Embroidered in gold in the center of the pillow was the logo of the *USS Rhind*, on the reverse side were the names, Katherine Rosemary McBride, and Lieutenant Baxter Underwood, and the date, May 11, 1940. It was the pillow Mikey had carried down the aisle as their ring boy over thirty years ago.

"I figured it was time you had it back," he said with a smile.

She walked around the car, threw her arms around him and kissed him on the cheek. "Thank you Mikey," she said, he just smiled. She turned and carefully put the pillow back in the box. Then she picked up the walking stick she had been carrying. She didn't know why she had brought it with her today, it just seemed like the right thing to do. It was made of a highly polished ebony, and was topped by a very large and ornate gold knob.

"That's quite lovely," he said. "Where did you get it?"

"It belonged to a man named Lord Northrup," she began. "He was the reason my great-great-great-grandfather Brian McBride had to flee Ireland in 1789, and come to America. In 1790, a man named Alexander Duckworth, the captain of the ship that brought my great-great-great grandparents to America, acquired it, and brought it to Rancocas, and presented it to great-great-great grandfather McBride. It's been in the family ever since.

"I suppose that it may actually be the property of my brother's father-in-law," she continued with a grin as she held the walking stick up and lovingly examined it, "but, I've no intention of ever giving it up."

Her attorney, Michael "Mikey" Simmons, esquire, looked across at his client and just smiled. "How are the boys?" He asked.

"Very well," she said beaming a great smile. "Ronny just turned 32, is still single, and is still out on the ranch. I think his Uncle Ted is grooming him to take it over. Michael, Sally, and the kids are doing well, and are still in D.C., so, at least we get to see them pretty regularly."

"So," he said, as they climbed into the car. "You and the Admiral are moving?"

"Yes," she said. "Virginia Beach is just becoming too crowded. We've bought a small place in one of those new retirement communities out near Princess Anne."

"What's the name of the place?" He asked.

"Creekbanks," she answered, as she turned her head and took one last look at the Rancocas that suddenly seemed to explode in shimmering light as the sun came out from behind a cloud and reflected off its choppy surface. "How wonderful is that," she asked, "that we're to be in a place called Creekbanks?"

Made in the USA
Middletown, DE
13 April 2021